MORIARTY'S MEN

THE COMPLETE SERIES

EVA CHASE

A STUDY IN SEDUCTION

MORIARTY'S MEN #1

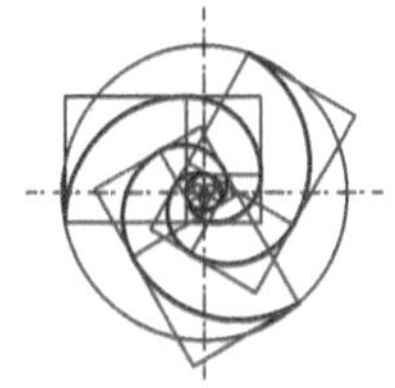

CHAPTER ONE

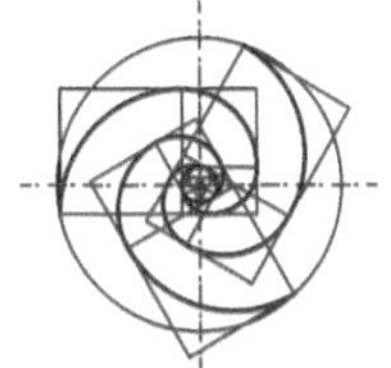

Jemma

I slipped into the reception hall crowd like a lover's hand easing up a skirt, half of my attention on the figures around me and half watching for the man I was going to ruin.

The finest investigative minds in the world filled the expansive room, all decked out in their cocktail best. The light from the crystal chandeliers shimmered off silk and satin. Voices bounced off the high molded ceiling, their tones bright thanks to the champagne that was flowing so freely I could taste the bubbles in the air.

The sequins on my violet evening gown whispered as I sidestepped between a few Australian sergeants and a couple of Peruvian detectives. I smiled demurely at the latter. One of the sergeants, who looked as though his suit was wearing him more than he the suit, took a surreptitious picture of the reception's finery with his phone. This gala was a pretty far cry from a normal day for a cop on the beat.

A waiter swept by with a platter of canapes, but I'd eaten before I arrived. The moment of action wasn't going to catch me with my hands full of poached pear on brioche. The wine glass in my hand served as a perfectly good prop—especially since I could transform it into a weapon with a quick smash, on the off-chance I needed one.

Even in distinguished company, you could never be sure. And not all of my company here was distinguished.

Ah, there was my man. If the cops and PIs around me had been half as good at their jobs as their being invited here should suggest, they'd have noted the recently released convict in their midst. The catering uniform fit the guy's stocky form just fine, but there were telltale signs a few months out of the clink could hardly come close to erasing. The marks on his shoes. The hang of his hair.

He'd been posted at the champagne table doling out glasses. That would make it easy to keep track of him.

The guy could have used some lessons in subtlety. I followed his gaze to the Glasgow commissioner. The woman was flicking back her fluffy blond bob as she chatted with a younger female officer who'd dabbed on enough face powder to turn an elephant Honey Beige. My convict was just barely restraining a glower at her.

The steady beat of my pulse picked up its pace in anticipation, but it wasn't time for either of us to make a move yet. I drifted in the commissioner's general direction. My mouth had gone a bit dry.

Everything was in place. There was no reason to get anxious, even if the consequences of failure would be devastating. Better to simply put that possibility out of my mind.

Another face caught my eye, this one from an interview I'd been perusing yesterday. I paused and turned toward it.

"Professor Charleston, isn't it?" I said, holding out my hand and beaming at the droopy-eyed man as if my life depended on this gambit. Which it very well might. "I've been following your work on trace evidence retrieval for years. It's an honor to be in the same room as you."

The professor made a pleased sound, with a twitch of his suit jacket like a bird ruffling its feathers to show off its plumage. As he shook my hand with a brisk pump, he peered at me, from my face down to the narrow but precipitous dip of my neckline, and then jerked his gaze back up. A little skin could make a large impression if you picked the right part of the landscape.

"I considered it an honor to be asked to lead one of the seminars here," he said. "It's good to know I have some wisdom worth imparting on the next generation."

"Absolutely! I'm dying to hear more about your recent strategies regarding gunshot residue. We'll see if I can't score a front row seat tomorrow."

My enthusiasm brought a flush to the professor's cheeks. "I'd save you one if I could."

I waggled a finger at him. "I'll just have to be resourceful. I'd better give the rest of the attendees a chance to talk to you before I embarrass myself with my gushing."

Professor Charleston chuckled as I gave him a little wave and glided onward. I continued smiling, now to myself. He might as well be tied up in a gift box with a bow on top.

Skirting a cluster of Japanese officers who'd gotten into a hushed debate, I checked that my convict had remained at his table. Indeed he had, with a little tug of his pants that told me in an instant where he'd hidden the pistol. Excellent. Every part of this plan was flowing along smoothly, except... where was the most important part of my audience?

A twinge of impatience had only just passed through me when the three I'd been waiting for strode into the reception hall. Half the heads in the room turned their way, which meant I could observe without looking unusually interested. This time I smiled only inwardly.

The trio of men who'd been selected for this conference from right here in London made odd companions. On the left, Garrett Lestrade was a little fox terrier of a man with dark eyes and boyishly angular features—the youngest detective inspector in Scotland Yard. On the right, John Watson, surgeon turned army medical officer turned forensics specialist, sported the bright hair and upbeat demeanor of a golden retriever. And looming tall between the two of them, his lean face as sharply alert as a deerhound, walked Sherlock Holmes, consulting detective, all of twenty-eight and already hailed in some circles as one of the greatest analytical minds of the century.

It might have been that reputation that drew so many gazes their way, but even an objective observer had to admit that the three of them were easy enough on the eyes in their differing ways. Watson bounded forward, a gleaming wooden walking stick offsetting his slight limp, already offering cheerful greetings and grasps of arms. Lestrade sauntered behind him, his hands slung in the pockets of his trousers and his chin raised at an angle that looked like a dare.

Holmes proceeded at a more leisurely pace, studying the room from beneath the messy dark waves of his hair, his stance aloof but a pleased smile curling his lips when a couple of lieutenants from Cardiff came over to compliment him on this or that brilliantly solved case. With the great height of his slender frame and that detached attitude, he might as well have been a king accepting the reverence of his subjects.

He had a dazzling mind to back up that confidence, absolutely, but even the mighty could falter. My heart thumped a little faster with a giddy shiver through my nerves.

I *would* have him, one way or another. The great Holmes hadn't yet tangled with the great Moriarty. Barely anyone even knew the great Moriarty existed, which was exactly how I liked it.

Possibly by design, the trio had timed their entrance perfectly. As the initial round of fawning wrapped itself up, a burly man with a pinstriped suit and a head like a turnip walked up to the podium at the head of the room and leaned toward the mounted microphone.

"Distinguished colleagues," he said with a faint whine of mic feedback. The conversations around the room quieted. "I'm overjoyed to welcome you all to London for our first International Conference of Investigative Skills."

I veered toward the fluffy-haired commissioner as we all moved closer to the podium. As if by chance, I came to a stop just a couple feet to her left. A quick glance toward the wine table told me that my convict was on the move too. I adjusted my weight on my feet, ready to spring.

Turnip-head at the podium went on with his speech. "I pride myself in thinking we've managed to assemble the top minds in criminal investigation from all across the world. You were invited because you're at the top of your field, but I'm sure you made it to those heights through the understanding that there's always more you can absorb. For the next ten days, you'll be able to learn from other investigators as skilled as yourself in their specific areas of expertise."

A flicker in the light over his head caught my eye. When I glanced up, the glow streaming down from the chandelier shimmered with a texture like a filmy piece of gauze. I didn't let myself visibly react, but inside my stomach tightened.

The shrouded one had already tracked me here. What was it doing, playing with light effects?

No one else appeared to have noticed anything off. It only wanted me to know it was here. Watching. Waiting.

My fingers curled toward my palm, not quite a fist. I wasn't letting that piece of supernatural excrement distract me from my mission.

Turnip-Head rambled on about how lucky, dedicated, and wise we all were—I could claim the latter two out of three; not bad—and the catering convict edged into view through the crowd. He had his hand tucked close to his waist, close to his pistol. Well, technically *my* pistol, since I'd contrived to get it into his hands. And to get him in here. And to give him this opening.

Fifteen years ago, Ms. Commissioner had been a sergeant who'd gotten him put away for killing a father of two in a bar brawl. The guy's long-time girlfriend had left him. He'd lost a job he liked to brag about. He'd been happy to take an opportunity to get revenge.

I couldn't really take credit for ruining him. That honor belonged to his poor life choices.

He could have ignored my offer. He could have walked away even now. But he didn't. Instead, he lunged, whipping the pistol forward at the same time.

All his attention had been focused on the commissioner, and none of it on me. Another poor choice.

A shout of warning rang out. The commissioner spun around, her face blanching. I sprang between the convict and her in one smooth movement guided by years of physical training.

Knee to the groin. Elbow to the ribs. My heel to his hand, kicking the gun out of his grasp.

I giveth, and I taketh away.

I pinned the convict to the ground, braced against his back. The flexible fabric of my violet evening gown pooled against his white catering shirt. Quite a few people were yelling. A security officer hustled through the throng and knelt down to snap a pair of handcuffs around the guy's wrists. We were in a room stuffed with cops, but this one night they'd all left their equipment behind.

"Oh my God," the commissioner said, holding out her hand to help me up, the other pressed to her chest. "Thank you so much—you moved so fast. He came out of nowhere."

I'd give too much away if I looked around to check, but I hoped the London trio had gotten a good view. I stood and squeezed the commissioner's hand with a small smile. "I saw the gun, and I just reacted. I'm glad you're okay."

~

After toasts and exclamations over my heroics, I welcomed the stillness of my hotel room. The grand establishment hosting the conference boasted worn historic limestone and ornate arched lintels on the outside, but the innards had been tastefully modernized. Ivory walls, thick slate-gray carpeting, a sleek ebony desk against one wall, a king-sized bed with matching ebony frame against the other, a little table in the corner near the window.

The window looked out over the back courtyard, dark now other than a few pools of light from the security lamps. I'd arranged a suite at the end of the hall on the second floor. The broad limestone sill outside would serve Bash just fine when he needed to drop in.

I turned away from the view, and all my satisfaction drained away.

A translucent white figure wavered in the glow of the bedside light. It formed a lumpy but vaguely humanoid shape beneath overlapping strips of ragged white fabric—at least, they looked like fabric. Sometimes I wondered if they weren't swaths of dead skin.

The only part the strips didn't totally cover was the area that should have been a face. There, amid the folds of cloth, a haze of mist stared back at me, so deep that if I looked at it for long, I'd feel I were staring clear across the continent into a realm where no human had ever ventured.

A chill raced over my skin, but I meandered across the room to the mirror over the desk as if I had no qualms about my visitor. "Hello, Bog," I said. "What brings you here?"

Bog wasn't really the thing's name. The shrouded folk had their own language that human ears couldn't properly decipher. Bog sounded somewhat right, and it gave me a tiny shred of amusement to call the monster after something repellant, if I had to address it at all.

I could still see it at the side of the mirror while I unpinned my hair. As the red waves spilled down over my narrow shoulders, the folds around Bog's face quivered.

"You are playing games," it said in a voice as dry as desert-bleached bone and as distant as the mist it came from. "I thought you might need reminding of our agreement."

A pinching sensation emanated from the spot on the back of my neck just below my hairline where the magic of our contract had marked me.

"Oh, I'm hardly going to forget that," I said. "I have a month longer. Why shouldn't I play during the time I have left?"

"Why play *here*, bloodling? You are no 'investigator'."

"Oh, I don't know. I think I've investigated plenty in my time."

"If that is what pleases you. Perhaps I will find something of interest in it too."

The shrouded one's tone stayed perfectly even, like mine had. We were playing a game right now — the game where I pretended I didn't plan to do everything in my power to escape the deal I'd made, and it pretended not to suspect me of that scheming. But those last words had been a warning.

I shrugged and picked up my brush. "You can spend your time however you want."

The mist stirred. I could almost have said I caught a glint of a smirk.

"Think more about how you wish to spend yours, bloodling. You received your ten years. In thirty days, your life is mine."

I smiled back at it through the mirror despite the tremor that ran through my chest. *We'll see about that.*

CHAPTER TWO

Sherlock

Halfway through the first morning of the International Conference of Investigative Skills, I had yet to be convinced that this wasn't an utter waste of my time. I wouldn't deny that it had been a badge of honor for the selection committee to have recognized my contributions despite my lack of formal credentials. They'd extended an invitation to John no doubt mainly in deference to how closely we worked together, and there was no denying *he* was enjoying the experience.

Nevertheless, so far the seminars had done nothing to alleviate my feeling that modern police work was woefully behind the times. I could have pointed out a dozen errors mentioned by the lecturer for our session on toxins—and would have, if John hadn't given me a pained look as if I were poisoning him with my initial clarifications. So far, our current session on the identification and analysis of trace evidence had revealed nothing I hadn't determined through my own work.

The trouble was, being permitted to solve crimes alongside the police required keeping the good will of the police. I could only imagine the offense that various parties would take if I removed myself, regardless of how much good I might do elsewhere during this time.

So, for now, I remained in the hard wooden chair in the fourth row of the bland beige room, letting Professor Charleston's baritone roll over me and resisting the urge to recommend to the woman sitting in front of me that she apply approximately thirty percent less of her jasmine-and-patchouli perfume out of consideration for the lungs of her colleagues.

From the worried strip of skin around her left ring finger, anyone should have been able to tell that she was recently and unhappily divorced. I probably ought to be considerate of her mental state. For John's sake, in any case.

As Charleston flipped through several crime scene photographs on a projector screen at the front of the room, Garrett shifted in his chair at my other side. This session might be of some use to my Scotland Yard associate, as loath as he'd be to admit it. He had his hands clamped together in his lap to keep from fidgeting. Sitting still and waiting for information to come to him had never been Detective Inspector Lestrade's forte.

"All right," Charleston said, rubbing his hands together. "I've laid out the scenario. Now why don't I give the rest of you a chance to weigh in? Would anyone like to volunteer what they would glean from the evidence offered so far?"

A hand shot up in the front row. I couldn't see the woman's face, and her casual blouse and slacks set a very different tone from her dress at the reception last night, but her flame-red hair and delicate build made her easy to identify. Yesterday's events had proven she wasn't as delicate as she looked. She'd thrown and pinned a man who had to weigh nearly twice what she did.

The reception had been all astir after that, even John and Garrett, as if they'd never witnessed an example of excellent physical conditioning before. You wouldn't think training in martial arts would be all that uncommon among the enforcers of justice. When dealing with criminals, it was careless not to be prepared for a situation to come to blows.

Several other hands lifted in the audience, but Charleston's face lit up when his gaze rested on the young woman in the front. He motioned for her to speak.

"What you were saying about the tire marks," she said in a voice that was soft yet precise enough to carry through the room. Her American-esque English was faintly accented with what sounded like a variety of mild influences rather than a single source I could pinpoint. "The obvious conclusion from the depth of the impressions and the drops of oil is that the perpetrator sat in the car for several hours waiting for the victim—not knowing her well enough to guess when she'd arrive."

I suppressed a sigh. Yes, that was the obvious conclusion, and the one almost anyone here could have drawn. It took *real* observation and insight to—

"I'd suggest that answer is misleadingly easy," the woman went on, to my surprise. She motioned to the photos. "In my opinion, it's more likely that the perp *did* know the victim and had parked there to visit her many times in the past, resulting in deepened impressions."

Charleston's eyebrows leapt up. "How would you support that conclusion?" he asked.

I found myself tilting forward slightly to make sure I caught every word of the woman's response.

"It's a very narrow turn into the driveway," she said confidently. "You can see the post has been scraped often—but there's no fresh marking, as though any recent visitors were practiced at avoiding it. The treads themselves look like the type to support an older car that might leak a few drops of oil in a short time. If I were investigating, I'd take soil samples to determine if the same oil lingered deeper in the earth and check the victim's friends and associates for anyone owning a leaky older car."

"Well." The professor blinked, and his lips twitched with amusement. "I'll have to give that take some thought. Anyone have another angle to offer?"

He called on some fellow farther down our row, but I was still watching the woman ahead of us. Her attention to detail and the swift leaps of her deductions—they almost reminded me of my own line of reasoning with...

I turned to John. "Did you write up any public accounts of the Yardsley murder?" Perhaps she wasn't particularly swift but merely remembering past investigations not her own.

John shook his head. His puzzled expression faded after a moment. "Her approach *was* quite a bit like yours there, wasn't it? She couldn't have read about it through any public channel that I know of."

The police records wouldn't have laid out my process either. She'd followed a similar train of thought through the adeptness of her own mind.

My gaze settled back on her bright hair. This conference might turn out to be more than mundane after all.

"You know," our little detective inspector said, trailing behind me as I strode into the hotel's library, "some people might call this stalking."

I dismissed Garrett's comment with a wave of my hand. "I'm merely looking to talk with a colleague of sorts. We're at a conference meant for the sharing of ideas. And I think *you* are just as interested to learn more about her as I am."

He didn't argue that point. John nodded toward a table at the back of the room just as I spotted that head of flaming red hair. We made our way over, past gleaming modern bookcases that held mostly recent volumes and none of the scent of stale binding glue and aged paper that belonged in a proper library.

The woman was poring over the contents of a folder, several photographs on one side and what looked like a police report on the other, glancing up only briefly to tap a few notes on a propped tablet. She was so absorbed in her study that she didn't notice our approach immediately, which gave me a moment to study *her*.

Other than that stark red hair, her eyes were her most striking feature: deep-set and the irises darkly ringed in a hue I couldn't determine at a distance. The rest of her pale face contained a mix of contradictory features. Her upturned nose and sharp chin gave an almost childlike impression that contrasted with those eyes and full lips and her overall bearing, which spoke of maturity beyond her apparent years. The set of her shoulders said they'd carried a lot but were prepared for more, as the chips fell.

Not a countenance one would soon forget.

Beyond her bearing, everything about her spoke of care and exactness. She kept her fingernails neatly trimmed and clean. Her clothes showed not the slightest stain or tear. She wore no accessories other than a simple but elegant silver ladies watch, not designed to draw attention but to keep time impeccably.

The entire effect revealed little about her history. She was unmarried and, to the best of my judgment, unattached. There were difficulties in her past she'd risen above—but what precisely I couldn't determine. Intriguing.

We were only a few feet from the table when she registered our footsteps. Her head jerked up, her slim hand automatically moving to flip the folder closed. Ah, that response I could read. She wasn't supposed to have brought the file here.

"My apologies for interrupting your work," I said, coming to a stop beside the table. "I'm Sherlock Holmes, and these are my colleagues, Dr. John Watson and Detective Inspector Garrett Lestrade. We were quite impressed by your analysis in the trace evidence seminar this morning. I was hoping we might get to know each other a little better."

The woman considered me for a moment, her hand still resting protectively on her folder. Her eyes were gray—the pale shade of a frozen lake bleeding into an outer ring that was dark as a thunderstorm. I'd imagine many men found them difficult to look away from.

After a few seconds, her shoulders eased down a smidgeon. "Jemma Moriarty," she said. "You... want to get to know *me*?"

She clearly recognized me, or at least my name. Whatever fame I'd earned could perhaps have its downsides if it intimidated her.

I propped myself against the table. John took the seat across from her, and Garrett stayed on his feet, gripping the back of the next chair over.

"I'll be honest," I said. "Even the experts assembled here tend to fall into the same tired patterns of thinking. You have a rare ingenuity. I like to cultivate as many inspired associates as I can."

"You were pretty impressive giving that gunman the smackdown," Garrett put in. "A bit of a firecracker, aren't you?"

"I guess you could say that." She flashed a smile. "I do my best."

"What made you focus on those details in the scene Professor Charleston laid out?" I asked.

"They were the details that were there," Jemma said matter-of-factly. "I've never believed in accepting the obvious answer from the most obvious evidence. You get to the truth faster if you take every available factor into account."

A spark of electricity raced through my nerves like it had when I'd listened to her speak in the seminar. She did have a mind, all right.

"I couldn't have said it much better myself." I dropped my gaze to her file folder, an itch of curiosity chasing the eager spark. I'd developed numerous strategies for coping with boredom in recent years, so no danger lurked in that area now, but I found it vastly more satisfying to avoid the sensation altogether.

It would be the perfect irony if the most stimulating part of this conference had nothing to do with the conference at all.

"What are you working on?" I asked.

Jemma tucked the folder a little closer to her. "Just a case from back home that's basically closed."

I judged her reaction. "But not solved."

She shrugged awkwardly. "We—I—ran out of leads. I thought being here in this atmosphere, something might click. No luck so far."

Her hesitation only made me more intrigued. I nodded to the folder. "I've yet to meet a case I couldn't crack. Why don't you let me put my mind to it and see if I can't shake something loose?"

"Well, I..." A bit of color rose in her pale cheeks. "I'm not actually supposed to have printed off the documents or brought them with me."

"I can manage discretion," I said.

"He isn't just full of himself, as much as he might sound like it," John said with a warm grin. "If there's a problem in existence Sherlock can't work out, I haven't seen it."

"Those of us at Scotland Yard have started to rely on him for our most complicated cases," Garrett added, more grudgingly.

Her hand stayed tensed on the folder. "We only just met. I couldn't ask you for a favor like that."

I waved off her concern. "You'd be doing *me* a favor. Alleviate the boredom of this humdrum symposium. What could it hurt? I swear I won't mention it to your superior officers back in…?"

"Freising," Jemma said. "It's a small city just outside of—"

"Munich," I filled in. "Are you German, then?" That could explain the softness of her Rs, but not much else in her accent.

In that moment, her smile looked almost sly. "For the time being. I wasn't born there."

The woman was a puzzle, but I could unravel that mystery soon enough. For now, I wanted to keep my primary goal in sight. I tapped the edge of the folder. "Five minutes. You can kick me off the case if I don't find anything."

Her eyebrows rose. She hesitated a second longer, and then she released the file to me. As I opened it, she crossed her arms over her chest, tension lingering in her shoulders. Garrett leaned over and John got up to peer at the folder's contents with me.

A city councilor had been found dead from a head wound on the side of a road on the outskirts of Freising—but one glimpse at the photo told me it hadn't been an encounter with a car. The side of the poor fellow's skull had been bashed open with a blunt rectangular instrument, the rest of him uninjured.

John grimaced. "With a hit like that, he'd have been gone so fast he wouldn't have suffered much."

"He was moved there," I said, glancing over the surroundings. "The murder happened at another site."

"We determined that," Jemma said quietly. "But not where."

Following that trail would be rather difficult at this distance. I considered the photograph again. "The assailant knew him—it was personal."

"How can you tell *that* from one picture?" Garrett said.

I pointed at the wound. "I expect John could follow my reasoning."

My friend considered the photograph. He'd struggled to piece together the blatant clues when he'd first begun assisting with my investigations, but in the past two years he'd proven himself a quick study.

"It was a crime of passion," he said. "You don't bludgeon someone that close up and that hard unless you're in the grip of strong emotion."

"Rage, most likely," I said with a satisfied nod.

Garrett grimaced. "Maybe this councilor was such an arsehole he could provoke rage in a stranger."

I ignored the off-the-cuff remark and flipped through the other photos from the scene. My fingers stilled around one near the back that showed what appeared to be a torn fragment of another photo.

"What's this?" I asked, setting it on the table.

Jemma peered at it and frowned. "We found that in his jacket pocket. Chances are it had nothing to do with his murder. Even if it does, it's impossible to determine what it was a picture of from just that piece."

A smile curled my lips. "Not at all," I said. "I can tell you exactly where you'd find that bit of stonework. It's just a quick jog across town. The real question is, why was your murdered councilor carrying a torn photo taken in London when he died?"

CHAPTER THREE

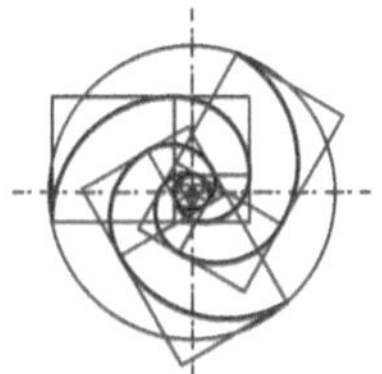

Jemma

It was a thrill to watch Sherlock Holmes at work—even more so because he clearly didn't suspect how much I'd engineered his current quest. I had to admit I hadn't expected him to identify the location in the scrap of photograph so quickly and from memory.

Now he strode briskly along the posh West London street without any concern that he was leaving John and me at his heels, taking the buildings and people around us in with his sharp gaze from beneath the fall of his dark hair. The crisp early spring breeze stirred the messy waves, and his trench coat billowed behind his lanky frame.

He thought he saw everything, picked up on every clue. He had no idea how much horror lurked at the edges of this world, hungry and conscienceless. Would he and his regular companions have believed that the things I knew even existed? Doubtful.

"From the way you handled the gunman at the reception, you've obviously done some combat training," John said to me, managing to keep up a pretty good pace and to still look relaxed about it despite his mild limp. His walking stick tapped against the pavement in an upbeat patter that fit his whole demeanor. "Do you have a preferred style?"

"I wanted to learn a variety of methods so I could apply whichever works best in any given situation," I said. "I started with Judo and Muay Thai and worked up to Krav Maga."

Holmes—well, Sherlock; we were all on a first name basis now— hummed to himself. He glanced back at me for a second before leading us across the street. "I'd have said there was some American military influence in your form as well."

Oh, he did see a lot, didn't he? An eager prickling ran through me at the thought of all those wits at my disposal.

"Funny you should mention that," I said, as if surprised. "While I was training, I'd often do some sparring with a friend of mine who served in the American army. I guess a few tics rubbed off on me."

A smile curled the corners of Sherlock's lips. That was how he got off: noticing and interpreting details other people didn't or couldn't. Every moment I spent in his presence was further confirmation of what I'd guessed—that his greatest point of weakness was his pride in his intellectual strengths. Did he care about my stakes in this supposed investigation? Not a chance. He'd come this far because of his need to show off his abilities at every turn.

He had an ego as big as an anaconda and equally difficult to shake. Play to that, and he'd dance, thinking it was all his idea. Like he was right now.

Arrogance aside, he *had* recognized exactly where that photo had been taken. He drew up short and pointed farther down the street to a stately bank building with a textured arc of stone along its top.

"This isn't the only building in the world or even this city designed in that style," he said. "But the combination of the texturing and the wear and the quality of the stone told the story clearly enough. Your dead councilor's photograph was taken within a foot of where we're standing right now."

Delight at the problem solved rang through his firm tenor. We'd only made it to the start of the trail, though. I peered at the bank building, choosing my words with care. If I gave him too large a shove in the right direction, he'd pick up on my intent, and then I'd be nowhere near getting him to the real goal.

"I can see it," I said. "But there's no way to tell what was in the rest of the photo—or whether it was something that led to the murder."

"We can tease out the possibilities and test our hypotheses." Sherlock steepled his hands together in front of him as if to hold his enthusiasm in check. "If it *did* prompt the murder, we have to assume it contained some sort of incriminating material, most likely as a point of blackmail. A photograph taken from this angle would have caught some of the neighboring buildings. Which of these do you think would be most likely to produce illicit behavior?"

I had to make it sound as if I were working through the options right now. "I suppose a bank robbery would be too convenient—and conventional. I don't notice anything particularly provocative about the boutique next door. And then…" I tipped forward to peer at the next sign. "Cavalier's. What kind of business is that?"

"I believe it's a gentlemen's club," John said in a wry tone.

"Indeed," Sherlock said. "One of the old-fashioned ones that still doesn't allow any gentle*women* as members."

"Exclusive clubs can be a hotbed for activity that skirts the law," I said. "I suppose if I were investigating I'd start there."

Sherlock's smile grew. "As would I. So, let us investigate. I'd like to get a look at their membership file to determine if any of those 'gentlemen' have recently been in the vicinity of Munich."

"Hold on," I said. "I don't have any jurisdiction here, and you're not even supposed to know about the crime. They aren't going to hand over their members' names to anyone who asks."

"Who says we're going to ask?" Sherlock said. "Sometimes bringing about justice requires a little bending of the law."

I'd already known he held that philosophy—no doubt it was another reason that Garrett Lestrade of Scotland Yard had begged off this little expedition, citing an appearance he was expected to make. But it wouldn't do to sound eager myself.

"Oh?" I said. "But if we're caught…"

A flicker of disappointment and maybe a little wariness crossed the detective's handsome face. His gaze turned downright piercing. He'd expected me to be committed enough to solving this crime to jump right in.

"If we play our cards right, we won't be caught," he said. "Unless you're not willing to take that gamble to find the answers you've been searching for?"

The question had the feel of a test. I had to walk a fine line between hiding my true motivations and keeping his good will. He'd be even *more* wary if I suddenly charged ahead after my initial hesitation.

"It's just not my usual approach," I hedged, buying myself a little time.

John grinned at his friend, his hazel eyes lit with fondness. It wasn't really me he was here to support—for him, this was all about his friend. "Sherlock's methods may not be entirely conventional, but he's never dragged me into danger we couldn't get out of. If you're not comfortable coming along, we can handle it between the two of us."

I pretended to waver for a moment longer. Then I exhaled in a sigh. "No. It's my case. If we're taking risks for it, I should be a part of that. What exactly is your plan, Sherlock?"

The detective studied me as if judging whether to accept my involvement after all. Then he shifted his attention to John. "Do you have a flash drive on you?"

At the other man's nod, Sherlock rubbed his hands together. "You'll be a gentleman interested in joining the club. His long-term girlfriend has her doubts. The management will bring you into the offices to see about registering, and then an unfortunate incident will draw them out of the room to make sure nothing jeopardizes the club's reputation in the eyes of the young lady. Simple as anything."

Exactly what I wanted to hear. And once he had the membership file, I could hope that it would be simple enough for him to identify my mark and dredge up one crime or another to pin him with. All I needed was the guy in custody for a day or two, and that would be enough of a window to make my real move, no further tactics necessary.

John set his broad hand on the small of my back. "Just follow my lead, and we'll be in and out in a matter of minutes," he said, so warmly confident I expected anyone would have gone along with him, a shrouded one's claim hanging over their heads or not.

I dragged in a breath as if from nerves. My actual nerves were tingling with exhilaration. In a matter of minutes, I might be nearly through with this mission. It'd be bye-bye to Bog without him or the men I'd used being any wiser.

Then I could get on with my real work. When I was finished with the shrouded folk, those ghostly creeps would never hurt another innocent soul like my sister again.

"All right," I said. "Let's do it."

Sherlock hung back as we started across the street. John whipped a strip of hair that matched the golden-blond stuff on his head out of his jacket pocket and patted it onto the skin beneath his nose. I arched an eyebrow at him with honest amusement.

"Do you always keep a fake moustache on you?"

He turned his grin on me. "Sometimes two or three. It has to be the right one for the occasion. Shall I take your arm? We'd better look the part."

I let him tuck his free hand around my elbow and dug into my purse so I could pop a sugar cube into my mouth. The pure sweetness dissolving over my tongue sharpened my concentration—and I wanted to be doubly sharp for this encounter.

We sauntered up the steps outside the club. Even from the door, the place stank of rich men: cigar smoke and fine scotch. The doorman held up his hand to stop us at the edge of the thick crimson carpet.

"I'm sorry, sir," he said, "but the lady may not enter."

"Well, now," John said in a snooty voice that matched the awful moustache. "I understand that she won't be joining me on regular occasions, but I've come to ask about acquiring a membership, and my darling has a few questions to set her mind at ease. Surely she can't harm anything by merely stepping over the threshold. We wished to speak to the manager—she won't stray beyond his office."

The doorman frowned, but he ducked inside. When he returned

a moment later with a gaunt man in a full suit, presumably the manager, John pulled his considerable frame taller with a raise of his chin.

"Is this how you treat all interested parties—leaving them to catch a chill on the doorstep? My cousin owns half the newspapers in this city, you know. I'm sure *he'd* like to hear about—"

"Sir, sir, no need for distress," the manager broke in, a hair shy of wringing his hands. He beckoned us in with a nervous glance around as if he thought my feminine presence in the front hall might bring the building collapsing down around our ears. "Cavalier's is pleased that you're considering joining our establishment. I'd be happy to address any concerns your charming partner has."

I stroked my hand down the side of John's arm as if in a loving caress. Whoa there. He might have looked like a sweet golden retriever of a man, but he was hiding a good bit of muscle under the softness.

He still had that pompous look pasted on his face, but I thought a glimmer of heat sparked in his eyes at my touch. An excellent start in case I did need to resort to my more complicated alternate plan.

"I just don't see how a place like this can be anything other than backwards when you have such outdated policies about women," I said, giving the manager a tight smile. "It's like you must be getting up to antics you wouldn't want us knowing about."

The manager smiled back just as tightly. He ushered us into his office where a laptop and various papers sat on a mahogany desk, surrounded by built-in bookshelves lined with leather-bound volumes I'd have bet half my accumulated fortune he'd never even opened. We sat on leather chairs that based on their patina were only slightly less old.

"I assure you, miss, that nothing at all inappropriate goes on within these walls," the manager said, sinking down across from us. "Our policy is simply a tradition that we've found many members enjoy keeping up. A sort of bonding within our gender. I'm sure you can understand that."

I rubbed my hand against my mouth. "I suppose. What sort of activities do you host here, then?"

"Most of our members simply stop by for a short span of relaxation—a drink, a smoke, a browse through the day's papers. We offer all the local publications as well as several international ones." His gaze flicked to John in memory of the comment about his supposed cousin. "We have a room for card games and another for watching sports matches. Our focus is the comfort of our clientele while they're with us."

"See, darling," John said, patting my hand. "There's nothing to worry about."

"Well, all right. Why don't you go ahead and do this registration —but I might think of more questions I want to ask."

The manager looked both relieved and horrified at the same time. He opened up his laptop and tapped on the keyboard. "Have you already been apprised of the fees, Mr…?"

"Yes," John said. "And it's Eric—Eric Freeman."

"Right. I'll need to see some ID, and then we'll go over the requirements. You may need to send in documentation of—"

A hoarse voice carried through the door, bellowing out a raunchy song that within its first few lines managed to describe a woman's genitalia and the uses the singer felt they might be put to solely through nautical metaphors. It was actually rather creative.

That had to be Sherlock providing our distraction. I made myself stiffen in my seat, and the manager blanched.

"What on Earth is *that*?" I demanded.

The manager shot out of his chair. "I assure you that cannot be anyone who ought to be in this building. I'll see that the disturbance is removed immediately."

I caught John's eye as the other man fled the room. He looked as if he was suppressing a laugh. The second the door had thumped shut behind the manager, he leapt around the desk so smoothly you could hardly tell he needed a cane. He whipped out a silver flash drive and plugged it in.

"Membership file… Bingo!" He beamed at me around the laptop. "You were perfect. Are you sure you haven't done this sort of thing before?"

I let myself offer a small smirk. "Not in the line of *duty* I haven't…"

He chuckled and clicked on the trackpad. The hoarse singer was still caterwauling away, but his voice was getting fainter. The club's security must be managing to oust him. We didn't have much more time.

"Have you got it?" I asked, with an urgency I didn't need to feign. If we were caught, he and Sherlock might give up on this line of inquiry. He *had* to get that list.

"There we go. But here's a folder of minutes from meetings of the board as well…" He dragged it over.

"John," I protested. "We didn't come here for that. The manager will be back any second."

John glanced up again, his face lit up in a way I hadn't seen before. For an instant, he had the look of a junkie who'd just shot up his favorite drug. Then it was gone, and he was his regular grinning self again.

Interesting. Despite the jangling of my nerves, I filed that moment away for future reference.

"There could be something useful in there," he said. "I don't want to leave until we have everything Sherlock needs to break open this case for you."

The floor creaked on the other side of the door. John sprang up. He yanked the drive from the computer and dropped into his chair beside me a second before the manager stalked inside.

"I do apologize for the disruption," the manager started, but John was already pushing back to his feet. I followed suit.

"I apologize too," John said, with a respectful bob of his head. "I may have wasted your time. I have to say I'm having doubts now about whether this establishment is quite the right fit. Good day to you."

As we hustled out, I could still see the excited light dancing in his eyes, bright as his hair.

Maybe his participation in this scheme wasn't just about his devotion to Sherlock. Maybe Dr. John Watson got off on investigations like this in ways all his own.

CHAPTER FOUR

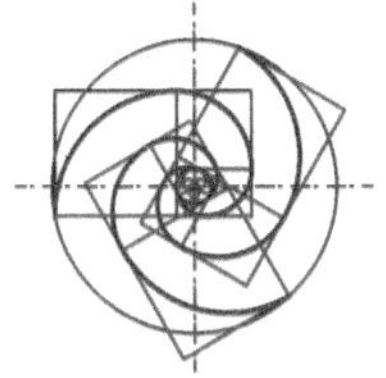

Jemma

I didn't have to wait long for results. The London trio caught up with me in the hotel dining room the next morning just as I'd reached the pastry table.

"You slept well enough," Sherlock said without preamble—not a question but a statement of fact. "Grab something quick for your breakfast. We have a lot to discuss."

That gave me an excuse to indulge my sweet tooth. Banana muffin? Raspberry sweet roll? Cinnamon-pecan bun? Yes, yes, yes, please.

I balanced my plate in one hand and gripped my mug of coffee with the other as the detective led the way out of the dining room and into a lounge area down the hall. There, a linen loveseat and armchairs surrounded a broad oak coffee table.

Sherlock dropped a bulging file folder onto the polished table top and paced from one end of the loveseat to the other. John propped himself against the loveseat's arm. Garrett took the nearest chair, sipping his own coffee and setting a small notepad on one knee.

I sank into one of the armchairs too, taking a bite of my

raspberry roll. Fuck, that was good—the perfect balance of doughy and fruitily sweet. Would it draw unwanted attention if I ate nothing but these for every meal?

"What's that?" I asked with a nod to the folder.

Sherlock set off on another pace back and forth, his hands clasped behind his back and his lean face solemn, though his cool blue eyes were starkly alert. "I went over the membership records for Cavalier's as soon as I had the chance. It took barely any time at all to narrow down the list to one name. A Stefan Richter has been a member there for twenty-three years. He also recently spent a few weeks in Munich, departing on the same night as your councilor was murdered."

Oh, good work, good work—all the applause. I restrained my smile and cocked my head. "That is a pretty big coincidence. Is there any other reason to suspect he'd commit a murder?"

Garrett motioned to the file folder with the pen he was holding. "Only the stack of reports I was able to dig up through police channels." He hadn't relaxed into the chair but sat there tensed. Something about this situation unsettled him. "This Richter has been on a lot of people's radar."

I widened my eyes. "If he's got that thick a record, why is he still walking free?"

"It's not a real record," Sherlock said. "No police department aware of his various exploits across Europe has ever been able to make a charge stick. I supplemented Garrett's findings with my own private research. The man has many hobbies—women, gambling, historic art and artifacts—and he tends to take first and make amends later if someone complains. Generally with a large pay-off to ensure no one presses charges."

Disgust colored his voice. Good to see we had similar feelings about our target.

Garrett gave Sherlock a disgruntled look as if he felt he'd been interrupted. He ran his hand—and the pen in it—through his short fawn-brown hair. "There have been investigations both here in London and in various cities abroad. He's been under suspicion of theft and extortion, but no one's been able to gather enough proof to really pin something on him. Evidence disappears, witnesses refuse to talk... He even sued the Paris police department once for supposed harassment to get them to back off."

"All that said, this is a little unusual, isn't it?" John said. "For a long-time criminal to suddenly leap from mainly property crimes to a violent act like murder?"

"Perhaps," Sherlock said, "but from what I gathered, there are plenty of women across the continent who could testify that he has no shortage of violent urges. If he was backed into a corner, he'd lash out however he could."

"Or he might not have committed the crime himself," Garrett pointed out. "It could have been a lackey."

The consulting detective made a dismissive sound. "As John pointed out so succinctly on examining the body, it was a crime of passion. A lackey with no personal stakes carrying out a premeditated murder would have used a method other than bludgeoning. Richter was provoked in some way and responded with a burst of rage. That much should be obvious to anyone."

John's posture pulled a little straighter at the recognition. Garrett's grew stiffer. He scribbled something in his notepad with terse jerks of his pen.

Watching the three of them, their working dynamic came into even sharper focus. Sherlock strode ahead in the lead with his arrogant certainty, John tagged along performing for scraps of praise, and Garrett trailed behind, not fully part of the team, always knowing that when he solved one of his cases, he couldn't take the full credit for the job well done.

The knowledge that Sherlock continually stayed a few steps ahead ate at him, didn't it? It wasn't enough for him to solve the crime and bring the perpetrator to justice—he wanted to have been the one with the right answers. I took that in with a stirring of uncomfortable memories.

I knew what it was like to feel every interaction with your peers was a competition. To be driven by the need to prove yourself better than all of them.

That need had nearly gotten me eaten alive.

I wet my lips. I might still find myself eaten alive if I didn't keep this trio on track. "Whatever Richter's reasons, is there any real chance of bringing him to justice for the murder while he's in London? I don't have any authorization to pursue him—and all the evidence of the murder is back in Freising."

Sherlock waved his hand dismissively and resumed his pacing. "Richter has had his fingers in enough corrupt pies right here that there must be some angle we can use to solidify a case. Bring him in on a local charge, and then 'discover' his connection to your case and reach out to your department. Nothing simpler."

"Sure," Garrett said. "And where are you going to start this incredibly simple process?"

Sherlock cocked his head. "I'd like to have a look inside his private offices. The police may not have managed to get access, but I'm sure it can be arranged with the right approach." He smiled like he had when he'd talked about conning Cavalier's to get their member list.

I clasped my hands together on my lap with a nervous twitch. "Are you sure that would be worth the risk? He's apparently killed one man who messed with him already."

"I know how to handle myself," Sherlock said.

"It's not just him... It sounds like you're talking about breaking the law."

His breath came out in a faint huff. "I take the chances I need to. Obtaining the facts is more important than any emotional concepts of morality."

A man after my own heart—or rather, my mind.

Sherlock cast his gaze toward Garrett. "No need for you to worry about that aspect, of course—your participation won't be necessary."

Garrett took a gulp of his coffee, his fingers gripping the handle tight. "I'm not completely seeing why *you* should be participating that far." He glanced at me. "The murder happened hundreds of miles away. Why are we getting so wrapped up in solving this woman's case for her?"

"Garrett," John said in a pacifying tone, but Sherlock had already raised his chin imperiously.

"The situation goes far beyond Miss Moriarty's case. This man has gotten away with innumerable crimes, and we have a chance to shut him down once and for all. You of all people should be concerned with that. If your police force had conducted itself more effectively, he wouldn't have been walking around Freising ready to murder a man in the first place."

A flush flooded Garrett's face. He slammed his mug down on the table so hard a little of the liquid sloshed over the sides. Shoving his notepad into his pocket, he sprang to his feet.

"Then I'll check in with you when you're in a less needling mood," he said, and stalked toward the doorway.

He would have marched right through it if a filmy white figure hadn't flickered into sight at exactly that moment. My heart lurched as a prickle ran down the back of my neck from my contract mark. Garrett stopped dead, staring. He rubbed his eyes.

"What is it?" John said, looking over. Bog's form was already fading. I blinked, and the shrouded one was gone.

What the hell was it doing? The shrouded folk had laws about their interactions with human society. To appear before the unknowing…

"I just—it must have been a trick of the light," Garrett said. "I thought I saw a flash of something in the doorway." He shook himself and marched on out.

I willed myself to relax in my chair. *I'd* seen Bog in full clarity, but my senses were attuned to its kind. It hadn't fully manifested on this plane. Toeing the line without quite crossing it.

Reminding me that it was still watching me, and that it could interfere in certain ways if it wanted to.

Sherlock and John didn't appear to have noticed anything at all. Sherlock was eyeing *me.*

Shit. I hadn't been able to completely control my reaction. This called for some redirection. Thankfully, I had an obvious route to restore my grip on the conversation.

"Detective Lestrade is a little prickly, isn't he?" I said with a shaky laugh, as if it were his abrupt exit that had unsettled me.

"He's very committed to his job," John said diplomatically.

"He has a temper, but he always sees reason quickly enough," Sherlock said. He swept up his file folder. "Now, I have work to do. I'll keep you apprised of my progress, Miss Moriarty."

Dusk fell early in London at this time of year. As the sun sank below the tops of the buildings across the courtyard, I tugged my window open and slid the gauzy curtain across it. A gust of cool air washed over me, but I could tolerate that for the moment. I turned on my reading lamp and set it on the little table where it would be visible through the curtain.

While I waited, I worked through a couple rounds of push-ups, sit-ups, and lunges, and then shifted into practicing some of the combat sequences from my training. I didn't get into physical altercations very often, and you lost your precision if you let your practice slide. Besides, keeping the body fit invigorated the mind as well.

I was halfway through a set of jab-cross-hook combos when the curtain whispered. I continued through the motions, snapping out my right fist, swiveling on my left leg. My visitor approached with a shift in the air and a wisp of warmth over my skin.

"This elbow could stand to be a little higher, Majesty," Bash said in his low smooth voice. He tapped my arm, bringing with him the familiar scent of gun oil mingled with a light tang of musk. After seven years in my service, Sebastian Moran trusted that I knew when he'd arrived even if I didn't let on—and that I wouldn't break his nose with one of these fists in a startled reflex.

I made a face at the wry nickname, nudged my elbow up, and threw another punch. "Better?" I asked with an arch of my eyebrow.

"Perfect." Bash offered his usual subtle smile. He'd worn a black turtleneck and black jeans for his foray up the hotel wall, setting off his tan skin and light green eyes. A little scruff had accumulated on his jaw since I'd seen him last week, nearly as thick as the wiry black hair he kept cropped close to his skull.

I'd asked him once about his background, and he'd told me he was a bit of this and a bit of that. *A Venezuelan lady on one side, a Turk on the other, and my grandma insists that if you go back a few generations there was a Kenyan prince in the mix somewhere. It makes it easy to blend in wherever I want to go. Although in my experience, people usually choose to see me as whatever option gives them the most excuse to be an asshole.*

He'd said that last bit with a hint of a smirk. If Bash wanted to, he could make any person regret being an asshole before they could so much as blink.

When he was standing this close to me, a part of me wanted to lean into him, to drink in his scent right up against his solidly muscled chest. But I had no shortage of practice at leashing that urge and sending it off to its kennel. Only an idiot would ruin the formidable partnership Bash and I had with a tumble between the sheets. He was the only person in the world *I* trusted. I wanted to keep him standing right here beside me.

I threw myself into the combination again with a little more force.

"And though she be but little, she is fierce," Bash said dryly.

I snorted at the Shakespearean quote and his pretense at irony. I'd somehow found myself with a hitman who was a sucker for historical dramas, no matter how much he made fun of them.

He stepped back, and I let my body fall out of the fighting stance. His gaze traveled to the dresser beneath the TV. The corner of his mouth quirked up, but he didn't comment on the odd arrangement of cosmetics bottles, notepapers, and TV remote spread out across it. My little Fibonacci sequence. It wouldn't stop Bog from dropping in if the shrouded one really wanted to, but it worked as a casual deterrent.

"I checked in with your local forgers and the new auto ring," he said. "The latest payments should be arriving shortly."

"Perfect. And I got out some more funds for you." I reached for my purse. Bash accepted the wad of cash without a word and tucked it into his wallet. I sat down on the edge of the bed. "Are you settling into the new place all right?"

I wasn't sure he'd have complained even if he wasn't, but he definitely wouldn't say a peep if I didn't ask. I'd have set him up right here in the hotel if there wouldn't have been so much risk of one of the trio bumping into him at the wrong time.

"It's not bad." Bash glanced toward the window. "Heat, decent water pressure, a TV—that's about all I need. Now if only there was any place in London that could deliver a proper pizza."

I laughed. "You survived years in Afghanistan without your beloved New York-style slices—I think you'll make it through a few more weeks here."

"Only in intense agony," Bash said, completely deadpan. "Where are we at with your plans, Mori?"

That nickname I didn't mind at all. He'd started using it after a couple years of working together, saying that "Moriarty" was starting to feel ridiculously formal.

"Everything's moving along even faster than I'd hoped," I said. "They're investigating Richter's local crimes already. But the way Sherlock is, I'm sure the murder mystery will keep niggling at him. He's going to do some more digging into that chain of events sooner or later."

"I'll be ready for your alert, then."

I nodded. "Let's make sure he doesn't end up going down any roads I'd rather leave closed."

CHAPTER FIVE

Garrett

My fingers twisted over the notepad I was gripping, pulling the pen in a winding line that made a caricature of the woman sitting rigidly behind her desk between stacks of framed paintings. At this point, it seemed incredibly unlikely that I was going to get any information from her worth writing down. The smell of oil and varnish that hung in the art dealership's back room seeped farther into my lungs, and my stomach turned.

"I hope you understand that any additional insight you can provide may help us stop an on-going series of crimes that have affected far more than just this dealership," I said, leaning on guilt as a last-ditch effort. "What you tell us could protect so many more people in the future."

"I really can't think of anything I didn't tell the police during the original investigation," the woman said. "I'm so sorry."

She didn't sound sorry at all. I restrained a sigh and flipped my notepad closed. The officers who'd been on this case had been almost certain that Stefan Richter had extorted early looks at and insanely cheap prices on valuable new acquisitions. Unfortunately, with the original tip anonymous, the sales records of any transactions with Richter mysteriously missing, and everyone at the dealership all clammed up, my colleagues hadn't been able to push the investigation very far.

Either this woman really didn't know anything, or she was a lot more afraid of Richter than she was of injustice going unpunished.

"Thank you for your time," I said, and left the place with gritted teeth. I'd set off yesterday morning determined to find just *one* fresh lead in all of the cases the department had on file—to come to Sherlock holding the key that would bring the villain to his knees, just this once. I'd skipped a seminar on interrogation techniques that I'd been looking forward to so I could hit the streets. All I'd come away with after two days' work was a notepad full of doodles.

This was ridiculous. We'd known Jemma Moriarty for all of ten minutes before Sherlock had been chomping at the bit to take on her problems. Weren't there enough crimes in London that needed solving?

The problem was I couldn't keep up that indignation for very long before I admitted that what I'd said to the dealership woman, as Sherlock himself had pointed out, was true. Richter was a menace. Why had I worked my arse off rising through the ranks if I didn't rise to an occasion like this? We had to put him out of commission. It would feel so satisfying when we did, like one huge piece of the balance had tipped in the right direction.

I couldn't rewrite my past, but I could do real good now. Had it been so much to ask that I turned up something remotely useful toward accomplishing that today?

Evening was setting in outside under the dreary sky. If I legged it, I could be back at the hotel in time for dinner.

I flagged a taxi. As it wove through traffic to where I was standing on the curb, an elderly woman walked by with a little Yorkie on a leash.

My skin tightened. I stepped as close to the road as I felt I could without risking the toes of my shoes, giving them plenty of space to pass, and trained my attention on following the taxi's path. The click of the dog's nails against the concrete made my nerves itch. When the taxi reached me, I hopped into the backseat and yanked shut the door, away from memories I'd rather not have dredged up.

Back at the hotel, I hustled into the lobby and spotted a bunch of the conference goers heading to the dining room. Maybe some good food would spark the inspiration I needed.

John was at the buffet table when I reached it. He ladled some buttered baby potatoes onto his plate and glanced over at me. "How was your day?"

"Not particularly productive," I admitted. My mouth watered at the smell of the roast beef. I carved myself off a piece. "I suppose your partner has already tied the whole Richter thing up."

John knit his brow as he turned toward the white-clothed tables. "Far from it, actually. He's been in one of his dark moods since around lunch time. I let him skip that meal, but I told him I was going to cart him down here on a luggage trolley if he didn't come get some kind of nourishment into him."

Sherlock was stumped? A twinge of victory that really should have been beneath me shivered through my chest. Not that I'd been victorious in any way myself. *I'd* been stumped too.

I followed John's gaze to where our renowned consulting detective was sitting. His thin form loomed over the table, one elbow propped on the edge, while he prodded his plate noncommittally with his fork. Even if he hadn't been frowning, I'd have known he was in that mood from the atmosphere of melancholy that had come over his whole demeanor. Sherlock in a funk might as well have his own personal storm cloud casting a shadow on him wherever he went.

"He'll come out of it," John said with typical optimism. "He always does." His gaze twitched to the side. "Jemma! Why don't you join us?"

He waved the young officer over. Wonderful—now dinner would definitely revolve around her unresolved case. Although I supposed it probably would have anyway.

Jemma's plate was already full—a bit of meat, a bit of vegetables, and the rest offerings from the dessert table she was still perusing.

She snatched up a lemon tart to add to her collection and swept her bright red hair back behind one ear as she joined us.

"Are we having our own little conference again?" she asked with a soft smile she aimed at John. I wouldn't have thought she was all that pretty just to glance over her in a room, but with the confident way she moved and that clear measured voice, something about her shone a little brighter. If I hadn't known Sherlock disdained anything to do with romance, I'd have thought we'd ended up on this crusade because he had a crush.

I certainly wasn't going to catch one. Even if, as we headed to the table, my gaze couldn't help straying just for a moment to the subtle sway of her slim hips in her tastefully fitted slacks.

"It seems that way," John said to her. "Although I'm not sure how much any of us have to contribute beyond what we discussed yesterday. I'm no detective in my own right—I fully accept my role as sidekick."

He grinned at her, she laughed, and I tried not to resent his easy good-naturedness. I benefitted from it often enough myself.

Sherlock barely stirred from his glum lethargy as we sat down around him. His blue eyes were always cool, but when they got this distant, they were outright chilly. He seemed to be looking a long way away through the centerpiece.

Some generous impulse compelled me to say, "I didn't have any luck either. That Richter fellow has every part of the city he's touched under lockdown."

Sherlock's lips pursed. His gaze didn't lift.

Jemma glanced from me to him. "You haven't been able to find enough grounds to arrest him for anything?"

"Not on my end," I said. "I dug into every old case I could. They couldn't be any colder."

"There will be a way," Sherlock said slowly. He blinked, and his eyes started to clear. "The man can't be clever enough to sow so much turmoil and cover his tracks successfully everywhere. But he has made it quite difficult. I'm not sure how long I'd have to stay on his trail to find a misstep."

Jemma bit her lip with obvious disappointment. "I can't ask you to put your other responsibilities aside to keep after him."

"Of course not." Sherlock tapped the tabletop, his energy coming back to him. "The answer is obvious. We follow the trail that's still warm—the murder he just committed. It may require some careful maneuvering of questions of jurisdiction and so forth, but we'll have our man much faster that way."

"Oh," Jemma said. "If you think that's our best option."

She wasn't fawning over him in adoring gratitude like the consulting detective's many professional fans tended to. Maybe I should cut her more slack—we'd come to her, after all.

On the other hand, who wouldn't jump for joy to have Sherlock Holmes personally investigating on their behalf?

I watched her as Sherlock poked at his already mangled green beans. "I think it's by far our best chance of putting him away for close to as long as he deserves," he said.

The smile she gave him looked genuine. "In that case, I can't thank you enough." She reached out and touched John's wrist where he was sitting next to Sherlock. "It means a lot to me that you'd both put your minds to this case."

Did John ease his arm a little closer to hers as he beamed back at her? Was it a little coy, the way she lowered her eyelids under his gaze?

Which one of us had been out there pounding the streets for her the last two days?

"I'll stay on the case too," I found myself blurting out. "I can get in touch with your local department over in Germany, see about setting up an exchange of information, and work through some of those jurisdiction concerns. Tomorrow, when they're out of bed."

"Of course," Jemma said. "I can get you their number. I have a card on me..." She opened her purse.

"That's all right," I said. "We've got a database at the department with the best contacts for international coordination."

"Right, of course you do." Jemma shook her head ruefully. "Maybe it would be helpful if I initiated the call?"

There was nothing about her tone or her expression that I could have pinpointed as disconcerting. All the same, while I knew I didn't have the same talent for quick analysis that Sherlock did, the impression prickled over me that for whatever reason, Jemma Moriarty was uneasy about me contacting her colleagues on my own.

Strange. Maybe I was reading too much into the exchange because I'd already been frustrated with how involved we'd gotten in her work. But my instincts had served me well before.

"I don't think that's necessary," I said. "It might even go over better for them to hear directly from us from the start, to reassure them that we're fully on board." Or, at least, that I was. I'd have to find out tomorrow what the chief was going to say about this.

Jemma leaned toward me, her distinctive gray eyes more intent than they'd been a moment ago. "You'll have a better idea than I do. I don't want you to think I'm ungrateful for the efforts you've already made, Garrett. Thank you so much for your dedication in following up on all those old cases—I know it must have been tedious. I never meant to derail anyone's plans by bringing that file here with me."

Under her gaze, with her that little bit closer to me, a flicker of heat raced over my skin. I couldn't deny that she cared a lot about the case, poring over it even during what should have been an escape from her regular work. Maybe she'd gotten the invitation to this conference thanks to her close-to-Sherlockian brilliance, but she had a sense of commitment I couldn't say very many of my colleagues in Scotland Yard shared.

I swallowed thickly. "We volunteered to pitch in. The man needs to be caught. I'm happy to contribute to the cause."

How true was that last comment? I couldn't have said. In that moment, I was happy to have her looking at me with so much appreciation... and possibly something more than that?

I tugged my gaze away and gave myself a mental smack upside the head. *Sherlock* would never have been distracted by a striking pair of eyes. I speared a piece of roast beef for something to do. My thoughts returned to the odd impression I'd had about her reaction.

"So, how long have you worked with the Freising police, Firecracker?" I asked, keeping my tone casual. We'd barely asked her anything about herself so far. Although maybe Sherlock had already catalogued her entire life history from the shape of her fingernails and the angle at which she tipped her head, so he hadn't felt the need to.

Jemma answered easily enough. "Coming up on three years — since I finished school. I've been based in Germany for five years altogether."

"And before that?"

She shrugged, swirling a chuck of potato in a pool of melted butter. "A little while here in the UK, in various parts of America, Portugal, Thailand, New Zealand... I've gotten around. My parents were roamers. I expect at some point I'll get restless and continue the tradition. It's useful having picked up the different languages and so on."

Being born and bred in London, I had trouble imagining a life that chaotic. How did you ever feel at home? Jemma didn't look fazed, though, and that hardly seemed like an appropriate question to ask a woman I was only just getting to know.

Before I could decide on a different angle from which to prod her, she glanced around the table. "I'm curious about the three of you. You seem to work together so well. How did you end up collaborating like this?"

"I found myself in London a couple years back, after my stint in the army ended for obvious reasons." John motioned to his leg. "I couldn't afford a place of my own, and a friend of mine knew this lunatic who was constantly over at the university experimenting with everything from poisons to bruising but who happened to need a roommate..." He raised his eyebrows at Sherlock.

"Oh, dear," Jemma said with a grin, brushing her fingers against his forearm again. "I suppose we should be glad you're still here and not dissected."

"I assure you, I have never dissected anyone who wasn't already dead," Sherlock said, straight-faced. "John proved a decent living companion and an excellent partner in the field. I can achieve a lot on my own, but I can't be everywhere, and some gambits are better pulled off with company."

I jumped in before they could continue their mutual adoration fest. "Sherlock has been offering Scotland Yard help with difficult cases for a few years. He… occasionally rubs some of the detectives the wrong way. He and I found we could cooperate without my wanting to strangle him—at least not very often. So, the commissioner often pairs us up."

"Garrett is the best of the lot over there," Sherlock said. "The police force truly is in a sorry state."

That was a backhanded compliment if I ever heard one. But Jemma was shaking her head at Sherlock and turning back to me. "Investigating can be a lot more difficult with the sorts of red tape we have to deal with. You must have quite the success rate with your own cases, or you wouldn't be here."

She wasn't even touching me, her hand lingering over the handle of her knife. I couldn't have called the blouse and slacks she was wearing anything but modest. So, why was my attention drawn more than before to the subtle curves beneath those clothes, to the fullness of her lips?

It'd been too long since I'd last had a shag, clearly.

I had to just ignore those impulses. And at the same time I desperately wanted to stop her from shifting her attention away from me again.

A couple of officers from one of the other tables sidled over, their hands twisted nervously in front of them. "Mr. Holmes?" the man said. "It's amazing to meet you in person. I've followed all of Dr. Watson's accounts of your investigations."

"They should have *you* giving all the talks here," the woman gushed. "Would you—is it too silly to ask you to autograph our program booklets?"

"I suppose I might as well," Sherlock said, bemused. As he brought pen to paper without a word of thanks for their compliments, John gave Jemma a nudge and rolled his eyes in mock exasperation.

"Poor you," she said, looking at him through her eyelashes. "The permanent bridesmaid?"

John chuckled, his face bright as he gazed back at her, and my stomach twisted the way it had right before I'd slammed my coffee mug on the table yesterday morning. Like a fool.

"Well," Sherlock said when his admirers had wandered off, "should we convene to discuss our next steps somewhere more private? Garrett, your room is the closest."

"It is," I agreed before I could think about whether I was being foolish now. "Why not? Let's go back to mine."

CHAPTER SIX

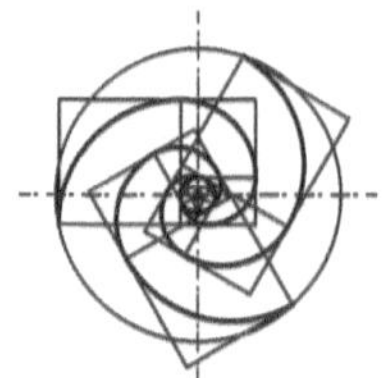

Jemma

After the four of us had talked for a while in Garrett's room, I'd flopped down on my back at the foot of the bed—not in a provocative pose, just as if the change in position and view might jog some new ideas loose. But when I propped myself up on one elbow as the conversation wound down, John's gaze lingered on the slope of my body for long enough to tell me the evening had been a success.

"All right then," the doctor said. "I'll see if there's anyone I know in the Munich area who could weigh in, and I guess we can make a final decision about how to proceed after we've slept on it." He stifled a yawn, his fingers clenching the handle of his walking stick a little tighter than usual. Even his grin looked a bit weary, though it was barely ten at night.

I knew from the medical records I'd dug up that he'd left his military service with more than just a limp. The infection he'd gotten while recovering from his initial wounds had left his whole body weakened. This was the first sign of that larger infirmity I'd seen in person. He held himself together rather well.

"Until tomorrow," Sherlock said in his lofty way, as if he thought he might have the whole case tied up by then. *His* gaze didn't linger on me at all, but I hadn't expected it to. He was above emotion, after all.

Imagine what I might find beneath that cool exterior if I managed to wake up a feeling or two.

That wasn't tonight's plan, though, as appealing as the idea was. As the two men left, I pushed myself upright and rolled my shoulders. Garrett glanced over at me with a flash of hunger in his eyes.

It didn't take much to generate that kind of reaction if you knew how to handle yourself. The slightest arch of my back, the angle of my face, the way I trailed my fingers here or there—I could have been dressed like a nun and still brought lust into a man's mind when I wanted to. Both John and Garrett were aware of me as a woman now in ways they hadn't quite been before. And I'd made sure Garrett had noticed John's awareness as much as his own.

I didn't think the detective inspector wanted to come in second place yet again.

Now that taking Richter down for his past crimes was off the table, I had to shift focus from the short con I'd hoped for to the long con I'd prepared. All three of the trio had to be totally invested if I was going to pull this off. Garrett appeared to be the best place to start, especially since I had another ruse I needed to carry out here.

"I suppose I should get going too," I said, standing up. To stay in the game, I was going to have to engage his sympathies as well as his desires. Not the easiest maneuver when he still seemed wary about the three of them being involved in my affairs at all.

I ambled toward the door and paused as if grappling with the question. "When do you think you'll put that call in to Freising?" I asked without quite meeting his eyes.

"First thing in the morning, I was planning," Garrett said.

I nodded stiffly, and that was enough, now that we were alone, to prompt the question he'd really wanted to ask.

He closed the notepad he'd been alternately scrawling and sketching in. "You don't like the idea of me talking to them, do you?"

I jerked around to face him. "Why would you say that?"

He tipped his head toward me. "Because you reacted like that to me saying it, Firecracker. Because you seem nervous about the subject every time it's come up." He folded his arms over his lean chest, drawing himself up a little taller. "What's going on?"

The woman he thought I was wouldn't give in that easily. My mouth twisted. "I don't know what you're talking about."

"You're hiding something. Don't you think it's going to come out, and sooner rather than later? Do you really think *Sherlock* won't figure out the whole story in five seconds flat?"

That last sentence held a touch of bitterness. Oh, yes, this man's competitive streak and the insecurities that fed it ran deep.

I stiffened as if the possibility hadn't occurred to me before and then sank into the chair at the desk, dropping my face into my hands. "It's nothing he'd even be concerned about. It's just embarrassing. It won't affect how you handle the case—I can promise you that."

"I'd be a lot more willing to believe that if you'd say what the problem is," Garrett said.

I took a deep breath and let my mind slip back to old childhood memories. All the jockeying for favor, the glares and the vicious sabotage, the desperation that had wrenched through me on the rare occasions I'd faltered and met my parents' glowers of disappointment. The fear that I'd also let down my little sister who couldn't quite keep up. The looming presence of the shrouded folk always watching, judging. Those tangled, fraught emotions prickled up to color my voice.

"It's been kind of tense at the department. I was at the top of my class, and I got a good position right out of the gate. A lot of the other officers resent that, I think. They hassle me and make sure the hardest cases end up on my desk. I work twice as hard as anyone there just to make sure I don't look like I'm falling behind."

"Go on," Garrett said—firmly but softer.

I let my head dip lower. "This case, the murder—I totally botched it. I ran down a lead I thought was good, and it went nowhere, and then the trail was getting cold. I couldn't get a foothold anywhere else… Everyone there has been sneering at me like I'm a failure, mocking the fact that I was picked for this conference, taking potshots at me every chance they get."

"That's ridiculous. No one solves every case."

"I was so sure with this one, though. I can handle the potshots. I'll survive. But I know when you call and tell them you're picking up the case, they're going to assume I went running to Scotland Yard to beg for help, and even my boss is going to lose all respect for me."

I tightened my voice on the last sentence, mastering the emotions I'd let leak out. When I raised my eyes, Garrett was staring at me. His jaw twitched as he grappled with the emotions my "confession" had stirred in him.

"I suppose I'm being as pathetic as they'd think I am if I let my worries affect how you handle the case," I said. "Forget I said anything. It's my problem to deal with. I'm sorry you had to listen to all that."

I got up from the chair and made for the door again, but Garrett reached for my arm.

"Hey." He eased me back around to face him. Whatever else he'd been feeling, compassion had won. It shone in his dark brown eyes, even if the rest of his expression had stayed tense.

"You don't have to apologize," he said. "I know what it's like to feel that no matter what you do, you can't quite earn the respect you want. I rose in the ranks quickly like you did, and it's a lot of weight knowing everyone's watching for proof that you didn't deserve the things you worked so hard for. Of course you're nervous. I'm sorry I pushed you into talking about it."

I gave him a pained smile. "Well, maybe it's better that you know. That way you won't be surprised about the attitude they might have about me when you call."

Garrett's fingers adjusted against my arm, but he didn't let go. The warmth of his hand bled through the thin cotton of my blouse. "What if... What if I didn't mention you at all?" he said. "Richter came here. We have every reason to be keeping an eye on him regardless. I can simply say that we heard about the murder and noticed that the timing of his visit to your area matched up, and we'd like to investigate further on our end."

My body relaxed. "That—that would be such a relief." Especially because if he did happen to mention an Officer Moriarty to any of the actual police in Freising, they'd have no clue who he was talking about. Bash had been meant to handle that call if it happened, but since Garrett had thwarted my earlier attempts to control the direction of the call, this was the most elegant possible solution. And he thought it was his idea.

He might not even have minded the deception if he'd known he was actually protecting me from a fate worse than death.

"It's easy enough," Garrett said with a rare smile. "Why should I let them think you came running to us when really it's that Sherlock badgered you into letting us on the case?"

"There is that too," I said, and laughed.

Garrett laughed too, looking more at ease in that moment than I'd ever seen him. He really was a rather good-looking man when he wasn't scowling or narrowing his eyes in skepticism. Which meant tonight's finale might be particularly enjoyable.

It was too bad the trio hadn't found a way to get Richter locked up quickly on some unrelated charge. That would have made saving my life so much easier. Now, to see the larger plan through, they were going to have to cross a lot more lines than a little play-acting in a gentleman's club. They were going to have to *want* to.

And the simplest way to get them invested in my case was to get them invested in *me*.

"Thank you," I said softly. "Really. You're a good man." I leaned in and brushed a kiss to his cheek.

As I eased back, Garrett swallowed audibly. I wet my lips, holding his gaze, as clear a come-on as I could make after the subtle tension I'd spent all evening building without outright jumping his bones. But he stayed where he was, frozen, his mouth slanting with indecision.

All right. There were ways I could make the decision even simpler for him.

I slipped my arm from his grasp and gave him a regretful smile. "It seems like I really should go. I'll drop in on John on my way up and see if he's gotten anywhere with his possible local connections."

I said John's name with an affectionate lilt, and a possessive spark lit in Garrett's eyes. He caught my arm again with a sudden intensity that set off a flare of heat right through me.

"You don't have to leave," he said in a low hoarse voice, and tugged me into a kiss.

He tasted like the sweet brandy John had passed around while we'd brainstormed, his mouth hot enough to burn. I slipped my arm around his neck and kissed him back hard, not wanting to leave any doubt that I was completely on board with wherever he wanted to take this next.

My body swayed against his. With a rough sound, he turned us and lifted me onto the desk, never breaking the kiss. My legs splayed around his hips. I gave myself over to the pulse of need spreading from my core.

It was the best kind of ploy, really. I got one step closer to freeing my soul and ridding the world of a much greater evil than I could ever claim to be. He got to feel he'd won the prize. We both got our rocks off, well. Wins all around.

Our mouths crashed even more urgently together. Garrett tangled his fingers in my hair, his other hand stroking up and down my side over my blouse. His scent filled my nose, as singeing sharp as a live wire.

Mmm, I liked that.

I scooted closer on the desk, bringing my body completely in line with his, shivering eagerly at the feel of him already hard behind the zipper of his slacks. Garrett let out a choked sort of groan and eased back from the kiss, but when I raised my chin to offer him access to my neck, he couldn't resist. He pressed his mouth to the sensitive skin along my throat. The flick of his hot tongue brought a pleased sigh to my lips.

"So you do have it in you after all," I murmured.

His mouth trailed down to my collarbone. His hand was working its way up under my blouse, stroking bare skin now. A shaky breath spilled over my flesh. "I don't normally think it's a good idea to mix work with—with, ah—"

"Pleasure?" I ran my fingertips down his chest, tracing the taut muscles there. "I find it's good to burn off the tensions of the job every now and then if I can find the right partner. Which isn't always easy, I'll admit. I was starting to think you weren't game."

He captured my mouth again, kissing me so intently and thoroughly that I lost my breath despite myself. Maybe he was aiming to top every man who'd ever kissed me before. I wasn't going to argue with that ambition.

"Are you convinced now?" he muttered against my skin. At the same moment, he unhooked my bra. As his hand cupped my breast, his thumb swiveling over the nipple, I leaned into his touch.

"I wouldn't mind if you convinced me a whole lot more."

He let out a ragged laugh and resumed his plunder of my mouth. I rocked against him, wanting even more than this.

Garrett took the hint. He tipped my head back, his tongue tangling with mine, and fingered the clasp on my dress pants until he'd dislodged it. I lifted my hips, he jerked, and my slacks slipped off to pool on the floor.

He pressed his fingers to my panties, but not to dislodge them yet. A hungry rumble escaped him at the dampness already forming there. He teased his thumb over my clit and down to my opening, forcing a whimper out of me.

I grasped the front of his slacks and popped the button free. At the yank of the zipper, he tore his lips from mine just for a second. "Do you have — ?"

"My purse." I reached for the bag where I'd dropped it on the desk beside me and fished out a foil packet.

There'd been men in the past who'd balked for a second at how readily I'd produced protection, who'd even sneered a bit. Garrett didn't so much as blink. With a few tugs of fabric, my panties were dangling from one ankle and his pants and boxers were at his feet. He sheathed himself in an instant. I arched toward him, and he plunged into me with a blissful groan.

And then he stayed there. Balls deep inside me, he eased his head back just far enough to meet my eyes. A strange tenderness had come over his face. My gut twisted.

That kind of look didn't have any place here. There was nothing like a hint of sappiness to ruin the mood.

I tilted forward, bringing my lips to his ear. "Fuck me," I said. "Fuck me until I can't see straight."

He exhaled with a stutter and started thrusting, harder and faster as I bucked to meet him. Oh, yes, this was what I needed. His thumb worked over my stiffened nipple, and his mouth crashed against mine, and for a few fleeting minutes everything in the world fell away except the swell of ecstasy building between my thighs.

He was awfully good at the whole fucking thing. Maybe we'd get the chance to take a second spin at it.

The pleasure sang through my nerves. I dug my fingers into Garrett's muscled back as my vision blurred. Then the searing sensation burst with a blissful shudder.

As I clenched around Garrett, he groaned and pounded into me a few more times. His breath hitched out of him as he came. I touched his cheek and drew him in for one more kiss.

Mine, I thought as my lips branded his. *From now until I'm done here, you're mine.*

CHAPTER SEVEN

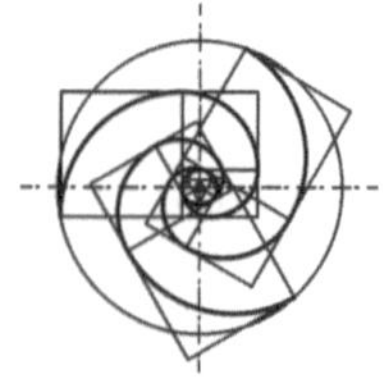

Jemma

The smell dragged me out of sleep—a parched scent carrying a taint of sickly decay, like bones flecked with flesh so ancient it'd rotted right into dust. I opened my eyes with the side of my face still burrowed into the pillow.

Bog's depthless mist of a face was hovering beside the bed just a few feet away. My pulse lurched. If I'd been anyone other than Jemma Moriarty, I would have screamed. As it was, I had to clamp my jaw tight.

The shrouded one would probably have liked it if I'd screamed. There wasn't any good reason for Bog to be lurking around watching me sleep.

I pushed myself upright in the hotel bed—my own, since staying in Garrett's would have skewed the feelings I was encouraging him to develop too far in the wrong direction. "Good morning to you too, Bog," I said flatly. "Get a good eyeful of my bedhead?" I fluffed my rumpled hair and resisted the urge to scratch at the mark on the back of my neck, which was itching at the shrouded one's presence.

Bog shifted. The floating swaths of white that shrouded it stirred as if in an underwater current. "In case you were starting to forget," it said in its husk of a voice. "Twenty-six days."

"Thank you so much for the reminder."

The shrouded one didn't answer, just faded from sight, leaving only that repulsive smell. I rubbed my nose. It was hard to imagine that I'd lived fourteen years immersed in the stink of the shrouded folk, barely noticing it.

The human body could adapt to an awful lot.

So much for my Fibonacci deterrent. I fiddled with the papers and bottles and added a handful of spare change to the sequence on the dresser, but who was I kidding? Bog had waited ten years to claim his reward. He was chomping at the bit to gobble me up. A little discomfort wasn't going to hold him back from his gloating.

Laying out the pattern did make me feel a little more in control, though, so I finished tweaking it anyway. Then I dug a sugar cube out of the baggie I kept in my purse and sucked on its clarifying sweetness while I got dressed.

Alerts on one of my phones informed me that the payments Bash had mentioned had gone through. Good—I wouldn't have to send him to crack any heads. My business was simple: I gave select criminal collectives a leg up with the insight and connections I'd cultivated over the years, helped keep the cops off their back as need be, and in thanks they passed on a nice percentage of their earnings. The arrangement worked out well for both sides as long as they held up their end.

Breakfast beckoned. Because Bog had woken me up earlier than usual, I was already through two cinnamon buns and one cup of coffee when my trio drifted into the dining room.

Sherlock came first, with an energetic stride and a brisk nod to me, emanating the air of a man about to get things done. As he shoveled eggs and ham onto his plate to join his toast, John ambled over and filled a bowl with cereal. They fell into step together as they approached my table, John grinning and giving his walking stick a quick flourish when he saw me watching. If yesterday's work had run him down, he appeared to have fully recovered.

The sweetness of the pastries lingered in my mouth. I smiled at both of them with nothing but genuine good will in my heart for that brief moment.

Garrett hustled in a minute later. His shoulders were already a little high, but they twitched up even more the second he glanced toward the table the three of us were sharing. I pretended to be absorbed in the last bite of my cinnamon bun so he wouldn't feel any need to make an immediate gesture of acknowledgement.

As he moved along the buffet, he appeared to get control of himself. He sauntered over to join us with a casual bob of his head and only the faintest flush in his cheeks. With extreme care, he didn't let his gaze linger on me any longer than on my companions.

"Good morning," he said evenly, and busied himself with his hash browns.

I licked sugar glaze off my fingers, suppressing my amusement. I'd had a feeling Garrett Lestrade was the type to get awkward the morning after. Did he think his colleagues would be able to sense what had happened between us? Was he afraid he'd overstepped some unspoken boundary?

It actually was somewhat possible that Sherlock would deduce what we'd gotten up to after he and John had left last night. He studied Garrett as the shorter man gulped his coffee. I didn't imagine he'd be particularly disturbed by that development, but Garrett might be by him knowing. The easiest way to redirect the one detective and reassure the other was to leap back into the case as if nothing at all had changed.

"Any responses to last night's inquiries?" I asked the table at large.

Of course, Sherlock was the one with a ready answer. "A contact of mine confirmed that Richter left by plane on the night of the murder from a private airfield near Freising, with a few crates of artistic artifacts as cargo. It seems he likes to show off his collection. He arranged an exhibit of the more valuable historic pieces in a gallery in Munich, like the one he's set up here in London."

Oh, excellent. I'd carefully nudged Sherlock toward that angle last night with an off-hand comment here and there.

"Were there any witnesses who could vouch for what time he got to the airfield and when the plane left?" I asked.

"I believe so," Sherlock said. "Richter has a manager who handles most of the logistics for his showings. It appears they both normally travel alongside the art when it's transported."

"You have the whole case wrapped up already, don't you?" Garrett said, but his tone was more wry than bitter. He was still avoiding looking too long in my direction, but perhaps the fun we'd had last night had loosened him up all the same now that he could see I wasn't going to make a big thing of it.

"The course of justice is rarely so smooth," Sherlock said, flexing his lithe hands. He sounded as if he enjoyed the prospect of a longer chase now that he felt he was on the right trail. "To speak to this manager, I need to track the man down, and he keeps himself rather incognito. But I managed to procure a photograph, and my Irregulars are on the look-out. I'd be surprised if they don't locate him before the end of the day."

"Irregulars?" I said.

John motioned to Sherlock with an amused look. "He's got a squad of delinquent youth who are happy to be his eyes and ears for a couple tenners when he needs them. The kinds of people we're often tracking down might dodge us, but they aren't so cautious around a kid shooting hoops or rambling around the streets."

"Over time I've narrowed them down to quite an effective force," Sherlock added.

Garrett glanced up at the ceiling. "I'm definitely not hearing any of this."

No, I supposed Scotland Yard might not approve of paying off street kids to act as unofficial informants. I'd gleaned some hints of that practice in my prep work, but I hadn't realized how organized Sherlock was in his marshalling of the resource. It really was a brilliant strategy, I'd give him that. And useful to know for my various other business endeavors.

Sherlock leaned his elbows onto the table. "In the meantime, I'll delve further into Richter's other recent dealings. Who knows what fruit that will bear?" A delighted smile crossed his face at the prospect.

"How historic are the artifacts he includes in his exhibit?" I asked. Best if Sherlock kept the art aspect at the front of his mind. "Does he even have the right to own all of them?"

"I'd bet he acquired some of those through questionable methods," Garrett put in. "He just always produces convincing enough papers if anyone questions him. We won't get far with that angle if no one involved in the acquisition is willing to talk."

Sherlock waved his fork in the air, his eyes lit with enthusiasm. "It's disappointing, really, that collectors focus on the aesthetic side of history when the antiquities are rife with real innovations. Take the Rama Empire, for example—when do they get credit for their civil engineering that in many ways puts our own to shame? Perfectly ordered roads, and plumbing all through every building. Do you know, there are archeologists who claim they had no concept of social class?"

He chattered on in a smooth and lively tone, the total opposite of the distant sullen mood I'd first found him in at dinner last night. The great Sherlock Holmes was a study in contrasts. Who would have thought he'd have read up on obscure ancient civilizations? I supposed he absorbed whatever struck his fancy—and once absorbed, facts stuck in that mind of his forever.

Imagine how quickly we could have conquered everything ahead of us working together if we really had the same goals. Instead I had to guide the knife of his mind indirectly, always a hair away from slicing my own fingers off.

John nodded along and interjected a question now and then to encourage his friend onward. A person would have had to be blind not to see the admiration that practically shone off him as he watched Sherlock. I almost wondered if it was more than admiration. Not that I'd seen any reason to believe the two had a more intimate relationship… but that didn't mean the desire wasn't there, admitted or not. For all his brilliance, I didn't think Sherlock had picked up on *that*.

A rising murmur in the dining room broke through Sherlock's

sparkling commentary. He trailed off at the same moment as I glanced around. The people at the tables around us were peering up over our heads with puzzled expressions that ranged between awed and frightened. I jerked my gaze upward.

Fucking hell. The light between the two fixtures on either side of us was flowing in a stream across the ceiling like a strip of cloth blown by the wind. Like several strips, actually, weaving together and fraying apart with an eerie shuddering. My skin crawled at the sight, and I at least knew where it came from. The mark on my neck pinched.

Stalking me in my sleep hadn't been enough for Bog this morning. The shrouded one had decided to put on a light show for the whole conference.

My trio was staring up at the display too, Garrett paling, John wide-eyed, Sherlock frowning. The last thing I needed was them wondering whether their new colleague had brought some sort of unearthly influence down on them.

A ghost of an impression whispered through my nerves, taking me back to the wrenching moment of pure icy panic when I'd discovered where all my childhood ambitions had been leading me and where they'd lead my sister too if I couldn't find a way out. When I'd seen that our parents and all the other adults in the cult of the shrouded folk were whipping us toward earning not some exhilarating honor but our deaths. We were sacrificial lambs vying for the slaughter.

It'd felt as if my whole life were slipping from my fingers too fast for me to catch it—but I had caught it. I'd bent circumstances to my control, and I'd kept doing that, over and over, to get to this moment right now. The shrouded folk might have won more than I could ever accept, but they'd lose in the end.

I clamped down on the panicked sensation with an iron grip. "It's ridiculous, isn't it?" I said, aiming for the dismissive attitude I'd seen Sherlock take on more than once. "The electrical systems act up for a minute, and the whole room devolves into a tizzy. The greatest analytical minds in the world, huh?"

"Indeed." Sherlock looked a bit distracted, but he drew his gaze away with a shake of his head. "The undisciplined human mind does love to leap to fantastical assumptions about the most mundane phenomena." His gaze fell on me for a moment as if considering my expression. I kept it as bland as possible.

To my relief, the light show was petering out as if to support my dismissal. Bog was *really* pushing the limits creating an effect that visible.

The shrouded one knew I was up to something. It *hated* the thought that I might slip from its grasp after all the time spent waiting, after the wrath it'd risked making the deal with me in the first place. So now Bog was pulling out all the stops to throw me off.

Too bad for it I was already three steps ahead.

My pulse beat a little faster as I caught John's eye across the table. He shot me a smile. "Apparently we needed some more excitement around here. The organizers should consider fireworks next year."

Or we could make a few of our own. I smiled back, grazing my fingers over my cheek.

John Watson might already be hooked on Sherlock, but I intended to hook him too. And after that little display, I meant to lock him down fast.

CHAPTER EIGHT

John

I'd had to accept, living and working with Sherlock, that he only revealed his plan and prep-work on a need to know basis. Unless he was fully confident that he was on the right track and that sharing the information wouldn't jeopardize his mission, even I wouldn't hear a peep.

I suspected he also enjoyed seeing the looks on people's faces when he unraveled an entire scheme with one grand flourish.

In any case, he hadn't needed me for whatever he was up to this morning, so I figured I might as well make the most of the conference we'd meant to attend. I was studying the schedule in the program booklet when an unassuming fellow with dark dreadlocks and startlingly blue eyes stopped beside me. He cleared his throat apologetically.

"Could you point me in the direction of Banquet Room B, mate?" he said with a mild Australian accent. "I seem to keep getting turned around."

"Let me have a look." I flipped to the map and tapped the right spot. "I was in there for a talk a couple days ago. It's just down this hall here and to your left around the corner."

"Thank you so much! I don't want to miss a word of Dr. Tanaka's talk—she's always leaps and bounds ahead of the rest when it comes to anything DNA."

He saluted me and loped off down the hall. I watched him go and grabbed my walking stick from where I'd leaned it against the wall. The bodily side of forensics was the one area where I could occasionally offer more insight than Sherlock. With a recommendation like that, how could I skip this talk?

Plenty of other attendees had felt the same way. When I reached the hall, one minute before the presentation was due to start, it took me a moment to spot an open seat in the rows of chairs. My gaze snagged on a now-familiar fall of ruddy hair halfway down. Jemma had decided to sit in on this session too—and no one had claimed the seat at the end of the row next to her.

I hustled over just fast enough to provoke a faint twinge in my hip and sank into the chair. "Brushing up on the forensic sciences too?" I said teasingly. "Are you working toward the day when you can run circles around even Sherlock?"

Jemma laughed. "I'm not quite that ambitious. But it seems to me I'm better off filling in the gaps in my knowledge than listening to people explain what I already know."

I wondered if she realized what a Sherlockian thing that was to say. My heart beat a little faster just sitting next to her, for reasons I didn't see any need to examine too closely. She was a pretty woman. She was an intelligent woman. There'd have been something wrong with me if I hadn't felt a brief crackle of attraction.

I might have asked more about what experience she did have on the forensic side, limited or no, but our speaker stepped up to the podium.

The Australian fellow hadn't steered me wrong. Dr. Tanaka breezed through several recent developments in DNA collection and testing—most of which I hadn't understood in a great deal of depth and a couple of which I hadn't been aware of at all—with crisp enthusiasm and a knack for translating the concepts into laymen's terms. The non-experts in the crowd should have been able to follow along without any trouble.

Jemma leaned forward, watching the doctor avidly. She wasn't taking notes like many of the attendees around us, but I had the feeling that sharp mind of hers was absorbing everything.

Sherlock didn't like to take notes either. He said it distracted from really hearing what a person was saying, with both their words and their behavior.

My memory wasn't quite on par with his, so when Dr. Tanaka launched into her top tips for officers on the scene, I jotted those down in my case journal. Anything I could contribute to wrapping up our cases faster, *I* wanted to absorb.

I left the seminar with Jemma a little lighter on my feet, eager to put the new techniques to the test. Too bad in our current case the victim and all available concrete evidence lay hundreds of miles away.

"That was inspiring, wasn't it?" Jemma said. "The intersection of science and policing—it's getting harder for criminals to cover their tracks all the time."

"Yes!" I said with a grin. "And it gives medical professionals a way to be useful on the crime-solving side of things. Although I can't see the kind of detective work Sherlock and Garrett do ever becoming less valuable."

"Oh, definitely not. After all, finding the right source to test in the first place is such a key factor. There was this one case, while I was still in training…" She paused with a rueful smile. "Never mind. You don't want to hear me ramble on about my minor victories as a cadet."

"Ramble away." I waved my walking stick at her encouragingly. Sherlock could be rather intimidating, especially when you weren't used to his attitudes and moods. The last thing I wanted was for Jemma to feel diminished by the time she'd spent around us. "You were already closer to being professional law enforcement back then than I am right now, so I'm hardly anyone to judge."

"Oh, well—we were investigating a murder with a few possible suspects but no clear evidence in any of the usual places. I happened to notice one guy had a fresh looking mud stain on the golf shoes he'd tucked away by the back door. It hadn't rained for days before the night of the murder, and he hadn't mentioned golfing in his account of where he'd been around the time of the crime. The senior officers thought I was bonkers, but they took the shoes in, and even though he'd tried to wash them, they found traces of the victim's blood in the cleats."

"Well done!" I said, clapping my hands. "There you go. You were running circles around those officers even then."

"I just follow what makes sense to me," Jemma said with a shrug, her cheeks slightly pink from the praise. "It doesn't seem all that extraordinary when I'm thinking about it."

Did she not see how extraordinary *she* was? My God.

"You know, I wasn't exaggerating comparing you to Sherlock," I said. "I never thought I'd meet anyone who came close to his analytical abilities, but here you are. He sees it too—that's the whole reason he wanted to approach you."

Jemma's mouth twitched into a smile. "And now I've given him a perfectly complicated case to relieve him of his boredom. I hope it won't be too much of a let-down when he solves it. I get the impression it's not going to take him long."

"You didn't have that one bit of key information. How could you be expected to have memorized every bit of architecture in London?" I shook my head.

She had the same crystalline intelligence Sherlock did, sharp as a scalpel, but with a much more charming disposition. I'd never fault my friend his moods—he could hardly help them—but he could be pretty callous without realizing it. Jemma obviously had more sensitivity to her than that.

In a few moments now and then, when I'd seen her standing apart from our group, I thought I'd caught a bit of sadness in her expression. I'd be willing to bet that she'd had a painful loss in her life, either recently or major or both. The impression resonated with my own various losses, even though most of them were long healed over.

We drifted down the hall, other conference attendees streaming past us in more of a hurry. I wasn't sure what sessions were running now, but having Jemma to myself for the first time, I couldn't think of anything I'd rather do than chat with her at least a little longer.

She swept her hair back over her shoulder in a careless gesture, and my gaze followed the graze of her fingers across the pale skin at the edge of her shirt's neckline. Interest stirred in other parts of me. No, it wasn't just her mind I found appealing. Who could blame me?

"You and Sherlock are very close, aren't you?" she said. "You seem rather attached at the hip."

"A fair observation." I rubbed my mouth, the question pricking at me despite the lightness of her tone. "It means a lot to me that he trusts me so much as a friend and colleague. He gave me a new life when I was starved for direction, you know. I was a surgeon, and now I can't trust my body to stay as steady as it'd need to be for that kind of work... This way I can still save lives by applying my knowledge from a different angle."

It would have been hard to put into words my gloomy state fresh off of my tour of duty—my body even weaker than it was now, the work I loved torn from me—or how collaborating with Sherlock had shone a light through that darkness. I wasn't sure I'd have wanted to express all that to Jemma anyway. I wasn't exactly proud of my first few useless months in London.

"I can see how he'd inspire devotion," she said.

"Well, I'm not sure I'd call it that, but—loyalty, certainly." I hesitated and decided I might as well mention this little fact and see what she made of it. I could determine in an instant whether there was any point in indulging the sparks I'd felt. "Not everyone understands our partnership. I had to break it off with a girlfriend I quite liked a few months ago. The longer we were together, the more critical Mary got of the time I spent with Sherlock. I don't think she'd have been happy unless I'd ended my collaboration with him completely."

"That's ridiculous," Jemma said without any thought at all. "The work you do with him makes you happy—I've only known you a few days, and I can see that. How much could she have cared about you if she'd ask you to give that up?"

Her answer sent a sharper rush of relief through me than I'd expected. "Exactly what I thought," I said.

We'd almost reached the dining room, but there was an hour left to go before lunch. Jemma looked around and wrinkled her nose. "It's a nice hotel, but I have to admit I'm starting to find it a bit stuffy."

"Why don't we get some fresh air?" I motioned her toward the lobby. "I could use some of that myself."

It was difficult to call any of the air in central London exactly *fresh*. The cool spring breeze we stepped out into carried a whiff of car exhaust and a waft of hot buttery grease from the Indian restaurant down the road. I did find it a little easier to breathe out there all the same. Restricting one's self to a hotel for days on end couldn't be good for the spirit.

"Should we take a turn around the corner and see where that leads us?" I said.

"Sounds good to me." Jemma tucked her hand around my elbow the way she had when we'd been putting on a show of being lovers, as if it were perfectly natural. Heat flowed through me from that point of contact.

I made an effort to walk as steadily as possible and lean on my walking stick as little as possible, not that Jemma had ever appeared bothered by my irregular gait. She peered through the window of the restaurant, sniffing the tang of curry that colored the air there, and commented that we should skip the hotel buffet to grab a bite there some evening. I was about to suggest that we do it tonight when we came around the corner to a clang and a muttered string of curses.

We jerked to a halt. A big guy, taller than me and with muscles flexing beneath his stained Henley, smacked the side of the newspaper box he was scuffling with farther down the road. His ragged blond hair shadowed his dark eyes.

He jammed a metal tool into the coin slot, trying to break it open. Here, in broad daylight—well, clouded dim daylight—without seeming to care who saw him. Figuring no one would dare challenge a guy who looked as tough as he did? I'd been around enough soldiers during my tour to know you couldn't judge fighting strength solely by appearances. A fact that applied to me as much as the man in front of me.

A tingle of adrenaline shot through my veins. I took a step toward him, and Jemma's grip on my arm tightened.

"We'll call the cops," she said. "He doesn't look like he's going to respond to a little friendly conversation. For all we know, he's armed."

Calling the police would be the wise thing to do. My pistol was back in my hotel room. Even if I'd had it on me, engaging with an already violent criminal could quickly cross the line from brave to brainless.

The guy glanced up and saw us watching him. He wrenched at the box, slammed it with his fist, and leered at Jemma. "Why don't you gawk a little closer, sweet stuff? Donate those tits to the cause."

Jemma's jaw clenched, but she turned away. "It's not worth it."

The fire that had flared up inside me said it was, though. No one should be allowed to talk to this woman like that.

I squeezed her hand. "I'll be fine," I said, and strode forward.

The guy straightened up as I approached. He took me in, and his leer turned into a sneer. He cracked his knuckles. "Think today is the day to prove yourself, huh?" he said.

"I think you'd better step away from that newspaper box and get going," I replied. The words tumbled out of my mouth automatically, propelled by the rush of adrenaline.

The guy guffawed. "That would be a no. Maybe I can break it open with that thick skull of yours."

I shifted my weight onto my good leg and adjusted my grip on my walking stick. When the guy swung a meaty fist at me, exactly as I'd expected him too, I dodged and jabbed my stick into the middle of his gut.

I knew how to deliver a good blow. The guy winced and stumbled, doubling over for a second before he lunged at me again, with a snarl this time. I couldn't yank myself out of the way fast enough.

His knuckles clipped the side of my head, sending my thoughts spinning. I gritted my teeth with a fresh flare of determination and whacked my stick across the guy's throat.

He sputtered and reeled back. The angry flush that had darkened his face faded. He spat out some incoherent insult, turned tail, and ran.

"John!" Jemma came to a stop beside me. She glanced me over as if checking for wounds. "You really didn't have to do that."

"I know," I said with a grin I couldn't restrain, my heart still thumping from the scuffle. It nearly drowned out the ache where the hooligan's fist had met my temple. "But so many of those guys are cowards. Show you can give them a proper fight, and they decide it's not worth the trouble."

From the look she gave me, she wasn't sure whether to thank me or keep berating me. I might have been fine with both. My pulse kicked up another notch as I gazed down into her cloud-gray eyes. A hint of her scent reached me, sweetly floral with a temptingly dark undertone. The impulse shot through me to trace my fingers along her delicate jaw and kiss her.

I balked, giving my passions a moment to cool. We were colleagues. She hadn't shown any definite signs of interest. She'd probably think I was taking advantage of the opportunity to play hero.

Before I could completely collect myself, my phone vibrated in my pocket. I fished it out, raising it faster when I saw the name on the text.

"Is that Sherlock?" Jemma asked.

I could give her news that I expected would be much more welcome than a kiss. "He's tracked down Richter's collection manager," I said with a nod. "We can talk to him this afternoon."

CHAPTER NINE

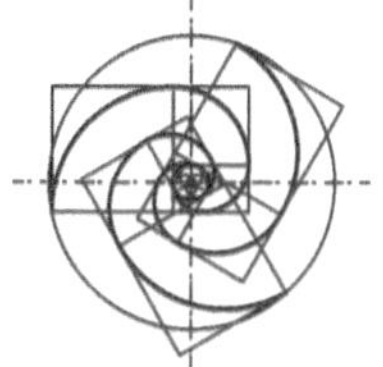

Jemma

My favorite kind of con hit two birds with one stone. Conveniently, John Watson had a complimentary pair of weaknesses.

As the four of us headed across the hotel's underground parking garage to John's car, I positioned myself at his side. Then I pressed my right heel into the concrete with slightly more pressure than before.

The heel snapped loose. I stumbled, and John caught my arm with his free hand. Savior impulse engaged.

"Whoa there," he said. "Are you all right?"

"Damned shoe." I examined the low heel dangling from the back of my practical black pump and sighed. "This brand usually holds up."

"We'll match," John said with his easy grin. "It's not so bad being a bit lopsided. On the other hand, I'm sure we've got time for you to run back to your room if you have another pair."

Sherlock made a disgruntled sound at the suggestion, already shifting his weight impatiently as if the interview he'd planned were a chemical reaction that would explode if the timing changed by a matter of seconds.

I patted my purse. "I always carry a little shoe glue just in case. I'll be lopsided the rest of the way to the car, and then I'll fix it up well enough to get through the day."

"Prepared for everything, hmm?" John said, with the admiring glint in his hazel eyes that I'd wanted to inspire. He liked saving me, but I got the impression he enjoyed watching my unwavering competence even more. Might as well appeal to both inclinations.

"Says the guy who carries multiple fake moustaches in his jacket pocket," I returned, and he chuckled.

He had another one on today, bushier than the one he'd used for the gentlemen's club, and a hat that hid his sandy blond hair. Sherlock had applied a full beard and dappled his messy waves with believable flecks of gray. They'd both dressed in scruffier clothes than usual too.

Only Garrett looked like his usual boyish self, but he was going to hang back in the car, both to stay out of any potentially illegal maneuvering we had to do and to be ready to call for back-up if Sherlock's plan went wrong.

I took the offending shoe off and walked with that foot on tiptoe, the pavement cold and unpleasantly damp through my sock. John kept his hand on my arm, more a touch than a hold, ready if I teetered. It was rather odd, really, to find a human being who both got off on coming to the rescue and applauded self-sufficiency. Most White Knight types preferred that their wounded birds stayed wounded.

You'd almost think the man was really as kind-hearted as he presented himself. But I'd seen how eagerly he'd leapt at the newspaper box guy this morning. Throw a reckless hankering for danger into the mix, and you got quite the stew.

At the silver Ford, John had to let go of me to head to the driver's seat. Garrett's glower followed him, one he wasn't making much effort to hide. Hmm. I should probably temper that jealousy before it sparked more of a fire. They did need to work *together*.

With his long legs, Sherlock naturally took the other front seat. I slid into the back next to Garrett. His expression stayed gloomy as he did up his seatbelt, but he didn't look at me.

John revved the Ford's engine and backed out of the spot with a smooth turn of the wheel and a burst of speed. I was glad for my own seatbelt as we zipped toward the exit. Apparently the good doctor enjoyed tempting danger on the road as well.

He and Sherlock fell into a conversation about another recent case a client had brought them. I dabbed the gummy glue onto my shoe, pressed the heel on tight, and turned toward Garrett. He wasn't so stoic that he could ignore my direct gaze. After a second, he glanced over at me, his mouth set at an angle that was tense but not hostile.

I brushed my fingers lightly over his forearm. "Hey," I said, softly enough to speak under the front seat chatter. "We're all right, aren't we? If things went farther than you'd have wanted— I know I can get carried away."

My touch brought a glimmer of hunger into Garrett's eyes. He appeared to gather himself. "We're fine. It was—ah, it was very nice. But you and John have something going now...?" His voice stayed carefully terse.

"Not at the moment," I said. "But I can't say it won't happen. I'm only here until the end of the week. It's not as if I could be looking to make any kind of commitment."

"Of course not. It isn't even my business."

"I do like you," I said. Sure, I could summon some appreciation for the man's dogged ambition. And for the competitive passion he'd unleashed last night. "If things were different, I wouldn't see any need to play the field."

A bit of light came into his face under the grimness. *You won,* I was telling him. *I'd want you more.* Which was exactly what he wanted to hear. From now through to the end, I needed all three of these men both invested and away from each other's throats. We had bigger villains to tackle—bigger than any of them knew.

Richter was just the gateway to a horde of monsters that ate children's souls.

When we parked a couple of blocks from the warehouse where

Sherlock was sure we'd find Richter's manager, Garrett leaned back in his seat, setting his police radio on his knee and taking out his ever-present notepad. He looked far more relaxed than he had when we'd gotten in. Good. My work here was done.

"I'll be watching for your signal," he said.

"I don't expect I'll need to give it," Sherlock said. "But in a case this volatile, it's worth taking the precaution." Both he and John were carrying pistols, just in case.

We set off past the dingy buildings toward the warehouse in question. This wasn't the sort of area where you'd expect a wealthy gent to have his lackeys working, but Richter had plenty of activities he'd rather keep far from curious eyes. My shoes tapped against the sidewalk. I dug my hands into the pockets of the worn jacket Sherlock had procured for my own "costume."

It was fascinating watching how the detective transformed. John had left his walking stick behind to move with a more definite hitch, and he slumped his shoulders a bit to change his posture, but I'd still have recognized him with a close glance. Sherlock, on the other hand, became an utterly different person.

Somehow with the bend of his legs, he affected a bowlegged gait and shaved a few inches off his considerable height. The swagger of his movements and the puff of his chest gave the impression of a much broader frame than he actually possessed. As we drove, he'd slicked back his hair with oil. Between all that and the beard, I had to peer to make out any hint of the man underneath.

Was that level of subterfuge really necessary for this lackey? I couldn't have said I was convinced, but Sherlock took pride in his disguise, and I enjoyed watching it, so I wasn't going to badger him about it.

At the warehouse, he shoved open the door, and we all marched in as if we belonged there. That was the core of his plan. Richter's manager wasn't likely to say much to strangers with detective airs. He'd be less on his guard with people he took to be colleagues.

As Sherlock had assured us, the slight man with a hawkish nose was puttering around by stacks of boxes at the far end of the main warehouse room. His ponytail, as much gray as it was dun brown, hissed against his shoulders when he spun around. His eyes narrowed.

"This is private property."

"Of course it is," Sherlock said in a boisterous voice that held no trace of his usual clear even tone. "You're Lenny, yeah? Richter passed on word for us to check that everything's in order for the new shipment."

Lenny frowned and reached for a clipboard he'd left on one of the boxes. "How new? I'm not expecting anything else until next week."

John's eyebrows leapt up. "Did you miss the message, then?" he asked, roughening his own voice. "Last-minute bid on some item that must be pretty special from how urgent he sounded about it. That's why he wanted everything double-checked."

Sherlock neatly picked up the thread. "Good thing we came by. Imagine how unhappy he'd be with you if he showed up tomorrow and you had no idea."

Lenny's skepticism hadn't totally faded, but he couldn't help paling at that suggestion. Richter didn't go easy on his employees.

"It's possible the manifest didn't come through," he said. "Do you have it?"

"We thought you'd have it. For fuck's sake, don't let on you missed this one. We can sort it out. You'll know the thing when it turns up."

That was my opening. I rolled my eyes. "If it even does. I wouldn't put it past him to back out on the bid after all this. The boss's moods have been all over the place lately."

"Tell me about it," Lenny muttered.

"That's true." Sherlock grimaced. "Ever since the guy got back from Germany, he's been on kind of a tear."

We were improvising now. If I let him keep going, no doubt Sherlock would have spun a good tale to lead Lenny down the right path. But if I wanted to keep the consulting detective invested in me and this case, I'd better appeal to him the right way too. Show I could play at the same level. Excite that intellectual ego of his.

"It started *before* he left Munich," I said. "He rang the office while I was in—I had to field the call. He asked some strange questions and sounded kind of odd too." I cocked my head at Lenny. "You were over there with him, weren't you?"

I knew he had been, and I knew Richter had been edgy, even if it hadn't been because he'd just committed a murder, which was what the guys would think I was extrapolating from.

Lenny nodded. It was always easier to get someone to simply confirm rather than to volunteer information outright. "He was a little... restless. He came by to check on the shipment a bunch of times before we flew out."

Sherlock waggled a finger. "Right. Do you have the crates from that lot around? We should take a look at their condition."

"They're right over there." Lenny pointed. "They were new ones for this trip—they should have at least a few more uses in them."

Several plywood boxes nearly as tall as me stood in one corner of the warehouse. A piney smell tickled my nose as we walked over.

Sherlock circled them and stopped by the third. He tapped one corner. "There's extra wear here compared to the others."

John considered it. "He must have opened it again at that end to pop something in last minute, don't you figure?"

A shade of Sherlock's usual knowing smile crossed his lips. "I think you've hit the nail on the head."

John's chin rose at the praise. Lenny sauntered over to see what we were talking about. Now was my chance to steer the great detective straight to our ultimate target.

"He *knew* he was going to stick something in at the last minute," I added. "Now the stuff he was talking about makes sense. He was carrying one of the pieces around with him until right before the plane was supposed to leave. One of the really valuable ones he was worried about getting nicked, I guess?"

Sherlock glanced at me, both wary and curious. Lenny stared at me for a few seconds, long enough to provoke a flicker of worry in me that I'd pushed too far. Then he let out a short ragged laugh.

"I don't know about the value, but you're right, he held onto the one thing until it was time to head out. Had it in an inside pocket on his jacket and kept his arm tucked over that spot the whole time. I'd never seen him that protective of one of the pieces before."

"Huh," Sherlock said with a casual air. "What, was it the Hope Diamond?"

"He'd wish. I don't know. He kept it so close I didn't even see it."

The detective snapped his fingers. "Maybe it was something about — I overheard him mentioning a call he sounded upset about."

Good man. He was following the assumption that something must have brought Richter and the murdered councilor together that night, throwing out a possibility so the manager had the opportunity to confirm or correct him. Leading him straight to the other clue I'd wanted him to stumble on.

"I don't know about a call," Lenny said. "He was only in the hangar briefly here and there. But there was — this messenger came in with a note. The boss left the airfield for a while after that. Who knows?"

He shrugged, his mouth flattening as if he'd realized he might have gotten talking a tad carelessly. That was fine. He'd delivered all the information I could have hoped for.

Sherlock veered back toward the topic of the supposed new shipment that might or might not arrive tomorrow, and after a quick back and forth, we were on our way again. The detective kept up his bowlegged gait all the way back to the car.

"Well, you all made it back in one piece," Garrett said as we climbed in. "Did the plan pan out?"

"I'm increasingly convinced that the situation was some sort of blackmail," Sherlock said. "A photograph that was torn up, a note that disturbed Richter and sent him running presumably to confront the man who sent it, all the crimes he's managed to suppress proof of..." He swiveled in his seat to peer at me, his gaze as sharp as ever within his disguise. "How did you make that leap about Richter carrying one particular item around with him?"

I wasn't going to tell him I'd seen it with my own eyes.

"The crate," I said. "The scrapes on the corner suggested it'd been opened at least three times. Something was packed and then removed and then put back in, I guessed. The marks of the nails supported that conclusion—it was only fully sealed once. He didn't close the lid tight right away because he knew he was going to be returning something there. If he was worried enough not to leave that artifact in the crate, why would he leave it somewhere else? It had to be on him."

"Yes," Sherlock said. "I came to the same conclusions myself, just not quite as quickly. You're a swift one with your observations." He sounded impressed, but at the same time his gaze felt more analytical than awed, as if he was searching for more to my answer.

"I do my best," I said, smiling innocently back at him. "I wasn't sure—it was only a possibility that seemed worth pursuing."

"Indeed." He eased back in his seat. "I would be highly surprised if all of Richter's unusual behavior isn't tied to the murder. I believe our next order of business should be getting our hands on a manifest listing the contents of that particular crate."

And that would lead him straight to the final, perilous prize.

CHAPTER TEN

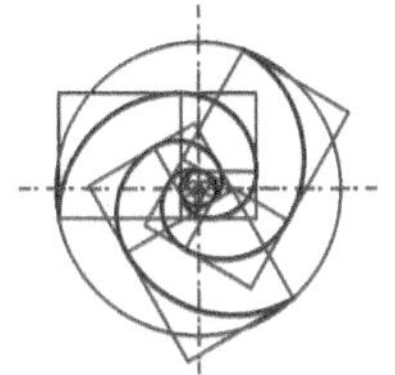

Jemma

A few sofas sat around the edges of the hotel lobby, and I'd positioned myself on the one that would be right in John's line of sight when he left the evening seminar he was attending. Tucking my legs up in front of me and resting my tablet on my knees, I nibbled on the sweet creaminess of a custard tart and checked the latest coded emails and bank transfers.

This chunk of money could go off to my account in Sweden, that one to the Cayman Islands. This contractor I'd send a little bonus to for a job well done. That one was going to need a visit from Bash if she strayed any farther.

Some people were just that stupid. As if they didn't realize I was paying enough attention to make sure they never got to make the actual attempt to screw me over. I hadn't built the most finely tuned network of illegal activity in the world by looking the other way.

For a few minutes, I skimmed through my database of contacts. This operation would be a lot more straight-forward if I hadn't needed to keep my trio of crime-fighters engaged but unaware. The trouble was, Stefan Richter had plenty of contacts and plenty of sway in the criminal underworld too.

The guy who'd been meant to pave the way to my score in Munich had flipped and gone to tattle to Richter at the last minute. Bash had gotten to him before he'd been able to say much, but I couldn't be completely sure of any of the lowlifes here either. Especially when Richter might have already spread the word that someone was out to steal from him.

I needed connections from the other side of the divide between criminal and crime-fighter. Sherlock and his friends were going to handle that for me as long as I played this right. I'd worked for nearly ten years to get to this point. I could be patient.

I switched to one of the local news sites in case I'd find something useful to riff off in the stories I was spinning. I'd made it through twelve pages of corrupt politicians, corporate negligence, and mass layoffs—who were the real villains in this world, exactly?—before the tap of John's walking stick reached my ears.

Keeping my gaze on the screen, I ran a hand through my hair so the waves rippled. The movement would catch his eye.

Sure enough, here came that soft tapping across the floor to my seat.

I glanced up when he was five feet away. John smiled down at me with the warmth that always made me feel he was actually glad to see me. Only because he didn't know what I really was, of course.

"What are you doing out here at this hour, Jemma?" he asked.

I rubbed my eyes. "I guess I lost track of time."

"Good book?"

"Something like that." I looked toward the elevators and hesitated, letting my mouth slant downward just slightly.

John caught even that small sign of discomfort, as I'd expected he would. He propped himself against the arm of the sofa. "Is something the matter?"

I produced an awkward laugh and waved off the question. "It's nothing. I'm being silly." I pushed myself to my feet, paused, and set off toward the elevators.

John kept pace with me. "I have trouble imagining you getting caught up in anything 'silly.' Maybe I can help. I promise I don't judge—and I've certainly gotten myself worried about plenty of things that seemed silly in the aftermath."

I stopped in front of the elevators and pushed the button. Then I exhaled as if overcoming my reluctance. "After going out and talking to that Lenny guy today, knowing that we're dealing with a murderer and a rapist who's very good at covering his tracks... I started feeling a little nervous about being in my room alone. If I were at home, the situation wouldn't get to me like this, but in an unfamiliar place—like I said, it's silly. This building is *more* secure than my apartment."

"Nope," John said with a playfully definitive air. "Definitely not silly. As a doctor, I declare that a totally reasonable worry considering the circumstances."

The elevator arrived with a ding. As we stepped on, I lowered my head with a swipe at my mouth.

"I feel guilty, too," I said. "I got the three of you wrapped up in the case. You're probably in danger because of me. The more we keep investigating, the more danger it'll be. This is my *job*; I'm supposed to face those threats. But you—"

"Hey." John set his hand on my shoulder with a gentle squeeze. "I carry out the work I do knowing there'll be threats along the way. Sherlock and I have tackled some pretty horrible characters before. I'm glad I got the chance to contribute to a case this big."

"We'll see how glad you are by the end of it," I muttered, but I gave him a hint of a smile at the same time.

The elevator whirred to a stop at the second floor. John's room was on the fourth. I tensed as the door slid open and then squared my shoulders.

"Why don't you come back to my room, just for a bit?" John said abruptly. He wet his lips. "A little friendly conversation might help settle your nerves. I mean, if you'd rather just get back to yours, that's completely fine—"

"You know, I think that would be just what I need," I said before he could stumble any further in clarifying his invitation. "Thank you."

He beamed at me, but he obviously wasn't sure of where this night might lead. I'd better make my interest a little more clear.

He jabbed the button to close the doors. As his hand dropped back to his side, I caught it in mine. My fingers tucked against his warm skin, and I stroked my thumb over his knuckles in a gentle caress.

John didn't say anything, but the air in the space between us warmed just a little. He adjusted his hand to twine his fingers with mine, like an answer to my proposition.

I suspected Garrett in the same situation would have tossed me on the bed—or maybe on the desk again—the second we walked into the room. John let go of me to amble over to his dresser.

"I picked up a bottle of sherry so I wouldn't be tempted by the mini bar. Would you like a drink?"

He couldn't help playing the gentleman, could he? I smiled in amusement and perched on the end of the bed. "Why not? I trust you chose good stuff."

John poured us each a dollop of amber liquid in the room's tumblers and handed one to me. Instead of sitting next to me on the bed, he turned the desk chair around to face me and sank onto that.

"You said before that you thought you might travel around like your parents did," he said in a casual conversational tone. "Where do you think you'd go first if you uprooted?"

A little more "getting to know you" before we got down to the fucking? His earnestness about this whole process was almost endearing. I could humor him.

"I'd like to spend more time in Iceland at some point," I said, somewhat at random. "And Peru—the little bit I saw of it was lovely."

"You really have been all over, huh?"

"I did tell you." I took a sip of the sherry, absorbing the rich nutty flavor. "What about you? Did the military take you many places?"

John's hand dropped instinctively to his hip. "I was only stationed in Iraq," he said. "A couple different bases. I'm sure if I'd been able to complete my tour, I'd have moved around more, but..." He shrugged. "These things happen."

He sounded genuinely regretful that he hadn't spent more time around bazookas and mines. "And now you have this," I said, gesturing at him to indicate his new career.

"Yes. It's hard to say I'd trade this life for another one. Maybe I missed my real calling until now."

He brought his glass to his lips, considering me. My gaze lingered on the ripple of his throat as he swallowed. How lucky I was to have my trio of crime-fighters made up of three such physically appealing men, as different as they were from each other.

"What drew *you* to this calling?" he asked. "Every police officer I've talked to has some kind of defining moment or urge they can point to."

I'd locked eyes with a lot of men over the years. I'd told lies to nearly all of them. But something about this man, in this moment, brought out an impulse to offer him an answer as close to the truth as I was capable of. I took a gulp of sherry to see if it would burn away the whim, but the sensation only prickled deeper.

Why not? It wouldn't hurt anything. He'd probably like the simplified version at least as well as anything I could make up.

"Someone who was very important to me died a long time ago," I said. "I've always felt like I should have been able to prevent it. I don't want anyone else to meet the fate she did if I can help it. So, here I am."

I held the memories at a distance where they couldn't hit me with more than a muted ache behind my sternum.

"I'm sorry," John said.

"*You've* got nothing to be sorry for." I drained the last of my sherry and set the glass down on the carpet. "Like I said, it was a long time ago."

"Still, that's the sort of experience that stays with you. And the sort no one should have to go through."

"And yet so many of us do." I leaned back on my hands, studying him, the alcohol having left me with a faint but pleasant tingling in my head. "Can I ask you a question now?"

The corners of his lips quirked up. "That seems only fair."

"The three of you have worked together all this time," I said. "And then suddenly you have this woman you hardly know tagging along everywhere you go. Sherlock is focused on the case, and Garrett has obviously had some concerns about some interloper crashing your party, but you've been nothing but welcoming right from the start. Why is that?"

John's smile turned uncharacteristically mysterious. "Maybe I recognized a kindred spirit."

If he'd known anything about the real Jemma Moriarty, he'd be aware that we couldn't have had less in common. I'd been more jaded than John Watson since the day I was born. I guessed his perceptions meant I'd done my job well.

I held out my hand. "If that's the case, kindred spirit, what are you doing all the way over there?"

Desire lit in his eyes. He set his glass, the sherry only half drunk, down on the desk and crossed the short distance to the bed without bothering with his walking stick. He stopped in front of me. Gazing down at me, he brought his hands to my face and teased them over my hair.

"Jemma," he said. "You are a gem. A brilliant jewel."

I trailed my fingers up his broad chest over his dress shirt. "You're pretty shiny yourself."

John laughed and lowered his head. His mouth found mine, careful and tender. So different from Garrett in this too, and yet with its own little thrill.

I gripped his shirt, urging him closer, and he deepened the kiss with a probe of his tongue. As we kissed and came up for air and kissed some more, one of his hands trailed down to trace the curve of my shoulder.

I yanked his shirt from his trousers. This position was perfect to get him panting with need.

When I unzipped his fly, his breath stuttered against my mouth. He kissed me harder, his fingers dipping to stroke over my breast, but I didn't miss the quiver of his thighs at the same time.

This wasn't the best position for *him* with that injured leg.

No need for that to stop me. I scooted back on the bed, tugging John with me, and he followed. He broke the kiss to ease my blouse up over my head. Then he was freeing my breasts from my bra, tipping one up to meet his descending mouth. His tongue swiped over my nipple, searing hot. I ran my fingers over his soft hair and hummed encouragingly.

His hands started to travel lower, reminding me of my earlier intentions. I nudged him down on his back on the fluffy bedspread and delved into the path I'd opened in his trousers.

"Fuck," John murmured as I closed my hand around his rigid cock. He was thick and silky and already beading precum at the tip. I flicked my thumb over the head and was rewarded with a groan.

Working him free from his boxers, I bent down at his side. I set my other hand carefully to avoid the jagged scar on his hip. A rough sound reverberated through his chest when my mouth closed over his cock.

His skin smelled clean and fresh like a light spring rain shower, with a hint of salt on my tongue as I swirled it around his cock. Alongside the bob of my head, I cupped his balls. John's hips bucked up encouragingly. Oh, yes, he liked that.

He was the kind of guy I could enjoy giving a blowjob too—responsive and eager but polite about it. He kept those hips in check while I sucked him down again, rocking with my motions but not jamming his dick down my throat. The panting I'd wanted to provoke rasped over his lips. The sound of it made me wet.

In this moment, you are mine. Mine, mine, mine. Just for this moment, this bright golden man wanted me more than anything else in the world.

John touched my waist and pulled at my body. It took me a few seconds to realize what he was after. I swiveled around, barely breaking my rhythm, until I straddled his shoulders. He eased my slacks and panties down and then pushed himself up to slick his tongue over my clit.

Oh, God Almighty. The number of guys who'd offer this generosity when I was already working them over was vanishingly slim. With my legs splayed over him, every part of my core felt doubly exposed and sensitive. The gentle pressure of his lips made me tremble. I wasn't going to last long like this.

I teased my teeth against the underside of his cock. John's hips jerked. He groaned against my core, the sound flooding me with pleasure. He was close too, but the throb of need inside me demanded more than this.

I slipped off of him and grabbed my purse to retrieve a condom. When I swung around to meet him face to face, John was waiting to draw me in for a kiss. Our breath mingled and our tongues collided as we kicked our pants and undergarments the rest of the way off. He slipped his hand between my thighs, one finger and then another slicking deep inside me until I couldn't have been readier.

At my tug, he rolled on top of me, bracing his weight on one elbow as he prepped himself. His mouth found mine for another kiss. I lifted my knees to his sides, and he slid right in, filling me with that perfect blissful pressure.

John's breath washed over my neck. He nibbled my clavicle, gripping my thigh at the same time, easing back and plunging even deeper. My head tipped back with a whimper.

"Your mouth felt fantastic, but this is even better," he mumbled against my bare skin.

A giggle escaped me. "My sentiments exactly."

I wouldn't have needed it, but he tucked his hand between us anyway. His thumb grazed over my clit and then pressed harder. His thrusts picked up speed. Pleasure flared from that little nub and seared along every nerve around my core, surging high and fast with the combined stimulation. I dug my fingers into the folds of his shirt and held on as ecstasy split me down the middle.

I came shaking and moaning, clinging on to him so tight my knuckles ached. John bucked into me faster still, sending another swell of sensation through me. Then he was biting down on my shoulder with a strangled sound.

He drove deep a few more times and swayed to a stop with a ragged exhalation. And in the aftermath as he sank down beside me, his arm looping around my waist, my mind leapt to the moment, soon, when I'd have to make my excuses and leave.

Bash

The moment I ducked through the window of Jemma's hotel room, I knew she'd just hooked up with one of her marks. I'd seen her post-seduction enough times to recognize the signs. Her hair hung straighter and darker than usual, damp from a recent shower, and her pose where she was sitting at the little table next to the window had the languid air of physical satisfaction.

She perked up in an instant at the sight of me, leaning her arms on the tabletop. The white hotel bathrobe she'd thrown on over her pajamas looked a little bulky on her slim figure, but the understated authority of her presence filled it out just fine.

"You got it?" she said.

I dropped into the chair across from her and pulled out the package I'd been carrying. "Exactly as you requested, Majesty."

Jemma gave me a mock grimace at the nickname and unwrapped the thin slab of metal. She ran her fingers over the etching on its surface, tracing the pattern of embedded gems.

"I doubt it'll fool the owner for more than a second," I said. "The forger said he needed to improvise some since you couldn't give him a visual reference."

She shrugged without any sign of concern. "I don't need to fool the owner. I just need to know my three do-gooders won't realize there's been a theft until I've had a chance to leave the building. They won't be paying attention to the details of this piece." She looked up at me with a sly smile. "Thank you. This is perfect."

Her damp hair made her deep-set eyes look even larger. That and the familiar smile took me back seven years to when I'd first met her. She'd been as scrawny as she was now and way too young to drink, but she'd tapped my shoulder in the middle of a rowdy bar in downtown Detroit and said with balls as big as Oberon's, "I hear you shoot people for pay."

How could I have said no to that?

"Your other plans are coming along well?" I asked, nodding to her get-up.

Jemma's smile widened, and my gut twinged with a little jab of the jealousy I'd thought I had reined in. "Very well, I think. Officer Moriarty of the Freising Police Department is much admired."

I'd seen the coy glances and flirty touches she used to work her wiles when she needed to. It wasn't as if, given the choice, I'd have traded places with any of those men. I got the real Jemma Moriarty, without pretense or artifice: focused, brilliant, and brutal. And in all that brilliance, she'd seen fit to rely on me above anyone else in her vast schemes.

No, being her right-hand man was the real honor.

She swept the replica engraving off the table and slipped it into a concealed compartment in her suitcase. "Was Corbin satisfied with his payment? I didn't expect the blows to land quite that hard."

I thought of the big Irish guy I'd handed off an envelope to this evening and chuckled. "He whinged a bit about having walking-stick bruises, but he looked very happy with the cash. He just made more in a day than I'd bet he usually does in a month. That's worth a few bruises. The good doctor has some spirit to him, does he?"

"Oh, he does," Jemma said, in a tone that told me exactly which of her marks she'd been with tonight. "His reaction to that little bit of theater was very enlightening. He's well on the hook now."

"How does our timeline look from here onward, Mori?"

That nickname brought a slight softness to her smile. I could have called her "Jemma" these days—she'd switched from "Moran" to "Sebastian" to "Bash" quickly enough the closer we'd worked together—but part of me liked having a name for her that was only mine.

"I expect we're only a few days from putting the heist into motion," she said. "They'll want to wrap things up for my sake before I have to go 'home' from the conference. You should get those rooms booked in Algiers—the second passport names."

"Right," I said, making a mental note. "And the flights?"

She shook her head. "I'll handle those. We'll want to take the first one out of here once I've got the prize. By the time they realize what idiots they've been and start looking for me, there won't be a trace left behind."

I gave her a teasing salute. "Your worthy deeds do claim no less than what you stand for."

Normally Jemma would have ribbed me about the bastardized quote, but her gaze had gone momentarily distant. She might not even have registered more than the gist of the words.

It took a lot to distract this woman. There were complexities to this latest scheme I didn't fully understand—stakes that for whatever reason she was keeping to herself. All she'd given me was a warning, a week ago. *In about a month, I might just... vanish. And if that happens, I won't be coming back. I'm only telling you because I need you to promise me something. Don't go looking for me, Bash. If I'm gone, I'm gone.*

She'd spoken as coolly and matter-of-factly as she normally did, but it wasn't like Jemma to talk fatalistically. She was a master at turning an impossible situation around to her favor. I'd only ever seen her falter once, years ago. She hadn't mentioned the possibility of her disappearing again, but the memory still left me uneasy.

I wouldn't pry. That wasn't how we operated. That wasn't how *I* operated. The fact that I cared about her at all, let alone as much as I did, still socked me in the gut with surprise sometimes.

I'd thought I'd been happy living out a life of random crimes for hire before I met her. No, I'd thought I couldn't be meant for more than that. But I was something more now. I might be joking when I called her "Majesty," but she ruled the world we moved through with the power of a queen, and fuck if I hadn't somehow become the dark knight who stood beside the throne and made sure the unworthy bowed down. Without her, I'd just be that guy who shot people for pay again.

So, if there was a way I could keep her out of that fatalistic place and be the rock-solid foundation beneath her if her balance got momentarily shaky, I'd lay down at her feet in an instant.

"Is there anything else you need me to put in place?" I asked.

Jemma's gaze snapped back to me, as alert as ever now. "I wouldn't be surprised if I need you to give another nudge or two during the conference. I can pass on those details online. And it's time to put that worm in the police chief's ear like we talked about. Otherwise, keep on as we discussed."

"Then I shouldn't keep you from your beauty rest," I said.

Jemma snorted at that comment and got up from the table as I did. I was just turning toward the window when an odd fluttering of light washed over the wall beside the bathroom door. It shivered and jerked like a body seizing—and then it flickered away.

When I glanced at Jemma, she had her gaze firmly on me, a hint of defiance in the set of her chin. I knew better than to ask any questions about the odd sight. The strangeness had popped up here and there across the time I'd worked for her, and she clearly didn't like it but didn't think it was worth bothering with. If she ever thought I could do something useful about it, she'd tell me more then.

"There is one other thing," she said abruptly. "I'd imagine our friend Richter suspects I've followed him to London. He'll have people on the lookout for me in case I reach out to the local element —word will have gotten around by now. Let's remind him of the dangers of meddling with my business."

I grinned, the implicit order perfectly clear. My work with Jemma was always steady and never dull. "A job I'm happy to do."

She shot a smile back at me, fierce in its warmth. "Thank you, Bash."

I went from Jemma's room to my own in a much smaller and shabbier hotel where no one asked very many questions and the cleaning staff had loads of respect for the Do Not Disturb sign. My ninth floor view looked out over the few buildings between this one and Jemma's, giving me a clear line of sight to her window if she needed to signal me surreptitiously.

It was a quick change: Bright orange rugby shirt, matching cap, contacts that turned my light green eyes a deep indigo. Give people parts of you to stare at and they won't remember the bits that could actually identify you the next day. The jersey had the extra benefit of easily concealing the holster I slid into my jeans against my hip.

Suitably prepared, I headed for the narrower, grittier streets of London's underbelly. Often the trick to getting what you want is making people think you're giving them what *they* want, a con I'd seen Jemma pull off more times than I could count. I might not be able to manage it with the same degree of polish, but I could put on a good front when I wanted to.

Along the way, I dialed up the police's media line on a burner phone. "Hello," I said in a brisk British accent I'd picked up from listening to a grifter in New York City. "I'm calling from the Telegraph. Can anyone there comment on what I'm hearing about a Stefan Richter suing Scotland Yard for their interference with his business affairs? I understand he opened a similar case against the Paris PD."

"I—ah—we don't have any official statement on that," the woman on the other end said, sounding bewildered. "I'm sure if there's anything to report, we'll share a press release shortly."

She hung up, presumably off to pass on word to the chief that someone believed a guy named Richter might be going to sue them. One of tonight's jobs done, one more to go.

In the first bar, I squeezed between the crowded stools and ordered a beer. As the bartender slid it across the counter, I leaned in and let my voice fall into a rolling Welsh accent courtesy of the owner of a different bar I'd spent a lot of time at some years back.

"I heard someone's asking after a woman just arrived in town, putting out feelers about a big venture. I've got information if you know who I should talk to."

"Can't help you there, mate," the bartender said.

I waited about twenty minutes, gulping the cool beer and tuning out the barrage of voices around me, just in case. Then I moved on.

In the third bar, I hit pay dirt. The bartender's eyes twitched. "I might have heard something about that," he said. "Stick around, and maybe the guy will turn up."

After he served a couple more customers, he stepped off to the side with his phone. I nursed the Jack and Coke I'd ordered like I wasn't in any hurry. It was maybe half an hour before I caught the bartender tipping his head in my direction for the benefit of someone who'd just come in the door.

A burly guy with a drooping jaw stopped by the bar and then pushed through the swarm of patrons to the spot where I was standing. He held up his own glass. "Cheers."

"Cheers," I replied, and clinked my glass to his. "What's the occasion?"

"You have information about a woman who's assembling a crew?"

"Who wants to know?"

The guy fixed me with a hard look. "My boss, who's got a generous reward for anyone who can point him in the right direction. Do you know something or not?"

I held up my hands. "Hey, give me a break. This isn't my usual scene. I'm just looking to make ends meet. It sounds like I ended up in the right place." I glanced at the people milling around us and tugged on my hat. "Should we take this outside? She's got a meeting place all set up for tomorrow — I can show you it."

The guy grunted and threw back the rest of his drink. "Come on then."

Perfect. He lumbered toward the back of the bar, and I followed, letting my wrist brush against the concealed holster at my hip. While

I was a rifle man by preference, a pistol worked just fine when circumstances called for it. My army superiors had called me the best distant shot in the forces, but they'd have hesitated to face off against me at short range too. I wouldn't be surprised if that'd contributed to the hurry with which they'd dishonorably discharged me.

Life didn't work the way Shakespeare and his type wrote it. They seemed to think no matter what else was going on, by the end of the drama everyone would have paid for their mistakes and flaws in systematic fashion. I watched those films for a laugh. It was fucking absurd how brutally fair they were.

In the life I knew, shitty people got away with shittier things the whole day long. But here and there, I could give them the shitty end they deserved. It might not be justice, but the act couldn't be more satisfying, especially when it served Jemma's unwavering sense of purpose.

We stepped out into the dank alley. I motioned to the guy, noting the pockets of noise and silence, judging the distance to the river. "It's just a few blocks over. She roped in a friend of mine. I didn't like the sound of it."

The guy guffawed. "Yeah, this crazy bint is a real piece of work, from what I hear."

I smiled tightly. In a few minutes, he'd be a piece of work—bloody artwork splattered all over a brick wall. And now I was going to enjoy it even more.

CHAPTER TWELVE

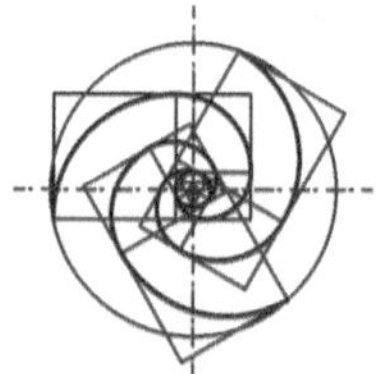

Jemma

In the car on the way to the gallery, I wound my hair into a loose braid. John must have caught a glimpse through the rearview mirror, even though he *should* have been keeping his eyes on the road.

"Felt the need to mix things up?" he said with a teasing lilt.

"I have the feeling I'm going to want it out of my face," I said, which wasn't exactly a lie. The larger truth, though, was the red waves could be rather attention-getting when allowed to flow freely. I didn't want anyone at the gallery taking particular note of me today.

I smoothed my hands over the skirt of my dress, feeling Garrett's gaze following the motion. It was a modest enough knee-length A-line, navy with a subtle quatrefoil pattern in a paler blue — the sort of thing Officer Moriarty would wear when trying to blend in with an arty crowd while casing a joint for evidence — but it was a lot more feminine than anything the trio had seen me in since the reception. Both Garrett's and John's eyes had shot to me the moment I'd stepped into the lobby to meet them for this field trip.

John roared through an intersection just before the light turned red and whipped us around a corner. He found a parking spot down the street from the building that was hosting Richter's exhibition. The gallery took up the whole other half of the block.

I studied the buildings as we walked over, noting the sleekness of the gallery's black marble-plated face and the narrow alley between it and the neighboring shoe shop. The edge of a fire escape leading to the apartment over the shop protruded from its rear.

"Those are our people," Garrett said with a subtle tilt of his head toward a tan sedan parked at the opposite corner. "Well, my people. The gallery put in a request to the department that we monitor the building the entire time the special exhibit is on—so obviously that order came via Richter."

The bigwig was stepping up his game from Munich. I prepared myself as we came up to the door.

Just like in Munich, Richter had demanded the highest level of security inside the gallery for his precious relics. I stood so the security camera just inside the door only caught the back of my head while the guard by the ticket booth pawed through my purse. More cameras were perched near the ceiling farther inside. I trod carefully between their lines of sight.

Reaching the two rooms that housed Richter's collection required a journey through the main gallery space, up a flight of stairs, and past a thick door with a keypad that clearly required a code for entry outside of visiting hours. Fixtures for motion detectors clung to the beige walls. From the warning lines laid on the floor around the display cases, I assumed pressure pads would set off an alarm if anyone stepped closer than Richter found comfortable.

Oh, he'd thought of just about everything. But I *would* have gotten the better of him in Munich if I'd had a little more time, if that pathetic excuse for an alarm hacker hadn't turned rat. Now Richter was up against not just me but Sherlock Holmes and company. We'd see how he enjoyed that challenge.

I meandered through the room, drawing a diagram of it in my head, letting my gaze skim over the displays on the wall as if I wasn't looking for anything in particular. I'd caught the gleam of gold from a case in the middle of the room. My heart thumped as I wandered closer to it.

I already knew what I was looking at. What I really needed was for the trio to see and to realize the significance, but the impact wouldn't land the same way unless they came on it themselves. I'd only nudge them if I had to.

Sherlock was examining the contents of each case with brisk efficiency, referencing the manifest he'd gotten his hands on by means he hadn't bothered to tell the rest of us. He indicated a bronze shield, a Grecian vase, and a statue lifted from this or that ancient temple, with John nodding along beside him. Then he turned toward the case I'd been working my way over to.

"It appears he organized his shipping containers to match the display layout," he murmured. "All four of these items were in that crate. Any of these are small enough that he could have carried them in a decent sized pocket."

"Sherlock." John came to an abrupt stop by the opposite end of the case. My pulse skipped a beat. *Yes.* He was staring through the glass.

"What is it?" the detective asked, his attention snapping to his friend. I moved to join them as if curious.

John pointed at a jade Buddha figurine about the height and width of his hand, carved up from a thick rectangular base. His arm trembled for a second, but he looked more giddy than anxious.

"The pattern along the base," he said. "Those ridges... I'd need to have it in my hands and to examine the victim's body in person to be sure, but I'd swear they match the head wound perfectly."

"From my memory, you're exactly right." Sherlock clapped the doctor on the back. "Well done, John."

Garrett hustled over, picking up on the momentous vibe. "What's going on?"

"John has found us the murder weapon," Sherlock said, still speaking under his breath. He must be thinking that the security cameras might be picking up sound as well as video.

I focused on the jade figure, schooling my gaze away from the strip of gold gleaming a foot away from it. "Would we be able to prove it? There might be other jade figures with the same construction, right? We don't have any proof that it was *this* one."

"We might, though," John said, excitement rippling through his voice even as he kept it low. "All we need is to find one bit of the victim's DNA on that statue. Obviously he took care to wash it off, but after the way he bashed that man's skull in, with ridges that deep—maybe a few years ago he'd have managed to destroy every usable shred, but now there'd have to be traces that the current techniques could lift, just like your golf shoes."

Thank you, Dr. Tanaka, for priming that epiphany.

"How can we get access to the figurine to lift evidence from it?" I asked. "Will your judgment based on sight be enough to get a warrant?"

Sherlock turned to Garrett. "I believe this is where you can be of great assistance. What can you work out with Scotland Yard? We'd want to move fast—have the warrant here with enough authority to confiscate the piece before Richter catches wind of the problem. He's slipped the police too many times before for us to risk giving him any leeway."

Garrett tore his gaze away from the figurine. "I'll talk to the chief and see what I can get in motion."

John passed him the car keys. "So you can have a private conversation. Just don't go driving off with her."

"That shouldn't be a problem," Garrett muttered, but he hurried out of the room with a spring in his step. Bringing down a man like Richter could make his career.

John frowned as he circled the case. "I wish I could get a better look at the entire bottom. The wound would have been from the edge, but the base made a large part of the mark. If I could see it, I'd be completely sure." A glint I recognized lit in his eyes. "This is a long shot, but... move back."

"John," I said with a nervous twist of my stomach as I eased away. Why did he have to pick right now to indulge his thrill addiction? I had to get him under control. "We don't want to do anything that'll draw attention. Like Sherlock said, if Richter gets any hint we're on to him—"

I'd meant to appeal to his loyalty to his friends and the case. Instead, my effort might have backfired by playing up the danger. John's mouth curved in a little grin. "This has nothing to do with any official business. Just a clumsy cripple whose walking stick slipped."

He turned and lifted his head as if catching sight of something that excited him. Sherlock opened his mouth to speak, but John was already moving. He lurched forward and let his walking stick fly out, sending him stumbling into the display case.

His shoulder hit the platform with a thump. It was so sturdily built the contents didn't so much as tremble.

As John groped for his fallen stick, two security guards barged into the room. I pretended to be fascinated by the vase Sherlock had been looking at earlier.

"Sorry!" John said. "So sorry! I'm still getting used to the stick— it gets away from me sometimes."

"Maybe you should steer clear of art galleries with precious artifacts on display, then, sir," one of the guards said gruffly. I swallowed a smile. That was a valid point, if not exactly presented with the most sensitivity. It sounded as if he'd bought John's lie.

Sherlock drifted past me. "Go out to the car first," he murmured from the side of his mouth. "We'll follow separately after. Better not to make it obvious we're together now that they'll be watching him."

I gazed at the vase for a few seconds longer and then ambled back the way we'd come. It wouldn't do to appear to be in a hurry, either. My slow pace also gave me the opportunity to scope out what looked like a maintenance door on the first floor toward the back, with a sign that said *Employees Only*. I added that to my mental blueprint of the building.

The guards by the front door didn't look twice at me. I strode by them, digging in my purse as an excuse to keep my head low as I passed the camera. On the street, I picked up my pace. My heartbeat sped up too.

I'd set all the pieces of this puzzle on a collision course to snap together, but there was always a small chance one gambit or another wouldn't work, that somewhere wires would be crossed...

Garrett was still on the phone when I opened the door to the backseat. He gave me a pained grimace that took the edge off my nerves. I made a face of sympathy and raised my eyebrows, but he held up his hand to hold off any questions.

"Yes, sir," he said into the phone. "I understand that. But I think considering the circumstances, it's worth taking that risk."

He paused while his chief said something on the other end. I settled into my seat, keeping an expression of concern on my face while the rest of me relaxed. One step closer.

Sherlock appeared a minute later as Garrett wrapped up the conversation. Garrett jammed the phone in his pocket, and Sherlock twisted around in his seat. "Are we set?"

Garrett's boyish face had turned stormy. "Let's wait until John gets here."

Our Dr. Watson walked into view a couple minutes later. He looked pleased with himself until he dropped into the driver's seat and caught sight of Garrett. "What happened?" he asked.

"The chief won't lift a finger," Garrett spat out. "He said to forget it, just drop it. Not our murder, not our problem. Bloody arsehole."

I widened my eyes. "*Why?* Shouldn't he be jumping at the chance to take down a menace like Richter?"

Garrett made an angry gesture with his hand. "Politics polluting real police work. It can be such a mess down there... He feels it would be too embarrassing for the force if we break apart the exhibit we've already agreed to protect and it turns out we're wrong, and he mentioned the way Richter sued that other police department. I told him both Sherlock and John were sure he was the perpetrator and that statue was the murder weapon, but even that didn't budge him."

My shoulders slumped. "Then Richter is going to get away with this crime too—and this time it's *murder.*"

"No," Sherlock said firmly. "We'll come up with another way. Let me think on it."

Yes, think on it plenty. This was the trickiest leap right here. It was more important than ever that they felt they'd come to the idea themselves. They'd never do it if they realized I was trying to push them into it.

I'd left my trail of bread crumbs. They'd followed it right up to the edge of the trap. All I needed was for them to take that final, crucial step inside.

CHAPTER THIRTEEN

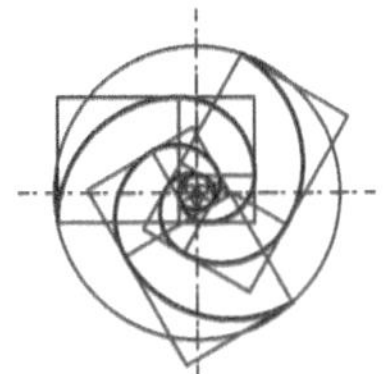

Jemma

I knew something was off before I'd even finished opening the door to my hotel room. A cool draft, a hint of a scent in the air—something my senses picked up on a level below consciousness, honed by fourteen years of living in close proximity to the shrouded folk. I eased inside, my body tensed.

There was no sign of Bog itself—no filmy figure floating around, no flashy lighting effects. My gaze swept the room and snagged on the items I'd laid out on top of the dresser. Two of the bottles had fallen over, breaking my Fibonacci sequence.

It could have been the cleaning staff. I eased up to the dresser and peered at the objects strewn there. Something about the clouded sides of the body wash and lotion bottles looked off. I picked up the body wash, and the contents made a soft hissing sound.

My skin prickled. I popped open the cap and tipped the bottle to squeeze a little of the gel out onto my fingers.

Before I could apply any pressure, a stream of fine gritty powder with the body wash's faint floral scent poured from the bottle's opening over my hand. I jerked the bottle upright, but not before a streak of the stuff had spilled onto the carpet.

My fingers curled with the urge to fling the substance off me, but I needed to examine it first. I rubbed a little between my thumb and forefinger.

Bog had turned the gel to dust, scouring all the moisture from it. The same way the shrouded one was looking forward to scouring all the life out of me? A shiver ran through me, and I stiffened my shoulders.

How had Bog even — I wouldn't have thought it was possible —

The doubts slid through my mind, and the powder on my hand quivered before my eyes. The particles melded back together into a pearly blue gel that dribbled across my skin in cool globs.

I exhaled through gritted teeth. Of course. The shrouded folk were limited in their abilities to affect our physical world unless people of this world gave them access. That was why they bothered with people like my parents in the first place. The pain the cultists drew from themselves and others in their rituals, the bodies offered up to the monsters' maws — it all opened a doorway.

Maybe long ago I'd been marked for the slaughter, but the bargain I'd made with Bog had freed me from that, and I wasn't giving it anything until I had to. Without a doorway, the shrouded folk's powers were restricted to illusions. Nothing solid, nothing permanent, no matter how real it felt in the moment.

Which didn't change the fact that now I had body wash all over my hand. Thanks for that, Bog.

With a sigh, I marched into the bathroom to rinse the stuff off — and stopped dead in my tracks.

The shrouded one hadn't been messing only with my Fibonacci sequence. My brush lay on the bathroom counter next to the sink, tendrils of wavy hair woven through the dark bristles. Normally the strands of red showed starkly against the black base of the brush. They still showed starkly right now, but because they'd been bleached pure white.

Fuck the shrouded folk and their misty heads. I strode to the sink, rinsed off my hand, and dried it on the towel. When I glanced at the brush again, my hairs there still gleamed pure white. I scowled at them, willing the illusion to fall away.

Maybe this one wasn't an illusion. The time limit on my contract with Bog was almost up. That might give it enough leeway to work a little magic on this fragment of me.

I touched one of the hairs that curled from the side of the brush, and it disintegrated in an instant. Not just bleached, but drained as dry as I'd thought the body wash had been.

My throat tightened. I snatched up the brush, and the rest of the hairs fragmented into dust as well.

With a jerk of my arm, I hurled the brush against the wall. It thumped there and clattered onto the tiled floor bristles first. A pattern of white dust flecked the turquoise glaze like ash. No matter how many times I blinked, it didn't fade.

All right. One point to Bog after all.

I walked back into the main room and sat on my bed, but my heart kept thumping at an uneasy rhythm. My trio of investigative geniuses had muttered some more about the police department's cowardice on the way back to the hotel, but no one had settled on any alternate course of action. Garrett had set off to Scotland Yard to speak to someone there in person, which I gathered had been a hopeless errand considering I hadn't gotten any word from him since. John had spent a while frowning at my crime scene photos and becoming even more convinced we'd identified the murder weapon, but scheming wasn't his area of expertise.

No, that talent was Sherlock's, and Mr. Sherlock Holmes had turned depressive and distant by lunchtime. He'd retreated to his room, and I hadn't seen him since.

I'd known it would take time. Making a decision to go this far over the line of legality couldn't be easy for any of them. But all I could feel right now was my time and my chance at escape slipping away from me.

I stood up again and paced the room in an attempt to wear down my nerves. The sugar cube I popped into my mouth seemed to turn sour on my tongue. I went through a series of punches and kicks, thinking over every piece I'd put in play to reach this moment to remind myself that they were all lined up perfectly.

The edgy sensation faded but didn't completely disappear. I stopped by the desk for a minute, torn by indecision, and then decided to hell with it. I'd feel better if I saw where Sherlock was at. I might be able to give him another nudge tonight. There wouldn't be anything odd about dropping in on him to talk after the day we'd had.

His room was two over from John's, right at the end of the hall. The Do Not Disturb sign was dangling from the handle. That was for hotel staff, not me. I knocked on the door lightly but insistently. "Sherlock? It's Jemma."

He took his time, but after several seconds, the door opened. Sherlock peered down at me from his great height, his piercing blue eyes shadowed and his whole demeanor rather sullen. You'd have thought it was his life riding on this "case" and not mine.

"You don't have news," he said, deducing that somehow or other from the once-over he gave me. He crossed his arms over the mouse-brown housecoat he'd put on over his dress shirt and slacks— apparently the hotel-issue bathrobe wasn't good enough for him. "What is it?"

From what John had said, he normally left Sherlock to stew in his thoughts when he got into these moods. That didn't mean I had to take the same tactic. It was ridiculous, really—a grown man older than I was all but sulking in his room because a problem had temporarily eluded his brilliant mind.

He should be better than that.

I motioned him away from the door to let me in. "I figured you've had enough time mulling things over on your own. Let's talk, and maybe we'll get somewhere."

Sherlock's mouth twisted, but he stepped aside and closed the door behind me.

He'd gotten himself a fancier suite than the standard rooms. The floor space was about a third larger than mine, making room for a sort of living room with a couple of armchairs around a sleek coffee table facing a gas fireplace. The fireplace was dark, reflecting his mood. An instrument case lay off to the side. I considered the size and shape.

"You play violin?"

Sherlock made a noise of agreement and sank into the farther of the two armchairs. "It keeps my mind well-tuned," he said, with no noticeable awareness of the pun. "I create my own compositions from time to time."

Of course he did. If I spent more time in his presence, I'd probably discover he baked pastries to rival Hermé, regularly swam the English channel in three hours, and found the time to persuade endangered animals to breed in between all that and his detective-ing.

As I sat in the other chair, he lifted an elegant wooden pipe from a side table and brought it to his lips. I raised my eyebrows at his pensive puff of smoke. "I wasn't aware the hotel allowed smoking."

He waved his hand dismissively. "A pipe is a far cry from cigarettes and cigars. It's a meditation."

From the earthy scent of the smoke, his meditation was Brazilian in origin. At least it was a reminder that he didn't feel many rules applied to him.

"And has your meditating taken you anywhere useful?" I asked, kicking my feet up on the edge of the coffee table, legs crossed for modesty in my dress.

"If it had, I'd hardly still be at it," he said in a sardonic tone. Then he sighed, rubbing his face. The dark brown waves of his hair fell across his high forehead in their usual disarray. "It really is a bitter irony that our efforts are so often hindered rather than helped by the police force employed to solve this city's crimes."

"Well, we know they're not giving us a warrant based on what we've got right now," I said. "So, how else can we make the case against Richter? Hashing it out between the two of us might spark an idea."

Sherlock's expression was doubtful, but he lowered his pipe. "There's no way to determine what was on the photograph that was likely blackmail material. No security cameras covering the area of road it would have shown. I've spoken with a few of our victim's colleagues, and they weren't aware of him carrying any photos or having any interactions with Richter, although he did make a phone call on the day of the murder that seemed to have him quite agitated. The number couldn't be traced. The councilor's behavior is a dead end."

"The shape of the blow—a forensic artist might be able to reconstruct the weapon from that to prove it's a match," I suggested.

Sherlock shook his head. "Only the base, and that base might belong to any number of objects when we can't bring in the one we believe it is for close examination. The only reason we'd assume that statue was the murder weapon is because of our other investigations, which are technically speculative in the eyes of the law."

I tapped the arm of the chair as if in thought. "If we could prove that the victim met up with Richter, then— But there wasn't enough evidence on the body to be sure of the murder site. There must be traces of blood wherever he was killed. It's almost impossible to fully clean a messy murder like that unless you've prepared for it, and Richter obviously acted in the heat of the moment."

"From your report, you had the dogs go out to try to pick up the victim's scent," Sherlock said. "They didn't discover any possible sites."

"They didn't. We could start from tracing *Richter's* movements, since we didn't have him to consider as a factor before..." I bit my lip. "His collection manager didn't seem to know where he went when he was away from the airfield, though. It sounds like he was on his own. We don't exactly have a plethora of traffic cams in Freising, but we might get lucky."

"I've already checked that angle. Another dead end. There is also no documentation connecting the two men. I determined that the victim dropped in on Cavalier's a few years ago while visiting London, but even if he saw Richter then, that's hardly the basis for a murder charge. There was no outside DNA found on the body. Believe me, I've looked at this from every angle a dozen times over."

I cocked my head at him. "Are you telling me that this brute of a man is smarter than the great Sherlock Holmes?"

"No," Sherlock said immediately, his ego ruffled. "His wariness simply gets in the way of many of my usual tactics. I would put out feelers about his connection to the victim or the blackmail to try to stir loose a telling response, but given his history, chances are he'll simply pack up his artifacts and leave, and then the one piece of evidence we do have will be completely out of our reach."

I made an irritated sound. "It's so frustrating to have that evidence *right there* and not be able to take it."

"Richter requires more subtlety than the average criminal, but the answer will come to me."

Sherlock said the last statement definitively, as if that were the end of any possible conversation on the subject. Then he settled deeper into his chair, his eyes going distant as he raised his pipe to his lips.

So very helpful. I leaned back in my own chair and found the thick line of my braid pressed uncomfortably against my spine. It wasn't as if I needed to keep my hair tied up any longer. I tugged off the elastic and ran my fingers through the strands to pull them loose across my shoulders.

When I glanced up again, Sherlock's gaze had refocused on me. There was something I couldn't quite pinpoint in his expression, curious but hesitant. I swiped a few stray waves behind my ear. "What?"

"Your relationship with both Garrett and John has become rather intimate in a short time," he said in that matter-of-fact way of his.

Ah. So he wasn't completely out of tune with those sorts of signs. I let the corner of my mouth lift in a slanted smile. "Given that we're all consenting adults, I'm not sure that's at all your concern."

Sherlock opened his mouth and paused for just a half a second, so briefly I wouldn't have noticed if I hadn't been studying his response. There was that hesitance again.

"I only hope you're taking care to ensure any emotions that arise don't interfere with our work," he said.

Was that really all he was thinking about? A niggling suspicion tingled over my skin. I shifted in my chair, slipping my legs off the coffee table in a way that let my skirt ride a couple inches higher above my knees. "We had sex, not a romance," I said. "There's no reason for any emotions to get involved except enjoyment in the moment."

There. He tried to school his expression impassive, but a flicker passed through it anyway. He *was* curious—curious about what his colleagues had seen in me? About what we'd gotten out of those encounters?

About what he was missing?

A giddy wave tickled through me, washing away any lingering uneasiness after Bog's tricks in my room. From all available evidence and my own observations, I'd believed that Sherlock Holmes was impervious to this particular temptation. It appeared there was a crack in his ascetic persona after all. A crack *I'd* opened up.

I'd hooked his mind—I could hook him right through his passions as well if I played this moment right.

It was a risk. Who could say how a man like Sherlock would respond if I outright shattered his sense of himself as a man without lust? But I needed him caught up in me, I needed him engrossed to the point of obsession, now more than ever.

And I also wanted this. I wanted to find out what I could experience with a man whose wits might match mine.

That thought sent another little thrill through me. Maybe I had more in common with John than I'd considered, even if our penchant for risk-taking wasn't what he'd meant when he'd mentioned kindred spirits.

"From my observations, human beings are rarely able to separate physical intimacy from tender emotions so neatly," Sherlock said. "And there are simpler ways of gaining bodily satisfaction."

"I suppose," I said, staying right where I was, my gaze holding his. "But it is a rather special sort of gratification. How much direct experience do you have on which to base that kind of judgment?"

"I had a few encounters in my college years. They were a lot of effort for little reward. There was nothing about them I'd recommend."

I smiled fully, just barely holding my lips back from a smirk. "I think you've missed out, then. A good 'encounter' can be incredibly stimulating to the mind as well. You'd have to recommend that."

"If I believed it," Sherlock said in a skeptical tone, but his eyes hadn't left mine. I was sure of the avidness I saw there now.

"So we have a difference of opinion," I said, resting my elbows on the arms of the chair. "What if I could prove it to you?"

CHAPTER FOURTEEN

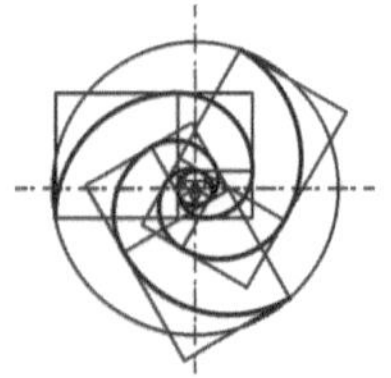

Jemma

Sherlock had been sitting nearly motionless before, but now he went completely still. "How would you expect to 'prove it'?"

Oh, he knew. I could see *that* in his face, in the brief bob of his throat.

"I don't think you're really so unaffected," I said, settling more languidly into the plump cushions of my chair. "I bet I could provoke a reaction from you without touching a single place we'd consider overtly sexual. Will you take that wager?"

"A reaction," Sherlock repeated.

"You'll be undeniably hard. And if I win that bet, I get to show you how much more you can feel, without restriction."

A faint smile crossed Sherlock's lips. He really thought I might not be able to live up to my word. "And if you don't?"

"I will," I said. "But for the sake of argument, what would you want? I've got a connection to a commissioner in Munich, if you want to take on more international consulting. I could write a report praising your talents."

"You'll end whatever you've started with John and Garrett beyond the work," Sherlock said abruptly.

I studied him. Interesting. Did my involvement with them bother him on some level, or did he simply figure that if I couldn't win this bet with him, I must be wrong about whether I was distracting them?

"Deal," I said, and stood up. "No time like the present."

It was rather gratifying simply seeing Sherlock so startled. "Now? I—" He recovered himself quickly. "Do you want me on the bed, then?"

"No," I said before he could do more than start to get up. "Right there will do. But... in the interests of ensuring we can confirm the results of this experiment, I will need you a little less dressed."

His eyes narrowed, but he eased out of his housecoat. "That does seem reasonable."

"Pants too," I said, gesturing. "The rest can stay on. I'll work around it."

He shed his slacks, revealing a pair of striped boxers. As he settled into the chair again, I came around the coffee table.

"Anything else?" he asked, in an impressively even tone.

"You're perfect," I said. "Stay exactly where you are."

I climbed onto the chair, straddling him with my knees on either side of his thighs. Lifting myself up a bit, I was face to face with him as I undid the top buttons on his shirt. This close, the blue of Sherlock's eyes was even more piercing. The earthy smell of his tobacco mingled with a sharp tang of aftershave. He put on such a cool demeanor, but everywhere our bodies touched, his felt blazing hot.

Fuck the risks. I wanted this man too damn much.

And I knew exactly how to get to him.

"It's fascinating how many nerve endings an earlobe has," I murmured, tracing my finger along the shell of his ear. I circled my thumb over the soft flesh at its base and leaned in to nip it between my lips, the smell of him filling my lungs. "Each one of them ready to light up at the right sort of touch."

Sherlock's pulse thumped under my palm where my other hand

rested just beneath his shoulder, only speeding up a smidge at my attentions. Not so much an ear man, apparently.

I tipped lower, my breasts just shy of brushing his chest, and kissed one side of his neck while I stroked my fingertips along the other. "The neck too. All that vulnerability tied directly to the brain, ready to go on the alert with pleasure just as much as it can with pain."

"Is this going to be a biology lesson?" Sherlock asked, but he couldn't mask the roughening of his voice. He was plenty sensitive here.

"I thought you might appreciate the scientific explanation, since you expressed so many doubts," I said, my voice still low, my breath grazing his throat.

"I'm aware of the basics of the physiological process already."

"But most lessons sink in better with an active demonstration, don't you think?" I smiled against his skin and tasted his smoky scent with a flick of my tongue. My fingers glided up to the crook of his jaw and down to his sternum. Sherlock drew in a breath with a slight hitch that set off an ache between my thighs.

"Those tingling nerves are encouraging the blood vessels to dilate all through your mind, urging the blood to flow faster." I kissed my way down to his collarbone, slow and lingering. Then I reached for his arm.

I caressed and then kissed the underside of his wrist as I unbuttoned the cuff of his sleeve and eased it up his arm. My fingers teased over the lean muscles to the inside of his elbow—and paused.

Most people would have taken the faint pink mottling there for normal skin variation. Would John even have noticed it? It didn't speak of an intensive habit—I'd seen what that looked like. But the pale impressions were just a little too regular to be natural discoloration.

I stroked my thumb over the area and looked at Sherlock. His eyes gleamed, a flush starting to seep over his cheeks. He hadn't conceded anything yet, but this moment felt more intimate than any I'd shared with Garrett or John.

He read the question in my eyes. "When the boredom becomes

too much between cases, I occasionally take cocaine by injection. I'm extremely careful with my dosing. The energizing and clarifying effect on the mind outweighs any ill effects."

That great mind of his didn't know how to deal with stillness, did it? I touched the side of his face with an unfamiliar twinge in my gut.

"All the better that we're having this... discussion, then," I said. "You can get just as good a high from the right sex with the right partner without burning out fragments of your beautiful brain."

How much less interesting would this world be without at least one man like him in it to challenge me?

Before he could argue against my claim, I turned my attention back to his arm. I traced up and down the sensitive skin with a feathered touch. "Those sparking nerves and that rush of blood heighten the senses, so that each new point of contact comes into sharper focus."

My lips followed my fingers with testing kisses. Sherlock's pulse fluttered, and his body seemed to sink deeper into the chair with ebbing resistance, but I wasn't quite satisfied yet.

I slipped my other hand under his shirt, careful to avoid the area of his boxers and his nipples so he couldn't claim I'd violated the terms of our wager. He might be slender, but compact muscles covered every inch of his frame. He didn't come by his knowledge of the martial arts just through observation. Maybe someday we'd get to spar in a more literal way.

I fanned my fingers against his taut abs, meeting them with tempting softness, and heard Sherlock swallow. His body shifted almost imperceptibly, as if it'd tried to rise to my touch but he'd held it back.

Very good. Neck and stomach. I could work with that.

I let my voice drop even lower. "The more aroused the body becomes, the more oxytocin floods the brain, relaxing and wiping away stress to clear the mind."

Drawing a gentle circle on his palm, I raised his hand to suck his thumb into my mouth. A quiver ran through his legs. I caught his gaze as I rolled my tongue around him and then released him.

"But the real high," I murmured, tipping to kiss his neck again, "comes from the dopamine that's being triggered too, lighting up all the best spots inside your skull—ones no drug is going to reach. And as all those effects come together and build, the high can carry on and on…"

I stroked his abdomen with both hands, switching to a teasing graze of my fingernails and back to feathered caresses as I nibbled along his jaw. Sherlock had barely stirred, but his skin felt twice as hot as it had before. His pulse stuttered against the press of my mouth. I drew every ounce of sensation I could from the side of his neck with lips and tongue and the tips of my teeth. Then I nipped him just above his collarbone.

Sherlock's hips jerked up, flooding my own body with arousal. I had him, as sure as anything. He went still again under me, but there was no mistaking that response or the growing raggedness he couldn't smooth from his breath.

I wasn't in a hurry. I licked the spot where I'd nipped him and sucked on the pulse point above it, just shy of leaving a mark. My hands eased a little higher beneath his shirt. Then I shifted backward to glance down between us. An erection I'd admit was rather impressive tented his striped boxers.

I looked at Sherlock with an arch of my eyebrows. "I trust we can agree on the winner of our bet?"

His cool blue eyes were outright glittering now, sharpened with desire. It sounded as if it took some strain for him to keep his voice steady. "It would be unjust for me to deny it."

A smile curled my lips. "Then this is mine."

I slipped my fingers around his erection through the cotton fabric. Sherlock's eyelids drifted shut. His cock twitched against my palm. Heat and need pooled at my core, but all my focus stayed on his responses. I stroked him from base to head, reveling in the desire that emanated from this one part of his body.

It wasn't good enough, touching him through a barrier. I dipped my hand beneath the waistband and eased his boxers down until I'd completely freed him. His cock rose rigid, almost parallel with his torso, the tip glistening.

I slicked that liquid over his length and leaned in. My other hand slid up to tease my thumb over one of his nipples, earning me a quiver that told me he was sensitive there too. I brought my mouth to the other side of his neck.

With each pump of my fingers around his hardened cock, Sherlock's heart thumped faster. I swiveled my thumb around his nipple and then flicked it right over, kissing every inch of his neck.

His hands stayed braced on the arms of the chair. A prickle of doubt ran through my mind. I didn't want this interlude to end with him feeling mauled rather than indulged. His body might be responding, but if his will still wasn't in it, I hadn't won after all.

I let go of him and pulled back far enough to watch his expression. Sherlock's eyes snapped open.

"I think I've made my point very thoroughly," I said. "If you want me to stop—"

"No," he said—one breathless, determined, perfect syllable—and yanked my mouth to his.

There was at least one thing in the world Sherlock Holmes wasn't an expert at. His kiss was unpracticed and sloppy in its wildness, but so raw with untapped potential that it sent a bolt of pleasure through me anyway. As I cupped his jaw to bring us together at a better angle, my own desire propelled me onward. My hips flexed, pressing my core to the solid member beneath me.

Sherlock groaned and ground into me. Kissing me harder, he jerked up the skirt of my dress to grasp my panties. I wriggled out of them with his impatient tug urging me on.

A tiny alert went off in my mind. But my purse was back by my chair, and I had my own internal means of protection, and Sherlock was both nearly abstinent and the most vigilant person I'd ever met. If I was going to break my rules for any man, it'd be this one.

His hips arched toward me. I gripped his straining length to position him. He bucked up as I sank down, filling me with a sudden sharp crackling of bliss that brought a gasp from my throat.

If the sex I'd had with Garrett had been urgent, this coming together was outright frantic. Our mouths parted and collided. Sherlock grasped my thigh tightly as he thrust into me hard and fast in pursuit of release. His cock jarred inside me, provoking a jolt of sensation that was more pain than pleasure. Another gasp hitched out of me.

He wasn't so lost in lust that he missed the difference in the sound. He shifted under me, filling me deeper and more smoothly.

"Right there," I mumbled as a fresh flare of pleasure seared through my core. "That's good, that's so —"

He brought my lips crashing into his again. Bliss shivered through me and spiraled higher. He had to be close after all my teasing, but that was okay, because I was almost there too.

We bucked against each other, almost violent in our need. I grazed my fingers down over Sherlock's chest to the dip of his belly again, and that caress propelled him over the edge. A choked sound escaped him as he drove into me even harder than before with a shudder. The feel of him bare inside me, flooding me with heat, sent me careening after him.

The final wave of pleasure shot through me. My body clenched. My mouth skidded across his jaw, my arm bracing against his shoulder as the burst of ecstasy turned my muscles to jelly.

We held like that for a minute or two, me kneeling over him with my head bent next to his, his hand clamped to my thigh. Our heartbeats slowed together.

"Well," Sherlock said in a voice that was still a little rough. "That experience was certainly… instructive."

I laughed, kissed his cheek, and straightened up. "You're going to have to work on your post-coital sweet-talk if you want to experience it again."

The corner of his mouth quirked up in amusement, but enough intensity lingered in his gaze to tell me that he did hope to repeat this experience. What a shame I might not be here long enough to take him up on that interest any time soon.

"I was under the impression that instructive was your goal," he said. "I suppose you'll go now?"

From any other man, the question would have come across as a cold dismissal, but Sherlock was merely asking me what my usual habits were.

"That's what I'd normally expect to do," I said. "Unless you'd rather I stayed longer?"

He paused, giving the idea genuine consideration as if he wasn't entirely sure of his preferences. Which I guessed he wouldn't be.

"No," he said. "That seems to be where the line between physical gratification and more tender emotions would be inclined to blur."

"Exactly my perspective." I grinned at him. "I appreciate that we're on the same page."

As I recovered my panties, Sherlock tucked himself away and pulled his housecoat back on. He saw me to the door. I stopped there and turned toward him to tap his jaw.

"Now that the rush has cleared our heads, let's see what solutions come to us after we've slept on the problem. We'll talk in the morning."

"Here's to a productive sleep, then," Sherlock said.

Another grin stretched across my face as I headed down the hall. I didn't know yet whether I'd just made the best decision of my life or the worst, but fuck, it had felt good.

CHAPTER FIFTEEN

Sherlock

Throughout my career thus far, I'd traced the threads of each case I pursued with the intention of contributing to justice and the safety of the general public. Personal concern for the client who brought the case to my attention, whether they were law enforcement or ordinary citizen, didn't enter the equation. Clients could lie or be misinformed, after all. The facts had to speak for themselves.

Yet now I found the Richter dilemma gnawed at me not only because of the array of crimes he'd already committed and the many more he'd likely commit in the future, but because of the woman sitting across the breakfast table from me, who was grinning at something John had said while taking a bite of one of those ridiculously sweet pastries. The thought of letting her down niggled at me like a second thorn in my side as a companion to the first born from my lack of progress.

I'd practically insisted that Jemma take me into her confidence on this matter. I'd dragged her away from the conference she'd been invited to as an honor to join me on quests that had gotten us nowhere. Her keen mind had seen a capacity in me that I hadn't known I possessed until last night, and I couldn't bring a murderer to justice with his crime spread out right in front of me.

It was bloody well unacceptable.

The combination of sex and sleep had left me invigorated yet steady in a way I wasn't used to but quite appreciated. Even so, my thoughts hadn't centered on a solution yet. They kept circling around to the stray comment Jemma had made in a moment of frustration about the evidence being so close but out of our grasp.

That was the key my mind kept returning to. The murder weapon was right there for the taking. If we could demonstrate its role in the murder, the police department would have to act. There *had* to be a way we could seize it even without a warrant on our side.

I scooped a spoonful of poached egg into my mouth. The salted yolk traveled stickily down my throat.

Perhaps if we slipped in when the relics were being packed up from the gallery? But last time Richter had been carrying that piece on him. He was particularly protective of it, and he might be even more so now that it could testify to his crime. I couldn't imagine him being careless with it in transit.

Jemma finished her sweet roll with a lick of her fingers. The gesture sent a tickle of sensation over my skin. If our encounter last night had brought my senses into sharper alertness, the effect was especially magnified when it came to her. Every movement she made in my presence echoed through me.

She was still a mystery, really, after all the time we'd spent together. How had she honed her mind to be nearly as incisive and pragmatic as mine was? Why on earth was she wasting her time in some tiny German city? If I could persuade her to consider uprooting, to making a go of it here—imagine how quickly her talents could develop working in tandem with me. Imagine the speed with which we could dispatch the country's, even the world's, most tenacious villains.

It would be a tremendous boon for *her* career, certainly, and a benefit to myself, John, and Scotland Yard as well. I hadn't given her much reason to trust that to be true yet, though, had I?

I swallowed the rest of my egg. Jemma and John were getting up, Garrett already scampering to the side table to pour himself another cup of coffee. I pushed back my chair.

"What are your plans for the morning, Sherlock?" Jemma asked. She smiled at me with the same friendly warmth she always had before, without any indication that the dynamic between us had shifted.

From what she'd said, I supposed it hadn't really. She'd been the same with John and Garrett. I'd only deduced the intimacy they'd shared from how *their* responses to her had subtly but unmistakably changed. John, for example, had suddenly taken up ironing his shirts with considerably more care, a task he hadn't been as attentive with since he'd parted ways with that last girlfriend of his.

"I hadn't settled on any yet," I admitted. I'd been considering returning to the gallery to study the murder weapon some more, but too much attention was likely to put Richter on the alert. After John's stunt there yesterday, we'd have to tread carefully. "Yourself?"

"I figured I might as well take a little more advantage of the conference while I'm here. Maybe one of the speakers will say something that inspires an idea." She glanced at her program booklet. "There's a seminar on criminal psychology this morning that I was looking forward to. In five minutes. I'd better get going!"

"I'll come with you," I said, because inspiration did sometimes work in strange ways. Also because John was clearly planning on tagging along, and the way his hand lingered on Jemma's arm as he encouraged her to lead the way made me wary. My friend and colleague was much more of a romantic than I was or Jemma had shown herself to be. If he'd gotten too caught up in her attentions, I'd like to determine that soon enough to effectively intervene.

The seminar was held in the same room as the first one I'd attended, larger than the others but with a staleness to the air that suggested the ventilation system wasn't working at full capacity. I'd need to give a word to the management about looking into some repairs. We couldn't find seats together, so the four of us—because Garrett had joined our expedition too—ended up spaced out by a row or two in a zigzag pattern near the edge of the rows. I watched Jemma's head and John watching her too as the doctor of psychiatry giving the talk took the podium.

It was not a particularly inspiring lecture. The subject of psychology tended to be rather wishy-washy in general, either common sense observations that anyone with a functioning brain should have been able to deduce or vague conjectures that were either useless or improvable—frequently both. This man's version of criminal psychology appeared to be no different. But the audience gazed at him avidly as he spun out this tale and that one about the mindsets that had led one person or another to commit various crimes, mostly rather mundane cases. Then he opened the discussion to questions, the first couple of which were even more mundane.

Was it worth the perceived rudeness to leave early and take a nice long walk through the city that was a lot more likely to jog some inspiration loose? I'd nearly decided in favor of that idea when Dr. Prashad nodded to someone a few rows behind me. With his attention in my general direction, I delayed.

The voice that spoke up had the lilt of an Australian accent—a somewhat muddy one, as if he'd spend a good deal of time in more than one province. "Is it true that criminals tend to continue down a path toward more severe crimes once they escalate their activities?"

A potentially intriguing concept. I glanced back and spotted a dreadlock-framed face with blue eyes so bright their color was clear even from a distance.

"I'm sorry," the doctor said. "I don't completely understand what you mean. Could you give an example?"

The man ducked his head as if embarrassed. "Sorry. I've just heard it said that if you have, say, a pickpocket, and he ends up getting in on a robbery, assuming he sees he can get away with it, he'll tend to keep on with robberies rather than going back to simple pickpocketing. Criminals tend to behave worse—or the same, I guess—over time, not better. Would you say that's true?"

I swiveled my head back toward the doctor, and my gaze snagged on Jemma's face. She'd looked toward the questioner too, and her mouth had drawn tight, her brow knit. She caught my glance and grimaced before turning to take in Dr. Prashad's answer.

My stomach tightened in turn. From pickpocketing to robbery. From assault to murder. Without listening to what the doctor was saying, I already knew that pattern existed.

Richter had been enough of a menace before. Now he'd learned he could kill a man with his own hands and face no consequences. How many more lives might he ruin in the most literal way if he slipped from our grasp?

A thought rose up with a new concrete certainty: We had to get our hands on that jade statue. We had to *literally* place our hands on it and whisk it to a lab, as soon as we humanly could.

Despite my skepticism of the utility of various laws in obtaining actual justice, part of me balked for a moment at the thought. I'd never gone to such lengths before… but when had I needed to?

My policy had always been to weigh the potential harm and follow the path that prevented more. No one at all would be harmed in a scheme to steal the statue except Richter—or myself and my colleagues, if I faltered.

So I wouldn't falter. Perhaps I wouldn't normally pursue a matter so boldly, but I wouldn't have believed I could feel what Jemma had brought out in me last night either until I'd been forced to recognize it. How could I truly call myself the world's greatest detective if I was afraid to do what needed to be done, to stretch myself beyond the strategies I found comfortable?

My heart picked up to a brisk but even beat. Yes, this was our solution. I only had to let myself accept it.

The rest of the seminar passed in a blur of voices and a whirl of silent planning. When the audience stood up, I motioned to my colleagues. John hurried to meet me in the aisle. Jemma and Garrett caught up with us in the hall just outside.

"What is it?" Jemma asked, studying my face. She must be able to tell I'd chosen a course of action. My confidence in that course lit me up all through my body. We had so much to do, but we *could* do this.

I would have to lead the way, even though this was Jemma's

case. She'd hesitated at my smaller ploys before, still a little too hesitant despite her brilliance. I could take the responsibility on my shoulders, and we'd both win out.

"Scotland Yard won't give us a warrant, so we'll just have to retrieve the statue by our own means," I said. "Once we can test it and confirm the evidence, any embarrassment or threat of lawsuit will be wiped away. We're going to break into that gallery and take it —simple as that."

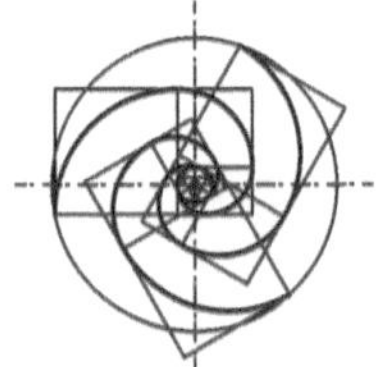

CHAPTER SIXTEEN

Jemma

I stopped on the narrower path where the park's trees hid me from view, confirming that my trio was already stationed by the tiered fountain up ahead. It was a typical early spring day in London, damp saturating the breeze that licked over me and a layer of hazy gray cloud blanketing the sky. I tugged my wool jacket close against the cold and pressed my phone to my ear.

"I'm almost there. Have you got eyes on the fountain?"

Bash's low dry voice carried through the speaker. "I'll be watching the whole time, Mori, ready to go if you need me."

"Let's hope there's no redirection required. It'll complicate things —but better to complicate them than to see them fall apart. If I rub my chin, you get in there as fast as you can."

"It shouldn't take me more than thirty seconds," Bash said. His confidence washed away the remaining chill. I could only imagine how much harder this entire scheme would have been to pull off without him. I'd managed all right during the few years before I'd connected with Bash, but having his help had elevated my reach so very far.

"Good," I said. "We'll talk again soon either way."

I ended the call, switched the phone to audio recording mode, and tucked it into the thin inner pocket I'd added to the jacket specifically for when I wanted to record a conversation. The fabric I'd picked still muffled voices a little, but they were recognizable. Useful if you wanted to double-check your memories later — or if you needed blackmail material down the road.

Having Bash standing by gave me an extra level of security right now. Sherlock had appeared to be determined to carry out his plan, and he'd won his colleagues over, but John and Garrett had shown even more hesitation than I'd allowed myself to. Whether they stayed on board might depend on how this security expert Sherlock knew reacted to his questions — and I was pretty sure I was going to need the entire trio to get us to my goal.

Tucking my hands into my pockets, I strode onto the wide paved path that led between two rows of cylindrical hedges toward the fountain. Dreary as the sky was, the newly grown leaves on the surrounding trees beamed in their fresh shades of green. They weren't going to be subdued by a little cloud cover.

Sherlock spotted me first and acknowledged me with a tip of his head. Garrett nodded too, his shoulders hunched inside his light linen jacket — he'd obviously underestimated the chill. John shot me a flash of a smile as he twirled his walking stick restlessly.

"Where is this guy?" Garrett demanded the second I joined them. "Wasn't he supposed to be here at one?"

"He's got a couple more minutes before he's even slightly late," Sherlock said evenly. "Considering what a last-minute request this was, I won't blame him if he isn't perfectly punctual."

"How can we be sure we can even trust him? You know how suspicious you'll sound with all these questions."

John hummed to himself. "More likely, he'll be wondering whether *he* can trust us."

Sherlock frowned at both of them. "He knows me. He's seen my integrity in action. I wouldn't be reaching out to him if I wasn't confident of his discretion and good faith."

"I trust *Sherlock*," I said in a mild tone. "Isn't that what really matters?"

Garrett scowled but didn't argue, and John looked chagrinned. The comment shut down their doubtful comments and made Sherlock stand even straighter, so that was a win all around.

Sherlock craned his neck. "Here he comes now. Right on time. I agreed to having you all here to ease your minds because of the enormity of the scheme we're putting together, but Neville is used to me working alone. I trust that *you* will let me do the talking and at least put on the appearance of a united front?"

I raised my chin. "Once I say I'm in, I'm in."

"Just pretend I'm not here," Garrett muttered.

John set the end of his walking stick firmly on the ground. "You know I'll stand with you through anything."

The man Sherlock had indicated was skirting a stone planter dotted with small shrubs. He was built rather like a shrub himself, short and portly with a sprig of curly dark hair down the middle of his head. Perhaps he'd sprout flowers later in the springtime too.

"Sherlock," he said with a hint of reverence when he reached us. His gaze slid over the rest of us. "And colleagues." He turned back to Sherlock. "We could have simply met at my office, you know."

"I wanted to avoid any visual record of this meeting, traffic cams and security videos and so on," Sherlock said, as if that were a perfectly normal concern for an everyday meeting. "For your sake at least as much as mine. The subjects I'd like to get your input on are rather… sensitive."

Neville raised his eyebrows. "Well, you've got me intrigued, that's for sure. Go ahead."

Sherlock fished in the pocket of his trench coat and produced a slip of paper. "First, could you tell me whether you know of any ways to break the code on this particular type of lock?"

He held the paper out so Neville could read it without Sherlock actually handing it over. The expert's eyebrows lifted higher. He scratched the corner of his jaw, his forehead furrowing.

"That's a top of the line system," he said. "With the newest models, you won't find many who could crack it. I could, with the right equipment, of course, but it wouldn't be terribly fast—at least a few minutes. Why do you want to know *that*?"

"It's better if you're not involved beyond the imparting of information and skills," Sherlock said. "And pointing us to the right equipment, unless you can lend me something that wouldn't be traceable. I'd like you to teach me how to use it."

He'd told us this was the plan when we'd discussed the meeting earlier. *This is our case. We can make the decision to take the necessary risks. I want to avoid all possible collateral damage. No one else should have to put their livelihoods on the line.*

"I'd say it's not the sort of thing I could teach very quickly, but I know what your mind is like. I could take you through the paces whenever you want." Neville cocked his head. "Is that all?"

"No." Sherlock flipped the paper around. "I also need to know how one would handle a motion sensor security system of this type. To shut it down, or at least avoid setting it off."

The other man hesitated. I balled my hands in my pockets, holding back the urge to jump in and steer the conversation myself. Sherlock knew this man, and I didn't. I *did* trust him at least as far as knowing what his allies would and wouldn't tolerate. A stranger jumping in might throw off a delicate balance I didn't fully understand.

Even if I did decide intervention was necessary, I'd let Bash handle that.

"It's pretty much impossible to tackle motion sensors of that type once they're running," Neville said slowly. "The only way you can disable them is if you can get at them before they're turned on or if you can cut the power."

"Then it is possible," Sherlock said. "Excellent, excellent."

"Sherlock… I'd really feel more comfortable if you told me what this was all for. I wouldn't even be talking about subjects like this with, well, almost anyone other than you."

"It's for a good cause. The best of causes, really."

Neville gave him a skeptical look. "How good a cause can it be if you can't tell me about it for my own protection?"

I held myself from shifting my weight restlessly. Garrett glanced at John surreptitiously with an expression that seemed to say, *I told you this was a bad idea.*

Sherlock simply gave the security expert a calm smile. "You remember Canterbury, don't you, Neville? I keep my cards close to my chest for a variety of reasons, but you can always be sure there *are* reasons. Consider: Sometimes to foil a criminal you must understand their potential methodology."

Well, that was a bald-faced lie. He was implying that we were trying to stop a break-in rather than plotting to commit one ourselves. Not that I hadn't seen Sherlock lie before, but it'd always been to people he disdained. He considered this man a trusted associate.

There was very little he wouldn't bend in pursuit of his victory, was there? Lucky for me. How many steps were there between criminal mastermind and crime-fighting consulting detective anyway? The things we could do together if he ever adjusted his morals completely...

His gambit worked. Neville visibly relaxed with a sigh of relief. "Of course. I'm sorry. Caution comes with the line of work, you know—it's difficult to turn that instinct off."

"And that fact does you credit," Sherlock assured him. "I won't keep you from your prior commitments any longer. When would be the soonest we could meet up for a lesson or two? The matter is rather urgent."

"My evening is free."

"Perfect. I'll call you when I have my own plans more settled, and we can arrange an exact time and place."

My hands unclenched. I eased them from my pockets as Neville ambled off.

One more piece of the puzzle was in place. We were getting so close I could almost taste my own victory.

"The motion sensors will require some thought," Sherlock said quietly. "The security company controls them and monitors the whole gallery from an external site. But we can work through one problem at a time."

"I have some experience with pressure sensitive devices," John said. "I can refresh my —"

He cut himself off just as a waft of deeper cold and the scent of parched rot washed over me. My stomach flipped. John's head had jerked up — and Sherlock's and Garrett's followed. I wrenched my own head back to see what they were staring at just above me, but the back of my neck was already prickling like a warning.

Bog floated there, filmy fabric drifting around it even more freely than usual, swaying up and down with an oddly stilted rhythm that jarred in my mind as I took it in. Ice shot down my spine.

My hand darted up in an instinctive gesture to try to ward the shrouded one away. I caught my arm at the last second and yanked it back down. Then my heart lurched for a completely different reason.

I'd caught my hand by my chin. From a distance, Bash might think I'd given him the signal to charge in. Shit.

"What the —" John said hoarsely, and Sherlock's gaze dropped from whatever he could make out above me to my face. Garrett took a step back. I didn't have time to juggle all of their reactions. If Bash rushed in with his ploy now, he could inadvertently throw off everything I'd gained — even more than it was already thrown off thanks to the creature fading away above me.

"Custard!" I snapped out, loud enough to be sure my voice would carry beyond the trees and hedges around us.

The apparently random word at least had the effect of interrupting the bewilderment of the men around me with a different sort of confusion. Sherlock knit his brow, still peering at me. "Custard?"

Bash and I had picked a code word that meant "Abort!" ages ago. In ideal circumstances, I'd have found a way to at least somewhat naturally work it into conversation. There was nothing ideal about this moment.

I swiped at my cheeks as if trying to wipe away a blush of embarrassment, raising their color as I did. "I just — I saw the weirdest thing — I must have eaten too much custard at lunch. There is an amount of sugar that can mess with your brain."

"*I* saw something too," Garrett said tersely. "I didn't eat any custard—or whatever. We all saw it, didn't we?"

I widened my eyes. "You saw it too? What exactly did you see?"

"It looked," Sherlock said with a frown, "like a ghost out of some sort of horror film. Pale and faded and vaguely humanoid." He swiveled on his feet, taking in the fountain, the path of hedges, the trees, as if trying to determine whether any of them might have been responsible.

Bog hadn't shown itself completely, but the shrouded one had revealed a lot more than a strange wavering of light. My fingers itched for one of my sugar cubes. This felt too familiar. It felt too much like that hopeless flailing sensation years ago when I'd discovered my expected fate. Panic trickled up through my chest.

"That's what I'd have said it looked like too," John said. "All sort of… streamy? Just floating there." He shook his head and touched his temple.

"It was fucking eerie," Garrett said.

Sherlock paced around me, studying the clouds overhead. "It was right above *you*, Jemma. Did you feel anything?"

"No," I said, grasping for some way, any way, to regain control here. I needed Sherlock focused on the gallery heist, not on supernatural beings following me around. I needed Garrett *not* to connect this spectacle to whatever oddity he'd witnessed from Bog in the doorway the other morning.

An idea clicked into place. I grabbed Sherlock's arm. "Maybe we should call off this heist idea. If our nerves are getting to us so much that we're imagining weird spirits—"

His ego kicked in before I had to go any farther. Sherlock Holmes didn't succumb to nerves.

"No," he said firmly. "There's nothing wrong with *us*. It had to be some sort of natural phenomenon. A sliver of sunlight cutting through the clouds at an odd angle, perhaps. We surely wouldn't all have seen the same thing if it hadn't been there."

And the last thing Sherlock would ever believe in was something beyond the world of the concrete and scientific. I'd read enough accounts where he scoffed at the idea of ghosts and spirits to be sure of that, thank all that was holy.

I exhaled slowly as if gathering myself. I'd gotten him back on course. This wasn't a catastrophe.

"You're right," I said. "We were probably all a little tense after this meeting."

"Easy to jump to an eerie interpretation when we're already keyed up," John said, although his expression was still wary.

Garrett motioned toward the path. "I don't know what the hell that was, but at this point I don't care. Can we just get out of here?"

"Yes," Sherlock said. "There's still much to be done."

But he kept frowning as he moved to walk away.

The second my hotel room door clicked shut behind me, I spun on my heel, glaring around the space.

"What the hell was that, Bog?" I said, raising my voice as loud as I dared, hotel walls being what they were. "If you want to give me a message, give it to me directly. Aren't you embarrassed to turn yourself into some kind of schlocky horror carnival trick?"

I hadn't known for sure that the shrouded one had followed me back here, but after the show Bog had just put on, I'd figured it'd want to watch my full reaction. The air near the window shimmered. The pale sunlight seeping through the glass partly solidified into Bog's wavering form.

"You seem very upset, bloodling. How unlike you."

I aimed my glare at the impenetrable mist of Bog's face. "I just can't believe how stupid you're being. How many of your kind's laws did you just break? You have business with *me*, not with anyone else around me."

"And yet your business with them seems so urgent as your days creep toward their end." Bog drifted over the table. "Very strange."

"I should be able to do whatever I want with those last few days, seeing as I still belong to myself for that time."

"I haven't prevented you from doing anything. You move about perfectly freely."

I gritted my teeth. "You know you're disrupting the human world. Do you really want me to report this to the rest of the shrouded folk? What will they do with you?"

The shrouded one made a sound like a creaky chuckle. "If they realize who you are, it will be just as bad for you as for me. If they don't, nothing they inflict would interfere with contracts already drawn. I doubt we will find out, will we, bloodling? You're in no hurry to place yourself before the ones you were once so desperate to escape."

The words made the back of my neck twitch. "There are ways I can tip them off without them knowing who pointed them in the right direction," I said. "Maybe I'd like to see justice carried out whether or not it affects what I owe you."

"Maybe," Bog said with hollow amusement. "Or maybe you would refuse to take even that chance."

It vanished like a streak of light swallowed up by a shadow, there and then gone. I stood scowling at the place where it'd been for several moments longer.

Maybe you would refuse to take even that chance. Bog was calling my bluff. A finger of cold prodded my stomach.

It *was* a bluff. I'd be worse off if the rest of the shrouded folk turned their attention on me than I was right now.

In the grand scheme of things, Bog was small potatoes. The only reason I'd been able to convince it to make the deal was that it'd never have gotten its maw on a human sacrifice in ten thousand years otherwise. What it'd said was true: If the higher folk found out Bog was the one that'd stolen their prized lamb, they might sever our contract, sure, but only so they could devour me for themselves.

There were certain lines Bog wouldn't cross. If it went too far, the shrouded folk would notice its antics on their own. But what it'd done already was bad enough. How many times could even Sherlock dismiss strange lights and figures he'd never seen before I'd come into his life as a mere coincidence?

There was nothing I could do to stop it. If I'd known a way to contain Bog, I wouldn't have been here in the first place.

CHAPTER SEVENTEEN

Garrett

One of the best things about Thompson was his predictability. He worked the same shift that ended in the mid-afternoon as often as he could get it, and after every shift he went straight to the pub down the road from the station for a beer before he headed home for dinner. He even had a favorite booth.

I spotted him there through the window—alone today, thankfully. Trying to divert more of my colleagues so I could have this conversation would have tied my stomach in twice as many knots.

Sherlock probably would have come in with a subtle ploy, pretending he'd just happened to pop in for a drink and, oh, why not stop by to chat with that coworker who coincidentally was in the same place? Deception wasn't really my style. The fact that I needed to do any at all had prompted those knots in my stomach. Normally Sherlock and John carried out their schemes while I looked the other way, and that suited all three of us just fine.

I pushed past the door into the pub. It wasn't a bad place, really —sure, the booziness in the air mingled with smell of frying oil from their famous wings, and as soon as you moved beyond the front windows it was rather dim, but the amber lighting created a warm atmosphere and the oak tables gleamed with recent polishing. Sprightly folk music played over the wall-mounted speakers.

When I reached his table, Thompson glanced up from the sports magazine he'd been flipping through. "Lestrade!" he said, a grin that looked a little too eager splitting his doughy face. "What brings you here? I thought you were all busy with that fancy conference."

Thompson had already been with the department two years when I'd started on. Three later, I'd become the youngest cop in Scotland Yard to earn detective inspector. Another three after that, Thompson was still on regular constable duty but chomping for the chance.

To be fair, he'd been friendly enough when I'd started. But that friendliness had ramped up several notches as I'd proven myself and then caught Sherlock Holmes' attention enough for me to start working with the consulting detective regularly. One time, I'd spent an hour recounting the not-particularly-sensational events of a two hour dinner at Sherlock and John's shared flat thanks to Thompson's avid questioning.

He played nice right now because he coveted what I had. The second he saw a chance to step in front of me, no doubt he would.

"Duty still calls," I said in a casual tone I had to force. "I've been looking into some things on the side. Do you mind if I join you for a few minutes?"

Thompson drew his elbows in, his gaze sharpening. He wasn't the swiftest bloke on the force, but he wasn't stupid either. And he kept his ear to the ground.

"Sure," he said. As I slid onto the opposite bench, he turned the beer glass in his hands and tilted his head to one side. "I heard you were hassling the chief for a warrant for the Richter exhibition."

"That's actually why I was hoping to talk with you," I said. "You've been assigned to the security detail keeping an eye on the gallery, haven't you?"

"I have." Thompson shifted in his seat, clearly unhappy with the fact. "Seems like Richter is more worried about being the victim of a crime than avoiding being caught for one. What got you all itchy about him?"

"It may not be him at all," I said. Lie number one. "Sherlock Holmes mentioned some concerns related to one of the relics, which are handled by various people, that I was hoping to follow up on. But the chief has to make his decisions as he feels is best." I spread my hands.

The mention of Sherlock automatically perked Thompson up. "This is one of Holmes' theories, is it?" he said. "What's he on the scent of?"

"He hasn't revealed very much yet," I said. Lie number two. "You know how he can be." That much, at least, would usually have been true.

"Well, I don't know much of anything about the stuff inside the gallery. I've been spending all my time stuck in the car watching the outside of the place."

I grimaced in sympathy that was honest enough. Being staked out like a guard dog on some rich man's whim wasn't a task I'd have wished on anyone.

"I had a few questions about the security set-up—ours, and the private company that's working with the gallery too."

Thompson eyed me. "Why are you still poking around there when the chief turned you down? You'll end up getting yourself in trouble if you keep pushing."

He didn't sound all that distressed about the idea, but he did have a point. I folded my hands together on the top of the table, willing down my growing queasiness.

How had I let Sherlock rope me into this? There were reasons I let him handle the more questionable strategies he liked to employ. If this scheme ended badly, if it came out that I'd helped him obtain confidential police information, I could lose everything.

I'd gone completely barmy, hadn't I?

I was already committed, though, and the words of lie number three tumbled out exactly the way I'd rehearsed them in my head.

"It's mainly to ease Holmes' mind. He wants to be sure there's nothing suspicious about the scheduled activity around the gallery.

You know how thoroughly he likes to analyze the details of a scene."

Thompson nodded, relaxing a little. In the past, he'd watched Sherlock spend ten minutes studying an apparently blank wall or a pattern of cigarette ash in an ashtray.

"All right. If it's just between you and him, I can't see how it hurts anything. We've got four shifts scheduled to cover the full twenty-four hours, plus doubling up overnight."

I had the urge to take out my notepad to jot down his answers, but that would make this supposedly friendly conversation feel too much like an interrogation. "What time are the shifts coming and going? Is there a specific spot you're supposed to stay parked?"

"The orders were close but not too close." Thompson ran his finger through the condensation on his glass, drawing the line of the road. "We stay on the opposite side. When it's just the one team, we park at the corner where we can see the entrance but not directly across from it. The second night shift takes the other corner. They're in from ten until six in the morning. The rest of us are doing midnight to eight, eight to four, four to midnight."

"I assume Richter let you know the private security team's schedule as well, so you wouldn't raise a false alarm because of them."

"Aye. He wanted us switching off at different times so there wasn't any moment when both us and them might be distracted in transition. They're doing seven in the morning to three in the afternoon, three to eleven, eleven to seven."

"And they come in the front?"

"Nah," Thompson said. "They go around back down the alley. But we can see the entrance to the alley from where we're parked, to keep an eye on who goes down there. It's easy to tell which is them, even at night. They've got a black van with the company logo stamped on the side in white."

"All right." I leaned back on the bench, a bead of sweat trickling down my back. "Nothing about that sounds like it should raise any concerns. I'll pass the information on to Holmes, but I'd imagine he'll drop that thread of inquiry. Thanks for lending a hand."

"Whatever I can do," Thompson said with a smile. I'd have to remember to figure out some favor to do for him before he called it in a way I didn't like.

I headed out and hailed a taxi—I avoided the hell that was driving in town unless on official business. My stomach churned away as I waited for the car to pull up to the curb.

I'd just baldly lied to a colleague multiple times to aid and abet a crime. Where the hell would I be if I blew up my career? I *loved* this job, jockeying for favor and petty in-fighting and all. I'd hardly had a chance to make a real name for myself without Sherlock's hanging over it.

As I got into the taxi, my phone chimed with a text—the consulting detective himself. *Have spoken to the fellow I know with camera experience. Will meet with you tomorrow, 11am, Fox & Crown.*

Right. Sherlock had grabbed hold of the fact that last year we'd worked a case where I'd had to do a lot of poking around with a shop's security cams. He'd decided in his authoritarian way that my task during our assault on the gallery should be rigging a camera loop. I'd imagine with some pointers from Sherlock's "fellow" I could manage it. Which would put me on the same level as the criminals we'd caught last year.

I shoved the phone into my pocket without answering.

The whole way to the hotel, the driver nattered on about the weather and a rugby game I hadn't watched, barely appearing to notice that I only responded with wordless sounds like "Hmm" and "Ah." My input wasn't required as long as I played my part.

I came into the lobby to find Jemma there waiting for me.

"Hey," she said with a smile, ambling over. "I saw you getting out of the cab while I was passing the window, figured I'd see how your talk went."

Somehow her presence made me feel better and worse at the same time. I found her striking face prettier every time I saw her, and her soft smile brought back the moment in John's car when she'd seemed sorry that our time together was limited. But it *was* limited— she'd be heading back to Germany in a few days now—and damned if she wasn't the first woman I'd met in years who stirred up an attraction that ran this deep.

On top of that, she was also the reason I'd gotten wrapped up in this crazy scheme of Sherlock's in the first place. If she *hadn't* been here, he never would have gotten onto the case and then apparently consumed by it.

The collision of emotions must have shown on my face. Jemma's smile faded. "Not so well?" she said. "Come on, let's grab coffees and you can tell me about it."

I wasn't sure how well coffee would mix with my unsettled stomach, but I followed her to the regularly refilled pots just inside the dining room anyway. It was kind of amusing watching her stir four spoonfuls of sugar into one mug. I didn't feel quite up to teasing her about it, though. Even the blissful look on her face when she took her first sip didn't quite penetrate my uneasiness.

We ended up in the little lounge room where the four of us had talked the first morning after we'd met her. Jemma sat next to me on the sofa, angled to face me, her knees just a couple inches shy of grazing mine.

How she could look so fucking sexy in loose slacks and a blouse buttoned up to her collarbone, I didn't know. Maybe it was just because I'd seen how much fire she could generate when those clothes came off.

"Did your colleague on the security detail not want to talk?" she asked. "It's all right. I'm sure we can figure out most of it through observation—it'll just take a little longer."

I shook my head. "No, he talked plenty. I got all the answers Sherlock wanted. I just…" I swept my hand over my face and into my hair. "This scheme Sherlock has dreamed up is so much crazier than anything he's even proposed, let alone seen through before. No one has to tell me how brilliant he is, but no one's infallible either. We're putting so much on the line. What if his ego has gotten the better of him, and his reach is exceeding his grasp?"

"I was nervous about it too when he first suggested it," Jemma said. "All right, I'm still a little nervous. But he sounds as though he's considered every angle. If we can't find an answer to every problem in the way, then we simply won't go through with it, right?"

"But I've already stuck my neck out, just digging for information the way I did today." I hated saying the words, especially to her, but the sick feeling inside me propelled them out. "I don't lie to people. I don't plan robberies. That's not—that's not who I want to be, even if it's for a good cause." I'd gone into policing specifically to prove to myself that I could be a person with real principles.

Jemma's expression twitched, her lips pursing tight. For a second I thought she was angry, but then I met her eyes again and saw nothing but sadness there.

"Garrett," she said in a voice that was slightly hoarse, "the last thing I'd want is for you to feel like you've been forced into something you don't agree with. I've felt guilty all along because of how dangerous Richter could be, what with everything he's shown he's willing to do to protect himself and all the crimes before that too. This wasn't your problem. You shouldn't have to take those risks."

The mention of Richter's extensive crimes made my throat tighten. "It's not that I don't want him caught," I started.

"I know. But you've already done so much for me… I'm sure the three of us could handle it on our own if you'd rather step back now. You don't even need to share what you found out from your friend, so you won't be complicit. Sherlock and John will figure out everything quickly enough. I can tell them we're going forward without you, and then you can get those worries off your back."

She was already getting to her feet, all determined compassion. My heart wrenched. Suddenly I was on my feet too, grasping her shoulder, not really sure what I was going to say but only that I needed to say something.

Was that really what I wanted—to watch Sherlock and John stride ahead with this plan, to see it unfold from the sidelines as if I hadn't made a difference anyway, as if I couldn't have contributed anything they couldn't do themselves? If they failed, I'd kick myself for abandoning them. If they succeeded, I'd kick myself for not having the guts to try.

The tricks with the security cameras—Sherlock could teach

himself those quickly enough, no doubt. But none of the others could handle the police side of the equation like I could. Without me, there'd be no one to ensure the evidence was even admissible. No one to finesse the situation with the chief. There were all kinds of elements to this operation that *only* I could handle.

This was about a man who'd terrorized countless people across this city and our best chance at bringing him to justice. Wasn't *that* what I'd gotten into this career for, really—to make the world better instead of worse? I should be at the front of the charge, not flailing around like an anxious child. For fuck's sake, John was in, and solving crimes wasn't even technically his job.

"No," I said. "I—I was just talking out loud, getting those doubts out. Maybe I've gotten too caught up in my own head. We're going to bring Richter down, and I'm going to be there to make sure it happens."

Jemma wavered. "Are you definitely okay? I wouldn't—"

"One hundred percent," I said, shoving my queasiness aside and setting my jaw. "I'm in, until the end."

CHAPTER EIGHTEEN

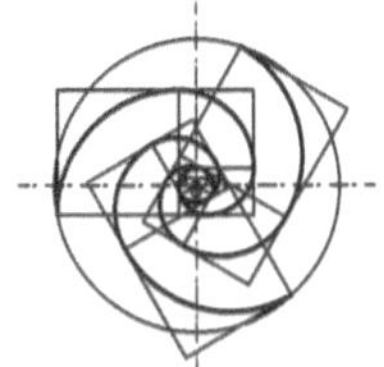

Jemma

Having fun?" John said, sounding amused.

I nudged the last few torn scraps of hotel notepaper into my Fibonacci sequence on John's desk. "It's something to pass the time," I said, keeping my tone casual as if I wasn't doing anything more meaningful than idle doodling.

The sight of the orderly spiral set my nerves slightly more at ease. I already knew the pattern wouldn't keep Bog out, but those scraps might delay the shrouded one from picking up on where I'd gone if it came looking for me. It couldn't keep too close a watch on me without raising questions with the rest of its kind.

I left the desk and dragged my chair over to where John was sitting at the room's small table. "How far off was Sherlock the last time he texted?"

"He said ten minutes, but he was relying on a taxi, so it depends some on the traffic." John looked at his phone. "Although I wouldn't be surprised if he walks in exactly at the time predicted. Which would be in about one more minute…"

I dropped into the chair, my ears pricked. I'd only taken a few more breaths when a knock sounded on the door. John chuckled and started to get up, but I waved him down since I could lope over there faster.

Sherlock strode into the hotel room looking wind-blown. I hadn't realized it was possible for his hair to get any more messy than it typically was. He shrugged off his trench coat, obviously having come up straight from the street, tossed it on the bed, and glanced at the three chairs around the table.

"Garrett isn't joining us?"

"He had more police business to look into," I said, taking my seat.

The truth was I hadn't mentioned the meeting to the detective inspector. After Garrett's near defection this afternoon, I suspected it'd be better to give him a breather from heist planning. Let the crime stay illusory and vague in his mind while he focused on the heroic underpinnings. And if he found out that we'd talked without him, chances were that would only feed his competitive desire to prove himself useful to the cause.

He'd looked so distraught when I'd talked to him that I hadn't been sure even my last-ditch gamble to suck him back in would work. The cop had more of a conscience than I'd anticipated. But his need for keep pace with his more daring colleagues had won out. For now.

Despite what I'd said to him, we did need him. He was the key to making the theft legitimate as evidence in the eyes of the police. Sherlock and John would never continue with the scheme without him. I'd known setting this plan in motion wouldn't be easy, but I didn't like walking a line this delicate.

I had to tense my leg to stop my foot from swinging restlessly as Sherlock sat down between John and me. Earlier, I'd groped in my purse for a sugar cube and discovered I'd nearly burned through my entire supply. As much as I tried to squash my emotions down, echoes of the helpless moments from my past gnawed at the edges of my consciousness.

I wasn't going to let this mission fall apart. I was stronger now — so much stronger.

"How did it go?" John asked his friend. "Are you now the city's foremost expert on lock cracking?"

Sherlock made a dismissive noise. "I may be the second highest expert on this particular lock. Neville took me through the paces. I've got the device and the connectors I'll need." He motioned to his coat. "We'll be able to get through the door to Richter's exhibit regardless of the hour."

"We know the hours we're working with now," I said. "Garrett got the full details of the various security schedules."

"Excellent." Sherlock glanced at John. "You were going to brush up on your understanding of pressure sensitivity."

"And I did." John leaned his elbows onto the table. His hazel eyes gleamed with eagerness to show off his knowledge. "As you can imagine, pressure-sensitive alarms are *somewhat* different in nature from the sorts of devices we had to worry about in the field in Iraq."

"Mines," I supplied.

"Yes. But the gist is essentially the same. The device is rigged to spark a chain reaction when a certain amount of weight is applied to it. In a mine field, that reaction results in an explosive blast, thanks to which my hip will never be the same—but at least I wasn't the poor soul who stepped right on the thing. Here, we only need to worry about the alarm system triggering."

"Though that would be equally catastrophic to our goal," Sherlock said.

"True. So, here's what we need to consider." John cast around and grabbed a deck of cards off the bedside table. He waggled it at me. "Always handy to keep around for impromptu entertaining of new friends and also as a prop for demonstrations. Let's say this is our display case."

He slipped several cards from the box and laid four of them together to make a large rectangle on the table in front of him. Then he built a smaller rectangular structure on top of that.

"Pressure here or here will trigger the alarm," he said, pointing to the area around the structure and then to the structure itself. "Where we have some wiggle room is that there's a lower limit to the weight that the device will register. Just as our enemy combatants don't want their mines exploding at a kicked rock or a fallen twig, the gallery doesn't want the alarm sounding because someone breathed too hard on the glass. As far as I can tell, it's incredibly unlikely they'd have set the lower limit at anything less than a few pounds. Ten is fairly standard."

"So, if we're careful, maybe swapping another object out that's close in weight, we should be able to remove the figurine without setting off the alarm," I said. "Getting *to* the display case is no problem. We can touch it without stepping on the pads—they're not that wide. The difficulty is going to be opening up the case to get to the figurine, isn't it?"

"Exactly. Only the base will be rigged, not the glass, but a significant amount of vibration in or pressure on the glass will trigger the system. I did think of a solution to that problem, though. We use heat." John drew his finger along the top of his model and down over the edge to the side. "Take a blowtorch and melt a line to cut out a chunk—along the edge, so we can easily 'fold' the piece out."

"Yes, that'll make handling it much easier," Sherlock said, his eyes distant but in an intent sort of way, probably picturing the actual display case we'd seen in the gallery.

John nodded. "And while one person handles the glass, another can slide an object we estimate to be around the same weight as the piece we're removing onto the top of the case to balance things out. I figure we should be able to make a guess that isn't more than a pound off. We can bring a hunk of jade to balance out the removed statue as well, like Jemma suggested."

"You've covered all the variables. Well done, John!" Sherlock smiled at his friend with genuine appreciation, and John's grin turned giddy at the praise.

My God, lovers in the fervor of a new relationship high gazed at each other with less adoration. And I was sure now I saw a little wistful hunger in John's expression when Sherlock glanced away.

An idea sparked in the back of my head with an eager quiver. How much passion could I spark in *them* if I guided them to the water's edge? Just the thought made the gnawing restlessness inside me ease back.

I was Jemma Moriarty. I could play the world like Sherlock played his fucking violin. Why not? I'd be giving them what they both might very well want if they'd let themselves admit it.

"Wow," I said with a breathless laugh. "We're almost there." I picked up one of the cards and tapped it thoughtfully against the others as if the idea were only just coming to me. "I don't know about the two of you, but I feel like I need a break from the planning and the worrying. Anyone up for a game of cards? We are new friends, after all."

John stretched his arms behind him and aimed his grin at me. "That sounds like just what I need to end off the day, actually."

"It's not a pastime I generally enjoy," Sherlock started.

I nudged his calf with my foot under the table, arching an eyebrow. "Now when have I heard *that* line before? You've got to know the basic rules of poker. We can play a simple five-card draw. To make things a little more interesting, we can play for dares instead of money."

"Dares?" John said. "That'd be a new one."

"We play it at the station sometimes back home," I improvised. "Kind of like strip poker, except safe for work." I winked at him. "Whoever wins gets to challenge the others to do something—within the same room, and nothing *too* extreme. It's all in good fun."

John laughed. "Somehow I think we'd better not let you win."

I spread my hands. "Well, if you don't think you can handle the heat…"

A sharper glint had lit in Sherlock's eyes at my nudge. Perfect. "All right. A few rounds won't hurt anything."

"Such an avid vote of enthusiasm," John teased. "I'll give it a shot. No bets and no folding, if we're not playing for money?"

"Exactly," I said. "We check our hands, exchange cards as we see fit, and then we discover who's made the right gamble. I'll deal first?"

John slid the deck toward me. I made a show of shuffling carefully. I couldn't guide the results of the hand completely, of course, since it was up to them whether they exchanged cards. But I could set one or another of us up in a good position with a bit of quick finger-work.

To start, it'd be better to let one of them win to warm them up to the game. And Sherlock clearly needed more warming. The cards flew between my hands. I tossed five each out across the table.

Despite his disinterest, Sherlock naturally had an excellent poker face. He looked at his hand in studied concentration, giving no sign of what he made of its contents. John let out a chuckle that might have been pleased or self-deprecating. From his swipe at his bright hair, I guessed the latter.

"One," Sherlock said blandly, discarding.

"Confident, aren't you," John remarked as I flicked a new card to his friend. "Ah… I'll take three."

"Two," I said, just to mix things up since I wasn't going to win anyway. I ended up with a rather nice three of a kind in nines. Not quite good enough to match Sherlock's three queens, though. John groaned as he laid down a hand with only a pair of sixes.

"What's the damage?" he asked Sherlock.

"Let me think." Sherlock steepled his forefingers against his mouth. "Ah. I'll have you both sample my pu-erh tea. I picked up a fresh bag while I was out." He pointed at John when the other man opened his mouth to protest. "You haven't given it a proper try yet."

He got up to fiddle with the tea kettle that came with the room. In a few minutes, he was setting down steaming cups of dark brown liquid in front of us, each only halfway full.

"No point in wasting it on the two of you if you don't enjoy it," he said. "But I expect you to drink everything I gave you."

An astringent scent carried on the steam. I let more heat rise off and then took a sip.

I'd tried pu-erh before, but there were quite a few variations. Sherlock favored one that leaned bitter and earthy, rather like his tobacco. He watched me as if daring me to try to pop a sugar cube in. I restrained myself, draining the cup slowly and steadily, but it did give me an idea for my first "dare." I was going to need to work up to the real challenge.

John set his cup down with a smack of his lips. "Yep, still not on the pu-erh train."

Sherlock looked satisfied anyway. "I suppose that means I can continue not to worry about you raiding it from the cabinet like you do my Colombian coffee."

"All right, let's get on with the next round," I said, clapping my hands.

Sherlock dealt, and I smiled inwardly when I lifted my cards. This was going to take a little luck but…

"One," I said, and then I had a flush.

"And I thought I was doing pretty well this time," John muttered, setting down a straight. Sherlock had nothing to speak of.

"You like to hassle me about my sugar habit," I said. "So you can both suck on a sugar cube." I handed over a couple from my remaining supply. A task both short and sweet, most literally. I took one myself to clear the bitterness of the tea from my mouth.

"You know," John said after he'd rolled it around with his tongue a few times, "I can see how this could grow on me."

"You would," Sherlock said fondly. "I'll stick to my tea."

I would have won again in the third round with a high straight of my own, but I swapped out a few cards and ended up with only a pair so as not to rush things. John crowed over his three aces.

"You," he said, with a pointed look at Sherlock, "have to listen to that new Burstback song you keep whingeing about. And actually listen to it, not just assume it must be awful." He glanced at me. "Obviously you'll listen to it too. If you're as snobby about music as he is, maybe it'll do you some good too."

"Play away," I said as Sherlock brought a hand to his agonized face.

The song that spilled from the speaker of John's phone was a bouncy pop anthem that wound into a more complex harmony made up of multiple guitars, a harp, and a rich cello. I got plenty of entertainment simply from tracing the different melodies. Sherlock's expression had mellowed by the time the melody wound down.

"Well," he said, which John seemed to consider a victory in itself.

All right, it was time to get things moving along. I dealt myself a nice full house and then kicked off my shoes.

"Since we aren't at work and we can get a tad racy, I would like a good foot rub," I announced. "Both at the same time. Five minutes, shall we say?"

John shook his head in amusement. He came around to sit on the edge of the bed and lifted one of my feet without argument. Sherlock went to work on the other.

John approached the task with the anatomical awareness I should have expected from a doctor, finding just the right angles to work the tension out of my arch, and Sherlock focused on a pressure point I hadn't known existed but that seemed to release a taut line that had stretched right up to my ribs. By the time my five minutes were up, I was quite pleased with my choice.

I'd been prepared to lose a couple rounds before I got the chance I'd been waiting for, but Sherlock's deal placed four tens in my hand. I certainly couldn't argue with that. And neither could the other two when they laid down their lesser offerings.

"Let's see," I said, drumming my fingers together. "I know. Kiss."

John blinked at me. I saw an inkling of understanding in his eyes, but he still asked, "Kiss *you*?"

I kept my voice perfectly calm, as if there were nothing at all unusual about what I was suggesting. "No. Kiss each other."

Sherlock had stiffened. John hesitated. A flush crept up his neck past the collar of his shirt.

"Is the idea really that horrifying?" I said. "I didn't ask for tongue." As enticing as that might be to watch. "You've shared a living space for two years; I'd imagine innumerable body parts have contacted other body parts without anyone going into fits."

"Not those particular body parts," Sherlock said, but his tone was more dry than defiant. The most obvious resistance had gone out of his posture. He glanced at John. "Would it make you terribly uncomfortable to indulge her?"

John's jaw worked as if he were grappling with the words. "Not if it wouldn't for you," he managed after a moment. He aimed for casual and didn't quite hit the mark, but the possibility that he might be excited by the prospect was clearly so far outside Sherlock's range of considerations that the detective didn't pick up on it.

Sherlock appeared to analyze their positions relative to the table and opted to stand up. John got up too. Even his cheeks were a bit ruddy now. I settled into my chair to watch, folding my hands on my lap.

Sherlock stepped toward John slowly enough. Then he leaned in faster than lightning and touched his lips to the other man's so briefly I'd have missed it if I'd blinked. He reached for his chair as if he figured that was the end of it, leaving John frozen in place.

"Hey!" I said. "I did say *kiss*, not barely perceptible peck. You didn't let us get away with one sip of your awful tea. Hold on right there." I hopped to my feet. "I'm sure you can do better than that. Let's see what we can produce with a little inspiration."

"Jemma," Sherlock said, like the start of an argument. I cut him off with the brush of my fingertips over the slanted trail down his neck where I'd determined his skin was most sensitive. All that came out then was a soft hitch of breath. I grasped the top of his shirt and tugged him back toward John.

The doctor was watching me with an expression that was almost pleading. Did he even know what he was pleading me for?

I tugged him closer too, staying partly between them. My hand glided down John's chest. I stroked Sherlock's neck again. My knuckles skimmed over John's belt and grazed his already hardening cock. He swallowed audibly.

I slipped my other hand down over Sherlock's body, tweaking my thumb across one of his nipples, fanning my fingers against his stomach the way I had yesterday. His only enjoyable sexual experience. I'd pretty much written the book on how to turn this man on. I let the heel of my hand reach his waistband and held it there without dipping lower. He needed a lighter touch.

"All right," I said in a low voice. "Let's try that again. Kiss."

Something had made up John's mind during my intervention. He didn't wait for Sherlock's cue. He reached for the other man, his hand settling on the same part of Sherlock's neck where he'd watched me caress him, and planted one on him.

I eased farther out of the way, my fingers stroking over both their sides. Sherlock hesitated, a shiver running through his body. Then he tilted his head just a smidge, leaning into the kiss.

Fuck, they looked gorgeous, bright- and dark-headed in the stark hotel light, John pressing the kiss a little more deeply at Sherlock's response, both of them giving themselves over to the moment. The sight sent heat flaring between my thighs. John raised his other hand as if to cup Sherlock's face completely, and—

Sherlock jerked back, his legs trembling for a second before he caught his balance.

"Well," he said, not quite meeting either of our gazes. "I think that's rather enough entertainment for one evening, considering the business ahead of us. I do have lock-breaking skills to practice."

He snatched his coat off the bed and fled the room in a rush of hastily summoned composure.

I winced inwardly. That hadn't exactly been the result I'd been hoping for. But then, had I really believed Sherlock would happily leap into making out with his long-time, utterly platonic friend with a few minutes of encouragement? I was smarter than that.

I hadn't been thinking with my smarts. I'd run with the idea to try to chase away the restless anxiety that had been nibbling at me. Now that uncomfortable sensation had returned. What if I'd just screwed up the dynamic I'd cultivated so carefully—the dynamic I needed for this scheme to work? Fuck.

John wet his lips, his hands having dropped awkwardly to his sides. He looked elated and gutted and startled all at once. Despite my frustration with myself, a little twinge of sympathy ran through me.

I could at least salvage things with him.

"I'm sorry," I said. "That wasn't— I shouldn't have pushed it that far. Maybe I shouldn't have suggested it at all."

"It's all right," John said raggedly. "It's not even really your fault. I mean, it wasn't as if we couldn't have called it off at any point." He gestured toward the door. "He'll be all right too, I'm sure. Sherlock deals with personal issues in a very predictable way. Come tomorrow morning, it might as well have never happened."

I studied his face. "Is that how *you'd* prefer to handle it?"

"I…" He couldn't seem to find the answer.

This poor sweet ridiculous man. I crossed my arms over my chest. "You really had no idea you wanted to do that, did you?"

"What? No. I—" His gaze jerked to me. "Did *you* know?"

The corner of my mouth quirked up even though my gut was still tight. "I saw a few signs. Call it an educated guess."

"Bloody hell. You're as bad as Sherlock with the mind-reading."

My lips stretched into a full smile. "Maybe that's why you wanted to kiss me too."

John laughed, and for the first time since Sherlock's departure, the tension ebbed from his stance. "Oh, no. You're something else altogether, Jemma the Jewel."

He dipped his head, and I bobbed up on my toes to meet him for a kiss that was nothing but enthusiastic on both sides. A trace of sweetness from the sugar cube lingered in his mouth, and I caught a smoky flavor that might have been Sherlock's. A thrill shot through me at the impression of kissing them both at the same time.

Any desire I'd been feeling had dampened with Sherlock's abrupt departure, though. I eased back with a softer smile to ease the rejection if John had hoped for more.

"I think we should all probably get some rest. We're going to want to be as alert as possible if we're going to pull off this plan."

John nodded with no hint of disappointment. I gave him one more quick kiss before heading out.

I shouldn't have let myself get carried away like that. From here on, no matter how precarious my situation seemed, I had to keep control of myself.

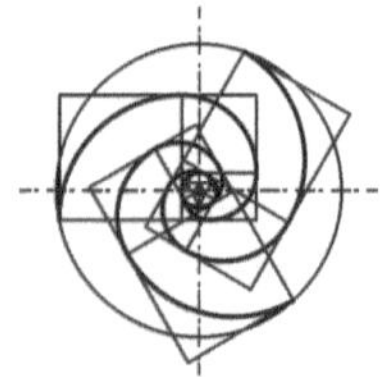

CHAPTER NINETEEN

Jemma

I was doing crunches at the base of my bed when the smell of desiccated rot quivered through the early morning sunlight. Resisting the urge to wrinkle my nose and the even stronger urge to snap around and find out what the asshole shrouded one wanted now, I finished my set of fifty reps. My abdominal muscles emanated a satisfying burn as I stretched them. Then I sat up and swiveled to look.

In the corner over the table, Bog was wafting its gauzy tendrils of fabric like a squid made out of spider-silk. I'd rather have talked to a squid.

"You know, I'm starting to think you're a little obsessed with me," I said.

The shrouded one ignored the remark. "You have been attempting to divert me," it said with a rasp in its distant voice that sounded almost angry. "Did you think I would not notice? Those wards will never be truly effective."

"I wouldn't bother with them if you'd leave me alone. While my life is still mine, I don't think it's unreasonable for me to aim for a little privacy."

Bog's body shuddered. "You're lucky you've had any extra time at all beyond the fate you were named for, bloodling. I'd like to hear gratitude, not complaints."

It wanted *gratitude*? I'd happily take a hunk of gratitude and shove it up Bog's ass. If the shrouded one even had an ass. It was kind of hard to tell.

In any case, I sure as hell wasn't in the mood to be lectured about my attitude from a creature who intended to shred apart my soul in less than a month's time.

I shrugged, pushing that irritation deep down inside. "A deal is a deal. You agreed to ten years. That's what I'm supposed to get."

"No part of that agreement forbade me from following your activities."

I ignored the growing itch of my contract mark. "And no part of it forbade *me* from making following me less comfortable for you."

The strips of Bog's covering swelled, its presence expanding until it looked twice as large as before. The mist where a face should have been clotted and churned.

"There is one fellow bloodling you've associated with for a long time. The darker male with little hair and many guns."

It didn't take a leap to realize the shrouded one meant Bash. My fingers started to curl into the thick carpeting before I caught them. "What about him?"

"I simply thought you should keep him in mind. Because if you do anything particularly stupid to hinder your association with *me*, there are ways I can appear to him. I can convince him that he can save you by giving up his own life. And then I will claim both of you."

Fear hit me in an icy wave. Would Bash really sacrifice himself if he thought it would save my life? We understood each other, we trusted each other, but it wasn't as if we ever talked about feelings of a tender sort.

I couldn't deny that he'd put his life on the line plenty of times over the seven years since I'd first hired him, though. Or that I knew he would again, the moment I asked him, without a second's hesitation. That was *why* I trusted him.

I didn't want to take Bash down with me. I'd done everything I could to keep him out of this part of my existence. If I failed, then the empire I'd been building, the money I'd amassed—it would all be his and deserved. That was the plan. That was the way it was supposed to happen.

How fucking *dare* Bog threaten to destroy the only person I gave a damn about who wasn't already gone.

The chill of my fear crackled into cold sharp rage. I held that in too, my hands braced against the floor beneath me, my heart thumping hard in my chest.

"I do business with the man," I said evenly. "We're hardly best buddies. If that threat is supposed to have me shaking in my boots, I apologize." I pushed myself to my feet. "Feel free to stop by if you come up with something better. I have to go get some breakfast."

I pulled a sweater on over my workout tee, not wanting to change in front of the shrouded one, and walked out the door without a backward glance.

The truth was my stomach was too full of that acrid mix of fear and rage for there to be any room for hunger. In an ideal world, I'd have found a punching bag on which to let out a lethal amount of force ten times over. But the hotel fitness center was a yuppie paradise of treadmills and exercise bikes in gleaming rows, and I'd probably burn through a few breakfast pastries' worth of calories just fuming on my way down.

If that fiend touched one particle of Bash's being—if it so much as whispered a word in my accomplice's ear—I'd find some way to tear *it* to shreds while I was going down its gullet. Just let it try me.

I hadn't slept all that well. The morning was still early, so not many of the conference goers had drifted into the hotel dining room yet. The pastry table waited for me, fully stocked with a fresh assortment—and Sherlock stood farther down the buffet line, decisively dropping a slab of French toast onto his plate.

He didn't look any worse for wear after our entertainment-turned-awkwardness last night. Well, perhaps a little. He held his shoulders a tad stiffly as he turned toward the tables, and I caught a nick from shaving on his jaw just beneath his ear. He'd never had anything but a steady hand with his razor before, from what I'd seen.

John hadn't arrived yet, or Garret either. That might be another sign in itself. Sherlock would know his roommate's usual morning habits. Was this the detective's usual breakfast time and he'd only delayed before for John's sake, or had his sleep been disturbed like mine?

I headed over to join him at the table he picked, keeping my expression blasé as I watched him. He gave me a mild smile and a nod as if it were a perfectly normal morning. Well, John *had* said Sherlock would simply erase the uncomfortable moment from his version of history.

"I see your tastes remain the same," he said, raising his eyebrows at my plate.

I might have gone slightly overboard with conveyances of sugar glaze. I considered my plate as I sat down. "I realize now my eyes may have been bigger than my stomach."

"I suppose the conference organizers would prefer we took too much rather than go the slightest bit unsatisfied. Have you had trouble this morning?"

I was starting to feel exhausted from how much emotion I'd had to squash down in the last half hour. Damn him and his perceptive eyes. I could already guess what he'd tell me if I asked how he knew —I'd normally have brushed my hair and dressed with more care before coming down for breakfast. He could tell I'd left the room in a hurry, driven out of my usual habits.

No point in denying it. I'd just have to give him an excuse he'd believe. He certainly wouldn't have been able to wrap his head around the truth. Let's see if I couldn't spin this slip in my favor.

"Not really trouble," I said. "I got woken up by a call from the front desk that a package had been delivered for me, and with everything that's been buzzing in my head and being half asleep, I thought it might be something to do with the case and rushed right down."

I shook my head at myself and tugged at the sleeve of my

sweater. "It was just this—my mom sent one of my old sweaters express because I mentioned how chilly it was here. Sweet, but I'd rather have a bunch of crime scene photos."

"A sentiment I can respect," Sherlock said. His gaze lingered on my face, and I'd have been surprised if he couldn't read signs there that I hadn't slept well even before the supposed phone call, but he didn't say anything about that. Because mentioning sleep, I guessed, would bring us too close to the other nighttime activities we'd been engaged in.

"Once I was down here, I figured I might as well eat." I tugged my hands inside the woolen sleeves as I hugged myself. "I'd just like the whole thing with Richter to be over. Have you seen Garrett—or John? We have so much more planning to do."

Sherlock held himself with admirable composure, but his eyes twitched at John's name. "I'd imagine they're still in bed," he said, his voice impassive. "I prefer to rise early, myself."

He gripped his fork and knife and sawed off a piece of French toast with a fair bit more force than it really required. Oh, yes, he was working very hard at willing last night away.

I didn't have much of a conscience left, if I'd ever had one. The upbringing I'd had wasn't structured to teach anything like empathy. Still, my stomach prickled with a faint sensation that might have been guilt. I appreciated Sherlock's unwavering intellect, and it appeared I'd shaken it. At the very least, that effect hadn't been my intention.

But it was what I had, so I might as well use it. Feeling unsettled, a man like him would commit twice as fast with twice as much determination to any task that would allow him to train all his focus on something concrete and separate from his emotions.

He wanted distractions. I'd point him toward one that would benefit me too.

"It seems like the most important factor we haven't really touched on is the motion sensors," I said, keeping my voice low in awareness of the other conference attendees breakfasting around us. "I've considered every angle, keeping in mind the elements we've already worked out and the layout of the place, and I can't see any way we could contrive to meddle with them before the security team turns them on at closing time."

"We'll have to let them go on and then interrupt their power supply before blocking them," Sherlock agreed.

"We can't turn them off directly from inside the gallery, right? You said you'd determined they're controlled from the security company's external site. I suppose we could cut off all the power to the building to give us time... but I have to think the police surveillance would immediately become suspicious. Can even you figure a way around that problem?"

Sherlock's posture straightened at the subtle dig at his ego. "There will be a way," he said. "I'll need to refresh my memory of the electrical layout around the gallery. Talk to me again later today and see if I don't have an answer for you."

He smiled, his pale blue eyes bright with the prospect of a challenge and his demeanor instantly more relaxed. I'd done him some good too.

If we pulled off this heist, it'd save Bash from the shrouded one as much as it would me. As soon as I could slip clear of Bog, it wouldn't know where to look for Bash either.

Invigorated by the work ahead, Sherlock polished off the rest of his breakfast in the time it took me to chew through one chocolate-filled croissant. The moment he'd left the dining room, I pulled out the phone I used for Bash.

He picked up after one ring, sounding ready for action. "What's the word, Majesty?"

The playful nickname made my lips twist. He had no idea how great a threat now hung over his head as well as mine. Not just one life but two might hang on this scheme's success—and on it succeeding soon.

I could cut him loose, couldn't I? Tell him I didn't need his services right now after all, transfer him the funds for a lovely, distant vacation, and order him to leave. Remove him from Bog's line of sight.

Only, if I was honest with myself, I wasn't entirely sure Bash *would* leave. He'd find the abrupt change odd—he'd suspect something else was wrong. Every instinct told me that he'd stick around surreptitiously, checking up on me.

The shrouded one would still find him. And taking on this challenge without him, I'd be so much more likely to fail, screwing over us both.

No, the only way through that I could tolerate was forward.

"Slight change in plan," I said. "The wiring gambit we talked about? I'll need you in place within the hour."

CHAPTER TWENTY

John

Driving made it easy to avoid uncomfortable subjects. I could completely occupy myself with navigating traffic while Sherlock flipped through textbooks about electrical systems on his phone. If we weren't talking about anything at all, of course we weren't talking about the fact that I'd been about ten seconds shy of slipping him tongue last night, even if at moments it felt as if I was thinking about it so loudly he should have been able to hear every word.

It probably would have been *easier* if Sherlock had gone off on this quest alone or with Garrett—or, hell, the Scarlet Pimpernel, as long as it wasn't me—but then he would have been admitting failure. Admitting that our kiss last night had mattered, somehow or other. The only way he knew how to make everything fine was to act as if everything *were* fine and assume all the things would sort themselves out in accordance with his will.

To be fair, I'd seen that strategy work several times in the past. He'd just never been erasing something that had happened with me.

The biggest trouble was, I was pretty sure the kiss did matter, at least to me. But I had the feeling trying to discuss that possibility with him might cause a meltdown of reality that wouldn't end well for either of us. Which was probably why I'd buried all hint of my apparent desire under several layers of plausible deniability until Jemma had yanked it blazing to the surface a little more than twelve hours ago.

If only those emotions had come with a manual on what the hell to do with them now that I'd admitted they existed.

"Park behind the blue sedan," Sherlock said, still so absorbed in his phone I didn't know how he'd managed to identify the open spot. "We'll walk the rest of the way."

I pulled in where he'd requested and checked my false beard. We hadn't gone for heavy disguises, just enough that the police wouldn't mark us as Holmes and Watson from a distance and that any internal security who noticed us passing by wouldn't connect us to recent visitors, one particularly clumsy.

Sherlock borrowed my walking stick and started tapping it ahead of him as though he were blind. My hand itched for the familiar surface as I ambled along beside him.

I could steady out my gait completely if I walked slowly enough, and the effort only provoked a slight prickling in my hip, but the walking stick had become about more than just balance. It was a weapon and sometimes a disguise in itself. No one expected much threat from a man who couldn't even walk without help.

While I was this close to him, Sherlock's pale eyes showed through the dim panes of his sunglasses. He used those to hide the darting of his gaze up the utility poles we passed and along the thick black wires that ran between them. Now and then, he murmured verbal notations into his phone.

I tugged my own gaze away from the furtive movements of his lips. I definitely shouldn't be looking at them.

"We'll circle the place," he said as we came up on the corner past the gallery. "If there's a trick we can employ, we're not likely to manage it in full view of the police. We just need to be sure we take into account the proper connections. Ah, there's the line directly into the building."

The cable ran by above our heads, just a few feet around the corner. "No chance we're messing with that unnoticed," I remarked.

"Indeed."

We rambled past the back of the gallery along the alley and then looped around to take in the adjacent road. Sherlock hummed to himself thoughtfully but didn't bother to mention any of his thoughts to me.

He stopped at the far end of the road, gazing up at the utility pole next to him and then frowning at the sidewalk.

"John," he said abruptly. "As a doctor, you'd have a reasonably accurate idea of the chances of pregnancy from a single unprotected encounter?"

Of all the personal questions he could have asked me, *that* was what he was going with? It wasn't a surprise that he'd deduced that something had happened between Jemma and me, but I'd have expected him to give me some credit for common sense. Did he have a reason for trying to imply I was careless, or was he just being irritatingly obtuse? If he'd made some observation that had worried him, he'd obviously been mistaken.

"Approximately zero, considering it was actually protected twice over," I said tersely. "We used a condom, and she has an IUD. I won't be procreating any time soon."

Sherlock's frown faded. "She told you about the IUD?"

Of all the ridiculous— He didn't know when to stop dogging a subject, did he?

I crossed my arms over my chest. "No. There are simply ways of noticing when one is intimate with a partner in particular ways. You'd think, considering that I *am* a doctor, and you…"

My agitation dwindled at the clear relief that washed over his expression. The phrasing of the questions and certain moments last night clicked together in my head.

God help me, was he asking for *himself*?

Watching the way Jemma had touched him last night, I'd assumed she'd been riffing off her general experience of what men responded to. It could actually had been the specific experience of having touched *him* before. It just hadn't occurred to me—for fuck's sake, the man sneered at the faintest whiff of romance or passions of the heart. He treated his body like a machine built for the sole purpose of carrying his brain around. When had *that* happened? *How* had that happened?

The idea that Sherlock might have had sex with Jemma was actually more boggling in itself than the possibility that he'd forgotten to take precautions. He could be rather… oblivious when it came to topics that didn't generally affect him. I'd once commented to him about whether we might ever see another man travel to the moon, and he'd expressed surprise at hearing any had gone there before.

It'd be pretty difficult to develop certain practical habits if you weren't practicing the act that went with them.

The image flashed through my mind of Jemma pressed up against Sherlock's tall frame, her lips on his, the sugared sweetness of her mouth and the bitter tartness his had held mingling together—and just like that, I was half hard.

Conveniently, Sherlock appeared to be just as thrown by the conversation as I'd been. He switched subjects at top speed with a jerk of the walking stick.

"It was rather strange, that vision we all had at the park yesterday, wasn't it?"

I blinked at him, needing a second to catch up. "The figure that seemed to appear over Jemma? Yes, I'd say so. I've never seen an effect of the light like that before."

"Two days before that, quite a few people in the dining room noticed other odd light effects," he said. "Which also appeared near her. And Garrett had an odd reaction Saturday morning while we were talking with her—he looked startled and said he'd thought he'd seen something in the doorway, 'a trick of the light'."

"Where are you going with this?" I asked. "Do you think she created those effects somehow?" I guessed it would be possible with a small but powerful projector that Jemma could have carried on her without us seeing it, but… "Why on Earth would she do that?"

"I don't know." Sherlock flexed his hand on the head of the walking stick as his gaze strayed into the distance. "In fact, every indication I've seen from her behavior would lead me to conclude that she wasn't at all pleased by the fact that they occurred. I started thinking about the repeated occurrences while I was doing my electrical research, and recalling each event, she's always been in quite a hurry to dismiss the strangeness and move on to other subjects."

Thinking back, I had to agree. "And it wouldn't make much sense for her to produce an effect she didn't want anyone to see."

"Precisely. Yet I can't shake the feeling that there's some connection between her and them." He paused. "I'd never seen light behave as it did in the dining room the other day either. Had you?"

I shook my head. "There was something unnerving about it, in a way I can't put into words. I'd remember if I'd experienced that before."

"Agreed. It seems too great a coincidence for us to have witnessed two such unique events—perhaps three, in Garrett's case —all within a week of meeting her and always in her presence. But, as you said, what could be the purpose? And why would she want to divert our attention from the very place she'd drawn it to?"

"Could it be someone else targeting her?" I said. "A strange intimidation tactic?"

He rubbed his mouth. "I considered that. It might have been the case with the instances in the hotel. But for an impression so precise and bright to appear directly over her the way it did in the park—the source would have to be quite close. We were in the middle of the broad courtyard around the fountain. I haven't been able to conceive of how it could have been done from farther afield."

"It must have been generated somehow or other," I said. "Unless you're going to tell me you think she's being haunted by a literal ghost, in which case I'll have to ask who you are and what you've done with my good friend Sherlock."

Sherlock's grim expression relaxed a little with a dry chuckle. "No, I'm not quite that far gone yet. I simply feel there's more to this matter than I can pin down, and that is not an ideal position to be in when we're planning a move this bold."

My mind leapt to last night, to Jemma's pained expression as she'd apologized for the dared kiss and the gentle humor with which she'd encouraged me to acknowledge my desire. She'd deciphered more about me than I'd realized about myself in the space of a week. Had she gotten to know all three of us that well that quickly? I hadn't seen any hint of maliciousness in her interest. If anything, she'd tried to rein us in from our riskier ideas in pursuing her case.

"Whatever's going on, I'd have trouble believing she wants to hurt us," I said.

"But harm can come as a secondary consequence as easily as the main goal." Sherlock tapped the walking stick against the sidewalk. "I'll speak with her and see what I can draw out before we see this plan through. We need to be sure of exactly what's at stake."

As we started along the road again, my heart sank. "Do you think we'll need to call the operation off?" I'd picked up a blowtorch this morning, and excitement had flickered through me when I'd pictured applying it to the display case. To snatch that statue right from under Richter's nose... "Richter needs to be caught at *something*. He's gotten away with too much already. We can't let him slip through our fingers when we're so close."

Sherlock's eyes gleamed behind the dark panes of his sunglasses. "We won't. One way or another, I intend to see him behind bars. The exhibit is scheduled to stay open until the end of next week. We have room to ensure our plans cover every possibility."

He was as eager to carry off this heist as I was, and damn if that enthusiasm didn't bring out everything that was most attractive in his face. I'd always loved seeing him caught up in a case. When had that enjoyment become more than friendly?

I honestly had no idea.

Sherlock waved the walking stick toward the buildings farther away from the gallery. "Hmm. What's that fellow over there up to?"

A man in a maintenance worker uniform, his neon yellow vest catching all of the midday light, was perched near the top of a utility pole down the road. Beside him, a dark cable dangled toward the sidewalk. He adjusted something on the metal outcroppings and then reeled that cable up slowly. It swayed back and forth against the pole as he formed it into a thick loop.

When I looked at Sherlock again, his lips had curled into a satisfied smile I recognized at once. My pulse beat faster. "What?"

"You never know where you'll find inspiration," he murmured. "What if we don't cut the power, John? What if we set up the police to do it for us?"

CHAPTER TWENTY-ONE

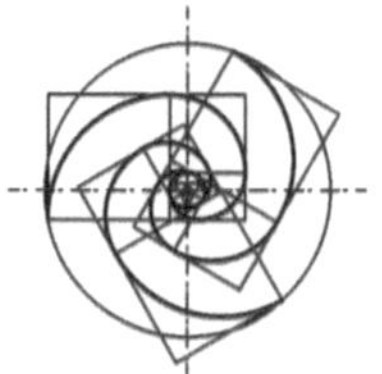

Jemma

The hotel lobby had the perfect little nook near the front windows where a stand of fake ferns hid me from the room, and the tint on the glass made me invisible to those outside. I'd been sitting there for a few hours, catching up on business through my tablet and setting new contracts into motion as if I could be sure of being around when they were fulfilled. Finally, John's silver Ford pulled up to the parking garage entrance.

Bash had texted to let me know that the doctor and Sherlock had left the gallery area a while back. They must have gotten started on whatever new strategies they'd thought up right away. I slung my purse over my shoulder and slipped across the room to one of the columns near the lobby elevators.

The savory buttery smell of shepherd's pie was already drifting from the dining room where the dinner buffet was about to open. Chances were good they'd come by this way.

I positioned myself where I couldn't see the elevator doors and no one coming off could see me, but I could hear just fine. The doors rasped open to Sherlock's voice in mid-sentence. "…should be quick enough to assemble," he was saying.

"It's good that it gets dark early at this time of year," John said. "At least we have a decent window in which to set things up."

They passed my column on the way to the dining room, their voices fading away alongside the tap of John's walking stick. I counted to ten in my head and then pushed off to follow them.

I'd nearly made it to the dining room doorway when the lobby door squeaked. I glanced over my shoulder out of habit and froze.

The man who strode in had a face so distinctive I recognized it in an instant. His rounded jaw jutted forward like that of an anglerfish, his ruddy skin gone leathery with too much sun over too much time. He'd combed and parted his white-blond hair neatly, and he'd decked out his bulky frame in a button-up shirt and dark jeans that didn't look totally out of place in this establishment, but I'd have marked him as a predator at a glance even if I hadn't tangled with him briefly before.

Anglerfish was one of the thugs Stefan Richter kept on his payroll. He'd come after me when the heist in Munich had gone sour. After a brief scuffle, I'd gotten away easily enough, and I'd been wearing a black wig and a lot more make-up, but he might still recognize *me*.

I crept back to the line of columns until I was close enough to the front desk to listen in. Anglerfish waited stiffly as the clerk helped the woman who'd already been in line. Then he marched over.

"I need to leave a message for John Watson—he's staying here."

"Just a second." The clerk tapped at her computer keyboard. "Yes, of course. What's the message you'd like to leave?"

"Let's see… Oh, hold on, I see him right over there. I'll go talk to him myself. Sorry for the trouble."

"Not at all," the clerk said blandly.

Anglerfish hustled away. As soon as the clerk was occupied with someone else, he headed out the door.

I darted across the lobby and ducked into my hidden nook. On the street outside, the thug crossed the road and got into the passenger seat of a car parked farther down the block. I watched for a few minutes, but the lights didn't come on.

Whoever else was in there, they were just sitting, watching the hotel like I was watching them. They must have followed Sherlock and John back here but only suspected who they were trailing. Now they'd gotten confirmation.

All the intimidated witnesses, all the destroyed evidence that stopped Richter's cases from going to trial—guys like these carried out that work. Richter wouldn't like a prominent detective and his partner hanging around his precious exhibit, whether or not he had any idea they were working with me. I wasn't sure if his thugs would dare take on Sherlock himself, but I wouldn't put it past them to try to put a whole lot of fear into John.

My throat tightened. I had practical reasons to want to keep all of my trio safe—the heist plan might fall apart if John was too injured to participate. But the thought of him being battered and bruised made me tense for other reasons as well.

He was only doing his job, and I could admit I was starting to believe he was a lot more earnest about it than most of the crime-fighters I'd encountered, even if he got off on the thrill too. There were a whole lot of people who deserved to be roughed up more than John Watson did.

My phone pinged with an incoming text. Garrett was asking whether I was coming to have dinner or at least dessert. I hesitated over the screen for a minute before answering.

Got some information from a friend back home that I'm following up on. Will check in with you all if it leads somewhere.

If Richter's men were planning on making a move, I wanted to know about it immediately.

I didn't see anyone stir inside or around the car for close to an hour. The sky darkened outside, the streetlamps glowing more starkly. I was debating alternate tactics when an all too familiar tapping reached my ears.

John was heading toward the front door, not in any great hurry but with a purposeful stride. Where the hell was he going on his own and on foot? Didn't he know there could be paid mercenaries waiting around to corner him in some dark alley?

No, that possibility clearly hadn't occurred to him.

I had only a couple seconds to grapple with my options. I could have reached out to Bash, but in the absence of other instructions from me, he'd have gone back to his hotel room. Even at his fastest, he couldn't make it here in time to follow John.

That left me. Fuck. Maybe if John had company, the thugs wouldn't hassle him in the first place, and Anglerfish wouldn't get close enough to have a chance at connecting me to the woman he'd chased through München Hauptbahnhof station.

I slipped between the ferns. "John!" I said as I caught up. "Are you heading out too? Good timing."

John blinked at me and then smiled. He held the door open. "Is your lead taking you anywhere useful?"

I made a face. "No, it ended up being a dead end, at least for now. Richter owns a large property in the councilor's district, so I'm thinking the blackmail might have been to pressure him into some decision regarding that, but I haven't found a clear link between the two of them there either."

"Well, it would give us a motive. Where are you off to, then?"

"I ran out of sugar cubes. Again. I figured I should buy my own stock before depleting the hotel's supply any more. What about you?"

John chuckled as we fell into step together on our way down the street, but he hesitated for a beat. "Just picking up some more tobacco for Sherlock."

Had he felt awkward admitting that? I raised an eyebrow at him as we passed Anglerfish's car and crossed the street. "Do you normally run his personal errands for him?"

"Only when it benefits me as well as him," John said, still smiling. "I noticed the tin is getting low, and Sherlock's too deep in planning mode to pay much attention. Halfway through the night, I expect he'll finish it off and then be irritable that more didn't magically appear. You really don't want to see him irritable. So, I'm making the magic happen." He waggled his fingers.

Car doors thumped softly behind us—two of them. From the sound, I guessed both Anglerfish and whoever had been in the driver's seat had gotten out. Their footsteps rasped against the sidewalk after us, no faster than we were walking. For now, they were just seeing where we went.

Waiting for a chance to attack.

My heart thumped, but I didn't let anxiety color my voice. "You really take care of him—Sherlock—don't you?"

"Oh, well, it's mutual, so I don't think it's so bad. Sometimes he notices when I've pushed myself too hard before I do and gets me to rest. He'll even play actual classical pieces on his violin to help me relax instead of insisting on his rather experimental compositions. There was one time he shot a guy who would have killed me. Little things like that."

His tone was light, but I caught just a hint of hesitation in it again. He looked at me with unusual intentness. A tingling of suspicion ran down my spine.

He'd spent a lot of time alone with Sherlock this afternoon. It was possible they'd compared notes about their experiences since meeting me and noticed something that had made them wary. Not incredibly so, or I didn't think we'd be having this conversation at all, but John wasn't quite as easy with me as he had been.

Maybe I should have intervened to reduce that alone time. I hadn't wanted to interrupt whatever schemes they were laying down. Well, I couldn't do anything about the past, but I could keep him distracted from speculating about me right now.

"I should be able to grab my sweet stuff in here," I said, pointing to a convenience shop up ahead, and then, as John followed me in under the bright lights, "Did you talk to Sherlock about last night?"

A faint flush crept over John's face. "No," he said. "You must have seen how he was this morning. He'd rather set it aside and move forward. I don't think there's any way I can bring it up without seeming 'dramatic' about it, and there's not much he hates more than unnecessary dramatics."

One man came into the shop behind us and sauntered down the aisle next to ours. I caught a glimpse of him between the shelves: not

Anglerfish but of similar stock, built like a truck with a forehead nearly as square as a windshield. A really friendly-looking guy. No doubt they only wanted to chat.

I grabbed a box of sugar cubes off the shelf and headed to the counter. "I have trouble picturing you being all that dramatic about it. But I've learned my lesson about meddling in whatever's going on between you two."

John was quiet while I paid. I scanned the street surreptitiously on our way out and spotted Anglerfish mostly obscured by cars on the other side of the street, a few down from us. The bell over the shop door sounded when we were several paces on our way—our other tail rejoining the chase.

"How did you do it?" John said, his gaze fixed on the street ahead. "Get him to… open up to that kind of experience?"

Ah, so he'd figured out that much. I suspected that had been deduction on his part more so than Sherlock admitting it. And now he wanted me to act as couples therapist? Dear lord.

I might as well be honest. "It was just sex. Purely physical, like a very enjoyable workout. I don't think I could give you any tips you could use. He can't be the same with you because he likes you."

John snorted. "And you're trying to tell me he *doesn't* like you?"

"He hardly *knows* me," I said. "He finds me intriguing. It's not the same thing. Your lives are entwined—you have a deep, life-saving, tobacco-fetching kind of loyalty. I doubt that kind of caring about another human being comes very easily to Sherlock in the first place, from what I've seen of him. It'd probably be even harder for him to detach those feelings from physical intimacy than it is for most people."

All the more reason why I'd been right to avoid that kind of complication between me and Bash, come to think of it.

"The intimacy wouldn't necessarily have to be *detached*." John paused. "But that's why your approach wouldn't work."

"I don't know. You could just talk to him about it and see what he says, dramatics or not."

"Yeah." He let out a sigh. "I should probably figure out exactly what I'd want out of that conversation first. I'm pretty sure I wouldn't want to actually *date* the guy. He's too... Sherlock. But maybe, if we stayed the way we are and just added in kissing and... whatever else, now and then—I don't know."

His befuddlement over the situation was kind of adorable. "Well, I don't get the impression he's going anywhere, so I'd imagine you have plenty of time to figure it out."

"Very true."

He led the way around the corner to a tobacco shop a couple blocks down. Truck-guy followed us in again. John poked through the offerings with practiced speed and made his purchase. We were partway back to the corner when he leaned close to my ear.

"As you may have already realized, we have extra company on our errand."

All his time in Sherlock's presence had clearly honed his own instincts. I nodded without glancing back.

John gave his walking stick a little twirl. "In situations like this I generally prefer to set up the ambush myself and turn the tables rather than waiting to see how my opponent would like to play things."

"What did you have in mind?" I asked. I couldn't say I'd complain about giving our followers some incentive to back off.

"Oh, maybe a shortcut down a darkened alley." He shot me a grin and caught my elbow to draw me with him down an alley that had presented itself. "The two of us against one—I don't think we have anything to worry about."

Against *one*? "John," I started with a lurch of my stomach. Before I could correct him in warning, the thugs charged into the narrow shadowed space after us.

They both barreled right at John. He was their real target, after all. I tossed myself into Anglerfish's path with a faked stumble, letting a gasp of surprise slip from my lips. Then I jammed my elbow as hard as I could into his gut.

You might think that it'd be easier to fight a massive dude from a distance, but I'd found with my particular skillset of speed and focused strength, I worked best when I was close enough to land my blows with maximum impact—especially in a space like this where there wasn't much room to maneuver anyway.

I slipped Anglerfish's attempt to catch me in a hold and socked him in the throat while kneeing him in the balls. He grunted but kept swinging.

He was going to regret that. I dodged to the left, and he grabbed my hair, yanking hard enough to send pain splintering through my scalp. For a second, he snapped my head around to face him. Our gazes locked, and then I was stabbing my fingers into his eyes.

With a choked sound, his grip loosened. I pulled free and slammed his legs out from under him with a sweep of my foot, adding a blow to his spine as he toppled. His head smacked the pavement, and he sprawled there in a half-conscious daze.

I spun around. John had been doing a decent job of holding his own against Truck-guy. The beefier man was favoring one foot, and a walking-stick shaped welt decorated his cheek. Apparently deciding he needed an extra advantage, the thug whipped out a knife.

That was hardly playing fair.

Before I could jump in, John lashed out with his stick and knocked the blade right out of the guy's hand. I snatched it up before it even hit the ground. Truck-guy glanced from John with his stick to me brandishing the knife and appeared to decide he'd had enough. He shoved past me on his way out of the alley.

John caught my arm to steady me. "Are you all right?" he asked.

He clearly was. His eyes were sparkling, elation emanating from every inch of his body. He'd enjoyed that fight for his life.

John Watson was an adorable sick fuck, and I liked it.

"I'm fine," I said, and nodded to Anglerfish, who'd found the wherewithal to roll onto his back. "Let's get out of here before they decide to make another go of it." As much as John might have enjoyed that, *I* wanted to get him back to the hotel in one piece.

John walked the rest of the way back at an energized pace. He burst into the lounge room, where apparently he and the rest of the trio had planned to meet. The moment Sherlock and Garrett ambled in several minutes later, he launched into an account of our adventure. I hung back by the door, watching the other two watch him.

"I don't know if we can even be sure they're Richter's people," he finished. "It's not as if we haven't pissed off plenty of other criminals and their associates."

"But most likely Richter," Sherlock said grimly. "They might have noticed us by the gallery today. I should have been more careful."

John waved his concern off. "If it is him, it'll be my own fault for that stunt trying to shake the display case."

Sherlock's gaze slid to me, and there was definitely a cooler edge to his penetrating stare than I'd felt before. "You're lucky Jemma happened to be with you."

Did he think I might have prompted the ambush somehow? Or just that I'd suspected it might happen?

Before I had to answer, Garrett's phone chimed. He woke up the screen and peered at it. A frustrated sound escaped him.

"What?" Sherlock said, his attention diverted.

"I set up alerts for any news about Richter," he said. "The gallery's just sent around a press release—he's pulling the exhibit early. Which means it's all getting packed up Saturday evening after closing."

The bottom of my stomach dropped out. It was Thursday. I didn't have to ask to know it was already too late for us to put any plan into action tonight.

Unless the men in front of me were ready and committed to go tomorrow, all this work had been for nothing. My last chance would slip right through my fingers.

I sank onto the sofa and tipped my face into my hands, not needing much imagination to appear distraught. "He must suspect something's in the works—how can we be ready in time? He's beaten us. Outsmarted us."

It was a shove more than a nudge, but it hit the mark. Sherlock's mouth twisted. "He hasn't. John and I hashed out the final necessary element this afternoon. We have all the pieces we need."

I glanced at him through my fingers. "Are you sure? If something goes wrong—"

"It won't," Sherlock said firmly. "We're bringing down that bastard once and for all." His gaze twitched toward John, and I realized my shove hadn't been the only thing that had pushed him. For all his cool composure, he was furious about the attack on his friend.

Thank you, Richter, for playing right into my hands, even if you had to fuck things up along the way.

Sherlock's coolness toward me hadn't slipped my mind. I had the feeling it would be wise for me to avoid giving him the chance to ask many questions before our pending heist.

"If we're going tomorrow, I'm going to practice the swaps some more," I said, getting up. "The last thing I want is to be the weak link. You know how to get a hold of me if you need anything else—don't hesitate."

Sherlock looked as though he might have protested, but John launched into an eager question about some plan involving a sign, and I ducked out unhindered. On my way down the hall to my room, I sent Bash a quick text.

We're a go for tomorrow night, but the situation is already dicey. Keep costume and stay ready.

Adrenaline quivered through my nerves as I slid the keycard into my door. In a little more than twenty four hours, I'd have achieved either my greatest victory or my most epic failure—and the balance between the two had never felt more precarious.

CHAPTER TWENTY-TWO

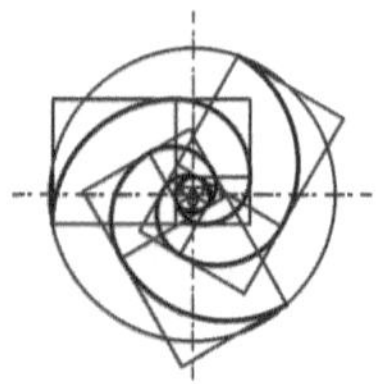

Jemma

Light was searing into my eyes from everywhere around me, and an icy chill jabbed into my skin. I spun around, my arms flailing, my throat closing against a swell of panic, my pulse thumping so hard the beat shuddered through my whole body. My fingers brushed a delicate shoulder.

"Jemma!" Olivia's thin voice wavered through the glaring light. I caught a glimpse of her face, the skin even paler than usual beneath her freckles. Her strawberry blonde hair whirled around her. Then the stark shine yanked her away from me and swallowed her up.

"No!" I threw myself after her, lashing out at the glow so forcefully the joints in my arms cracked.

My body jerked forward, my eyes popped open, and I found myself sitting up in the hotel bed in my pitch-black room, sweat-damp and shaking. My pulse raced on through my veins.

A dream. A horrible fucking dream.

I dragged in a rough breath, and a stench that was all too real flooded my lungs. Cloying and metallic with a sour undertone, it coated my mouth with the impression that I'd bitten my tongue raw.

My chest constricted. I groped for the bedside lamp.

The glazed bulb came on with a click, and all I could see was red.

Blood drenched the bed from head to foot, punctuated by chunks of gristle and severed bits of human flesh: a finger, an ear, a hunk of hair with scalp still attached. It drenched *me*. That wasn't sweat but blood seeping all down the front of my nightshirt, drying cool on my skin from hands to armpits as if I'd dunked them in a barrel of gore.

The surge of scarlet had washed over the entire room. Blood spattered the floor, the furniture, the mirror, the walls. An arm lay beside the desk, wrist wrapped in a heavy watch I recognized. Over there, a booted foot. And there on the dresser, hair slicked ruddy to the sides of her face and lips parted over crimson-stained teeth, Olivia's head stared at me with gouged out eyes.

A scream ripped out of my throat. My arm swung instinctively and smacked into the lamp. The impact sent pain spiking up from my wrist as the lamp flew off the bedside table. It smashed onto the floor, and the light snapped out.

Everything was dark again. The bloody stench congealed deeper into my lungs.

What had I done? What could I do? Oh, fuck, fuck, fuck.

My stomach knotted tight. My mind balked at even thinking about the scene that had been laid out in front of me. I sat there frozen, willing myself to move but not quite managing it.

Footsteps hustled down the hall outside. A sharp knock rang through the door, and a woman's voice came with it. "Hello? Is everything all right in there?"

I choked on a horrified laugh that almost turned into vomit. My head was still numb, but my body finally got the message to get moving. I peeled off the wet covers and crawled out of the bed. Walked across the soaked carpet, tuning out the faint squelching sounds beneath my feet, to the bathroom door where the carnage stopped. Wrenched on the bathrobe to cover myself.

Was there any blood on my face? I couldn't tell. I didn't dare touch it to try to find out, my hands were so smeared. I tucked them inside my sleeves as I eased open the door just a few inches.

The bright hall light left me blinking. A woman in the hotel uniform of white dress shirt and forest-green vest and slacks was standing just outside, her mouth set in a tight frown.

One clear thought pierced through the mess of my mind: I had to get her out of here. I couldn't let her see what I'd done.

"One of the other guests reported hearing some sounds of distress from your room," the woman said. "Is something wrong?"

"No," I said quickly, ducking my head. "I get nightmares every now and then—it's a PTSD thing—I'm so sorry I disturbed anyone. It shouldn't happen again. They don't—they don't come that often."

My halting embarrassment and the mention of a mental condition were enough to diffuse the woman's inquiry. She backed up a step. "My apologies. You understand, we have to check when there's a report..."

"Of course," I said. "You're just doing your job. I really thought I was past this." I let out a weak chuckle.

She had no idea what to say to that at all. "I hope the rest of your night is more restful," she managed, and hightailed it out of there.

I pushed the door shut and flipped the door guard over to prevent any sudden intrusions. Then I turned around, gripping the cuffs of the bathrobe. The numbers on the digital clock gleamed through the darkness—it was just after midnight.

My night wasn't going to be restful at all. I had to deal with this, clean it up, something, somehow.

Bracing myself, I flicked the switch for the main light. It washed over the same gruesome scene I'd been met with before. My bare feet had left bloody footprints across the carpet from the bathroom to the door; my fingers had streaked the doorknob. So much fucking blood. And the bits and pieces—the head on the dresser—

My stomach clenched. I wasn't going to let myself look at that again, not yet.

Where did I even begin?

I wavered at the edge of the chaos, my mind freezing up again. My eyelids were heavy with exhaustion. This didn't even make *sense*, did it? How could I have— These people were—

Across the room, the window pane I'd left a crack open rasped up. My heart stuttered. I started forward and then stalled as Bash's muscular form eased past the blind.

I'd told him to "keep costume." He had on his wig with the dreadlocks and those shockingly blue contacts that drew a person's gaze straight to his eyes. He stepped onto the bloody carpet without any hint of disgust or horror, *his* gaze fixed on me.

"Are you okay, Mori?" he asked, worry coloring his tone as he took in my expression. "I saw a light flash and go out—it looked like some kind of struggle."

My voice came out hoarse. "I… It's everywhere. I don't know what happened. I don't know how to get rid of it."

Bash's forehead furrowed. He glanced around me, and I winced inwardly in anticipation of his reaction. But he only looked confused.

"What do you have to get rid of?"

Understanding sank through the muddle of shock and panic in my head.

He couldn't see it. It wasn't really there. None of it—the blood, the body parts. It was a hallucination to outdo any hallucination I'd experienced before.

Of course it was. That arm and that watch belonged to a Chicago mobster whose death I'd ordered months ago. That booted foot belonged to a deceased loan shark who'd tried to screw me over. And Olivia…

Bog had collected mementos from my memories and strewn the wreckage around me. The shrouded one had probably provoked that horrible dream too, the asshole.

I inhaled slowly and deeply, but the butcher-shop stench stayed just as thick. The red splattered all around me didn't fade.

Bog had put a hell of a lot of power into this illusion. I'd have taken a little satisfaction knowing the shrouded one must have exhausted itself so much I'd have a temporary reprieve from its presence if I hadn't wanted so much to erase *this* evidence of its presence from my senses. I rubbed my eyes, but that didn't help either.

"Mori?" Bash said again. What the hell would he be making of his boss apparently losing her mind?

"It's okay," I said, as convincingly as I could manage. Olivia's gouged face stared at me from the corner of my vision. I took a step forward to put it out of my line of sight, but I could still *feel* it, even though it wasn't even there. "There's no real trouble. I just have to sort this out."

"Sort *what* out?"

How could I explain it to him when I could hardly explain it to myself? I drew my spine straighter, but I couldn't quite stop a tremor from running through my limbs.

This wasn't how I wanted him seeing me. He couldn't do anything here anyway.

"I'll take care of it," I said. "Don't worry about it. You should go."

Bash's mouth twisted. With a jerk and a couple quick flicks of his hands, he'd tossed his wig on the table and popped out the contacts so he looked only like himself. He crossed the room and grasped my shoulders, his natural light green eyes fixed on mine.

"I'm not leaving you when something's obviously wrong. It's my job to protect *you*, not the other way around."

"Bash…"

I meant to protest, but as I stared back at him, the heat of his hands soaking through the cotton fabric of the bathrobe, the imaginary stink retreated. The scarlet splashes around us hazed.

He was real. He was pushing the horror back. My hands rose of their own accord to clasp his arms, to increase that contact.

His grip on my shoulders tightened, his gaze searching my face. "What do you need? Whatever it is, I'll get it. I'll tear apart the world if I have to. Just say the word."

I believed him. A devotion I'd suspected but never let myself assume thrummed through his voice. It woke up an ache in my chest, an echo of all the moments when I'd wanted but not let myself have, not let myself see, not let myself feel.

If I had my way, we'd get to tear down the worst horrors in this world together, Bash and me—if my fucked up past didn't tear him to pieces first. He didn't even understand what he was up against.

I closed my eyes, but the image of Olivia's mutilated head swam up, merging with her frightened face from my dream. I swallowed hard.

"It's my fault," I said. "It was all my fault."

Bash's hands shifted from my shoulders to the sides of my face. The firm but gentle pressure of his fingers drove more of the carnage away, replacing the stench with the smell of gun oil and the tang of his natural musk. When I opened my eyes, all I could see was him.

"I don't know what you're caught up in, Jemma, but I know whatever it is, you're fighting it as hard as you can," he said. "Because that's what you've always done for as long as I've known you."

I couldn't remember if I'd ever heard my first name in that low smooth voice. It turned the ache inside me into an eager pang that spread low in my belly.

"You know me," I said.

His lips formed a tight but definite smile. "I do."

"And you're still here even though you know what I am. A liar. A villain. A murderer."

"Who do you think you're talking to?" Bash said. "I wouldn't have you any other way."

He sounded so certain, so full of faith in me. The fervent sensation inside me swelled through my chest. In that moment, it felt more powerful than anything I'd ever experienced, stronger than the guilt and the fear that never quite stopped nipping at my heels, stronger than anything the shrouded folk had ever thrown at me.

I wanted to grab hold of the sensation with both hands and hang on tight. I wanted to wrap it around Bash too to shield us both. But I didn't know how. I didn't know what to do with myself or this rush of emotion.

My fingers curled into the front of his shirt. I brought him to me the only way that seemed right, with my mouth pressing hard against his.

Bash's breath caught, and then he kissed me back with so much intensity my head spun. I tugged him even closer, melding my body to his, and kissed him just as fiercely, as if I could conduct the rush of power into him just by touching him.

There were too many layers of clothing between us. I dislodged the buttons down the front of his shirt and let go of him just long enough to yank the belt of my bathrobe loose. Both shirt and robe fell to the floor without us needing to break the kiss. I trailed my fingers down Bash's sculpted chest, following every curve of muscle, every dip and ridge of a combat scar.

"Mori." Bash's mouth slid from my lips to brand the corner of my jaw, the side of my neck. He held himself back for a second with an effort that tensed the muscles beneath my hands. "You were upset."

"That's gone," I said, willing the words to be true. "It's all right. I needed *you*."

He brought his mouth back to mine, tender and insistent all at once. I jerked open the fly of his jeans. He snatched out his wallet before kicking them off and dropping it onto the bed. Which would be an excellent place for us to find ourselves too.

I pushed him around and onto his back on the mattress. As he eased himself farther up, I climbed over him and straddled his hips while I reclaimed his lips.

Bash propped himself up on one elbow to meet my kiss even more avidly. His free hand teased up my thigh and under my sleep shirt. His thumb traced the hem of my panties, and I couldn't stop myself from grinding into the erection that was stretching his boxer-briefs.

He growled, his teeth nicking my lower lip with a perfect jolt of painful pleasure. Then he was rolling us over to pin me beneath him. His mouth traveled over my throat.

"I don't want to rush this," he muttered against my skin, "but all I can think about is getting inside you."

A breathless laugh escaped me. "So why aren't you there?"

He gave another growl and wrenched at my panties. I yanked his boxer-briefs down too. He paused to grab a packet from his wallet, stroking my clit at the same time so I wasn't left unattended. I squirmed against his touch, wanting more, wanting him everywhere.

He eased up over me again, slicking the condom over his jutting cock. I took advantage of his momentary distraction to flip us with a strategic heave, landing back on top of him. His sound of protest was lost in a groan as I sank onto his erection.

His thick length filled me, stretched me, sparking pleasure all through my core. I took him in completely and lifted up with a flex of my hips, leaning forward in search of the best angle. He rocked up to meet me, and bliss quivered through me. Mmm, right there would do fine.

No amount of training would have put me on par with Bash's corded soldier's body. He could have taken back control if he'd wanted to, but he let me set the rhythm, caressing my breasts and my thighs, his mouth curving into that quiet little smile when I gasped.

I dug my fingers into the bedspread beside him and tugged his head up with my other hand. As I kissed him, pleasure hummed from my core all the way to the top of my head. It raced farther with each pump of my hips until it shot through me in a crackling wave of ecstasy.

I bowed over Bash as my orgasm crashed through me, and he looped his arm around my waist. With one careful but powerful motion, his cock still hard inside me, he rolled me beneath him again.

Raising my hips up to meet him, he thrust into me so hard the burn sent my release soaring even higher. My head tipped back against the sheets. A cry of pleasure broke from my lips. Bash's chest hitched, and his rhythm broke apart with the groan of his own peak.

In the hazy afterglow, Bash tucked me against him, my back to his front, his breath on my shoulder and his hand on my belly. I tucked my arm over his instinctively. The stress of the horrors before we'd come together and the intensity of our collision had left me drained.

A vague sense of uneasiness crept up over me, but before it could sink in its claws, exhaustion dragged me down into sleep.

CHAPTER TWENTY-THREE

Bash

I woke to a softer light than I'd been used to the last several nights, the patter of bare feet on carpet, and the swish of Jemma's hair. She'd pulled the red waves back into a ponytail for her training. Right now she was repeating a kick-cross-hook-roundhouse combo that I could easily imagine toppling her imaginary opponent. Her breath sounded steady enough, but from the gleam of sweat on the back of her neck, she'd been at it for a while.

She held so much controlled but ruthless power in that slender body. I could have watched her work it for hours. Whatever had shaken her yesterday, she'd bashed its head in and thrown it out the window.

That same woman had softened enough to come apart under me last night, to curl up against me and fall asleep. But as much as I'd enjoyed that, I had to say I enjoyed this side of her even better.

She was seeing her mission through today, with her trio of dupes that she'd wrapped around her finger. I'd be waiting on the sidelines, but it'd still be quite the show.

I sat up, reaching for the right wry quote to make her roll her eyes at me, and she whirled at the movement. The look on her face—jaw tight, eyes clouded—stopped me. Her shoulders tensed and then came down as she consciously willed herself to relax.

"Bash," she said, evenly enough. "We should talk."

"Talk away," I said, but my stomach had sunk. She was upset.

She sucked in a sharp breath, somehow looking fiercer than most of the soldiers I'd faced off against even in her loose sleepshirt and leggings. "This can't happen again. I'm sorry I let it happen at all. Last night—I didn't rein myself in when I should have. I hope we can move forward as we were."

Did she really think I'd abandon the seven years of work we'd done together because she didn't want to fuck again? A prickle of jealousy might have run through part of my mind thinking about the other men she'd recently slept with without expressing any of the same qualms, but I'd taken this leap knowing who she was. It wasn't as if I'd have even wanted a grand romance. I'd be here for her however she needed me.

It'd just seemed for a moment there that she did need me that way. To hold her, to adore her, to make her cry out with bliss.

"If I overstepped at all," I started cautiously.

"No," Jemma said quickly. "You were—You did everything right. It's on me."

She closed her eyes for a second as if gathering herself and crossed her arms over her chest. Then she looked straight at me with a determined expression.

"The thing is, I use sex as a tool to maneuver people for whatever ends. I've *only* ever used it as a tool—and if I happen to get off, great. I don't know if I can turn off that mindset and just be with someone honestly. And I never want to find myself using you like that. You mean too much to me to risk it. All right?"

Whatever niggling jealousy I'd felt disintegrated with those words. We didn't talk about the various ways our relationship had warped far beyond simple employer and employee across the years. I never acknowledged that there wasn't anyone I felt closer to in the world, and she'd never indicated it was the same for her. Until now.

Maybe she saw the acknowledgment as payback for the devotion

I'd admitted last night, but I could tell from her tone and her eyes that she meant it. I'd take that over another hot-and-heavy session any day.

"Of course it's all right," I said. "If that's how you feel, then nothing has to change from how it was at this time yesterday. I'll have your back like I always have, we'll topple the assholes who think they run the show, and it'll be great."

She relaxed completely then, with a small but relieved smile that —damn it—made me want to kiss her. I'd gotten awfully good at roping in those urges, though. So what if it might be a little harder now that I knew what I was missing? I'd hone my self-discipline even more.

Apparently it did need a little more honing, because I couldn't help adding, "But I meant it when I said it's not your job to protect me."

The corner of her mouth twitched as if she'd caught it from turning into a frown. "Then don't think of my decision as being for your protection. Think of it as being for mine. I don't have much conscience to go around—I'd like to keep any weight off it that I can."

She turned and knelt down beside her suitcase. Her agile fingers unearthed a plastic envelope from a hidden compartment I'd never seen her open before. "That's also why I think it's time I told you a little bit more about what I'm—what we're—doing here."

She sat down on the edge of the bed, and I eased over to join her, keeping the sheet spread over my lap. Carefully, she opened the envelope and slid out a faded photograph, the edges creased.

The picture showed two young girls sitting side by side on a wrought-iron bench with a ratty shrub looming behind them. The older girl couldn't have been more than nine or ten, but I could easily recognize her as Jemma. She'd had the same penetrating gaze and thick red hair back then, her face and limbs just as pale and angular in the sack-like dress she was wearing. Her arm was slung around the younger girl, who was equally pale and skinny, but with softer eyes and hair somewhere between blonde and red.

"They didn't take many pictures," Jemma said. "This is the only one I got to call mine." She slid her thumb along the bottom of the photo to rest beneath the younger girl. "This was my little sister, Olivia. Four years younger. The only thing that mattered to me other than—other than living up to expectations was taking care of her."

Her use of the past tense hadn't escaped me. "What kind of expectations?" I asked instead, because that seemed like a safer question.

"That part isn't important," Jemma said in a tone that told me we weren't touching on that subject at all. "The gist of it is, we were trapped in a place run by a sort of monsters. Monsters that sometimes ate kids when they got to be a certain age. I got out of there the only way I could find how, and I did everything I could to be ready to come back and get her out too…"

I knew something about growing up with a monster, but I could tell she didn't mean quite the same thing I would have. She paused for a second, but when she spoke again, her voice was just as steady as before. "Do you remember the mountain village you came with me to in Utah?"

Six years ago. I couldn't see how I'd ever forget it, even though she'd left me behind for whatever quest she'd been on, staked out partway along the path. She'd made it back to me hours later clutching a swelling wrist to her stomach, her eyes as glazed and face as drained of color as a corpse.

I'd seen that vacant hopeless look on men who'd just glanced down and seen that a blast had taken their lower half straight off. It'd never bothered me half as much on my fellow soldiers as it had on her.

"I remember it was bad," I said.

"Well, yes." Her fingers pinched the photograph. "That was where they'd moved to. Our family and the monsters. She should have had almost another year before they'd have taken her, but—the one that wanted me, it must have been pissed off that I slipped out of its grasp. So it took her early. She was already gone. I didn't make it back in time."

My mind leapt to my siblings—to hustling them out of our parents' house and hitchhiking across three states to the grandparents we'd never met. Promising my grandmother that I'd go back home, that they wouldn't have to deal with some thirteen-year-old delinquent as long as they took in the little ones.

It'd hurt, leaving my brother and sister behind, going years before I saw them again, and I'd known they were safe. I'd known I'd gotten them out.

How agonizing would it have been if I'd lost them along the way?

It's my fault, Jemma had said last night, looking like she'd seen a ghost.

"You did everything you could," I said. "I *know*. I was there with you helping you prepare. You were practically still a kid yourself, Mori."

"I was eighteen."

"And already pulling off more than anyone I knew three times that age. You had to balance being ready enough to really save her with getting there in time." I remembered my own childhood tightrope walk with a twist of my gut. "Was there any way you could have tackled the 'monsters' if you'd gone there earlier, before they took her?"

Her jaw worked. "I don't know," she said. "At least I could have tried. But that's not the point. That's the past. Since then, I've had to — To get out, I made a deal with one of the monsters. I bought myself ten years. That time's almost up. What we're doing here, it'll help me break that tie so I'm free of it. I just need to do that, and then I'm going to destroy all of them, with all the means I have. If I have to burn down the rest of the world in the process, I don't really care—but I don't want you getting burned. That's not what you signed up for."

"I signed up to kick all the ass you need kicking and to pitch in whatever other ways I can," I said. "If some of those asses belong to some kind of monsters, it doesn't really matter to me. The lines of work I've been in, there's always a chance of getting burned. It comes with the business."

"This isn't like any business you've ever been involved with before. These things are... worse."

I held her gaze. "I don't fucking care. Okay? If there's something I need to know to help me stay ahead of them, by all means tell me, but I'm not going to run."

She looked away for a moment and then glanced back at me, her eyes fiercer than before. "They can't touch you, not really. All you need to remember is not to make any deals. Even if you think it could save me. It won't. If I'm gone, then I'm gone."

"Fair enough," I said with a nod.

The answer appeared to reassure her. She slipped the photo back into its envelope and tucked it away in her suitcase. "If everything goes well tonight, I'll have that worry off my back."

"Have your detectives come up with a solid plan?" I asked. "You sounded a little concerned in your last text."

"Oh, that. I think we can pull it off. Garrett's determination, John's optimism, and Sherlock's genius make a pretty potent combination, exactly as I expected. No, the problem is more that the damned genius seems like he might be forming suspicions I'd rather not have to tackle. But with the heist moving forward this quickly, I think I can dodge them."

Her tone had softened with something like fondness as she'd mentioned the three men's names. Not an emotion I was used to hearing from her.

"You're starting to like them," I said.

"What?" Her head jerked up, and she blinked at me. Then she laughed. "I don't like people. It's not my style."

I raised my eyebrows at her. "Oh, really."

"You're an exception. They're..." She waved her hand vaguely. "I don't know. They're interesting. That's not the same thing."

Jemma didn't tend to care about things she didn't find interesting anyway. I leaned back on my hands, watching her with curiosity. "What's interesting? You didn't think they'd be as good as they act, but you've discovered they actually are?" What were the chances of that?

Her gaze went distant for a second, with a hint of longing that woke up my earlier jealousy despite everything she'd just shared with me.

"No," she said with a crooked smile. "Although they might be. It's more that I'm starting to see how much they might be like me."

CHAPTER TWENTY-FOUR

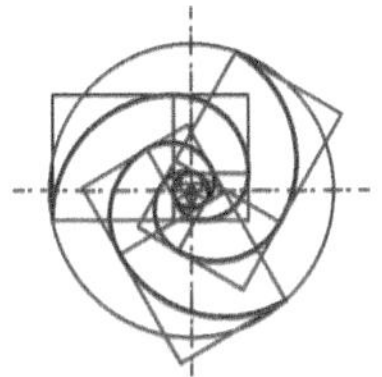

Jemma

H e's just getting the check," Bash said over the phone. "The way service has been going in there, I'd say we're waiting another ten minutes."

"Great. Just enough time to finish my coffee." Stretching out my legs beneath the little glass-topped table I was sitting at in a café around the corner from Richter's chosen lunch spot, I plopped another sugar cube into the mug for good measure. Then I took a gulp of the bittersweet liquid. The bitter side woke up my brain a little more, and the sweet side smoothed out my nerves. My head still felt slightly fuzzy from two nights of disturbed sleep in a row, but I could work around that.

Bash shifted on the other end of the line with a rustle of his down jacket. "Shouldn't you let me handle this? Richter knows you—or at least he knows about you."

"It's a two person job. I don't trust anyone else with it. If you do your part right, he won't even notice I'm there."

"When we were working out the London plan ahead of time, you said we weren't going to need a sample."

Bash's tone was mild, but there was a hint of a question in it. I wet my lips.

"I always knew we might want to doctor the real figurine. That's why I had you take the sample from our departed friend in Freising. This way the trio will get what they wanted, no embarrassment, no need to worry too much about my role in the whole thing. Now that I've seen them in action, I got thinking that if I leave them in the lurch, they won't let it go. I'd rather not have to deal with vengeful criminal investigators on my tail."

Bash hummed to himself. The sound might have been skeptical, or maybe I was reading too much into it.

My answer had been pretty much the whole truth. Since arriving here, I hadn't really thought about where I'd be leaving Sherlock, John, and Garrett at the end of my plan. I'd been too focused on getting us to that end and trusting that I'd worked everything out. The jade figurine they'd end up with didn't have the slightest trace of DNA on it, because it wasn't a murder weapon. The real murder weapon was an excellent copy that Bash had since tossed in the Pullinger Weiher lake.

When I'd decided on that outcome, I'd had a laugh to myself imagining the three most brilliant crime-fighters in London fumbling to explain themselves after the proof didn't present itself as expected. Now the thought had become less satisfying. I *wasn't* a monster like Bog, spreading misery for the pleasure of it. All of my plans had a purpose.

Whatever their flaws, the three men did by all appearances care about bringing Richter to justice. And there was plenty of justice that Richter was due. On the balance, it now seemed more prudent to throw him under the bus rather than them.

Which meant I needed a little piece of him to plant.

"The waiter has brought the check," Bash reported. "Target getting his coat on. I'm moving into position now."

"Same here." I got up. "After this, I'll see you tonight."

"Everything's ready to go."

"Perfect." I paused. "Thank you, Bash."

"I am made of faith and service, Majesty," Bash said in his wry Shakespeare-quoting voice.

The comment settled my nerves more than the sugar had. When I'd first woken up this morning nestled against him, I'd been afraid that I'd completely fucked up the one good sure thing I had in my life by, well, fucking him. But he'd taken my concerns in stride. He'd listened to my story about Olivia and the shrouded folk without badgering me with questions I didn't know how to answer yet. Exactly as I should have expected him to.

I'd yet to see anything really shake Sebastian Moran. It was too bad that was such a turn-on as well as being an excellent quality in a right-hand man.

It was so absurd that he'd suggested I was starting to care about my trio of investigators. It didn't matter how appealing they could each be in their own ways—they were a means to an end. When I slipped out of their lives, when they realized I'd used them, they'd be glad to see the back of me. Bash was my constant, my rock in the rapids.

Although if he ever did leave, I could go it without him too. I had to remember that.

I left a fiver on the table and tugged my hood up over my hair as I headed out. We'd gotten another damp dim day, but at least it wasn't outright raining like it had been this morning. I dodged the shallow puddles on the sidewalk.

When I turned the corner, Bash came into view at the other end of the block. He walked with a brisk stride, the collar of his puffy jacket pushed to the bottoms of his ears. I picked up my pace to be ready for the interception and curled my fingers around the little scalpel inside my sleeve. He tipped his chin in a slight nod before he started jogging.

Richter strode out the restaurant door—a tall, broad-shouldered man with eyes sunk as deep as his nose protruded out. Bash ran right into him, their shoulders colliding.

"Hey, watch it!" Richter shouted as he swayed backward.

I ducked past the two of them with a flick of my scalpel. There and then gone, so shallow and swift a scratch that Richter wouldn't see it had happened until he was sitting in his car. A papercut he hadn't noticed at the time, he'd have to guess.

A tiny splatter of blood was all I needed.

I dropped the blade into the baggie in my pocket and hurried on down the street. "Watch where *you're* going," Bash was saying in a belligerent voice. As soon as I'd slipped around the next corner, he'd back off and end the distraction.

A few paces down the nearest cross-street, I waved over a cab and hopped in. My pulse thumped at an eager tempo as I gave the driver the name of the hotel.

I'd done it. The last piece was in place. Now all that mattered was making sure tonight didn't fall apart before it happened.

The trio had made plans to hole up in Sherlock's room for most of the day, hashing out the final details. I stopped by my room to drop off my illicit acquisition and pick up the morning's purchases before heading upstairs.

John answered my knock. He ushered me in, excitement beaming from every inch of him like lights on a Christmas tree. Clearly I didn't have to worry about *him* getting the last-minute jitters. Last-minute boners was more likely.

"You're absolutely sure they won't get hurt?" Garrett was saying to Sherlock where they were bent over the table looking at a diagram Sherlock had drawn.

"The last thing I want to do is electrocute a member of our precious Scotland Yard," Sherlock replied. "I've studied the matter thoroughly."

"Only you would consider a twenty-four hour education to be 'thorough'," Garrett retorted, but with half a smile. He glanced up, and his smile touched both sides of his mouth while also becoming more hesitant. "And here's our Firecracker. How did the shopping go?"

I tossed a couple bags onto the bed from the errands I'd run while Bash had tracked Richter to a convenient location. "Four blue jackets, to your exact specifications. I bought them each at different stores so no one would think a batch purchase was odd."

"Exactly what I should have suggested," Sherlock said with a snap of his fingers.

"I think you sent me to do it so you wouldn't need to figure out all the necessary suggestions." I winked at him and dropped onto the edge of the bed next to my loot. "Where are we at?"

"All things considered, I believe we're remarkably well-prepared. I got the call that the van was ready about an hour ago." His gaze lingered on me for a beat too long to be totally relaxed. He motioned to John. "Did you want to get in a little more practice with the blowtorch? We have that spare pane."

All right. I had two potential stumbling blocks left in front of me. No need to get fancy. I could tackle them one at a time.

"There's a disturbing lack of coffee in this room," I said. "I feel I can best contribute by getting some of the good stuff from downstairs. Garrett, help me carry?"

It was a bit of a weak excuse, but I'd wanted it to be. I wanted him to pick up on the fact that I was angling for a conversation.

"Sure," he said with an expression somewhere between curious and wary, and followed me out.

I waited until we'd almost reached the elevators. "How are you doing with all of this?"

Garrett shrugged, but his shoulders tensed. "It's fine. The plan is coming together. Sherlock is… He's Sherlock, but not really all that much more so than usual. I'll just be glad when we're done."

The elevator arrived with a chime. I gripped Garrett's arm gently as we stepped on and turned to face him.

"I hope you know how much I appreciate the way all three of you have taken on this case as if it's your own—you especially. You have so much on the line. I don't see that kind of courage or commitment to justice very often."

I really did appreciate those qualities in him, whatever had stirred them to the surface in this particular situation. He was helping save my life, even if he didn't know it. A little honesty helped sell the words.

The tension in Garrett's body ebbed. "That's why I picked this job," he said. "So I could contribute something good to the world while other people are doing their best to destroy it."

"Evil doers beware," I said in a teasing tone. My fingers trailed over his wrist. He gazed into my eyes and grasped my hand abruptly, leaning in at the same moment. His mouth caught mine with all the determination he'd had that first night.

A second later, the elevator chimed at the ground floor. Garrett pulled back as the doors slid open with a curse under his breath. "Elevators," he muttered.

As we headed toward the dining room, I twined my fingers with his and let my voice dip low. "I'm here until Sunday. Maybe tomorrow, after the farewell dinner, we could... celebrate a very successful conference, just the two of us?"

A smile that was nothing but pleased crossed Garrett's face. I'd picked him for my last night here. He'd won twice over.

"I'd like that," he said, his gaze lingering on my face. "And if you ever happen to be in the city again..."

Or maybe he simply enjoyed being around me.

I shoved that thought away. He enjoyed the woman I'd shown him, a woman I'd catered to his tastes. That was the whole point, after all.

"Let's hope I have the opportunity," I said.

Now I had two secure on the line, with one still in danger of wriggling off the hook.

By the time we returned with the coffee mugs, my third fish had apparently decided to take matters into his own, er, fins.

"Sorry to send you off again," Sherlock said, aiming his piercing gaze at Garrett, "but John would like to work with a structure as close to the actual display case as we can find. He won't be able to carry it alone, and I need to get the emblems on." He tapped the jacket he'd spread on the table. "Will you lend him a hand?"

"As long as I can bring my coffee with me," the detective inspector said, looking pleased to have something else to do to distract him from the looming heist. John met him at the door with a clap to his back, and then Sherlock and I were alone.

My first instinct was to toss out an excuse and get the hell out of there, but I stood my ground. If he was going to insist on working through whatever was nagging at him, it was better that we did it now rather than half an hour before go-time.

I ambled over to the table and nodded at the thin metal contraption in the corner. "So, that's going to cut the power for us?"

"Assuming we set the cable up properly, but I don't expect that'll be too difficult." Sherlock placed the replica of the security company's badge he'd had some associate manufacture on the jacket's breast and raised the hotel iron with a faint hiss of steam. "Jemma," he added, looking at the task in front of him rather than at me, "can you think of anyone who would have known you were heading out to Regent's Park the other day?"

He asked in an off-hand way, but my skin prickled with the importance of the question. This was his first feint. He was feeling me out.

And his main concern was Bog's brief haunting by the fountain. Damned shrouded one.

Sherlock must be trying to put together the pieces of how that hazy figure could have appeared. I couldn't blame him for not being convinced it was yet another trick of the light. Either I'd created it or someone else had. So I'd give him an imaginary someone else.

"It's possible," I said slowly, as if thinking back to that afternoon. "When I requested at reception for them to have a taxi there for me, the concierge asked where I was off to, and I told him the truth. I didn't want to risk him hearing me direct the cabbie and wondering why I lied. There might have been someone else in the lobby close enough to overhear."

"Did you see anyone lingering near the fountain courtyard when you came to meet us?"

I frowned. "No. I checked as I approached to make sure no one looked to be close enough to overhear us, and I kept an eye out through the whole conversation." I let my eyes widen. He knew I was smart enough to follow his thread by now. "This isn't about our plans. You think someone might have followed us there and… created that weird lit-up figure we all saw?"

"The thought had crossed my mind," Sherlock said calmly.

"Considering the number of events in close succession. Have you experienced strange light effects like that or the one in the dining room before?"

I shook my head. "No. It *is* strange. But it seems even stranger to think someone would be doing it on purpose. What possible reason could they have?"

"That was where I was hoping you might enlighten the rest of us. You have a quick mind, and you know your situation better than any of us could." He set aside the first jacket and laid out the second.

I sank into the chair opposite him and brought my hand to my mouth in thought. I needed a story he'd accept that wouldn't incriminate me or make him too nervous about my involvement in the heist tonight. It wasn't hard to think of one. All I had to do was remember why I'd picked this trio in the first place.

"I'm not sure if there's anything specific to me," I said. "I came on my own, and I'd be surprised if there's anyone here who already knew me. But an awful lot of people here know *you*, and presumably John and Garrett in relation to you. If I were going to pick a most likely possibility, I'd say one of the other attendees has seen how closely I've ended up associating with the three of you, and they tried to disrupt that closeness out of jealousy. I find the idea pretty far-fetched, though."

A waft of steam rose off the iron as Sherlock finished the second jacket. Heat tickled over my skin. He set the iron down and rubbed his chin. "It is," he said. "But the explanation would fit with human nature of a certain sort. I'd hardly assume that every individual here is of the most stable emotional makeup."

He was buying the ploy. With a little more of a nudge, we'd be back on solid ground.

I wet my lips. "You don't think someone like that could compromise our plans tonight, do you? I'd swear no one could have been close enough to overhear us, especially with the sound of the fountain—that was why you picked that spot, wasn't it?"

"Indeed. And I've been extremely careful while arranging our supplies." He paused and raised his head to meet my gaze. "I'd hoped I could have said the same of you."

A chill quivered through my chest. I wasn't sure what he was talking about now. "Of course I've been careful," I said. "I haven't mentioned the gallery or Richter in public. I kept an eye out during every errand I've run. I want to see him caught and brought to justice at least as much as any of you do."

"Then why did you arrange to cross paths with him today?"

Shit. I held my face impassive, my mind whirling. How could he know about that one brief instant? Did he know what I'd done beyond simply "cross paths" with Richter?

His street-kid squad. There might have been a homeless teen I hadn't noticed tucked away at the edge of some alley. The informer couldn't have been close then—no one had heard my conversation with Bash or seen the scalpel. All they could know was that I'd gotten close to Richter.

"Did you have me followed?" I demanded with what felt like appropriately righteous indignation.

"For good reason, it seems," Sherlock said. "Although no, you weren't followed per say. I simply put out the word to certain parties to keep an eye out if they saw you on the streets, to see if anyone *else* was following. Why would you risk drawing Richter's attention when we're so close to our goal?"

His eyes stayed fixed on me, analyzing every particle of my response. I folded my hands together on the table.

My poker face was at least as good as his. I could navigate this unexpected storm.

"I kept my hood up and my head low so he wouldn't get a good look at me, which would only matter if he's seen me in the German news reports about the investigation. I just wanted to see *him*, once —to get a proper measure of him. When you three break the case and have him in custody, Freising will probably pass it over to your jurisdiction. I'll be heading home. I might not get any other chance to even look at the man I've been chasing for three weeks."

"So you let ego guide you."

He was one to talk about ego. I drew myself up straighter. "I thought it was possible I might notice something about him that would help tonight as well. But maybe that was ego too."

It was ego Sherlock could relate to better. He was still frowning, though. I'd given him the best possible answers, but he wasn't happy with them. It couldn't sit well with him that he'd misjudged the situation. Any second now, he was going to suggest they could go through with the heist without me, that it was safer that way.

I had to head him off at the pass with something that made him even more uneasy. I tossed out the trick I'd been holding in my back pocket.

"Are you trying to suggest that I should back out of helping tonight? If I really thought our plans were at all compromised, I swear to you I would. This whole effort has been built on my work — I should at least *be* there — I've been practicing for the switch-offs." I sucked in a breath. "If this is really because of the other night and the dare thing, I'm so sorry. I got a little carried away — the last thing I wanted was to offend you. I hope you won't dismiss my contributions over that."

Sherlock's posture stiffened as the jab landed. Mine relaxed a smidge in turn. Whatever gods there were, let that be enough.

He opened and closed his mouth a few times before he worked words out of it. Funny how mentioning the dared kiss opened John up but shut Sherlock down.

"I've put that incident completely out of my mind," he said finally in an equally stiff voice. "And I can assure you that I would never let some sort of petty retaliation guide my decisions. *I* apologize if I've given the impression that was my intent. I agree, I've seen no indication that our plans are compromised. We're more likely to succeed with you than without. I'd only ask, steer clear of our target for the rest of the day?" He managed a small smile.

My lips quirked upward in return. "I can make that promise without any trouble at all. Here's to bringing the bastard down."

Both Richter and the shrouded one who'd better not come any closer to ruining my plans.

CHAPTER TWENTY-FIVE

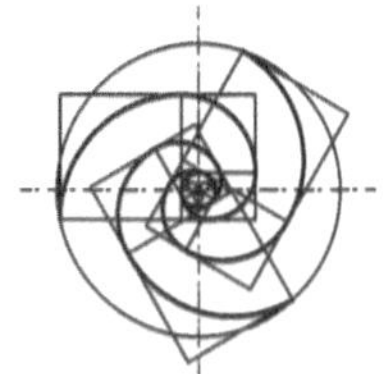

Jemma

That should do it," the kid said, looking up from the receiver box he'd been fiddling with in the back of the van. He couldn't have been more than thirteen, his hair cut ragged and his too-small jacket going threadbare at the elbows, but apparently he knew radios —or at least certain tricks you could play with radios—better than anyone else Sherlock knew. "You'll catch the call from that frequency, and the other place will be blocked. All you've got to do is answer."

Right now the box was only emitting a static crackle, but Sherlock looked satisfied with that. "Your assistance is greatly appreciated," he said, and handed over a few tenners.

From his seat at the front, Garrett watched the kid scamper out the back. "Are you sure we can trust him not to shoot his mouth off?" he asked when Sherlock had closed the doors.

"He doesn't know enough to have much to say," Sherlock said. "But yes, I'm sure. I'm a rather good judge of character."

I had to catch my lips from twitching into a grin. A giddying combination of excitement and anxiety jittered through my nerves. I curled my fingers around the cuffs of my security guard jacket sleeves, itching for a sugar cube, but I'd left everything with Bash except the absolute essentials.

"There isn't much time left for anyone to interrupt us anyway," I said.

John glanced at his watch. He'd taken the driver's seat, naturally. "With the way we placed the spikes in the driveway, if they're on schedule they should be calling in the delay in just a couple minutes."

Sherlock held up his hand, cloaked in the same flexible leather gloves we all wore, and hunched over the receiver. "Quiet, then."

We sat there, braced in the dark of the van with only the thin light of the streetlamps seeping through the tinted windows, listening to the wavering static. I leaned into the firmly padded seat and clasped my hands together on my lap. My heartbeat counted out the seconds until a blunt voice broke from the hiss.

"Team Three, we're having a little van trouble. Can you hold off departure? Over."

Sherlock grasped the mic. "We hear you, Team One," he said in a brusque tone. "We can hold. How long do you expect to need? Over."

"I'm hoping no more than half an hour. We'll call in on thirty if it looks like longer. Over."

Sherlock motioned to me. I already had my hand on the door handle. I darted out and yanked off the black sheet that had been covering the copied logo. John started the engine as I hopped back in.

"Half an hour," he said with a breathless laugh.

"If we do this right, we'll only need three quarters of that," Sherlock said.

The van lurched forward and roared along the city streets. We'd parked in waiting only a few blocks from the gallery. I pulled the scratchy curls of the light brown wig Sherlock had offered me over my head and adjusted my prescription-less glasses on my nose.

Sherlock had gone darker, with a unibrow and a beard to match the team leader of the real security detail. John's blond locks were tucked under a chestnut fringe with a coordinating moustache. Garrett had gone coppery auburn.

"Time to make the call?" the detective inspector asked, holding up his phone.

Sherlock paused until we'd turned the corner toward the gallery's back alley. "Now."

We cruised into the alley past the police surveillance, looking for all the world like the team they'd been expecting. Garrett brought the phone to his ear. He pitched his voice higher with a distressed strain.

"Yes, I'd like to report a hate poster I just saw. It's truly horrible —I can't imagine if my children saw the picture they've printed on it. I wrote down the exact post. Can you get someone out there to take it down as soon as possible? I thought I saw a police car already nearby."

As he gave the details to the dispatcher, John parked beside the matching van that Team Three had arrived in. He slung his duffel bag over his shoulder. Garrett flashed a grin at me as he hung up the phone. For all his hesitations, he couldn't help enjoying getting one up on his Scotland Yard colleagues.

And I couldn't help returning his grin. Yeah, I might miss that competitive determination a little after this was done. Who knew if I'd ever see it again?

Sherlock leapt out of the van first. He keyed in the passcode another of his young allies had spied out for us, and we strode behind him into the gallery's back rooms before spreading out as if beginning our patrol. Only Sherlock passed the departing team with a salute that partly hid his face.

"Quiet night, as usual," the other team leader said. "Try not to get bored out of your minds."

Then they were gone, and the gallery was ours.

Garrett hustled off to loop the camera feeds pointed at the Richter exhibit. The rest of us waited for his signal and then hurried to the exhibit's doors. John handed Sherlock the code-breaking device from his bag.

He had to get this done and get us into the exhibit room before the power cut out. Otherwise we'd lose our chance to stimmy the motion detectors.

Sherlock opened up the side of the keypad and fiddled with the wires. Garrett pinged us that he'd gotten in place standing watch by the back door. Numbers flickered on the device's screen. I resisted the urge to shift on my feet.

A tendril of scent crept into my nose: a dry sour smell like old rot. My heartbeat stuttered. I glanced around surreptitiously, but my eyes couldn't make out even a glimmer of the shrouded one in the darkened gallery room. That reassurance didn't stop my chest from constricting.

Bog was here. Too weakened from the massive hallucination he'd wrapped me in yesterday night to make much of an appearance, maybe, but the fact that he'd followed me this far from the hotel through the mortal world meant he'd gotten some strength back. If he recovered enough before we were finished…

I couldn't afford to let that fear distract me.

Sherlock peered at the device's screen as several more seconds slipped by. Finally, the numbers froze on a code. I held my breath as he tapped it in. With a sigh, the steel door slid open.

We'd only just crossed the threshold when the security lights blinked out. "Quick, now!" Sherlock said, flicking on an electric lantern and setting it in the middle of the floor.

We all had squares of the thick black material in our jacket pockets, designed to block the sensor functions so they wouldn't pick up the heat of our bodies. John boosted me up to fix one and then another over the devices high on the walls, keeping his weight on his good leg. Sherlock managed to reach them on his own with his great height. We moved through both rooms, covering all of them.

A sliver of my attention lingered on the glass case that held my prize. A tingle raced over my skin. So fucking close now. I could almost feel it in my hand, feel the relief of its release.

But Bog's scent trailed after me too. A glimmering streak of movement caught my eye in a corner. My head jerked around, but at the same moment, the lights gleamed back on, dimmer than before. The building had a backup generator someone off-site had turned on.

John drew the blowtorch from his bag. Nothing that generator was powering could tip the security team off now as long as we handled the display case just right. He braced himself in front of the section where the jade figurine lay, his shoulders loose but the muscles in his forearms tensed, exactly like when he'd practiced.

He'd insisted that he be the one to carry out this part of the heist since he was the one who'd suggested it. His eyes glinted with anticipation, but his jaw had tightened.

For him, taking on this task wasn't just about pulling off this one heist, was it? It was about proving he could play an equal part despite his lingering injury in everything he and Sherlock did together.

The spurt of the torch's fire made his eyes spark even brighter. I readied myself with the chunk of glass we were going to use to offset the removed weight, watching him and the line of flame. A thin pang of emotion fluttered through my chest.

I was going to miss his earnest recklessness too, just a bit.

Heat grazed my face. John drew the lines of the rectangle again and again, a sheen of sweat forming on his forehead. Then he stopped, set the blowtorch aside, and nodded to me.

He tugged, and the edge of the case gave. As he tipped that chunk out, I slid my piece onto the top of the case at exactly the same speed. Then I slipped closer beside him, a piece of jade in one hand, a fake golden etching tucked inside my other sleeve. Fixed to my baby finger, I held a metal pick coated in two different sets of blood, just out of view.

I moved even faster than I had in practice. One hunk of jade swapped for another, two quick swipes of the pick inside the grooves, flicking the pick back into the nook in my sleeve as I handed the figurine to John. Sherlock stepped closer to him, his face lit with eagerness now. As I turned, I dipped my other hand into the case behind my back to complete the second switch.

My fingers closed around a cool gold surface marked with lines etched with mathematical precision and speckled jewels perfect in their symmetry. Joy trembled up my sternum as I tucked my real reward away as quickly as I'd taken it. The shrouded one's smell touched my nose a little more strongly, and the lights overhead wavered faintly, but the men were too absorbed in their score to think it was anything other than a fault of the generator.

The relic I'd needed was mine. Bog's tricks, the trio's smarts—none of it had stopped me. All I had left to do was complete my escape.

John eased the piece of the display case back into place while I removed the extra weight. We gathered our things in a concentrated flurry of movement and hustled to the back door where Garrett was waiting.

"Call it in," Sherlock said. We all shed our wigs and security uniform jackets and stuffed them into John's duffel bag. He handed the bag to me. I was the only one unneeded for the last part of their plan; I was the ideal person to dispose of the evidence. Which worked out perfectly for me.

As Garrett pulled out his phone, I raised my hand in friendly farewell and set off around the van.

"Jemma," Sherlock called after me, keeping his voice low. I stopped just past the van with a hitch of my pulse and turned as he caught up with me. Had he noticed part of my larger ploy or caught on to Bog's attempts at signaling them? Did he suspect something?

He reached toward my face and eased off the glasses that had been part of my disguise. "You were in such a hurry you forgot about removing these," he said.

He didn't miss much even in the middle of the craziest scheme he'd ever gotten wrapped up in. I gazed into his sharp blue eyes and wondered once more what it might be like to work *with* a man with a mind like that instead of against him.

I was never going to know.

"You pulled it off," I said. "It was brilliant. I guess I got too focused on making sure the rest goes off without a hitch."

"There's always a necessary balance between caution and speed," he said, so perfectly Sherlock that an unexpected urge rose up inside me despite my sense of the time slipping away. Then a waft of Bog's scent filled my nose, giving me the perfect excuse to indulge myself. Just as another streak of light shuddered into being above us, I bobbed up on my toes and brushed my lips to Sherlock's.

When I released him a second later, Bog's final effort had faded. "Thank you," I said, meaning it for far more than he could guess right now.

Sherlock blinked at me, momentarily startled—not a look I saw on him often. My throat tightened, but his hesitation gave me just enough opening to pat his arm and lope away.

John had left his car at the other end of the alley for me to use. I dropped the fob he'd given me on the pavement just behind one of the front wheels, where I expected Sherlock would spot it easily enough in the morning, and headed in the opposite direction from what we'd planned.

The farther I got from the gallery, the faster I picked up my pace. The desiccated shrouded folk scent licked after me, growing thicker by the moment. When I switched to breathing through my nose, it coated my mouth.

I came up on the shadowy spot of bank I'd picked, the darkly glinting waters of the Thames ready to meet me. The weight of the piece of glass should be enough to sink the bag, but I stuffed in a few large rocks for good measure while retrieving a couple items from my jacket. Then I hurled the whole lot as far as I could over the depths. The bag hit the surface with a splash and dropped like a stone.

I couldn't wait any longer, not with Bog hovering nearby trying every play it could. I dug into the pouch I'd fastened under my sweatpants and drew out the three other etched golden shapes I'd collected over the last year.

As I tugged down my pants, another wave of the shrouded one stink washed over me. A glow crackled through the air. I fumbled with the pieces. They fit together, end to end, around my mid-thigh like a metal cuff. Bog's light seared brighter as it closed around me, the mark on the back of my neck burned—and I clicked the last section, the one that had once belonged to Richter, into place.

The supernatural glow vanished into the night, and the burning faded away. A quiver of energy raced over my skin from the cuff. It lingered there, a gentle tickle that brought a choked but ecstatic laugh to my lips.

Bog couldn't find me now, couldn't reach me now. Not one of its shrouded one skills could penetrate the cloak this relic gave me. I'd just bought myself my freedom.

With a smile stretching my lips, I tugged my pants back up and loped off toward the spot where Bash would be waiting to drive us to the airport. In a few short hours, I'd be far away from here. Far from anywhere Bog knew to look for me, and far from the three men who'd helped me in more ways than they knew.

They might not have known how final that farewell was at the time, but I'd even gotten to wave my trio good-bye.

CHAPTER TWENTY-SIX

Sherlock

Sometimes I enjoyed taking the lead with an interrogation, but often it was more instructive to stand back and watch the questioning play out, studying the suspect's reactions. Especially today.

On the other side of the one-way glass, Garrett leaned his hands onto the interrogation room table. Richter sat across from him, his hands in cuffs, his long-nosed face held at a haughty angle.

"If you didn't have anything to do with the murder, then how did your DNA and the victim's end up on an object you own that's a perfect match for the killing blow?" Garrett said, his voice turned slightly tinny by the speaker system. "Please, let's hear your explanation."

He might not have as incisive a mind as some, but our little detective inspector made up for it in tenacity. Richter scowled at him. His lawyer in the chair beside him, a stout mole-faced man, started to raise a protest, but Richer waved him quiet. When he replied, he sounded just as certain as he had before.

"I don't know. Maybe you planted it there. Maybe *she* did. I didn't even know this councilor who apparently died, and that statue was packed away in its crate for hours before the plane took off."

Garrett raised his eyebrows. "Who's this 'she'?"

"I don't know that either," Richter snapped. "There's a woman who's been trying to steal one of my pieces since my last exhibit—and not that jade one. I haven't had a chance to sit down and chat about it with her. Why do you think I had so much security set up?"

Beside me, John shifted his weight to lean on his walking stick. "I suppose some criminals will do whatever they can to displace the blame."

"I'm not so sure that's what's happening here." I wrinkled my nose against the lingering odor of sweat and stale coffee in the room—and against what my instincts were telling me. "His body language suggests he's telling the truth."

John stared at me. "What? You don't think he's our murderer, after all this?"

"I'm still forming my impressions. Watch, and see what you make of him."

Richter had switched to a different tactic. He was nodding to his lawyer, who shuffled his papers. "Your evidence will be inadmissible in court regardless of the details. My client can attest that you or a Sherlock Holmes broke into the gallery and stole the artifact from its display case, eliminating the correct chain of custody completely."

Garrett chuckled. We'd worked out our story together, and I'd heard him give it to his colleagues more than once since last night without missing a beat.

"You're going to have a hard time swinging that as your defense." He fixed his gaze on Richter. "Sure, the gallery was robbed. You're lucky my esteemed colleague Mr. Holmes happened to be passing through the area and noticed the warning signs. He alerted the police, but the robbers fled before we arrived. They dropped the statue they'd stolen, so we took it back to the lab for testing, and it was a total surprise when it matched up with an unsolved crime all the way over in Germany. Pretty ballsy, leaving your murder weapon out in plain view, I've got to say."

Richter glanced toward us—toward what to him would look like a mirror. He was familiar enough with police investigations to be aware someone was on the other side. If he'd expected an interruption declaring Garrett's story untrue and releasing him from custody, he was disappointed. His posture deflated, but he jerked his chin up even higher.

"I'd like to consult with my lawyer before I answer any further questions."

John tapped his stick against the linoleum floor. "We should ask him about Jemma. If one of his men was watching the area around the gallery and spotted her leaving, who knows what they've done to her. We shouldn't have let her go alone."

The concern in his voice snagged sharp as a hook on something inside me. It dredged up a flash of memory: her sly smile, sitting at the table in John's hotel room. A hand on my —

I shoved that fragment back into the compartment I was keeping sealed tight. It wasn't important and certainly didn't bear any relevance to our current situation.

"If Richter caught her, we wouldn't be having this conversation, because he'd have all the evidence *he* needs," I said. But perhaps Jemma had seen reason to fear for her safety and had gone to ground. She hadn't returned to her hotel room last night. We hadn't received a single text or call. The more hours passed, the more her disappearance weighed on my gut.

I knew how sharp *she* was. Surely she'd have found some way to contact us?

If she wanted to, that was.

One of Garrett's colleagues ambled past us. "Did you hear the latest about his victim?" he remarked, nodding to Richter through the window.

"His victim?" I repeated.

"Yeah." He worked his jaw as if chewing on something. "This morning, someone raised a complaint out in Germany that this city councilor abused him as a kid when he was part of a youth program. Seems like a few have come forward now. Maybe this knob here did us a favor twice over, taking that guy out of commission and then getting caught for it."

John frowned as the officer sauntered off. "Richter's older than the councilor, and he has no children. This couldn't be revenge. Do you think he might have been a partner in the abuse? That would be blackmail worthy."

The threads of suspicion that had been unfurling in my mind tightened into a starker image. "I think our councilor died in part because no one would end up sorry to have seen him gone."

Before John could ask what I meant, Garrett emerged from the interrogation room. "What a piece of work Richter is," he said. "But we've got him. He hasn't produced an alibi, and with the circumstantial evidence alongside the DNA and his history—I doubt he'll even get bail."

"I'd like to take another look at the gallery," I said.

The detective investigator gave me a puzzled look. "Right now?" he said, in a milder tone than I expect he'd have used if there hadn't been officers around who might overhear.

"If they can spare you. Or if you can arrange official permission for us to enter the crime scene without accompaniment."

"No, if you're tracking down an additional lead, I want to be there for it too." He ducked out of the room to speak to one of his superiors and returned a few minutes later. "All right, let's go."

This once, Garrett drove in his official duty vehicle, leaving John to tap his walking stick restlessly in the back seat.

"What's this about?" Garrett said as soon as we'd pulled out of the parking lot. "What the hell could you possibly want to look at there now?"

"Richter is claiming that someone was targeting his gallery," I said. "Trying to steal a different one of his artifacts. Indulge my curiosity."

The gallery's entrances were taped off, with no one inside other than one officer ensuring the crime scene remained secure. She exchanged a nod with Garrett. We walked straight to the rooms that housed Richter's special exhibit.

I studied the area around the display case that had held the jade statue and then stepped closer. With the pressure alarms off, I could come right up to the glass.

The cut piece of the case had been removed, along with the piece of uncarved jade we'd used to balance the statue's weight. My gaze came to rest on an object farther down the display: a rectangular strip of etched gold set with tiny gemstones.

My heart sank as I studied it. "I'm going to take a closer look at this," I said to Garrett, pointing to it and then pulling on my gloves.

"What does that have to do with anything?" he muttered, but he didn't try to stop me.

I eased the piece out and turned it to catch the light. My thumb rubbed one corner. I lowered it with a grimace.

"This is a fake. Plated gold—cheaply done, even. Richter couldn't have missed the signs. It's been switched since he last saw this display."

John went still. Garrett's eyes widened. "What?" the smaller man said.

"I think we'd better discuss this matter in more detail in private."

My thoughts whipped through my head as we headed back to the car. I sank into the passenger seat and got out my phone. As before, when I dialed the number Jemma had given me days ago, the phone on the other end rang and rang. No voicemail. No indication of its owner. Just a blank.

"What's going on?" Garrett demanded. "Who are you calling?"

"I'm not sure," I said slowly.

"Sherlock thinks Richter might be telling the truth," John put in. "He might not have been involved in the murder."

"*What?* But we have all the pieces—all the evidence leads to him."

"Where did we get most of that evidence?" I said. "Or at least the start of the trail, like that scrap of photograph?"

"From Jemma," Garrett said. "What does that have to do with anything? Of course she—"

"Did you ever confirm with the Freising police that they have an officer on staff by the name of Jemma Moriarty?"

He hesitated. "Well, no—she was worried there'd be repercussions for her if they thought she'd asked the London police to get involved. I made it sound as if we stumbled on the case ourselves. But there was an article about her in the internet, with a photograph and everything. Some award she'd won. You said you'd seen it too."

There'd been a few mentions of Jemma in articles I'd had to translate from German. "See if you can find it now," I suggested.

Garrett took out his phone and typed in a search. I watched him, nearly certain of the results, as he scanned his screen. He clicked through to another page and then another before raising his head. "It's gone. Hold on. Maybe I only searched her name, not the city too, and that's how it came up."

He typed again and paused. Then he handed his phone to me, the color starting to drain from his face.

The top search result for simply "Jemma Moriarty" was a profile for a math tutor based in Oxford. Her credentials included an impressive list of publications and honors, but none of them had anything to do with policing or criminal investigation. The photo on the page showed a meek woman with pale auburn hair pulled back in a loose bun, her lips so pale they nearly blended into the rest of her face, her eyes obscured by thick rimmed glasses.

I'd trained myself in the art of facial recognition. I could draw the features of the Jemma I'd known over this woman's cheekbones, the angle of her nose, the depth of her eyes, the slant of her neck. But I knew at the same time that no one at the conference would believe this woman was the one who'd toppled a gunman in our midst nine days ago.

John confirmed it. "That can't be her," he said, peering over the back of my seat.

"It is," I said quietly. "The articles we found before were a ploy."

"But—why—"

"She wanted to steal that trinket from Richter?" Garrett filled in. "*She's* the woman he's talking about? How much could that little thing be worth that she'd go to those lengths..." He trailed off, looking even more sick than before.

"She fooled all of us," I said with a strange mix of revulsion and admiration.

How had I let myself be led astray? How quick a mind must she have to have managed it?

I thought I'd seen a woman on the verge of greatness, close to matching my skills. She'd just given a demonstration in how to run circles around me. It was close to being both the most shameful and the most stimulating thing that had ever happened in my life.

Most importantly, where the hell had she gone now?

"All of that subterfuge, all of the pieces she must have set up to get us into the gallery..." John rubbed his face. "I agree with Garrett. I can't see the point of risking all that if it was only about that one piece."

"Unless that piece had some value we're unaware of," I said.

"If she set up Richter," Garrett said slowly, "then who murdered the Freising councilor?"

I glanced at him pointedly. "How could she have set up the details so perfectly to point us—and only us—toward him if she didn't have a hand in it?"

We were all quiet for a moment. "He was a child molester," John pointed out in a rough voice. "But it is still murder. What do we do now?"

That was the question I'd been turning over in the back of my head from my first inklings of the truth. I exhaled and flexed my hands. "Before I give my opinion on that, I'd like to talk to a few people at our hotel while the conference is still running."

Garrett started the engine. "She lied about everything," he said.

"Possibly. At the very least, she lied about a lot." My mind darted back to that moment just before she'd left last night, when she'd given me a quick kiss and thanked me.

I'd have sworn as readily that she'd meant those two words as I'd have sworn that Richter's indignation was legitimate.

At the hotel, we marched up to the front desk. Garrett flashed his badge. "Official business," he said. "We need to know what information you have on file for one of the guests, who may be involved in a major crime."

The clerk blanched. "Which guest, sir?"

"A Jemma Moriarty," I said. "She was staying in room 247."

The clerk brought up the record on her computer and frowned. "Do you mean Jena Morisarti? That's the name we have for that room." She turned the screen so I could see the spelling.

I almost laughed. How neatly Jemma had played that gambit. If we'd overheard the staff calling her "Miss Morisarti," we'd have thought we'd misheard or they'd simply mispronounced her name. But it meant there was no record of any Moriarty, including the Oxford math tutor, staying here this week.

"Perhaps we were mistaken," I said. "Thank you for your assistance."

Dinner was being served. I walked into the dining room and spotted the Glasgow commissioner Jemma had saved at a nearby table. John and Garrett trailed behind me as I sidled over.

"I'm sorry to bother you, ma'am," I said. "I just had a quick question. Did you get the name of the young lady who subdued your attacker during the welcome reception?"

The older woman brightened at the memory. "Yes, of course. Jemina Moriety. What a promising officer. She does Dover credit."

The other two and I exchanged a look. Another name, another story. How many had she used throughout the conference?

Had any of them been real?

We retreated to the lounge room where we'd spent quite a few hours of the conference in discussion—most of it with the woman we'd known as Jemma. Garrett paced for a few seconds and then threw himself down onto one of the chairs. John leaned against the arm of the sofa.

"I ask again," Garrett said. "What now? Do we throw out the entire case against Richter?"

I paused. "No," I said. "I think... whatever her many crimes, Miss Moriarty—or Morisarti, or Moriety, as the case may be—has given us a gift. We *know* Richter was a terror. We have a solid case where we never did before. A sentence for murder won't cover half his previous transgressions. No one has to know what we do."

John nodded. Garrett gnawed at his lip, but I could tell he wasn't against the idea, even if it didn't entirely sit right with him.

"It's still justice," John said to him. "Just arrived at in a pretty convoluted way."

"And we could be wrong about Jemma," Garrett put in. "It's possible we're conjuring this entire conspiracy, and he really *did* murder that man."

I'd have placed the chances of that at approximately one in a million at this point, but I couldn't see the benefit in saying as much.

"What do we do about Jemma?" John said, his gaze on me.

"We couldn't charge her with anything even if we wanted to," I said. "We can't explain how we know she took that relic without admitting our own crime. We can't even prove the woman we knew *exists*. At least, not yet."

Garrett perked up. "Not yet?" he prompted.

Despite my tangled emotions, a smile crossed my face. I knew what I was up against now. The game was afoot.

I leaned forward, resting my hands on the top of the sofa. "There are a few answers I'd like to obtain before I settle the matter completely. Wouldn't you say the same?"

CHAPTER TWENTY-SEVEN

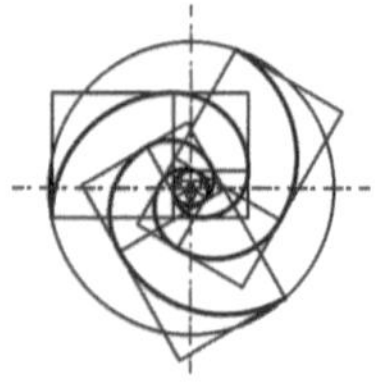

Six weeks later

Jemma

"Forget Shakespeare," I said, pointing my fork at Bash's plate. "*That* is an absolute tragedy."

He lifted his eyes from his coffee to consider the quarter of pancake that he'd abandoned under its dollop of whipped cream and drizzle of syrup. It was the only surviving piece of the room service breakfast I'd ordered for us after he'd stopped by to discuss the day's plans. His gaze rose farther to meet mine.

"Are you asking permission to steal it?" he asked with a hint of a smirk.

"Only if you're not going to eat it. It would be a horrible waste, is all I'm saying."

He pushed the plate toward me. "By all means, Majesty."

I wrinkled my nose at him for a split-second before scooping the fluffy creamy goodness into my mouth. Okay, now back to business. After I licked the traces of syrup from my fork.

Bash made a not very convincing show of restraining an eyeroll, but his smile had that fond quirk to it that would have stirred up other sorts of hungers if I'd let it.

"When we're done here," I said, "I promise we'll go to Italy next, and you can eat the most authentic pizza in existence every day while I see what I can make of the mob."

"I look forward to it." Bash flipped the page of one of the national papers. "I'm not seeing any useful articles today, as per usual."

"We might as well keep looking, just in case." I skimmed a little farther through my tablet's map of Croatia. "There are too many fucking mountains in this country. None of the feelers you've put out have turned up anything?"

"Not so far," Bash said.

I grimaced. I was starting to think I was going to have to climb to each peak and circle around it for good measure just to find the place I needed. "Why don't we give a helicopter rental another try? We can cover a couple of the slopes. Even if these people are hiding, they can't cover a whole village perfectly."

"If that's what you'd like to do, I can arrange it," Bash said. "Which part of the country?"

"Hmm... How about up here?" I swirled my finger over the northwestern edge of the map.

He nodded and pulled out his phone to look into making arrangements. I tossed my napkin onto the table and got up to stretch my legs.

When we'd picked up this trail a couple weeks ago, I'd known this process might take a while, and it was a lot easier with Bog's threats so distant. But damn, a careful search of an entire country could be mind-numbing.

One of my phones rang—one of the urgent business lines. I scooped it out of my purse and yanked it to my ear.

"Hello?"

"Ms. Matthams?" a reedy voice said, using the name I'd signed into the hotel with.

"Jakov," I said with a skip of my pulse. I'd learned a thing or two during my stint in London, one of which was the usefulness of employing the local youth. Although in my case I'd gone a step above street kids and slipped some cash to the needier looking porters who worked in the lobby. "What have you got for me?"

"Well," the young man said, his accented English slightly muffled as if he'd huddled away in a corner, "you said to call you if anyone came in asking about a woman and showing photos. An old man did a few minutes ago. The people at the front desk didn't say anything, but I followed him a little ways outside, and he met up with two other men, younger guys, like you said might happen. So I called."

A jolt of adrenaline tingled through my veins. "Thank you, Jakov," I said. "You did wonderfully. I'll leave an envelope for you with the front desk when I come down."

"Thank you very much, Ms. Matthams!"

When I turned around, Bash was on his phone. I made a slicing gesture, and he ended the call.

"What?" he asked, cocking his head.

I tapped my phone against my palm. The corner of my mouth curled up. "Change of plans. We have company."

THE TEMPTATION OF FOUR

MORIARTY'S MEN #2

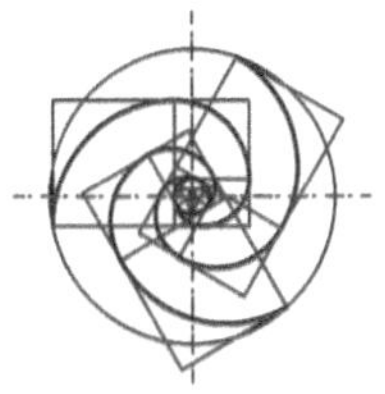

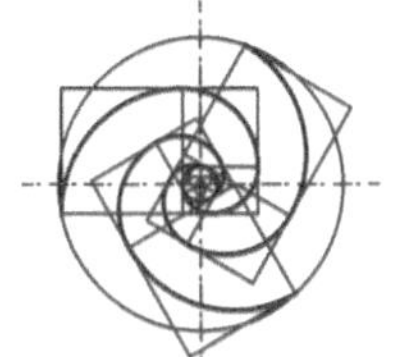

Jemma

Hidden by the velvety folds of the brocade curtain, I peered out my hotel room window. Shoppers and tourists strolled through the mid-morning sunlight along the road below. One of Zagreb's bright blue trams whirred past. The glossy signs at street level, nearly as many of them in English as in Croatian, stood out against the aged stone that rose two or three stories above them.

The hotel rose taller still, but even from my sixth floor vantage point, I should have been able to recognize the men I was searching for if they'd been in view. I'd gotten to know Sherlock Holmes, John Watson, and Garrett Lestrade rather intimately during the time I'd spent with them in London weeks ago.

"Do you have eyes on them?" Bash asked. My right-hand man had gotten up from the table where we'd been enjoying a room service breakfast, his newspaper discarded. His fingers veered instinctively toward the pistol I knew he was wearing in a concealed holster at his hip.

"Not from here." I drew back from the window. Honestly, I'd have been a little disappointed if the trio of London's top criminal investigators had tracked me all this way only to carelessly reveal themselves that quickly.

They might not even realize I was in this hotel. The porter who'd called to warn me that an "old man" had come in asking about me had said the staff at the front desk had denied any knowledge. But that man had almost certainly been Sherlock in one of his elaborate disguises, and if anyone in the lobby had given a hint that they knew more than they were letting on, he'd have picked up on it.

I hadn't exactly left the three of them in the lurch when I'd vanished from London, but I *had* lured them into committing a heist that would have cost them all their careers if they'd fumbled. And I'd told them plenty of lies along the way. After realizing that, they might not be in the friendliest mood toward me.

I turned to Bash. "There's no way they could charge me with any crime they know of without revealing their own. They don't even know *you* exist. So they don't pose any real threat, as long as they keep out of my other business. I'm thinking we head off potential interruptions by finding out what exactly they want."

Bash raised an eyebrow. Otherwise his tan face was as deadpan as usual. "It looks like giving them their evidence didn't stop them from wanting revenge after all."

I'd gone a little out of my way to ensure the trio didn't end up embarrassed after the heist was over. At the time, I'd told Bash it was to protect myself. They'd gotten their man, even if he hadn't actually committed the one crime I'd planted evidence of. Stefan Richter had been guilty of plenty of other indiscretions. If Sherlock and company had figured out his innocence in that one murder, they'd decided to let him hang for it anyway.

"Maybe they'd have caught up with us three weeks sooner if they'd been angrier," I said. "And we might have had Richter's people harassing us on top of that. Let's go. You take the front, and I'll take the back—we'll meet up at Franjo's. Watch from the back room?"

"Of course. I'll be there before you walk in, Majesty." Bash gave me a mock salute, swiped his hand over the black stubble of his hair, and headed out the door. With well-honed self-control, I avoided spending more than a second admiring the sculpted muscle of his backside.

I took more time than he had with my own preparations, pulling my thick red waves into a braid and covering my head with a gauzy scarf as if I wanted to hide it. The casual cotton dress I'd put on would work well enough.

When I'd given Bash a couple minutes' head start, I slipped out into the hall and made for the staircase at the back of the building. If the trio suspected I was staying there, they'd be watching that exit.

In the alley, I let the warm spring breeze tug a strand of my hair from beneath the scarf and paused to put on a pair of sunglasses before I emerged. I hadn't heard any definite signs of pursuit, but these three were better than that. My heart thumped at a pace that might have been slightly giddy as I wove through the streets to the pub Bash and I had been frequenting.

Franjo's held an eclectic mix of styles and offerings. I stepped inside to exposed brick walls and a buoyant Europop song. The tables scattered throughout the middle of the room were old wood carved with a checkerboard pattern, but the bar on one side and the booths on the other shone with slick indigo laminate. The smell of pickles, barbeque wings, and fine wine mingled in the air.

I slid onto one of the padded booth benches in view of both the entrance and the black curtain that hung over the doorway to the back room. Franjo Junior, the grizzled son of the original Franjo who'd established the pub decades ago, nodded to me from behind the counter, where he acted as primary bartender as well as owner. Bash and I had gotten ourselves into his very good graces by handling an extortion racket that'd been breathing down his neck.

It always paid to make friends with the locals.

The waitress brought over my usual, a sidecar. It might have been early in the day for alcohol, but there was a little orange in it, and anyway, I deserved a drink. As invigorating as the prospect of tangling with the London trio again was, especially after the dull drudgery of the last six weeks, it was also a hassle.

Where had I slipped up to allow them to track me here? What the hell were they hoping to get out of following me?

I didn't have to wait long for the opportunity to ask those questions directly. I'd just taken my first sip of the sidecar's tangy sweetness when a stooped figure with shaggy gray hair came in. The man took a seat at the bar—not directly across from my booth but close enough that he could easily keep an eye on it—and ordered a local beer.

Sherlock truly was a master of disguise. I wasn't completely sure it was him and not a regular getting started on his daily boozing until he dropped his napkin and reached down to pick it up, giving him the perfect excuse to steal a surreptitious glance my way. His long lithe fingers confirmed my suspicions. I restrained a smile, pretending to be absorbed in my drink. When he'd gotten back on his stool, I ambled over with my glass.

"Hello, Sherlock," I said, sliding onto the stool one over from him. "What a coincidence, bumping into you here."

Sherlock's hand tightened around his beer mug, just slightly. He rubbed his narrow face, his posture straightening to reach his full remarkable height, and suddenly it wasn't so hard to see the man I knew within the disguise. His cool blue eyes studied me with their usual penetrating sharpness. He gave me a crooked smile.

"Hello, Jemma," he said evenly. "I'm guessing it isn't such a coincidence on either of our sides after all."

"I'll give credit where it's due," I said. "I don't think I'd have seen through the disguise if I hadn't been waiting for you."

He made a dismissive sound that seemed to say he wasn't going to be mollified in his failure and took a sip of his beer. His lips twisted with a grimace. Sherlock was more the brandy type.

I leaned back against the bar. "Should we invite John and Garrett in too? Make it a full reunion?"

"I think it's probably best to keep the conversation simple. One-to-one."

"All right. Let's converse then. How did you track me to Zagreb?"

A hint of his earlier smile came back. "If I tell you that, you'll know how to cover your tracks better next time."

He did enjoy being able to hold his superior strategizing over a person. I set aside that question. I'd find out eventually if I needed to. "Fine. I assume you'll at least tell me *why* you tracked me here. This is an awfully long way to come just to have a drink together."

Sherlock turned toward me on his stool as if he could read my reactions better that way, which maybe he could. A whole lot went on in that admittedly brilliant mind of his that I couldn't entirely follow. His thoughts and deductions moved in patterns different from my own. Which was part of what had made him so fascinating from the start.

"I'm surprised you'd even ask that," he said. "Did you really think I wouldn't realize how thoroughly you deceived us? It took less than a day for me to put the pieces together, in case you wondered."

The corner of my lips quirked up. "Less than a day after I'd already left. Not less than a day after the scheme began."

"Fair." He nudged his beer mug but appeared to decide against trying to drink any more of it. "You pulled off a crime under our noses and escaped with the spoils. You couldn't expect me to ignore that."

I shrugged. "There isn't much else you *can* do about it. You can't even prove I did it in any way a court of law will accept."

"I don't understand why you did it at all." His gaze searched mine even more intently than before. "That piece you took was valued at a few thousand dollars. Hardly worth the lengths you went to in order to obtain it. Unless you have some personal stake in it."

The piece I'd taken was now part of a gold cuff, etched with mathematical patterns that were punctuated by perfectly symmetrical gemstones, currently wrapped around the middle of my right thigh as it had been since I'd snapped it into place right after the heist. Thinking about it, I had the urge to rub the spot on the back of my neck where the ghostly fiend I'd bartered my soul to years ago had marked me.

The gold cuff was the only thing keeping me out of that fiend's maw. I'd made the deal with it for reasons Sherlock could never have understood. He'd never have believed the shrouded folk with their haunting visages and unsettling powers even existed.

"I can't see that there's any benefit in discussing that," I said.

"How about something even more basic: who exactly *are* you?"

I brushed off the question with a wave of my hand. "The same answer applies."

Sherlock didn't look perturbed. "The benefit is that if I'm satisfied with your answers, I'll go home. Whatever schemes you're attempting to enact here, I assure you I can be very disruptive."

I didn't doubt it. "Hasn't the greatest consulting detective in the world got better things to do with his time than dog one woman over a single theft you admit wasn't that shocking in value?"

"No," Sherlock said. "Because everything I know about you tells me it's impossible you *aren't* carrying out other schemes of one sort or another. The one I do know about involved at least one man's death. I wouldn't be surprised if you're the greatest danger the world currently faces."

Ha. Let me introduce him to the shrouded folk and see what he thought then. They ate his version of dangerous for breakfast. There was one still hoping to eat *me*.

"So, you're going to follow me around until the end of time?" I said. "That sounds rather tedious."

He gave me his first real smile of the conversation. "I'm counting on it being considerably more tedious for you than for me."

He was very pleased with himself to have found me at all, wasn't he? That would have been amusing to see if it hadn't been equally annoying that he was here at all. I wet my lips, and Sherlock shifted an inch toward me. His voice dropped.

"Jemma, you'll notice I didn't say I'm *sure* you're the greatest danger the world faces. The pieces of the puzzle I do have make me wonder if you weren't in some kind of trouble back in London. Have you escaped it yet?"

A chill tickled over my skin, seeping deep enough to make my fingers itch for one of the sugar cubes I kept in my purse. He did notice more than any man had a right to. Did he think I'd turn to *him* for help if I needed it?

I pulled back and took a swallow of my drink. When I answered, I kept my voice as bland as possible.

"I can assure you that I'm perfectly fine."

Right now, it wasn't even a lie. Sherlock looked skeptical, though. "And how long can that last? One trinket won't hold off a debt collector in perpetuity."

It could if it was more than a simple trinket. But at that moment, the chill that had washed over me a moment ago condensed around my thigh—around the gold cuff. An icy tingling shot through my nerves from around the metal surface.

The cuff had set off that sensation a few times in the last couple weeks. I'd tried not to make much of it. This time the tingling quivered right up into my chest. I inhaled, and the scents of the pub turned frigid in my lungs. Cold fingers squeezed around my gut.

For an instant, everything inside me felt frozen, like the instant when I'd peeked out from my hiding place on that high plateau near the cult commune where I'd grown up and discovered what happened to kids like me. Kids who impressed the shrouded folk with their drive and their wildness year after year, spurred on by our parents to prove their loyalty to the creatures they worshipped. The "lucky" ones like that boy just a couple years older than me were chosen—chosen to be swallowed screaming into the fathomless mists of the creatures' mouths.

His screams had gone on for the longest time after he'd disappeared down the shrouded one's gullet, growing fainter as if spiraling into the distance, with hitches and tremors that suggested something inside the fiend was ripping him apart piece by tiny piece. It was the most horrible sound I'd ever heard then or since.

"Jemma?" Sherlock said.

I wrenched myself back to the present. The icy tingling had faded, and the world's most brilliant detective was watching me with eyes that saw too much. I shook off the last of the chill and gathered my ample composure.

"I'm fine," I said, "and I expect to remain fine for the foreseeable future. I don't owe any debts." That deserved to be paid, at least.

Maybe it was time to turn this scenario more in my favor. My trio was here and insistent on staying. Why shouldn't I make use of them?

CHAPTER TWO

Garrett

Normally I found John's easy-going demeanor much more enjoyable to be around than Sherlock's arrogant intensity. But as we waited, watching the pub the consulting detective had headed into after Jemma, the doctor's apparent lack of concern was becoming incredibly irritating.

"I wonder why Croatia?" he said in an offhand way, swiveling the handle of his walking stick where we were standing a little back from the front window of an electronics shop.

Of the questions I'd like answers to, that was pretty far down the list.

I shoved my hands in my pockets to stop them from fidgeting. I'd have taken out my notepad and jotted down observations of the road if that wouldn't have made it even more obvious to the store's staff that we weren't actually browsing their merchandise. It was a good thing they were mostly occupied with the soccer game showing on one of their display TVs. Cheers echoed through the speakers as someone must have scored a goal.

"Why London?" I said. "Why Richter? Why string *us* along?"

John shrugged. "She wanted to get that relic for whatever reason. Maybe we should be flattered that she decided we were her best chance at getting to it."

"That's assuming she picked us because of our skills and not our gullibility," I muttered, although to be fair, no one I was aware of had ever accused Sherlock of being gullible.

She'd pulled the wool over *my* eyes easily enough. I'd been starting to care about her, to think about how I might arrange to see her again.

And now she was sitting less than a hundred feet away, doing God knew what. The restless tremor that ran through me carried a jumble of emotions with it. I wanted to see her. I wanted to touch her again. I wanted to demand an explanation for why she'd done it and have her make some kind of amends. I wanted to never have met her in the first place.

Up until now, I'd been so focused on finding her that I guessed I hadn't given myself enough room to sort out my varying reactions.

"That's why we're here, isn't it?" John said, still way too calm about the whole scenario. "To find out what she's up to and what her grand plan is. Sherlock may very well be right that she was under external pressures."

"That doesn't absolve her of the crimes she committed," I said. And I was pretty sure no "external pressures" had forced her to seduce me. But at the same time the thought that she might have been escaping some kind of danger brought a sympathetic twinge into my chest.

I just had to keep reminding myself that the woman I'd met wasn't real. The Jemma Moriarty I'd gotten to know was a figment she'd created to con us. The true Jemma Moriarty—

I hesitated, leaning closer to the glass and narrowing my eyes. The shade of the awning over the pub's window made it possible to see inside, all the way to where the overhead lights gleamed off bright red hair.

The true Jemma Moriarty was sitting on a stool just a couple feet away from Sherlock.

I stiffened. "They're talking to each other. That wasn't the plan.

He said he was just going to watch her and see what she did and who she was meeting."

John followed my gaze. His stance didn't change, but his hand tightened around his walking stick. "She must have recognized him. He was so pleased with that disguise too."

"He shouldn't have gotten that close." She hadn't been conning us about how sharp she was, clearly. I shifted my weight from one foot to the other. I couldn't make out much from this distance, but it looked like they were just sitting there chatting. "If she's made him, she'll know we're here too. Why the hell are we hanging around over here like a couple of idiots?"

"Garrett," John said in protest, but I was already heading out the door. Halfway across the sun-drenched road, he caught up with his slightly uneven gait, his stick tapping against the pavement. "I'm not sure this is the best idea."

"I don't want Sherlock doing all the talking for me," I replied. "Especially when he couldn't even manage to keep up his ploy for five minutes. It's about time *we* put some pressure on her."

I had to see her as she really was, face to face, and then maybe any other feelings still lingering would burn away.

That was the plan, anyway. I stepped into the dimmer space of the bar ahead of John, sour and weirdly savory smells washing over me, and Jemma looked up. She smiled.

Just like that, I was seeing double: the woman who'd told me so earnestly how much she appreciated the risks I was taking and what I now recognized as the sly confidence of a master grifter. My feet stalled for a second before I pushed myself onward.

Other than the air of confidence that came across a little more overtly than it had in London, she looked essentially the same. The scarf she'd pulled over her head had fallen to her angular shoulders, exposing her scarlet hair that caught the eye even when pulled back into a braid. The banded light-and-dark gray of her deep-set eyes stood out as starkly as ever against her pale skin.

It didn't matter that the fullness of her lips didn't totally match that pert nose and pointy chin, or that I knew her deceptively slim frame could topple a man twice her size—I couldn't turn off the part of me that sparked to life at the sight of her. That insisted I'd never met another woman quite so appealing.

"Look who's joined the party," Jemma said in her soft but precise voice, sounding unruffled and if anything mildly amused. "Scotland Yard could spare even you, Garrett?"

"These two wouldn't be here either if it wasn't for me," I found myself saying. I snapped my mouth shut before any other careless remarks could slip out. That competitive impulse, the urge to show I was better than my much-celebrated colleagues, was what had made me so vulnerable to her machinations.

I had to be better than that. I'd thought I was better, at least enough to put the past behind me, until six weeks ago.

Jemma arched an eyebrow at Sherlock, who was still wearing his wig and his droopy moustache.

He raised his shoulder in a light shrug. "Garrett found one of the key pieces of info that allowed us to narrow down your location. It wouldn't have been fair to exclude him from the expedition."

His tone made it clear that he would probably have excluded me if given the option. Sherlock might have preferred to work with me above any of my police colleagues, but mostly he preferred to work alone.

"You don't need to worry about me," I allowed myself to add. "I had plenty of vacation days saved up."

The chief hadn't minded me taking off on a vacation of indeterminate length in large part because of my role in bringing down Stefan Richter. He didn't know that Jemma had handed the international menace to us on a silver platter. The fact that I couldn't really take credit for even that victory niggled at me too.

We needed to sort things out with her, figure out how much of a threat she was and deal with any other crimes she was involved in, and then I could go home and put her behind me like I had all the transgressions of my youth.

"I'd still like to know what the three of you are hoping to accomplish by dropping in on me." Jemma cocked her head. "You have no legal footing to arrest me. If you were hoping to carry out a less official sort of revenge, I should mention that I have a colleague with a pistol watching right now to make sure nothing happens to me."

Sherlock's gaze darted to the back of the pub. A curtain hung over the doorway there, just enough ajar that someone could have gotten a clear shot at any of us if they'd wanted to.

I couldn't make out any figure standing in the shadows there, but a prickle quivered through my nerves. I didn't think she was lying.

"Do you really think I'd come here to rough you up?" Sherlock said incredulously. Revulsion at the idea congealed in my stomach, but it sat uneasily next to the churn of my anger.

"We don't really know each other all that well, do we?" Jemma took a sip of her drink. "I've already told you I've got nothing to discuss with you."

Sherlock shook his head. "That's not a good enough answer."

"*You* involved us," John said. "We need to know exactly what you've gotten us mixed up in."

She flicked her hand dismissively. "Your part in any of my plans is completely behind us. I know you're smart enough to understand what already happened."

As if it were that simple. As if she couldn't have taped our conversations or gathered other evidence of the crime we'd committed—as if all our livelihoods might not rest on whether or not she decided to dabble in blackmail sometime in the future. Did she really think we could forget about that looming possibility?

Did she really think we could just shrug off the way she'd used us, pretend it hadn't mattered at all?

Jemma's eyes found mine as if she'd read my thoughts. Her expression wasn't quite the same as when she'd glanced at me as I'd come in; something more studied and pensive had come into it. Her gaze stayed on me even when Sherlock spoke again.

"I think you're smart enough to know we won't be shaken that easily."

"Well, if you're going to insist on sticking around..." She slid off the stool and slung her purse over her shoulder. "I'll have to get on with my responsibilities as if you're not here. Do whatever you want in Zagreb. It's a lovely city. Just keep away from Pametno Pohranjivanje."

She turned to head out the back. To simply walk away from us after we'd spent six weeks chasing her down. My gut twisted, and my body moved, stepping forward so I could catch her arm.

Jemma's slim forearm was warm against my hand. She stopped and studied me. "I wasn't bluffing about my friend with the gun. What do you think you're going to do with me, Garrett?"

I couldn't have said there was anything suggestive in her voice, but somehow just those words sent my thoughts spinning back to the things we'd done together before—in my hotel room, up against the desk with her legs splayed around me and her gasps in my ear. A different sort of heat flooded me from the groin up.

Before I could figure out how to answer her, she swiveled her arm in my grasp, curling her fingers around my wrist in turn. With a little tug, she leaned in to speak close to my ear.

"You've got nothing here to prove," she murmured. "I've known from the start that the work matters more to you than it does to those two adventurers."

That wasn't at all what I'd been thinking about, and yet somehow the words cut straight to my core. "Jemma," I said, still groping for that perfect verbal blow to knock her down, to shake her confidence the way she'd just shaken me.

She slipped my hold and strode past the curtain with an insistent swish of fabric.

"What was that about?" John asked behind me.

I jerked back around. "Nothing. More of her games." Telling me what she'd managed to determine was exactly what I needed to hear. "Are we just going to let her leave?"

Sherlock showed no sign of concern. He motioned for us to follow him out to the road. On the sidewalk, he glanced around and spoke in a low voice.

"I've seen to it that we'll know if she leaves the city—but I very much got the impression that she has unfinished business she needs to attend to here. I'd like to know what it is. It may provide us with the leverage we need to get our answers."

"She warned us away from Pametno Pohranjivanje," Watson said, his Croatian pronunciation much more badly accented than Jemma's had been.

"That's obviously a ploy," I said. "She *wants* us to look into them for whatever reason. She wouldn't give away a detail that specific otherwise."

Sherlock nodded. "Garrett has it exactly right. Unfortunately, it's for that exact reason I think we should investigate. Not because we assume she doesn't want us to, but to determine why she'd have wanted to point us in that direction. It's a lead in its own way."

I couldn't deny with the logic of that. "What about keeping an eye on her?"

A smile crept across Sherlock's face. "I have a few ideas, one of which is already in motion. But if we do our work right, next time she'll be the one coming to us."

CHAPTER THREE

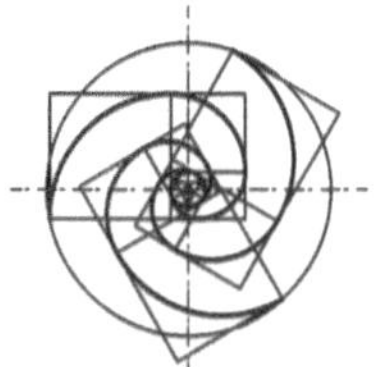

Jemma

The helicopter jerked with a gust of wind as the pilot guided it along the mountain's slope. "This is as close as we can safely get," he hollered back to Bash and me over the stuttered roar of the whirling blades.

"I guess we don't have to worry about those three Londoners trailing you up here," Bash said dryly, his light green eyes trained on the treetops beneath us. They formed a blanket of green across the range we were cruising over, only a few peaks of pale gray rock poking up through the vegetation. Not even hikers came out to this isolated stretch.

"I gave them something to keep them busy." A smile curled my lips at the thought of Sherlock and the others grappling with the piece of information I'd so blatantly handed them. They wouldn't trust it, but they wouldn't be able to stop themselves from investigating either.

"You don't think we need to worry about them making trouble with any of our business?"

"I've always been very careful that nothing can be traced back to me." I turned my smile on him. "Don't tell me you're worried about them after how easily we played them back in London."

"They seem pretty determined to make things more difficult for you, that's all. They're not going to want to head home empty-handed after working so hard to find you."

The evenness of his voice, more careful than it usually sounded, made me wonder if there wasn't more to his concern. He knew I could handle myself.

Back in London, he'd suggested I was starting to like the trio. Was he more worried about what *I'd* do with them around than what they would?

"They can't be more determined to pin something on me than I am to see through this task," I said. "I don't plan on letting anything distract me." My scheme in London had bought me temporary freedom. If I succeeded here, I'd end any connection between me and the shrouded folk completely.

Then I could get on with crushing their misty asses.

"I don't doubt that," Bash said easily enough, so maybe I'd misread his tone with the racket the chopper was making. He cocked his head, still gazing out the window. "What exactly are we looking for down there?"

I leaned close in case I could spot something right now to point out. No luck. "Anything that could indicate human habitation," I said. "There isn't likely to be anything as obvious as smoke from a fire, but a hint of a building between the trees, or a glimpse of a color you wouldn't expect to be there naturally… Anything that looks like more than part of the wilderness."

Bash nodded. We both wore jackets against the cooler air at this elevation, but the warmth of his body seeped through to mine where my shoulder touched his solidly muscled arm. I couldn't linger in it, though. I scooted over to the far seat to peer out the other side.

My colleague hadn't asked why I thought there might be people living secretly on one of these slopes, or what I wanted with them when we found them. That was the simple unspoken faith he had in me—that I had good reasons, and that when he needed to know, I'd tell him. Just as I had the simple, unspoken faith that when I did need him, he'd act without hesitation.

It was hard to make out anything below through the dense forest. Of course, the people I was looking for would have picked a place with that kind of cover specifically for that reason. That was probably why they'd settled in a country where most of the mountain ranges didn't tower too high above the tree line in the first place. Those sporadic peaks served the cult's purposes just fine while their communes stayed hidden.

Even if I spotted a hint of their presence, we'd have to proceed carefully. We weren't equipped to storm in just yet. I was hoping a little more research would smooth my way there—the task I'd sent my trio on might help.

The helicopter droned on. Nothing passed by beneath us other than rippling green. My body started to tense. The pilot had said that with the travel time out to this range and back, he could give us an hour in the air at most. At the slow pace I'd asked him to keep so we could really eyeball the terrain, we wouldn't cover even half of this side of the range.

That was all right. I had time. I'd bought myself that time by stealing the pieces of the gold cuff still clamped around my thigh. And even though I was ever aware of the mark on the back of my neck, it hadn't prickled with Bog's insistent presence since I'd put the cuff on. The shrouded one couldn't reach me as long as I wore it.

Bash tapped his window, but by the time I'd rejoined him, he was shaking his head. "Just a lightning scar on a tree," he said. "Nothing man-made."

As I slid back into my seat, the helicopter veered a little higher. My gaze rose too, over the forest to the rocky ground above. The cult of the shrouded folk wouldn't be so careless as to leave clear evidence out in the open. There was nothing up there but scattered shrubs amid the scree, a few patches of grass, and—

And a sun-scorched slab of stone that would have looked like nothing but naturally bleached rock to anyone normal. Anyone who hadn't seen those specific ragged markings come into being with the blaze of a shrouded one's satisfied hunger, long ago.

My pulse hiccupped. "Can you take us down over there?" I asked the pilot, pointing through the windshield. "As close as you can get to that smooth patch on the slope. I need to take a closer look."

"I'll do my best."

As he took the chopper around in a slow circle, checking for a stable place to land, I studied the forest below the bleached slab. It looked as lonely as the rest of this strip.

The helicopter finally touched down on a flat plateau about a ten-minute walk from the bare stone. I hopped out the second the engine had stopped. At the edge of the plateau, I braced my feet on the rough pebble-strewn ground and pitched my way toward the spot more carefully, one hand clutching my purse strap.

Bash followed with heavier steps, his head swiveling as he scanned our surroundings. "What did you see, Mori?"

"I'm not totally sure yet." The chilly wind tossed my hair into my face, and I swept it back, tugging up my hood. "It might not be anything all that helpful."

As we approached the stone, which pointed like a tongue toward the forest farther down the slope, a deeper chill sank into my skin. The mountain air smelled crisp and clean with a hint of evergreen, but an echo of a memory tainted my senses with dry rot and seared skin. I swallowed hard, but I couldn't clear the awful flavor from my mouth. My hand fumbled in my purse for a sugar cube.

With the pure sweetness melting over my tongue, my chest loosened a little. I inhaled fully as I reached the edge of the stone.

For a second, I doubted my senses. Maybe the sun *did* just happen to hit the rock here at the right angle to make those streaks naturally.

I circled the smooth patch and stopped by a boulder near the tip of the "tongue." My throat closed up, the last fragments of sugar souring in my mouth.

No, I hadn't seen wrong. From this angle, from nearly the same angle as where I'd crouched all those years ago, I could see how the ritual had played out all too clearly. The memory that had hit me when I'd spoken to Sherlock yesterday swelled up from the back of my mind again. The blaze of supernatural light, the unending scream as the shrouded one had consumed the boy bit by bit…

I shut my eyes. Bash came up beside me, his faint heat cutting through the chill.

"Something happened here," he said. Not a question. I wasn't controlling my reaction as well as I'd have liked. But it was Bash seeing me, and Bash knew enough now that I could be at least partly honest with him.

"Do you remember the story I told you about my sister?" I asked, more rhetorically than anything else. Of course he did. "The monsters that took her—they took someone else right here. Maybe more than one someones. Kids. It's always kids."

My hitman let out a sharp sound and glanced around. "On horror's head horrors accumulate," he murmured in a more serious tone than he usually used when he quoted the Shakespearean dramas he refused to admit he loved. "Do you think those monsters are here? Is *that* what we're looking for?"

The shrouded folk were everywhere and nowhere all at the same time. I didn't see how it'd be helpful to tell him that, though.

"There are people who worship the monsters like gods in a sort of cult," I said, forcing myself to open my eyes again. To edge farther around the stone, checking the ground for other signs. "My parents were like that. The cult has little communes set up here and there, mostly at high elevations. The things thrive on our sunlight. One of those communes has something I need, and my research suggests they're in this country. That's who we're looking for."

Bash took this information in stride without hesitation, although I noticed his hand came to rest on his hip holster. "The people from the commune would have arranged the… sacrifice? That happened here?"

"Maybe. Or maybe there's more than one group around. And the fact that they held a sacrifice here doesn't necessarily mean they're living anywhere all that nearby."

They liked to give the shrouded folk plenty of room for their feeding. I'd slunk along for five hours following the little procession that had led that boy to his doom.

If the cultists who'd arranged the sacrifice had left any signs of their passage at the time, the weather had washed it all away. I turned rocks with my foot, finding bleached streaks on the bottoms of a few that must have been dislodged since the shrouded one had set off its blaze of energy. My meandering path took me down toward the trees.

A hunched pine had sprung up among the rocks a little higher than the line of the forest, almost directly beneath the sloping stone. I studied it, ducking low to check the branches. A dimpled line across one made me grimace.

"Found something?" Bash asked.

"It looks like there's been at least a couple decades' growth since the last time anyone used this spot." I backed away from the tree. They might not do sacrifices often, or they might have moved farther afield. "We're following an old trail."

"One of your sources was more recent than that, wasn't it?" Bash said. "You were sure they'd still be in the country."

That was true. "They had deep roots here. It'd have been difficult for them to completely move. But I don't think this spot is going to help us find them."

Just in case, I eased several paces into the forest, studying the ground and the vegetation. The place looked undisturbed. Not even an oddly snapped twig or a scuffed footprint in the dirt.

I started back up the slope toward the helicopter. "We'll take the rest of this area even slower than before." I wanted to think this meant we could at least narrow down our area to the highlands on the interior of the country, ignoring the peaks along the coast, but this group had kept themselves hidden around their object of worship for centuries if not millennia. Who knew how far they'd go to obscure their location?

I picked up my pace to get past the horrible memories the slab stirred up—to get on with this search—and my foot came down hard on a jagged edge in the rocky ground. The rock snapped and crumbled under the sole of my boot.

Years of martial arts training had given me excellent reflexes and even better balance. I half stumbled, half leapt to the side, catching my footing on more stable ground. I was already perfectly steady when Bash touched my arm.

"Just the mountain keeping me on my toes," I said. "I'm okay."

The corner of his mouth quirked up. "Of course you are. When aren't you?"

Standing this close to him, I couldn't help thinking back to the one time recently I hadn't been okay at all. When the shrouded one that had a claim on my soul had filled my head with a hallucination of blood and gore I couldn't shake, and only Bash's presence, Bash's devotion, had driven it back. From the way his gaze strayed for a second to my mouth, I suspected my right-hand man was thinking of the same night.

That night I'd given in to the attraction that had always simmered between us. I'd nearly fucked up all the faith and trust we'd built between us. Even if the memory of the unexpected tenderness he'd shown alongside his strength sent an eager pang through me, I couldn't risk making that mistake again.

I stepped away, maybe a little more abruptly than was natural. Bash's hand fell. The awkwardness my first mistake had already created hung in the air for an instant before I swatted his shoulder.

"I'll beat you to the chopper, hitman."

He laughed. "Only if you watch your footing better, Majesty."

We scrambled up the slope, leaving the traces of the shrouded folk's horror behind us—for now.

CHAPTER FOUR

John

I wouldn't say I was religious, but I experienced a certain awe stepping into a building like Zagreb's famous cathedral. Huge fluted columns rose up to the breathtakingly high vaulted ceiling alongside the rows of dark wooden benches. The midday sun beamed through the stained glass windows around the vast altar, filling the space with a warm glow and rendering the intricate gold chandeliers unnecessary. The scent of the place spoke of history: candle wax and varnished wood.

I kept my walking stick tucked under my arm as I walked slowly and therefore mostly evenly up to the table near the front with its stacks of booklets. The chances that Jemma *wouldn't* notice my presence seemed highly unlikely, but the tap of that stick would be an automatic giveaway I could avoid. Only a tiny bit of pain nibbled at my hip.

Several tourists were perusing the central aisle. More had taken at least a brief seat on the benches' red-padded seats. Jemma sat about halfway down the rows at the far end of her bench, where a marble angel seemed to peer down at her. She'd braided her bright hair again, but it was still easy to pick out the back of her head.

Sherlock had been sure she was going to meet someone here around this time. He hadn't said how he'd determined that, but I'd leave my friend a few secrets since he enjoyed them so much. Clearly his intel had been correct. He hadn't known who she might be planning to see or why, though.

Observe what you can, and if you interrupt the meeting, that's fine too, he'd said when he sent me off. *The sooner she realizes she can't simply ignore us, the sooner we'll get some real answers.*

He and Garrett had gone to look at the main storage warehouse belonging to Pametno Pohranjivanje, which had turned out to be a local storage company. We'd taken a quick look around yesterday under the guise of customers needing a tour, but Sherlock had wanted to return for a more in-depth exploration while they were closed over the weekend.

I was going to look odd if I stayed at this table much longer. I wavered, considering my options. Sit at the back where I wouldn't be as visible but also wouldn't be able to hear any conversations Jemma had, or risk a closer approach?

Well, Sherlock had said it wouldn't be a horrible thing even if I simply interrupted her plans. The spoils rarely went to the cautious. I meandered along the aisle, aiming for the bench two rows behind her.

My gamble didn't even succeed long enough for me to get in place. Jemma's head turned as another gaggle of tourists jostled past me, and her gaze immediately locked with mine. I had the ridiculous urge to duck as if she'd somehow forget she'd seen me if I dropped out of sight.

Her mouth tightened, just for an instant. That was the only sign that my arrival bothered her. Then she raised an eyebrow as if to say, *Are you just going to stand there or what?*

Maybe I could observe something useful even after she'd noticed me. Letting my walking stick touch the floor now that there wasn't any point in attempting subterfuge, I headed over to her bench at a faster pace. She got up at the same time. Meeting me at the edge of the aisle, she tucked her hand around my elbow like she had more than once back in London. Her touch set my pulse off-kilter in a way that was both disturbing and exhilarating.

I shouldn't let myself be affected by her like that. I had no idea whether any part of the woman I'd admired in London was even real. Okay, that wasn't entirely true—she was even *more* brilliant than I'd thought. But the other parts that had drawn me to her: the sense of strength in the face of loss, the easy way she'd shared her feelings with me… Those aspects had been a ploy, at least in part.

So why did a large part of *me* want to go head-to-head—and, ah, other bits to other bits, if I was being totally honest—all over again?

Jemma nudged me toward the altar, and I ambled along at her direction. "Taking in the sights?" she said.

"Sherlock said I shouldn't miss this place."

"Hmm. Another coincidence then." She shook her head and dipped her other hand into her purse. Her phone's screen glowed on for a few seconds as she must have diverted her intended companion. "Do you really think this is the best use of your time—following me around?"

"You could always answer our questions and set our minds at ease," I pointed out.

"That's assuming you'd find the answers I could give you at all reassuring." She flashed me a coy smile. "Are you sure you didn't just want to see me?"

We came to a stop at the foot of the main altar. The candles stood unlit, but a spark lit in my chest as Jemma trailed her fingers over my forearm before releasing me.

"What for?" I asked, keeping my voice steady. "So you can wrap me up in an even crazier scheme? I think the once was enough."

"Do you?" Both eyebrows rose this time. "Let's not pretend you didn't love every minute of that adventure, John. When was the last time you'd had as much fun as you did during that week with me? I gave you a gift."

"I usually like to be aware of any ulterior motives that come with a gift."

She poked my chest lightly with her forefinger. "Oh, really? I'd be willing to bet you're also enjoying the fact that you have no idea how much I'm capable of."

Fucking hell, just those words turned the earlier spark into a flame. I had to focus on what I was here for. Which wasn't dragging her off into the nearest private room and rediscovering how good her body felt against mine. Definitely not an appropriate line of thinking for our current situation or our current location.

"Why don't you tell me more about it, then?" I suggested. "What other thrilling deeds have you gotten up to?"

"Ah, no. I didn't come here to share stories with you."

"But you were hoping to meet up with someone else."

"Another part of my business I'm not planning to share." She wandered to the other side of the aisle, and I followed. "We had some fun together, and we both got something we wanted. Now we're done."

Every part of me rejected that statement. I grasped her shoulder and waited until she glanced at me again. Her expression stayed mild, but I'd be damned if I couldn't still see that hint of sorrow in her fathomless gray eyes.

"No," I said. "We're not done. I'm not leaving until I understand what it was you got out of that bargain."

She shrugged. "A pretty trinket. Why does it need to have more explanation than that?"

"Because it obviously does. Because it wouldn't make sense otherwise."

"Maybe I'm not the most sensible person in the world." She folded her arms over her chest and looked at me through her eyelashes. "I think you've just been bored since I left town. You're looking for stimulation. Is Sherlock still giving you the cold shoulder?"

That question sent a very different twang of emotion through me. "We're working together as well as we always have," I said, as if I didn't know what she was talking about.

"Still pretending that kiss didn't happen, then, is he? It amazes me he manages to see as much as he does while purposefully blinding himself."

In the weeks since it'd happened, I'd thought I'd managed to suppress all thought and feeling related to the kiss I'd shared with Sherlock nearly as well as he had. One flippant comment from Jemma brought the tangled mix of desire, uncertainty, and frustration rushing right back to the surface.

It was because of her we'd kissed at all—because of her I'd realized that maybe I'd wanted to for a while and very much wanted to again. After nearly two months of Sherlock studiously avoiding acknowledging the event, *that* revelation didn't feel anything like a gift.

Jemma was smiling at the emotions that must have been playing across my face. "Oh, John," she said. "He's your best friend, isn't he? Where did you get the idea that you don't have the right to ask people for things that you want?"

That question caught me like a swift jab to the gut. *You wouldn't understand. You don't even* ask, *you just take.* But the thought of continuing any conversation on that subject made my stomach clench.

"What does it matter to you anyway?" I said, a little more brusquely than I normally would have spoken. "I thought you were done with us."

Jemma paused. I caught another hint of a deeper emotion that might lie behind the nonchalant airs she was putting on—a twitch of her mouth, there and gone.

No, I didn't believe it. She wasn't as detached as she wanted to seem. Maybe she wasn't the woman I'd found myself so drawn to in London, but she was more than a conniving con artist too.

Which only made her more dangerous. Everything about this talk told me how much I should be on my guard with her.

"Maybe I just think it's a waste, all that pent-up longing with no way to apply it." She brushed her hand over my arm again. "I suppose I might as well get going. Enjoy your sightseeing."

I didn't intend to let her wander off to resume her original plans. I tagged along several feet behind her, watching her braid sway against the thin ivory fabric of her sleeveless blouse, which was only a few shades paler than her lightly freckled shoulders.

Jemma must have heard me behind her, but she didn't glance back. She strode out of the cathedral and through the streets to the tram line. One of the long blue vehicles was just pulling up at the stop.

I got on after her. Jemma saved me from having to decide whether to sit next to her or keep my distance by picking a spot between two other passengers. Ignoring me, she pulled her tablet out of her purse and flicked through something on its screen.

If we could get our hands on that device, we could find out so much more about what she was up to. I couldn't imagine her making that kind of theft easy, though.

She got off down the road from her hotel and headed straight there. After I watched her disappear inside with a thump of the glass doors, I lingered outside, not entirely sure what to do with myself now. I couldn't pursue her all the way to her room. If I'd tried, I imagined she'd have hotel security on me before I'd so much as crossed the lobby.

My phone vibrated in my pocket. I fished it out.

"How did it go?" Sherlock said without preamble.

I sighed. "She spotted me early on, so I didn't find out much, but I did give her a bit of hassle. It looked like she canceled her meeting. She's gone back to the hotel now."

He made an approving sound. "Can you get over to the warehouse? It appears we have a large job here—your assistance would be appreciated."

"Sure, as long as you don't think I should watch the hotel," I said.

"No," he said immediately. "We've done enough there for now. When you get here, come around to the green door on the side."

I took a taxi most of the way there and walked the last short distance out of practiced caution. The padlock that I assumed had been on the side door now lay broken on the driveway's cracked pavement. Sherlock opened the door at the sound of my footsteps and caught my glance.

"Such a shame," he said with a small grin. "We showed up and the door had clearly been forced open, so of course we felt compelled to investigate."

"Of course," I said, unable to stop myself from smiling back at his self-satisfied expression. In the middle of a successful enterprise, Sherlock took on a buoyant energy you wouldn't have believed he was capable of from seeing him in his more serious moments. His cool blue eyes twinkled. He spun, beckoning for me to follow him and swiping stray waves of his dark brown hair away from his forehead as he strode down the hall.

If you'd asked me two months ago whether Sherlock was a good-looking man, I'd have told you I hadn't really thought about it, and that would have been true. Now I'd have to admit, *Hell, yes.*

"What's going on?" I asked him.

"It appears my earlier suspicions were correct," Sherlock said, as if he'd bothered to tell me about those earlier suspicions. "We even saw a van bringing around a new lot. This business is a front for a cartel of robbers and black market dealers."

We came out into a wider hall that smelled sharply chalky. Three of the locker doors were open. Garrett was peering into a plastic crate inside one and jotting notes.

"I've matched up items in a few of the lockers with recently reported robberies," Sherlock went on. "We'll notify the local police, naturally. But first I'd like to document exactly what was stolen—and to get that done fast. You can take that locker. Do you have something to write on?"

"I have my case journal."

"Excellent. Make note of everything. Let's see if we can't find a pattern that'll reveal Miss Moriarty's intentions."

CHAPTER FIVE

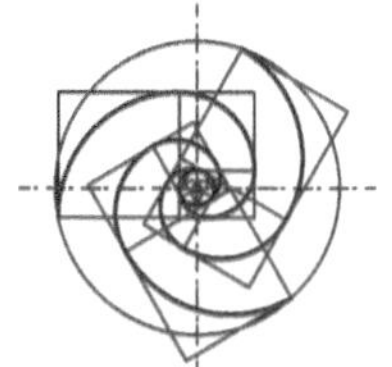

Now that the London trio was in town, I wasn't making much use of the hotel elevators. Taking the stairs down offered a little extra workout, and it meant I could scope out the lobby surreptitiously for anyone who might be keeping an eye on those elevators.

Like today. I spotted the familiar head of short-cropped fawn-brown hair almost instantly. Garrett wasn't making any particular effort to hide where he was leaning against the wall near the front doors, his boyishly handsome face stern with concentration as he jotted something in his ever-present notepad. Every few seconds, he glanced toward the elevators and then around the room with its marble-tiled walls and little burbling fountain.

He was taking this job very seriously. I supposed he had to be to take time off from his actual job to track me across the continent. None of the three were happy with me, but the vibe he'd given off the other day in the pub had been outright angry.

I *had* strung him along a little more than the others, even if I hadn't promised him anything. I'd only led him on as much as was necessary, though. He could keep his hurt feelings, and I'd keep my freedom from being devoured by a shrouded one, thank you.

If he'd been assigned to watch the front entrance, what were the chances no one was staked out in back? I wet my lips, considering. Just then, one of the young porters I'd been paying off, Jakov, pushed a cart stacked with luggage into view.

Perfect. I caught his eye with a quick gesture and waved him over, producing a reasonable tip in kuna from my wallet.

"Do me a quick favor?" I said, showing him the money. "One of the men who've been hassling me is over near the entrance. You see him, the one with the notepad? I don't want to make a fuss, but if you could push your cart over there and act like you want to help him, ask him if there's anything you can do for him, whatever you can think of to keep him occupied so I have a chance to leave without him bothering me, I'd really appreciate it."

"Of course, Ms. Matthams," Jakov said with a smile, using the name I'd given the hotel. He looked a little guilty taking the money for that bit of work, but he did take it. It was business, after all, whether he totally understood the extent of it or not.

Jakov set off with his cart. The second the stack of suitcases blocked Garrett's view of the lobby, I slipped through the room and out the door. All I heard from the inspector detective was his frazzled voice saying, "No, really, I'm fine right here. I'm just waiting for someone."

I went the wrong way on the street, heading around the next block and doubling back, just to avoid him getting a glimpse of me out the lobby window. No one followed me. I wandered farther until I was sure I wasn't being tailed, and then I plucked my main phone out of my purse.

"Bash," I said, keeping my voice low as I dodged a pack of morning shoppers. "Did you get confirmation?"

"You were right," Bash said on the other end. "A truck came by around two in the morning and unloaded a bunch of boxes. Novak came down to collect them personally. From the way he handled them, they were heavy."

I smiled. "Boxes of books would be." A wealthy collector of rare texts, Mr. Novak placed his hobby over the law. He'd had a hand in funding the syndicate of thieves who'd been breaking into homes and shops all across the city and the surrounding county. They grabbed plenty of valuable items for themselves, but their targets always just happened to have a special book or five that they lifted too. Those never made it to the black market—they were set aside for Novak.

Yesterday the local police had rounded up most of that gang, thanks to the trio's meddling. They'd worked as quickly as I'd hoped. Novak had hidden his recent acquisitions in storage somewhere I hadn't been able to determine, but the arrests had made him nervous, as intended. He'd brought all his precious texts into the safety of his home.

Safe from police confiscation, maybe. Not safe from me.

"Do you need any support on this one?" Bash asked.

"No, I think it's a one-person con," I said. "Keep your phone where you can hear it, just in case."

I tucked mine away with a rush of heightened spirits. The cult of the shrouded folk kept to themselves and rarely let any record slip out of their hands, but they'd been around long enough and orchestrated enough strangeness that accounts of their activity existed here and there. I'd followed a trail of increasingly clearer references from one book to another until I'd been pointed to a book on Croatian myth and superstition of which only a handful of copies had been printed.

The only one of those I'd been able to locate had belonged to a rare books and antiquities shop on the outskirts of Zagreb until Novak's gang had hit it a few months ago. The volume I wanted was one of those reported stolen.

Now I'd just have to steal it back from him. Considering I'd grown up in the damned cult and as far as I could tell he was only a dabbler in the dark arts, I had more of a right to the information than he did anyway. Taking on the commune wasn't going to help me if I didn't know how to use the prize they were protecting.

I stopped at a corner to wait for an approaching tram and take another look around. The Londoners had helped my mission along, but they'd also thrown a spanner or two into the works. Thanks to

John's interruption in the cathedral, the woman I'd spent months finding and weeks coaxing into a conversation had gotten gun-shy all over again. From what I could tell from a few vague comments I'd uncovered on the internet, she'd heard stories about the commune directly, but she wasn't willing to discuss the subject in any more depth by email or phone.

If one of my temporary pseudo-colleagues got in my way today, I might lose my chance with Novak too. I still wasn't sure how the trio had figured out I'd be at the cathedral in the first place.

No one else got on the tram when I did. I watched the street behind me as I walked to a seat. They couldn't even know I'd left the hotel. Even three against one, I could out-scheme them any day.

In the middle of a commercial strip, I had to switch tram lines. I let the crowd of other departing passengers hustle on down the street ahead of me, leaving me some breathing room.

As I strode past the darkened windows of a movie theater, a prickling chill raced up and down my thigh where the gold cuff was clamped around it.

The muscle seized. My lungs constricted at the sudden shock of cold. I stumbled, and at the same moment, a gaggle of elementary school-aged kids brushed past me, one of them bumping my shoulder where I'd bent over.

I jerked my purse close to my chest instinctively. The sensation faded like it had before, but more slowly this time. It took me several seconds before I could straighten up and keep walking, and even then my leg wobbled.

It was getting worse. Whoever had constructed the gold cuff had designed its patterns and gems to disrupt the shrouded folk's senses, but they hadn't meant it to be worn for months at a time. I'd already known I didn't want to rely on a piece of metal as a lifelong solution, but clearly I had less time to find a more permanent fix than I'd assumed.

The brush with the kids had left my nerves jangling too. Sherlock had tracked me using his contingent of street youth back in London. What was to stop him from using similar tactics here?

The first chance I got, I ducked into the shadows of a dusty alley where I'd be out of view from the street. First I patted down the pockets on my slacks. Then I riffled through my purse.

There was nothing in there I didn't recognize — not even a spare coin. And I'd done a thorough accounting after that first meeting with Sherlock at Franjo's. I hadn't found anything then either except a stray sugar cube that had escaped its plastic bag...

My shoulders stiffened. It had seemed so innocuous at the time, and I hadn't seen Sherlock get his hands anywhere near my purse besides, but maybe I'd underestimated him.

I pulled out the baggie of sugar cubes and turned it in the thin sunlight that reached into the alley, studying them. I had a couple dozen on hand, all of which had been in my purse for at least a week. The corners of the cubes no longer poked sharply into the plastic but had dulled from scraping against each other.

The corners on all of them, that was, except one that was still as crisply cubic as any popped fresh from the box.

I dug it out and rubbed my thumb against the gritty surface. It didn't crumble the way a regular sugar cube would have. The glinting crystals didn't give way until I scraped them against the brick wall beside me.

I licked the other side and found it tasted as sweet as usual. Whatever substance Sherlock had used to keep the cube intact, it was probably sugar-based too. He'd been prepared that I might try to eat this one.

And if I had, I might very well have simply swallowed the device inside without realizing. The sugar coated a little gelatin pill. I broke it open to find a tiny rectangle of metal that I had to assume was some kind of tracking device.

For a minute, I just stood there staring at it. For fuck's sake. I'd had my purse on me with the bag of sugar cubes in it every time I'd left the hotel since that first meeting with Sherlock. He'd know that I'd gone to rent the helicopter and then taken it out into the mountains. He'd be able to see where I was right now. I'd almost led him straight to Novak.

The balls on that man. I wanted to both scream in frustration and laugh at his genius.

My fingers tensed around the device with the longing to crush it, to destroy his ploy. I held myself back.

No. If the signal cut out, he'd know I was on to him, and he'd turn to other tactics. Tactics I also might not pick up on right away. Better the enemy I knew than one I didn't.

He'd used this trick against me. Now how could I use it against him?

A plan sprang up in my mind from the soil of everything I'd experienced in the last few days.

My time was running out again. I didn't know how much longer I could wear the cuff without it causing me permanent harm, and the second I took it off, Bog would zip straight over to claim the soul I was already late handing over. My own investigations into the commune had been going too slowly—but my trio had just proven that they had the connections and resources to get things done even here in Croatia. Different connections and resources than I had access to. I wouldn't mind borrowing those.

They'd think they were on *my* trail, but instead I'd put them on the trail of the place I wanted to find. Then, when they found it, I'd hop over their heads and be on my way before they knew it, just like before.

I couldn't have managed it by manipulating them to their faces like I had in London. They'd be too skeptical now. But if they thought they were gathering information I didn't want them to know, they'd jump on a new lead without hesitation.

A smile curled my lips. While no doubt applauding his own cleverness, Sherlock had handed me exactly the tool I needed.

How could I point them in the right direction without giving too much away? They should already know I'd been scoping out the mountains for some reason. Ah, yes. That would come together nicely.

I caught another tram, this one traveling in the opposite direction from where I'd originally been heading. In twenty minutes, I was stepping off just down the street from a small moving company with three trucks in its back lot. I circled the place and peered at the trucks for a little while so anyone tracking the device I'd tucked back into my purse had plenty of time to narrow down my location. Then I stepped into the scruffy looking building.

The room inside and the guy behind the counter looked scruffy too. The floor creaked under my feet. The guy pushed himself straighter where he'd been leaning on his elbows reading a magazine.

"Can I help you?" he asked in Croatian.

I was hardly fluent, but I'd made a quick study of the language when it'd become clear this country would be our next destination. Most of the people in the city spoke decent English, but not all, and plenty in the smaller towns relied on their native language.

"Yes, please," I said, smoothing out my accent as much as I could. "I have a somewhat odd question to ask. It needs to be kept discrete —no talk of the job with other people. Is that possible?"

The guy looked a little puzzled and a little curious. "I don't see why not. What's the job?"

I tapped my fingers against the counter, managing not to grimace at the gritty texture. "I want to know if it's possible to transport an entire small community across a fairly significant distance. The contents of several houses and other buildings packed up together. Much of it would need to be moved across some distance by hand. The locations are quite isolated and at a high elevation—the roads won't reach far enough."

The guy's expression shifted all the way to puzzled. "That sounds like a much larger effort than we're equipped to handle. Where is this community?"

"Never mind about it then," I said quickly, taking a step back. "I thought it was worth checking. Do me a favor and forget I asked."

I hustled out of the office with enough speed to hopefully take him from puzzled to suspicious. Suspicious enough to not feel guilty mentioning what I'd asked him to anyone who came calling to inquire about the visit.

Where to now? A few blocks down the street, I came across a little café wafting a sweet scent that made my stomach twinge. I bought myself a piece of custard cream cake and ate it at one of the spindly-legged tables while I contemplated my next move.

The seed I'd just planted wasn't likely to be enough on its own. I didn't want to head to Novak's today now that Sherlock might have tracked me partway there, even if I stopped back at the hotel to leave the tracking device behind. Better to let that trail go colder.

Why not throw out a little more fishing line and see who came to play? I licked my fingers and dug out my phone again.

"Bash—me again. I had a new thought. Meet me at the zoo? I'll explain along the way."

CHAPTER SIX

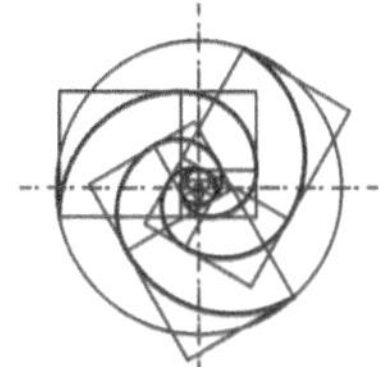

Jemma

The perfect meeting spot presented itself the moment I came through the zoo's gates. One of the first enclosures stood off to one side, partly hidden by a high stone wall. Just the kind of wall someone could sneak up behind to listen to a conversation unnoticed.

I took my place at the railing along the edge of the enclosure where I'd be in view of anyone coming into the zoo. As I took out my phone, a snow leopard prowled by on the other side of the fence. Another sprawled on a wide boulder, washing its paw and shooting wary glances toward the visitors.

How did they feel about being stuck in that little space instead of having a whole forest to roam around in? The pacing one gave off a restless tension that resonated through me.

Maybe someday you'll get a chance to escape and run free too, I thought at it.

Not that I'd completely shed my wall-less prison yet.

Tourists and maybe a few locals drifted by with a rhythmic shuffling of feet and oohs and ahs. A little boy lost the ice cream off his cone and started sobbing. I popped an undoctored sugar cube into my mouth. As I rolled its sweetness over my tongue, I switched my phone to selfie mode and held it so I could watch the entrance behind me covertly on its screen.

How long would it take Sherlock to send someone to check up on me? John had gotten to the cathedral no more than twenty minutes after I'd arrived. If I hadn't gone early to scope out the layout and reassure my contact that everything looked safe, I might have been able to meet with her. But then, if I hadn't, he might have shown up when I was still talking with her, and that would have compromised my goals so much more.

Maybe Sherlock would come himself this time. I could turn the tables on his ploy right in front of his face.

The thought sent a little thrill through me, but when the sunlight glanced off a strong brow and swept-back blond hair passing the gate, I smiled. John would do just fine too. As far as I could tell from the way he'd responded to me in the cathedral, he wasn't entirely sure whether he should be hunting me or helping me. Of course he'd be the fastest out of the trio to consider forgiving.

I saw him note my presence and then the wall behind me. Faster than anyone who used a walking stick had a right to move, he slipped out of sight. Good man.

He'd be sidling over to the opposite side of that wall right now. I could picture him: his careful steps to avoid alerting me, his hazel eyes lighting up with the excitement of playing spy, like a golden retriever ready to bound after a tossed ball.

Except a golden retriever couldn't batter a thug into running for his life. I'd rather that I never provoked the more ferocious side of Dr. John Watson that he'd shown a couple times in London, but knowing it was there made me enjoy the game even more.

I stepped closer to my side of the wall as if to ease apart from the other zoo-goers. That was Bash's cue to approach. He sauntered around the enclosure a minute later, his eyes shaded by a wig of distinctive bowl-cut black hair and thick sunglasses. Baggy sweats and his loose gait downplayed his muscular frame. He sure as hell wouldn't strike anyone as a former special ops sniper right now.

"Did you have any luck?" I asked him when he reached me,

pitching my voice low but keeping it loud enough that I expected someone listening closely by the wall would make out the words.

Bash shook his head. We'd worked out a loose script over the phone on my way here. "It's a big job. Not the kind of thing these companies are used to dealing with — especially the ones we can trust to keep quiet about it."

"Damn it."

"Are you sure we have to move them? They've been running things out of that little village for ages without anyone noticing."

"My 'friends' from London weren't here poking around before," I said. "If they stumble on the commune, we're screwed. A few dozen people can't support themselves on a mountainside without leaving some kind of trail. Better to relocate them ASAP than wish we had after it's too late."

"I'll start reaching out to possibilities farther afield then," Bash said. "You're sure of where you want to relocate them *to* now?"

"Yeah. Here are the coordinates. I found a good spot. Equally isolated." I crinkled a slip of paper as if I were passing it to him. "We'll need some construction work too to set up new buildings."

"I'll add that to the list." Bash smirked at me, enjoying the con. "Is there anything else you need from me right now?"

"Just lay low. They've been sticking close to me — I'm not sure how they're managing it. I don't even trust my phones anymore. I'll signal you the usual way if we need to talk again."

"It's a pleasure to work with you as always."

He tipped his head to me, and I nodded to give him the go-ahead to leave. As he walked away, I glanced toward the wall.

I *could* wander off myself and let John head back to report on what he'd heard unhindered. But it would be a lot more fun to keep him on his toes. We wouldn't want him to feel he'd gotten what he wanted too easily, would we?

I suppressed a smirk of my own and let out a sigh, deliberately letting my feet scrape against the ground as I headed around the wall so he'd have a little warning.

John's walking stick knocked the stone in his haste to hustle away. When I came around the wall, he was standing by a map of the park several feet closer to the gate, his face only slightly flushed. Not a bad feint—not bad at all. I pushed my mouth into a frown and marched over.

"Hello again," I said, propping myself against the sign. "I'm starting to think you've signed up as my new shadow. The old one does work just fine."

John blinked at me, doing a decent job of pretending surprise, even if he didn't quite have Sherlock's poker face. He was rather terribly adorable.

"Jemma!" he said. "I was just passing the time while Sherlock's off on some mission he didn't want to explain." He hesitated. "Oh, that's very clever. You followed *me* here and managed to slip in ahead, didn't you?"

He shook his head with a wry smile, and, okay, I could give him credit for an excellent gambit. Spinning the situation so the accuser suddenly became the accused was one of my favorite tactics too.

I raised my eyebrows at him. "Oh, no, don't try to turn this around on me. Why would I need to follow you around when your only business here is messing with me?"

"Maybe it's a real coincidence then," John said, still smiling. "What are you doing here, then? Playing tourist?"

I shrugged. "I like watching animals when I have a spare hour or two. They're so much simpler than human beings. It looks like you just got here. What were you looking to see first?"

He glanced back at the map, which I suspected he hadn't really studied in his hurry to look as if he were studying it and not eavesdropping. "Ah, I've always been fond of the chimps. Mainly because they aren't all that simple."

"I hadn't made it that far yet," I said. "Why don't I join you? And you can buy me an ice cream to make up for acting like a stalker."

"Of course you would want an ice cream," John said, sounding amused, but he was studying me at the same time. Wondering what my intentions were, no doubt. Eager to get back to report to Sherlock, but also probably hoping he might catch me in a tiny slip that would give him even more to report. And he might have another reason or two to like the thought of sticking around.

I wet my lips. "I didn't leave my sweet tooth behind in London. Come on." I gave his arm a gentle shove, and he went, twirling his walking stick before applying it to the ground.

It wasn't far to the nearest ice cream stand. I asked for chocolate and grinned while John dug out the cash to pay. He couldn't quite manage to look disgruntled about it.

He also couldn't quite manage to stop his gaze from twitching to my mouth as I gave the creamy chocolate scoop a generous swipe of my tongue. The flicker of hunger in his eyes was almost as delicious as the treat in my hand.

It might have been too long since I'd gotten to act on my own carnal appetites. My work over the last several weeks hadn't required any intimate encounters—and, to be honest, the thought of picking up some random man in a bar just to scratch an itch hadn't been all that appealing after the very satisfying time I'd had in London. Where was I going to find anyone with Garrett's passionate determination, or John's earnest enthusiasm, or Sherlock's unplumbed depths of desire?

It wasn't safe to let myself even consider Bash.

Better that I let those memories fade a little longer. As fun as it was to tease, what were the chances any of the trio was going to give me another shot between the sheets now that they had some idea of who I really was?

"So, you like chimps, hmm?" I said as we strolled that way. I slipped my hand around John's elbow and licked the ice cream again, feeling the thump of his pulse under my fingers.

"They say the apes have an almost human-like intelligence," John said, keeping his tone casual enough. "I always wonder what they'd tell us if we could properly communicate."

"Probably to leave them the hell alone already," I remarked, and John chuckled. "Speaking of human intelligence, what *did* Sherlock tell you about this mission he's abandoned you for?"

John's fading chuckle turned into a cough. "I think I'm offended that you figured there was any chance I might answer that."

"Nothing ventured, nothing gained." I patted his arm soothingly. "I have no doubts about your loyalties. Presumably he's investigating something to do with me, so perhaps if you told me I could offer some assistance."

John outright laughed at that. "Oh, I'm sure you would. Assistance in pointing him in completely the wrong direction."

"I didn't lead you *that* far astray in London, did I? You got your man."

"I guess we did." He stopped at the edge of the path between two of the enclosures and turned to face me. His expression had become abruptly intent. "Who are you really, Jemma? Is this you, the way you're talking with me now, or is it just another mask you're putting on?"

The unexpected question pricked at me. "What makes you think any of it is a mask?" I said tartly. "I was the woman you got to know in London, the one you believed was a 'kindred spirit.' I'm the woman I am now. I'm whoever I need to be as the situation requires it."

He held my gaze as if trying to read more than I'd said from my eyes. "No one's just a collection of appearances. There has to be something you want, something that drives you, beneath all that."

"I never said there wasn't."

He shifted his arm, freeing it from my grasp and cupping my elbow in his own hand. "When we were talking that one night in London, you told me you lost someone important to you a long time ago. That was true, wasn't it?"

An uneasy shiver ran through my chest to my gut. This wasn't where I'd intended this conversation to go. I should never have shared that with him.

"I told you a lot of stories," I said.

"Yes," he said. "But I know what real grief looks like. I lost my older brother, years ago—to carelessness and alcohol, but he used to be the person I looked up to most." He swallowed the roughness from his voice. "The way that feels, I could see in you."

Kindred spirits indeed. Except he'd lost the sibling who should have been protecting him, and I'd lost the one I should have protected.

My stomach had tightened into a ball, but I kept my smile on my face and grasped onto the one thing I could control. I couldn't let him see he'd put me off balance, so I'd have to throw him off just as much. And I knew exactly the way to spin this conversation around.

I rested my hand on his broad chest, lowering my eyes to look at him through my lashes. "Are you trying to turn me into a fair maiden who needs to be rescued, John? You don't need to go to that much trouble. You're sweet, and I do love sweet things. We could go back to wherever you're staying right now, and I'd happily show you how much."

I slicked my tongue over my nearly finished ice cream. A flush raced up John's neck with a slight hitch of his breath. He stepped back, and I let my hand fall.

"I don't think that would be a good idea," he said.

"Maybe not," I said agreeably, already feeling steadier on my feet. "But doesn't that make you want to do it more? What could it hurt, really? You don't honestly think another little dalliance with me would put you in any danger, do you?"

His jaw worked. "I don't know."

"You want to know the truth?" I eased a tad closer and let my voice drop as low as a caress. "I am fucking dangerous. I can kill a man with my bare hands, and I know because I've done it. But I haven't needed to go to those lengths in years, and I'd like to keep it that way for as long as possible. So really, you're perfectly safe."

John's lips parted, but he didn't appear to know what to say. For all his body had tensed, his pupils had dilated while I'd spoken. I'd frightened him a little, and oh, how that turned him on.

He didn't want a damsel half as much as he wanted to tempt peril, and he could see both in me, wrapped up in one neat bow. I'd give him some time to stew on that.

Before he'd recovered himself, I bobbed up to kiss his cheek. "Enjoy the apes. You know where to come looking for me when you make up your mind."

I slipped away and headed for the entrance. If he made any move to follow, it wasn't fast enough. I strode past the gates and on down the street to hail a cab.

I could almost call checkmate. We'd see where the game led next.

CHAPTER SEVEN

Sherlock

"I don't know what this all adds up to other than it's very, very weird." Garrett jabbed his kebab skewer toward the end of the table where I'd laid out a map of the country. He'd brought take-out dinner for the three of us to the two-bedroom suite John and I had managed to obtain across the hall from his own room. The common living-dining space gave us plenty of room to discuss our discoveries and strategy.

The sharp flavor of the meat lingered in my mouth, a little heavier on the spice than I generally preferred, but I didn't see the value in complaining to the inspector detective. He'd been in a rather combative mood since we'd first seen Jemma.

I pressed down on the last bit of tobacco I'd scooped into my pipe and brought the stem to my mouth to take a few puffs while I lit it. The rich earthy smoke filled my lungs and smoothed out my thoughts into clearer lines.

"Perhaps 'weird,' but we can piece together a decent picture from the evidence we've gathered." I tapped the map. "She's gone off surveying the less-traversed areas of the country's mountain ranges.

She expressed interest in moving a small community from an isolated spot of high elevation to another. Whatever that community means to her, it's something important and that she believes our involvement would interrupt. I think we can safely assume local law enforcement wouldn't be pleased if they found out either."

"What could she have an entire village doing for her?" John asked, leaning back in his chair. He hadn't completely sat still since he'd returned from his mission to observe Jemma's secretive meeting at the zoo. Normally I wouldn't have paid his restlessness much mind, but it was becoming unusually prolonged.

I studied his expression. "I'd imagine there are any number of illicit ventures she could be involved in. Obviously our next task is to locate this 'commune' before she can relocate their base of operations and determine what work they're doing for her. Did she say anything while you were with her that gave even a small hint?"

"No," my friend said. "Not that I caught on to, anyway. She's very careful about what she says." He paused, rocking the chair's front feet a little off the floor. "It did seem like something had changed since we last talked, though."

Garrett's head jerked up. "In what way?"

John twisted the handle of his walking stick in his grasp, his mouth slanting at an awkward angle. He looked at the map rather than either of us. "When I spoke to her a few days ago at the cathedral, she made a point of saying that we were 'done'—that she wasn't going to have anything more to do with us if she had her way. Today… She suggested I take her back to my room so we could, ah, pick up where we left off."

He'd kept his voice reasonably even, but the tips of his ears had flared. That explained a few things.

It shouldn't have mattered—it didn't matter—and yet a little spark of irritation flickered up inside me. That she was still coming on to him that way? That he had clearly been tempted?

No, it didn't matter *at all*. I snuffed out the spark and made myself chuckle. "She's certainly never been shy."

"But that means something has changed," Garrett said. His shoulders had tensed, but his tone was almost hopeful. He tossed his cleaned skewer onto his plate. "She wants something from us—maybe just to know how close we are on her trail. She's willing to get close to us to accomplish her ends. We could use that willingness, couldn't we?"

I shifted my full attention to him. He hadn't talked quite like that before. "What do you mean?"

He spread his hands. "Turn her tactics around on her. If we can get into *her* room, we'd have a chance at lifting one of those phones or her tablet where she's doing so much of her planning. We might see something useful, or she might give away something in the heat of the moment."

He paused and seemed to notice for the first time that both John and I were staring at him. His mouth tightened. "What? It isn't as if we haven't already crossed a hell of a lot of lines dealing with her. If you don't want to sleep with her, then don't sleep with her. I was just making a point."

"A fair point," I said mildly. "I'm only wondering whether you could be dispassionate enough to come out unscathed. She got under your skin quite a bit on our first run around."

Garrett glowered at me, but he couldn't argue that fact. "I'd know what I'm getting into this time," he insisted.

He'd have to forgive me for not being entirely convinced. "Your line of thinking is solid, all the same," I said. "Putting aside physical intimacy, her overture to John suggests she'll be more open to entertaining conversation—flirting, as it were, with possibilities."

I took another puff on my pipe and nodded to myself. Garrett and John were too romantic by nature to stay detached when Jemma had already stirred up their emotions. What she and I had exchanged had only ever really been a quid pro quo transaction.

I straightened up. "I think it's time I spoke with her directly again. Perhaps I can tease out a few answers—ones she might not even realize she's giving me." A quick check of the tracking app on my phone showed me she was currently at her hotel a quarter mile away.

"You're going now?" John said, looking as if he were about to get up and then catching himself.

"No time like the present. From the conversation you overheard, covering up her activities will be difficult, but she's pursuing the options with some urgency."

Garrett crossed his arms. "And we should just sit around here while you have your chat with her?"

"No," I said. "You can get to work searching for signs of small secluded habitations in Croatia's areas of higher elevation. Between the two of you, you should have enough knowledge and connections to come up with a few avenues of inquiry."

"Sherlock," John started, with a note in his voice that made something twinge low in my gut, like—like a moment it wouldn't do either of us any use to think about. I glanced at him, and he gave me a sheepish smile. "Be careful."

"I think I can hold my own against one woman, brilliant as she may be," I said.

It was hardly worth summoning a taxi when my destination was less than a ten-minute walk away. This section of Zagreb didn't have quite the same austere quality as the streets I'd often roamed through in London while sorting through my thoughts, but stretching my legs as I passed the modern storefronts still brought a certain calm. I tuned out the jangling of the radio playing through an open car window and focused on the task ahead of me.

In Jemma's hotel, I strode up to the front desk with an ingratiating smile. The only time they'd seen me before, I'd been in full disguise—I didn't expect anyone here would recognize me. Thankfully, we'd managed to determine what name Jemma had checked in with through a brief comment overheard.

"One of your guests asked me to have you call up when I'd arrived to meet with her. Ms. Matthams. You can tell her Sherlock Holmes will be waiting for her in the bar."

"Of course, sir," the woman behind the desk said. She looked at her computer and picked up the phone to convey my message. I was trusting that Jemma would be curious enough about my intentions to come down.

"I will. Thank you," the clerk said to whatever Jemma had responded, and hung up. "She says she'll be down shortly, sir."

I tipped my head to her in thanks and headed into the bar. At this time in the evening, the stools along the slick glass counter were mostly taken, no two free side-by-side. I found an empty table in a corner that wasn't too noisy, ordered a martini, and sat back to watch for Jemma's arrival.

Several minutes passed. I sipped my martini and tried not to dwell too much on the growing possibility that she was toying with me. I was ninety-nine percent certain she'd make her appearance. Well, perhaps ninety-five, at this point.

I was down to the vicinity of eighty percent when Jemma's slim form emerged under the bar's glaring lights. The red waves of her hair drifted over her shoulders in stark contrast with the dusty rose hue of her silk blouse. Her slacks looked neatly pressed. She'd changed since this morning's outings. Earlier, or just now, for me?

She wasn't carrying her usual large leather purse but a simple cloth clutch a slightly deeper shade of pink than her blouse. The color in her cheeks as she dropped into the seat across from me suggested she'd rushed some coming down. I certainly didn't imagine the thought of meeting me had provoked that reaction on its own.

"I hope you weren't too bothered by the wait," she said in that sweet yet assured voice of hers. "I was in the middle of something when I got your call."

I'd managed to disrupt her planning again at least somewhat, then, had I? A minor victory in itself.

"I can't complain, knowing how unexpected this visit was," I said easily. "It's good to see you're not having any trouble keeping yourself occupied here."

She made a humming sound, faintly amused. "And I'm sure you'd like to know what I'm occupying myself with. We'll skip that part of the conversation. What did you want, Sherlock?"

"I can't simply stop by to catch up with a friend?"

She cocked her head with a sly glint in her gray eyes, and the curl of her lips brought back a tingle of sensation—the memory of those lips trailing down my neck, the slender hand she was now raising to her chin tracing over my stomach.

"Is that what we are—friends?"

"We could be," I tossed out.

Her smile grew. "I don't think so. I suspect that being merely your friend would be distinctly unsatisfying—possibly for both of us. Well, if that's all you had to say…"

She pushed back her chair, and my pulse stuttered. I'd expected more time and more interest than that. I opened my mouth, and my mind shot to Garrett's suggestion, wrapped up in the echo of feeling and the suggestive lilt to her words.

"That isn't all," I said. "I wanted to ask you something."

Jemma paused and leaned her arms on the table. The fabric of her blouse slid against the curves of her breasts. I'd never paid much attention to the bodies of the women around me before, but it suddenly struck me as a ridiculous shame that despite the intense physical intimacy we'd shared that one night in London, I hadn't the slightest idea what that part of her felt like or even looked like unclothed.

"Here I am," she said. "Ask away."

A question I hadn't known had been stewing in the back of my head until just now fell from my lips. "What happened between us in London—was that simply a means to an end, or did you actually enjoy it?"

Her eyebrows twitched. I'd managed to surprise her. I'd have had an easier time calling that a victory if the room hadn't turned inexplicably hot at the same time.

"Why does it have to be an *or*?" she asked. "It served my purposes—I won't deny that—but I also enjoyed it. Every moment of it."

Ah. Well, then. I resisted the urge to adjust my collar, as if that would help at all when a significant portion of the heat was being generated within me.

It was an uncomfortable feeling at least in part because it was still so unfamiliar. Jemma Moriarty was the only woman who'd ever provoked this reaction in me. She'd been right at the time, whatever her larger motives—the physical release had cleared my mind and swept lingering tensions away, at least as well as any high I'd ever gotten. She'd promised me that was possible, with the right partner.

I'd tried a couple times since then to recreate the same effect with women who'd appeared to find me attractive in the bars back home. Those efforts had been as unsatisfying as the few forays of my youth.

Perhaps it was simply that whatever differences formed a gulf between us, Jemma had a mind like mine, and she knew how to cater to my needs in a way no one else I'd ever known could. But that meant I should be able to do as much for her, didn't it?

I could learn about her just as she'd studied me and built off my responses. Lull her the way I'd been lulled. Or perhaps I'd discover even that spark was deadened now that the novelty had worn off, and the temptation would die with it.

In a way, this was exactly what I'd come here for.

"Would you like to enjoy it again?" I said.

Jemma ran her thumb over her full lips. I couldn't help tracking the gesture. She beamed at me. "Are you propositioning me, Mr. Holmes?"

"Are you accepting, Miss Moriarty?"

She paused for a moment, just long enough for a pang of disappointment to shoot through me, and then she extended her hand to me. "Why don't we continue this conversation in my room?"

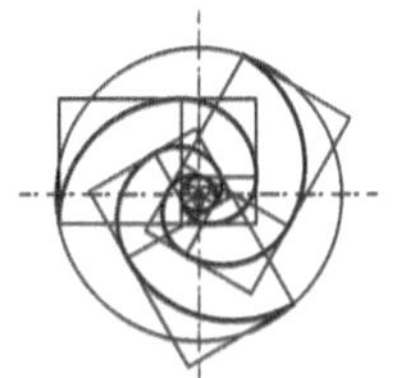

Jemma

Sherlock stopped just behind me at the hotel room door, close enough that a wisp of tobacco scent reached my nose. He'd been smoking his pipe not long before he'd come calling.

Very, very soon I might be tasting that flavor on his skin. The prospect thrilled me enough to swing me right back to caution.

I glanced up at him, seeking out the cool blue eyes that now gleamed with restrained heat. Heat that radiated off every inch of his lanky frame. It took a lot of effort not to lick my lips.

I'd woken up that passion in him. I'd taught him that he could feel it. And he'd come back for more.

"Are you sure about this?" I asked, keeping my tone casual. "I thought you saw me as some incredible threat to the world at large."

His hand came to rest on the small of my back—tentatively, as if he were testing what he wanted, what he was capable of. His voice came out wry. "Are *you* sure about this? The last time we spoke you seemed to think you needed an armed guard to ensure your safety."

"An initial precaution," I said, "as I judged your intentions. While you seem determined to present as much of an obstacle to my work as you can, dragging me off to interrogate me through torture doesn't appear to be your style. Or am I mistaken?"

The corner of his mouth twitched upward. "I can't make any promises about what methods I'd be willing to resort to were they deemed effective, but information obtained through torture is notoriously unreliable."

"Well, that's reassuring." I tipped my head to the side coyly. "Then I don't see why we shouldn't put our differences aside temporarily to fulfill desires we happen to share. A few hours of truce, and then you can go back to making yourself a nuisance."

"And you can go back to your current schemes. At least I can rest easy knowing you aren't committing any crimes during the time we spend together."

I rolled my eyes at him. "It's a deal, then."

I didn't have any illusions that he was going to turn off the analytical side of his brain. No doubt this sudden interest had been sparked by John reporting the come on I'd made to him. Sherlock had realized the avenue might be open to him too. He might want me and the pleasure I'd summoned in him, but he also would be taking in my accommodations, listening for stray comments. Which was why I'd left my purse two floors up in my main room and only brought a few essentials in this clutch.

The lock beeped at my swipe of the keycard. The lights blinked on automatically as we stepped inside. The second hotel room I'd paid for looked lived in enough—I'd left an extra suitcase, closed, against one wall, squeezed some of the toiletries out, and placed some spare change on the top of the dresser. The scarf I'd worn over my hair the first day the trio had found me hung over one of the bed posts. But the detective would observe nothing in here that would tell him about my recent activities.

I'd booked this room the afternoon after they'd arrived, knowing there was a chance I'd have to entertain them here one way or another, wanting a place that could serve as proper neutral ground.

It was a good thing I'd made other preparations tonight as well. When I'd set off from the hotel, leaving Sherlock's tracking device behind upstairs, I'd asked the hotel clerk to call my cell phone if anyone asked for me while I was out. When she'd rung me up, I'd been a five-minute tram ride away, preparing to make another stab at getting that book from Novak.

Based on his tracker, Sherlock would assume I'd been here the whole time, and thankfully I'd still been close enough to return without too much of a delay. He'd managed to be a nuisance already.

Still, having him like this might be the best thing that could have happened. Novak could wait. The questions Sherlock was sure to ask me once he thought my guard was down might tell me all kinds of interesting things about what he'd discovered from the clues I'd doled out.

The door clicked shut. Sherlock swept his hand across his forehead, scattering the messy dark brown waves of his hair, looking abruptly uncertain as he took in the room.

"Cold feet?" I said.

His gaze jerked back to me. "No," he said firmly. His hands rose to his shirt collar. He undid the buttons with deft jerks of his fingers, gradually baring the chest I'd only felt the last time. He'd already made it most of the way down before I caught his hands with mine.

"You know, normally people fool around a little and take their clothes off as it goes rather than stripping right down from the get-go."

Sherlock peered at me. His clear tenor dropped low. "Is that what you want? Something normal?"

If my panties hadn't been melting in anticipation of this encounter already, they would have then. "No," I said. "Not particularly."

He clasped my wrists and tugged me closer, bending to kiss me at the same time. Like before, it came without warning and there wasn't much art to it, but I'd been ready anyway. His lips were a little rough where they collided with mine, the earthy flavor of his tobacco lingering on them, and just like that I was twice as hungry.

I gripped the loose front of his shirt and pressed into him. My mouth slid against his, finding the place where we could fit together perfectly.

Sherlock cupped the back of my head and kissed me harder.

Mmm, yes, that was good. He eased me backward, moving us toward the bed. When we reached it, he pulled back with a tight sound as if breaking away from me even for a moment had been a strain.

"Last time you found all the most effective ways to arouse me," he said. "I want to learn what works for you. What *your* body responds to." He touched my cheek and trailed his fingers down the side of my neck. "Will you let me do that?"

How could I resist that offer from this man? "Be my guest," I said.

We eased onto the bed, him looming over me, his gaze traveling over my body still fully clothed. The smile that curved his lips reminded me of his expression when faced with an unsolved case he was sure he could crack open.

"This will be my first real experiment in this domain. I'll endeavor to do well by my subject."

"I have full faith in your investigative abilities," I said, and he kissed me again.

This time he leaned in, shifting the angle of his mouth just slightly, and just slightly again, until my lips parted. His fingers teased down my side to tug my blouse loose from my slacks. I raised my arms to make it easier for him to slide it off me.

He studied me for a second, considering the swell of my breasts filling out the small cups of my bra. My pulse sped up waiting for his next move.

As if deciding we needed to be at an approximately equal state of undress, he plucked the last couple buttons of his shirt free and tossed it aside after mine. My fingers itched to trace the compact muscles etched across his lean torso.

Before I could reach for him, he ducked his head and brought his lips to my neck. With softly peppered kisses, he tested every bit of my skin, pausing when my breath shifted as he grazed a particularly tender spot.

He stayed there and kissed harder. Pleasure tingled over my skin. A flick of his tongue drew an encouraging sound from my throat.

He kissed lower, across my collarbone and down to the edge of my bra. I ran my hands over his shoulders, but before I got any farther, he caught one of my palms and started working his way down the underside of my arm. He hadn't proved all that sensitive to my ministrations there, but the nerves in my arms responded readily. Giddy quivers of sensation ran over my skin.

Sherlock followed the same path I had on him, all the way to my inner elbow. He tested the tips of his teeth there, and my breath outright hitched. A self-satisfied smile crossed his face.

This slow careful seduction was a certain kind of torture when I didn't *need* to be seduced. A needy ache swelled between my thighs. "Come here," I growled, gripping his neck with my free hand, but Sherlock simply caught that wrist instead.

"I intend to be thorough," he said with a mischievous glint in his eyes that made me want him even more. I let out an impatient sound, but I submitted to his attentions down my other arm, settling for stroking my fingers over his taut chest.

I circled my thumb around one of his small nipples and then swept it straight over. The heat of Sherlock's breath trembled against my arm.

"You're distracting me," he murmured.

"But it's a good distraction, isn't it?" I said. "There are plenty of things *I* haven't gotten to try yet. Like this."

I pushed myself upright and gave his neck a teasing caress while I brought my mouth to the same nipple. A hum reverberated through Sherlock's chest as I applied my tongue to the pert nub. He needed more than that, though. He liked a little force.

I swiped my tongue faster, and then I nipped him between my teeth. With a choked noise, Sherlock's fingers tightened where they'd tangled in my hair.

"I wasn't finished yet," he said with a rasp, and tugged my shoulders to turn me around. He pressed a kiss to my shoulder as he unclasped my bra. Sweeping my hair to one side, he charted a path to my neck and then up to my hairline. The pleasure of his touch mingled with a twinge of awareness from Bog's mark.

Before he could reach the signifier of my deal with the shrouded one, I shook my head, letting my hair fall back into place. Sherlock took the rebuff in stride. He slid his hands around to my breasts and cupped them. His long hands covered them completely.

I relaxed into his narrow but solid chest as he explored them, first with broad strokes that sent muted waves of pleasure through my torso, then focusing in on the peaks. He tucked his head over my shoulder to watch my nipples stiffen to meet the careful flicks of his fingers.

He pinched one between his thumb and forefinger, and I let out another growl at the jolt of pleasure. With a soft chuckle, he repeated the gesture on the other side.

I could pay that pleasure back. I tipped to the side and leaned back my head to kiss the spot on his neck where I'd gotten the most reaction before. Then I shifted one hand backward into his lap. His cock jumped at my touch, already hard enough to make my mouth water.

Sherlock stifled a groan. He caught the side of my face and swiveled us enough to recapture my mouth with his. As I stroked him through his pants, his breath broke with a stutter. He kissed me harder, welcoming my tongue, squeezing my breast in an echo of my hand on his cock.

The hunger in me expanded through my whole body. I'd never met anything sexier in the entire world than this analytically detached man turned wild by my touch.

He had some self-control left. "Still. Not. Finished," he muttered against my lips, and managed to tear away from me. He nudged me down on my back, gazing down at me with eyes as bright as blue flames. "Keep your hands to yourself."

"I'll give you five more minutes," I said. "After that, no promises."

He made a faint sound of protest, but his hands leapt to the fly of my slacks at the same time. As he tugged my pants down, he leaned over to suck my nipple into his mouth as I had his.

At the forceful slick of his tongue, a gasp tumbled out of me. My hands moved instinctively, but I drew them back, giving in to the blissful torture. I dug my fingers into the covers instead.

I had to hold on tight. Shivers of pleasure raced to my core as Sherlock experimented with the movement of his tongue and the pressure of his lips and teeth. He might not have been practiced in the ecstatic arts, but he was a quick study in this as with all things. Every eager twitch of my body had him amplifying the gesture that had provoked it.

My hips arched toward him, and he appeared to take the hint that my patience wasn't going to last much longer. He yanked my slacks the rest of the way down and paused for just a moment as his gaze found the gold cuff that circled the middle of my thigh. The gold cuff made in part of the etching I'd stolen out from under his nose.

"Truce," I reminded him. Dear God, he'd better not change his mind now. "We set all those matters aside."

His gaze held as much inquisitiveness as it did lust, but he inclined his head in a slight nod. I didn't doubt there'd be questions about that discovery later, but right now I didn't much care.

He hooked his fingers around the hem of my panties, and I squirmed to help him slide them off. Then he was bending down again to kiss the plane of my stomach, the dip of my belly button, the slope of my hipbones.

His thumb traced over the mound between my thighs. He watched its passage with more intentness than any lover I'd ever taken before. I had to clench my muscles to keep from bucking up to bring his touch to the place I most wanted it.

When he grazed my clit, a blissful tremor raced through me. He looked up to meet my eyes.

"Here?"

"That would be the spot." I couldn't help amusement from creeping into my voice even as longing twanged through my body. "There are men with multitudes of experience who have trouble identifying it that readily."

Sherlock gave me a smile that was a shade shy of a smirk. "I found the opportunity to do some reading after our last encounter."

A laugh spilled out of me. "Of course you did." My voice broke with a moan as he pressed down on that spot with careful precision. My hips jerked up despite my best intentions.

I eased my legs farther apart so Sherlock could kneel between them. My hands balled around the covers. It'd been well over five minutes now, but I was enjoying his "experiment" too much to risk interrupting him.

He worked over my clit slower and faster, softer and harder, taking in every gasp and sigh. Then he lowered his mouth to me. The first swipe of his tongue had me quaking with need.

The kind of whimper I rarely let myself make slipped out of me as he licked and sucked. Pleasure knotted all through my core up into my belly. So close. So fucking close.

"Your fingers," I said raggedly. "Inside me."

Sherlock obliged in an instant. He traced two fingers down over my slit, drenched with my arousal, and eased them inside. Just a few inches of that pressure inside was all I needed to tip me over the edge with the next flick of his tongue.

I arched up with a gasp and a shiver of bliss that wracked my whole body. Sherlock's breath caught audibly. He kissed me again, covering my entire core with his mouth as I rode out the wave. I cried out at the fresh burst of pleasure.

I sagged back into the covers with a near-delirious grin. Sherlock looked at me, his mouth deliciously flushed and his expression tight with desire. His erection strained against his slacks. He hesitated for a second with that rare uncertainty that somehow turned me on twice as much as before.

"Can you—can that happen for you again?" he ventured. "Right away?"

I laughed and shoved myself upright to pull him into a kiss. "Fuck, yes."

My tart flavor mixed with the smokiness that had laced Sherlock's mouth. Between the two of us, we peeled his pants and boxers off in about five seconds flat. I grasped his cock, reveling in the smooth solid length of it, and his mouth crashed into mine again.

I ached to have him in me, now. "Purse," I mumbled in an instant between kisses, groping across the bed. He caught the clutch and passed it to me, and I dug out the condom I always kept in the inner pocket, just in case. I certainly hadn't expected I'd be needing it tonight.

"Right," Sherlock said, taking it from me. "Naturally."

I touched his jaw as he ripped it open, seeking out his gaze. "I normally do," I said. In that moment, it seemed important that he understand this one fact. We might be enemies in essence, but I wouldn't have wanted to strike out at him that way, a careless passing on of some venereal disease. That wasn't how I worked. "Last time—last time was the only time I haven't. Special circumstances."

Some unfamiliar emotion flickered across his face and was gone. He opened his mouth, but words didn't come. Instead he kissed me again. As his mouth melded with mine, he lowered his body to mine. I opened my thighs to welcome him. He thrust into me, finally blissfully pressing his cock into me to the brim.

I was so primed he could have fucked me just about any which way and I'd have come again. But Sherlock was committed to his experiment to the end. As he plunged in and out of me, his hand slid over my ass. He lifted me, fitting me against him until he found the angle that made me not just gasp but sob with the shock of pleasure that hit me.

When I clutched his shoulders and bit his lip, he groaned into my mouth. He drove into me again and again with sharply powerful strokes. The force of his cock sent my head spinning with bliss.

I scraped my fingernails over his back, he tweaked my nipple tightly, and ecstasy flooded me. We toppled together over the edge in a surge of shudders, sweat-slick skin, and broken breath.

After a minute, Sherlock withdrew and eased down onto his side next to me. I glanced over at him, my limbs boneless with release, not possessing the will to send him off quite yet. I really ought to give him a chance to make his informative inquiries, after all. There wasn't anything wrong with basking in the heat of his body in the meantime.

He grazed a fingertip over my ribs just below by breasts where a faint scar marked my skin. "This was a knife," he said. "A few years ago? It looks as though it should fade away completely before much longer."

The thin pale nick was the only remnant of the second to last man

I'd killed with my bare hands, four and a half years ago to be exact. The last person other than Bash I'd ever had business dealings with directly, face-to-face. The head of a criminal syndicate had paid him off to take me down. He hadn't stood a chance.

"You've probably faced off against more knives than I have," I said blandly.

Sherlock's hand traveled from my side to my arm between us. His thumb swept over the point of my elbow. "A childhood scrape, deep. You grew up somewhere with a lot of rocky terrain?"

That observation sent a quiver that was uneasy rather than pleasurable through my nerves. "It wasn't a place with no rocks. I'm sure that narrows it down ever so much."

Sherlock smiled faintly. His fingers skimmed up over my shoulder to my neck. He knit his brow. "Did you know you have an imprint just at the top of your spine here? It doesn't have quite the qualities of a birthmark—somewhat closer to a tattoo, but—"

My jaw clenched for a second before I caught my reaction. I'd expected him to be watching for clues, yes—but with the intent to figure out my current plans, not to dredge up my distant past. A sharper sense of nakedness prickled over my body.

There wasn't anything he could really learn from me without my consent. Not when he wouldn't have believed in the things I'd grown up with, the things I'd made deals with and run from.

I rolled onto my side to fully face him and grasped his wrist. As I pushed his hand away from me, I gave him a pointed look. "Was *tonight* just a means to an end, or did you actually enjoy it?"

The corner of his mouth quirked up. "If it could be both for you, can't it be both for me as well?"

Somehow that response made me want to strangle him and also kiss him until he was hard enough to slide inside me again. Either would have shut him up.

"Fine," I said. "But then you've overstayed your welcome."

"And if I don't happen to feel like leaving yet?"

I let out a huff and sat up to shove him off the bed. Sherlock slipped out of my grasp and swung on top of me. Before he could get a good enough grip on my arms to pin me down, I gave him a light knee to the side that pushed him aside enough for me to scoot free. That worked for all of three seconds before he caught me around the waist. He rolled me over him and then rolled back on top of me.

Sherlock grinned down at me, holding my hands above my head and locking my legs under his, clearly having an excellent time. Also clearly not expending *that* much energy. I had to extend a little respect to his physical prowess and to admit it had aroused me all over again, and both of those facts left me disgruntled.

"I could get you off me," I informed him. "I just don't want to hurt you."

He cocked his head with apparently genuine curiosity. "Why not?"

I grimaced at him. The answer that tripped off my tongue was maybe more genuine than I'd have given if he hadn't appeared to truly want to understand. And if he hadn't just given me the most satisfying sexual experience of my life so far.

"Because in spite of you being a meddling, arrogant know-it-all, I like you."

Sherlock blinked at me. *That* comment was apparently enough to shut him up. My throat tightened. After a moment, I added dryly, "That would generally be your cue to tell me you like me too."

He chuckled, his grip loosening as he shifted his weight. "I'm not sure that 'like' is quite the word."

I'd thought we were bantering. I'd never had any intention of caring what this man or any other thought of me. All the same, the answer felt like a slap across the face.

An uncomfortable sort of heat flashed through my chest. I squirmed out from under Sherlock and grabbed my blouse. "Go whenever you like, then."

I pulled the blouse over my head on my way to the bathroom, not entirely sure what I was going to do in there, but there were plenty of possibilities for occupying myself away from the jackass on the bed. Wash my face. Brush my hair. Run a bath and drown myself in it for my idiocy.

The mattress squeaked as Sherlock righted himself. "Jemma," he said. "Wait."

I stopped, crossed my arms, and turned partway back, looking at him sideways. "What do you want?"

He sat in the middle of the bed without any self-consciousness about his nudity in his posture, though that earlier awkwardness had come back into his expression. His gaze stayed fixed on me, as intent as ever. I didn't know what he was trying to read now.

He inhaled slowly. "Saying that was difficult for you, wasn't it? I didn't realize. I'm sorry."

The great Sherlock Holmes was apologizing for hurting my feelings. Was that a win or a loss? I wasn't totally sure. I didn't answer, just watched him as he was watching me.

His mouth twisted. He set his hand on the covers beside him. "Will you come back here?"

"Why?" I asked.

His lips parted, and he paused. Then he said, a little haltingly, "So I can tell you what I meant."

Well, God damn it, if Sherlock was going to admit he had feelings, I supposed I could acknowledge them. I allowed myself to return to the bed and sat on the corner. "Tell me, then."

He looked far more pleased that I'd come than he had any right to, and the look gave me far more pleasure than *it* had any right to. I clasped my hands in my lap.

"I don't think," he said, "that anyone examining my thoughts and behavior since I met you would consider 'liking' a potent enough term to encapsulate those. If I'm being purely objective, I'd have to admit that something along the lines of 'fascination' or perhaps even 'obsession' would be more accurate."

The sharp edges that had risen up inside me softened with a flicker of surprise. "Oh," was all I managed to say.

He ran a hand through his now thoroughly mussed hair. "This isn't my forte," he said. "I can analyze people and their motives and all the rest, but when it comes to the interplay between myself and them, absorbing and responding—I've never really known what to do there. So I generally go forth with whatever I was going to do anyway and let whoever's around me make of it what they will."

I shrugged. "Why shouldn't you?"

"Well, exactly. It's served me perfectly well so far. I've accepted it as who I am."

Had it really served him well, though? For a second, looking at him, I imagined I could see through the man to the boy he must have once been—still an arrogant know-it-all, lurking on the fringes of the posh school his well-to-do parents had sent him off to, which I knew from seeing the records. Had he never felt the slightest pang of childhood loneliness?

I had, and I'd grown up in a community where friendship was never more than a means to an end for anyone anyway. I'd had my sister.

"Never underestimate people's capacity to change," I said with half a smile. "Although in my experience, they generally change for the worse. I'm not complaining about who you are."

"You're not," he agreed. He sighed and folded his hands over his raised knee. "I've never met anyone like you, Jemma. Anyone who reminds me so much... of me. I don't know how you spend your time, why you dream up schemes to steal things like that." He motioned to the cuff around my thigh. "But you're clearly not a common criminal."

"You wouldn't be here if you thought I was."

"No. But you are— We are at odds." He met my eyes again. "Is there no middle ground where we could meet beyond this temporary truce? Do your goals *have* to clash with mine? Perhaps if we talked it through..."

I shook my head. "Do *your* goals have to clash with mine?" I asked lightly. "Why not come all the way over to the dark side, Sherlock? You wouldn't, would you, because of the principles that matter to you? I have guiding principles too." Survival. Security. Vengeance. "I can't throw mine away any more than you can yours."

"Then we're at an impasse."

"And when the truce is over, may the best of us win." A strange prickly affection stirred inside me, more thorns than blooming rose. I eased across the bed to join him. His gaze had become wary, but when I raised my hand to stroke my knuckles against the side of his neck, he leaned toward my touch. "Your consolation prize is getting to go up against a worthy opponent."

"There is that." He took my hand in his. "How much longer is this truce designed to last?"

I had to smile. "I'm sure we could stretch it out a *little* longer." I rose up on my knees and kissed him, this man both fascinating and fascinated. Already he knew how to shift instinctively to align our mouths just a little more pleasurably.

But there were other games we could play even while we were pretending to ignore them. I brushed my lips over his cheek and tipped my head toward his ear. "I'm sure you have many more questions clamoring for attention. Ask, and let's see if there are any I'm willing to answer."

CHAPTER NINE

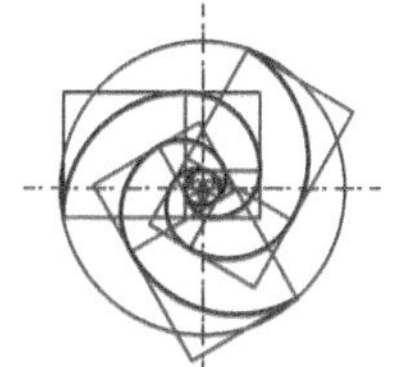

Jemma

On my third attempt at retrieving the book I needed from Novak, I finally made it all the way to his street in the falling dusk. And there was Garrett Lestrade, so hidden in the thick shadow of the wall around the house opposite that I only noticed him because I scanned the area with particular care. He stood watching the blocky modern mansion that belonged to my mark, notepad and pen in hand.

I could say one thing in favor of the geometric monstrosities that Zagreb's nouveau rich gravitated to: Their built-up front yards and parking pads offered plenty of shelter. I crept behind a concrete pillar and peered up the street toward the detective inspector.

The streetlamps gave off only a thin glow against the deepening twilight, but there was no way I could walk up to the Novaks' front door and spin out my planned story without Garrett spotting me. Only an occasional car had rumbled by as I'd walked the last couple blocks here. The warm breeze carried the scent of lilies from someone's private garden. It was all very peaceful.

Too peaceful. I needed a distraction.

If I'd managed to get here the first time I'd set out, I might have avoided this problem. The trio wouldn't have connected the crime ring they'd taken down to Novak instantly. He kept himself detached enough from the thieving syndicate that the Londoners probably weren't sure even now; they just wanted to take the lay of the land. I could head back to the hotel empty-handed *again* and give them a few days to give up on him...

No. I was here now. The longer I waited, the more chance there was that Novak would stash some of his collection elsewhere. I'd play with the hand I'd been dealt.

It'd have been easier if I'd had Bash to act as wingman, but he was staked out at the trio's hotel keeping an eye on their comings and goings, ready to jump in if the right opportunity presented itself. I'd simply have to be careful.

Leaning against the post, I took out one of my more disposable phones and tapped in a number I'd memorized weeks ago. Might as well see what kind of mood Garrett was in tonight.

I was far enough away that I only heard the faintest quaver of Garrett's ringtone. He took out his phone, frowned at the caller display that would have told him nothing, and rocked back on his feet as he answered. A stream of lamplight cut across his face, highlighting one eye, a cheek, the corner of his mouth.

"Hello?"

"Hello, Garrett. Is this a good time to talk?"

He stiffened instantly at the sound of my voice. "Jemma. Why are you calling me?"

I didn't want him to think it had anything to do with his current assignment, but it shouldn't be hard to imply that I was simply digging for general information about their investigations. I wet my lips as if I were a little uneasy. "I just wondered what you're up to."

"Wonder away. That doesn't mean I'm going to tell you anything. Fool me once and all that?"

"I didn't give you such a bad time in London, did I? Can't we have a friendly chat for old time's sake?"

He let out a laugh, but he hesitated before he answered. When he spoke again, some of the tension had smoothed from his imposing voice. "All right. Chat away. What are *you* up to?"

"I just got back from dinner," I said. "I had a very good steak at the place next to Franjo's. You should try it sometime. You seem like a steak man."

"Do I? Are you a steak woman?"

"When I'm in the right mood. I wouldn't mind some dessert though. I'm *always* a dessert woman. How'd you like to join me—or are you too busy with whatever you're doing that you don't want to tell me about?"

"Maybe I've just settled into my room and can't be bothered to leave. You've got actual friends here you can call up to invite, don't you?"

He was doing an admirable job of keeping the tone light while insistently turning the conversation back to questioning me. No doubt he'd realized he should use this opportunity to dig for whatever dirt he could. If I hadn't been able to see him, I might have thought he was cool as a cucumber. But right now the metal fixtures on his pen were flashing in and out of the streetlamp light as he spun it with agitated jerks of his fingers.

Just talking to me was hard for him. Apparently my conversation with Sherlock last night had left prickly thorns of affection sprouting in all sorts of unexpected places, because a twinge of regret ran through my chest.

I could have handled Garrett differently. I'd taken the strategy that was easiest for me without worrying about how it would affect him.

And why should I have worried? I had monsters to vanquish and promises to keep, and all that required a whole lot of money and the right sort of connections. I did what I had to do.

It was possible I could do a little more, though, without hindering my work—just for the sake of reducing the inspector detective's vengeful urges. And making this offering might put him off-balance enough to help along the next part of my gambit.

I drew back from the column and ducked down a side street to circle around behind the Novaks' house. "Oh, I have plenty of friends," I said. "But here you are in town, and I feel like we haven't really talked."

"I'm still not sure what you think we'd talk about."

"Maybe what happened in London? I'm sure there are all sorts of things you're dying to say about that. We should hash things out properly sometime, in person. You can tell me how horrible I am to my face in as many ways as you like, and we'll have cleared the air."

He laughed again, more hesitantly. "Sounds wonderful. Not tonight. But... maybe some other time."

"I'll leave you to it, then," I said. "Your Firecracker wishes you good night."

I hung up and picked up my pace. He'd always said the nickname he'd given me with a mix of awe and apprehension, as if he appreciated my gutsiness but was wary of how far I'd take it. Let him think about that, about the intrepid police prodigy he'd thought I was, while I did... this.

I scooped up a polished quartz stone from the base of someone's yard. Just around the corner from Novak's house, I spotted a Mercedes that was guaranteed to have an alarm system. I flung the stone onto the hood.

The alarm blared. I slipped behind a neighbor's shed as Garrett intrepidly loped around the corner. The moment his attention focused in on the source of the noise, I crossed the yard and made for the Novaks' house, slapping a patch on my button-up shirt as I went and pulling a clipboard from my purse.

I rang the doorbell and pasted a smile on my face, trying not to think about the number of seconds it might take for Garrett to decide the possible intruder a few homes away had nothing to do with his mission.

Mr. Novak was out, as he was most evenings—this was literature and academics night at his favorite auction house just outside of town. He went as much to scope out potential scores to send his minions after as to bid on items, I'd bet. It was his wife, nearly twenty years his junior, who answered the door.

"Hello?" she said in Croatian, her brow furrowing.

"Hello, Mrs... Novak?" I said with the most precise accent I could summon, and handed her the card I'd made up a few days ago for this purpose. "So sorry to disturb your evening. I'm with Grand Pest Control, on behalf of the city. It appears there's been an infestation in this part of your neighborhood, and we've been asked to check the surrounding buildings to ensure it doesn't spread farther."

The woman's delicate wan face tensed. "Infestation?"

I nodded briskly. "It shouldn't take more than ten, fifteen minutes to give the house a quick examination. I'll be out of your way in no time, I promise."

"I guess you'd better come in then."

She stepped back, and just like that, I was walking into the house invited.

I paused in the hall with its ornate rug and knocked on the wall beside me. Mrs. Novak went even more rigid. I glanced at her apologetically.

"If the pests have spread this far, sometimes they come right out of the woodwork while I'm searching. They don't like tile, though. If you want to make sure they don't come near you, you'll be safest in the kitchen or perhaps a bathroom."

She nodded with a quick jerk and vanished into a room farther down the hall.

I made a show of working my way through the first floor, murmuring to myself and knocking here and there loud enough that the wife would hear my progress. Despite the modern trappings on the outside of the house, which I supposed was meant to impress the neighbors more than follow Novak's sensibilities, he'd designed the interior with fine hardwood and old-fashioned moldings like a place from earlier times.

I knocked on up to the second floor, where my real goal lay. A solid oak door there led to Mr. Novak's study. I pulled out a couple of lock picks and made short work of the deadbolt, with a couple knocks for good measure along the way.

The smell of aged leather permeated the dark room. I switched on the lamp near the door. Its light glowed across built-in shelves on every wall and a couple of armchairs facing a round wooden table in the center. Every piece of furniture was stacked with old books, even one of the chairs. Here and there between the rare volumes lay other curiosities of the supposedly supernatural variety: an oddly shaped animal skull, a jar of viscous liquid, and a bundle of partly charred twigs tied with a silk ribbon.

Novak was one of the many who helped keep the cult of the shrouded ones in business. He didn't have a clue who they were or what they stood for; he just purchased their objects of pseudo-power through the back channels where they peddled them with enough gravitas to convince an amateur dabbler in the dark arts. I doubted a single item they distributed had a scrap of actual significance.

The books Novak had amassed were another story. The cult wouldn't have liked any outsider having even the small amount of information contained in the text I was looking for.

Several boxes stood in a stack at the back of the room. He hadn't unpacked yet. I hurried over and started sorting through their contents.

My fingers leapt over the spines. It wasn't in this box. No, nothing in this one either. My heart was pounding by the time I set my hand on the title I was looking for in the fifth box I'd checked. I yanked it out.

Pages fifty-six to fifty-eight. I'd committed the numbers to memory. It was possible the treatise on Croatian folklore held a few other useful tidbits mixed in with the rest, but my life would be easier if Novak never realized he'd been robbed.

I tore the two pages from their binding with a wince, stuffed the book back into its spot, and folded the papers so I could tuck them into my purse.

I was just setting the boxes back into their stack when the creak of the stairs reached my ears. Shit.

I dashed out of the study, snapping off the light and jerking the door shut behind me. When Mrs. Novak reached the upstairs hall, I was knocking on the wall a couple doors down.

"Are you almost done?" she asked, with a nervous glance that darted along the baseboards. "Do we have any?"

"It's looking clear," I said with a smile. "I've just finished up."

She led the way back down the stairs.

"You call the number on that card if you notice any worrisome signs in the next few weeks," I told her, and looked around. "Do you have a back fence? I should take a look at that too before I move on."

"Yes, of course," Mrs. Novak said, all hasty relief. I knocked on a few spots on the fence, declared it pest-free too, and gave the woman my thanks as I headed out the back gate, far from Garrett's watching eyes.

My awareness of my prize tingled through me, but I forced myself to wait until I was tucked in the back of a cab before I drew out the pages. My gaze skimmed over the yellowed paper until I found the lines I was looking for.

One of the most obscure legends of this sort I've encountered is that of the shrouded dagger. The few references I've come across claim this magical weapon was a gift from the fae realm into this one, to solidify the association between those beings and their human allies. It is said to imbue the powers of a fae on any person who brandishes it under the right circumstances.

Fae. Ha. If he'd ever met an actual shrouded one, he wouldn't have placed them in the same category as Tinkerbell.

This all fell in line with what I'd already heard. If the dagger could give me the power of a shrouded one, then I could hope it would allow me to sever the pact I'd made with Bog, just as consenting to that deal with him had freed me from my more general bond to the cult and his kind. But what were the "right" damned circumstances?

The author rambled on for a few paragraphs about how much was unknown about this specific "faerie" people and the humans who associated with them, including why the dagger was referred to as "shrouded," before he finally got to the point. My fingers tightened around the paper, my pulse lurching with a bump of the cab's tires over a pothole.

The best understanding I've arrived at is that adherents believed this faerie people derived their power in our world from sunlight. Thus, a human wielder of the shrouded dagger could only take on full fae potential when the powers of the real fae were muted. A couple of references suggest that night or a place in shadow might be enough to evoke the dagger's supposed magic, but this seems overly simplistic considering how easily one could test the possibility.

One account, though brief, strikes me as having the most validity. It claims that tapping into the power can only happen in the moment the sun is abruptly yet fully interrupted by a solar eclipse. This idea has the ring of proper legend to it.

A giddy rush washed over me. Yes. That *felt* right, down to the core of my being where I'd been shaped by the shrouded folk across the first fourteen years of my life. I dug out my phone and tapped out a search for the next full solar eclipse.

It was just a few weeks away, the full effect visible from certain parts of South America. And there wouldn't be another until next year.

The giddiness faded, replaced by a more uneasy sense of anticipation. If I was ready in time, I could sever the contract between Bog and me in less than a month. If I didn't find all the pieces quickly enough... either the cuff around my leg or the shrouded one I'd bound myself to would destroy me before I got another chance to save myself.

CHAPTER TEN

Bash

I was sitting with a book on the bench outside the hotel when two of my targets emerged from the elevator. Adjusting my position just slightly, I pushed a button on the little receiver in my pocket.

John Watson and Garrett Lestrade made an even odder match without Sherlock between them to balance things out. As they headed to the front desk, the doctor's sweep of blond hair hovered nearly half a foot higher than the detective's close-cropped brown, the former's frame as broad as the latter's was wiry. If Watson had stood directly in front of Lestrade, you wouldn't have caught a glimpse of the smaller guy. But even though he was bigger, there was a softness to the way Watson carried himself that matched what Jemma had told me about his personality.

Neither of them looked like a very formidable foe, even taking into account walking stick combat skills.

My earphones crackled as the clerk at the front desk shuffled a few papers. Watson and Lestrade came to a stop there, and the bug I'd planted transmitted the clerk's thin voice into my ear, just a little louder than the growl of the passing traffic.

"How can I help you this morning?"

Watson was looking at something on his phone. Lestrade spoke first, a little too loud, a little too forceful for the situation—the tone of a guy with too much to prove. "We need a couple of taxis."

That was my cue. I left the receiver on as I got up from the bench and crossed the street to the spot where I'd stashed my mocked-up cab.

"Maybe just one," Watson said in his lighter voice. "It looks like the station is on the way to the hospital. We might as well share."

"Well, you'll be the one who ends up paying then."

"I'll have one around for you in just a few minutes," the clerk said.

I had quite a good stash of disguise options in the trunk, many brought with me, a few obtained here in Zagreb. For this... I tugged a stark white prayer cap over my head and fixed a thick beard that was as much gray as black to my jaw. The coarse hair itched at my skin, but the chances Watson would connect me to the bowl-haired man he'd seen briefly talking to Jemma were essentially nil.

The engine sputtered as I reversed out of the tight, secluded nook. It wasn't the finest car I'd ever driven. Jemma would have given me more cash if I'd asked, but a posh new model would have stood out more than I wanted.

I pulled my fake taxi up in front of the hotel less than two minutes after my targets had requested it and got out to beckon them over. "Mr. Watson and Mr. Lestrade?" I asked, putting on a thick Bosnian accent.

I opened the back, and they got in without more than a glance at me. It was almost too easy. I smiled to myself as I got back into the driver's seat.

"We've got two stops," Lestrade said. "The central police station first."

"Not a problem," I said, and gunned the engine before the taxi that had actually been called could arrive.

"It's really not that far," Watson said to his companion.

Through the rearview mirror, I watched Lestrade lean over,

presumably to check the other man's phone. He let out a huff of breath. "I could have walked that."

"Maybe it was better to take a taxi anyway. It'll be harder for her to have anyone follow us in a vehicle than on foot."

"True."

I held back a full smirk. They thought they were pretty smart, didn't they? You'd think they'd have realized by now that Jemma would always be at least two steps ahead of them.

She'd started to find the three of them intriguing while she'd conned them in London. Now that she didn't have to play along with their restrictive ideas about morality, it must be so obvious to her that she could outpace them in an instant. Nothing to admire there. She and I controlled the playing field, and they were just dupes fumbling their way across it. Foolish knights that she brought in one night, Shakespeare might have said. He'd have had a field day with this bunch.

"She's certainly holding her cards close," Watson went on. "Sherlock didn't get much out of her the other night."

Lestrade made a snorting sound. "It depends on what he was looking to get. You know he slept with her, don't you?"

My fingers tightened around the steering wheel.

Watson raised his eyebrows at the other man. "What makes you say that?"

"I saw him right after, when he got back to the hotel. He had this energy to him—it wasn't how a man looks when he's just been foiled in a simple conversation, I can tell you that much."

"I suppose it doesn't really matter."

Lestrade slumped down his seat. "No. I just can't help noticing it was *you* she came on to and *me* who suggested using that angle while he dismissed the possibility, and somehow *he's* the one who ended up in her bed."

He was trying to keep his voice nonchalant, but a ripple of jealousy ran through it. I'd have been more amused if a similar prickling hadn't shot up inside me.

It wasn't any of my business how Jemma conducted her personal affairs. She'd gotten plenty of mileage out of her seductive charms in the past. It was all part of the game.

Did it bother me that she'd gone after them at all or that she hadn't mentioned either incident to me—making a move on Watson, hooking up with Holmes? It wasn't as if she normally gave me a detailed account of her every maneuver… but I suspected she'd made a conscious decision to keep this to herself. I could even understand why. Things hadn't been quite as steady between the two of us since the night *we'd* shared together in London.

It was harder to tamp down desires after they'd had a little room to breathe and grow.

Jemma had made the boundaries of our partnership clear. Any trouble I had with maintaining that distance was on me.

I forced my hands to relax on the wheel. Lestrade was flipping through a notepad.

"You know, we haven't seen any more of those strange light effects around her this time around. What do you make of that?"

Watson cocked his head. "We did conclude they had to be coming from someone other than her. That someone probably stayed in London. Maybe it really was some conference-goer who was envious of the time she was spending with us—nothing to do with her personally at all."

"Maybe," Lestrade said with a frown. I'd have liked to see the look on their faces if they'd had to deal with the actual monsters Jemma was taking on. Maybe the things would eat the two of them, and Holmes too, and save us any more hassle.

The police station came into view up ahead. "Here we are," I said.

"Good luck with the lab coats," Lestrade said to Watson flippantly. The detective inspector climbed out.

Watson leaned forward. "I need to get to the university hospital now."

"Of course."

I pulled back into traffic, needing a few seconds to work out the best route based on my memory of the city maps. The police station had made sense. What information did the Londoners think they were going to get out of the city's main hospital that would help them figure out Jemma's plans?

I'd just have to find out. That was what she needed from me. These three would outlive their usefulness soon enough, and then we could move on completely.

"Are you sick?" I asked. "I have lived here a long time. If there's something specific you need, I might be able to suggest a place not so busy as the hospital."

"That's all right, but thank you," Watson said. "I'm not going for treatment, just to look at some records. I understand the hospital is associated with the Ministry of Health."

"Ah, I see, indeed," I said with an agreeable bob of my head. "Well, if there is anything else you're looking to know—even about areas farther abroad. Before I settled down here, I lived many places around the country."

Watson stayed quiet for long enough that I thought I hadn't hooked him. But he was obviously a little desperate for information. I could only imagine what they'd made of the odd story Jemma had slyly laid out for them.

"Have you always lived in cities?" he asked. "Did you ever spend much time in the countryside—near the mountains, maybe?"

"Oh, yes. In my younger days I liked to adventure. I've been many places, talked to many people."

He worried at his lower lip for a moment. "Did you ever hear any strange stories—about things happening on or near any of the mountains?"

"Hmm." I sucked in a breath slowly as if thinking it over. I couldn't point him in the right direction since I didn't know what that was. Jemma and I were counting on his bunch figuring that out. I could at least give him an encouraging nudge that there was something to find.

"There was one place, years ago, people in town talked about things disappearing now and then," I said. "They didn't know why. The custom was to say the fae folk from the mountain took it. Silly tales. Not what you're looking for."

"There might be something to it," Watson said, eagerly enough that I had to suppress another smile. "Which town was that?"

"I can't remember for sure. I moved around so much back then. It was very close to the foot of the mountain—that much I can picture."

Watson fell into silent contemplation for the rest of the drive. I stopped at the main hospital building where panes of glass melded with slabs of graying concrete, and he handed me a handful of cash that had a significant tip on top of the amount showing on the price meter I'd rigged. The man wasn't a cheapskate, anyway. One small point in his favor.

As he disappeared through the glass doors, I drove off—around the complex to the first out-of-the-way driveway I could find. I had another disguise that would work in the trunk. Yes, here, one of the lab coats Garrett had poked fun at.

I yanked that on, tugged off the beard, swapped my prayer cap for a tawny brown wig, and magically I was a white guy with a tan instead of a vaguely Middle Eastern-ish immigrant. Many thanks to my ancestors and their diverse tastes in lovers.

I'd shaved close this morning to remove my usual shadow of stubble, but Watson had seen me several times in the last couple months. For extra security, I popped in contacts that were a much brighter green than my natural color and slid on a pair of thick-paned glasses after them.

The main reception area was crowded, voices bouncing off the high ceiling and blurring together. Watson was only just leaving the room, following a young nurse who must have been summoned to assist him. I swiped an ID card from a brown-haired intern I brushed past and clipped it to my pocket. All anyone needed to see was the hospital logo and a picture that looked like a match at a distance.

I ambled behind Watson and his helper at a careful distance, fixing my face in an expression of intense concentration to discourage anyone from bothering me. Let them think I was in the middle of working out the world's first true cure for cancer. Finally, the nurse ushered the visiting doctor into a room. I loped over and caught the door just before it clicked.

The space on the other side held several desks and a row of computer stations along the far wall. The nurse led Watson to one of the computers. As he sat down, I eased inside.

Getting into place unseen was easy. I could sneak up on an enemy target to put a bullet in his head without him knowing I was there until his skull cracked open. I moved to one of the desks without so much as a whisper of sound and positioned myself as if I'd been standing there working all along. Neither Watson nor the nurse looked up.

"These are the main databases here," the nurse was saying. "We have English versions for sharing information internationally. Let me see..." She clicked on a few things and nodded. "That should get you started. Is there anything else I can help with?"

"No, I think I mostly need to browse through the data for a while," Watson said. "Thank you so much for your assistance."

What story had he offered up to convince the hospital staff to give him access to government data? Had word of Sherlock Holmes' exploits with his sidekick spread all the way out here? Maybe he'd played up his medical career and military service. Or maybe he'd spun as much of a story for them as I had for him in the cab.

He and his consulting detective thought they were such paragons of justice, but they broke the rules left and right when they felt like it.

As Watson got to work, I eased open a folder that had been left on the desk. If he did happen to glance over and notice me, I needed to look as though I had actually been working myself. Once I had the chart spread out in front of me though, I mostly watched the other man. What data was he sifting through that he thought would lead him to Jemma's mountain commune?

Half of the left pane of my glasses contained a magnifying lens. When I angled my head, I could make out some of the larger text on John's computer screen. He tapped in one search inquiry and another, scrolling through reams of records, not looking particularly satisfied with any of it. A pattern gradually emerged.

He was looking for evidence of covert medical activity. Stolen supplies, undocumented patients coming in for treatment. It wasn't a bad line of thought. A small secret community would have to find ways to stealthily look after its members' health.

I couldn't follow everything. Watson seemed to go back and forth between different threads without any obvious connection. I'd been standing, watching over him, for nearly two hours—not nearly long enough for my well-trained body to raise any protest—when a smile crossed his lips. I peered closer.

He'd brought up a bunch of figures from coastal communities. Why was he focused on them rather than the mountains on the interior? Had he seen something that had pointed to the coast as the more likely region?

Two hours. Jemma and I had been in the country for nearly a month without narrowing down our search that much. It had simply never occurred to me to check medical records for clues.

A jab of annoyance ran through my gut at Watson's smug smile. In that second, my hand twitched toward my hidden holster. It would be so very easy to shatter *this* man's skull. I could have my pistol out and my finger squeezing the trigger in the space of a heartbeat. He'd never even know he was in the slightest danger.

The impulse only lasted a second, though, followed by a jolt of shame. Who the hell would that help? Not me, not Jemma. I shifted my weight—and in my distraction I didn't hold myself perfectly quiet.

The floor creaked faintly. Watson startled and jerked around. I raised my head as if I were only just looking up at him.

"Are you all right?" I asked him in a bland voice.

He rubbed his face. "My God, I didn't even realize anyone else was in here."

I gave him a small smile. "You looked very absorbed with your work. I didn't want to interrupt you."

"Yes, of course, that's fine." He shook his head at himself with a sheepish expression.

"Have you found everything you were looking for?" I asked.

"I think so. I actually... I'd like to print some of this information off, but I'm not sure how to handle that with this database. Do you have a moment?"

"I can spare one." I came over, adrenaline pulsing through my veins. "Let me see."

With a quick examination, I found the most likely option. Watson didn't need to know that I was guessing as much as he would have been. When I clicked the command, a machine across the room hummed to life.

"Much appreciated," Watson said.

I pretended to go back to my work. He grabbed his papers from the printer and left. As soon as the door had shut behind him, I stalked back to his computer and drew up the print history. I'd take one more set of those pages for me, thank you.

I tucked the print-off under my lab coat and headed out, watching to make sure I didn't accidentally cross paths with Watson again. Near the back exit, I tossed the ID on a trolley. I shed my lab coat as I came up on my car.

Jemma would be happy about this find. As I dropped into the driver's seat, I could already picture the way she'd beam when I gave her the papers.

I grinned at the thought, and the image shifted. She'd been with Holmes the other night—he'd had his hands on her body, his mouth on hers—

I shut my eyes, inhaled, and exhaled slowly. For fuck's sake, Moran, get a grip on yourself.

The fresh flicker of jealousy faded, but my cock had stirred at the same time. I couldn't completely wipe the memories of the scent of her skin, the feel of her against *me*, from my mind.

I'd have to make a stop at my own hotel room before I went to deliver these. Time to burn off some of that libido by hand—if that would even be enough. I'd almost shot a man half out of jealousy a few minutes ago. Soon I was going to need to turn to a more concrete source of satisfaction.

CHAPTER ELEVEN

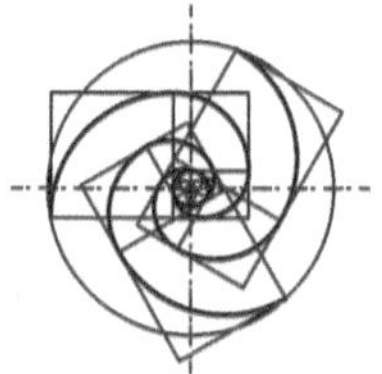

Jemma

My contact, the woman I only knew as Zena67 from her online posts and her email account, was late. We were supposed to meet in one of the display rooms of the city's Museum of Broken Relationships, and I'd been meandering between the bright white walls and display stands for nearly half an hour.

The stories of the various artifacts of love gone wrong weren't exactly dull, but they weren't what I was here for. The faint hum of the many lights was starting to niggle at my nerves.

She might have already come and gone, losing her nerve at the last second. I wouldn't have known her on sight.

I frowned at the chipped garden gnome on the stand in front of me. If anything, this museum stood as a testament to the stupidity of falling in love in the first place. Too much messy emotion, too little self-awareness. If you knew yourself well enough to recognize what you wanted, then you could simply take it, no need for sweeping promises or fanciful dreams.

But then, the only committed romantic relationship I'd ever gotten to see up close was my parents', and most of their adoration had been focused not on each other or even their children but the shrouded folk they worshipped. They got along because they barely had any selves left. That wasn't an example I could apply widely.

I drifted across the room to a pair of red stilettos I couldn't help thinking it was a shame to have shut away here instead of on someone's feet. The scuff of hesitant footsteps reached my ears. I kept my face turned toward the shoes, but I tracked the figure who entered the room from the corner of my eye.

The woman was short and a little plump, with a bob of graying curls that stirred restlessly around her prominent ears. Mid-fifties to early sixties in age. She wore a drab tan tunic that hung nearly to her knees with equally dull gray pants showing underneath, her small feet tucked into flat leather sandals. The sort of person you'd easily glance over and barely notice was there. Which was, based on how she'd interacted with me so far, exactly how she liked it.

She stiffened a little when she looked at me, but she made her way over as if compelled. Coming to a stop beside me, she folded her arms over her low bosom.

"They might as well have gotten a cat," she said quietly. Her English was good, her accent faint. The sentence had been her idea, part of a coded exchange to confirm we had the right person. I suspected Zena67 had watched too many spy movies in her time.

"Two would have been even better," I said on cue. I felt a bit ridiculous, but Zena's stance relaxed.

"Have you seen the other rooms yet?" she asked now that the brief pre-arranged script was done.

"No. Why don't we have a look?"

We wandered past a wall tacked with bras in various colors. Zena swallowed audibly.

"I'm not sure how much I have to tell you," she said, her voice still so low the soft tap of our shoes nearly drowned it out. Her thick rosy perfume trailed off her as she moved. It fit the mood of this place so well I wondered if she'd picked it for thematic resonance. She obviously enjoyed a little drama.

"That's fine," I said. "As I've said, I don't have high expectations.

I'll be happy to hear whatever you're able to tell me, even if it isn't a lot."

"You don't have any reason to think you were followed?"

"No. Believe me, I know how to be careful." I glanced sideways at her. "Do you really think someone might hurt you over this?"

Her mouth tightened. "I wish I hadn't even hinted at what happened in those posts. I'd delete them if I could. It'd been so long, and I'd never talked to anyone about it, so it felt good to let a little out, but... I've gotten calls since then, where I pick up and no one answers. Sometimes I see a man watching me when I'm doing my grocery shopping."

I highly doubted that any of the shrouded folk's minions had tracked this woman down. *I* hadn't even been able to determine her exact location or identity from those few forum posts and her email address. Whatever she'd experienced, it had clearly left her haunted, though. Haunted to the point of paranoia.

"I have people who can look out for you," I said, improvising. "The more you can help me, the more I'll be able to help you." That sounded like a suitably covert thing to say.

"It has been a long time. I'm sure I've forgotten some details."

I softened my tone as much as I could. "Whatever you remember. Whatever you feel comfortable telling me. You can take your time."

Just hurry up and spit it out already.

My fingers curled around the strap of my purse, but I resisted the urge to pop a sugar cube into my mouth. The less strange she thought *I* was, the less hesitant she'd be to share her story of the strangeness that had shaken her. I shouldn't have to worry about the time — I'd left Sherlock's tracker in my hotel room while I slipped out for this meeting — but he'd already proven capable of interfering with my subterfuge without even meaning to.

Even if I had enjoyed his most recent interference quite a bit in the end.

"I guess I should start from the beginning." Zena dragged in a breath. "It was about thirty-five years ago. I was working in a hospital in Split, just an assistant. A woman came in who wasn't much older than me — definitely not more than thirty — all scraped and scratched up, wearing odd clothes, and in a total panic. She was so weak she could hardly stand up, but she didn't want to sit still. She seemed like she was trying to run away from something."

Split—down near the coast. Some of the cases John had found suspicious had been clustered in that area. I'd have to take another look at the print-out Bash had brought me yesterday.

"That must have been unnerving to see," I prompted with a show of sympathy.

Zena nodded again, her head moving with a sharper jerk this time. She hugged herself tighter. "I was alone in the room with her for a few minutes. She seemed to go... delirious. Saying things that didn't make any sense. But she was obviously scared and in pain—and a little angry too, I thought."

She paused, rubbing her mouth with a nervous hand. I had to ease her along, not scare *her* off. You'd almost have thought that long-ago woman's panic had infected her.

"Were the doctors able to help her?" I asked, even though I already knew the answer to that. If fleeing the cult of the shrouded folk was as simple as running as fast as you could, I'd never have needed to make a bargain for my soul.

Zena's voice dropped to a whisper. "No. She seized up, all of a sudden, clawing at her chest and her throat. It seemed like only a few seconds—I shouted for the doctor, and he hadn't made it yet even though he hurried—and then she was gone. He said her heart stopped."

Everyone in the cult agreed to a sort of contract for the "honor" of living alongside the shrouded folk. My parents had sworn my sister and me into that fealty within hours of our birth. Stray too far from our loyalties, and our own bodies would betray us. Only a contract with a single shrouded one could override that broader pact.

This woman, whoever she'd been, hadn't been sly enough or brave enough—or maybe, from her perspective, stupid enough—to make the necessary trade. She'd taken her chances in a mad dash, and her fate had come chomping at her heels.

Of course, I couldn't really judge. Mine would have chomped me down already if not for the cuff around my leg. I adjusted my purse, the bottom of it brushing the edge of the gold band through my cotton dress.

"She claimed she'd come from a group that worshiped some kind of supernatural beings, from what you wrote," I said. "Something about 'shrouds.'"

"That was something she said. That the shrouds would come for her. That they didn't let anyone go lightly."

That much certainly was true, but it didn't help me. I ambled on toward another display, and Zena trailed behind me. "What else did she say?" I asked when we'd come to a stop. "Even the parts that didn't make sense... They might be useful somehow or other."

"Those are the parts I don't remember all that well, because of how crazed she sounded." Zena exhaled raggedly. "She said something about people searching for her, and about blood, and... tunnels. The tunnels took her almost all the way, but they were still over her when she came out. I couldn't figure out what she meant by that, but she sounded so tortured when she said it, it stuck with me."

My pulse beat a little faster. Tunnels. The woman had escaped from the commune through some sort of tunnels. Which meant I might be able to use the same ones to enter the place without being noticed on the way up.

"It sounds as though she was nearly insensible," I said. "Difficult to know what she could have been talking about without any context."

"She might have imagined it all, for all I know. Hallucinations or what have you. Obviously she wasn't really serving magical creatures." Zena shook her head. "Someone treated her very badly; that's all I know for sure."

I swallowed hard. "Yes."

I took another step through the museum room, and a stabbing sensation shot up through my hip as if I'd been speared by a blade of ice. My foot went numb beneath me. I stumbled and caught one of the display stands for balance with a rasp of breath. Then my whole body froze as I stared at my hand in front of me.

Where my fingers gripped the sleek white surface, the tips of them were fading away. The gleaming white shone right through them as if they'd turned translucent. Pain echoed from my hand all the way to the clamp of the cuff on my thigh.

I jerked my hand back before anyone else could notice. My fingertips tingled and then steadied against my belly. My thigh throbbed, but the chill was easing back, inch by inch. I managed to recover my balance on my feet, gritting my teeth against the pain.

Zena was staring at me. Her face had blanched. Maybe I hadn't hidden my hand quickly enough.

"Wait a moment," I said as calmly as I could, holding my hand out to her to show her it was perfectly normal now, but she'd been shaky enough already. Without another word, she spun and dashed away, her curls bouncing behind her.

And I was left with the sinking sensation that as far as I'd come, as much knowledge as I'd gathered, I might still be too late.

CHAPTER TWELVE

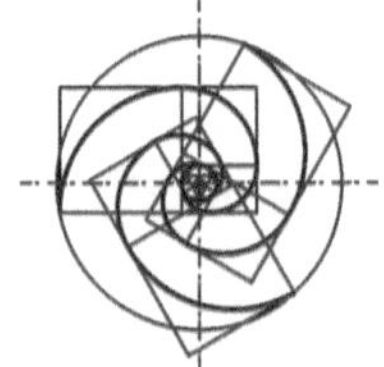

Jemma

I came back to the hotel the next afternoon with my stomach pleasantly full and my mouth laced with the doughy sweetness of the pastry I'd just eaten. This time I could walk right through the lobby without any subterfuge, because I'd taken Sherlock's tracker out for a walk. I'd rambled around one of the city's larger parks for a couple hours before stopping by Franjo's.

None of the trio had bothered to follow the tracker to see what I was up to, though—or if they had, they'd been stealthier about it than usual. I'd been hoping I might be able to catch one of them in a conversation and find out what else they'd learned, but no dice.

Maybe it was time I moved on to making my own investigations around Split. I had a fair bit of information to work with. The only question was whether I could make the move there without the trio trailing along behind me, their investigation changing from a help to a hindrance.

Jakov hustled over to me as I stopped by the elevators. "Ms. Matthams," he said in a low urgent voice.

Or perhaps I had more business to attend to here. I gave the porter my full attention. "What is it?"

"One of the men you asked me to watch for—the tall one with the dark hair—he came through the hotel this morning. I didn't see exactly where he went, but I thought you'd want to know. You said it was better not to call anymore, or I'd have told you right away."

"That's fine, Jakov," I said despite a prickle of irritation. I hadn't wanted any unexpected phone calls interrupting my various activities, but in this one case, it would have been nice to get the information immediately. "Thank you for telling me now."

What had Sherlock been doing here? A quiver shot through my nerves as the elevator jerked upward. If he'd determined the main room I was staying in...

When I reached the door, I eased it open carefully with a rustle of the Do Not Disturb sign. No prints marked the sprinkling of face powder I'd left on the carpet just inside the door. I exhaled in relief. It looked as though no one had come through here, including any obnoxiously nosy consulting detectives.

I ducked inside anyway, quickly checking over my things. I hadn't been leaving anything in the room when I went out that would be of much use to Sherlock, but I didn't want him meddling in here anyway. Who knew what his penetrating mind might be able to deduce that I wouldn't have expected?

There was no indication anyone had been in here since I'd left, not a thing missing or out of place. Good. I headed out and down to the other room in my name—the one where Sherlock and I had entertained ourselves the other night.

The moment I stepped through that doorway, I knew. He was too careful to leave any obvious sign of his investigation, but I caught the faintest whiff of that sharp aftershave he wore. In another hour or two, it would have faded. I might not have noticed it at all if I hadn't been searching for it.

One of the screws fastening the grill on the air vent showed a tiny scratch that hadn't been there before. He must have opened it up to check for hidden materials. No doubt he'd riffled through my suitcase and the few articles of clothing I'd left around the room too, though he'd managed to put them back exactly as they'd been before.

Had he been able to conclude that I wasn't really staying in this room? I wasn't sure he'd gleaned enough about my usual habits to know what was typical versus uncharacteristically spartan.

The truce was definitely off. My attempt to draw them out this morning hadn't worked. Let's see if I couldn't find a more successful angle for the afternoon.

I sucked my lower lip under my teeth as I sat on the end of the bed. *What's the latest on our friends?* I texted to Bash.

I'm staked out by a government building right now, he wrote back. *H and W just headed in ten minutes ago. L left the hotel at the same time, in a different direction.*

Good. Let me know when they leave?

On it.

Do you have any more of those audio bugs? I might have the opportunity to place one in a good spot.

In the bag next to the bedside table in my room. Help yourself, Majesty.

The corner of my lips quirked up. Let's see if Sherlock hadn't left me a little more of a reward than I'd given him.

Half an hour later, I got onto the elevator of the trio's hotel next to a cleaning woman and her trolley. With a feigned stumble and a flick of my fingers, I swapped her master keycard for a standard one I'd nabbed off the check-out desk downstairs. When her new one didn't work, she'd just think she'd grabbed the wrong one by mistake.

She got off on the third floor. I continued up to Sherlock and John's suite. The bug Bash had already placed by the front desk had gotten us their exact room number days ago. Reasons to never order in delivery when you're facing off against a criminal mastermind.

I squinted at the edge of the door before I tried it. A tiny scrap of paper showed between the door and the frame, several inches above my line of sight. Did Sherlock really think a gambit like that would escape me?

The door opened with a swipe of the card. I slipped inside,

scanning the floor and the walls for any other subtle protective measures. Then I snatched up the paper that had fluttered to the floor and tucked it back into place so there was no chance of my forgetting to place it in the right spot on my way out.

The earthy smoky smell of Sherlock's tobacco met me as I slunk through the living area. His wooden pipe and tobacco box lay on the coffee table. A few glasses with a ring of amber liquid I'd be willing to bet was sherry, courtesy of John, scattered the full-sized dining room table. Someone had stuffed several take-out containers into a plastic bag by the wall. They'd left the air conditioning on, the unit making a soft whirring sound as it dampened the late spring heat.

That might suggest they hadn't expected their government meeting to take very long. Bash would warn me when they headed back, but I needed to move quickly if I was going to make a thorough search of the place.

I scanned the table, lifting a napkin here and a receipt there to check for handwriting. A map lay on the kitchen counter, but when I unfolded it to the full spread of Croatia, I didn't find any personalized markings. The drawers held only the hotel-standard offerings.

Damn it. They couldn't have left out even one little note about how they were narrowing down their search for my mountain village?

The dining table appeared to be their center of operations. I knelt down and pressed Bash's bug into a nook where one of the legs met the hardwood top. Then I moved to the bedrooms.

The first one I entered was clearly John's—not at all smoky, with a deck of cards sitting on the side table. He'd set a few small rocks of no discernable value on top of the dresser. I studied them for a second and moved on.

The drawers in there turned up a Western novel with a faded cover, a sleep mask, and a prescription bottle of mild pain pills. His hip must still hurt him enough that he needed those now and then to sleep. I set them back carefully.

John's clothes spilled out of his suitcase haphazardly. I sifted through them and turned up nothing of interest except for a torn notepaper in one shirt pocket that said only *Antibiotics—frequency?* and a few numbers with no clear significance. I took a picture of it with my phone just in case it could lead me somewhere, but it didn't look terribly promising.

Sherlock's bedroom was tidy to a fault. His shirts and slacks hung in a well-pressed row in the closet, his sparse toiletries—toothpaste and brush, shaving kit, and a block of soap with a scent as sharp as his aftershave and a London company name printed on it—set in a semi-circle around the sink. John's covers had been tangled; Sherlock's were pulled crisply straight.

Unfortunately he appeared to be equally fastidious about his work paraphernalia. If he'd made any record of his mental workings outside his head, he had those notes with him or had hidden them away somewhere I couldn't see.

I was just about to drag the chair over to start checking out the air vents, since he'd thought that was a worthy consideration in my hotel room, when the lock on the suite door beeped. I froze.

One set of footsteps came in, with a short sigh and a rustle of clothing as the new arrival must have scooped up the paper from the door. The sigh told me why Bash hadn't signaled me. I hadn't been joined by either of the suite's regular inhabitants but by Garrett. They must have given him an extra key card so he could enjoy the larger living space whenever he wanted to.

I crept to Sherlock's bedroom door, which stood a few inches ajar. Garrett was pushing something into the kitchenette's fridge with a clinking of glass. Then he hunkered down at the dining table. He pulled out his notepad and jotted something in it. Frowning, he considered the page.

A tingle of anticipation quivered through my chest. There'd be something useful in that notepad—I'd be willing to bet on that. He had a tendency to hold onto it though, and right now he was sitting between me and my only escape route. I didn't like the odds of surviving a jump down from an eighth-floor window.

So, why not kill two birds with one stone? I'd won Sherlock over enough to get him into my bed. It'd be useful to know whether the detective inspector's new armor had its chinks too.

I'd be highly surprised if it didn't.

A smile curled my lips. I nudged open the door and sauntered across the room as if it were perfectly natural that I should happen to be there.

Garrett startled and bolted out of his chair. "Hello, Garret," I said, dropping into the seat across from his. "You look like you could use a little company."

He stared at me. "How did *you* get in here?"

I shrugged, leaning my elbows onto the table. "Not so differently, I'd imagine, from however Sherlock got into my room this morning. Since he seemed to consider an uninvited visit fair play, I didn't see why I shouldn't return the favor."

From the tightening of Garrett's mouth, he'd known that Sherlock had searched my room. He didn't have much of a leg to stand on if he wanted to accuse me of shady practices. He stayed standing, his hand clenched around his notepad.

"What do you want?"

"Well, we did discuss the possibility of having a proper conversation, just the two of us. This seems like an excellent time for it, since our paths happened to cross. Why don't you sit down?"

He sat, but he didn't look happy about it. I pretended not to be interested in his notepad as he set it down in front of him. He paused for a moment and then said, "You took me by surprise—that's all. We can talk."

He'd smoothed out most of the tension from his voice, just as he had when we'd spoken on the phone a few days ago. Making a conscious effort to engage with me. That attitude felt different from the brusque energy he'd given off when we'd faced each other in Franjo's that first time since the trio had caught up with me.

Bash had said that Garrett had mentioned something about "using" the fact that I'd propositioned John. Maybe he thought he could get more out of me by playing sweet than Sherlock had. Wouldn't he love that—to score both between the sheets and by outdoing the great consulting detective in their investigation?

He didn't wear the friendlier attitude well, though. Sherlock had been honestly willing to offer the sort-of truce, to indulge his "fascination" despite his wariness. Garrett's uncertainty showed in the flex of his shoulders, in the twitch of his eyes as I gazed back at him. He was holding back a mass of bottled emotion I'd have loved to uncork and drink down.

"I haven't seen much of you since you three showed up in town," I said casually, aiming a subtle jab at his pride. "Are you letting Sherlock and John take the lead?"

Garrett's jaw worked. "We're all contributing the best way we can. You don't need to worry about that."

"Of course not. You aren't really the type to stand back and let others do all the heavy lifting. Very admirable."

"Am I supposed to believe that you admire me?" he said, managing to sound amused.

"Why not? Am I supposed to believe that you *don't* admire me, at least a little bit?" I tapped his calf with my toes under the table. "There's no shame in it. I'm very good at what I do, even if it's not exactly what you thought I did."

He sputtered a laugh. "That's the understatement of the year."

"Which part? That I'm very good?" I touched his leg again, just enough to move the tap to a caress this time.

"Is that what you wanted to talk about?" Garrett asked. He leaned toward me, with a flicker of hunger in his expression that I didn't think was an act. "How admirable we both are?"

"Well, if you don't want to talk about it, maybe I should see what wonderful things you've been writing about me."

My hand darted across the table to snatch up the notepad. Garrett sprang after it with a noise of protest, too late. I sat back in my chair and flipped through the many marked up pages.

"You do draw a lot too, don't you?" Words and images fluttered past. I stopped on one that showed a woman with long wavy hair from behind, with careful attention to both the hair and the ass. I grinned. "Is this me?"

Garrett came around the table to make a grab at the notepad. I slipped off the other side of my chair. We studied each other from either side of it, shifting weight one way and then the other to feel each other out, his expression lit with determination.

I could have run for the door, but that would have given away that I wanted the notepad for more than just to tease him. I dashed for the kitchenette instead, brandishing it like a trophy. Garrett leapt after me. He caught my arm, and I spun us around with a laugh. Pushing into the turn instead of fighting it, he pinned me against the counter and plucked the pad from my hands.

"That," he said, close enough that his breath grazed my cheek, "is mine."

He shoved it into the pocket of his jeans. His other hand was still gripping my wrist, his arm flush with mine, the rise and fall of his chest echoing into my body where I was trapped between his wiry frame and the counter.

I raised my eyebrows at him as if to ask, *What now?* For an instant, I thought I felt him about to push away from me. Then his dark brown eyes flashed, and he pressed his mouth to mine.

Garrett Lestrade knew how to kiss. *I* knew that because of the intensity with which he'd met that challenge back in London. Now, he nudged a little closer, his hand rising to grasp my shoulder, but his lips moved awkwardly, hard but hesitant. I felt his reluctance all through the set of his shoulders and the tension in his touch. That wasn't at all the emotion I'd wanted to liberate.

I ducked my head, breaking the kiss, and brought my fingers to his cheek to ease him away from me. "No. We're not going there if you don't really want it."

Garrett backed up a step, his arms jerking up to fold over his chest. In that moment, he looked only furious. "Pardon me? Since when have you ever cared what *I* want?"

I straightened up against the counter, a jab of annoyance stiffening my spine. "Are we going to talk about what happened in London, then? Because I gave you exactly what you wanted. You can't pretend I forced you into a single thing we did together."

"I don't really see how that matters when you were lying to me the whole time." He exhaled sharply and dropped his hands to his sides. "Forget it. It's not as if there's any point in discussing it. I—I do still find you attractive, regardless."

He eyed me as if he were trying to figure out just how convincing he had to be about that for me to accept his advances. Or maybe he was trying to figure out whether the plan he'd decided on really was the best idea. I wasn't sure what would play into my hands most effectively. The one clear thing that had rung through his voice in those first forceful remarks was pain.

I'd known he was angry with me from the start, but I'd thought it was wounded pride. I hadn't realized I might have wounded him more deeply than that. My approach might require some recalculations. And perhaps some strategic honesty, if I was going to get what I wanted from him now.

I held his gaze. "Garrett, I can understand why you're pissed off at me. I wouldn't expect anything else. But you know, everything in London — I made the moves that would get me to what I needed. I maneuver people as it suits my ends, and, yes, sometimes I get some gratification out of that. But I'm not some kind of sadist who enjoys tormenting people just for the sake of it. I didn't have anything against *you*."

"I was just in your way?" Garrett supplied.

"More like you *were* the way to get where I needed to go." I wet my lips, and he followed the movement of my tongue. Part of him did still want me despite everything he knew, despite everything I'd just told him, even if a larger part of him was balking. "You were brilliant, you know. I knew you would be. That's why I turned to you. I could have stuck to Sherlock and John, but they wouldn't have been enough."

"Am I supposed to be flattered by that?" he asked, as if I couldn't tell he was.

"If you want to be." I eased half a step toward him, not daring to try to touch him yet. "You were a pretty brilliant fuck too. I'd have done *that* again just for fun, if there'd been the time for it. We could. Why not? You know what you're getting into this time, and it doesn't have to mean anything more than what it is. You almost went for it just now. What's holding you back?"

His gaze slipped back to my mouth. His throat bobbed. "There are a lot of bad choices in the world and not so many good ones. Somehow you make it hard for me to tell which is which."

I had to smile. So, underneath the passionate competitor, Garrett was a moralist. Who would have guessed? Sherlock must have led him down more questionable paths than I had so far, but this wasn't the time to argue about it.

"I happen to think that most choices aren't inherently good or bad," I said, letting my voice drop lower. "It's what you make of them that matters."

His tone softened. "I don't know what to make of you."

"You can make this the first time I've ever been fucked in this suite, even though it's not yours."

He made a tight sound in his throat, but he moved to meet me at the same time, one hand catching my waist, the other tracing my jaw. His mouth claimed mine.

This was the kiss I remembered, so intent it seemed determined to erase every other lover from my mind. I looped my arm around Garrett's neck as I kissed him back, trailing my fingers down his side at the same time. He nudged me back to the counter again, already hard as he pressed against me.

I let my breath stutter over my lips at the feel of him. Garrett kissed me more deeply, his tongue teasing into my mouth, his hand hot on my hip—

And then he was shoving himself back from me with a heave of his chest. He shook his head.

"No. Fucking hell. No. Every fucking time, you bring out the worst in me."

That last comment stung. He hadn't seen anything like the worst yet.

I wiped my mouth and raised my chin. "Then I guess we're done here. I'm sorry you feel that way."

He didn't try to stop me when I headed out the door. I strode to the elevator, my fingers brushing over the notepad I'd freed from his pocket and stuffed into mine.

I'd come out on top. I should be pleased. So why was my gut twisted into a knot that only lurched tighter with the elevator's descent?

CHAPTER THIRTEEN

Garrett

Pebbles rattled in a frenetic rhythm against the undercarriage of the rental car. As usual, John was driving a bit too fast for comfort as he navigated the road between Split and a smaller town further north where Sherlock had decided we should make inquiries. I wondered if I had any chance of taking the wheel on the way back. My stomach would definitely appreciate a less death-defying pace.

"Do you think she's fallen for the trick?" I asked, glancing out the back window as if I might see Jemma speeding along after us.

"I can't imagine her failing to follow up on a lead like the one we gave her," Sherlock said with his usual confident air. "We all played our parts well."

I'd texted John as soon as Jemma had left their suite, and Sherlock had been in full-out precautionary mode when they'd returned. He'd looked a little ridiculous examining every surface in the suite as if it were a crime scene, but his vigilance had rewarded us, because he'd spotted the bug she must have placed before any of us had said anything we wouldn't have wanted her overhearing.

I'd said she must have placed it before I'd gotten to the suite.

That had better be true, because if she'd done it under my nose, I'd have to be doubly humiliated. It'd been bad enough forcing myself to admit to the loss of my notepad she must have lifted off me.

I'd had to grit my teeth, but the boy I'd been ten or fifteen years ago would have hidden the mistake automatically, regardless of the damage it could do. I'd grown up. The man I'd become was better than that.

For the most part.

I *hadn't* mentioned how I might have failed to notice her taking the notepad or anything else that had happened between us other than conversation. My bungled attempt at possibly-seducing-or-maybe-being-seduced didn't seem all that relevant to the case. Why bring it up and have them think I was an idiot as much as I did?

I still wasn't completely sure which had been the more idiotic move: going for that last kiss or pulling away from it.

In any case, after he'd discovered the bug, Sherlock had come up with a plan that I had to admit was solid. We'd hashed out our actual findings of the day in my room, which Sherlock had determined was bug-free, and then returned to the suite's living area to discuss a modified version including supposed follow-up plans. Plans which involved driving into Zadar and heading north from there, rather than flying into Split and heading south like we'd actually done.

Sherlock had fully committed to the deception. We'd rented a different car for our supposed road-trip, set off as if for the coast, and then doubled back through a series of hasty maneuvers that John had way too much fun pulling off. He'd parked that car at the Zagreb airport, where we'd caught a flight to Split.

We hadn't seen any hint that we were being followed, but Sherlock took a lot of delight in his precautions, and since he *had* found the bug, I wasn't going to hassle him about it.

If Jemma tried to interfere with our investigations, she'd have her people looking for us many miles distant. Or she might not have bothered, amusing herself thinking that we were on completely the wrong track.

I really shouldn't be imagining her lounging on her hotel bed right now smiling that sly grin of hers. I'd thought a lot about

Jemma over the last several weeks, but after kissing her yesterday, after the way she'd talked to me, she kept popping up when I was trying to focus on other things.

"It's quite the view," John remarked, not that he showed any sign of slowing down to take it in. On the left, we sped by pale buildings made out of stone or plaster, surrounded by green shrubs. Gray mountains speckled with vegetation loomed beyond the shallowly slanted rooftops. At our right, blue-green expanse of ocean stretched out toward the horizon. The air that the car's hitching air conditioning system drew in smelled of sand and salt.

"Too bad we're not here to take in the scenery." I stretched my legs as well as I could in the back seat. "We've found plenty of evidence that there's *some* small group of people operating undercover out here, but it's only traces. Do you really think we've got enough to find a community that's been hiding this well for so long?"

"I'd have preferred to wait until we could trace Jemma more directly to them," Sherlock said, "but her recent activities haven't pointed us any closer. We know she means to move them and to cover up their operations here as soon as she can. I have several possibilities for the location, areas away from the usual tourist routes but within a reasonable range for hospital access and the other unusual reports. I expect the locals will be able to give us a good sense of when we're close."

He ordered John off the paved road onto a dirt one that wound through the countryside toward the line of mountains. We stopped at a country house where Sherlock knocked on the door and explained to the owner in rough Croatian that we wanted to explore a nearby section of the mountain despite the lack of paths. When the man responded with brusque enthusiasm, as if he appreciated our daring even if he'd rather we got out of his face, we returned to the car.

Sherlock crossed an item off his list. "He said the local teenagers roam through the woods there all the time. I'm sure a secretive commune would have found some way to discourage that activity."

Three stops later, I was starting to think we were barking up the wrong mountains. No one had appeared at all concerned about our various supposed uphill jaunts. Even Sherlock was getting a grim look I recognized. If we'd been back in London, it would have meant he'd take to his sofa in his house coat for hours examining his ceiling until I turned up with a case intriguing enough to prod him out of his stupor.

We pulled up outside a stone farmhouse at the edge of a few scruffy fields. A tractor puttered in the distance. An elderly woman with her sleeves rolled up over brawny forearms came out and frowned as Sherlock gestured toward the gray peak jutting in the near distance.

"English, yes?" she said when he was about halfway through his usual spiel.

Sherlock paused. "Yes."

"I speak some. Enough." She waved her hand at the mountain. "No. You don't go there."

She turned as if she thought that answer alone would satisfy us. She'd clearly never met Sherlock Holmes before.

"I'm sorry," he said in a conciliatory tone that was ruined somewhat by the eager light that had sparked in his eyes. "Why not? It doesn't look all that dangerous. I don't believe it's private property."

"Bad things happen there," the woman said. "All around. Last month, a farm even closer, they found half their chickens torn to pieces on the roof of the coop. A few years before, a man came up from town with his dog, the dog ran off, next day we find it at the bottom of the mountain, its skin…" She made a folding motion. "Turned inside out."

My stomach clenched. John looked rather green around the gills too. We'd gotten this far based on stolen medications and odd hospital visits, missing equipment and strange deliveries. We hadn't expected stories of mutilated animals.

"There weren't any police reports," I said. "Haven't you told anyone?"

She raised her hands. "What would they do? People don't live too close. The ones with the chickens, they left. Everyone just knows, anything that goes up the mountain there, don't expect to get it back."

A queasy chill pooled in my belly. I didn't want to ask this, but I had to. "There *was* one report. Five years ago, a little boy who was climbing near here fell. Broke his spine. The account said it was an accident?"

The woman pursed her lips. "The city people, they don't want to think it could be more. He went too close. My husband is the one who found him. The way he was twisted up, his waist bent right around... No one could fall like that. They took his eyes and scraped his hair off to his skull. No accident. Don't go there. Leave the mountain alone, or the mountain takes."

We walked back to the car in silence. My stomach kept churning. There hadn't been any pictures of the boy in the report I'd seen, but the woman's words had drawn a clear enough picture. The kid had been only eight years old.

When we reached the car, John looked at Sherlock. "We're going up, aren't we." It wasn't even a question.

Sherlock dropped into the front passenger seat. "We appear to have found the place we were looking for. There's a road farther along that will take us closer. I don't want any locals running after us trying to save us from ourselves now that we've made our intentions known."

"Are you sure this is a good idea?" I said as John started the engine. "Just the three of us? We're talking about people who'd kill and disfigure a *child*. They're not going to hesitate to come after us."

"A child is easier to kill," Sherlock said matter-of-factly. "I have my pistol, and Watson has his. We'll tread carefully, but there was no point in coming out here if we don't investigate the exact location."

My fingers itched for my own police-issue gun, but I'd had to leave that behind in London since I wasn't here on any official business. Just chasing a woman who'd worked her way too far into my head.

That thought brought a fresh wave of nausea. I rubbed my mouth. "We assumed Jemma had to be the one calling the shots with this group—directing whatever they're doing. This isn't about just stealing pretty artifacts or making money. These people are *sick*."

"We don't know exactly how she's involved," John said, but the protest sounded weak.

Sherlock's jaw had set. "Whatever she's had a part in, she'll face the consequences for her crimes."

What did it say about her that she was willing to work with people who'd torment children and animals? God, what if she'd been the one to give *those* orders? The same woman who'd looked me in the eyes yesterday and told me without a hint of guile that everything she did served a purpose, that she never acted purely to cause pain.

I'm not some kind of sadist...

What did it say about me that I'd believed her, at least in part? That I'd wanted to believe her? Because even though she'd wrapped me around her finger and then flicked me aside in London, I couldn't seem to shake the hold she had over me.

Maybe I hadn't left behind the boy I'd been as far as I'd thought. The boy who'd acted out his frustrations through cruelty. With every case solved, with every bid for justice fulfilled, I'd buried my past deeper, but something in me, something strong, found her compelling. She'd drawn that jealous, resentful side of me out with her teasing encouragement as recently as yesterday.

My hands balled where they were resting on my thighs. Now I knew what she really was. I wouldn't forget it. And this was a reminder not to forget who I could be either, as sick as the memories made me feel.

John parked on a grassy shoulder where the road curved to veer past the steeper slope. My feet felt heavy as I clambered out, but I tramped after the other two into the dense forest that hugged the mountain's base. Every snapped twig, every waver of sunlight piercing through the leaves overhead, made my skin twitch.

The ground grew steeper and rockier, pale gray chunks of rock protruding between roots and shrubs. The trees thinned, letting more sunlight stream through to balance out the cooling air. Sweat streaked down my back. John and Sherlock veered to the right, and I followed them automatically.

After several paces, Sherlock stopped abruptly. He peered around himself and backtracked. I moved to follow him, but the impression gripped me that heading upward would be completely the wrong way.

I hesitated, John beside me. His knuckles had blanched where he clutched his walking stick, his blond hair sticking to his sweat-damp forehead. His expression was tight. The hike had been tiring for me —I couldn't imagine how rough it had been on the doctor's shaky constitution.

A short scramble higher up, Sherlock knelt down and prodded a tiny impression in the dirt.

"What is it?" John asked.

"Only the slightest edge of a footprint, but I believe someone has walked here. Heading down from higher above." Sherlock raised his head and then glanced at his partner. "Perhaps you should stay here with Garrett while I continue investigating."

"No," John said firmly. "You're not wandering off on your own to tangle with child murderers. We go together."

I pushed myself after Sherlock. We climbed farther, leaving the trees for ground that was now all rock spotted with pockets of earth that allowed grass, wildflowers, and the occasional coarse bush. Within a minute, the sense hit me even harder that we were heading the wrong way.

I stopped. "This doesn't seem quite right."

"I agree," John said. "I think we've gotten ourselves off course."

Sherlock knit his brow. He scanned the terrain around us. "I am certain," he said, "if a community such as this exists…" He strode up the rocky slope abruptly as if pushing against the same resistance I felt.

I was watching him—I saw it happen. One moment he was marching along in his obstinate way, and the next, with a shiver of the sunlight, his body buckled as if something had battered his abdomen. He tumbled backward, his feet flying out from under him, his arms wheeling.

"Sherlock!" John cried. He threw himself forward with a lurch of his weaker leg.

Sherlock managed to spin himself around to protect his head, but his ankle slammed into a jutting rock just as John reached him. The thump made me shudder as I rushed over too.

John crouched next to his friend. Sherlock shoved himself upright, straightening his left leg. His ankle was already swelling where the leg of his trousers had ridden up. His normally impassive face pinched with pain.

"You've probably sprained it," John said. "Don't put any weight on that foot, or you'll make it worse." Gripping Sherlock's shoulder, he glanced around us, his other hand going to the pistol in his pocket. "It looked like you were pushed, but there's no one around."

"It *felt* as if I was pushed," Sherlock said. "Hard. But I agree—I was looking straight ahead, and nothing moved at me. Perhaps an impactful projectile?"

"I was looking right at you, and I didn't see anything." I paused. "The light moved strangely right when it happened, that's all. Nothing fell with you that could have hit you."

The light. I paused. It hadn't looked like any of the effects I'd seen around Jemma back in London. She wasn't even here—she *couldn't* be, could she?

John handed me his pistol. "Have a look around while I make him a temporary splint so he doesn't hurt himself even more on the way down. Then we're getting out of here."

"John," Sherlock started to protest.

John stared at him defiantly. "If you've ever trusted me for anything, Sherlock, it's my medical opinion. And I'm telling you this investigation is finished for the day."

I scanned the forest below us, but there was no sign of anyone. Still, I didn't like it. I didn't like any of this.

Evening was falling by the time we left the hospital. I walked behind the other two, John with his rhythmic limp, Sherlock hobbling with a brace around his sprained ankle and a single crutch, which was all the assistance he'd been willing to tolerate. As we reached the rental car, I brought up the subject we'd set aside during the wretched climb down the mountain and the bustle of the hospital.

"Now what?"

"We aren't climbing any more mountains, not for a few days at least," John said before Sherlock could answer.

Sherlock's mouth tightened. "Whoever and whatever is up there, they're dangerous," he said. "And they're tied to Jemma. If we can't tackle the mountain, then we'll tackle her. We have to go back to Zagreb."

"And then do what?" I demanded. "We don't have any more evidence of a concrete crime to charge her with than we did before."

"Perhaps we cut her too much slack. Perhaps we were more swayed by her charms than we should have been." He rubbed his jaw. "Anything more she orchestrates under our watch is on our consciences too. We have evidence. We have proof of a relic she stole from a major London art gallery."

"We don't know where it is. We don't even know if she brought it with her to Croatia."

Sherlock's lips curved into a bittersweet smile. "I do."

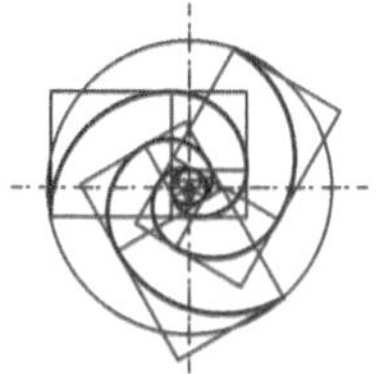

CHAPTER FOURTEEN

Jemma

I flopped back on my bed with a stifled groan, holding my phone to my ear. "So there's nothing? No sign they were ever anywhere near Zadar?"

"Our contact there had several of his people on it as soon as I gave him the heads up yesterday," Bash said on the other end. "They paid especially close attention to the roads heading into the mountains. Nothing unusual. No sightings of the car the Londoners left in. And there's something else."

At his grim tone, I braced myself. "What?"

"I put some pressure on a guy with access at the airport here. Three men booked tickets together from Zagreb to Split at the last minute yesterday morning. Under different names, but they've used covert tactics in the past. You thought they might be focusing on Split, didn't you?"

"Yes," I muttered. "Before I heard them talking about their travel plans the other night. Fuck. You know what it is? They found the bug, and they decided to jerk us around like we've jerked them."

Garrett's notepad hadn't been specific enough to tip me off. He'd jotted down information that I guessed must have come from conversations with various police officials here, but he'd been looking into thefts and similar crimes all along the coastal mountains. There'd been a few more pages devoted to the Split area than to Zadar, but it hadn't been totally unbelievable they might have found out something else that had tipped them the other way.

I let out a growl of frustration. Bash gave a dry chuckle. "How should we pay them back, Mori?"

"I need to know what they were doing in Split. They might have found the place already. If they stick their noses any more into this situation…"

Bash diplomatically avoided reminding me that I was the one who'd pointed the trio toward a possible mountain-side commune in the first place. "We'll find a way to redirect them."

"Yes, yes." I glared at the ceiling, and the ping of an incoming text on one of my other phones carried from my purse. I reached for it, and my eyebrows jumped up. "Well, isn't this interesting. Inspector Detective Lestrade just reached out. They want me to come by their hotel for a chat."

Bash made a skeptical noise. "I don't like the sound of that. Either they want something out of you, or they think they've got something on you."

"I might as well play ball to see what they're up to. One can hope they'll have their guard down a bit if I seem to be cooperating by coming to them. Are you in your spot near the hotel?"

"I've got eyes on the lobby and the audio coming through."

"All right. I'll tell them I'll meet them in the lobby, and I'll stay close to the windows once I get there. On the off-chance I should need backup, I'll signal you."

"I'll be watching."

I texted Garrett with the lobby suggestion. He agreed readily enough. I studied the phone for a moment longer, debating calling him up just to hear the tone of his voice. The written word was such an opaque medium.

Well, I'd get an even better read on the three of them in person. It wasn't as if they could be arranging to arrest me or anything that involved. Even if they had found the commune of the shrouded dagger, they couldn't have connected the place to anything I'd done, since I'd never been near the place. At this point they might know more about it than I did.

I hadn't even eaten breakfast yet, so I ordered room service and took a quick shower, and then downed eggs and pastries while pulling on a simple smock dress that gave me plenty of room to maneuver. I hadn't made any promises about exactly *when* I'd meet Garrett and the others.

By the time I reached their hotel lobby, the trio was already standing near the elevators. Too tight a spot for my tastes. I ambled along the broad front window where Bash would have a view of us and waited for the three men to come to me.

Sherlock swiveled, revealing a padded plastic brace around his foot and a crutch tucked under his arm. As he made his way over with a swaying gait, something in my chest twisted. Had those perverse bastards managed to hurt him while he was just poking around? I'd wring all their psychopathic necks on my way to that dagger.

But I wasn't supposed to know where they'd been or even that they'd left town. Better to let them think they had me fooled a little longer.

I cocked my head as they reached me. "What happened to you? A little too much breaking and entering?"

Sherlock gave me a thin smile. His expression struck me as cooler than usual. "I never *break* and enter," he said. "It's hardly my fault if a door just happens to open for me."

I restrained myself from rolling my eyes. John looked more tense than usual too, which I'd have put down to concern over Sherlock's injury if it had been the only change. Garrett had his hands slung in his pockets, his mouth set in a scowl, but that was pretty standard from him these days. He probably wasn't all that happy about the stolen notepad.

I glanced around the little semi-circle they'd formed. "I'm here. What important matters did you need to discuss?"

"I think this is the sort of conversation it'd be better not to have in public," John said. "Come up to our rooms?"

A warning prickle crept up my spine. "No, that's all right, I'm perfectly happy here," I said. "Or we could head down the street to Franjo's. I did just eat, but I can always find room for a little extra dessert."

Sherlock shifted to the side. If he hadn't been on the damned crutch, I might have marked the movement faster, but my first instinct was to assume he was simply adjusting his balance. The next second, the blunt metal muzzle of a gun pressed into my back, just below my shoulder blades. Right where a bullet could shatter through my ribs to puncture my heart.

John rapped his walking stick against the ground in additional warning. Garrett's expression tightened even more.

"We're going to the elevators," Sherlock said in a flat, measured voice that had more steel to it than I'd ever heard before, "or the three of us will be carrying out the rest of this investigation without any assistance from the late Jemma Moriarty. Are we clear?"

My pulse stuttered. I hadn't pictured this possibility, and if I had, I'd have said they'd never have been fully committed, that they'd have been bluffing enough that I could have slipped their grasp with a few well-placed blows and a fast dash.

There was no bluff at all in Sherlock's tone or the others' eyes. No hint of the desire I'd managed to stir in them before. If I played this wrong, the man at my side would kill me, clean and simple.

What the hell had happened yesterday to harden them like this?

It was my fucking fault for underestimating them. I should have watched my back better; I should have read their mood faster. I shouldn't have let myself get so damned cocky.

I wasn't alone, though. I gave a slight nod and turned toward the elevators, splaying my hand against the side of my purse where it'd be visible through the window.

Bash would follow. Between the two of us, we'd get me out of this mess.

"This is a rather different reception than you've generally given me," I said as we marched across the lobby, Garrett falling in behind me to block anyone else from seeing Sherlock's gun. "Would someone like to fill me in on why you feel this is necessary?"

Garrett guffawed roughly. "Give it a little thought, and I'm sure you can think of a few dozen reasons."

His pocket rustled with a metallic rasp. As the elevator door hummed closed, he tugged my arms back behind me.

Panic flashed through me. I dropped my purse and jabbed out with a knee, an elbow, not thinking, just drawing on years of physical training.

Those years might have given me the upper hand against one of those men, but three—it was a desperate gamble. My heel smacked Sherlock's calf just above his ankle brace. He hissed, but he stayed on his feet, shoving me hard against the elevator wall with the muzzle of the gun digging deep. John let out a grunt from the impact of my elbow, but he wrenched my hand back into Garrett's grasp. His walking stick shot up to jab my throat.

The solid bite of a pair of handcuffs clicked around my wrists. I jerked back from John's stick, my throat aching where he'd hit me. "What the *fuck*?" I sputtered.

"We've become better acquainted with the full extent of your criminal activities," Sherlock said. "I'm afraid it no longer seems wise to let you roam around freely."

"So, what? You're going to chain me up in your hotel room like a dog?" I summoned the composure I'd momentarily lost and twisted my head to catch Sherlock's gaze. "Maybe you get off on that idea."

A flicker of discomfort crossed his face, but the gun didn't waver. "Believe me, I don't take any pleasure from this at all."

John scooped up my purse as the elevator stopped at their floor. They hustled me off and escorted me straight to their suite.

"I'd still like to know what it is you're expecting to get out of doing this," I said. "You obviously don't have any grounds to arrest me, or you'd be taking me to the police."

Sherlock pushed open the door. "I don't trust the local law enforcement to take a deft enough hand with your dealings. You might improve your situation by talking to us. When we've seen where you stand, you can be assured you'll be delivered to the appropriate authorities."

"For what? What do you think I've done? Isn't there some rule about informing people what you're arresting them for?"

"We're not arresting you," Garrett said. "We're just asking some questions."

John pawed through my purse and came up with a single phone —a new burner I hadn't used yet. I'd at least been wary enough not to cart all my devices to this meeting. "There's nothing on here," he said to Sherlock, who made a dismissive gesture.

They'd been set up for this capture. The three of them ushered me through the living area into Sherlock's bedroom, where a wooden chair was already poised by the foot of the bed. The covers lay neatly tucked and a hint of tobacco laced the air, just like when I'd snuck in here two days ago. Otherwise everything felt totally different. The taste of blood lingered in my mouth, sharp and metallic, from biting my lip when Sherlock had shoved me in the elevator.

Garrett pushed me into the chair. The hard back jarred against my spine. He secured the chain of the handcuffs to a wooden rung with a plastic restraint. I sat there awkwardly, my calves braced against the chair's legs, an uncomfortable burn already pinching the muscles in my shoulders.

I sought out John's eyes. Of the three, he'd always had the softest touch. He'd warmed up to me first and resisted me the least.

"You can't really think this is okay. It's not as if I've hurt anyone." Recently, anyway.

He dropped his gaze. "We don't know that," he said stiffly.

The others had stepped back to stand in a slightly looser semi-circle than they'd formed around me downstairs. Sherlock stood in the middle, right in front of me, his pistol still clutched in his free hand. He leaned his weight on his crutch. I had the urge to suggest he get himself a chair too, but mouthing off at him in his current state didn't strike me as all that wise.

"The first part is simple," he said. "We've seen indications that you're not working entirely for yourself but under the duress of a higher power. Tell us who has given you orders or directed your activities, however they have, and we may be able to end this unfortunate confrontation right now."

I glared at him. "I don't work for anyone. I don't take orders. When I meet a 'higher power,' I hand it its ass."

"All right. Then what orders have you given to your group operating out of the mountains near Split."

If he expected me to look shocked that he'd figured that out, I didn't see any point in giving him the satisfaction. "I don't know what you're talking about. What are they doing that you're all up in arms about?"

The three men exchanged a glance. Fucking shrouded folk. Fucking cult. The trio had obviously seen or heard *something* out there yesterday that had shifted me in their minds from tempting shades of gray to pure menace to society. What were those deluded assholes up to other than protecting their beloved dagger?

"There's no way she doesn't know," Garrett said.

"I concur." Sherlock shifted his cool blue gaze back to me. "From the time I've spent in your presence, I can't believe you wouldn't be keeping strict control over any operations carried out on your behalf."

If they wouldn't tell me what the problem was, I couldn't explain it away. I might end up telling them more than I wanted to at the same time. I dragged in a breath, and the air conditioner thrummed on. With that sound, the bedroom door eased open just an inch, so smoothly none of the men facing me noticed.

My spirits leapt. Bash had made it. I had to give him an opening, had to turn this situation around so we could break me out of it.

My fingers shifted against the back of the chair, feeling for where I could grip it. Even attached to my rear, it could make an effective weapon if I swung it well. All I needed was to batter my way through the trio to the door, and then it'd be Bash's gun against Sherlock's. A fair stand-off.

"I think you've been talking to the wrong people," I said to buy myself a little more time as I readied for my charge. "I can't think of anything I've done or ordered done that should be such a shock to you after what you already knew. Nothing worse than what you're doing to me right now, so I guess that makes you a bunch of hypocrites."

"Nothing worse—are you joking?" Garrett snapped. He motioned to Sherlock. "She isn't going to say anything. This is pointless. We should just arrange to turn her over and figure out the rest on our own."

"Turn me over?" I said. "I still haven't heard how you're going to accomplish that."

Sherlock stepped closer and crouched down in front of me. Too close for me to whip my chair around without him catching the signs and stopping me before I could land a real blow. My fingers tightened around the rungs I'd gripped. The second he stepped back—

"By proving you're in possession of not one but multiple stolen artifacts," he said, and tugged the skirt of my dress high enough to reveal the gold cuff. He met my eyes pointedly. "I did some more research. You have four major thefts on your rap sheet just with this."

John mumbled a curse behind him. My bared skin tingled with the cooling air. The blood vessels around the cuff showed starkly through my flesh, as if my thigh was starting to turn as translucent as my fingers had the other day.

He reached for it, and my heart stopped.

"Don't touch it!" I said, instinctively jerking back in the chair. The movement sent a pulse of pain up my bound arms.

Sherlock ignored my protest. His fingers slid along the cuff searching for a connective seam. "We need it disassembled so we can confirm each stolen item with the original owners."

My chest constricted so abruptly I couldn't breathe. The second he detached that thing, Bog would sense my presence, no matter where in its world the shrouded one was. It would descend on me like the demonic fiend it was and shred my soul. In one instant, everything I'd done, everything I'd fought for, would shatter.

I whipped up my foot, catching Sherlock in the jaw. He reeled back, his gun hand jerked up, and in that instant I knew there were two ways this could go. I could die in a pool of blood or a shrouded one's gullet, or I could scream and bring Bash blasting in, taking all three of the men around me down.

My blood or theirs.

My throat clenched around the scream. I didn't want either of those choices. But Bash didn't wait for more than the sounds of scuffle he'd already heard. The door slammed open.

The words broke from my mouth. "No! No, Bash, don't."

My hitman halted on the threshold, his hand quivering as if it'd taken a concentrated effort to hold himself back from squeezing the trigger. Garrett and John jerked out of the way, John fumbling a pistol out of his own pocket. Sherlock's head jerked around to take in the new arrival. He kept his gun aimed at my head.

"I can still take them, Mori," Bash said, his voice raw. "Piece of cake."

"No," I said again. The decision I'd made without much chance to think it over reverberated through me. I dragged in a breath. "I don't want them dead. They're just doing their job." Too fucking well.

He grimaced. "Fine. But if anyone shoots her, she won't be able to tell me to stand down anymore, so you'd better be ready to lose your own life over that choice."

"Who the hell are you?" Garrett said, braced as if he wanted to fight but didn't know how to start. As the only man in the room not holding a firearm, he couldn't be blamed for a little uncertainty.

Bash didn't answer.

"He's the guy who would have killed all three of you if I hadn't stopped him," I said, managing to keep my voice steady. "That's not how I want to leave this room. Please don't make me regret it."

Garrett let out a choked sound. "So you'll kill kids, but we're somehow exempt?"

"Who said anything about killing *kids*?" I said, my gut wrenching, and then I knew with a punch of cold right through my chest. The shrouded folk and their brutal rituals, their sadistic ideas of fun. They hadn't been quite discrete enough down near Split.

My whole body tensed. I'd like to strangle the fiends—and then rip their misty heads from their bodies and dropkick them off a cliff.

Too bad that might not even hurt them.

Sherlock looked back at me, at the rage that must have crossed my face, and his own cold expression faltered with a hint of uncertainty. His hand adjusted its grip on the gun, and Bash cleared his throat.

"Get that thing away from her head, *now*."

Sherlock eased back, groping for the crutch he'd set down. My gaze slid from him to Garrett and John standing rigid at opposite ends of the room, then to Bash in the doorway between us. What an epic mess I'd made. And if I didn't want it to still end up with a whole lot of blood on the floor, I was going to have to talk my way out of it.

I'd decided the trio's lives were worth something. Worth enough to trust that they wouldn't take mine. Why should I even care?

Because they were different. Because out of all the people I'd dealt with, bargained with, or conned, they were the only ones I'd ever met who I could believe might put a greater cause than themselves over their own desires when the chips were down. Because the world was already a shitty place, and while I was happy to make use of that, I didn't want to be the one to make it even worse.

Because in their own small ways, they'd made me happy.

They'd found the commune anyway. It wasn't as if they could screw me over *more* than they were right now.

"You found a group of people in the mountains near Split yesterday," I said. "They seem to be associated with some kids dying?"

The trio didn't react. Sherlock straightened up with his crutch, his gun partly lowered but still at the ready.

"You think I orchestrated that somehow," I went on. "And that's fair. I *wanted* you to think the commune was part of my business. I wanted you to find them, because it was taking me too damn long to do it myself. I don't work with them. I'm planning on stopping them. I just had to figure out where the hell they were first."

"That's a little difficult to believe," John said quietly.

"Is it?" I focused on Sherlock. "I found your little tracking device, hidden in your doctored sugar cube. I went to that transport company with weird requests on purpose. I 'set up' a meeting for one of you to overhear. You didn't discover my plans. I fed false ones to you, just like you did to me yesterday with your little trip. Do you have *any* other proof that I'm connected to the commune? You haven't come across a single shred of evidence that I didn't hand to you, have you? Because there isn't any."

I could practically see the gears turning in the detective's head. His gun hand bobbed down a few inches further. "And you handed us that information because you wanted us to find the 'commune' for you?"

"Yes. I'd already been scouting around for them for weeks when you three turned up. I figured with your smarts and resources you could fast-track the process, and then I'd reap the rewards."

"What rewards are those?" Garrett asked, his tone skeptical. "What does it matter to you what these people are doing if you don't have any connection to them?"

I sat up a little straighter in my chair. "I didn't say I'm not connected to them. I know... people like them. They're part of a larger organization—a sort of cult. I know the kind of horrors they celebrate, and it makes me sick. They have something I need, something that'll help me take down not just them but everyone like them."

"So, this is all selfless generosity?" John said with his eyebrow slightly raised.

"No," I admitted. "It's also self-preservation. If I don't get the thing I need from them, I'm probably going to die. Maybe not for another few months, maybe as soon as one. I've got a chain you can't see dragging me down, and they have my only chance at severing it."

Bash's expression tensed where he was still braced in the doorway. I hadn't told him that much. I'd have delivered the revelation more gently if I'd had the time.

"What is this thing you need?" Sherlock asked.

He'd never believe the story about the dagger. I improvised. "Their people poisoned me with a slow acting toxin. They cultivate an incredibly rare plant there that'll serve as an antidote."

He studied me for a long moment. He'd seen me under the effects of the cuff's powers at least once. I knew from my glance in the mirror this morning that I was looking paler than usual overall. Bog's claim on me and the aura that protected me from the shrouded one might as well have been a poison.

Whatever Sherlock was looking for, my explanation appeared to convince him. He gestured toward the room at large. "Why are you telling us this now?"

"Because it seems to be either that or watch Bash put a bullet in your brain," I said. "And it turns out I like that brain of yours enough that I don't want to see it splattered on a wall. What would be the good in that? We both want those assholes on the mountain to stop all the shit they're up to. I'll get us in there without them killing us first, you take them down, arrest them, shoot them—I don't fucking care—and let me get what I need, and we all come out ahead."

"We don't know that a single word she's saying is true," Garrett protested.

Sherlock sighed. "Yes, we do. I did plant a tracker on her that I contrived to disguise in a sugar cube. We did manage to hear about her plans in very convenient ways. We haven't seen any evidence that she already knew the whereabouts of this commune, let alone that she had any control over their activities." He paused. "And from the bearing of our friend at the door, I have no doubt we *would* all be dead if Jemma preferred we were out of the way."

The hostility in Garrett's stance deflated.

"As far as I can see it, it's pretty simple," I said. "You can stop them, or you can stop me. If they're the ones you have the bigger problem with…"

Sherlock's mouth twisted. He looked at Bash. "You follow her orders, I take it."

Bash smiled grimly. "Even when it would give me plenty of satisfaction not to."

The detective tossed his gun on the bed. "Then I assume if the three of us retire unarmed to the other room to discuss how we'd like to proceed, we can count on our heads staying intact?"

"Yes," I said firmly, and Bash nodded.

"Sherlock," John said.

His friend motioned to him. "We were mistaken. We need to reevaluate the situation. I think, given the circumstances and the faith shown in us, we can offer faith a little in return."

John hesitated a second longer and then set his gun on the bed next to Sherlock's.

"Phones too," Bash said. "I don't want to see you making any calls to the police."

"Fair enough." Sherlock fished out his and set it down, and the other two followed in turn. Bash stepped to the side so they could file out into the living area. They gathered around the table and started talking in voices too low for me to make out.

Bash stayed on the threshold, his gaze sliding between them and me. "Are you all right?"

"I've been in more comfortable seats in my life, but it appears I'll survive."

He glowered at me. "I don't think you should be joking about that right now."

"Sorry. I should have been more careful in the first place." I paused. "Thank you for coming to my rescue."

The corner of Bash's mouth quirked up at the wry note I'd let creep into my voice. "My pleasure to be of service, Majesty." He eyed the trio again. "Are you really sure we can't just get rid of them?"

"Yes," I said. "As obnoxious as they've been for the last half hour, I was the one who gave them the idea I was in charge of the damned commune in the first place."

"A little personal responsibility never stopped you from clearing the way before," Bash remarked.

Before I could answer that, the trio returned.

"We have a few conditions," Sherlock said. He strode past the bed to his suitcase, where he retrieved what looked like a thin silver bracelet. "Namely, we want some guarantee that you'll keep to your word. An associate of mine at Cambridge designed this. It's a subtle version of ankle monitor. He thought I might have opportunity to try it out. We'll know your whereabouts—or know if you break it to remove it. This goes on, the handcuffs come off."

I could accept that. I shifted my arms. "Well, get on with it then."

"You'll share everything you know about the commune with us?" John said.

"If you're going to use it to take them down, absolutely."

Sherlock snapped the bracelet into place around my wrist, feeding one end into the other until it was tight enough that I couldn't wriggle it off.

Garrett came over and cut the tie holding the handcuffs to the back of the chair. He hesitated beside me as I stood up. "The key for the cuffs is in my room. I'll go—"

"I'll come with you," I interrupted. "And Bash too, to make sure you do find that key." I studied him and then the other two men. "Are you all on board with this temporary alliance? You don't have any lingering doubts that I'm a child-murdering psychopath? I'd rather avoid being shoved around like this again in the near future."

John's gaze settled on my throat. I could tell from the twinge when I swallowed that a bruise was forming where he'd hit me. "I'm sorry," he said. "It was a defensive reflex. I'm all for an alliance if you are."

"It's fine," I told him. "At least you didn't jab a gun into my back."

"That was a reasonable reaction given the information we had at the time," Sherlock said with a lift of his chin. "A reaction I've adjusted in light of new information."

I gave him a thin smile. "I've decided I'll forgive you."

Garrett just stood there with his hands jammed into his pockets, his gaze wary. He didn't protest the alliance, anyway. I could feel him out one-on-one.

I turned back to Sherlock. "I'm a little shaken up by this whole adventure, and I could use a few hours to assemble the details I have. You know I'm not going far." I tipped my head toward his tracking bracelet. "Meet me at my hotel this afternoon—let's say two—and we'll go over what we all know? Or would you rather talk here?"

"Let's say here," Sherlock said, his eyes glinting. "And I expect you to be prompt."

CHAPTER FIFTEEN

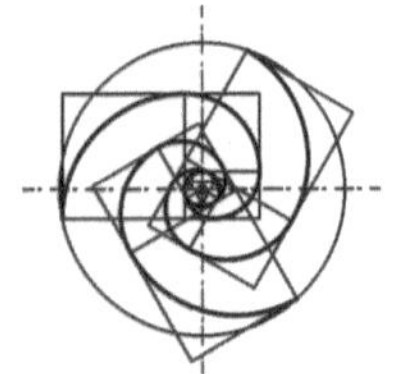

Jemma

On our way out of the suite, I glanced toward the purse John had left on the dining table. "Can you grab that for me, Bash?"

He caught the leather strap without a word. Garrett watched him with particular attention to the pistol still poised in my hitman's grasp.

Bash gave the detective inspector a particularly unfriendly glower. "Let's get on with getting that key."

He held the gun close to his side as we crossed the hall, but no one came out to notice us anyway. My mind flashed back to the massacre I'd pictured in Sherlock's bedroom, and my stomach turned.

If I'd let Bash blow the three of them away, the scene might not have looked so different from the gory hallucination Bog had forced into my head back in London.

Depending on how well the trio played along, my plans might have just become ten times more complicated. I couldn't say I regretted the choice I'd made, though. I was a liar and a criminal, but I wasn't a monster. A person had to have *some* standards.

Garrett's room was a much simpler affair than Sherlock and John's suite: a bed, an armchair, and a dresser that held a small flat screen TV. The accordion blind was pulled down over the window.

He punched a code into the safe in the closet and retrieved a small key. His thumb slid over the inside of my wrist as he moved to unlock the handcuffs, and a shiver traveled up my arm that wasn't entirely unpleasant. I might have suggested he leave the cuffs on a little longer for the conversation we were about to have if I hadn't known there was no way Bash would leave me like that.

The cuffs clicked free. I pulled my arms around in front of me and rubbed the reddened skin. Garrett's mouth slanted in a way that looked vaguely repentant and vaguely disgruntled by that repentance.

"It's all right," I told him. "You did what you had to do."

Bash snorted. "And he can stew about it while you get your bearings again."

He set a protective hand on my upper arm, but I clasped it and eased it away. "I think I should stay and talk with Garrett a bit," I said, holding Bash's gaze. "We have some unfinished business. I'm all right now. You can wait downstairs for me if you want."

Bash frowned. "Mori..." He didn't quite want to overtly argue with me, but he didn't want to accept the suggestion either.

I turned to Garrett. "Should I be worried for my life or safety in your presence?"

The slant of his mouth shifted into half a smile, even if it was a tight one. "Don't reveal that you're actually a child murderer after all, and I think we'll make it through one conversation unscathed."

Bash exhaled roughly, but he bobbed his head to me and handed me my purse. "You know what you're doing," he said, managing to sound as if he really did mean that without any *I hope* tacked in front.

He went out, his footsteps fading as he headed down the hall. Garrett set the handcuffs on top of the safe. His gaze skimmed over me as if searching for something.

"You're really dying?" he said.

Oh, yes, I had mentioned that, hadn't I? "Not if I have any say in it," I said, spreading my hands. "These people can be vicious, as you've obviously already found out."

"Does it… hurt? The poison?" A flicker of concern passed through his eyes despite his stiff tone.

"A little," I said honestly, other than the fact that the problem wasn't a literal poison. "I'm managing. If we can get to the commune in the next few days, it'll never be more than a little discomfort." Relative to what I'd face if Bog caught up with me, anyway.

That wasn't what I wanted to talk about, though. I reached into my purse, detached the false bottom, and pulled out Garrett's notepad from the narrow compartment there. "I figured I should give this back. Since we're allies and all for now."

"I suppose we are," he said, not sounding all that convinced, but he accepted the pad and flicked through it briefly as if checking to see if I'd defaced it somehow.

"You doodle a lot," I remarked. "I think quite a few of these drawings are me."

That tight smile came back. He tucked the notepad into his pocket. "I think you know you make a striking visual, Jemma. Why did you tell Bash to take off? Do we really need a repeat of the conversation when you stole that?"

"I was hoping for something a little better."

He sat down on the edge of the bed, watching me. "Why don't you start then?"

He might have been a physically smaller man than his two colleagues, but his presence was plenty potent. Garrett Lestrade had worked his way up through the ranks at Scotland Yard faster than any man his age. He'd managed to impress Sherlock despite his adherence, until recently, to the word of the law.

And there was still a little anger burning in those dark brown eyes when he looked at me.

I believed that Sherlock and John would stick to our deal for the next little while, as long as I didn't do anything epically stupid.

Garrett, on the other hand… Something in him was still raw and sore. I needed to know that anger wasn't going to spark at the wrong moment and burn me.

It was possible I also wanted to know that I *could* douse that anger. That he wouldn't always think of me as the woman who'd brought out the worst in him.

I propped myself against the wall a few feet away from him and felt for the right words.

"I'm sorry. I didn't really say that before, did I?"

Surprise darted across Garrett's face—and vanished into suspicion. "Do you mean it?"

"About working that scheme in London? No. But I didn't mean to hurt you as badly as I obviously did, and I don't enjoy seeing it." I couldn't help making a face. "Do I really seem to you like someone who'd kill a child—or ask someone else to?"

"I don't know, Jemma," Garrett said, sounding weary. "We don't really know you at all. For all I can tell, we could be falling deeper into the rabbit hole with this 'alliance' rather than finding our way back out. Hell, Jemma isn't even really your name, is it?"

"Actually, it is. I was born Jemma Marie Moriarty."

He raised his eyebrows at me. "I'm supposed to believe you gave us your real name back when you were only around to con us?"

I shrugged. "I wasn't sure I was going to make it out of London alive. Maybe it was vanity, but I liked the idea that someone other than Bash would know Jemma Moriarty existed—someone who might appreciate how much I'd accomplished even if they didn't approve of it—if my run ended there."

Garrett stared at me for a second. Then he tipped his head back with a groan. "I don't know when to trust my instincts around you. You lied so easily before."

"What reason do I have to lie now?"

"I don't know. Because you want to be sure I won't screw you over?"

That guess was close enough to the truth to make my skin twitch. I wasn't lying, though.

"There are easier stories I could tell you," I said. "Stories you'd be more likely to believe. Stories you'd want to hear more. Would it make you feel better if I said that you were the only one of the three of you it was hard to leave behind?"

A hint of longing crossed his face before he caught it. He studied me again. "You know it would—if *that* was true. But it's not, is it?"

"No," I said. "That's what I mean. I'm trying to make peace with you here, not play a game. If I had a game in mind, this isn't how I'd play it. All right?"

"What is the truth, then? How do you feel about me—about any of us?"

A lump rose in my throat with the words. It felt like cutting open my skin and displaying my nerves, admitting this. But it was what he needed.

"I ended up liking all of you more than I should. More than I've liked just about anyone. Which may not be a lot compared to the average person, but… I should have been annoyed when you three showed up here to get in my way, and I was, but I was also stupidly glad to have you around again, as ridiculous as that might sound."

Garrett's voice dropped. "It doesn't sound all that ridiculous." The skepticism in his eyes hadn't totally faded, though. He curled his fingers around the edge of the bed. "What's one thing you like about me, then?"

That question wasn't at all hard to answer. I smiled as I trailed my hand over the faint rippling of paint on the wall. "You have that drive to be the best—to be better than everyone around you—but you have it under control. You make the urge work *for* you instead of you working for it."

Garrett gave a startled laugh. "Not always. I've let it ride me more times than I'd like to admit. I'm not any paragon of self-control."

I waved his objection away. "When is anyone absolutely perfect at anything? You found a middle ground. You leveraged that drive into being spectacular at your career. I—" I paused. "The way I grew up, we were raised to jockey for a spot at the top, no matter who it hurt. No matter what it cost. You weren't worth anything unless you could prove yourself." Prove that the highest among the shrouded folk would deem you a delectable meal, it'd turned out.

"When I got out of there, I learned pretty quickly that I couldn't trust that impulse in myself," I went on. "I have no sense of when to rein it in. I have to focus on practicalities and numbers and facts, or it'll lead me away from my goals. You turned the same feeling into fuel to get you where you wanted to go. I think I'm allowed to like that."

"I've never really thought about it like that. As something good." Garrett hesitated. "No one pushed me to feel that way when I was a kid, but I had three older brothers who were all 'better' in pretty much every way, and I don't think my parents really knew what to do with me. I did some rotten things when I was younger, thinking I was just evening the playing field. It got… bad. I couldn't stand to keep going like that. I've turned it around as well as I can."

"And look at you now," I said teasingly with a gesture to myself. "Tracking down master criminals all across the world."

The smile he gave me in return was a little more relaxed in its wryness. "Bringing said master criminals to justice is another matter."

"Oh, maybe you'll catch me yet."

Silence settled between us for a moment, me by the wall and him on the bed. Something shifted in his expression.

"I haven't been able to stop thinking about you," he said quietly. "Even after we realized how you played us. It's hard to trust you when I know that I want to in spite of all available evidence."

The admission tugged at some part of my heart I hadn't known still worked. "Maybe you don't have to trust me," I suggested. "Maybe this can just be whatever it is, and if I fuck up enough, you can toss me behind bars and throw away the key, but until then… until then we take what's in each moment as it comes."

"I don't know."

He didn't look angry anymore, but the pain hadn't completely vanished. I didn't know what to do with that. Maybe I'd gotten as far as I could.

I straightened up, nudging myself off the wall. "Look. I have no agenda right now, in this moment. I still owe you a night. We can make it a morning instead if you want. You call the shots. Get me out of your system. It's up to you. I'll walk out of the room while you think about it so you can be sure I'm not working some kind of voodoo on you. Just don't leave me hanging too long or the housekeeping staff will chase me off."

I didn't wait to try to prompt an immediate answer. I grabbed my purse and went right out. In the brighter lights of the hall, with the door clicking shut behind me, my breath came out in a rush.

When was the last time I'd talked that openly with anyone? I wasn't sure I had ever—not since Olivia. Not even with Bash. I hadn't told Garrett anything he could use against me, but waiting to see what he'd do, my innards seemed to have twisted together.

It was all right. Even if this interlude didn't go any farther—it was all right. He wasn't angry anymore, at least.

I was starting to consider that maybe I should just leave when the door jerked open. Garrett blinked at me as if he hadn't really expected me to still be there. He wet his lips. Then he eased back to make room. "Come in?"

My heart thumped with anticipation as I stepped back inside. Garrett flipped the security latch over. He turned to face me, close enough that the heat of his body grazed my skin.

"Just this once," he said with a rasp in his voice. "To get it out of my system."

"Nothing wrong with that," I said.

He touched my cheek, his fingertips gliding over it and into my hair. "How should we do this?"

"You were supposed to get Jemma Moriarty the rising star of the Friesing Police Department. I can give you her if you want."

He shook his head. "I want Jemma Moriarty, criminal mastermind. How does she fuck?"

I grinned. "To tell you the truth, she liked the desk quite a bit. Two thumbs up."

"Well, then..." He led me into the main part of the room. "No desk this time, but there is this handy dresser."

He shoved the TV over to the far end so we had plenty of room and rested his hand on my hip as I hopped up. The way he'd talked, I'd expected a quick wham-bang-thank-you-ma'am, not so different from our first encounter. Instead he leaned in slowly to catch my mouth with his.

He kissed me at a measured pace, not touching me otherwise except the circle of his thumb over my hipbone and his fingers steady in my hair. When I ran my hands down his chest, he deepened the kiss with a pleased hum.

Hunger welled up inside me at the heat of his mouth, the crackling electric smell of him filling my nose. Every lingering shift of his lips, as if he were absorbing all the pleasure he could from each simple sensation, left my nerves quivering eagerly.

I teased my tongue across the seam of his mouth. He nudged closer and tugged me to him at the same time, his groin settling flush between my legs. The bulge of his erection sent a fresh wave of exhilaration through me. I couldn't help rocking into him as he opened his mouth so our tongues could dance.

"You feel so fucking good already, Firecracker," he murmured, ducking his head to kiss my neck next, careful of the forming bruise.

I sighed in agreement, grinding against him harder until he groaned. He slid my dress up my thighs and tugged it over my head, making quick work of my bra while he reclaimed my mouth. Our tongues slicked together as I ran my fingers through his tawny hair. I couldn't hold back the motion of my hips. *That* felt fucking good. The friction of his jeans through my panties already had me soaking.

Garrett caressed my breasts with both hands and then held me more firmly in place to lower his mouth to one. I tipped my head back against the wall as his lips closed around the nipple and sucked hard.

A gasp shuddered out of me. Pleasure raced through my chest with each lap of his tongue. He devoured me with the intentness of a man enjoying his last meal.

Bliss was building between my thighs too. I grasped Garrett's shoulder, lost between his mouth on my breast and his cock still three layers of fabric away from where I wanted it to be. I couldn't remember the last time I'd come from nothing but contact through clothes, but oh —fuck —

The orgasm caught me like a wave from my core. I arched against Garrett, and he yanked my mouth to his again. We kissed and kissed again, until I was losing myself in that sensation too.

My hunger wasn't sated yet, and I couldn't believe he was anywhere close to satisfied either. I fumbled with his shirt, and he yanked it off. We collided again, his bare chest searing hot against mine, the urgency I'd remembered coming back into his kiss.

I flicked open the button of his fly, and he shed his jeans, groaning when I gripped his cock through his boxers. I rubbed it against me as our kisses grew sloppier, our breath ragged.

He wrenched off my panties. I snatched a condom from my purse and shoved it into his hand. With a rough chuckle, he dropped his boxers and prepared himself. Then he kissed me again, stroking my breast, massaging my hip, until I growled insistently.

"You want this?" he said, running the head of his cock over my opening.

"Yes. Please. Fuck me."

The last word had barely left my lips when he thrust inside me. I couldn't hold back a moan.

Maybe that was what he needed to know more than anything else —that I wanted *him*, that this meant at least a little more to me than mashing genitals with any decently good-looking man who happened to be in the vicinity.

"Garrett," I mumbled around a hitch of breath. He plunged into me even deeper, and I dug my fingernails into his shoulder at the burst of pleasure. "Just like that. Please, Garrett."

At the plea and his repeated name, his thrusts turned wilder. His lips pressed against my jaw and then the side of my neck with a nick of teeth. His cock hit the most sensitive spot inside me. I cried out, arching up to meet him. He hammered into me, and I hung on through the surge of ecstasy that swept over me and crashed with a shimmer of stars behind my eyes.

"Jemma," Garrett muttered. He came with a choked sound,

holding me tight. Before the impact had even quite rippled from his body, he drew me into one last kiss.

The kiss went on and on, oddly gentle after the last frantic pounding of our coming together, but perfectly sweet. *Just this once,* I found myself thinking. *To get it out of his system.*

I didn't know what to do with the pang of mourning that came with that thought.

CHAPTER SIXTEEN

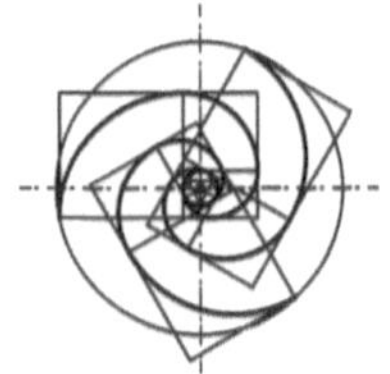

Jemma

Even though I'd encouraged Bash to pick a hotel as nice as mine, he'd gone with an older, more modest building a couple blocks outside of the downtown core. It had only eight rooms per floor, which meant it wasn't hard to tell that the woman just emerging into the hall was coming out of his.

I paused for a second on the worn carpet outside the elevator and then pushed myself to start walking again. The woman brushed past me without a hint of concern. Her bleached hair hung slightly damp from a recent shower, but the clothes on her skinny frame suggested a walk of shame — a little too rumpled to be fresh. I caught a whiff of orchid-and-amber perfume she must have recently reapplied, no doubt from that massive rhinestone studded purse.

A sharp-edged sensation wound through my gut. I waited until the woman had vanished onto the elevator before I knocked on Bash's door.

"Just a second," he called, and opened it shirtless with jeans slung low on his hips like he'd barely managed to tug them on. His blasé expression stuttered at the sight of me.

He'd thought the knock was his recent playmate coming back for something she'd forgotten.

"I see you had a good night," I said with a smile that formed a little stiffly. "Now put on a shirt, and we'll get down to work."

It wasn't that I objected to his bare chest per say. Bash's military training and the physical regimen he'd kept up since that time had bulked him out with an impressive array of muscle. The smooth light brown of his skin was broken here and there by darker scars that only added to the visual appeal.

Right now, though, the visual reminded me a little too starkly of running my hands over those muscles while he'd thrust inside me weeks ago. The memory mingling with the sight of the woman in the hall provoked a trickle of nausea.

I shouldn't be bothered by it. We were better as colleagues —*safer* as colleagues, with the rules cut and dried, knowing exactly what we could expect from each other. I'd never had an honest romantic relationship, open and giving without any ulterior motives, with anyone. It wasn't in me. I had no playbook for that.

Still, my gut stayed clenched as I sat down at the table by the window. The warm mid-morning sun streamed across two glasses and an empty bottle of whisky from the mini-bar. Crimson lipstick marked the rim of one of the glasses. I clamped down on the urge to toss it out the window and enjoy the smash of it shattering on the driveway below.

Bash yanked on a T-shirt that only partly disguised his impressive physique and sat down across from me, studying my face with what looked like wariness. "I didn't realize you'd come by this early."

Somehow both the fact that he was apologizing at all and the fact that he was apologizing in such a half-assed way irritated me beyond measure. I shoved the glasses to the side, maybe with a little more force than was necessary, and set my tablet in front of me.

"I'd like to move quickly now that Sherlock and the others know the score. The less time we're reliant on their goodwill, the better. Your contacts here who can get us military-grade equipment are still good, right?"

"Absolutely. I can reach out as soon as I know what we need."

"Good. I've got a list. Feel free to add anything else you think would help with a covert operation. The budget is no object. I'll need to get as close as possible to the village without them knowing I'm there—probably making use of some natural caves—and then I'll need to keep them diverted so I can get what I need."

"Which isn't any special plant," Bash said. "That whole story about you being poisoned—you made that up to get Sherlock off your back."

"Yes," I said. There wasn't any point in mentioning that my life was still on the line here. Bash couldn't do anything about that. "They have a dagger with supposed magical powers… If I'm lucky, it works as advertised. With that, I should be able to sever the pact I made, and none of those monsters will have any claim on me."

"Sounds good to me."

Bash leaned back in his chair. A hint of orchid-and-amber perfume reached my nose, and my gaze slid past him to the bed with its strewn covers. An image popped up in the back of my head of him bending over that woman there, fucking her the way he'd fucked me.

Sleeping next to her the way he'd slept next to me. The way I hadn't slept next to *any* other man I'd ever fucked.

Why should I expect that part to have meant anything to him? Pleasure and proximity and convenience—nothing more.

I jerked my attention back to my tablet. "We're moving to Split as soon as you have the equipment. It'll be easier to plan our approach from closer by. We'll need a truck or a van to transport everything, since we can't take the equipment by plane without raising some eyebrows. I was going to set us up in the same hotel this time for ease of communication, since we'll need to work together closely for most of this." I paused and glanced up at him. "Unless that would cramp your style."

He looked back at me evenly. "I don't think it'll be a problem."

"Good. And I trust you won't allow any of your extracurricular activities to interfere with our plans."

His jaw tightened at that remark. "Of course not. What we're doing is my first priority."

"Glad to hear it." I stood up abruptly. The jagged feeling inside me had twisted around too much. I didn't like it, and I didn't totally trust my own reactions.

More of that orchid-and-amber scent flooded my lungs as I inhaled. It was all too here, too in my face. A little distance, and I'd have my tangled emotions under control.

"I don't think there's anything else we need to talk about right now," I said. "I'll leave you to it—and whatever else you're occupying yourself with."

As I headed for the door, Bash pushed back his chair, its legs scraping against the tiled floor. "Mori."

"You know," I said without looking back, "you should probably stop calling me that. It's hardly professional."

I grasped the handle. Bash caught up with me at the same moment. He leaned his hand against the doorframe, not exactly blocking my exit—I might have taken a shot at breaking his *fingers* if he'd gone that far—but with the clear implication that he didn't want me leaving. "Jemma."

I looked up at him, willing myself not to glare. The only other time he'd used my first name was right before we'd fallen into bed together. "Moriarty works just fine. I'll even still accept 'Majesty' if you insist. I was on my way out."

"I'd rather you didn't leave angry."

"Who says I'm angry?" I said, with an edge creeping into my voice that I couldn't quite rein in.

His gaze bored into me. "We don't normally talk like this. I know you well enough to tell."

I sidestepped, folding my arms over my chest. "Well, you don't normally act like this." All the tiny details that had been irritating me collided in a surge of—all right, anger. The words burst out.

"I'm not stupid. I know you have your own needs, and I've assumed you fulfill them as it suits you. But in seven years, you've managed to keep that side of your life totally separate from anything we're doing. I've never seen even a hint of a fling. Somehow today, when you knew I'd be coming by, you just *happened* to have someone here, you let her spend the night, leave her scent all over the place, when we just—when I—" I cut myself off, swallowing thickly.

A shadow had crossed Bash's eyes. "You can't act as if I've done something wrong when just yesterday you told me to take a hike so you could put moves on the prince of Scotland Yard," he said. "You didn't hide that. Why the hell should you be jealous now?"

"It's not the same," I said, my throat constricting. "And this isn't about jealousy. Every man I've ever been with, it's been a means to an end, part of the business—except for you. You know that. I *told* you that. And then you... Tell me it's a total coincidence. Tell me you didn't want me to react. Can you? Because as far as I can tell, this wasn't a mistake. It was a low blow from the one person I trusted to have my back."

Bash winced. His hand fell from the doorframe, but I stayed where I was. I needed to hear his answer.

"Maybe you're right," he said after a minute, hoarsely. "I promise you it wasn't something I consciously planned, but I wasn't thinking —if I'd let myself think about it, this wouldn't have happened. I'm sorry. I've been trying not to let what happened between us change anything, but it's changed already, hasn't it?"

"What do you mean?"

"When you told me you wanted things to stay the way they'd been, you said that you didn't trust yourself to have that kind of relationship honestly. Because I meant something to you, and you didn't know how to handle that. But the Londoners, now... It's not just business with them. You have to admit that they mean something too—they mean enough that you risked your whole plan just to keep them alive!"

My chest clenched. "Bash," I started.

He shook his head. "Maybe I've been angry too. Because you're willing to trust yourself with them but not with me, even though I *am* the one who's always had your back. Unless it's really that you don't trust *me*."

I didn't know what to say to that. Part of me screamed to reach out to him, as if the feel of his skin against mine would somehow heal this rift, but the rest of me balked. I'd only end up complicating our relationship even more.

When he met my eyes again, his were less stormy. His voice came out quiet. "They still don't really know you. The first chance they had, they jumped to the worse possible conclusions about you. They're never going to appreciate how fucking brilliantly incredible you are. I do, so it's hard for me to watch, but that's my shit to handle. I'm sorry I let it affect our partnership."

"Okay." I dragged in a breath. "I'm sorry I didn't realize this was hard for you."

"You know that woman, and any others there've been like her, doesn't matter, right? I'd rather it was you."

I'd rather it'd been me too, but that didn't seem like a helpful thing to say when I wasn't going to follow it up by volunteering. "I don't know exactly what's different with Sherlock and the others," I said. "But even if something is—as soon as we're done here, I'm smashing this tracking bracelet and we're moving on without them. We'll cover our tracks even better. They'll give up on trying to follow soon enough. They're not going to matter either."

His lips twitched into a shade of a smile. "I guess I can grit my teeth for another few days then. And—I promise you won't have to see anything from that side of my life again."

I inclined my head in acknowledgment. "I'm sure I can manage to be more discrete too."

"It really isn't— I know you already have—"

"I'll do better," I said firmly. "Are we good?"

Bash nodded. "I am if you are."

"Then we're good," I said, willing that answer to be true. "And we still have work to do."

CHAPTER SEVENTEEN

John

Jemma crouched close to me and peered at the handheld screens I'd propped up in the back of the helicopter. "Are we getting any useful readings yet?" she asked over the roar of the blades.

"We might need to get a little closer," I said. "Are you worried that these people will get suspicious?"

"I think it'll be all right. They don't know anyone's looking for them." She leaned over to give a few instructions to the pilot whose chopper we'd hired and turned back to the screens. One was lighting up with a blotchy rainbow of bright colors; the other showed undulating bands of gray broken by paler lines. "Quite the set-up your army friends arranged for you."

I shifted against the padded but stiff seat to find an angle where I could study both images without my hip starting to ache. The helicopter dipped slightly, making my breath catch.

"I was lucky one of the fellows at the British embassy did time in Iraq," I said. "Although it's hard to say whether that got me the favor as much as the thought of being part of one of Sherlock's investigations. He has become awfully famous even among the expats. I'm not sure what the Croatian army made of the equipment request, but I guess they figured we couldn't do much harm with a couple of scanners."

"Oh, they of little faith," Jemma murmured.

My attention jerked to her face, but she was smiling in what looked like only amusement, nothing more malicious. Her gaze slipped away from the scanners to the landscape beyond the window, and even that faded. For a second, her brow knit. From the distance in her eyes, I didn't think it was anything here that was bothering her. She'd seemed a little distracted ever since she'd come to meet me for this venture.

I couldn't help looking at the bruise at the side of her throat, the previous purple now faded into a dull brown, where I'd smacked her with my walking stick just a few days ago.

It wasn't as if I couldn't do harm too.

"I got the impression you have some connections of your own, considering the haul you brought with you," I said. I hadn't gotten a close look at the contents of the van she'd driven down in with that associate of hers—Moran, he'd told us to call him in a brief exchange after we'd arrived in Split—but from a few of her comments since then, I'd gathered she expected to go into this commune well-equipped.

Jemma's focus came back to me, and she shrugged. "Maybe, with enough lead time, we could have come up with something like this—but close-range scanners wouldn't have done me much good before we had the location narrowed down. It's easier to find the simpler stuff on the black market anyway. There isn't a whole lot of demand for top-of-the-line infrared scanners among criminals like me." She glanced at me as if daring me to be offended, still smiling. "Why do you think I kept you around?"

That intent gaze sent a nervous shiver through my pulse and a jolt of lust to my groin at the same time. I couldn't forget that even if she'd spared our lives after we'd threatened to kill her, even if her intentions appeared to align with ours right now, she'd told me to my face how dangerous she was.

The trouble was, I also couldn't deny that walking the risky line of being around her appealed to me at least as much as it unnerved me.

"And what will you do with me when I outlive my usefulness?" I asked, mostly joking but with maybe a little genuine curiosity.

Her smile widened, and she gave my shoulder a playful shove. "Don't you worry about that. I've decided the world is better off with Dr. John Watson in it, so far be it from me to remove you."

From what she'd said about the poison she needed the antidote to, she might find herself removed from this world if we couldn't pull this mission off. It was becoming hard for me to imagine a world without Jemma Moriarty in it too, even if I wasn't going to admit that right now. Even if it was driving me barmy that she'd refused my offers to look into alternate treatments.

"How incredibly comforting," I said instead.

"Stop worrying about that and focus on all this fancy monitoring equipment." She motioned to the screens. "I get that 'hotter' colors means more heat. That's pretty simple. You said we should be able to use the radar system to figure out where the caves are? Do you even know how to read it?"

I squinted at the screen with the undulating lines. "The tech guy walked me through the basics. I think I should be able to recognize when we pass over any significant underground crevices. Look, right there!"

I waved toward a sharper jump along some of the lines. Jemma cocked her head and then peered out the helicopter window toward the ground. "You can get exact coordinates from that, I assume?"

"Yes, naturally. And I can double-check with someone who has more experience." I clicked a button on one of the controllers to take a screenshot, and another, and another as the helicopter eased up over the forested slope that Sherlock, Garrett, and I had climbed on foot not so long ago. "If I'm reading this right, the caves start pretty close to the foot of the mountain. I'm not sure we'll be able to tell whether they're wide enough to move through all the way up."

"At least one woman managed to come down the mountain that way." Jemma sucked her lower lip into her mouth, all her attention on the screens now. "If she could do that, I can figure out a way to go up. The most important question is where exactly the people she was running from have set down roots."

"I'm surprised they could live this close to so many towns and tourist areas without anyone stumbling on them," I said. "That one boy aside, they've hardly been murdering trespassers left and right."

"It is a little odd." She paused. "How did you feel when you got higher up the mountain? You said when Sherlock fell, he'd walked up ahead of you and Garrett—why weren't the two of you right there with him?"

I thought back to the moments before Sherlock's tumble. "I'm not sure," I said. "I just had the sense that we weren't heading in the right direction—an instinct, I suppose. Maybe a wrong one, since Sherlock's pointed him differently."

Jemma made a soft humming sound. If she'd made something of that response, she didn't share the significance with me. She took another look out the window and opened the topographical map we'd gotten of the area on her lap.

"The tree line is inconsistent," she said. "You came out here, where there's this secondary peak, but the forest spreads out around that and continues about another half a mile up the mountain before it falls away completely. They'll probably be as high up as they could get while staying sheltered."

"We're coming up over that area now."

"Keep a close eye on the infrared screen." She eased over to say something else to the pilot—asking him to chart a path just below that tree line across the mountain, from the shift in the helicopter's course.

I studied the fuzzy patches of yellows, greens, and blues. If we'd been closer, we might have picked up larger animals as speckles of orange or red, but at this distance the technician who'd prepped me had said we weren't likely to see signs of life unless there were several large bodies in close proximity. These people had to have additional sources of heat too—fires or gas for cooking, battery-powered devices. If more than a couple of them were living together, we should be able to spot them.

Jemma hunkered down on the floor next to the row of seats,

leaning her shoulder against my thigh in a companionable way as she watched the shifting colors. The warmth of her body sparked another flash of arousal, but one I could ignore.

For reasons I didn't totally understand, the dynamic between us —between her and our whole group—had felt less fraught since the whole nearly-killing-each-other episode. Less a game of cat-and-mouse and more a simple collaboration.

We knew, in essence, what she was, what she did, and where she drew the line. She was offering enough trust to include us in her scheme rather than weaving it around us. It still left me slightly unbalanced when I considered that we were throwing our lot in with a self-proclaimed criminal who'd no doubt orchestrated plenty more schemes than the ones we were directly aware of, but I'd felt plenty off-balance when we'd been actively at odds too. I'd take this.

Her spine jerked a little straighter as a flutter of orange appeared on the right side of the screen. I inhaled slowly as the patch flowed across the image, dappled with bits of red. A picture—couldn't forget to take a picture to fix the coordinates.

The edges of the shape trembled and blurred. For a second, it contracted, bleeding back into yellow. I hesitated. "Maybe that was just a glitch."

Jemma shook her head. "No. That's them. It has to be. I didn't realize— They must have more ways of disguising themselves than occurred to me before. I wonder if… I found signs of their activity on another mountain across the country. It could be they traveled all the way over there for the event, or maybe there's another settlement over there too, managing to stay hidden." She sucked her lower lip under her teeth in thought, and then looked up at me. "You recorded it?"

"I got the screenshot."

"All right. Let's take a quick scan around to make sure we haven't missed anything, and then we'll head back to earth." Her gray eyes sparkled. "We've got them now."

I took shots of what I believed to be some more cave formations as the helicopter veered back down the mountain, but nothing particularly striking presented itself. Our pilot set down in the parking lot where we'd left my rented pick-up truck. Clouds were starting to roll across the sky overhead, a thicker dampness congealing in the salty air. I had the feeling it was going to be a wet night.

The pilot helped us detach the external scanners from the body of the chopper. I tucked the tarp wrapping that had come with them tightly around them in the truck's bed and pulled the bed's cover into place as well. Sherlock and I were never getting any more technological favors if we returned these pieces ruined.

The helicopter took off with a gust of wind. Jemma helped me snap the cover securely on and then moved toward the passenger door. I was halfway around the driver's side when there was a pained gasp and the thump of knees hitting pavement.

"Jemma?" I hustled around to the other side of the truck with a lurch of my weak hip.

Jemma was crouched on her hands and knees, her fingers tensed against the asphalt, a tremor rippling through her as she got her rasps of breath under control. I knelt down to help her up—or whatever she needed—and my body stiffened.

Her hands were fading away. Literally *fading*, the black of the pavement showing through her pale skin and the flesh beneath. In that moment, in the space of several heartbeats, only the outlines of them and the wan shadows of bones shimmered visibly against the dark surface, all the way up to her wrists.

I blinked and blinked again, but the sight in front of me didn't change. Jemma yanked her hands closer to her, managing to sit up on her knees. She pushed her hair back from her now sallow face and drew in a lungful of air. When she gripped the side of the truck to heave herself upright, her fingers looked solid again.

"Jemma," I started.

She motioned me away. "Don't. There's no point in going there."

"I think there is. What the hell just happened to you? There isn't any toxin in the world that could affect your hands like that."

"You don't think there are things in this world beyond what you know?"

"I don't think basic human biology and physics could suddenly turn on their heads."

I stared at her, and all the other eerie moments of the last two months came back to me. The invisible shove that had propelled Sherlock down the mountainside. The ghostly figure we'd seen hovering over Jemma in London, and the strange lights that had dogged her before that.

"What are you really mixed up in?" I said. "Who are these people we're after? And don't tell me the same story you already gave us."

Her mouth set in a pained line. "What's the point when there's no way you'd believe me? What I told you was accurate enough. I need something there that'll save my life. Why do you need to know more than that?"

"How about because we're staking our careers and maybe our lives on this scheme too?" I swiveled my walking stick restlessly. "I know something unnatural is going on. I've seen enough strangeness to be convinced it's beyond the realms of science. I can't promise I'll believe everything, but I'll listen with an open mind. Also, we're not leaving this parking lot until you explain something."

She looked at me balefully, and the awareness prickled over me that if she *really* wanted to leave, there wasn't much I'd have been able to do to stop her. On the other hand, if I told Sherlock and Garrett to call off any arrangements we'd made to help her, they'd almost definitely agree. I did have some leverage.

"I told you this commune is part of a larger cult," she said. "They serve beings that live in their own realm alongside ours, but with the right impetus, they can cross over and have their fun here. Like vicious demonic faerie creatures... It sounds crazy. That's why I skipped that part. But you've pretty much seen one—that day in the park in London."

Demonic faerie creatures. The idea sounded so ridiculous I wanted to laugh, but Jemma looked deathly serious, and we never had been able to explain the strange glowing figure we'd all witnessed.

"And one of those things is hurting you?" I ventured.

"In a roundabout way." She swept up her hair with one hand and turned to show me the back of her neck as she lifted it. A jagged white blotch stood out against her skin at the base of her scalp. "I made a contract with one a long time ago. A sort of deal with the devil, if you like."

She dropped her hair and faced me again, hugging herself. "That cuff I made with the gold artifacts—it's the only thing stopping the thing from collecting me, but apparently it wasn't meant to be used for long periods of time. Now the cure is starting to kill me. What I can get in that commune, it'll help me arrange a more permanent solution."

"What happened just now, you think it's because of the gold band around your leg." Poisoning by percutaneous absorption wasn't unheard of. If I thought of it in those terms and didn't focus on the supernatural elements, I felt steadier. "Would you let me examine you? Just your leg? Maybe there's some way I can help."

Jemma's lips quirked upward. "You really want to play doctor, don't you, John?"

"I *am* a doctor, practicing or not. Come on, get in the truck for a little privacy and let me have a look."

She chuckled under her breath, but she took her seat and pushed it as far back as it would go so she had plenty of space. As I slid in on the driver's side, she tugged her loose pantleg up to mid-thigh.

The gold band and the gems imbedded in it gleamed in the dwindling sunlight. The skin around its edges did have an odd pearly quality to it, the blood vessels showing more starkly than they naturally should.

I reached to touch the spot, and Jemma tensed. I remembered how she'd reacted when Sherlock had put his hands on the band the other day.

"I'm not going to take it off," I said. "I just want to check your leg. All right?"

"All right." She tipped her head back against the seat and managed a grin, even if this one was tight. "Have your way with me, Dr. Watson."

I ran my thumb gently over the thigh muscle below and then above the gold band. For a second, when I applied a little more pressure, I thought I could see straight through to her femur. Nausea pinched at my stomach. This thing was definitely affecting her body in some bizarre way.

"Does it hurt?" I asked.

"Not really. Most of the time I don't even think about how it's there. But every now and then—more often, recently—it sets off this overpowering chill… It's supposed to wipe all trace of me from the creatures' senses. I think it's decided to wipe me out completely."

"And you can't take this off?"

"Not unless I want to go in an even more painful fashion."

I had to ask. "Are you going to be okay to see this whole operation through?"

"I'll have to be," she said matter-of-factly, giving me a smile like I'd never seen from her before, sharp and a shade wild. When I raised my hand, she straightened up. "I should be fine for long enough to crash the commune. After that, I won't need the cuff anymore. No problem."

Jemma Moriarty wasn't just the boldly confident woman who never ran out of sly remarks. This was her too—stoic and determined and maybe just a little scared.

"I wish there was something I could do in the meantime," I said. "It might help if you put some material between the gold and your skin… I don't know how the effect functions."

"I don't think that would cut it. But thank you." She pulled her pantleg down. "I know this is probably too much to ask, but if you can bring yourself to keep a secret for a little while, I'd rather you didn't mention this to Sherlock."

I hadn't thought that far ahead. The request automatically made me balk. "Why not?"

Jemma looked at me, her expression both fond and weary. "You know him a lot better than I do, and even I can see he'd sooner eat his own hand than admit to anything supernatural existing. It was convenient when the thing was trying to mess with us in London, but now, not so much. He wouldn't be helping if he thought this was about some 'superstitious nonsense'."

She was quoting a comment I'd recorded in one of my published accounts of the cases Sherlock and I had worked on. And her evaluation of him wasn't *wrong*, exactly.

"He puts proof above everything else," I said. "If you just show him, he'll have to accept it."

"Show him what? Do you really think this is enough to convince him that paranormal beings exist?" She motioned to her thigh.

"No," I had to admit.

"I can't make one of those attacks come on at will to provide a demonstration. The only concrete proof I could give him would be to remove the cuff in front of him and let him watch one of the fiends devour me bit by bit, but unfortunately that would defeat the purpose of proving it."

I didn't know what else to say. I didn't know what to think about the crazier parts of her story. Maybe she was partly insane—maybe there was some other explanation... but with all my medical training, I couldn't think of one.

Did it matter? She'd given me the answers I'd asked for without any obvious guile, simply and straightforwardly. She didn't expect even me to believe them. I could tell that from the set of her jaw. If this was one more deception, I had to think she'd have chosen one easier to swallow.

I wouldn't have thought of Jemma as a woman in need of defending, but a protective urge rose up in me as she waited for me to lay out my judgment. Whatever she'd been through, regardless of what she'd done before or after, it'd been terrible. I could at least believe that right now she was struggling simply to survive.

I could offer her this one small thing. I didn't know what I'd tell Sherlock anyway. Did it make any difference why she wanted access to the commune? He and I were doing this to take down people who'd been involved in the murder of a child, animal mutilations, and who knew what else. That hadn't changed.

"In that case, I think I can manage to keep it to myself for the time being," I said.

Her gaze snapped to me with blatant surprise. "Thank you," she said. Then a hint of her usual slyness came back. "I knew there was some reason I liked you."

I raised my eyebrows at her. "Is that the only one?"

"Of course not."

She raised her hand to trail her fingers down the side of my face, and my heart jumped. I caught her hand, thinking I was going to ease it away, but somehow instead my body leaned in as she moved to meet me.

The soft press of her lips was just as sweet as I remembered, even if she wasn't the woman I'd thought she was the last time I'd experienced it. She kissed me again, a little harder, but then her body tensed.

She pulled back with a squeeze of my hand. "Let's leave it there. I think I've made things complicated enough already."

Even if she was right, I found myself thinking as I started the truck's ignition that I wouldn't have minded another complication or two if they came in the form of Jemma Moriarty.

CHAPTER EIGHTEEN

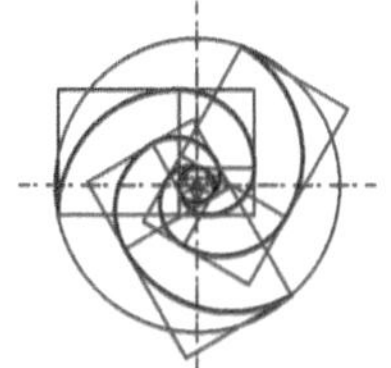

Jemma

The growl of my car's engine faded out into the whistling of the breeze at the base of the mountain. Bash parked his van next to me. We got out at the same time, him coming around to meet me at the back of the van.

"I could come with you, just to the caves," he said as he pulled open the doors to the storage area.

I shook my head. "The less activity on the ground around here, the better." The gold cuff might be wearing away at my body, but it also meant any shrouded folk keeping watch over the commune wouldn't see I was skulking around. Bash didn't have the same advantage.

They *were* keeping a close eye on this little village — I was sure of it. From what John had told me, they were using their illusory abilities to discourage people from coming too close, giving them the sense that they were going the wrong way. If a shrouded one could make me see, feel, and smell a room drenched in blood like Bog had in London, the occasional nudge of a stray hiker wouldn't be hard at all.

And if that hiker proved as persistent as Sherlock had, the nudge became a heave.

The way the infrared display had fogged confirmed it for me. Maybe the shrouded folk protected all of the cult's communities that way. There could be another out there by that sacrifice spot we'd found in the interior mountains. For all I knew, there could be a dozen settlements just here in Croatia. I'd never needed to think about details like that while I was living in the commune I'd grown up in.

"You're the boss, Majesty," Bash said. He pulled out the climbing gear he'd assembled. "Oversuit so you don't scratch yourself up. Knee and elbow pads. Rubber-soled boots. Helmet with headlamp. Rope. Waist belt with a bottle of water and a spare headlamp in case they mess with your first one." He elbowed me lightly. "I don't want you getting lost in the dark."

"I think I'll manage to find my way." How much equipment had Zena's patient had when she'd made her desperate scramble away from the commune? Probably none.

Having all this stuff almost felt like cheating. But against these fiends and the people who worshiped them, we needed all the advantage we could get.

I pulled on the oversuit, the thick fabric making my skin heat up within seconds, and attached the various accessories. The rope had a hook to attach it to the side of the belt. As I fixed the helmet on my head, its strap bit into the fading bruise on my throat. Bash frowned, looking at it.

"Are you sure Dr. Watson's technician friend gave you the right directions? The Londoners and their people haven't always been all that concerned about accuracy or your safety."

"I was there. I went over all the radar images with them." I touched Bash's arm. "You don't have to worry. This is just a scouting mission. I'm not planning on getting into anything dangerous."

"Only you would say that right before you race off into unmapped caves on a mountain that seems determined to kick people off it," he said dryly, but he couldn't mask the concern in his eyes. He turned to the van and handed me a couple of metal tools about the size of my hand, shaped like blunt knives. "Pitons, in case you have to clamber up any steep parts. Wedge the narrow end into a crack and use them to lever yourself up."

"Excellent." Going up was almost certainly going to be harder than coming down. I stuffed those into the hip pockets of my oversuit.

Bash reached a little farther into the back of the van. "Here, there's something else I picked up for you. I don't know if you'll end up needing it, but it might come in handy."

He drew out a black metal rod about an inch thick and slightly shorter than my forearm. With a flick of his wrist, two extra segments snapped out, nearly tripling its length. Bash made a few quick jabs with it and tossed it to me.

"Collapsible baton," he said. "The most lightweight one I could find that's still high quality. The steel in that will stand up to just about anything. You could say the good doctor inspired me with his walking stick antics."

I twirled the rod in my hand with amusement. "Did you think I was planning on fighting the caves?"

He chuckled. "No, but it'll give you some maneuverability if you do have to fend off an attacker while you're in there, regardless of the range. And it might be useful for climbing too if you can wedge it across a passage you want to scramble up. You can clip it inside your sleeve so you can whip it out in an instant. I know how fast those hands are."

He gave me a teasing wink as he motioned to my arm, but a little ache formed in my chest. I ducked my head as I attached the clip to my sleeve as he'd suggested. With a quick snatch, I could slip it off and extend it in less than a second. I tried the maneuver a few times before I looked at him again.

"Thank you," I said. The weight on my arm was a testament to how determined he was to protect me, even when I insisted on running off into harm's way alone.

How much longer would I have that?

I knew how human emotion worked even if I hadn't experienced a full range all that deeply myself. I'd watched enough people interacting during my business dealings. Even after Bash and I left the London trio behind, the night we'd shared and the fact that I'd refused any further intimacy would be hanging there between us. It had already been gnawing at him, and it'd keep gnawing at him until the downsides of working with me outweighed whatever he liked about the job.

He could say he accepted my decision, but I didn't know if he could really promise he'd always feel that way. I didn't know if I'd have wanted him to promise something like that. If he had to back off, I'd let him go, and then I'd make my own way again like I had before. It was fine. I'd manage.

It was only the thought of getting to that point that sent a brief jab through my gut.

I went back to my car and retrieved my phone and my written coordinates from my purse. "All right. Off I go."

Bash saluted me and got in behind the wheel of the van. He had other business to look into while I was exploring, but I knew he wouldn't leave until he'd made sure I at least got into the forest without incident. With his eyes on my back, I set off into the brush.

Every few minutes, I checked the GPS display on my phone to make sure I was on track. The forest became denser, fallen sticks cracking under my feet. I wasn't too worried about being noticed this far down. Sherlock and the others had made it a lot higher before the shrouded folk had intervened, and they couldn't detect me. I planned on getting as close to the actual human habitation as I could.

When I came for the dagger properly, I'd want to make my approach at night. There'd be less energy for the shrouded folk without immediate sunlight, and more chance that most of the cultists would be sleeping. I'd like to be totally familiar with my route before I navigated it by starlight.

I'd walked for about twenty minutes before I came on the first point where the radar had shown underground passages near the surface. Other than a crack I could barely fit my fingers through in the rocky shell of the ground, it didn't offer any access. I headed on up to the second location, about five minutes farther.

The commune clearly knew about the cave system beneath them.

I found a crevice just wide enough for me to slip through—and a bear trap fixed to the rock right in front of it. They might not venture down this far very often themselves, but they didn't want anyone wandering up and finding them either.

I studied the trap. I might have been able to safely spring it with a branch, but then they'd suspect someone had come through if they checked the trap before I returned. There had to be another option.

I eased up over the loose dirt that covered the ground beside the crevice. The opening wasn't very wide, but it was pretty tall. And there was this handy tree looming right over the top...

With a swing of my arm, I tossed my rope over the lowest branch, tied it firmly near the base, and dangled the rest into the crevice, letting the end fall just beyond the trap. Then I gripped it and jumped through the opening.

The momentum carried me past the trap. I loosened my hold and landed on the uneven turf inside, catching the rope before it could smack into the trap. I was going to need it to get back out again.

I wedged part of the rope into a crack in the edge of the crevice, switched on the lamp on my helmet, and set off into the cave.

The bear trap meant there might be other traps—of that sort or other kinds—along the way. I trod carefully over the dry rock, the cool still air grazing my face as I moved. A faint mineral flavor laced my tongue, like a muted version of the ocean's salt. The white glow of the lamp lit up bulges and dips of rock that wound deeper into the mountain's face and then veered upward with the slope.

Despite the cool dry atmosphere, sweat started to bead on my skin from the climb. I ducked under a low chunk of ceiling and at the last second spotted a patch of floor that didn't look quite right. A thin slab of rock sat in the middle of the passage. I nudged the edge with my toe, and a few pebbles crumbled off it.

A pit trap, I'd bet. I backed up a couple steps and dove over it through the cramped space. A jolt of pain ran through my shoulder as I rolled my landing on the uneven rock on the other side, but the trap stayed undisturbed.

A short climb farther, a streak of natural light coursed down from above. A gap in the ceiling emitted the faint shine, wavering with the movement of distant leaves. I eyeballed the space with an idea unfurling in my head. The gap was big enough that there were quite a few things I could shoot through it. I did still need a distraction as part of my plan.

I made a note of the spot in the rough map I'd been sketching on my phone and continued on. When a side passage twisted away from the main cave, I peered down it and decided to skip it—it looked like it fell away deeper into the mountain rather than offering access upward.

The cave I was moving through widened and tightened again. It wound back and forth through the rough stone and then shot up in a passage that was almost totally vertical. I grasped the pitons and drove them into the cracks, bracing myself with my feet and back between each shuffle upward. This part was definitely going to be easier on the way down.

The ponytail I'd pulled my hair into stuck damp to the back of my neck as I emerged. I paused there for a moment to catch my breath and crept on up the steep incline of the cave.

I squeezed through a particularly narrow section and edged across a patch of more level floor. A shuffling sound overhead made me freeze.

It came again. I held my breath, listening as carefully as I could.

I'd swear that was someone dragging something heavy—the rasp of the friction and the thump as they lowered it between heaves. Another sound wavered down with the texture of a voice speaking, even if I couldn't make out a single word. Another warbled in return.

My heart thumped faster. I'd made it to the commune. Or nearly made it. Knowing I was right beneath the settlement didn't do me much good if I couldn't figure out how to get aboveground.

I slunk along the passage, searching the ceiling and the walls for any sort of opening. Around a curve in the cave, my headlamp picked up a jaggedly circular outline where the ceiling dipped to a little lower than my height. It looked as though a huge rock had been set there to cover the entrance.

The boulder would be heavy, but the people up there must still be able to move it if they needed to. If I dragged the right tools up here, I could heave it out of the way.

I eased closer, meaning to test it gently with my hands. My gaze snagged on a thin cable that stretched across the floor just an inch off the ground. I jerked backward, propelling myself away from whatever trap the trip wire activated—and the ground under my heel crumbled.

My heart lurched into my throat as I reeled backward. One clear impression sprang into my mind: the snicker of Bash's baton snapping to full length. I wrenched the tool from my sleeve and whipped it out just as my body dropped through the chasm that had opened in the floor.

The steel bar jarred against both sides of the chasm. I swung my other hand up to grasp it. My feet dangled beneath me for several aching moments, flailing for purchase and finding none, before I managed to yank them up and plant them on one side of the narrow space.

Ignoring the strain in my shoulders, I glanced down. Only darkness met the stream of my headlamp. My breath snagged in my throat.

I'd almost fallen into nothingness.

I would have, if it wasn't for Bash. He'd managed to have my back even all the way up here, even though I'd pushed him away and denied him my full trust twice now.

The breath in my throat solidified into a lump. I swallowed hard. Flexing my arms, I managed to walk my feet up the side of the chasm and pull my torso higher at the same time. I swung one leg and then the other over the edge onto the cave floor and wrenched the rest of me up to follow them. Then I lay on my back, one hand still clutched around the baton, my pulse thudding with the memory of that fathomless drop.

The next time I came up here, I'd better stick to the right side of the cave. Good to know. I eyed the stone surface that had crumbled so easily, but I couldn't see any way to cover up the hole I'd broken in it. I'd just have to hope that if anyone checked in the next few days, they'd assume it'd given way on its own.

Shoving myself upright, I checked the floor for any marks I might have left that would reveal my presence. I scuffed away the edge of a footprint. After I'd marked the apparent entrance on my digital map, I headed back the way I'd come.

I didn't let go of the baton the whole journey down.

Evening was falling by the time I made it back to my car. I peeled off my equipment, dropped into the driver's seat, and sent a quick text to Bash. *Have returned alive. Located commune.* Then I tipped the seat back to let myself rest for a few minutes before heading back to the city.

My chest still felt tight, even though the scouting mission had gone perfectly. I'd survived. I'd found a route through the caves to the commune. I had a reasonable expectation of breaking my way the rest of the way through when I needed to.

But for some reason a hole almost as deep as that chasm had opened up inside me.

I needed to put that close call behind me. Move forward, move onward. I'd feel better once I got away from this place.

It was full-out night when I reached Split. I slipped between cheerful friends and couples strolling along the sidewalks to grab a seat in the first bar I spotted. The bartender brought me a burger and then a couple of beers with professional politeness. The alcohol added a slight fizz to my thoughts but didn't really dull my uneasiness.

Keep moving. I left the bar and meandered around the downtown strip until I spotted an asshole spewing drunken pick-up lines at every woman who passed him. I sidled over from behind and neatly lifted his wallet.

Looking at the contents around a corner didn't give me even a little spark of satisfaction. Thirty dollars' worth of local currency and a few credit cards I had no real use for. What the fuck was I doing?

Trying to be okay. Trying to walk far enough to walk *away* from things I hadn't wanted to feel.

But I did feel them. They were part of me. What was the point in denying myself something I wanted that I could have? If it crashed and burned, I wouldn't be any worse off than I was right now.

I wove through the streets to my hotel with a knot in my stomach but resolve swelling around it. When I reached my floor, I pulled the second keycard out of my purse. Bash and I had exchanged our extra copies in case we needed quick access to each other's belongings.

I eased his door open to find the room dark, the blackout curtain pulled, and the slow rasp of sleeping breath drifting through the air. With silent footsteps, I crossed the room to the bed.

Bash was sprawled there on his back, a little off to one side, his face tipped to the pillow.

My body balked for a second. Then, ever so carefully, I sat on the opposite edge of the bed and lay down on top of the covers.

Bash stirred and settled. I closed my eyes and dragged in my first truly full breath since my fall in the caves. With the scent of gun oil seeping into my lungs, my limbs relaxed into the bed.

I was here. We could deal with the rest in the morning.

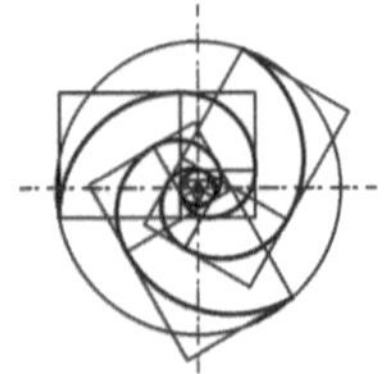

Jemma

A hitch of the mattress snapped me out of sleep. My head jerked up.

Bash was staring at me, sitting half upright where he must have startled to see me in his bed, the covers sliding down his brawny torso. As the initial surprise faded from his expression, his jaw tightened with concern.

"Are you all right, Mori? If you didn't think you were safe to stay in your room, why didn't you wake me up?"

I stretched and pushed myself upright, yesterday's blouse and pants shifting against my body in their wrinkled state. Last night, coming here had felt so complicated. Now, with Bash's musky scent surrounding me and his instinctive protectiveness immediately on display, all my anxieties seemed ridiculous.

This was Sebastian Moran. I knew him better than I'd ever known anyone, and he knew me like no one else. If I wanted to take this step without it ending in a mess, he was as close as I was going to get to a sure thing.

"There's nothing wrong with my room," I said, meeting his gaze.

"I've been thinking about what you said the other morning and how I feel, and I've changed my mind. We should take it slow, but I'd like to give us a try. As lovers."

Bash blinked as he straightened up, but in spite of his apparent bemusement, an eager warmth had lit in his light green eyes. He glanced from me to the door. "And you figured the best way to tell me that was by sneaking into my room in the middle of the night?"

The corner of my lips twitched upward. "I thought I should make some demonstration of being good to my word. I… I haven't trusted anyone enough to sleep next to them in ten years, other than you. And this time I was thinking clearly about it."

He didn't seem to know what to say about that. He edged his hand across the bed to rest at the small of my back, his thumb tracing an arc over my spine. "What changed your mind?"

The lump that had filled my throat yesterday in the caves returned. I willed it down. "I *can* do this alone," I said, because it suddenly felt very important to make that clear. "But I don't want to. Pretending there's nothing more between us than business is just as likely to fuck things up as, well, fucking."

I don't want to lose you. That understanding sat in my gut, too heavy for me to propel into words, but maybe he could hear it in what I did say.

Bash scooted closer to loop his arm right around my waist. "Sounds perfectly reasonable to me."

I raised an eyebrow at him. "Like I said, I want to take things slow. We're not jumping right to the fucking part. I want to be sure my intentions are in the right place when it comes to you. And—if we're doing this, you have to accept that sometimes I'm going to be with other men too, when I need to."

"And when you want to," he said, as a statement of fact rather than a judgment.

My shoulders came up a bit. "Just because I've enjoyed some of those encounters—"

"It's all right," Bash said. He pressed a kiss to the corner of my jaw that sparked desire all through my body. "I'm not saying the jealousy is gone, but I don't know if I'd really want you to restrict yourself like that. I like the energy you get when you've been 'enjoying' yourself with other people. And I'll definitely like knowing that no matter who you play around with, it can be me you come back to, every time. So, if you get the urge to, say, have a last hurrah with the Londoners before we leave them in our dust, just promise me you'll milk them for everything they're worth." He smirked at me.

I grinned back at him. "That's a promise I have no trouble making."

I couldn't have asked for more than what he'd offered in his response. I leaned into him, inhaling the tang of his natural scent. Wanting to taste him. Wanting to throw the principles I'd decided on out the window and explore every inch of his body at my leisure.

But was that an urge born from honest attraction, or an impulse to tie him to me, to lock down his devotion and appease my sense of control? I wasn't sure I could tell the difference, so I held myself back.

Bash was obviously thinking along similar lines. "When you say we'll take it slow, how slow is 'slow'?"

I wet my lips and looked at his. "Well, I'm not saying we should become monks."

I raised my head and he lowered his at the same time. He claimed my mouth with a firm certainty, as if he knew exactly how I'd want to be kissed even though we barely had before this moment.

He did know, though. The heat of his lips flooded me from head to toe, and I shifted even closer, my hand coming to rest on his bare abs.

Bash let out a faint groan, his arm tightening around me. He deepened the kiss until his tongue twined with mine, and a bolt of lust shot to my core. My self-control started to fray.

I eased away from him, breathless. "Maybe we should put a pin in it for now."

Bash laughed, his fingers stroking over my side. "You're going to be the death of me."

I stiffened automatically. Bash's hand stilled, and he pulled back far enough to meet my eyes. "I didn't mean that literally, Mori."

I let out a breath. "No, but you could have. There's a pretty good chance that's true."

"Hey." He touched the side of my face, all his attention focused on me. "I'm fine with that. I've been tempting death my whole life. I'd sure as hell rather it happened at your side, taking on your monsters, than in the army or doing shitty jobs for the random assholes I worked for before you. I'm where I want to be."

"Okay." I believed him, even if the idea of my mission leading him to his death made my stomach clench. I rubbed my mouth. "We're supposed to meet with Sherlock and the others soon. I should shower and get changed into clothes that aren't clearly slept in, or they'll think I'm losing my touch."

Bash snorted and released my waist. I couldn't help turning to plant one more kiss on him. It went on a little longer than I'd been planning before I managed to wrench myself away. I flashed him another grin and hopped off the bed.

"It's going to be *cold* showers around here," he muttered to himself as I slipped out the door, but it was the happiest muttering I'd ever heard.

Our hotel had a few meeting rooms that could be reserved for private use. The trio arrived right on schedule from the place where they were staying down the street. Sherlock strode right in with a thump of his crutch and a dip of his head in acknowledgment, John and Garrett trailing behind him. We sat around the boardroom-sized table, Bash and me on one side and the three of them on the other.

I leaned back in my chair with a faint creak. "On my side of things, I'm basically ready to go. I've planned a route through the cave system, and I have the gear I need. All we need to figure out is how you're going to put your raid into motion."

"I'm still not entirely sure why you feel you can take on this entire cult group by yourself, but we'll need extensive help," Sherlock said.

"Oh, you're going to help me," I said. "I'm pretty sure I can make it to their stash, but getting off the mountain unscathed would be trickier. That's why I need to be sure you'll come storming into the place not too long after I get there."

"Also," Bash said, "you didn't even make it halfway up that mountain last time without ending up in a cast."

"It's a brace," Sherlock said tartly. "Only a sprain."

"My point stands."

"Unless I've read the situation wrong, you're the muscle here, not the brains. Perhaps you should leave the discussion to the rest of us."

Bash shifted forward in his seat, and I cleared my throat. "I'm sure I don't have to remind you that Bash very considerately did *not* shoot you the other day when you were threatening me at gun point. So maybe we could keep this conversation considerate as well?"

Sherlock looked a tad chagrinned. "Yes. Well. More to the matter at hand, why should you go ahead of us at all? Why not arrive as part of the raid? I'm sure whatever force we can assemble would overlook the lifting of a small item or two."

"Unless there's something else you have planned before we get there," Garrett put in, his gaze suspicious but his tone more curious, as if he couldn't help wondering how I might pull the rug out from under them yet again.

"No," I said honestly. "All I want to do is grab my cure and get the hell out. But I'll be helping you too on my way up. I'll provide a little distraction, get them stirred up about that, and then it'll be easier for you to swarm the place... without any more turned ankles."

"You could do that just as easily with us," Sherlock said.

"No, I couldn't. I know how to get past their warning systems. I'm the only one who can get close enough to cause enough chaos to open the way."

"You *could* share those strategies with the rest of us."

I gave Sherlock a firm look. "Sorry. I can't do that either. There are certain things that can't be taught." Like the power of a gold cuff to hide one's presence from the shrouded folk he'd scoff at the very idea of.

His eyebrows jumped up. "I'd expect you know by now that I can pick up nearly—"

John knuckled his arm. "Sherlock, *we* know that Jemma has a lot more experience with the cult than we do. If she thinks this approach will be safest for all of us, I say we listen. I don't think she protected us four days ago just to get us killed now."

"That might make a very convenient distraction," Garrett remarked.

I glowered at him, but Sherlock's expression softened a little as he looked at John. "Perhaps we should work out the rest of the plan and see if it hangs together before drawing judgments," he allowed.

John smiled, lighting up the way he always did when Sherlock showed how much he valued his opinion. Watching them, a flutter passed through my chest, like an echo of the longing that had brought me to Bash's bed last night.

They'd developed the same understanding and trust that Bash and I had between us, as clear as anything. It really was a shame that Sherlock couldn't seem to wrap his head around seeing anything more than platonic affection from his friend. Would that friction end up breaking their bond apart the same way I'd been worried Bash and I might fall out?

It wasn't my concern, not really. I drew my attention back to our strategizing.

"I know you don't approve of my usual methods," I said, "but I'd like to see you take down those psychopaths as much as you would, so we really do have the same goal here. If you've changed your mind about believing that, then I'll figure out something on my own. The door's right there." I motioned to it.

"No, no," Sherlock said briskly, as if he could speak for all three of them. "Let's carry on."

Garrett tapped the edge of the table. "We don't have the legal authority to do anything about these people anyway, do we? If the idea is to shut down whatever operations they have running and make sure they don't hurt any more kids or animals, we need to get the local police involved."

"Indeed." Sherlock pulled a slight grimace. "I have less faith in them than your Scotland Yard colleagues back home, Garrett, but I don't see how that can be helped."

"They've ignored the situation for years—maybe decades," John pointed out. "They brushed off that boy's death as an accident."

"And we don't have any proof of more recent crimes."

I rested my hands on my stomach, interlacing my fingers. "We don't need a real crime, do we? We just need a story to get them riled up—or at least feeling like they have to act like they are."

The consulting detective hummed to himself. "That's true. I do have a little sway here. We could appeal to the General Police Directorate. If we convinced them that international relations were at stake rather than merely the concerns of a handful of farmers and countryfolk, that should stir them."

"I'm not going to make up an official case," Garret said. "That could come back to bite me too easily."

"Of course not. Don't worry yourself about crossing those lines. We can make it a private matter. It's simple enough. What innocent British citizen might venture up the mountain?"

Sherlock glanced around looking for suggestions like a professor testing his class.

"A tourist?" John said. "There are always adventurous types looking to go off the beaten track."

"Exactly my thought. This imaginary tourist—we'll make her a woman, that always draws more sympathy, no offense meant to present company—"

"None taken," I said with amusement.

"—she mentioned to relatives back home that she was going to attempt a climb of this mountain, and then they never heard from her again." Sherlock spread his hands. "Not having any contacts in the area, they turned to me for my services. And during my investigations here, I discovered a small hidden community engaged in illegal dealings who almost certainly did away with the young lady."

Garrett nodded. "That hangs together pretty well. They might not be too motivated by the concerns of a couple of independent detectives, though." He paused, and a sly glint lit in his dark eyes. "John, it is the sort of case you might decide to write about. You could tell them you're planning on publishing an account."

"That does sound plausible," John said with a grin. "I'll make sure to emphasize how many people enjoy those accounts, to rub it in that their response will be scrutinized by the public eye."

Sherlock snapped his fingers. "Perfect. We'll hit two points of pressure at once. The potential shame of being revealed to have ignored horrific criminal activity going on under their noses, and the ego stroking of being asked for assistance where my means are not enough. Law enforcement officials are so often guided by pride."

I suppressed a smile, and Garrett caught my eye with a glance of conspiratorial exasperation. As if Sherlock wasn't guided equally well by a good ego-stroking.

"That's all very impressive," I said, "but I have to think the Police Directorate has enough common sense to look into your missing persons case before sending a SWAT team up the mountain. Give me the rest of the day, and I'll have a nice trail of online breadcrumbs for you. Articles, a family website asking for help, social media presence for your supposed tourist. We'll want this to look authentic."

"Right," John said. "You can do that?"

I smirked at him. "I convinced you all that a police officer from Friesing named Jemma Moriarty existed, didn't I?"

Next to me, Bash chuckled.

"Fair," Sherlock said. "Fair enough." He looked as though he wasn't sure whether to be impressed or horrified by my professed efficiency. "It would be good to have all our bases covered."

"It sounds like we have a plan, then. You'll find plenty of evidence to place charges once you're in there." Since the cult of the shrouded folk avoided contact with outsiders, I knew from past experience that they didn't take all that much care to hide their activities inside the settlements.

The trio might have been a little unsettled, but as my gaze slid around the table, an air of triumph came over the room. They worked well together—I'd seen that right in front of me many times now—and I worked well with them, didn't I? Putting our minds and our resources together, we were finding a way to unseat the commune so much faster than I could have without them.

The real shame was that we'd only get to do this once, and then we'd be enemies again. I supposed I should enjoy the collaboration while it lasted.

We talked for a while longer, hashing out the details of the missing person story, and then we parted ways. In the elevator, Bash got out his phone. "Should I reach out to Nikolev?"

"Not yet. When I have the materials put together, I'll give you a shout. I don't want him any more involved than he needs to be. In the meantime, I do have a few more things I'd like you to pick up for my next mountain expedition."

He set off to round up the remaining equipment, and I stepped into my room.

The second the door closed behind me, a knife of pain sliced up through my hip and abdomen from my thigh. I staggered, my lungs squeezing tight.

My breath rattled in my throat. My hand, groping along the wall, washed out from the fingers to halfway up my forearm. For a few seconds, even staring at it, I couldn't feel the texture of the plaster beneath my palm.

I closed my eyes, and sensation gradually seeped back through my body. Fuck. I'd had an episode yesterday morning right before I'd left with Bash too. They were coming on more frequently now.

John's question from two days ago came back to me. *Are you going to be okay to see this whole operation through?*

The answer was the same: I had to be.

CHAPTER TWENTY

Sherlock

I opened the door to my hotel room at a knock, expecting to see one of my colleagues. Instead, Jemma stood on the other side, already dressed in cargo pants and a thin tank top as if ready to set off on her mission right now. She placed her hands on her hips.

"Well, are we good to go?"

It took me a moment to recalibrate my reaction. I supposed, in a way—temporarily—this woman *was* one of my colleagues. "You could have simply phoned," I said.

"I wanted to go for a walk anyway." She cocked her head at me. "Should I head back to my hotel and get on my phone if I want an actual answer?"

"No, no, but I'm not sure it's the best subject to be discussing out here in the hall."

I stepped back to let her come in, and my point was proven before she'd even finished entering. John poked his head out of his room next door, clearly having heard her voice.

"Is there news?"

"For you? Not unless Sherlock's been keeping quiet with you

too," Jemma called over her shoulder. She sank down on the edge of my bed.

John came over anyway. The last few days, he'd been more attentive of Jemma than he had been even when she'd first charmed him back in London. The change had happened after they'd gone out on that helicopter flight, to be precise. Something must have happened between them then.

I hadn't asked because I suspected it was the sort of thing John would rather keep private. It wasn't as if I could fault him if he'd continued to indulge in her charms, any more than I could deny that I'd gotten more than professional satisfaction out of the recent truce I'd shared with her. All the same, watching his gaze sweep over her body made my skin tighten.

It wasn't so strange that I'd be concerned about him, was it? This woman *had* tricked the three of us into committing a major crime not that long ago. Her current story lined up with the evidence I'd seen with my own eyes, and I hadn't caught any inconsistencies or unusual occurrences to make me question her true situation as I had last time, but she'd proven her wits were as sharp as mine. I couldn't take anything I thought was true for granted.

"We made our arrangements after you sent along your online work," I said. "Garrett went back to speak with one of the police chiefs after lunch to finalize the details of tonight's raid, but they are committed now."

"And very interested in making a heroic showing in my report," John added with a grin.

"All right. That's good." Jemma leaned back on her hands, denting the bedspread I'd pulled flat a few hours ago, but a tension lingered in her shoulders that offset her casual pose and tone. "You'll be able to keep them on a leash until I set off the flare, I assume. That should give me just enough time to take care of my part."

We were bringing two squads of special officers by helicopter to plateaus in the rocky mountainside above the commune's forest location. On that terrain, with the distance we'd have to cover, I expected it'd take us at least twenty minutes to reach the village. The fastest among us, anyway. John had tried to insist that I stay back on account of my ankle, but the sprain was healing quickly. I didn't need the crutch anymore to move around this room.

And I'd be damned if I wasn't there to take responsibility for the mission I'd agreed to orchestrate.

"We've told them we have an associate who's gotten close to the commune to gather evidence, and that you'll signal us when it's the best time to rush in," I said. "I don't think they'll be in any hurry to go charging off into the woods without that confirmation."

"Everything's ready then." She let out a breath and smiled, but the set of her lips looked tense too.

She was still human, after all. In less than twelve hours, she was going up against enemies far more personal to her than to us, enemies who'd already made an attempt at killing her. She'd be going in alone.

I felt reasonably certain I'd survive the night. Jemma might not have the same expectation.

"I know I've said this before," I said, "but are you sure you shouldn't have some sort of backup with you? Can't that Moran fellow follow your lead?" What was she going to do if the entire commune converged on her with assorted weaponry?

"Bash will be waiting to help me get back off the mountain," Jemma said. "Believe me, if I could have him covering me, I would."

I still didn't understand her insistence on going solo, but I'd decided by now there wasn't any benefit in arguing about it. "Well, if there's any additional equipment you think would help your efforts that your own connections haven't been able to provide..."

Amusement glittered in her gray eyes. "Are you worried about me, Mr. Holmes?"

For some reason, her use of my last name sparked a flicker of heat inside me. Perhaps because the only other time she'd used it recently, in the same teasing tone, we'd been talking about propositions.

"Not so much worried as aware of the magnitude of the danger you're insisting on throwing yourself into," I hedged.

A smile curved her lips. She pushed herself off the bed and sauntered up to me where I'd stayed standing not far from the door.

Close enough that her coolly sweet scent, like violets blooming by moonlight, reached my nose.

"I'm flattered that I'm worthy of your concern," she said. Then she bobbed up to brush a kiss to my lips, so soft it reminded me of the peck she'd given me right before she took off on us in London. As if she were saying good-bye with it.

The thought made something clench in my chest. She touched my neck to lean into the kiss, letting it linger on longer than that past one. Despite the hunger that stirred in me, my nerves twitched with the awareness that John was standing just a few feet away.

I pulled back. "Perhaps this isn't the time."

Jemma glanced from me to John, who was standing by the narrow desk with his face set in an uncertain expression, and returned her gaze to me with a laugh.

"Do you think John minds? He probably likes watching, and he's welcome to join in if he wants. He'd like to be kissing you too, you know—and everything else from that to fucking."

"Er," John said, his cheeks flushing.

My spine had gone rigid, my thoughts scattering. I managed to say, "Perhaps we should leave behind this subject entirely."

Jemma rolled her eyes. "My God, you are hopeless. You do remember what happened in London, don't you? You recall that you have kissed him before? I'm assuming you haven't really completely erased that moment from your mind."

I'd buried it very, very deep. Even the brief flicker of memory that rose in the back of my head—the firm pressure of his mouth, not at all like Jemma and somehow provoking a reaction so similar— tipped my sense of balance. Suddenly I wished I hadn't left my crutch leaning against the headboard.

"I remember," I said, looking only at her.

She raised her chin impertinently. "Then you might as well put him out of his misery already. Did you run away because it was so horrifyingly unpleasant?"

Heat started to collect around my collar. I didn't know what to make of what I'd felt during that kiss; I didn't want to talk about it at all. It had been so much easier not having to think about it, setting it aside as irrelevant data. A momentary whim spurred on by Jemma's coaxing… Nothing worth shaking the foundations of our partnership —our *friendship*—over.

John was the only bloody friend I'd ever had, if I was being honest. The only person in my life who'd observed my peculiarities and wanted to immerse himself in them rather than backing away. He'd seemed happy enough to set the incident aside too.

He wasn't arguing with her assessment of the situation, though. I might not be ready to meet his eyes, but I could feel him standing there, waiting on my answer as much as she was.

We could end this conversation right now if I said yes, but I wasn't going to tell a lie that might wound him.

"No," I said. "It was not horrifyingly unpleasant."

"How would you describe it, then?" Jemma asked.

I shifted my weight. Standing here still favoring my ankle in its brace was starting to strain my other leg. "I'm going to sit down," I said.

She swept her arm toward the spot on the bed she'd vacated. "Be my guest, as long as you answer the question too."

I settled myself on the covers and braced my hands against the edge of the bed. "I'm not sure how to describe it, because there was rather a lot going on around that moment, and it's difficult to pick apart what—and who—caused which sensations."

"But there wasn't any part of it you found off-putting."

"No," I admitted, and then I finally found the wherewithal to look at John again.

His flush had faded, but his eyes held a slightly feverish light. "It wasn't at all off-putting to me either."

"Wow. Such enthusiastic declarations." Jemma shook her head, her ruddy waves skipping over her shoulders. She paused to consider us both in turn. "I don't suppose you'd like to try it again and see if we can come up with words beyond 'not off-putting'?"

John shifted forward and hesitated. My shoulders tensed.

Jemma sighed. "We can start with this then." She glanced toward John. "Would you like *me* to kiss him?"

Half a smile curled his lips. "Absolutely."

I might have protested that surely I should have some say in the matter, but Jemma had already cupped my jaw and leaned down to make good on that offer. The conversation we'd just had seemed to have stripped my nerves bare. The simple touch of her mouth sent my whole body tingling, in part because of John's gaze on us.

"We'll want to be clear-headed for tonight, don't you think?" Jemma murmured, her lips still grazing mine. "Are you game?"

My head certainly didn't feel at all clear right now. My cock was already starting to rise. The urge for release twisted through me.

It was a diversion. A way to pass the time somewhat productively while we waited to see our plan through. I could focus on that and not whatever else this might be.

"What did you have in mind?" I asked.

"This is a good start." She looked John's way again. "Feel free to join us whenever the mood strikes you."

She reclaimed my mouth, and this time I met her with equal ardor. I raised my hand to trace my fingers over her scalp, tangling them in her hair. She trailed her thumb along the sensitive path down the side of my neck that she'd gotten such delight out of stimulating. A quiver of pleasure raced over my skin in the wake of her touch.

John had come up behind her. He set his hands on her waist, watching us, and then kissed her spine where the neckline of her tank top dipped low. At her eager sound, he slid his hands higher under the thin fabric.

Jemma's mouth caught mine with a hum and a nip of teeth. My fingers tightened in her hair. We were all one being generating pleasure together, and it felt perfectly natural.

I reached for her breast, wanting to tweak her nipple the way she'd responded so eagerly to during our truce, and my fingers brushed John's. We jerked apart.

Jemma kissed me harder, and the awkwardness melted away. He shifted his attentions to snapping open the back of her bra. I slid my hand under one cup to caress the soft mound that could provoke such thrilling reactions.

Jemma swayed with our attentions. I squeezed her nipple, and she growled against my lips. That sound and the feel of her was enough to harden my cock completely. The crotch of my pants had become uncomfortably tight.

With a pleased sigh, Jemma pulled back and motioned me farther up the bed. She followed, prowling after me with a passionate fierceness I had to admit made me even harder. As she knelt beside me, she ran her hands over my chest. In a few seconds, she'd loosened my trousers.

"A little help?" she said to John, who was still standing by the end of the bed. My mouth went dry as he tugged the pants the rest of the way off.

Then Jemma was bending over me to ease her lips over my cock, and I didn't have the capacity to feel anything but ecstatic. The hot slickness of her mouth and the swirl of her tongue sparked to life places in me I hadn't known existed.

A curse tumbled from my lips. She smiled around me and licked me from base to tip with a force that echoed bliss through every inch of my body.

John came around the bed to stroke Jemma's back and chest again. She practically purred, her breath spilling over my groin in the most exhilarating way. When she eased up, her tongue flicking around the head of my cock, my body screamed for her to take me back down again.

"You could feel even better than this," she said to me with a teasing lilt. "I've gotten to enjoy the benefit of two mouths, two sets of hands. Wouldn't you like to discover that experience, Sherlock?"

My gaze jumped to John's face. He met my eyes, his expression hesitant but… hopeful?

The longing I read in his eyes made my own hesitation seem ridiculous. What was there really to be afraid of here? I was master over my emotions, not the other way around. Why shouldn't I accept what he so clearly wanted to offer and see where it would bring us?

I extended my hand tentatively. If I'd had any doubts about how eager John was, they'd have been erased by the way he beamed in response. He shifted onto the bed, searching my face. My heart thumped faster, but I tipped my head toward him. He bent down and let his mouth come to rest on mine.

Oh, it was good. Awkward but somehow just right, his lips carefully adjusting against mine until my head twitched upward to solidify the kiss, the fervent tremor of his breath in response. His fingers traced along my jaw.

Jemma bowed over me, and my nerves flooded with sensation like a candle burning at both ends. My hips arched up at the swivel of her tongue. My mouth collided with John's again. The pulsing build of my release swelled at the base of my cock.

At the rasp of a zipper, my eyelids fluttered open. Jemma had yanked down the fly of John's khakis. While she teased one hand over my balls, she dipped the other into that opening to grip his erection.

He groaned against my lips, and they parted as if to accept the sound. Our mouths melded together even more avidly than before. It felt *too* good, between him and her—overwhelmingly so. I turned my head to break the kiss, my breath ragged.

Jemma sucked me hard, and I let out a groan of my own. She released me with a rough gasp.

"My turn again. John, my purse—condom."

When he glanced at me as if worried he'd misstepped, I nodded to say we were all right, as coherently as I was able to. Without another second's hesitation, he fumbled for her purse.

I'd seen other men naked before—at the gym, in the sauna—and John was still mostly clothed, but I'd never seen an erect cock other than my own. I couldn't help watching as he unrolled the condom over his rigid length. Then he was yanking Jemma's pants and panties down and tucking his hand between her legs in a way that made her lips squeeze around my own cock. My vision hazed with pleasure.

John closed his eyes as he thrust into her. He pumped in and out with a shaky exhalation, and Jemma rocked with him. The motion rippled into me with the rhythm of her sucking and the swipe of her tongue, as if he were fucking me through her as well.

My balls contracted. I came with a blaze of bliss that seared through all the scattered emotions I'd been grappling with, every bit of concern I might have had about the mission ahead of us. Burning me clean so my thoughts could regather in better order. It was the best kind of high I'd ever felt. Jemma hadn't lied when she'd promised me that all those weeks ago.

She licked me clean as I softened in her mouth and then ducked her head against my thigh with a moan provoked by John's thrusts.

"Fuck," John said hoarsely.

"So close," Jemma muttered, her fingers curling into the bedspread like they had when I'd worked her over last week. A fresh flare of desire shot through me. I could make her release as dazzling as mine had been.

I turned on the bed as swiftly as I could and pulled her into a kiss, ignoring the salty musky flavor that must be mine on her lips. My other hand traveled to fondle her breast exactly the way that had made her moan before. A cry broke from her throat as my thumb swept over the peak. Her lips mashed into mine with the trembling of her own climax.

John's breath hitched, and he bowed over her with a shudder.

Jemma sagged onto the bed, and John sank down so we formed a sort of triangle between us, a careless assortment of limbs. As my breath evened out, my gaze lingered on my friend's face, the fall of his light hair around it, the broad brow and the soft cheekbones I'd seen thousands of times without really paying attention to them. The mouth that had met mine so eagerly.

His gaze lifted and found mine. My throat closed for a second. Then I said, "Come here?"

He eased up on one elbow. "What is it?" His earlier tentativeness had returned.

I licked my lips. His eyes tracked the movement. Fresh heat quivered through me, but I needed to know for sure.

"I'd like to kiss you once with no other variables involved," I said. "To see... to see what it is when it's only us."

Something shifted in his expression. As he swiveled around to face me properly, Jemma eased back, watching us. John definitely looked nervous again. My own body tensed now that the rush of passion had faded.

"You don't have to if—"

"It's all right," he said. "I want to."

He brought his lips to mine like that first gentle kiss. The quiver of heat turned into a wave. I kissed him back, reveling in the unexpected sensation, until we eased apart again.

"Well," I said, "that was definitely not off-putting at all."

Jemma let out a guffaw and sat up, swatting my back. "Hopeless," she said. "Totally hopeless." But she was grinning with an air that I'd have called joy, as if seeing John and I unearth this new possible realm of our partnership gave her genuine satisfaction.

She'd led us to this discovery. Shoved me would really be more accurate. Just for the selfless enjoyment of watching us find our way there.

This woman was a puzzle. A thief. A murderer, if only of other criminals—as far as we knew. The most gifted liar I'd ever met. Yet beyond my fascination with her brilliance, perhaps I was coming to simply *like* her too, for reasons I couldn't argue away.

And tonight, we might lose her.

CHAPTER TWENTY-ONE

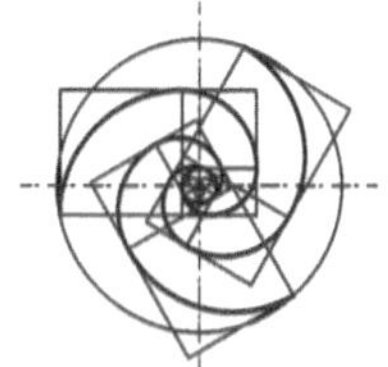

Jemma

Technically, the caves weren't any darker at night than they had been when I'd explored them the other afternoon. No sunlight penetrated solid stone either way. They *felt* darker, though—the shadows around the beam of my headlamp denser, the chill in the dry air thicker—as I picked my way toward my destination.

My load definitely weighed heavier on my back. I had to brace my hands against the rough stone walls to keep my balance with the pack Bash had loaded up for me. The sugar cube I'd popped into my mouth at the entrance had long since dissolved, leaving my mouth faintly sticky. I wasn't even halfway to the top yet, and my back was already damp with sweat.

The trio and their band of police should be waiting higher up on the mountain by now. What would they be talking about to pass the time? I distracted myself from the strain of the climb by thinking back to Sherlock and John's fumbling negotiations after our interlude in Sherlock's hotel room.

Just to be clear, I'm not looking to make some big romantic thing out of this, John had said as he'd straightened out his clothes. *It just *might be nice to, er, kiss or whatever else fits the occasion, when the right moment comes up.*

Sherlock had managed to look lofty even while he was tucking himself back into his pants. *That sounds like a reasonable proposition.*

I had to smile at the memory. They really were ridiculous. It was a good thing they'd found each other in their roundabout way. I could even take a little pride in having given them a kick on the ass to help them get there.

When I reached the first pit trap, I had to toss my pack over the thin slab of stone before I hurled myself. After I'd heaved the bag back over my shoulders, I had just a brief climb to reach the small gap in the ceiling I'd noted before.

That spot was definitely darker than last time, the hole barely discernible against the dimpled rock even with my headlamp pointing at it.

I pulled the four flare guns out of the pack. The first one was to get the commune's attention. The others were to convince them something major was going on that they'd better investigate—and a backup in case one or another hit a tree branch on the way up.

Positioning myself beneath the gap, I angled my arms so the flare should shoot out at a slight angle and burst even closer to the commune. They had to feel the potential threat was nearby to guarantee that some of them would leave to investigate.

I squeezed the trigger, and the first shot crackled through the air. My ears rang, but I listened as closely as I could. A sound like a thunderclap and a distant blaze of light penetrated the cave through the gap. Grinning, I reached for the next gun.

The second one blasted off without a hitch. With the third, I must have shifted my angle by accident, because all I heard was the thunk of it hitting something above. I adjusted my position again, and the fourth one sparked another stream of light high above.

I tossed the used guns aside. It didn't matter if the commune found them now. Either I'd be long gone with the dagger by the time anyone from the cult had a chance to search around here, or I'd be dead. Simple as that.

The flares were also the signal for the police to start down the mountain toward the commune. I had to make sure I got there first. I scrambled on up through the narrowing passages.

My arms strained to pull me up the particularly steep section. I gritted my teeth and shoved myself onward. A strand of my hair got caught in a jagged bit of rock and yanked out from the roots, leaving me wincing. I rubbed the stinging spot as I hustled along.

The beam of my headlamp bounced over the uneven walls and ceiling in a way that looked much more eerie than before. I pushed myself faster.

There. My gaze caught on the outline of the wide opening and the boulder sealing it where the cave narrowed to nearly a tunnel up ahead.

I hadn't forgotten my close call the other day. I treaded carefully along the edge of the still partly hidden chasm and stepped gingerly over the tripwire—and another tripwire a few feet after that.

The area right beneath the entrance looked clear. Dragging in a breath, I reached into the pack and took out the rectangular thing Bash had called a "minor explosive." With a wiggle of my hand, I wedged it as far into a crevice between the boulder and the opening as I could. Then I lit the fuse and darted back the way I'd come, shutting off my headlamp.

Even several feet away, I crouched down to shield my body in case the explosive did more than propel the boulder off its seat as Bash had said it would. *This little thing shouldn't do more than crack the ceiling a bit*, he'd told me, but explosives in caves seemed like exactly the right moment for a little extra caution.

The flame hissed up the fuse. Then the explosive blasted apart with a wallop of sound. The rock around me trembled—and the boulder flew off its resting place.

My heart skipped a beat. I leapt forward, covering both trip wires at once, listening for sounds of approach. The whole commune wouldn't have gone down the mountain to check out the flares, and whoever was left here wouldn't ignore a noise like that.

Peeking out through the opening, I found nothing but trees looming all around. The caves must open up beyond the edge of the actual settlement. A few shouts were carrying from somewhere to my right.

With my pulse pounding through my chest and limbs, I hauled myself out through the opening and ducked behind a tree. My hands wrenched the pack open. I grabbed the grenades stashed near the bottom, flicked the pins, and hurled them off into the forest. With the first fiery *boom*, I dashed in the opposite direction through the trees.

Footsteps hammered across the ground and veered to the side to track the impact of the grenades.

"What the hell was *that*?"

"We'll check it out. Shine the lights down there. And keep your guns ready."

I slunk away as they headed deeper into the forest. With a little luck, my gambit would stop them from even noticing the open cave until I'd gotten out of here.

Some of the cultists would be investigating the flares. I'd drawn a few more away with the grenades. Now I just needed to tackle however many had stayed behind to guard their great prize.

I took out my own gun, a light pistol Bash had picked up for me years ago, and kept it raised as I eased toward sparser woods up ahead. More moonlight streaked through the forest there.

The outline of a wooden hut came into view, the roof draped with fresh branches to blend it in with the canopy. Others lay beyond it, scattered haphazardly between the trees. Any sort of pattern to a layout made the shrouded folk uneasy. They liked randomness, wildness, like the flaring of a fire, like the searing of the sun they fed off.

A couple of figures moved between the buildings. I froze, watching them as they peered after the departed cultists. They murmured to each other in voices too low for me to make out.

I peered into the space beyond them. Where would they keep the dagger? Definitely toward the middle of the settlement, so it was protected on all sides. And no doubt they had a few people standing guard right by it at any given time. I wasn't making it to my prize through stealth alone.

Stealth could take me pretty far, though. I slipped behind one of the huts and eased around the back. The scent of the shrouded folk, dry and sour like long-rotted meat, wafted over me.

My stomach turned. I'd gotten several weeks without having to taste that stench since I'd left Bog behind. Now it seemed to pool in my lungs, congealing into bile.

The people around me didn't even notice the stink anymore. When you grew up in it or gave yourself over to it for years on end, it was the fresh air beyond the boundaries of the commune that tasted off. It'd taken me months to totally adapt to the regular scents of human life after I'd escaped my parents' settlement in New Mexico.

I darted from one hut to another. Someone on the other side of those walls was humming to themselves in an erratic rhythm that told me they were probably swaying with periodic jerks in a reverence meditation. Even though I'd fallen into that trace nearly every day until I was fourteen, even though I'd *wanted* to align my soul more closely with the shrouded folk, it'd always unnerved me watching other people at it.

I'd navigated about half of the perimeter before I felt certain of the village's layout. Seventeen huts stood sporadically throughout a rough circle about a quarter of a mile across. One just off-center had even more branches heaped on top of it than the others, and now and then the moonlight caught on random dents and slashes on the walls where they'd been carved in deference to the shrouded folk. The dagger had to be in there.

The doorway was so narrow I'd barely fit without turning sideways, hung with a burlap curtain. Three cultists in brown robes stood just outside it. I had to go through them.

I didn't have much time left. I eased closer, grimacing at the sight of their faces, which were smeared with dark smudges of blood. Possibly their own, possibly that of another person or an animal — one way or another, obtained through pain. The shrouded folk liked that kind of burning too. *By hurting, you make holy,* one of the elders in my settlement used to say.

I guessed they were going to be particularly holy after tonight.

With my fingers tight around the pistol, I braced myself. Then I dashed across the last short distance to fling myself at the guards.

My knee caught the nearest one in the gut before he had a chance to react. He doubled over, and I fired a bullet into the side of his head.

The woman next to him whipped around with a submachine gun. Adrenaline spiked through my veins. I slammed my elbow into her wrist and dispatched her with a shot to the forehead.

As she slumped, I caught her just in time to make her a living shield. The third guard fired a couple shots. I shoved her backward into him and blasted the back of his head off as he stumbled. Before he even hit the ground, I was hurtling through the doorway.

The stink of the shrouded folk hung so thickly in the air inside that I could almost feel its texture, like shreds of dry flesh. The room was empty other than a wooden altar just off-center. The dagger, curved and gleaming silver with pure gold strands randomly crisscrossing its hilt, lay on a pool of white velvet in a bowl of carved moonstone.

Yes. I snatched it up and threw myself back out of the hut, jamming the dagger into the belted pouch at my waist as I went.

The curved metal shape bumped against my belly—and a spear of pain rammed through my chest from the protective cuff around my thigh. The sensation in the lower part of that leg and my forearms numbed. I staggered, falling to my hands and knees on the well-trodden forest floor. A choked croak escaped my lips as I fought to draw breath.

Fuck. I had to get out of here. Figures were racing through the trees, brought by the gunshots from just a few seconds ago. I heaved forward, swaying back onto my feet.

With my strained attempt at inhaling, only a trickle of air reached my lungs. The worst of the pain was easing back like it always had before, but the numbness was holding on, seeping deeper with a chill I couldn't shake.

A woman charged at me with a knife. I yanked my gun hand up, much slower than it should have moved. Her blade raked through my oversuit and my bicep all the way to the bone before I managed to squeeze the trigger.

Blood soaked down my sleeve with an even sharper pain. My right foot still couldn't quite find purchase on the ground, prickling tingles racing through it. My head was spinning with the lack of oxygen.

I lurched across the village toward the shelter of the thicker forest. Toward Bash waiting for me at the base of the mountain.

I had the dagger. I had my permanent escape, my chance to turn this all around against the shrouded folk and watch *them* burn. No fucking way was I failing this close to my goal.

A shot rang out just as I ducked farther forward. It clipped my shoulder deep enough to make my flesh flare with agony. I gritted my teeth and stumbled onward.

Then a sound I'd never thought I'd welcome rang out from behind me: a voice speaking strident Croatian, raised to a bellow by a megaphone.

"Down on the ground and stay where you are, by the order of the police!"

The beam of a searchlight swept the village grounds. I was already staggering past the last of the huts into the dense forest that would lead me down to safety.

I made it ten more steps before my half-numbed foot snagged on a root I hadn't seen. I pitched forward into the darkness.

CHAPTER TWENTY-TWO

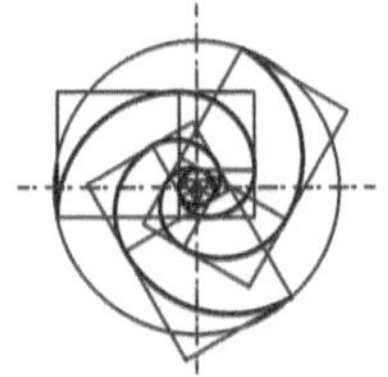

Jemma

Lights came and went farther up the slope. Voices echoed. Something crashed to the ground. One shot split the air, but I didn't hear any gunfire after that.

The members of the shrouded folk's cult were obsessed, but they'd know when they were outnumbered. When they'd seen the number of police coming at them, their first priority would have been to destroy as much evidence of their activities as they could. I had faith that my trio would ferret out enough to put the cultists they rounded up away for one crime or another even if the police weren't as adept.

I had less faith in my ability to make it down the mountain to Bash. I'd been counting on having two working legs and also two functioning lungs. After my fall, which I believed had left me with many bruises but nothing worse, I'd managed to scoot into a dip sheltered by shrubs to try to recover.

What felt like at least an hour later, my chest still strained to drag in even half a breath. My right leg prickled with rising and ebbing waves of numbness. Despite the strips of cloth I'd torn from my oversuit's sleeves to wrap around my wounds, my head was only getting dizzier from lack of blood.

The gold cuff around my thigh set off periodic jabs of pain. The damned thing that was supposed to be protecting me had fucked me over even worse tonight. I had to assume it was reacting badly to the shrouded dagger, but I couldn't exactly leave that behind.

I couldn't call Bash to come collect me either. My phone had been in the pouch with the dagger, and the fall had crushed the screen against the metal blade.

My best option seemed to be staying huddled there like a wounded deer and hoping the cuff would cut me a break sometime soon. Going down the slope wasn't going to take as much energy as coming up had, but I did need to be able to count on both my legs staying in this realm of existence.

The sharp spruce-like scent of the shrubs tickled my nose. I teased my lower lip under my teeth, wishing I had another sugar cube.

A crunch of footsteps in the brush reached my ears, much closer than any had come before.

I stiffened in the moment before a familiar voice called out, low but loud enough to carry. "Jemma?"

It was Sherlock, a fact confirmed by the shuffling gait with which he continued to move toward me, back on his crutch under duress but refusing to let that slow him down. A couple other figures moved through the forest with him. I could guess well enough who they were.

I stayed tensed for a few seconds, my heart thudding, debating my options. I'd wanted to be well on my journey away from the London trio by now. I'd expected the interlude in Sherlock's hotel room would be our last hurrah. But he'd clearly picked up on some clue that had suggested to him I needed help, and, frankly, I wanted to get off this fucking mountain. Keeping the rest of my blood in my body would also be nice.

They'd helped me get this far. I could rely on them a tiny bit farther.

Sherlock was only a few feet away now, pausing to crouch down by the ground with a flashlight. I eased myself upright.

"I'm here."

The beam flashed across my face and hit on my shoulder. Someone—I thought Garrett—sucked in a breath. Then John was pushing forward, one hand tight around his walking stick, the other groping into the messenger bag he was carrying.

Sherlock kept his flashlight trained on me as John produced antiseptic ointment and a roll of gauze.

"Well, you didn't do that bad a job bandaging yourself up for someone bleeding out and one-armed," the doctor muttered, packing and binding my wounds with professional efficiency. "Are you hurt anywhere else?"

He could probably tell those injuries weren't enough to have kept me so close to the village. I caught his eyes. "I fell. Hurt my leg. It's not bleeding or broken, I don't think, just hard to walk on."

From the brief tightening on his face, I could tell he'd followed my hint. He knew what kind of trouble I'd had with my leg before.

"I guess we can thank you for thinning the herd up there before we showed up?" Garrett said, in a tone that suggested he wasn't sure whether to be impressed or horrified by the short work I'd made of however many cultists I'd dispatched. Four? Five?

He grimaced. "Bunch of sick lunatics. I can't believe some of the things they had stashed away."

Good. They'd gotten what they'd come for, then. I glanced at Sherlock, little more than a tall lanky silhouette behind the glow of the flashlight. "How did you know I was here? I'd have thought you had better things to do than track that bracelet."

"I did." He lowered the light enough for me to make out the curl of his lips into a wry smile. "But one distinctive red hair snagged on a twig, an unusual scuffing in the dirt, and a bit of blood told the story well enough."

"Good thing," John said. With his help, I pushed myself onto my feet. The right one met the ground with a sensation as if it was sifting through sand. That wasn't promising at all.

"We could bring you up back to the choppers," Garrett said.

My chest twisted even tighter. I shook my head. "No. Bash is waiting for me. He'll already be worried." I could have asked for one of their phones to relieve a few of those worries, but I didn't want to give them his number. Who knew what information Sherlock could turn up from that.

Besides, the thought of squeezing into a vehicle full of cops and members of the cult I'd spent the last ten years fighting made my skin itch.

John looked to Sherlock. "We could help her make the walk down. It's not that much farther than we came before."

"By daylight," Garrett muttered.

"We wouldn't *all* have to make the trip," Sherlock said, in a tone that placed immediate judgment on anyone unwilling to.

Garrett's jaw clenched. "We're in this together, aren't we? I'll tell the squad leader that we need to meet up with our operative. It'll fit the story we gave them well enough."

He set off toward the village. Sherlock maneuvered down over the rocky ground with swings of his crutch.

I eyed him skeptically. "Are you sure *you* shouldn't be going back for that helicopter ride?"

"I made it this far," Sherlock said. "Between the four of us, we have five good legs. That seems like plenty."

If a fresh burst of pain hadn't flared around my cuff, I would have laughed. As it was, I had to grit my teeth to keep from gasping. My fingers tightened where I was gripping John's elbow. He looked at me in concern.

"I'll be fine," I said. "I just want to get away from this place."

"You found what you needed?" he asked.

"My mission was successful."

Garrett returned a moment later with a flashlight of his own. "All right," he said. "Let's see if we can make it to the bottom without any more injuries."

It was an awkward, rambling descent, veering back and forth as we followed the most even patches of ground. Insects hummed in the brush, and twigs crackled under our feet. My discomfort clung on, but with each step away from the commune, it eased a fraction more.

It hadn't been just the dagger but that whole place setting the cuff's effects into overdrive.

John chuckled to himself and glanced at the other men. "Doesn't this remind you of that case where we spent the whole night wandering around the hilly part of Greenwich Park checking the angles of a bike light around the trees?"

"Lord, don't remind me," Garrett said. "At least tonight we know we accomplished something. I swear Sherlock had that case figured out three days before he let the rest of us in on it—he just likes ordering us around."

"We *did* narrow down the suspects with the information we gleaned with that activity," Sherlock reminded them. "It was a lovely night—rather refreshing, as I recall it."

John outright laughed at that, and a moment later Garrett joined in. Sherlock glowered at them, but he couldn't completely suppress a smile.

Their easy comradery flowed around me with a different sort of warmth than I was usually looking to spark. The kind of warmth that made me want to toss in a clever remark of my own, to become a part of that connection.

A pang spread through my chest. I set my jaw against it. It didn't matter if I liked these men. No, that was all the more reason I had to move on. They could accept me for the moment while we had the same goals, but in the long run? Ha. I'd find myself in handcuffs again.

They'd just have to find new ways to entertain themselves without me.

When we finally emerged from the trees near the pull-off where Bash was waiting, he strode to meet us with a ferocity in his eyes I wouldn't have wanted to be at the wrong end of.

"What happened?" he demanded.

"I had an unfortunate encounter with a knife and then a bullet," I said in the most carefree voice I could summon. "My doctor friend patched them up very nicely, though."

Bash studied me. He could probably tell I was suffering more than just that. The long clamber down had left me exhausted on top of everything else. All I wanted to do was fall into the seat of the van and shut my eyes.

"We should get you to the hospital," John said.

I waved him off. "It's nothing a little rest can't cure." And whatever doctors my upcoming travels could provide.

"Jemma," Garrett started.

I fixed him with a firm look. "I know myself better than anyone does. Besides, you've got this big case to assist with now. There are worse things in this world than me."

"That wasn't —"

"Maybe they're right," Bash said, to my surprise. "We still have a few loose ends to tie up. Why don't we see if they can contribute?"

I raised an eyebrow at him. We'd arrived here separately in the van and the car so we'd have two vehicles in case things turned dire, but the plan had been to hop in the van and floor it to the airport the second I showed up. Granted, I had meant to show up a couple hours earlier. That shouldn't change things all that much.

Did he think I wasn't fit to fly? I took a couple steps, if wobbly ones, on my own and moved my arm while restraining a wince. "What's there to contribute to? I'm good. I bounce back fast. Give me my hotel bed, and I'll have all I need."

He gazed back at me steadily. "It seems like you've run into more complications than you expected."

When had I ever not wriggled my way back out of a situation like that? I tapped his chest. "Into the van with you." I turned to the trio and fished the car's keys out of my pocket. "Since I took you away from your chopper, why don't the three of you drive my car back? If there's anything else you think we absolutely *have* to talk about tonight, you can meet us in the lobby. I'll give you ten minutes. You can even have a head start."

My blasé attitude must have been convincing enough. I tossed the keys to John, who snatched them out of the air with a smile. "Don't burn any rubber," I warned him.

"There are a few matters I would like to discuss, if not tonight then in the morning," Sherlock said, but when I nodded, he moved with the others to the car.

I hopped into the van next to Bash. "Let them go first," I said. "I did promise them their head start."

"What are you up to, Mori?"

I watched as the car's headlights blinked on, swept across the dirt road, and pulled ahead of us on their way back to the city. The pang came back, digging deeper. I shook it away.

"As soon as we're close enough to the city, lose them and get us to the airport. We're still flying out tonight."

CHAPTER TWENTY-THREE

Bash

It wasn't hard to lose the Londoners. I let the van drift several car lengths back as if by chance so we weren't directly in their rearview mirror. Then, when they turned off the highway into the city, we roared on by.

Jemma had borrowed my phone to check flight times. The electronic light reflected off her face, which was a sicklier shade of pale than I'd seen it any time except that one panicked night in London and the night six years ago when she'd gone to rescue her sister and failed. She didn't look up, but the corner of her mouth tightened as we left the three behind. She was paying attention, even if she didn't want to show it.

"Swing around to head back south as soon as you can," she said. "They'll expect us to head for the local airport or to Zagreb. We're going to Dubrovnik instead. We should get there right in time for the first morning flights. This exit up here should let you loop around fast."

She set down the phone for long enough to saw through the silver tracking bracelet Sherlock had fastened around her wrist. As soon as she'd snapped it free, she tossed it and the little hand-saw out the window. They crunched under the tires of a car the next lane over.

I swerved around at the exit she'd indicated, watching her in moments between watching the road.

It wasn't just her paleness that worried me. Now and then her hand trembled where she'd picked up the phone again. The set of her jaw told me she wasn't just focused but mastering the pain that must still be wracking her shoulder and arm. The pungent scent of the antiseptic Watson had applied tainted the air along with a metallic hint of blood. We had Vicodin in the van, but she'd refused it, saying she wanted her mind sharp.

I was pretty sure she was suffering from more than just the obvious wounds too. It took a lot to shake Jemma Moriarty's composure this clearly. Her confrontation with the cult had hurt her in other ways too, ways I couldn't entirely understand.

Ways I didn't think even she had been prepared for. Would she have made it down the mountain at all if Sherlock hadn't found her? The question sent an uneasy jab through my chest. I'd have gone looking for her eventually, orders be damned, but I couldn't say for sure I'd have found her in time.

"Where are we flying into?" I asked.

"I'll take the earliest one—that'll get me to Dusseldorf. There's one a little later into Istanbul that we'll put you on. From there, I think our easiest meet-up point will be Paris. Maybe we'll take a day or two there before we embark on our ocean crossing."

"You said we're going to Chile?"

She nodded. "That's the end point. But I'm thinking word will spread about our adventure tonight, and my monsters might figure out what I'm planning. There's going to be a solar eclipse over part of Chile next week—that's what I need to get there for. It's probably better if we don't arrive until just before I can use it."

Lowering the phone into her lap, she closed her eyes. It was just past four in the morning, and she looked as if she needed a few days' worth of sleep. Maybe she could catch a couple hours during the drive to the airport.

Five minutes later, her whole body tensed with a breath sucked through her teeth. I winced, my hands clenching around the steering wheel.

"Mori?"

"It's okay," she said in an unnaturally hollow voice. "It's getting better now that the fucking dagger is stashed in the back."

In the entire seven years I'd worked for and alongside Jemma, I'd never once doubted that she could pull off whatever scheme she set her mind to—not even in those sick-with-anguish moments in the past. Those, she'd barreled through with her usual force of will. Right now, looking at her, hearing her, the suspicion niggled at me that something tonight had attacked her right down to her strength of will.

Whatever she had to do in Chile, it was even more important than this mission tonight had been. She'd just told me she expected the monsters she was battling to track her there. Tonight they hadn't been ready for her. How much worse was the fight going to be when they were?

If she'd been one of my early clients, this would have been the moment where I'd have backed out. A client wavering on the edge put everyone around them at risk. I wasn't in this for thrills. I had no interest in gambling with my life just for a little extra money.

But I hadn't been in this for the money for a long time. The idea of abandoning Jemma didn't even feel like an *idea*, just a concept as bizarre as turning my gun collection into an art installation or running away to join the goddamn circus.

I'd meant it every time I told her I'd have her back through anything. But I'd been saying that to the Jemma I knew, the Jemma who always came out on top. I still meant it now, though, didn't I? Even if she faltered, even if she stumbled right into some monster's maw, I'd be right there with her.

I cared about this woman too fucking much, and I didn't even mind.

I cared about her enough that I couldn't help saying, even though she'd shot down my earlier hints, "Your London friends did end up coming in handy. Are you sure we couldn't put them to some good use overseas?"

Jemma snorted softly. "You should be glad we're rid of them," she teased. "No more competition." Her eyes turned more serious as she contemplated the landscape beyond the window. Dark waves undulated across the moonlit ocean at our right. "Anyway, they're more hassle than they're worth. They might make more of a mess rather than less of one. We can handle this just the two of us."

Did she completely believe that, or was she trying to convince herself as well as me? For just a second, before she rubbed her hand over her face and closed her eyes again, I'd have sworn she looked sad.

"They seemed to handle the mess tonight just fine," I said, because apparently I didn't know when to quit.

Jemma opened her eyes to shoot me a narrow look. "What is it with you right now? You don't even like them."

But you do. And maybe what she'd said about me wasn't entirely true. All three of them could be jackasses in their assorted ways, Sherlock especially, and I wasn't absolving them of dragging her off at gunpoint any time soon, but I'd seen the way they responded to her during our planning. It was hard to completely hate anyone who'd give this woman all the respect she was due, even if they gave it somewhat begrudgingly.

"I know how important this last operation is," I said instead. "Anything that could swing the situation more in our favor sounds good to me. We've gotten a lot of mileage out of them so far."

Jemma smirked for a moment before that good humor faded. "We did. But convincing them to travel halfway across the world and battle monsters is a very different thing. I'm not going to count on that kind of commitment."

Maybe she should, though—or at least give it a shot. If they didn't turn up, we weren't any worse off than otherwise. After everything I'd seen, I couldn't believe she really thought they'd screw things up more than they'd contribute, unwittingly or not.

I drove in silence for a while, mulling that over, trying to find the right words to frame around the growing knot of uneasiness in my chest. Finally, I said, "I've never told you about my father."

"Not enough that I know more than that he was an asshole," Jemma said.

"That would be phrasing it mildly. He put on a good front—had a nice white-collar job, sniveled to his bosses like a loyal lackey—but he hated being ordered around. He got back at them by skimming profits out from under them, and he took out the rest of his frustration by pushing us around—me and my brother and sister, and sometimes my mom too if she tried to stop him."

Those memories didn't bring up any emotion now other than a dull resignation. That was what normal had looked like for the first sixteen years of my existence: cutting insults and barked criticisms, a shove, a smack. And I didn't see any need to think back on the even darker moments when his frustration had tipped over into fury.

Jemma's full attention was on me now. "Well, he sounds like a prime candidate for getting a bullet in the brain."

I had to laugh, without much humor. "That's what I thought. I got the younger ones out of there to our grandparents when I could, and then I conned my way into army training early. The whole time I was out there in the field, I knew I was coming back for him. It was the only thing I was sure of."

"Then he got what he deserved."

"I think so, but not exactly like that." I paused. "When I went back for him, I hadn't been in touch for years. It turned out my mom had finally kicked him out of the house. He'd gotten caught at his job, fired and blacklisted. He was working at some shitty diner serving coffee and going home alone to a dingy roach-infested apartment. He couldn't have been more miserable. I watched him for a while, and all I could think was, why would I want to put him *out* of his misery? He earned that. Let him stew in it. So, I left with the bullet still in my gun."

Jemma smiled. "My earlier comment still stands, then."

"It does," I agreed. "My point is—I've only spared someone's life once, and that was to leave him worse off than if I'd killed him. I've *never* seen you back down from a necessary hit. But you trusted those three enough that you decided you were better off with them still living, even after what they did to you, even with them being on the other side of the law. It's up to you what we do about them now. I won't bring it up again. I just thought I should point that out."

Jemma was quiet for a long moment. When she spoke again, her voice came out a little stiffly. "I think I'm in the best position to make judgments on how we go forward. The less said about the London trio from here on, the better. Understood?"

I dipped my head, the knot in my chest hardening into something more pointedly uncomfortable. "Understood."

We didn't speak any more after that. She might have slept for a half hour or so as I drove on along the coast. The sun started to rise, streaking pale pink across the scattered clouds in the sky. Jemma shifted and undid her seatbelt as the city came into view up ahead.

"Drive carefully," she said in a wry tone that said we were putting any previous tension behind us. "We're cutting it close for that first flight. I'm going to get changed."

She squeezed into the back and returned in slacks and a loose blouse that covered her bandages. I parked the van in the airport parking lot, and we grabbed our remaining bags from the back. At a kiosk, Jemma picked up the tickets she'd purchased via my phone and handed my boarding pass to me as we hustled toward security.

Just before we reached the line, she stiffened. "Shit, I almost forgot." She turned to me and passed over a plastic bag from her purse. "I didn't want to get rid of these until we were on our way. You know what to do with them."

"Of course."

She smiled up at me, briefly radiant despite her exhaustion. "I'll see you in Paris later this afternoon."

"Enjoy your flight," I said with a crooked smile in return, avoiding the impulse to tell her to take care of herself as if she wouldn't.

As well as she could. She rose up to kiss me steadily enough, and for the few seconds her lips lingered against mine, it was hard to feel anything but awed that this woman had decided to lower her guard so far for me. But I couldn't miss the wobble she quickly controlled as she walked to the end of the line. I forced myself to turn away as if I had nothing but total confidence that she'd reach our distant meeting point in full health.

The bag contained several burner phones that Jemma had used for various purposes across our stay in Croatia. I ducked into a stall in the restroom and set about disassembling them and crushing the chips that held the information about who they'd been used to contact or what about.

One of the phones I recognized as the silver flip phone she'd texted the Londoners on a few times. I saved that for last. As I curled my fingers around its cool surface, the knot inside me tugged my ribs tight.

I didn't like that Holmes, Watson, and Lestrade had earned some of Jemma's respect in turn. I didn't like that it obviously bothered her to put an end to whatever they'd had. My job was to look out for her, though, not wallow in my own petty feelings. I was important to her… and there was no denying that they'd become important too.

If they were loyal enough to deserve her affection, let them come and prove it. Making sure she made it through the next week alive was a hell of a lot more important to *me* than how pissed off I might make her.

Technically, she'd only told me not to talk *about* them, not *to* them.

I checked that the restroom was otherwise empty, pulled up the text history, and found Sherlock's number. The line rang as I raised the phone to my ear. I'd rather not leave him with a visual record of this conversation—and I wanted him to know for sure the tip had come from a legitimate source.

He picked up on the third ring. "Jemma, what are you up to now?"

"This isn't Jemma," I said quietly. "It's Moran. We're leaving to take on even bigger monsters than you did last night."

Sherlock's tone turned more urgent. "Where are you going?"

"There's an eclipse she needs to use. I'm sure if you care to be there, the three of you can figure out the rest."

I ended the call and crushed that phone's inner workings like I had the others. On my way out of the restroom, I tossed the bag in the garbage bin.

The pressure in my chest had released a little with those few sentences. Not the way I'd felt when I'd walked away from my father with my gun unfired. No, more like when I'd waved good-bye to Mike and Sara while they'd watched from our grandparents' window.

I'd done the right thing by them then. Here was hoping I'd done the right thing by Jemma now.

CHAPTER TWENTY-FOUR

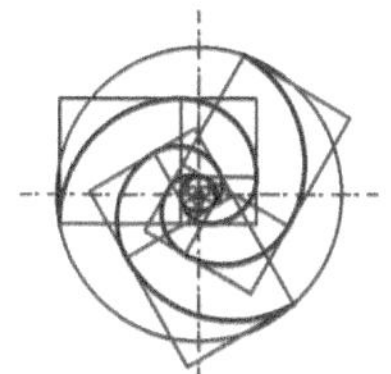

Jemma

There's one," I said to Bash as we eased through the town marketplace. I gestured surreptitiously to a woman standing by a fruit stand.

He made note of her with a glance. "How can you tell?"

"They stand out in the sun for hours sometimes in meditation—there's a specific pose. I can see it in her posture. The way she lifted her face toward the sky for a second."

I veered away from the cultist toward a stall selling stuffed tomatoes. The smells of grilled meat and vegetables and a cacophony of spices tickled my nose. I'd have enjoyed it if it hadn't been for the hints of the shrouded folk's dryly rancid scent mingling with the local atmosphere. Some of the folk were prowling alongside their sycophants, invisible yet leaving a trace I could recognize.

The street ahead of us sloped slightly downward. I walked carefully, wary of my wobbly right leg, not wanting to draw any attention by falling. This place wasn't exactly the best environment for someone who had enchanted jewelry gradually wearing away at her thigh.

The whole town sprawled across the side of a low mountain, turning into a patchwork of brightly colored buildings when viewed from above. We'd just come down from the open area along the mountain's peak where I'd been scouting out the best spot to complete the bond-breaking ritual during the eclipse. The dagger was supposed to give me the powers of a shrouded one, and the shrouded folk liked to be close to the sky.

Since I wasn't sure if this ritual was going to work at all, I figured I'd better increase the odds as much as I could. All I had to go on in my planning was what I'd observed of Bog when we'd made our pact, the part I'd had to play in it, and the fealty rituals I'd witnessed for the younger cult children.

It was going to be harder getting up to the mountaintop this evening with shrouded folk and their cultists prowling the place. I'd spotted a couple of men who'd rubbed my instincts the wrong way outside a church on our way back into town. Now, ducking past a shoe shop, I noticed another woman, this one swaying in a slight erratic rhythm for a second before she caught herself.

If I'd already seen four on our first real jaunt through town, how many more were wandering through here? The shrouded folk who'd been hanging around the commune might not have been able to see who'd stolen the dagger, but they'd know someone had and where a person could use it. And if even one of the cultists who'd gotten a glimpse at me had managed to pass on word to another settlement, all of them would know to look for a slim woman with bright red hair.

Which was why I'd picked up a wig on our rambling travels across the last week. I gave the dark strands a brief tug to confirm it was still secure after our hike, wishing I'd gone blond instead of black. The bright sun was turning my head into a sauna. At least it'd keep anyone from noticing me as long as I didn't do anything eye-catching.

Bash leaned close to me as we left the marketplace behind for less crowded streets. "How do they know to look for you here? It's a big country."

"It is, but there's only a narrow strip where the full eclipse will be visible. They're probably watching for me all along that strip, but this is the only town completely centered along the path."

"Are you sure we should do this here, then?"

My mouth tightened grimly. "I need civilization around to blend into as soon as I'm finished. Once I take off the cuff, even after my contract with the monster is severed, they'll be able to sense me again, affect me again, with whatever power the cultists are giving them. On some lonely mountaintop, they'd break my body on the rocks, lickety split. But they're very cautious about revealing themselves to the rest of human society. They'd sooner let me escape than put their magic on display right in the middle of all these people."

Bash nodded, but his forehead was furrowed. I touched his arm, a simple gesture that felt weirdly intimate now that we'd started touching each other in a whole lot of other ways, but it was getting more normal with each passing day.

"I know this is a lot to take in," I said. "You can let me worry about the supernatural stuff. The cultists—they're just regular humans who think they're something special. You won't have any trouble taking them on."

"I'm not worried, Mori," he said. "It's those bastards who should be."

I wished I felt as confident as he sounded. My leg was throbbing from the long walk, even worse today than yesterday, and too many factors drifted beyond my control.

I'd never known anyone who'd challenged the shrouded folk at all, let alone like this. I had no guidelines for the right approach. I was winging it, and I vastly preferred being prepared.

Especially when Bash's life might very well be on the line as much as my soul was.

An icy jolt shot up from my thigh. I stumbled, and Bash caught me around the waist. He dipped his head toward mine at the same time to give the impression he was tugging me close for romantic reasons rather than to stop me from toppling over on the slanted street, in case any suspicious eyes were watching.

"Okay?" he murmured, a much more pleasant heat washing over me where his body pressed against mine.

"Just a minute." I gritted my teeth, willing the pain back. The cuff had been acting up more and more in the week since we'd left Split, hitting me harder at least a few times a day and continuing to jab at me for minutes at a time instead of seconds. If the eclipse had been farther off, I'd have hung in there even if I'd had to crawl my way to the ritual spot. Thank God I didn't have to find out just how bad it could get.

A dog trotted past us down the road—a stray with notched ears and patchy fur. My gaze followed it as it disappeared down a side street. Blood and anguish helped the shrouded folk transition their powers into this world. A creature like Bog would have delighted in having an animal as aware as a dog used in its honor.

My gut twisted, and not from the pain in my leg. It might have been effective to use one of the town's many strays to boost the dagger's magic, but I wasn't going to give the shrouded folk the satisfaction of having turned me into a monster like them. There'd be blood and pain this evening, but it'd all be mine.

Bash's thumb stroked up and down my side. The jagged ache the gold cuff had sent through me gradually retreated. I tested my leg, and we walked on.

We'd rented a second floor apartment in a little house with beaming yellow walls and a crimson roof. I'd paid for a month upfront on a one-year lease even though we'd only arrived here last night and didn't plan on sticking around more than a day. Our enemies—and anyone else who might be trying to track our movements—wouldn't be looking for apparently long-term renters.

Money couldn't fix all one's problems, but it certainly made tackling some of them easier.

We'd spent each night in a different city before arriving here just in time for the eclipse, even making a stop in Naples so Bash could get himself some one hundred percent authentic pizza—after which he'd informed me that he still liked the New York stuff the best. Through a truly valiant effort, I hadn't rolled my eyes.

If the London trio had bothered trying to trace our movements, they'd have had a long trail to unravel. I didn't think they'd make it very far. How far would they really want to chase me at this point?

Before, they'd been confused and uneasy about who I was and why I'd roped them into the heist. Now, they pretty much had their answers. They had the commune to finish dealing with and cases back home in London waiting for them. Our paths might cross if mine took me back to the UK, but I wasn't posing any threat to them at the moment.

Even thinking that, though, I couldn't help scanning the street before we stepped into the house, not just for any cultish figures but for a familiar tall lanky form, head of golden hair, or boyishly handsome face. Even though we had technically been enemies most of the time I'd known them, I'd worked with the three of them more closely than anyone other than Bash. I'd told them things I'd never *told* anyone other than Bash.

Maybe I was just a little uneasy knowing they were roaming around out there in the world with that knowledge, outside my control. Yes, the pinch in my chest couldn't be more than that.

Bash kept his arm around me as we climbed up the stairs. I stepped away from him once we reached our apartment, but only to walk as far as the bedroom. I flopped down on the light duvet with a sigh as the tension in my thigh eased.

Bash sat down on the end of the bed beside me. He rested his hand gently on my knee, bare where my tourist-y sundress had ridden up a little. "Would a massage help?"

The dip of his voice promised attentions even more enjoyable than just a massage. Desire sparked low in my belly, but I didn't want him seeing my upper leg right now. The flesh around the cuff had become almost completely translucent. I could easily see the outline of my femur through it. I felt nauseated looking at myself like that—not really the reaction I wanted to provoke in my right-hand man turned lover.

"I think it's better just to leave it alone," I said, and sat up to take his hand in mine. I hesitated before tipping my head against his shoulder. So many tiny gestures of affection I'd only ever used as a ploy before.

"Are you ready for tonight?" he asked.

"As much as I can be. It'll mostly be a matter of getting to that spot on the mountain. The cultists are going to be on the alert when it gets close to eclipse time. And they can probably guess I'd head for higher ground."

"I'll have your back all the way there." Bash lifted his chin toward the bag in the corner that held a rifle, a couple pistols, and plenty of ammunition. "Anyone comes at you, I'll take them down."

Until the shrouded folk realize what you're doing and take you *down*, I thought, my chest clenching. Bullets couldn't hurt those misty fiends.

The shrouded folk would have encouraged their followers to feed their power with everything they could. If their rulers had decided I was fair game for a hunt, then anyone helping me would be too.

"I don't want you sacrificing yourself," I said. "If the odds go against us, you get out of there. If I'm dead, I'm dead anyway, so there's no point in you dying too in the process."

"Mori." Bash touched my jaw and turned my face so he could meet my gaze. "There's no way in hell I'm bailing on you. What kind of asshole would I be if I took off to save my own hide while I might still make a difference? We're breaking this thing's claim on you together. And then you know I'm ready to go tear all the rest of those monsters apart for you."

I couldn't help smiling at his vehemence. "*I'm* going to tear them apart," I corrected him. "But I'll let you help."

The corner of his lips curled up. "Then I'll be there, by my faith and honor."

I poked his chest. "And *then* you can take up your true calling as a Shakespearean actor."

Bash laughed and tugged me closer. We'd explored the uncertain space between us enough that he felt comfortable going straight for a kiss. I kissed him back, letting the heat of his mouth wash away any lingering pain.

That kiss bled into another and another, until all I could smell was his perfect musky scent, until all I could feel was that heat and the flex of his muscular shoulders beneath my roaming hands. He was a perfect pocket of someplace else in the middle of the horrors both behind and ahead of me.

Longing unfurled from my core up through my chest. It hadn't exactly been easy moderating my interludes with Bash over the last week, despite my best intentions. We'd reached the point of getting each other off with a well-placed hand. All that hesitation felt a little silly now.

Since I'd met him, I'd never been closer to dying than I would be tonight. I knew I wasn't seducing him into staying or fulfilling some other selfish need. I just wanted him. I wanted the thrill of his cock inside me, the total release and the sensation of him following me over that edge.

I wanted to have sex with this man clear-headed and open-eyed, for no reason other than because of how much we'd both enjoy it, and this might be my last chance.

I shifted around to settle myself on his lap. Bash scooted back on the bed, one hand coming to rest on my side to steady me. I kissed him again and again as he eased down the flexible straps of my dress.

When he slid his hand beneath the fabric to cup my breast, I made an encouraging sound. My teeth grazed his lower lip, and he pressed his other hand to my back, kissing me harder.

As his thumb flicked over my nipple with increasing pressure, our tongues tangled between our mouths. I rocked against his growing erection, and he groaned. My hands found the bottom hem of his shirt and yanked it up. While I peeled it off of him, he yanked the bodice of my dress all the way down and tossed my bra aside.

For a second, as he palmed both my breasts, I could only gasp. I tilted forward, my lips brushing his cheek.

"I think we've done enough waiting."

He gave a ragged laugh and kissed me before saying, "I couldn't agree more, Majesty." He teased his hands down my torso and back to my breasts, studying my expression. "I don't want to hurt your leg even more than it already is. Is this a good position?"

"Mmm, I think this works just fine." I sank so my core grazed his cock. With him sitting up, supporting part of my weight, I didn't have to flex my thigh too much, and I could keep the skirt of my dress pooled over the unnerving section of flesh around the cuff. Having him on top of me could quickly turn from *ooooh* to *ouch!* "Let's stay right here."

I reached for the fly of his jeans, but he caught my hand and eased me back so he could bring his mouth to my breast. His tongue swiped over the already taut nipple, and a little growl escaped me. My hips rocked impatiently, but his mouth felt so good I couldn't bear to tell him to stop.

Bash took his time, working over one side to send a rush of pleasure through my chest, and then repeating his attentions on the other. My fingernails dug into his shoulders. Need pulsed between my legs. When he finally raised his head, I yanked his mouth back to my lips and jerked open his jeans at the same time.

His cock sprang free with a few tugs. Bash grabbed my purse and retrieved a condom. I bobbed eagerly as he slicked it over his erection. Then I was sinking *all* the way down, whimpering as the head of his cock pushed past my opening, letting out a shaky sigh when he filled me completely with that blissful burn.

"Mori," Bash said softly, touching my cheek. His light green eyes were soft too as he gazed back at me. The tenderness I saw in his expression would have made me retreat any other time. Even now, my lungs started to clench up.

I inhaled slowly, leaning into the feeling. The knowledge that this man cared more about standing by my side than keeping himself alive. The knowledge that I was willing to put my own life at even greater risk if it meant seeing him safely away.

I didn't know if I was capable of the sort of love his Shakespeare wrote about. I'd never felt that strongly about anyone except Olivia. But this was something—something good, something I'd never had before. As I relaxed into the sensation, the pleasure building inside me shimmered giddily.

"Until the end?" I said.

Bash's voice rasped. "Until the end."

His mouth captured mine as he lifted his hips to meet me. A breath shuddered out of me at that first sharper burst of bliss. I ground down against him, and he urged me on with his hand gripping my ass.

You'd have thought I'd gone a year without sex rather than a week. With just a few thrusts, I could already feel my peak on the horizon. A twinge shot through my thigh, but I ignored it, pumping faster over him.

My lips tore from his. He kissed my neck as he fondled my breast with his other hand. His cock plunged into me over and over, so hard and fast and *right*—

I moaned as ecstasy swelled and crashed inside me. Bash's breath spilled harsh against my skin. As I clenched around him, he held me tight and came with a groan that reverberated through us both.

My head dipped to rest on his shoulder. His arms wrapped around me, hugging me to him. As we lingered there in the moment after the first time I'd done anything remotely close to "making love," an ache formed around my heart.

There were so many things I hadn't known I was capable of doing, capable of feeling, before the last few weeks. Before just now. What a shame that unless a whole lot of luck was with me tonight, I'd never get the chance to make the most of them.

CHAPTER TWENTY-FIVE

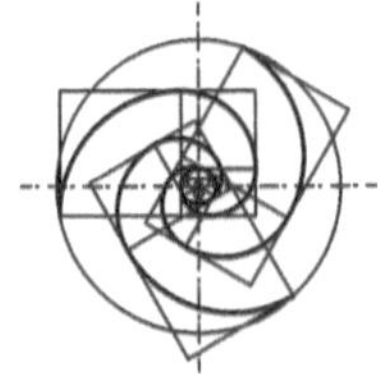

Jemma

The day had wound down, but the sun still seared along the rooftops across the town. Slowly but surely, the moon edged closer to covering it. From my mountain perch, the eclipse would be completely visible.

And it was going to be a perch in a very literal sense, because I clearly needed to adjust my plans. I hadn't realized how many tourists would come even to this small-ish town, eager just to get a glimpse of the eclipse at its fullest.

Bash and I wove through the growing crowd on the sparsely treed slope above the edge of the town. Groups of people clustered together talking in excited voices and waving their viewing devices.

They gave us cover, and the shrouded folk weren't likely to strike out at us with so many witnesses this close. Unfortunately, the crowd also hid our human enemies. They might become enemies themselves if they freaked out once I started cutting myself to bring forth the dagger's power. I wasn't going to get through this night if a bunch of good Samaritans jumped in thinking they were saving me from myself.

So, rather than bracing myself on the barren patch right at the peak, where a bunch of locals had set up folding chairs amid the tourists, I was going to make use of the slab of rock that jutted from the slope a little farther down. Its uneven, weed-dotted surface loomed a few feet over the heads of those passing by, and it looked like a tough enough climb to dissuade any adventurers from taking a seat on its narrow top. I could manage it, though.

As long as my leg didn't totally fail me.

A sharp prickling ran through my limb from knee to hip, deepening to a now-constant throbbing around my joints. I had the dagger tucked in my purse, and the cuff's protective magic was working overtime to defend against the shrouded folk's essence imbued in the blade. I'd wrapped the weapon in a silk scarf with a geometric pattern that dulled the affect a little — but not enough to spare me the discomfort.

The hike wasn't too difficult, at least. I'd picked another summery dress so I could snap off the gold cuff beneath it quickly, but I had practical walking shoes on my feet. Among the tourists, I was far from the most haphazardly dressed.

The summer heat was starting to wane, but the wind that licked over the gathered spectators still warmed my skin. At the same time, it chilled my gut. The sour smell of the shrouded folk hung thicker in the air now.

They knew where I was most likely to make my stand. They and their followers would be gathering around this crowd while I moved through it.

I glanced at Bash to indicate the perch I'd chosen. He nodded in return, his face shaded by a red baseball cap. As we meandered toward the slab, his hand hovered close to the holster hidden under his touristy polo shirt. As soon as we'd seen the growing crowd, he'd known he wasn't getting any use out of his rifle, but a pistol could take down any cultist who got too close to me just fine.

The crowd was thinner around my slab, the ground near it rockier and less comfortable for standing. I circled around to the spot where I could most easily clamber up to the top, smiling at people we passed as if I were just another friendly sightseer.

A gasp nearby made my head jerk up, but the sunlight was only just starting to waver as the moon drifted along its path. I checked my watch. We had several minutes left before totality.

When I lowered my eyes, they landed on a head of messy dark waves that stood out in the middle of the shorter figures all around it. My body stiffened for a second before I caught my reaction.

It was Sherlock. He proceeded methodically through the crowd, his piercing blue eyes scanning the faces around him. I shifted on my feet to ease a little farther behind a nearby couple and spotted Garrett prowling along the edge of the spectators on the other side. No doubt John was around here somewhere too, then.

I ducked my head to let the sleek black strands of my wig shield my face. "What is it?" Bash murmured, tensing, and then relaxed a little with a soft chuckle. "They made an appearance after all."

"Just as long as they don't get in my way," I said.

"I'll pull back. I can cover you better from a little farther away anyway, and it might not take them long to recognize me without a full disguise."

I grabbed his hand to squeeze it. "Whatever happens, we've had a good run of it."

He smiled. "Absolutely."

A tugging sensation ran through my chest as he walked away. Not just to stay close to *him*—I had the urge to stride on over to the London trio and ask what exactly they thought they were doing here. To see the interest that would light in their faces no matter how they felt about my giving them the slip last week. To banter with them one last time.

They really might try to get in my way, though. I only had a few minutes left before I made my move. I had to stay here, braced and ready and beyond their notice.

A fresh pain stabbed down to my ankle and up behind my ribs. I sucked in a shallow breath. Yes, I needed every shred of energy and control I had just to get this chance.

The light was dimming faster now. The voices around me quieted to awed murmurs. Through the fall of my false hair, I saw Sherlock's gaze lock on Bash where my hitman had stationed himself in the crowd. The detective tapped something into his phone as he headed that way. Summoning the other members of the trio, I assumed.

If I'd had more time, I might have tried to interfere. But Bash could handle himself—and the moon was creeping toward the far edge of the sun now. Shadows sharpened against the ground.

I couldn't delay any longer. I had to be at the top of that slab by the time the eclipse was complete. The moon's position would only give me one minute to finish my task.

Clenching my jaw against the pain radiating from my thigh, I marched up to the jutting protrusion of rock and leapt to plant my feet on a bulge on its side. A knife of agony speared through me, but I clutched onto the best handholds I could find and hauled myself upward. My elbow scraped against the rough stone.

Shouts rang across the slope. I had to keep all my concentration on the climb, but the rancid scent of the shrouded folk congealed around me as I yanked myself closer to the top of the slab. Scrambling for another foothold, I banged my right knee and bit my lip to hold in a cry as the impact amplified the cuff's painful effect. My fingers caught hold of the slab's upper edge.

Movement flickered at the edges of my vision. Bash's striped shirt flashed in the dwindling light as he threw himself into someone —one of the cultists, I assumed. A length of dark brown that might have been John's walking stick whipped through the air. Someone grunted, someone hollered. I heaved myself onto my perch—and the click of a gun made my blood turn to ice.

I ducked down instinctively. The shot crackled through the air close enough that the air rippled against my face. Screams echoed across the mountainside. There was a thump, and another shot nowhere near me.

I couldn't wait. The light around us had turned to dusk. With a choked gasp, I shoved myself upright.

My leg wobbled under me but held despite the agony of the climb. Below my perch, the eclipse spectators were milling around, most of them streaming back toward the city's buildings. Well, that would give Bash a clearer shot at any cultist who came at me now.

It'd also mean that the shrouded folk could attack with less caution, but I couldn't worry about that yet.

The wind cooled as the moon slid over the last bit of sun. The tone of a sunrise lit the horizon all around me. A tiny line of brilliance shone around the dark circle in the sky.

It was time.

I dug the dagger out of my purse with one hand while I yanked up my dress with the other. My fingers flicked the snaps on the cuff, and the gold pieces dropped onto the stone.

Bog's mark on the back of my neck flared as if prodded with a searing brand. The glimmering streaks that showed at least a dozen shrouded folk wavered into view around me, but whatever energy they'd been fed by their sycophants, their light was dimmed to near transparency with the blocking of the sun.

That didn't stop them from flinging themselves at me.

"Back!" I shouted, and sliced the dagger in two swift strokes across the inside of my elbow and wrist where the flesh was most sensitive. The pain that flared through my arm immediately overtook the throbbing that was fading from my leg.

"I claim this pain, I claim this blood," I called out, brandishing the dagger. "I am shrouded, and you may not touch me."

A wave of power washed over me from the blade, dizzying and vast. The glimmers of the shrouded folk flinched back.

In that instant, the landscape around me dulled like a sepia photo. The sense of an immense space beyond it rang through my body down to the bones—a space that belonged to me. A space from which I could rule.

No, it didn't belong to me. That was the realm of the shrouded folk, and it only belonged to this dagger. The seconds while I could wield its magic were slipping away from me.

"There is no one more powerful than me," I declared, hoping that in this moment while the sun was swallowed, it was true. "I sever the claim of another on this human soul and stake my own claim. She belongs to me."

I wrenched my wig off my coiled hair and brought the dagger to the base of my scalp. Bog's mark was still burning away. I dug the blade into it, splitting the mark with an X. The pain of the cut skin and the dribble of blood wiped away the sear of my former contract.

"I give myself freely to myself," I said, in case that side needed to be covered too. "I accept Jemma Moriarty's claim."

My voice sounded warbled to my own ears, as if I were falling away from it into that eerily vast space. Another flare of sensation raced over my skin, this one bright and binding. A rush of exhilaration chased after it.

I was mine now. I belonged only to me, for the first time since my birth. None of the shrouded folk could overstep the claim I'd made while I held more power than any of them with this dagger and the dimmed sun.

They couldn't stake a claim, but they could affect me in other ways. As I dropped the dagger onto the wad of silk in my purse, the blade's purpose fulfilled, the moon edged a little away from the sun. Starker beams of light shot from around its edge. The early dusk began to brighten, and the glimmers of light that showed the shrouded folk's presence quivered into clearer focus.

The sense of power slipped away from me, leaving me with only my totally human joy at my victory and the ache spreading from my wounds. I was no longer the creature with the most authority here, and the cultists had made their own sacrifices for their pseudo gods.

I crouched to slide down off the slab—not fast enough. A whirl of bright streaks flung itself at me and slammed into my side with enough force to break a rib. With a hitch of breath, I skidded off the side of the protrusion and plummeted toward the rocky ground below.

CHAPTER TWENTY-SIX

Garrett

We left the Chilean town behind, following the locals and tourists who were spreading out across the mountaintop. There were dozens of people ahead of us, but I didn't catch a single glimpse of Jemma's flaming hair. I glanced at Sherlock as we started up the slope.

"Are you sure she'll be here?"

Sherlock gave me the haughty look that often came over him when anyone questioned his reasoning. "It wasn't as if I needed to consider the entire world or even a large portion of it. Narrowing down my range of inquiry to the path of the eclipse, I should hope I'd be able to locate two reasonably distinctive travelers."

"They're not looking all that distinct to me right now." I eyed the crowd ahead of us. "What the hell would she even be doing here?"

"All her man told you is that she needed to watch the eclipse, right?" John said at Sherlock's other side, leaning a little more than usual on his walking stick as we hit a steeper section.

Sherlock kept a slightly slower pace than usual too, sans ankle brace but wary of turning his recovering foot again. He frowned at John's question.

"That's the gist of it. He didn't say why. And this appears to be the ideal location for those in town to observe. The fact that he shared that information does still concern me, though."

"That and the fact that she left us in the lurch *again* back in Split?" I said.

John's gaze roved over the sightseers nearly as intently as Sherlock's, twitching here and there at sudden movements. What was he worried about?

"It was hardly 'in the lurch'," he said without looking at me. "There was nothing fake about the evidence we found in that commune. If she hadn't looped us in, the cult would have kept up all the torture and the thefts and—everything."

He was right. And it was because of that I couldn't summon any real anger about Jemma's second disappearance. Had I really expected her to sit around and have tea with us after she'd gotten what she needed? She was still an admitted criminal, and we were still men sworn to bring criminals down. Which led me to my main concern.

"All right. Then why are we here at all? To finally bring her in for stealing that relic? Because we don't have evidence of any other crime *she's* committed, and last time I checked, there weren't any laws against watching an eclipse."

John's mouth tightened. "It might be an opportunity for someone to commit a crime *against* her. She said that this cult is widespread. They've already tried to kill her at least once. Whether she put Moran up to the call or he made it of his own accord, it could have been for her protection."

"The whole thing seems too complicated to me," I muttered. Poisonings, psychotic cults, random trips across the ocean… I could have been spending the rest of my vacation on a beach someplace where I wouldn't have to beware of anything worse than a sunburn.

I could have been, but when Sherlock and John had picked up the chase, I'd come here anyway. Maybe it was because when I thought of Jemma, what I remembered first was seeing her huddled weak among the trees outside the commune. And then my mind went to the efforts she'd taken to clear the air between us back in Zagreb.

She'd needed me for her plans in London. I hadn't really served much use in her operations in Croatia—nothing Sherlock or John couldn't have taken over. Nonetheless it had mattered to her to make peace, even after the rough way we'd treated her when we'd assumed she was leading the cult rather than fighting them. Wasn't it all right then for it to matter a little to me what happened to her?

I didn't have a solid answer, but it'd been enough justification to get me on the plane.

That morning with her in my hotel room, she'd suggested I could get her out of my system. Clearly I hadn't managed that yet.

"No matter what her reasons are, we'll be on our guard for whatever comes," Sherlock said. "Come on, let's split up to cover more area at once. Your phones still have a signal? We can alert each other that way if we spot either of them."

Without waiting for our agreement, Sherlock strode off to the right, so I headed left, leaving John to take the middle route. The sightseers looked excited, grins and upbeat chatter all around me. I forced my mouth into a smile so I didn't look too out of place.

Jemma wasn't a stranger to disguises. She could be anywhere here. I eyed every woman—and even some of the men—checking for signs that their appearance was only a front.

My gaze settled on a couple at the edge of the crowd, and my instincts tingled uneasily. They weren't chattering happily, just standing there rather stiffly with their eyes fixed on the crowd. They were looking across the mountainside rather than down toward the dimming sun.

What—or who—were they watching for? What was about to happen here? I couldn't think of any crime it would make sense to commit at this specific moment in the middle of this event.

My phone chimed in my pocket. I glanced up without checking it, my gaze finding Sherlock across the way with no trouble thanks to his height. He was cutting through the crowd with all the intensity of a homing missile.

I managed to follow his gaze to a guy in a baseball cap and polo shirt standing higher up the slope. A guy with enough bulk to fill out that shirt with muscle and a strong tanned jaw beneath the cap's shade. Moran.

My attention skittered across the crowd around him with a lurch of my heart. If he was here, then Jemma almost certainly was. Probably close. But with the sunlight dwindling even more as the moon drifted across it, it was getting harder to make out faces at a distance.

I set off to join Sherlock. He might need backup.

John clearly had the same idea. His bright hair glinted in the lingering sunlight just ahead of me. Then he froze, his head snapping toward a thick spear of rock that thrust up from the earth just below the mountain's peak.

A woman was scrambling up the side of the rock. The wind tossed black hair across her face, and it was so dark now I might not have been able to make out much of her features anyway, but seeing that slim frame move with such strength and speed, I knew it was Jemma just as John must have.

She swayed for a second as her right leg bowed, and a pang of concern shot through my chest. Whatever injuries she'd had before, she hadn't completely recovered.

What the hell was she doing?

I started forward again, and several other figures made a beeline toward her through the crowd at the same time, including the couple I'd seen staring on the fringes. Apprehension prickled down my spine. One of the figures, closer to her than I was, sped up to a run with the flash of something metal in his hand. He raised his weapon as he charged at Jemma.

Moran leapt out of the crowd and tackled the attacker to the ground. "We've got to help her," he shouted. "They'll try to kill her."

We. He was speaking to us. He'd either seen us here or assumed we'd make it.

I didn't have time to think about that. John had hustled ahead of me to the base of the stone. He whacked his walking stick into the gut of a woman who was jumping after Jemma. Jemma was just reaching for the peak of the rock, her face pale and stiff with controlled pain.

As I hurried toward the stone, my gut wrenched between two opposing instincts. She was wounded and under attack yet unwilling to back down, and part of me longed to protect that determined, defiant spirit. But we had no idea about her plans here, who these people were, or what she intended. What if they had a good reason to try to stop her?

I couldn't let my emotions rule my mind yet again.

One thing I was sure of: I had to at least help my friends. John was springing at another guy who'd run at the looming stone. Bash lunged around to punch someone in the face. Sherlock had grabbed a man by the collar. I hustled the rest of the way to John's side, even though he didn't look as if he needed a whole lot of assistance at the moment.

Just as I reached him, a strangled squeak reached my ears. My gaze jerked around.

A man stalking toward me had a furry lump clutched in his hand. A mouse, I realized with a jab of queasiness. He'd crushed it in his grasp. He raised its mangled body toward the sky, blood streaking down his forearm. "For the shrouded folk!"

An invisible force that felt more solid than the wind whipped past me. Streaks of gauzy light that couldn't have come from the nearly covered sun slashed through the air around the rock. And a woman several paces away came to an abrupt halt and raised a pistol toward Jemma.

Resolve hardened in my chest. Whatever Jemma had done, whatever she was doing now, these people were worse than her. I'd never tackled an evil like this. I didn't understand the cult we'd uncovered in Croatia, but these were clearly the same brand of lunatics. If only in this one conflict, Jemma's side was the only side I wanted to be on.

I threw myself at the woman with the gun, wincing as her first shot split the air. She managed to pull the trigger a second time just as I barreled into her. I shoved her to the ground, and the shot went wild. With a kick, I sent the gun spinning from her hand.

The sightseers around us were shrieking and shoving away from us now, scattering across the lower slope. Everyone except the deranged cultists. The man who'd crushed the mouse dove for the gun, and I threw myself at him. As I shouldered him to the side and snatched up the pistol, a billow of filmy light blasted into me, knocking the breath from my lungs. I crashed onto the ground on my back.

I started up at the wavering form descending on me, and a rush of cold arrived with the fall of an even deeper darkness. The eclipse was full.

Jemma stood at the top of the stone, stabbing a curved silver knife toward the sky. She yanked at something on her leg—the gold cuff—and its pieces clattered onto the rock beneath her feet.

Several of those strange billows of light, fainter now despite the darkness around us, converged on Jemma. The one over me whipped around to follow them. I blinked hard, trying to wrap my head around what I was seeing. When I squinted at them, they looked almost like—like *ghosts*, for fuck's sake. Like that creepy form that had appeared over Jemma in the park back in—

Oh. Ice formed around my stomach. What if that hadn't been a projection from some source we'd never determined. What if... that had been an actual *creature*, appearing and moving by some will of its own, like the patches of hazy light flying toward Jemma were giving every appearance of being?

I didn't believe in ghosts. Since I was ten, I'd rolled my eyes at my gran leaving milk out for the "wee folk." But I couldn't deny that something very real and not of the world I knew had appeared in front of me.

Jemma slashed the curved knife across her arm. I shoved myself back onto my feet, swallowing back queasiness at the sight of blood streaking over her pale skin. I wanted to run to her, to wrench the blade from her hands, but at the same moment the filmy beings that had been racing toward her flinched back.

Her voice rang out, strained but clear. "I claim this pain; I claim this blood!" Light flared around her, silhouetting her slim form, brighter than the things that circled her. A quivering energy radiated from her perch and washed over my skin. It warbled in my ears so loudly I lost the next few things she said.

Jemma tossed off her wig. The unnatural light burned even sharper around her pinned-up red hair. My stomach lurched as she brought the knife to the back of her neck.

What the *fuck*?

I couldn't help stepping forward, my hands opening and closing, grasping for something to do but not knowing what. As crazy as this situation looked, as unnerving as Jemma's actions were, her voice and her stance spoke of total control.

She knew what she was doing, and I sure as hell didn't.

I couldn't see the back of her neck, but I could tell she'd dug in the blade from the way her jaw clenched. "I give myself freely to myself," she called out. "I accept Jemma Moriarty's claim."

I didn't know what that meant either, but it must have been enough to accomplish her ends. She dropped the knife into her purse.

Daylight glimmered brighter over the mountainside as the moon edged away from the sun. Jemma's glow faded, and the gauzy patches around her shimmered a touch brighter.

They whipped toward her in an instant. She bent down—and a force with a flicker of light rammed into her, sending her tumbling over the side of the stone. Like the wallop that had thrown Sherlock on the mountain near Split.

I ran to her as she hit the ground, her arm braced protectively around her head. Sherlock, John, and Moran dashed over too. Glowing streaks seared the air around her, and she flinched, jabbing out with her hand as if fighting against something.

Another flash of light punched me in the chest. I reeled back for a second and then sprang at her.

The air around Jemma had turned frigid enough to bite into my skin. Her head lolled to the side, a welt from a blow I hadn't seen forming across her forehead.

"We have to get her out of here," Moran said, dropping next to her across from me. "She'll be safe in the town. Those things won't follow us there. Cover me!"

He hauled her up, slinging her quickly but carefully over his shoulder as if she weighed nothing, and launched himself down the slope. The three of us raced after him, Sherlock's expression tight, John wide-eyed and pale.

A shimmering streak battered me to the side, but I shoved back to block it from getting at Moran and Jemma. John flailed his walking stick, the wood reverberating as it struck or was struck by something none of us could see beyond a glimmering patch of air.

My heart pounded hard and heavy in my chest. Another blow smacked me across the face. I swore and jabbed out my elbow instinctively, light sparking around the filmy surface I hit.

Then we were stumbling into the midst of the sightseers who'd congregated at the edge of the town. Shouts carried after us, but Moran kept hurtling onward with Jemma, and the three of us charged after him.

The air didn't attack me again. The wavering light effects faded away. But my pulse kept thudding and my skin kept crawling as we hustled through the streets.

I didn't know what we'd tangled with on that mountaintop, but clearly the world contained villains more terrifying than I'd ever imagined could exist. And the woman now crumpled on Bash's shoulder not only knew but had dared to stand up to them.

CHAPTER TWENTY-SEVEN

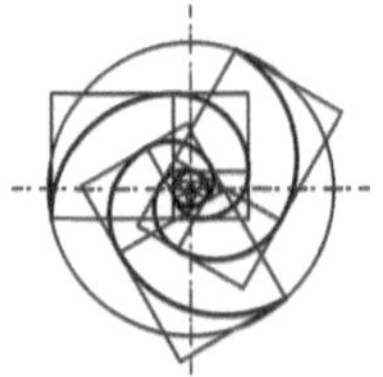

Jemma

I woke up on a soft bed in an unfamiliar room. Sunlight streamed through a wide window, lighting up the pale yellow walls and white furniture. A warm breeze rippled the curtain. A distant jangle of music carried with it, much more perky than I felt.

"Mori!" Bash had been sitting in a wicker chair on the other side of the bed. He leapt up and rested his hands on the sheet next to me, his eyes intent. From the dark smudges under them, *he* hadn't gotten much sleep. "How are you feeling?" he asked.

I shifted against the mattress, taking stock. A dull ache spread across my forehead. I touched the spot and found it bandaged. My arm was bandaged too—pads and swaths of gauze wrapped around my wrist and elbow where I'd sliced myself open with the shrouded dagger.

"I've been better, but I've also been worse," I said. Tentatively, I pushed myself into a sitting position. My shoulder and my hip throbbed. The gold cuff no longer weighed on my thigh, but the muscle there felt tender. I lifted the sheet, eased up the skirt of my dress, and winced. Purple bruises mottled the skin from knee to hipbone.

But I'd take that over turning translucent any day.

I turned back to Bash. "Where are we? What happened after the eclipse?" I had a blurry memory of falling, flares of light and pain and voices shouting around me, but I couldn't piece together more than that.

"Your monsters took a good stab at getting you, but we were faster," Bash said. "You were banged up pretty bad, though. The good doctor did what he could for you, and I managed to arrange a private flight pretty quick. I figured the sooner we put distance between those things and the last place they found you, the better." He motioned to the window. "Rio de Janeiro. Not too far a hop but big and busy enough for us to go unnoticed."

"Good choice," I said. "It's only—that was all yesterday?"

He nodded. From the quality of the sunlight, I'd guess it was early afternoon now. I hadn't even been out for a whole twenty-four hours. Our Chilean adventure definitely could have gone a lot worse.

"John should probably take another look at you now that you're awake," Bash said. Apparently he'd gotten on a first name basis with at least one of the trio while I'd been unconscious. "Do you mind if I go get him?"

"If it'll make you feel better." I waved him off.

He went to the bedroom door and leaned out. "Hey, doc, your patient is awake."

John came striding in a few seconds later, and Sherlock and Garrett trailed behind him. It was kind of amusing seeing someone other than Sherlock taking the lead for once. The other two stood awkwardly near the end of the bed while John sat on the edge beside me.

"Hey," he said. "It's good to have you back with us."

"It's good to be back, considering I wasn't sure I was even going to make it through the eclipse alive." I raised my bandaged arm. "You do neat work."

He laughed, but concern still shone in his hazel eyes. "I haven't completely lost my touch. Can you move all right? Is your vision clear?"

"Everything feels pretty normal, just achy here and there. I think I'm through the worst. I wouldn't mind a painkiller if we've got any around. Not the heavy stuff, just to take the edge off."

Bash tossed over a bottle of over-the-counter pills and went to get me a glass of water. I gulped a couple down and turned my attention to the two men still standing vigil at the end of the bed.

"Can I assume that since we're in an apartment and not a prison hospital that you're not here to arrest me for something or other?"

Garrett shot Bash a wary look, maybe in recognition that even if they'd wanted to, they'd have had a tough time taking me into custody under my hitman's watch. Sherlock tucked his hands into the pockets of his trousers, studying me with his incisive gaze.

"I have no grounds on which to arrest you at the moment, Miss Moriarty," he said. "But I was rather hoping you could provide some illumination on the events during the eclipse. What exactly did you accomplish there, for example?"

"And what the hell were those things that were trying to stop you?" Garrett put in.

John hadn't told them the extra details I'd shared with him about the cult, then, even now that they'd seen plenty of evidence. I couldn't blame him for leaving that task to me—they'd have thought *he* was crazy.

An urge to lie coiled around my chest. My hands balled on top of the sheet. But what could I tell them that would sound any less crazy than the truth? What would it hurt for them to know?

These men had turned up and fought in my battle alongside me without any need to. They might very well have saved my life twice over now.

I wet my lips and looked at Sherlock. "Are you sure you're going to believe what I tell you? I think you know I'm not going to say it was an elaborate electronic light show. If you're only going to scoff, I'd rather skip that."

He shifted his weight, his mouth twisting into something between a smile and a grimace. "I was present for everything that happened. I can admit that the phenomena I observed cannot be explained by any scientific means I'm aware of. It may pain me to consider a less grounded explanation, but I can hardly call myself an objective observer of facts if I refuse the most fitting account simply because I find it difficult to accept."

Spoken like only Sherlock would. The fact that he was even willing to entertain the idea of something supernatural sent a flutter of affection through me for the proud, brilliant man in front of me. I had discovered many things I hadn't expected about myself in the last several weeks. Perhaps he hadn't come through that time unchanged either.

"I don't understand exactly what they are either." I leaned back on my hands as I chose my words. "There are beings with powers most people would call magic. They like our world—they like our sun. Left to their own devices, they can only create illusions, making themselves or other things visible but not really affecting anything. But if they can find people willing to worship them, to feed them with pain and blood, that gives them enough energy to have an impact on our world."

Garrett looked ill. "That's why the mutilated animals—the boy— all the things we found in the commune…"

I nodded. "Some of that might have been the fiends themselves, enjoying themselves after they'd been let loose. Their tastes tend toward the violent. But yes. Wherever they can find people who get off on being near creatures that much more powerful, they've fostered their cult of worship. We call them the shrouded folk. I grew up in one of their communes. I was still tied to them even after I escaped, but that ritual with the dagger means they have no more claim on me."

"Are you done with them?" John asked.

A laugh sputtered out of me. "Hardly. They—they killed my sister. They would have torn me apart and enjoyed it. And the people in the cult, like my parents, might as well be monsters too, considering the lengths they're willing to go to in service of those things. Now that I can take them on freely, I'm going to destroy every commune there is by whatever means necessary until there's no one left giving reverence. Until the fiends can't touch anyone here ever again."

The men around me were silent for a long moment. Garrett drew in a breath.

"These 'fiends'—they're what you meant," he said. "Before you took off on us in Split, you said there were worse things in the world than you."

The corner of my mouth quirked up. "Yes. So, I wouldn't ask you to stick your necks out again. I don't plan on setting up any schemes that would conflict with your work. I just hope you'll agree that letting me go to deal with these fiends is in everyone's best interests —not just ours, but every human being out there." I motioned to the world beyond the walls.

Garrett looked at the floor and then back at me. A fierceness had come over his expression. "What if we want to stick our necks out? I got into this line of work to make the world better. If those *things* are out there, killing and warping people to their wills… I don't know how I can manage it around the job once I have to go back—"

"I can handle that," Sherlock broke in. When Garrett's gaze snapped to him, he smiled thinly. "Your chief appreciates how many cases I manage to smooth along for Scotland Yard. I'm sure I could convince him that I had a great need of you being assigned to an undercover detail for an indeterminate length of time. No need to be on hand in the station." He turned his attention to me. "We might not even need to go very far to start, if this cult operates in Britain as well."

I stared at the two of them. A strangely bubbly sensation emerged from my gut.

"It operates pretty much everywhere," I said. "I'd be surprised if there isn't at least one settlement in the Highlands. It *would* be easier to tackle them with more minds and resources put toward the cause… Are you sure?"

"Take on the most challenging enemy I've ever faced or go back to the hum-drum grind of petty crimes." Sherlock arched his eyebrows. "The decision is hardly difficult."

John grinned. "If he's in, you know I am."

I felt I needed to clarify, just for the record: "You'd have to let me direct our moves—and not ask too many questions about how I acquire my own resources. I've been working toward this from the moment I understood what monsters the shrouded folk truly are. I'm not compromising this mission for anyone's morals."

John tipped his head to the other two. "I'm sure we can avoid prying when it serves the greater good, can't we?"

A sly glint sparked in Sherlock's eyes. "As long as your means never appear more of a concern than the enemy we intend to eliminate, I don't think that should be a problem."

Garrett cleared his throat. "Yeah. What he said."

I glanced at Bash in case he had an opinion about bringing the trio into the mix. I wasn't taking them on if it meant losing him.

He simply shrugged with a hint of a wry smile. "I can tolerate them if they're making themselves useful. It's up to you, Majesty."

I sat up straighter with a smile of my own, an energy flowing through me that was even more potent than what I'd felt in the grip of the dagger's power. "All right then. Let's take the bastards down."

THE HOUNDS OF DEVOTION

MORIARTY'S MEN #3

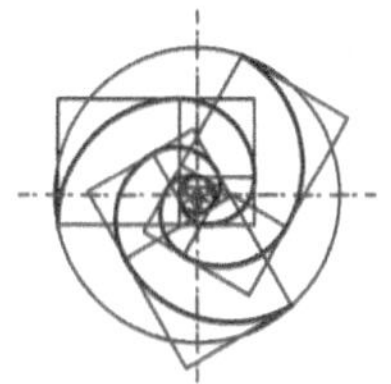

CHAPTER ONE

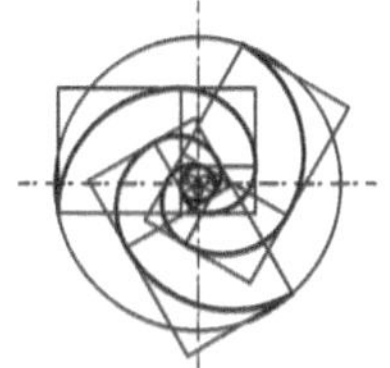

Jemma

Throughout my career, from when I'd first struck out on my own at fourteen years old and started carving a space for myself, officers of the law had been people to avoid or overcome. I certainly never expected to find myself sitting at a table with three of the most esteemed crime-fighters in the world, all of them aiming to help me.

Garrett Lestrade took a swig from his beer and motioned to the tablet he'd set on the table, looking perfectly at home even though the apartment belonged to his two colleagues. I'd gathered that Scotland Yard's youngest detective inspector had joined Sherlock and John for many a dinner over the last few years. Despite being only a smidge taller than me and wiry in frame, the intensity in his pose and boyish face gave him just as much presence as the other two.

"Looking for similar patterns of crimes to what we saw when locating the commune in Croatia, I'd say that cult of yours has some sort of base over here in the Lake District." He motioned to the map he'd brought up on the tablet's screen. "Somewhere along the outskirts, I'd assume, away from the popular hiking paths. They do seem to like their mountainous areas, don't they?"

"They do." I leaned forward to consider the spot he'd indicated and took another bite from the cinnamon cookie I'd been nibbling on, which was the best dessert I'd been able to scrounge up here. Sherlock and John had a disturbing lack of sweets in their apartment. "The shrouded folk draw on the sun for energy, and the higher the elevation, the more they can absorb."

The corner of Garrett's mouth twitched downward at the comment, just for a second. My trio of criminal investigators was only starting to fully wrap their heads around the idea that a sort of demonic faerie creatures existed and spread their malicious influence through our world. It was easy enough for me to believe, having grown up with the monsters.

The thought of those early childhood rituals, swaying in the sun while drawing lines of blood into my skin with a tiny blade, sent a cold shudder through me that I held tightly inside.

Sherlock Holmes, both the most skeptical and the keenest thinker among the trio, tapped his narrow chin with a distant expression as if absorbing that fact for later analysis. He took a puff from his pipe, thickening the earthy smoky smell in the air, and tugged the tablet closer. "Would we assume the cult has only *one* base of operations in all of England? You gave the impression they were rather more widespread than that, Jemma."

"There might be others," Garrett said quickly. "That was only the spot with the clearest pattern. I have other possibilities as well, but we decided we'd start with the most likely, didn't we?"

Sherlock regarded him evenly, his pale blue eyes sharp beneath the messy fall of his wavy dark brown hair. As well as they worked together, I'd had many opportunities to observe the tension that existed between the two men, Garrett always striving to prove himself just as adept as the brilliant and widely lauded Sherlock.

"I find it best to have all the potential threads at my disposal," the consulting detective said.

As so often, it was John Watson who eased that tension, with all the warmth he must have brought to his medical practice before his stint in the army had brought that career to an end. He shook his blond head ruefully. "I'm sure Garrett can go over all the patterns he found in the police records later. The location he named does match up with our suspicions from our own investigations. Why don't we focus on our next steps for now?"

"Yes," I said, with a drumming of my fingers on the table's edge. I wasn't used to collaborating with so many people directly. While our alliance was clearly working to my benefit—the trio had access to resources it'd be much harder for me to get my hands on—I couldn't say the extended back-and-forth felt exactly comfortable. "We can only tackle one of these communes at a time. And while I'd be surprised if there weren't at least two or three in the whole of this country, whichever one's showing the most obvious markers ought to be the largest and the one it's most important to take down."

The other man at the table, the one who'd always been on my side, lifted his jaw toward me. He spoke low and firm. "This is Jemma's operation. We go by what she says."

Sebastian Moran knew how to cut to the chase. The hitman who'd become my right-hand man—and closest confidant, and recently lover—also exuded power with his presence. Just a few weeks ago, he'd been perfectly ready to shoot all three of our London trio rather than debate with them to save my life. A fact I doubted any of the three would soon forget. His brawny arms flexed as he shifted in his seat as if to provide an additional reminder.

Most of Bash was dark, from the stubble of black hair on his tan scalp to the glower he could turn on in an instant, but a spark of admiration lit in his light green eyes as he fixed his gaze on me.

"How can we best go about taking down these monsters?" he said. "It's not like Croatia—you were mostly looking to get that knife from the commune there."

"Although it was a welcome addition that our strategy meant the arrest of most of the cult members as well." I exhaled slowly. I'd had years to plan for this moment, but I'd planned for going it alone. In the last several days, as the men around me had begun their investigations and I'd recuperated from the ceremony that had freed me from my deal with one of the shrouded folk, I'd had plenty of time to think about other approaches that would better utilize the keenness now at my disposal.

"I actually think that the approach we used before might be adapted quite well to other circumstances," I went on. "The short of it is, I want the shrouded folk cut off from this world. Let them skulk around in their own realm, wherever that may be, so no person here ever has a reason to offer up the bloody sacrifices they demand. And it's the people in those communes, making those sacrifices, who open the doorway for the shrouded folk to come here."

Sherlock nodded, understanding sparking in his eyes. He might still find it hard to believe in my supernatural beasts, but he could follow a chain of logic nonetheless. "If you can eliminate their avenues of support, you eliminate their access. We need to prevent these people from conducting the rituals that give these... things their power."

"Exactly." I shot him a smile as a little thrill tingled through me. Perhaps there was something strange about this man devoted to dealing out justice allying himself with a consummate criminal, but I couldn't help enjoying the sharpness of his wits. Sherlock was the only man who'd ever gotten the better of me, if merely temporarily. The challenge had been exhilarating, and having him put those skills to work on my behalf might have been even more so.

"And root out their accursed line," Bash murmured with a dark smile of his own. Even though he often mocked the Shakespearean dramas he liked to watch, they stuck with him well enough to give him quotes at the ready.

"If all goes well," I said. "I think we need to be clear on one thing. These cultists—the ones who are adults, anyway—are hardly victims. They know full well the horrors the shrouded folk require, and they go along with them in exchange for existing near beings with that much unearthly power. Frankly, if I could simply have them all slaughtered and eliminate the folk's basis of support that way, I wouldn't see any problem with that."

John turned a bit green. "Well, I mean, they *are* people, even if they've been swayed by—"

I waved off his protest. "Don't worry. I'm not saying we

slaughter them all. I just wanted to make the point that we can't let *ourselves* be swayed by misguided pity. Every person in those cults has been an accomplice to murder and has carried out torture, often of children. Keep that in mind when we're tackling this problem."

The doctor's mouth tightened. I could tell from the resolve in his expression that it wasn't my behavior he was objecting to the thought of now. I did enjoy John's softer side, especially when I got to experience it in intimate fashion, but I appreciated the strength he could summon underneath it just as much.

Bash chuckled. "If slaughter's off the table—more's the pity— you're thinking we sic the cops on them, Mori?"

"They *are* criminals, all of them," I said. "There'll be evidence of those crimes in every commune if we can justify a search like we did in Croatia. The cultists won't be able to conduct their rituals from a jail cell. But we need to arrange our police raids so they come by surprise, sweeping through swiftly and effectively."

"Any cult members who escape the sweep could go on with their practices elsewhere," Garrett filled in. He might not have quite the crystalline brilliance Sherlock possessed, but he was sharp in his own right—and full of a delicious passionate determination as well. "We cracked down on them easily before, and we've got better contacts and more clout here. We just need an urgent justification, like that kidnapping story we came up with."

Sherlock frowned. "As well as that gambit worked, we can't simply go around conjuring false crimes if we're going to be tackling several of these communes. Our credibility will take a beating before we're even a fraction of the way through this mission."

"I agree." I might not have any need to worry about my own credibility with the police—we wouldn't get into how many times I'd pulled the wool over their eyes or misdirected them before—but my trio of detectives wouldn't be much use to me if they lost their standing. "But the cult commits plenty of real crimes. We'll need to set them up for an illicit act where we're pulling the strings, and then we can tip off the local cops."

"Presumably we're not going to set up a murder," John said.

I patted his arm. "Don't you worry about that either, my dear doctor," I said teasingly. "They've got a perfect weakness for us to exploit that doesn't involve any blood spilled at all."

"Their penchant for theft," Sherlock said.

"There you have it." A sly grin curled my lips. "In particular, the communes always need medical supplies to offset their bloodletting and other horrific rituals. They can hardly bring a sliced-up child into a hospital without provoking an instant investigation. So we'll dangle a jackpot they can't resist: a large shipment of antibiotics and other essentials that'd last them for years. We don't even need an actual shipment—they just need to believe we have one."

Bash straightened up. "I assume that's where I come in."

My gut pinched with a hint of guilt as I shook my head. Normally, spreading any kind of public information would have been my hitman's job, while I orchestrated events in the background. But I had to take full advantage of all my allies' strengths.

"I may want you in there later," I said. "But Sherlock and John know their way around a disguise and can play off each other well. Better to start spreading the word with conversations simply overhead rather than making any direct inquiries."

John's eyes gleamed with the prospect of getting down to work. "I'd imagine we could arrange to be overheard all over the Lake District."

"What do you need on the official side of things?" Garrett asked, his stance tensed as if he was afraid I wasn't going to need him at all.

I caressed his hand reassuringly, a flicker of heat racing through me at the desire that simple touch could light in his eyes. Garrett could be passionate about all sorts of things, but I loved it most when he aimed that passion at me.

"You'll have plenty to keep you busy," I said. "I think we should start spreading the word about the cult within law enforcement circles. The news isn't likely to have traveled all the way from Croatia, but you've got a perfectly good reason to talk about it, since you were there. If everyone is primed for a cult full of horrors, we'll be able to push them into action faster."

He tipped his head to me, looking satisfied.

I turned to Bash. "You and I are going to do some covert

scouting out around the Lake District to see if we can't narrow down the commune's location."

Bash gave me his slow smile. "I'm up for that." He paused. "How careful do you need to be around these things? You broke whatever contract you had with that one, but some of them would recognize you, wouldn't they?"

"Maybe. I don't know exactly how they move around our world, whether all of them draw on all the communes or whether they stick mainly to certain locations." I rubbed my mouth. "Most of my association with them happened in the United States. But those ones may have a presence here too—and the one I had the contract with may have spread a general warning."

The shrouded folk had rules about impinging on the natives of this world. They wanted to keep their presence reasonably secret from those unaware of them. But they already knew *I* was aware of them. If they caught me in isolation, I wouldn't put it past them to attempt to kill me. They'd already done that once just after I'd severed the contract.

Sherlock got up from the table. "I might have something that can help with that concern."

He ducked into his bedroom and emerged holding four gleaming gold pieces etched with mathematical patterns and embedded with tiny gems. A laugh tumbled from my lips.

"You picked it up during that dash for your lives."

He shrugged with his usual confidence. "It seemed the sort of thing that might come in handy again."

It certainly was. Those gold pieces could connect together into a cuff that prevented the shrouded folk from detecting a person. It'd kept me hidden from the fiend that wanted to claim my soul for weeks until I'd been able to free myself from that contract.

Bash's forehead furrowed. "That relic made you sick when you were wearing it before."

"Only after I'd had it on much longer than it was ever intended to be used for. I'm back to full health now. I can't imagine it'll hurt to wear it for a few hours here and there while we get the lay of the land." I accepted the gold pieces from Sherlock and raised an eyebrow at him. "I trust there won't be any trouble over the acquiring of the one piece?"

I'd stolen the final piece I needed from under the trio's noses — and with their unwitting help — months ago.

The corner of Sherlock's mouth quirked upward. "I find I can overlook the theft of an item stolen from a long-time thief and miscreant."

"All right then." My fingers closed around the smooth metal. My gaze slid over the men assembled around me, and a quiver of excitement raced through my chest. "Let's destroy those bastards."

CHAPTER TWO

John

Our fifth pub of the day was the kind of place I'd call "colorful" if I was being generous. In a less optimistic mood, I'd probably have gone with "sleazy." The lights were dim, the booths shadowy, the tables a hotchpotch of garish reds and oranges. The tang of alcohol hung in the air so thick you could practically get tipsy simply by breathing, and from the raucous laughter that pealed out every few seconds, everyone in here other than Sherlock and me was already at least that drunk.

The laughter mixed with the lively rock song that was playing, which meant our voices weren't going to carry far. We'd picked a table close to a couple of booths full of the people Sherlock had deemed most likely to be criminal types through his various methods of deduction.

"We'll get the whole truck," he said to me in an affected accent, pitching his voice loud enough to rise over the music but not so loud it'd sound as if he meant to be overhead. "The driver's ready to step back and let us at it without raising a fuss. As long as he can claim robbery and get a small cut for his trouble, it's all ours."

"How much do you figure we can make off that kind of medical stuff?" I replied, doing my best to match his tone in my own altered voice.

"Ah, there's always need for antibiotics and the like. We'll make a good profit, don't you worry."

"Have you got a buyer lined up already? I don't want to try to be selling this load bit by bit. We'll need someone eager for the whole thing."

Sherlock shrugged with a grin that showed all his enjoyment at getting to put on a performance like this. We'd both donned disguises for this bit of subterfuge, but while most of his face was hidden behind a false beard and makeup, his light blue eyes remained the same. When they gleamed as brightly as they were right now, I found it hard to look away.

"I know how it goes," he said. "I'm sure I can find someone quickly enough. We'll have plenty of room to be flexible with the price and still have it be worth our while."

I couldn't tell if any of the blokes sitting in the booths were paying attention to our conversation, but reading people wasn't my specialty. Sherlock shifted back in his chair, giving every sign of satisfaction. If our gambit was going to land with anyone here, I supposed we'd said enough.

I edged my chair a tad closer to Sherlock's so we could talk without being overhead now. He reached for his whisky, neat, at the same time as I reached for my beer, and our elbows brushed against each other.

A few weeks ago, the jolt of electricity that shot through my nerves at the contact would have set me off-kilter. A few months before that, I'd have denied it even existed. Somehow or other, with her wiles and her all-too-perceptive gaze, Jemma had changed that.

Yes, I found the man in front of me as immensely attractive as he could be incredibly infuriating. Yes, I had acted on that attraction not just once but twice now. The first time might have been a disaster, but the second…

The memory of our mouths colliding sent another jolt straight to my groin. Sherlock hadn't run away that time. He'd met me halfway, and afterward he'd found it in him to admit he'd liked it, as awkwardly as he might have gotten that across.

Having any sort of relationship, even platonic, with my roommate, best friend, and colleague had never been simple. I'd intertwined my life with his knowing that, and I hadn't regretted it once. Now there was one more dimension to our partnership. So what if I'd never been attracted to any man other than him, and he'd never seemed much attracted to *anyone* before we encountered Jemma Moriarty? Navigating this new dimension might be awkward, but the feelings themselves were perfectly straightforward.

I took a gulp of my beer, an ale with a lot less body than I'd been able to get in the last pub. "I still find it hard to believe that Jemma's 'folk' influenced so many people without you catching on that there was something wrong. Do you think they're really as widespread as she suggests?"

Sherlock raised his shoulders again, but this time there was a hint of stiffness to his shrug. "I expect with her experience she'd be a much better judge of the particulars than we are. I've certainly known that various supernaturally focused cults exist. It simply never would have entered my mind that the supernatural aspect of their worship had any basis in reality."

"It's not just the supernatural, though, but the intersection with the real world. The thefts, the torture, the killings…"

"From what she's said, the sacrifices usually are made by the cult's own people. When they live so far apart from society, there's no way for any official body to keep track of possible crimes. They hardly pilfer enough medical supplies and the like to draw national, let alone international attention."

"No, I suppose that would go against their need for secrecy." I let out a wry laugh. "Even having seen them—having witnessed their attack on us and Jemma—it's hard to wrap my head around the fact that these things *do* exist. You don't think we could have—"

"I'm quite sure there is a ponderance of evidence in support of the creatures being real—I would never have so much as entertained the idea otherwise," Sherlock cut in, his normally smooth tenor going sharp.

I blinked at him. It wasn't like Sherlock to lose even a little of his temper—certainly not in the middle of a calm conversation with *me* of all people. Which meant, knowing him, it wasn't me or the conversation he was really irritated about.

"Do you think there's a factor we haven't considered that could become a problem?" I asked. "Or is this whole endeavor taking too much time away from your usual cases?"

Sherlock's stance had relaxed again. He turned his sweating glass between his slender fingers. "Oh, no. I suspect this will be the greatest case of my entire career, even if it'll also be the most secretive. Onward we go, and we'll deal with any unexpected factors as they arrive. It's an adventure, isn't it?"

I wasn't sure I totally believed the smile he aimed at me, but there was no point in pushing a subject if Sherlock had decided he didn't want to talk about it. He could lock himself up as tight as a bank vault.

I was reaching for a change of subject with a burly guy with a yellow bandana tied around his head jerked out the other chair at our small table, spun it around, and dropped into it with a decisive thump. He crossed his arms over the back and gave us a narrow stare. My pulse immediately kicked up a notch with a rush of adrenaline.

"You don't look like much for a couple of guys who talk a blue streak," the new arrival said in a growl of a voice. "But obviously you don't have much smarts twice over."

"I'm not sure I understand your meaning," Sherlock said evenly. "Care to explain?"

The tough guy counted off his point points on his meaty fingers. "First, you come in here blathering about your plans so's half the place knows about it already. Second, you didn't bother to ask around before you started nosing around here with your schemes. This territory is covered. Any deals you want to make, they go through my boss. Any deals you've already made, we take double for the disrespect."

I reached for my walking stick instinctively where I'd leaned it against the side of the table. The cool firm surface against my fingers solidified my confidence. The thump of my pulse propelled the words from my throat.

"I don't think you can lay dibs on a whole area like that. We'll talk about what we want where we want, and we'll make our deals without any payoffs."

The man focused his dark glower completely on me. His gaze slid to the stick for a second, and his lip curled with a sneer. He had no idea that I could use that tool as effectively in a skirmish as any weapon he might be carrying on him.

"I don't think you want to be picking fights you can't see through," he said.

Another burst of adrenaline flooded my veins. In that instant, I could taste how good it would feel to take this jerk on, to flex the combat muscles I rarely got to use, to see the shock on his face when I toppled him. It'd teach him a lesson about judging by appearances, and it'd give an extra gossip factor to help our story spread. I started to shift my weight onto my feet—

—and Sherlock set a hand on my thigh under the table, warning me to stay in place.

"We're not looking for any fight," he said, holding up his other hand in a gesture of submission. "No deals have been made yet. If you object to them happening around here, I'm sure we can take our business elsewhere."

The man scowled at him. "You'd better keep your partner in line. And if you're going to be messing around in these parts, you ask after Mick first. Got it?"

"Absolutely. I'm sorry for the confusion. In fact, I'd imagine we should be on our way now."

He let go of my leg and stood up, and there was nothing for me to do but follow him.

I started to reach for my glass to toss back the rest of my beer but decided the mediocre stuff wasn't worth it. Hefting my walking stick, I let it rap hard against the wooden floor just for the pleasure of watching the guy's muscles twitch. Then I stalked out of the pub after Sherlock, walking slowly so I could keep my pace perfectly even despite the twinge of my war injury in my hip. I'd rather the thug never realized I needed the stick for anything other than an affectation.

Sherlock headed straight to the car. Without any discussion, he got in on the passenger side, leaving the driving to me. I sank into the seat, but I didn't turn on the engine right away.

"I could have handled him," I felt the need to say.

"Of course you could have," Sherlock said. "But that's not what we're here for. A bar brawl hardly seems like the type of behavior that would enamor us to a group aiming to keep as low a profile as possible. We're looking to spread the word, not bruises."

I hadn't thought about that angle. A prickle of shame ran through me. "Right. Of course. I must have gotten a little too caught up in playacting the crook."

Sherlock chuckled. "Well, now you can work out some of that aggression by tackling the road with much vehemence, as you're so fond of doing." He consulted the map on his phone in the waning evening light. "I think we can manage one more stop before we turn in for the day. Do you figure you can cover fifty miles in half an hour?"

A different sort of thrill tingled through me. "You'd better believe it. Just remember that I haven't gotten us into an accident yet." In the grip of a sudden impulse, I leaned across the seats and planted a quick kiss on his lips. The feel of them, warm and dry and instinctively pressing back against mine, melted the last of my agitation.

When I pulled back, Sherlock blinked at me, startled but with a faint flush to his cheeks that didn't look displeased. "What was that about?" he said mildly.

"To clear our heads?" I suggested. That was the excuse Sherlock most often turned to when he allowed himself to indulge in sexual pleasure. The thought of all the ways Jemma had heightened that pleasure made me momentarily giddy. I knew better than to push Sherlock very far, but maybe eventually we'd explore some of those avenues just the two of us.

"I suppose that's as good a reason as any," Sherlock said with a glint in his eyes that looked a tad mischievous.

I grinned back and gunned the engine.

CHAPTER THREE

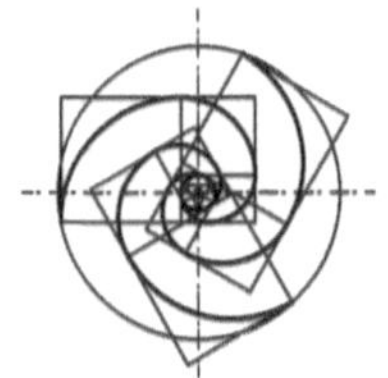

Jemma

The wind rustled through the treetops as I studied the laptop's screen where I was sitting on the hood of the rental car, connecting the final pieces of a perfect scheme. The internet connection wasn't great here on the side of a lonely country road, but I got enough to both text with our prospective buyer and use the tracking software to confirm his general location.

I just needed to keep the guy communicating a bit longer. That was fine. I'd like to get a little more out of him to ensure this plan's success.

You've got the numbers, I wrote. *It's a great stash. Let's talk payment.*

My texting partner named a figure that brought a smile to my lips. Not that I needed the money, but clearly the cultist recognized the value of getting this large a collection of supplies all at once. *I need a full guarantee that this deal will stay completely anonymous,* he added. *Only the driver and the truck—one of us will arrive to hand off the payment. If we see anyone else around, everything's off.*

Of course. I totally understand. That's a good amount of cash, but we've had other similar offers. Care to sweeten the pot? My boss is a collector as well as an investor. Art, historic relics, any sort of curiosities—if you've got anything like that you could add as a trade, I can make sure the goods go to you.

That request would be all too easy for the shrouded folk's people. One of the main ways they made money was creating and selling unusual artifacts to black magic aficionados and students of the occult. As far as I knew, most of those artifacts didn't contain any real magic—the shrouded folk rarely imbued a permanent object with their power the way they had the dagger that had severed my contract—but hobbyists couldn't get enough of them.

As expected, the guy wrote back just a few seconds later. *I have a friend who deals in supposedly supernatural items. Would something like that appeal?*

Oh, absolutely. He's fascinated by the paranormal. What kind of items are we talking about?

I could include a talisman for good fortune and a protective brooch.

My computer pinged, the app showing a fuzzy ring on the map, from which the texts were being sent. My initial forays had been correct, then. We'd be able to sic the local police on these people without any problem now.

Excellent. Consider the deal made, then. We'll have the shipment tomorrow night around 11pm. Can do the exchange at midnight. Why don't you pick the spot to ease your worries?

The cultist mentioned a half-constructed townhouse development about fifty miles out from where I estimated the commune to be. Close but not too close. As I tapped in my agreement, a muscular figure slipped from between the trees by the car, so stealthily I only heard the faintest rasp of his feet over the ground.

"We've got to get going," Bash said, yanking open the car door on the driver's side. With his khaki pants and broad-brimmed hat, meant to make him look like a mere hiker, you wouldn't have thought he could pull off much gravitas, but his expression was deadly serious. "I think I got a little too close. A sentry started heading my way as if he'd heard something. I'd rather he thinks it was his imagination."

"Shit." I slid off the hood of the car with a lurch of my heart and dropped into the passenger seat an instant later. Bash tossed his hat in the back and gunned the engine. He yanked the wheel to swing the car around. We roared off, back toward civilization.

"Anyone nearby is definitely going to hear *that*," I said with a teasing arch of my eyebrow.

Bash chuckled. "I got a good head start on that amateur. No point in waiting until someone's close enough that they *would* hear, that's all."

"So you had me terrified for nothing." I shook my head at him.

His chuckle turned into a full-out laugh. "As if you're ever really scared of anything, Majesty."

"You obviously don't know me as well as you should if you say that." I could remember with all too much vivid clarity the panicked thump of my heart as I'd scrambled onto a tall boulder on the Chilean mountainside, knowing I'd either free myself from the fiends that had owned me my whole life or die in the next few minutes.

"Maybe I shouldn't have said that, then. More accurately, you're the bravest person I know."

That kind of compliment coming from a man who'd been through military combat as a sniper and all sorts of disreputable dealings since then was enough to send a flutter of warmth through me. "All right. That I'll accept."

Bash turned the car onto the main highway. "Where are we heading? The hotel here or all the way back to London?"

I shifted lower in the leather seat, getting comfortable. "We'll stay here. The deal's going through tomorrow night. No point in going to the city just to turn around and come back."

"Is everything set up, then?"

"Just about. I think Garrett still has a few strings to pull, but it sounded as if everything's going smoothly on his end too." I folded my arms behind my head and allowed myself a satisfied smile. "I had no idea how easy a scheme like this could be to pull off with the right talents at my disposal. Maybe I should have brought cops into the operation sooner."

Bash let out a snort. "I think we've had plenty of police presence as it is the last few months. We got lots done when it was just you running the show and me taking care of everything else."

His tone was casual, but a thread of tension ran through it. I glanced over at him, noting the tightening of his hands on the steering wheel. This merging of resources hadn't come easily to him. It *had* been just the two of us working in close partnership for a long time. I couldn't blame him for being hesitant—I'd certainly hesitated to put any trust in our trio at all. On the other hand...

"I'm not sure you should be criticizing the approach when you're the one who arranged it."

Bash's gaze jerked from the road to me. "What?" he said, but there was a hint of guilt in the flex of his jaw.

I waved my hand vaguely at him. "Don't give me that. Did you think I wouldn't figure out that you tipped the three of them off at least partly so they could find us in Chile? I've had plenty of time to think over every step we made and the precautions I took. They definitely didn't track us all that way in the space of a week because *I* let anything slip. Are you going to deny it now?"

His jaw worked again, and then he sighed. "Are you going to be angry? I saw how the situation was wearing on you. I wanted you to have as much backup as possible for your big plan. And after seeing how things went down during the eclipse, I still don't think I could have protected you by myself."

"Maybe not." The events after I'd concluded my ritual with the dagger were kind of a blur, but I knew the shrouded folk who'd turned up had come close to killing me. "You trusted the trio that much. Don't you trust them now?"

"It's not so much about trust," he muttered. "They just don't have the same perspective we do. We'll never be able to talk openly about half the things we're working on. It was only..." He sighed, and his voice gentled. "*I* was scared, all right. I was terrified of seeing anything happen to you. So I pulled out all the stops. That doesn't mean I can't want to push them back in now that they've done their job."

The words sent a softer wash of warmth through me. My hitman and I didn't discuss emotions very often. Until recently, we hadn't discussed them at all. Our loyalty to each other had been solid but unspoken.

Given recent events, the way Bash had stepped up for me, and the way my own perspective had shifted when it came to both the people in this world and what I might be capable of… I'd found I might have more capacity for caring in me than I'd ever have believed even half a year ago.

"I worry too, you know," I said. "About you and the others—about the danger I'm putting you in getting you involved in this mess with the shrouded folk. You've only scratched the surface of the sorts of horrors they enjoy."

"You focus on keeping yourself safe," Bash said firmly. "Let us decide for ourselves what we can handle—and I think we can handle a lot."

I gave him a crooked grin. "Do you want me to send them off or keep them a part of this, then? You can't have it both ways."

"Maybe not. I reserve the right to grumble about them anyway."

"Fair enough." His musky smell filled my lungs with my next breath, and I decided I could give him a larger show of devotion than simple words. I set my hand on his thigh and let my smile turn coy. "I can tell you that you're the only one *I'd* trust to stay steady while I do this."

"Do wha—fuck." His voice dropped to a whisper with the curse as my fingers brushed over his cock through his pants. With another stroke, he was already getting hard, swelling and stiffening at my touch.

The thrill made my smile stretch wider. Bash was the most unflappable person I'd ever met. I knew he could keep enough of his attention on the road even during my attentions to avoid a crash. But damn if it didn't turn me on a hundredfold to know how much of a thrill I could give *him*.

I gripped him harder, and he swallowed audibly, his gaze trained straight ahead. He shifted a couple inches lower in his seat to give me a better angle for access. I took advantage of the new position to pop open his fly. My hand delved beneath the fabric to uncover his rigid length, and Bash let out a low groan.

"There are still plenty of things we can do, just the two of us," I murmured, clicking open my seatbelt. Then I bent over and slicked my tongue around the head of his cock.

"God, Mori," Bash said in a ragged voice. Strength radiated all through his well-built body. I took him all the way into my mouth, reveling in the rough sound he made, in the slight buck of his hips toward me.

There'd been a time when I'd been afraid to give in to my attraction to Bash, even after I'd been sure he returned it. I'd only ever called on physical intimacy as one tool in my repertoire for getting what I wanted. I'd been afraid I might end up using him rather than being a real partner to him, falling into old habits. But in a moment like this, I knew there was no intention in me other than to show him just how happy I was to have him in my life.

The engine thrummed, and I moved my mouth in time, swirling my tongue over his silky skin and gripping the base of his cock. The salty, musky flavor of him flooded my mouth. I sucked him harder, and his elbow quivered where he'd let it rest lightly on my shoulder. With the pump of my hand and a swift flick across his tip, his breath hitched.

Heat pooled between my own legs. I pressed my thighs together as I took Bash down to the back of my throat. There'd be plenty of time to think about my own pleasure after I'd given him every bit I —

Bash's arm dropped abruptly, shielding my head as he yanked the wheel with his other hand. With a screech of tires, he pulled the car onto the shoulder. As I raised my head in confusion, he slammed on the parking brake and shoved his seat back. Then he tugged me all the way onto him, pulling my mouth to his.

Our lips collided in a mad crash. He tangled his fingers in my hair, tilting my head so he could kiss me even more deeply, while his other hand wrenched up my skirt and made short work of my panties. He caressed his thumb over my clit, sending a jolt of pleasure through me, and then dipped lower. At the slickness that spoke of my own desire, he growled against my mouth.

"If I'm going to come inside you, it's going to be here," he said, cupping my sex.

I gasped my giddy agreement. "Do you have—"

"I've decided to always be prepared." He dug a foil packet out of his pocket and ripped it open at lightning speed. I kissed him again, my tongue teasing over his, as he readied himself. The second I felt his hand draw back, I gripped him like I had when I'd been pleasuring him earlier and lowered myself onto his cock.

That first burn of bliss as he filled me was always a rush. Bash groaned again and kissed me with even more fervor. He'd almost been at the point of release already, and it didn't take more than a few thrusts to get me close too.

I fumbled for the seat control and tipped it all the way back so he was nearly lying down. As I braced my hands on either side, rocking up and down over him, he massaged my breasts through my blouse. Pleasure shot through my chest to meet the wave rising from my core.

The first time we'd had sex, he'd let me have my fun on top and then rolled me over to take charge. Today, he let me set the pace the whole way through. As the bliss rushed higher and my eyes started to roll back, his breath broke into panting, but he didn't make the slightest move toward unseating me.

That realization tipped me over the edge. As I careened into ecstasy, I tightened the muscles inside me to squeeze him harder. Bash grunted and pumped up to meet me, spilling himself alongside my peak.

I sagged over him, resting my forehead against his, and he gave me the most brilliant grin I'd ever seen cross his face. My heart sang and ached at the same time.

He was the most unflappable man I'd ever met, but he was willing to hand all control over to me. It *was* a little scary, no matter what he said. He'd given himself over to me completely in so many ways.

I had to make sure he never regretted it.

CHAPTER FOUR

Garrett

There were some things I loved about Scotland Yard. It was one place that was truly my own, for example. No matter how many cases Sherlock and John had a hand—or even the lion's share—in solving, I had my badge and they didn't. I'd put in the time and training to earn a spot here, and that meant something. For the most part, the people here believed in bringing crooks to justice by following the letter as well as the intention of the law, with a lot less of the moral blurring that the independent detectives dabbled in.

That said, sometimes I wished the place were a little less rigid and conformist—and that so many of my colleagues, stung by the fact that I'd been promoted ahead of them, weren't so eager to point out any area where I'd misstepped.

Thompson was still friendly enough, but I'd seen that jealous gleam in his eyes now and then, getting starker with each year that passed while he was still only detective constable. He ambled over to my desk as I finished up my phone call, his doughy face set with anticipation. My stomach twisted.

"Perfect," I said to the inspector on the other end. "It sounds like you've got everything in order there. I'm glad we could help."

Thompson propped himself against the side of my desk as I hung up. "Were you on the phone with Cumbria again?"

"Just passing on a few final details," I said briskly. "My informant heard a couple more things I thought they'd find useful in their sting operation."

"Seems like you've been spending more time fighting their crimes for them than working on troubles here in London." He straightened up and gave me a playful cuff to the shoulder. "Remember your holiday is over, Lestrade. We need you on the cases here. I wouldn't be surprised if that's what the chief wants to talk to you about."

"He asked to see me?" Damn. I'd hoped I could sail through this initial scheme without involving any of my higher-ups.

Thompson motioned toward the chief's office with a jab of his thumb. "He said you should head on in as soon as you were off the phone."

Well, the mission I'd gotten myself wrapped up in was only going to get more complicated as we continued rooting out Jemma's cult. I couldn't even say it was Jemma's mission now. From what I'd seen of her shrouded folk, the creatures stirred up far more violence and horror than any human criminal I'd ever encountered. I'd gone into this line of work to make a difference for good in the world. I couldn't have asked for a clearer opportunity.

And if I also found it hard to walk away from the woman who both fascinated and unnerved me, no one else needed to know that part of the story.

Chief Higgins looked up from the report on his desk as I stepped into the office. He gestured for me to close the door. He'd been the chief as long as I'd worked at Scotland Yard, but he looked more the stereotypical brute enforcer than an administrative type, built like an ox, his ginger curls cropped close to his head. He was almost always frowning. You basically had to hang the moon—and the perpetrator of a decades-old unsolved case—before the man would crack a smile.

"Lestrade," he said. "I gather you've been coordinating rather a lot with the Cumbria Constabulary in the last few days."

"I have, sir," I said with a respectful bob of my head. The chief might be dour-faced most of the time, but in my experience, he was generally even-handed. "I came across information regarding a crime that I felt they should be aware of."

"You seem to have taken a particular interest in that crime. Is there some sort of personal stake I should be aware of?"

The memory of Jemma pressed up against me, her gasp in my ear, flickered through my mind with a flush of heat I managed to suppress. This was the perfect opening to start warming the chief up to the sort of cases I hoped to continue pursuing from my position here.

"Not personal," I said. "But I do feel a sort of responsibility. As the details came together, I realized this case appears to connect to that crime Holmes and I ended up investigating during our travels."

"Just like the both of you to go on vacation and end up working harder than ever," Higgins muttered. "What was that again—a kidnapping?"

I hadn't gone into much detail about our exploits in Croatia with the department on my return, wanting to wait for the most strategic timing. This would appear to be it.

"We were looking into a missing persons case," I said, "but we ended up uncovering a far bigger problem. There was a cult operating in an area of wilderness near the coast—they'd been responsible for the murder of multiple children as well as more minor crimes like thefts."

The chief sat up straighter at my words. "A cult murdering children? That sounds like something out of a penny thriller."

"I know. I wish it hadn't been real." I still did. The thought of the evidence we'd uncovered about the commune's activities sent a chill through me even now.

"How does that relate to this crime in the Lake District?"

"We've seen a few similar patterns, sir. Certain types of thefts at a certain frequency, unusual disturbances in the same general area... We have reason to believe that the sect we stumbled on in Croatia was only one pocket of the cult, not the entire thing. Now Holmes and I suspect there may be at least one sect of the same group here in England."

Higgins' frown pulled deeper. "I can see why you'd have taken an interest, then. Not the sort of types we want in this country, that's for sure. Are there any signs we should keep an eye out for here in the city?"

"Not as far as I know yet," I said. "They seem to prefer to live in isolation. If something comes up, though, I'll let you know."

We could eventually let police departments all across the world know, couldn't we? Why should the five of us be the only ones tracking down signs of the cult? The clues were simple enough to follow once you were familiar with the pattern.

Once we took down this sect here on home ground—once we'd proven they had a presence everywhere from here to Croatia—those other departments would have to take notice. We could send out briefs all over the place, and they'd do most of our work for us.

Of course, we couldn't trust that they'd all take the same sort of care that Jemma wanted. Simply sending the cultists on the run wouldn't do the job, from what she'd said—they needed to be caught and confined. But perhaps we could come up with strategies for ensuring the right approach was taken even if we weren't directly involved. Surely she didn't expect to personally tackle every single commune of the dozens or even hundreds she'd indicated might exist?

"Well," the chief said. "I'm glad you're keeping an ear to the ground on this subject. It does your policing instincts credit."

I couldn't stop a smile from springing to my lips at the praise, which Higgins doled out only sparingly. I might have proven myself quite a bit by earning the position of detective inspector at a younger age than anyone else currently working here had, but this was an entirely different level of policing. My scope had shifted from merely the city to a threat that encompassed the world—and I was bringing Scotland Yard on board with it.

At least, I'd made a *small step* toward bringing the Yard on board. Higgins followed up his praise with a firm stare. "It sounds as though you've done all you can for Cumbria now. I want your focus back on your regular duties from here on. We have no shortage of our own cases that need tending to."

"Yes," I said, my smile faltering. "Absolutely. I was just looking through the Shawfend file a few minutes ago, actually."

"See if you can't crack that one, then. And feel free to rope Holmes in if you take a mind to. Heaven knows if you can catch his interest with a crime, he'll find his way to the answer faster than any of us could."

My tone flattened slightly. "Yes. I'm not sure it's quite unusual enough to pique his interest. I can sort it out without the extra help."

"I know you can," the chief said, easing the sting of his earlier remark. "Well, what are you waiting for? Get on with it."

He sent me from his office with a shooing motion. I managed not to grimace as I headed out. Several pairs of eyes watched me return to my desk. A prickle ran down my back.

There was taking policing to a higher level and tackling widespread brutality, and then there was looking like an obsessed lunatic. I was going to have to be careful I didn't stray into the latter territory.

There was so much I couldn't tell anyone here: not my colleagues, not the chief. Keeping the supernatural elements they'd never believe—that I barely believed even having experienced them directly—a secret was only going to get harder as the five of us dug deeper into this hornets' nest. I'd often prided myself on being straightforward, a man you could assume would cut to the chase. My association with Jemma had turned me into a conspirator.

All the same, the current London cases were hardly gripping enough to hold *my* attention all that well when I had demonic beings and murderous cults on the brain. I took some notes and talked to the constable who'd interviewed a couple of the witnesses, and then set off to consider the scene of the robbery myself. By the time my shift was over, I was itching to be off in the Lake District with the others.

They were meant to be closing in on the commune there tonight, and I couldn't have any direct part in it. I'd already stretched the department's patience with my extended vacation.

My phone rang just as I came into my flat. I glanced at the number with a jolt of excitement that quickly faded.

"Hello, Mum," I said as I answered it.

My mother's high voice carried through the line. "Garrett! I hope I'm not interrupting anything. I know how busy you get."

"I'm done work for the day," I told her, sinking down onto my sofa—which was starting to get rather threadbare in spots, I noticed. I really ought to find the time to go shopping for a new one. "How are you?"

She rambled on for a few minutes about her garden, her book club, and the nurse at her medical practice, and I hummed encouragingly at appropriate moments. I'd never totally felt like a part of the Lestrade family, if I was being honest. Even to look at the lot of us, you'd see me as cut from a different cloth. My parents and older brothers were all blond and brighter eyed, and they'd gravitated toward the sorts of professions that elegant people at the dinner parties they often held would exclaim admiringly over.

I'd turned out darker and wiry and often sullen. I hadn't excelled in school. No one in the house had really known what to do with me. And I'd felt it, so deeply something sharp still stirred inside me if I let myself linger on that thought too long.

"Anyway," Mum said finally, "we were thinking we'd have all of you over the weekend after next for dinner. Can you make it on the Saturday?"

It took me a second to catch up. "All of us?"

"You and your brothers," she said in a familiar faintly exasperated tone.

"Oh. Yes—yes, I should be able to manage that."

Even as I said the words, my heart was sinking. It was ridiculous. Any wrongs I'd done were well over a decade ago. None of my brothers had any idea I'd ever caused them any harm with my childhood pranks anyway.

I knew, though. I knew they'd been not so much pranks but

malicious acts propelled by jealousy. I'd been as bad as the colleagues who watched my moves in the office so carefully.

That was why I worked so bloody hard, wasn't it? Surely I'd made enough amends to counterbalance the pain I'd brought into the world by now.

And if I hadn't, destroying a realm's worth of demons should do the trick all right.

CHAPTER FIVE

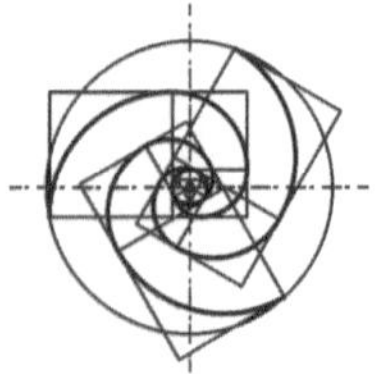

Jemma

The gold cuff formed a constant pressure around my thigh as Bash and I crept through the dark forest. The metal artifact wasn't diminishing my body the way it had when I'd been wearing it for weeks before, but the feel of it summoned the memory of the shocks of pain and the fading of my skin.

Thank goodness for Sherlock's coolheadedness in grabbing the pieces, because it would keep me undetected by our supernatural foes during our schemes, but I couldn't wait to take it off. I didn't expect any of the folk to be prowling around at night, when their powers in this world were at their weakest, but I wasn't taking any chances.

Only slivers of moonlight and my memory of my earlier scouting missions guided our way. I stopped at the sight of a small notch in the bark of a tree. It easily passed for the scrape of some small animal's claws, but I'd marked it there yesterday with a pocket knife.

"Start here," I whispered to Bash, and pointed to the notch. "You'll find a mark about every ten feet. We want this whole end of the perimeter covered."

He nodded, shifting the large knapsack he'd been carrying off his back. It was full of coils of wire, so thin and dark it wouldn't show up against the night's thick shadows, twisted and barbed to not just trip but snare anyone who ran into it.

The cultists would flee when the police arrived. I aimed to be sure they didn't make their escape successfully.

I touched Bash's arm briefly as I moved to leave, and he gave me the small knowing smile I'd only ever seen aimed at me. The smile that said he had no doubt I'd accomplish exactly what I was setting out to do, and he was looking forward to celebrating my victory on the other side.

He started fixing the end of the wire around the base of the tree trunk. I slunk on, closer to the spot where the commune's farthest sentries would be lurking. As I went, I slid on the night vision goggles Bash had obtained for me.

This cult settlement appeared to be a fairly subdued one, no major troubles recently, so they probably wouldn't have had a substantial guard most of the time. Tonight, though, with one of their own off arranging a criminal deal, I'd expect their security to be doubled.

I didn't want the inhabitants getting much in the way of advance warning of the raid. My job was to dispatch the sentries quickly and quietly. As a bonus, I could plant a few clues on their body to help speed justice along once the police found them.

I set my feet down with care, avoiding twigs and loose rocks, keeping close to the trees. My stark red hair might have drawn attention even in the dim moonlight, but I'd tucked it under the hood of my light jacket. My skin was starting to sweat with the late summer heat, still present in the middle of the night, but I kept all my attention focused on the forest ahead of me.

There. The goggles picked up the form of a middle-aged man with a holster at his hip as he shifted his weight at the edge of a little clearing up ahead. I paused for a moment, taking in his stance, the position of his gun, and the movement of his attention. Then I slipped closer.

No one else moved in the woods as I circled around him. I eased across the uneven ground until I was just a short leap away. He raised his gun hand to scratch at his scalp, and I sprang.

I'd told the trio that I wasn't going to try to kill *all* of the cultists, but I hadn't made any promises about a handful here and there. This guy would only cease to be a threat if I put him totally out of commission.

As I caught him, I grasped his jaw and the side of his head. Before he could let out more than a grunt of surprise, I wrenched my arms. His neck snapped, and his body slumped. I lowered him to the ground.

One down, I'd guess at least four more to go.

I stuffed my bit of "evidence" in his shirt pocket and stalked on. The guards closest to the dirt road that led into the commune were my main concern. I found another posted by a garage building where the road petered out, and dispatched her as swiftly as the first guy.

I didn't have much space in me for conscience, given the life I'd led and the things I'd had to do to make sure I stayed alive. The people whose lives *I* was taking tonight had sacrificed children to monsters and encouraged everyone around them to carve themselves up in worship. Still, a twinge that felt almost like guilt passed through my gut as I came up on the third guard, a young man with fawn-brown hair like Garrett's.

What would my trio have thought if they'd witnessed the crimes I was committing tonight? They'd seen the results of my efforts when they'd stormed the commune in Croatia, but only after a shoot-out between the police and the cultists. There wouldn't have been any telling which bodies were my fault.

If they'd watched me walk up to this guy, slam my knuckles into the back of his head, and crack his neck as coolly as if he were a chicken for a roast, would they have looked at me with anything other than horror?

Possibly not. That was why Bash balked at keeping them around, wasn't it? He trusted them to help but not to understand, and he was right. If they'd been through what I had—if they'd understood how the shrouded folk had taken over these people and how many more lives would be lost if I couldn't see through my mission—

It didn't do me any good thinking about it.

The thought lingered with me, though—enough that I paused when I spotted the next sentry. This one was a young woman, barely more than a girl really. Only a few years older than I'd been when I'd fled my family's commune back in Utah. Old enough to have survived past the sacrificial age and to have become fully complicit, of course. Still, something clenched in my chest as I studied her. She rubbed her thin lips, scanning the forest around her with a twitchy gaze.

It wasn't as if I *enjoyed* killing. Take the shrouded folk out of the picture, and I'd have been perfectly happy never harming another human being—other than separating the undeserving from some of their money every now and then as need be—for the rest of eternity.

I hadn't spent much time considering what my life might look like after I removed the shrouded folk from this world. It was hard to imagine that time or that I'd make it through the entire mission alive. But survival seemed a little more likely now. I might be able to look forward to much less fraught times in the distant future.

I shouldn't have let myself dwell on those ideas. They threw off my concentration. This time, even though the girl was clearly the least experienced of the guards I'd tackled, I held back just a little as I grabbed her from behind. The tiny hesitation left just enough of an opening for her to cry out and jab her elbow into my stomach.

Pain burst through my abdomen. My body reacted on pure instinct after that. I slapped my hand over her mouth to prevent any louder shouts for help or of warning and yanked her head to the side so fast my shoulders burned with the effort.

Her spine snapped. Her body sagged like all the others. I laid her down with a trickle of queasiness both at the task I'd had to carry out and my own momentary faltering.

What good was it being human, caring about other humans, if that would mean the shrouded folk kept strewing their misery and violence? No, I was exactly the way I needed to be right now, and if my trio ended up having a problem with that, the door was always open for them to leave.

I turned on my heel, studying the woods around me, my ears

perked for any sound—any indication that the girl's brief cry had drawn attention. Nothing stirred. The next sentry, if there even was another, must have been far enough away. I exhaled in relief and was just moving on in my sweep of the forest when engines rumbled behind me.

I spun with a lurch of my heart, but my pulse settled in an instant. The flash of headlights carried from the road I'd passed, showing the colors of a line of police cars arriving. The cavalry was here.

That was my cue to fade away. The local police didn't know anything about my involvement in this sting operation, and it was better for everyone if we kept it that way.

I turned to head for the spot where I was supposed to meet Bash at the car, and a whiff of a scent reached my nose that set the hairs on the back of my neck on end. Dry and sour like something dead so long it'd mummified—that was the smell that clung to the shrouded folk. None of those fiends could sense my presence with the gold cuff shielding me, but I could pick up on theirs just fine.

The odor could have simply lingered from when the folk had moved through and around the commune during the previous day, but I hadn't noticed it earlier. That suggested this waft was fresh. Despite the lack of sunlight, at least one shrouded one's attention had been drawn back to our world by the growing commotion descending on their worshippers.

What the hell did it mean to do?

The police cars had parked around the garage. Officers poured out of them and hustled with guns drawn along the narrower footpath that led to the commune. I made out Sherlock's tall, thin frame and John's broader form amid the uniforms.

Another whisper of the shrouded-folk scent drifted past me. I grimaced and treaded carefully after the flood of cops.

The fiends *shouldn't* interfere with this operation. There were too many witnesses; the risk of discovery too high. But they'd been desperate enough in Chile to attack me in front of the crowd that had gathered to watch the eclipse. I wasn't sure I trusted them to follow their own laws at this point. And if one of them was up to something, none of the officers who were storming the compound had any idea how to deal with them.

Shouts were ringing out now. A couple of cops led figures in handcuffs back to the cars. The crack of a gunshot split the air, and I restrained a flinch. Oh, yes, the police were convinced this commune was a den of criminals now.

I stopped several feet back from the sparser patch of forest where the commune had set up their cabins. Flashlights cast their beams all through the area, catching on the walls and the nauseated faces of the cops making gruesome discoveries. As they hustled more people off, one of them emerged from a building and promptly vomited beside the doorway. I was going to guess that was the bloodletting room.

I edged around the settlement until I spotted my consulting detective and his sidekick again. Sherlock was motioning to something on the ground while a few of the cops looked on, John nodding enthusiastically as if his show of agreement would make whatever the other man was saying easier to swallow. One of the cops knelt down—and a flicker of light that hadn't come from any flashlight glanced off the leaves over Sherlock's head.

A cry of warning caught in my throat. If I rushed in there without any good reason to be in the area, I'd force my two allies to make up a big story about what I was doing at the commune that would complicate everything. I tensed, watching to see if the shrouded one would actually make a move.

The light wavered and then vanished. I'd just started to relax when Sherlock's arm twitched. He slapped his forearm as if to catch a mosquito, and I sprang a few steps forward before I realized there was nothing more to the apparent "attack." If he'd been reacting to the shrouded one, it'd barely touched him.

I stayed there, braced to leap in if the fiends made another move, as Sherlock returned to his work. He didn't pay his arm any more mind. But even from where I stood, I could see a purplish mark coming into focus on the skin just below his wrist. My hands clenched at my sides.

The shrouded one *had* touched him. What were the fiends playing at now?

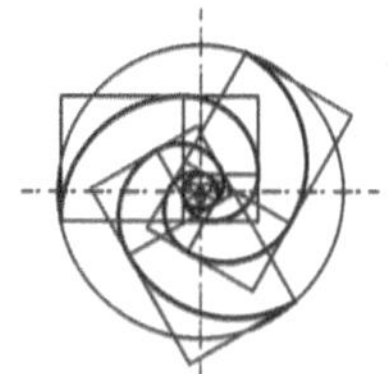

Jemma

Garrett made a disgruntled sound and sprawled deeper into the corner of Sherlock and John's sofa. "I wish I could have made it up there for the takedown."

"No, you don't," John said from the other end of the sofa, with an uncharacteristically grim expression. "The things those people do, the evidence we uncovered just in the initial sweep..." His lips twisted at a sickly angle. "And all this time these creatures have been pushing people to savage each other right under our noses."

Sherlock had stayed on his feet for this meeting, pacing now with a soft rasp of his shoes over the rug. In the early afternoon light steaming through the living room's two narrow windows, his light blue eyes glittered even more coolly than usual. "Not any longer. We're bringing them to justice just as we've gone so many other criminals, even if the others were human. It makes no difference."

I shifted in the stiffly padded armchair I'd taken — I could tell just from the rigid feel of it that it was probably Sherlock's usual perch. "That's not entirely true. Let me see your right arm?"

He hesitated for a second before moving toward me when I

beckoned him over. That was enough to tell me that he already knew what I was after. Even though it was another warm summer day and only a whirring fan added any relief to the heat in the apartment, he'd chosen a long-sleeved button-up to wear today. With a pointed look, I motioned for him to roll up the sleeve.

"I bumped my arm against something while we were searching the commune," he said briskly. "I suppose you saw that from the outskirts before you left."

"You didn't bump it against something," I informed him. "Something bumped against you. More specifically, a shrouded one."

I took his wrist gingerly, studying the mark that had formed like a bruise on his forearm. If I hadn't seen it happen, I might have taken it for an actual bruise. Because I knew to look for the signs, I noticed the faint, erratic dappling along the edges.

And when I breathed in, the dry rotten scent I'd first picked up in the forest still tainted the air.

"One of them marked you," I said. "I don't know why, but it'll have left a little of its energy in you so it can track you down again."

Bash leaned farther over the back of my chair, where he'd propped his sculpted arms. "Why would they want to do that? Why him?"

"Maybe word has spread enough that it recognized you had something to do with the incident in Chile," I said to Sherlock. "Or in Croatia, for that matter. They'd have wanted an easy way to trace you back to me, or at least to keep an eye on you even if you didn't. Hold on."

I got up and moved to the dining table. One of the napkins from our takeout lunch would do. I ripped it into even pieces and started spreading them across the wooden surface of the sideboard in a Fibonacci pattern.

John got up from the sofa to watch my progress. "You did that in my hotel room during the conference."

I nodded. "The shrouded folk thrive on pain and unpredictability. The certainty of mathematical patterns throws them off. This won't stop one that's particularly determined, but it'll act as a general deterrent—and it may even interfere somewhat with their ability to tune into the energy in that mark. Leave this here."

"I suppose it makes for an interesting decoration," Sherlock said with a lift of his eyebrows.

He wasn't taking this problem seriously enough. I went back to the chair and grabbed my purse. "I also think that for the time being, you should wear this. You should be fine for a week or two without any ill effects, and maybe that'll be long enough for them to give up on you."

I offered him the pieces of the gold cuff. Sherlock blinked at them and raised his gaze to my face.

"You need these," he said. "You're their primary target."

"Yeah," Garrett said. "We already know they'll try to hurt *you*, even with the contract broken."

"They came after all of you when you were getting me out of the way after the ritual, didn't they?" I shook the pieces at Sherlock. "You're the one they're the most interested in right now. If they follow you to me, then I'm screwed anyway."

The detective's lips pursed, but he accepted the cuff. After examining the pieces, he rolled up his pantleg and fiddled with them until he'd secured them around his lower thigh. Then he raised his eyebrows at me. "Satisfied?"

"Reasonably. Make sure it stays there."

Garret shot Sherlock a quick glower as if he blamed the other man for giving in to my demand. "What are the next steps, then?" he asked me.

"Last night's raid will have stirred things up all through the cult, especially any other local sects," I said. "For a few days, we can monitor the various types of activity around the other locations you thought looked like possibilities. I suspect we'll see some indications confirming one or more of those, and then we can move ahead from there."

We discussed who would collect which data for several more minutes. By the time I got up to leave, the rancid scent had faded from the air. The cuff and my sequence must have been enough to put off any shrouded folk hanging around here, if one had stuck around after following Sherlock to the apartment at all.

Garrett looked as though he intended to stick around, but he caught my arm before I headed out after Bash. His dark brown eyes searched mine. "Are you sure *you* have enough protections, firecracker? If I can get you anything…"

I didn't know if there *was* anything a police officer had access to that would fend off the shrouded folk, and from his pained expression he didn't either. But the offer and the affectionately admiring nickname softened the tension inside me anyway.

"I've been keeping myself safe for ten years," I reminded him. "I've got all the methods down pat. But thank you."

I tugged him a little closer to kiss him as consolation for my refusal. Garrett stiffened for a second, most likely in awareness of his friends still in the room, but it wasn't as if my widespread affections were any secret among this bunch.

He'd been the first of the trio I'd drawn in, the first who'd really cared about me, and as silly as the consideration sometimes seemed, part of me was determined never to make him feel he came in second place.

He relaxed into the kiss, touching the side of my face as he kissed me back hard. The heat of his mouth sang through me. It was an awful shame I had illicit activities to plan right now that my police officer wouldn't want to be privy to.

"To be continued," I told him in a teasing voice as I drew back, and headed out with a smile on my lips.

Bash had waited for me in the hall outside. "Where are you off to now, Majesty?" he asked in a dry tone as we headed for the stairs, but his eyes studied me with concern. Apparently all my men were in protective mode at the moment.

"Back to my place and the computer for at least the next little bit," I said. "I'll let you know if I think we need to take another field trip."

A hint of acrid rot touched my nose, and I tried not to let him see me tense. Oh, one of the fiends had stuck around, clearly. And now it was following me.

"Why don't I join you?" Bash tipped his head toward the street. "Two minds accomplish more than one?"

They might, but whatever the shrouded folk might intend for me, he didn't have anywhere near the practice at defending himself that I did. Neither did Sherlock, which was why I'd insisted he take the cuff. If the fiends were going to break their rules and make themselves known, dealing with them was my responsibility. My allies had already put themselves in plenty of danger as it was.

I tapped Bash's solid chest. "I suspect in this particular case it'd be more a matter of two bodies creating too many distractions. Besides, I need you to follow up with our forger about that payment."

Bash's jaw tightened. I grasped his arm and bobbed up to give him a quick kiss, heading off any further argument he might have made. "I'll see you soon," I said. "You know how to reach me if anything urgent comes up."

I hailed a taxi in the vague hope that a car might throw the fiend off, but I didn't really expect that to work. The shrouded folk scent met me as soon as I stepped out onto the sidewalk outside the posh modern apartment building where I'd gotten a short-term, furnished rental unit. I pretended not to notice and marched on inside.

I quite liked the place I'd gotten with its clean simple lines and muted color palette of ivory and soft grays, but it was hard to get comfortable knowing I had an unwelcome visitor. I'd already laid out a few Fibonacci sequences in the decorative stones that had come in a glass bowl on the hall table. They obviously hadn't been enough to shake my follower. I tweaked them slightly in at attempt to improve their accuracy and wandered into the bedroom to grab my laptop.

When I came back into the open-concept main room, a hazy figure shrouded in strips of pale streamers was waiting for me, hovering over the coffee table. I stopped dead in my tracks, my heart lurching even though I'd been expecting something like this.

It was impossible to tell the shrouded folk apart by physical characteristics. They didn't have much of a bodily presence in our world at all. With a person, I'd have considered the facial features, but all the shrouded folk had where their faces should be was a gaping black void amid the folds of tattered fabric—or perhaps it was swaths of dead skin. What a pleasant thought.

Still, in the first instant as I took in the visitor, I knew it wasn't the one I'd called Bog—the one I'd made a deal with to get me out of my commune in the first place. The quiver of energy in the air and the exact taint of the dryly putrid scent wasn't quite the same. When you'd lived among the fiends for fourteen years of your life, you learned other ways of identifying them.

"Not much for manners, are you?" I said to this one in the most flippant tone I could summon. "Guests are generally supposed to wait for an invitation. A knock would have been a good start too."

The shrouded one spoke with a voice as dry as its scent and utterly emotionless. "We do not bother with doors."

"Clearly." I flopped down on the linen sofa. "What do you want, then? I don't owe any of you anything now. All contracts have been voided."

"Indeed." Its form shifted as if it were gathering itself. "But you voided them by way of a trick. And even if we might have ignored that and left you alone, *you* have not left *us* alone."

"I don't recall doing anything to any shrouded folk."

"Do not play games. You are interfering with our worshippers and drawing other humans into this purpose. To what end?"

I fixed my gaze on the area where its eyes should have been. "What do you *think*?"

"You will not stop then."

Its tone was too flat for the sentence to be a question, but I answered it anyway. "I'll do whatever the hell I want, and none of you get to have any say in it. Not so fun being on the receiving end of that treatment, is it?"

The shrouded one quivered. "I think you are mistaken in how much control you have over this situation."

"I know your laws. I know the ones who came at me and my colleagues with physical force two weeks ago will have been sanctioned. I'm not the one who revealed that you exist to them— you all did that by yourselves."

"Yes, but there are forces other than the physical, as you should well know. I don't intend to leave you alone, not at all, not for as long as you still exist."

I tensed instinctively as the words drifted out into the air. The room around me was already mutating. A red slick spread across the peachy hardwood floor like a pool of blood, and then another formed on the other side of the coffee table, then another by kitchen island.

A metallic scent filled the air. But Bog had tried a bloody hallucination on me before, and I'd survived that. I fixed my gaze on the shrouded one in front of me.

"Is that the best you've got?"

It didn't speak, didn't move other than the erratic wavering of its covering as if the fabric were floating in an uncertain current, but I could have sworn I tasted a smile in that instant.

The puddles rippled. A bulge formed in the tops of them. It rose larger, the blood streaking down the emerging form until my spine stiffened in recognition.

My sister's face. Olivia's head—no, her whole body—was emerging from each of the crimson pools. Just as young as she'd been the last time I'd seen her, when she'd been ten and I'd been fourteen and I'd given her one last desperate kiss to the cheek before I'd fled, promising her I'd come back for her.

I'd been too late. The guilt of that fact never left me, and right now it knotted tight all through my chest.

There were five of her—no, six, seven, eight—rising up like cherubic demons summoned from the underworld. Her blood-streaked eyelids opened. Her bright blue eyes fixed on me from all sides. Her lips pulled back in a horrifying grimace.

"You did this to me," she wailed, all of her at once. "You killed me. It was you."

One of the heads popped off with a nauseating squelch. Another spun around as her neck purpled with bruises. One dug her hand right into her blood-splattered dress and gouged her heart out of her chest. Bile shot up my throat.

I closed my eyes and covered my face, focusing on the pattern of my breathing, but the rasp in and out had turned shaky.

"You. Murderer. I hate you!" she ranted, her thin voice carrying on and on. Something wet and squishy smacked into my hair—for fuck's sake, had one of the illusions thrown her own heart at my head?

Under my breath, I started reciting the decimals of pi. I'd made it to the seventh when one of my sister's bodies flung itself right into me.

CHAPTER SEVEN

Sherlock

I'd followed a rather incredible number of individuals in my time, both outright criminals and ordinary people who simply had something to hide. Technically, Jemma was the former, as much as I disliked that fact. She was certainly the most formidable target I'd ever tailed.

I'd made a couple of hasty changes to my appearance before I'd headed out after her: a swipe of gel through my hair to both darken it and slick it back, a pair of prescriptionless glasses from one of the drawers in the side table. As I ambled out onto the street, I let my posture slouch to disguise my height and thinness. My stride took on the rolling gait of a much portlier man.

Very few people who'd ever met me would have recognized me in passing, and I doubted even Jemma would have identified me on first glance. There was a much higher chance that she'd realize *someone* was following her, regardless of whom, and so when I spotted her flaming red hair just a few dozen feet farther up the street where she was speaking with Moran, I turned and began sauntering in the opposite direction.

A tiny mirror embedded in one side of the glasses allowed me to keep an eye on her even from behind. Her conversation with her associate ended quickly. As she hailed a cab, I beckoned for one of my own.

"Follow that car there," I instructed the driver as soon as I'd slid into the back. "Police business."

I'd learned over the years that those last two words could prevent all sorts of hesitation, even if I wasn't officially employed by the police. Few people bothered to check. This fellow pulled away from the curb without a single question and kept on Jemma's trail as her cab wove through London's chaotic streets.

The gold artifact she'd insisted I put on pressed against my thigh. The thin metal wasn't exactly *un*comfortable, but I didn't feel entirely comfortable wearing it. The symbols etched in it and the gems embedded in the thin metal surface had some esoteric power that I barely understood—that a few weeks ago I wouldn't have believed was anything more than superstition.

I hadn't liked the impression I'd gotten from Jemma as she'd made to leave. She'd had an air of apprehension I doubted anyone else in the room had picked up on, she was so skilled at moderating her emotions and distracting those around her by stirring up other feelings. Nevertheless, the subtle signs had been noticeable enough to me now that I'd had ample time to observe her over recent months.

Something had been worrying her. She wouldn't have told me what if I'd asked. So I would find out the way I found out many things, through further observation and deduction.

I might have volunteered my support to her cause, and I might appreciate her dedication to ending the horrors we'd witnessed from this cult twice now, but that didn't mean I was going to trust her completely. I highly doubted her faith in the three of us on the right side of the law was anywhere close to unwavering.

Jemma didn't appear to be heading anywhere unusual at the moment. Her cab led us from Westminster into East London and stopped outside a posh white apartment building that rose several stories higher than its nearest neighbor. I'd already determined she'd rented a flat in the place. She'd only been returning to it.

I might have headed home myself then if I hadn't caught a glimpse of her face on her way out of the cab while my own idled farther down the street. Now that she believed she had no witnesses, her mouth was set in a tense line, and her gaze darted around her warily—not along the sidewalk or across the road but higher along the buildings.

She was watching for some threat she expected to come from above. I waited until she'd gone into the building, and then I handed the driver his payment and went after her.

I didn't know precisely which flat she was renting, but the elevator indicator helpfully told me which floor she'd gotten off on, and a quick sweep of that hallway gave me enough clues to deduce which door she'd gone through. I hesitated there, momentarily unsure of myself.

Jemma understood how I worked. If I knocked and explained myself, she'd almost certainly laugh and perhaps admit to the problem if I insisted. Although perhaps I should take a turn around the building first to see if I could unearth any signs of a potential threat for myself.

Before I'd quite decided, Jemma's voice carried through the door. The building was well-constructed enough to hold sound within each flat, but even though I couldn't make out the words, the sound had the tenor of a rising yell. I might have even detected an edge of panic to it.

My instincts kicked in. Without a second thought, I yanked out my wallet, grabbed a keycard one of my less reputable sources had provided me with some years ago, shoved it into the slot, and jammed on the handle at the same time.

The building might have been solid, but it was hardly military-level secure. Hitting the handle with the right angle and pressure in combination with the signal on the card disengaged the lock in an instant. I shoved the door open and hurtled inside.

Jemma was standing at the edge of her living room, her eyes

closed, her hands thrust out at either side, her face sickly pale. Her yell was already fading, but her voice kept on chanting a stream of numbers I recognized as digits of pi. She motioned with her hands, and her shoulders came down a tad. She recited more digits even faster.

The sight of her so frantic set my own mind off-kilter. Jemma was the most self-possessed person I'd ever encountered. For something to have shaken her this badly—

It had to be something to do with those creatures, her shrouded folk.

My thoughts were still whirling, but there was one certain way I knew to combat the monsters. After all, she'd given it to me just an hour ago. I yanked up my trouser leg to snap open the gold cuff and rushed the rest of the way to her.

Jemma's eyes popped open as I knelt in front of her. I closed the cuff around her thigh over the fabric of her slacks, where it fit snugly. If I'd needed proof of the artifact's efficacy, it came with the rush of relief in her exhalation. She peered at me as I straightened up, the color already starting to come back into her cheeks, her eyebrows arching.

"Where did you come from all of a sudden, Sherlock?"

"I got the impression you might need some assistance." I studied the room around us, my stance tensing. Jemma might be protected now, but I no longer was. The bruise on my arm was evidence enough that the creatures were willing to affect me at least in small ways. "What happened?"

"One of the fiends showed up and tried to make me regret taking them on. It didn't work. I *was* getting a handle on the situation by myself, just so you know."

"By reciting numbers."

She ran her fingers through her hair, which had fallen astray during her distress. "Yes. I told you the shrouded folk don't like mathematical certainties." She dragged in a deep breath. "It made the hallucination the thing created ease off, and I think the fiend is gone now."

She had ways of detecting it beyond anything she could teach us or that I could fully understand. That knowledge made me shift restlessly on my feet, my own lungs tightening. These creatures exerted their horrible influence on our world in so many ways, could bring this magnificent woman to a state of panic in a matter of minutes, and even after tangling with them and their worshippers multiple times, they were still the biggest mystery I'd ever encountered, a vast blank in my understanding.

They left me little to observe, next to nothing to deduce from, and the deductions I could make jarred against everything logic and common sense offered.

"Are you safe to stay here?" I asked, with a prickle of frustration that I had no idea what the answer to that question might be.

"They can't affect me while the cuff is around my body," Jemma said. "Although of course that's why I gave it to *you*. I can fend for myself."

She bent down to remove it, clearly with the intention of giving it back to me. I caught her arm before she could.

"No," I said firmly when she glanced up at me. This much, at least, I was utterly certain of. "The things marked me yesterday, and they haven't harmed me in any way since then. The moment you no longer had that artifact in your possession, they came at you. There's nothing you can say that will convince me that I need it more than you do."

She sighed. "Fine. Let me at least put it out of sight. It's more effective skin to skin anyway."

I let go of her so she could unclasp the cuff and slip it under her slacks. The sight of her leg bare halfway up her thigh set off a flicker of heat that shot from my chest to my groin. The sensation of lust wasn't one I was especially familiar with either, but at least it wasn't a mystery. On the contrary, it was a human weakness so commonplace I'd once prided myself in being above it.

Jemma had shown me the productive side of physical satisfaction. And I couldn't say there wasn't a certain sense of accomplishment in bringing a woman this brilliant and assured to the heights of pleasure.

Her eyebrow rose again as she let her pant leg slip back down, as if she suspected my reaction. Perhaps I'd given off some hint of it that she could read as easily as I read so much else. She looked around the room as if confirming there was no sign of whatever the creature had been tormenting her with, and another pinch of restlessness nipped at me.

This was the greatest case of my career by far. My opponent couldn't remain this opaque to me. Otherwise I'd be little more use in bringing the things to justice than a constable straight out of school.

"Will the same trick with the numbers work for anyone, should the creatures attempt a similar assault on the rest of us?" I asked.

"Yes, for anyone who has plenty of pi memorized." She grinned at me. "I suppose you've got it to the thousandth digit or so."

"Somewhere around there."

"I don't think we'll need to put that possibility to the test, though. They aren't afraid to hit me with the worst they can conjure up because I'm a known quantity—I used to belong to them. With the rest of you, they'll be more careful to follow their rules. If they come after you, it may be in ways so subtle you don't realize there's any supernatural influence at all."

She folded her arms over her chest. "I think I'd better come back to your apartment with you, if you're going to insist on leaving the cuff with me."

"I'd imagine John and I can take care of ourselves, especially if the effect would be so small."

"You of all people should know that subtle doesn't have to mean small. The shrouded folk only followed you there recently. I don't think I should leave you and John alone on your first night afterward, not until I see if they're planning anything more than just following."

I opened my mouth to protest again and paused. Why dismiss her help? It would be easier to learn the ways of these things with her there to guide us if one of them acted on us. I might have my pride, but only a stupid man would wave off the chance to learn vital information.

"All right," I said. "I suppose there's the couch, if you can accept sleeping there."

"I think I'll manage just fine," she said, with a glint in her eye that suggested she expected she'd make it into one or the other of our beds if only for a portion of the night. "Let me get a few things, and then we can start our monster watch."

CHAPTER EIGHT

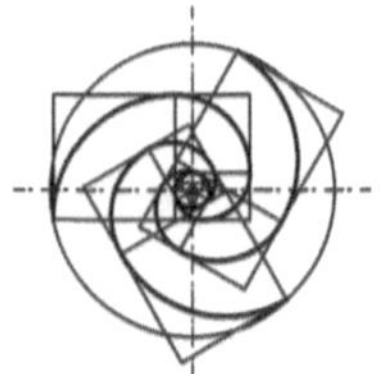

Jemma

"Oooh, right *there*," I said, letting myself sink deeper into the sofa cushion.

John chuckled at the other end of the sofa, where he was massaging my foot with skilled strokes of his thumb. Each press sent a pleasant burn and a trickle of relaxation through the muscles all the way up my leg. Between that and the Indian takeout filling my belly, I couldn't imagine a much more enjoyable way to spend an evening. Perhaps I should look into bringing on the doctor as a full-time foot masseuse.

"Ready for the other one yet?" he asked with a lift of one eyebrow. I hadn't asked for the massage, but I had sprawled out on the sofa with my feet on his lap when we'd retired to the living room after dinner, so I supposed that'd seemed like enough of a prompt.

"No, I'll take a little more on the arch before you move on," I said with a grin.

Sherlock shook his head where he was sitting in the armchair next to the sofa, pipe in hand and tablet propped on one knee, but the corners of his lips had quirked upward as well. "You'd better not let word get out how easily won over you are by a little foot rub. What will become of the brilliant Jemma Moriarty then?"

"She'll have incredibly well-tended-to feet," I shot back, and let out another encouraging hum as John dug his thumb in a little deeper just above my heel. The rich smell of Sherlock's pipe smoke mingled with the honey sweetness lingering in my mouth from the extensive dessert I'd ensured the takeout meal included, making another sort of heaven all on its own. Who needed a criminal empire when you could have this?

The thought had passed through my mind in jest, but a twinge followed it. My life *could* have looked something like this if I'd been born into a normal family, not one devoted to the shrouded folk and offering up their children as further sacrifice. If I'd had a chance to learn how to really connect with people instead of seeing them all as competition... If I hadn't been left with my sister's murder hanging over my head...

But then the world wouldn't have any Jemma Moriarty to carry out her avenging mission. The shrouded folk would still have existed, still have killed other children. On the balance, everyone else was better off for my fraught early years.

I wouldn't have minded a taste of that imaginary alternate life, though. This might be one right here. No unsettling scent had returned to the apartment to indicate a shrouded one had returned to survey it. There wasn't anything wrong in indulging in the illusion of normality for one night.

The fiends had stolen so much from me. I deserved a chance to be *completely* free for them, if only for a brief moment before my responsibilities called once more.

Unfortunately, John had clearly been thinking about my early years too. He shifted to my other foot automatically, but his expression went serious, his mind on something other than my appendage.

"You lived in one of those communes for fourteen years, you said."

I nodded. To fill in the most essential blanks in their

understanding, I'd told the trio the basic details of my history over the week when I'd been recovering.

"I can see why you needed to build up a certain amount of wealth and influence so that you'd be able to take on these creatures," he went on. I hadn't mentioned Olivia at all, but the scenes they'd witnessed in that other commune had shown them plenty of motivation for anyone to want to put an end to the shrouded folk's reign. "Why is it that you took the criminal route? Why not put your skills toward a legitimate business?"

His tone didn't reveal any judgment of my chosen line of work, but knowing John, the fact of it niggled at him. He was, really, the most *good* of the trio, his adrenaline junkie tendencies aside. The three of them all had their own motivations for coming to their lines of work. Sherlock liked to solve puzzles. Garrett had something to prove.

John... He cared about people, pure and simple. Which I supposed was an excellent quality for a doctor to have, and often useful for a consulting detective's partner as well, but it also meant he cared about all the people I'd conned over the years.

A little tension wound back through my gut. I ignored it. I could give him an honest and reasonably complete answer.

"Growing up in a place like that," I said, "everything was out of our control. The adults pushed us into our various sacrifices and spats with each other. The shrouded folk directed the adults. I never even knew what the supposed 'high honor' I was competing for was until I snuck out to watch one of the older kids taken..." A shiver ran down my back at the memory of the blaze of light, the awful screams that had seemed to go on forever.

Sherlock was watching me intently now, but John's hand paused against my foot. "If you'd rather not talk about it—if it's too painful—"

I waved off his concern. "I can manage my own discomfort. I don't resent the question. Anyway, fourteen years of that left me with a deep need for control. I function best when I can direct as many pieces of a scheme as possible by my own will."

"And how does that need interfere with having a legitimate business that you own and operate yourself?"

I gave him a pointed look. "How do you think? Any completely legal way of making money involves all sorts of permissions and restrictions from outside parties—people I don't trust not to screw me over. If you want full control, it's easiest to simply ignore the law completely."

"Easiest for the perpetrator," Sherlock said wryly. "Not so much the victims."

My gaze shifted to him, the twinge I'd felt earlier digging more sharply into my chest. "I'm not going to tell you about all the things I've done, because I don't think you'd enjoy hearing them. But I hope you know me well enough by now to be able to 'deduce' that I don't hurt people for some sick enjoyment but only when it's necessary—and generally only those who have it coming. If I can rid this world of the shrouded folk, then I'll have ended a lot more misery than I've ever caused."

John started to rub my foot again with a gentle pressure. He spoke quietly, like an apology. "It's amazing that you made it through the childhood you had as strong as you are. I realize I can't really know what it was like, and I can't say what I might have felt I needed to do if I'd gone through the same thing."

I accepted that sentiment, but I didn't want to dwell on the past anymore. I wanted to get back to that warm, contented moment of a few minutes ago when it'd almost seemed that past had never existed. With a shove against the cushions and a bend of my knees, I scooted closer to him. "So, you're not going to chuck me out the door just yet, then?"

I'd never seen anything quite like the eagerly kind smile John Watson could produce, as bright as his blond hair. "I know you wouldn't hurt us."

He said it like a simple statement of fact when really it was all faith. My throat tightened at the words. Garrett had felt plenty hurt by the way I'd deceived him when we'd first met. During that early scheme, I could have ruined all of their careers if I'd wanted to—that had been my original plan.

But then, maybe I'd earned a bit of John's faith after all. I *had* changed my plans once I'd gotten to know the trio face to face. I'd saved their lives later on when Bash had come to my rescue, ready to set his gun blazing.

"No, I wouldn't," I said, bringing my fingers to his cheek. There was one thing I could get from these men that topped every other enjoyment I'd had tonight. "I have much better things to do with you."

I slipped my foot out of his grasp so I could lean the rest of the way to kiss him. He moved to meet me, one hand coming to rest on my waist as if to steady me—as if I needed steadying. As soon as our mouths collided, a rush of heat and assurance swept through me.

I wouldn't have these men forever. I might not even have them for the entirety of my mission. But damn, they did spark something deep during the time they were around. Right now, I wanted to take all the bliss of this sensation and see how high I could fan the flames, as if they might burn away everything awful in my life.

John kissed me tenderly and then with more passion, his other hand coming up to tangle in my hair. I devoured the sweetness of his mouth. He paused for a second, keeping his head close to mine, and glanced toward Sherlock as if in question.

The other man's posture had stiffened, but I recognized the hungry light in the back of Sherlock's eyes. Hunger both of us could provoke, it turned out. But the consulting detective didn't like to give in to carnal impulses simply for the sake of it. I could give him an excuse to justify the idea.

"I think we deserve a reward after the first part of the job well done," I said with a sly smile. "To clarify our thoughts for the rest to come, from tomorrow onward?"

He wet his lips, and I tracked the movement with another flash of heat. Then he got up without a word, set his pipe on the end table, and came to sit on the sofa at my other side. He traced the curve of my hip, and John pulled me into another kiss, and oh yes, this was bliss, all right. A joy no shrouded one could possibly conquer. The fiends wouldn't have had the slightest clue what to make of this encounter or what the purpose of it could possibly be.

Sherlock eased my hair to the side and kissed my neck, finding the sensitive spot he'd discovered I responded to well before. I growled at the bolt of pleasure that intensified with the nip of his teeth.

My fingers trailed down John's broad chest, and he teased his thumb over the peak of my breast. Sherlock dipped his hand right between my legs. My breath stuttered as he trailed it along my inner thigh to the spot that burned for contact. His lips seared a path of their own to the crook of my shoulder.

I kissed John long and hard, and then I nudged him back just far enough to allow me to speak. "I think we should take this to a bed. The only question is which one."

"Sherlock's," John said with a breathless laugh. "Much less of a mess."

Sherlock looked as if he might object to the mess *we* might end up making there, but when I caressed his lean torso through his linen shirt, desire overcame any resistance in his expression. "What are we waiting for, then?" he said matter-of-factly.

Having seen the way he kept his hotel rooms, I knew what to expect from Sherlock's bedroom, but walking into a place so entirely *him* still sent a happy quiver through me. Everything from the bedcovers to the books on the shelves along one wall was perfectly orderly, as John had suggested. The smoky tang of his pipe smoke lingered in the air.

John looked affected by it too. His pupils dilated, and he rested a tentative hand on his friend's shoulder. Sherlock glanced at him. Some silent communication seemed to pass between them before Sherlock leaned in and captured John's mouth with his own.

They kept touching me as they kissed each other, John's hand on my back and Sherlock's on my hip. I simply watched the pleasure they took from each other for a moment, and then added to it by grazing my lips against Sherlock's skin just below his ear.

A few weeks ago, Sherlock had barely been able to admit his attraction to his long-time friend. Now, the two of them getting intimate looked as natural as breathing. Maybe I had hurt them in little ways before we'd gotten to this point, but I'd given them that gift too, hadn't I?

Sherlock pulled away from John to kiss me next. As he claimed my lips, John eased his hand up under my blouse. He loosened my bra. A moan slipped from my throat as he stroked my bare breast, sending a wash of giddy sensation through me.

Sherlock took the opportunity to kiss me even more deeply, taking the initiative with his tongue this time. I grasped the fly of his pants and yanked. The first couple times we'd come together like this, it'd been a slowly building seduction. Tonight I was ready to get to the best parts fast.

I pushed Sherlock onto the bed, tugging John with us too. His leg would bother him if he was standing for long without support. As he clambered onto the covers after me, the good doctor lifted my blouse right up over my head. Sherlock reached for the clasp of my pants, and I yanked his down. He cupped me through my panties with a skillful precision that brought a gasp to my lips. A hunger for even more flared all through my body.

As Sherlock and I kissed again, John brought his mouth to my breast. I nearly bit Sherlock's lip at the jolt of pleasure. I shifted my attention from one man to the other, stripping John of his collared shirt. While I claimed his mouth in turn, Sherlock fondled my breasts from behind, circling both nipples deftly and flicking his thumbs over them with little jolts of pleasure.

I dawdled on that bliss for a minute, kissing John as thoroughly as I was capable of. Then I swiveled and gave Sherlock a light shove as I kicked my pants the rest of the way off. He sank back on the bed, his long cock standing rigid at attention. My sex throbbed at the sight of it. I stroked the velvety skin from base to head, rewarded by the hitch of his chest.

"I need you inside me *now*."

Sherlock's eyes gleamed with a delight he couldn't hide. John pitched in by divesting me of my panties while I ripped open the condom packet I'd grabbed from my purse. I worked Sherlock over a few more times, slicking precum down his length. The second after

I'd prepared him, I straddled him and sank down onto him, my eyes rolling back with the fresh burn of bliss.

John sprawled beside us, fondling my breast with one hand. I meant to urge him up the bed so I could take him in my mouth while I rode his friend, but at the same moment, Sherlock reached toward the other man. As I rose and eased down again over him, he traced the lines of John's chest tentatively. His gaze stayed fixed on his companion's face as if waiting for some sort of rejection.

John simply gazed back at him, a flush seeping up his neck and onto his cheeks.

Somewhere in our eager groping, I'd undone the fly of John's pants, even if I hadn't managed to get them off. Sherlock's hand hesitated at his friend's waist. His throat bobbed with an audible swallow. "John," he said in his overly formal way, "I would— That is, if you—"

"Yes," John said softly.

I stilled over Sherlock as he dipped his hand inside John's pants. John closed his eyes, his lips parting. His expression was so ecstatic I practically came just watching him.

He rolled farther onto his side toward us. Sherlock began a careful but steady pumping. His gaze came back to me, and I bent down to kiss him, hoping I could convey just how very okay I was with this mutual adoration-fest. I caressed John's side, and he resumed his attentions to my breast, even as his hips started to twitch with the rhythm of Sherlock's helping hand.

I couldn't bear to stay still any longer. I started to ride Sherlock again, and he rolled his hips to meet me, filling me even deeper than I'd managed on my own. He gripped my thigh with his free hand, shifting his position slightly beneath me, and his cock hit a spot deep inside that sent pleasure pulsing through every part of my body. I couldn't hold in a whimper.

"There?" Sherlock said, sounding both eager and self-satisfied. He bucked to meet me, and I trembled with the sensation.

"Fuck, yes," was all I managed to reply. I rocked over him faster, and his hand on John sped up at the same time. We all moved together, sparking pleasure between the three of us in a weird unity that was nonetheless the most wonderful thing I'd ever experienced.

"Christ, Sherlock," John said in a strained voice, so clearly close to the edge that the words sent me tumbling right over. As Sherlock plunged into me, I cried out with the burst of my orgasm through my core. John groaned as he followed me. I kept bobbing up and down over Sherlock in my blissful haze until his grip on my thigh tightened. He came with a choked sound.

We collapsed into a warm, gleefully sweaty heap of limbs. As I nestled there between the two men who should have been my enemies, an odd sense of peace spread through my chest.

I didn't know if I'd ever feel actual love in my life, for someone else or from them to me, but just now, in this moment, I caught a glimmer of what it might be like.

CHAPTER NINE

Bash

An engine roared beneath me, and dust kicked up in clouds beyond the open back of the army truck. Jemma's trio of London crime-fighters closed in around me, all of them decked out in full military fatigues.

Garrett grabbed my arm where I was sitting on the bench and wrenched me up so hard my shoulder nearly popped from its socket. I moved to resist, and my wrists jarred against a binding that bit into my skin. When I drew in a breath, the air crackled into my mouth, dry and gritty.

"Out you go!" Sherlock hollered, and pushed me toward the open door. "We don't need your kind around here."

John smacked his walking stick across my face. As my head spun, he shoved me even closer to the edge. "People like you don't deserve anything."

"Get the hell out of our lives!" Garrett snapped.

I tried to throw myself farther into the truck, and they all heaved at me at the same time. I stumbled over the edge. The sensation of falling only lasted one lurching second before my head smacked into the hard-packed earth with an explosion of pain that —

I flinched awake in my bed. My heart thumped on and I could have sworn a dull ache lingered, creeping through the side of my head, but I wasn't in Afghanistan. I was in the bedroom of the temporary apartment I'd rented near Baker St. The plain white ceiling loomed over me as I swallowed to clear the taste of sand from my mouth.

Of course I was in my apartment in London. I'd left Afghanistan and the army nearly nine years ago. Jemma's trio had never been over there in the first place. It'd been a dream — a stupidly unsettling dream that I still couldn't quite shake the memory off as I got up and went to take a shower.

It might have been a dream, but it hadn't been entirely inaccurate, had it? Those three would have tossed me out of Jemma's mission in an instant if they could. I didn't figure any of them would forget the moment in Split when I'd been a twitch of my trigger finger away from killing the bunch of them.

I *had* been the one who'd invited them back into our lives, if only to save Jemma's. Maybe I should have killed them back then and spared us all the trouble. Jemma had charmed them, but in their eyes I was only the hired help, and a thug on top of that.

Jemma had offered to get me a rental in the same place she was staying, but I'd wanted to stay close to the main two in the trio in case this alliance went sour. The upside was it only took me five minutes to get from the apartment to Sherlock and John's for our planned morning meeting.

John was the one who answered the door. He smiled at me like he seemed to smile at just about everybody, but the expression he aimed at me didn't have quite the same warmth. The image flashed through my mind of his face in my dream, lip curled with disgust. I blinked it away, dipped my head to him, and came in without bothering with greetings.

Despite my close proximity, I was the last one to show up. The others were already sitting around the dining table, Jemma tucked in between Sherlock and Garrett, her hand brushing Garrett's arm as the cop said something she chuckled at. For all her cool collectedness, *she* had plenty of warmth for all three men now. As if Detective Inspector Lestrade wouldn't just have soon have seen all of the rest of us out of the picture so he could have her to himself.

The thought came with an uncomfortable prickling. As I took my seat, I exhaled, willing myself to focus.

Jemma flashed me a grin. "Right on time. Let's get started." She gave Garrett's shoulder a light poke. "You've been following up on the local investigation in the aftermath of the raid on the Lake District commune, haven't you?"

"Of course," the slight man said, his chin coming up. "A lot of horrifying stuff, as we'd all have expected. There was one kid they found in a hollowed-out room under one of the cabins…" His mouth twisted. "Anyway, these people don't seem to keep a whole lot of written records, but the local department turned up a few things that might point us in the right direction. At least I hope so, considering the hassle my own coworkers are giving me over my interest in the case."

"Does it bother them that you're following up?" Sherlock said with a frown. "Surely they can understand why you'd check in, what with my own involvement and your key role in directing the investigation?"

Garrett tossed up his hands in an unexpectedly violent motion. "I don't know what goes through their heads. Most likely their heads are all full of rocks, the way they go around. More interested in gossip than actually getting any work done. They're all bloody useless fuckers."

There was a momentary silence around the table as we all hesitated. The cop had a temper, but he didn't usually shoot off his mouth to that extent out of the blue. Jemma peered at Garrett, knitting her brow. "Did something particularly bad happen when you were at work yesterday?"

The man rubbed his mouth, his expression still tight, his posture defensive. "No. I just—I get sick of them. That's all. Nothing so strange about that. You hear the way Sherlock talks about them."

The explanation didn't ring totally true to me, but I didn't really give a shit what bee the cop had in his bonnet anyway. "What's the useful evidence you got?" I said. "That's the important part." Not his petty grievances.

Garrett shot me a look as if he were going to snap at me too, but his voice came out even enough now. "They found some sort of order invoice with an address that just led to a farm down near Dover. They left it at that, but the data we got together earlier suggests there's been other activity in that general area. This address completes a sort of ring that I'd expect a commune or similar is sitting in the middle of. Not a very large one, though, from the level of activity."

"That's a start," John said briskly. He drummed his hands on the edge of the table. "We can pursue that."

"Is that all?" Sherlock asked. "As enjoyable as your enthusiasm is, my dear Watson, I think we should hear all the possibilities before leaping ahead."

Garrett shook his head. "On top of that, they found items they were able to determine came from a couple areas in the Scottish Highlands. Also near some points of activity we observed earlier—a little more there. Although it's been harder to get clear data because the departments in Scotland aren't always so keen on cooperating with London... I'm planning on doing some further digging as I can."

"It sounds like there must be some association between the different communes here," Jemma said with a cock of her head. "I don't remember mine being in communication with other settlements, but then, at my age, they probably wouldn't have shared that kind of information with me. It'd certainty help with ensuring all the nearby communes had enough supplies and support if they ran into trouble."

"The Highlands location has shown evidence of being a larger target," Sherlock said. "Why don't we continue our own investigations from a distance and see what we come up with in a few days' time before taking any more direct steps?"

John looked at him, his hand still shifting restlessly. "Can we really afford to wait? The crimes they're committing on a regular basis…"

"We need to be fully prepared," Sherlock said firmly. "We can't afford to step wrong and throw the whole operation against this menace off."

"The place in Dover isn't that far from here," Garrett said. "It wouldn't be difficult to scout out more closely."

"If we're going to look more closely, I say we go straight to the bigger commune," John said.

Sherlock raised his eyebrows. "We don't even know for certain that it is larger. I'd say—"

A tension I hadn't fully registered building inside me suddenly overflowed. I smacked my hands down on the table. "I say you all shut up and let's get something done. What the hell is the point of all this arguing?"

Sherlock stiffened. "Determining the best course of action is an essential part of any—"

"Not when you're going in circles. Here's a simple plan: We investigate everything and every way we can investigate. That matters more than any of you being 'right' or whatever you're trying to prove."

"Bash," Jemma said quietly, and my gaze jerked to her. She was watching me much the same way she'd looked at Garrett a few minutes ago, her forehead lightly furrowed, concern shining in her blue-gray eyes. As the prickle of frustration eased off, I realized I'd just said more in the space of a minute than I'd generally contributed to these discussions at all. I let the rest of them do their talking, and then I carried out what Jemma needed doing. That was my role.

They just were getting on my nerves today.

Jemma's intervention cooled my jets, though. I let out a huff of breath. "Do what you want," I said to the others. "But what I said stands."

"I would like to take some actual action," John said, glancing around the table. "I suppose Dover *is* closer… It couldn't hurt to go out and take a careful scope around the area today, could it?"

Yes. Let's get away from this table and their constant discussion and crack a few heads. "I'll go with you," I said. "Strength in numbers. And I know enough to make sure you don't screw everything up."

I looked to Jemma again, wondering if she'd insist on joining us, but she simply nodded. Maybe she was glad to see me outright offering to collaborate with one of her trio.

"Let me quickly go over all the information we already have on that spot and see if I have any pointers," she said. "Then it's all yours."

"Not so much a ring as a semi-circle," John said, studying the map. He'd made a similar comment earlier in the drive, but at least when he was talking he wasn't moving about restlessly in the passenger seat. Maybe I'd let him drive on the way back. I'd preferred to have primary control over our route, but it might be worth the trade-off to have him fully occupied.

"That still makes it easy to narrow down where the place might be," I said. The data the trio had gathered from their various sources pointed us to a section of the country's southern coastline, high up on a cliff over the sea. Jemma's cult did have a thing for elevation. "How much farther to that farm now?"

"Ten miles. How close do you think we should go to the likely area?"

"Close enough to see where the edge of their surveillance is. That's the most important factor if we're going to crash their party."

John nodded with a knowing expression. "Any facility's security is only as good as the men on guard." He paused. "Or women, I suppose. We didn't have many of those in our unit in Iraq, so sometimes my phrasing is a little skewed."

I glanced away from the road to briefly study his face. I'd known John had been in the field overseas from Jemma's preliminary research on the Londoners, but there was so little military in his demeanor I hadn't thought about it in a while. Beneath that apparently soft exterior was a man who'd endured a similar environment to the one I had. It could be that the only reason he wasn't still out there was the blast that had left him needing that walking stick.

"Do you regret joining the service?" I asked abruptly. "If you hadn't, you'd still be a surgeon, right?"

John blinked at me. He might not realize just how much intel Jemma had shared. "No," he said after a moment, with what sounded like honest thoughtfulness. "And not just because I'm very happy with the career I have now. Going over there gave me a sense of a higher purpose on a broader level that I hadn't really felt before. I'm glad I have that, however I'm going to apply it." He smiled. "And it's always good to test your limits and discover how much you can survive."

I had to chuckle at that. "No kidding."

I returned my focus to the road, but I felt him studying me in turn. "Where were you stationed?" he ventured.

Was he guessing or had Jemma mentioned my time in the army? I guessed it didn't matter for him to know. "Afghanistan. Pretty brutal. I don't regret going either, because of the things it taught me about myself and everyone else, but I sure as hell wouldn't go back."

"No. I think once is enough."

The set of John's mouth resonated with something inside me. As huge a distance as there was between me and the three of them, he and I at least had more common understanding than I'd considered. I didn't want to be best pals with the guy, but the prickly sensation that had lingered since my dream eased with a touch of warmth.

He might have overly grandiose ideas about good and evil, but John Watson was okay. He'd gotten his hands dirty—he'd put in the work.

He shifted in his seat. "Here's the farm. Take a right at the crossroad."

I followed his directions, easing up on the gas with each passing mile, until the road turned into a dirt track and a metal gate came into view another half a mile up ahead. At the sight of it, I pulled the car over to the side of the road.

The track led on past the gate across a short stretch of field and then on into hilly woodland. The cult liked the cover of forests as much as they liked to be high above sea level. I scanned the area but didn't see any sign of security other than that gate. There might not even be a commune beyond it—it could be another farm or country property for all we knew.

"Should we go on foot from here?" John asked.

"I think that makes the most sense." I shoved open the door. "Better make it look like we're wandering tourists in case anyone's watching from the woods. If they don't want us to get that close, they'll turn us back quickly enough, and that'll tell us something right there."

I had to admit that John knew how to play a part well when he needed to. He got out of the car with that entitled vacationer air already in place, giving his walking stick a quick whirl. We approached the gate without incident. A padlock hung from the chain that held it closed, so I clambered over and helped John follow me.

We ambled along as if sightseeing until we reached the cover of the forest. No one stepped out to shoo us away. I started scanning our surroundings more warily, watching for any human movement or other sign of habitation. John shifted the branches of a shrub with his stick here, peered down at the dirt track there. The third time he knelt down, he stayed there.

"Someone drove through here recently?"

I crouched across from him. "How can you tell?"

He motioned to a tiny blotch in the dirt. "Oil. Still on the surface, not quite dry yet. Sherlock probably could have given you an accurate estimate to the hour—the best I can say is I think it couldn't have been more than a day ago they went through. It doesn't tell us a lot, but there's obviously someone who's been active out this way."

I straightened up. "Let's see if we can find out what they've been up to."

John spotted a few more specks of oil as we walked on. Birds chattered in the trees, and the warm summer breeze erased any coolness the shadows might have provided. We'd been on the trail maybe an hour without encountering anyone or anything human-made when a hint of a scent reached my nose. I stopped in my tracks.

"Do you smell that?" I said quietly.

John had come to a halt when I had. He took a breath, and his eyebrows rose. "Smoke," he said. "Not just ordinary wood smoke either. Something's been burning that wasn't meant to be burnt."

Yes, I'd caught the chemical flavor to the smoke too. My nerves on edge, I set off again a little faster than before. Something about this whole situation didn't feel right.

The smell thickened as we hurried on. The track came to an abrupt end—and we found ourselves looking at what I assumed had once been a garage, now nothing more than a few pieces of charred walls and a heap of burnt rubble.

"What the hell happened here?" John said under his breath. "Do these people have enemies other than Jemma?"

"Not that she's ever mentioned to me. And I'm sure she would have made use of them if they existed." I peered between the trees and thought I made out a dark shape up ahead that wasn't a tree. "Come on."

We crept along cautiously at first and then with more confidence as it became clear no one at all was left in this godforsaken place. Eight cabins scattered the woods about a mile from the garage, but all of them had been burned, roofs crumbled, innards hollowed out, what remained of the wooden walls little more than cinders. Many of the trees near them were charred as well. I wouldn't be surprised if the only reason there hadn't been a huge forest fire was the recent rains.

The smoky stench hung thick in the air here. A huge pile of ash with no sign of walls or anything to mark it as a building lay in the approximate middle of the settlement. I walked up to it and poked it with a broken branch I picked up, sifting through fragments of blackened paper and melted bits of plastic. Understanding rose up inside me.

"This wasn't something some enemy did to them. They did it to themselves. They were getting rid of evidence. This must have been the stuff they particularly wanted to destroy."

John let out a low whistle. "Do you think they heard about the raid and figured they might be next?"

"Who knows? These people are insane, and I'm not sure the creatures that direct them are any less crazy." I dug deeper into the pile of ash, hoping I might find some shred of evidence to bring back to Jemma, but they'd done a thorough job. The chemical smell was at least partly kerosene, I recognized now. The stuff had been doused to make sure it burned. Probably the buildings had been too.

"We check all the cabins," I said. "Grab anything that's got any kind of identifying mark on it, any text, anything we might be able to get information out of. Jemma won't be happy if we lose this bunch completely."

CHAPTER TEN

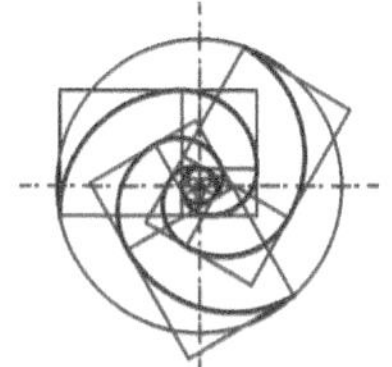

Jemma

The woman behind the reception desk gave the four of us a bemused look. "What are you here about again?"

"The parent company hired us to take a look at your computer security systems," Sherlock said in a clipped voice that didn't sound at all like his own. "All we need is a station with internet capability, ideally in an office we can have to ourselves for the hour or so the testing will take. I have the work order right here."

He produced a paper I'd had one of my many contacts in the forging business put together for us. The receptionist glanced at it and then at us again.

We'd gone for the most clear computer-geek stereotypes, all of us in one sort of glasses or another, slacks and plain button-up shirts, my bright hair hidden under a much dowdier wig. The only one who stuck out a bit was Sherlock's Irregular addition to our crew—a girl named Marissa who couldn't have been more than eighteen but who apparently could hack circles around just about anyone. But she mustn't have looked ridiculously young, because the receptionist picked up her phone.

"Let me see what I can do," she said, and five minutes later one of the staff escorted us into a small but private room with a few desks and a couple of laptops.

"Is there anything else you need?" the guy said.

"I think we're good to go," John replied, keeping his own voice flatter than usual. None of us wanted to be recognized if we had to make another appearance here in a more official capacity. Not that I expected that would be very likely.

The guy left, I locked the door behind him, and Marissa dropped into a chair in front of one of the computers with a crack of her knuckles. "Give me five, maybe ten minutes," she said, her gaze already intent on the screen. "I'll have it all laid out for you by then."

"We'll leave you to it," Sherlock said in his usual dry tone.

The three of us wandered through the room while Marissa's fingers clattered over the keys. The florescent light overhead gave off a faint buzzing, and the air had a lemony waxy smell as if someone had recently polished the floor, but I'd been in worse spots.

John leaned against the far end of the table. He lowered his voice so as not to disturb Marissa's work. "We're only looking for the details of a theft, right?"

"If it even exists." I fished in my purse for the pen that had been among the seemingly random assortment of items he and Bash had brought back from the burnt-out commune near Dover. The tip was scorched and the body partly melted, but not so much that we hadn't been able to make out the company logo printed on the side: Havenboard Foods. The business stocked a variety of grocery and corner stores throughout southern England.

Sherlock nodded. "There are many ways that pen could have ended up in the commune other than by the theft of a shipment. Businesses give out promotional materials of that sort in large quantities. It'd have been easy enough for a cultist who temporarily left the settlement to happen to pick one up any number of places."

He spoke evenly, but his expression was darker than usual. A bit of a cloud had been hanging over him since we'd rounded up the group this morning. I hadn't seen him in one of his morose moods since that first week we'd spent together when he'd been temporarily stumped by the case I'd presented the trio with.

It didn't make sense for him to be withdrawing in frustration now. We had plenty of leads and had hardly exhausted any of them.

"Have any other cases come up while you've been working on this?" I asked, taking a roundabout route to getting at my real question. Sherlock had ego to spare. If I suggested that he was behaving irrationally or overly affected by emotion, his kneejerk reaction would be denial.

He gave me a look that was almost a glower. "Don't worry, all my attention has been on these operations."

I was a little stung by his assumption that I'd meant to question his dedication. "That wasn't the point I was getting at. You seem... more preoccupied than usual this morning, and I wondered why."

"I'm merely eager to gather more information so that we can arrive at clearer conclusions," Sherlock said.

Eager wasn't at all the word I'd have used to describe his demeanor. Apparently Watson was on my side. "Perhaps we both had a restless night," he said in his gentle way. "Everything we've seen and had to think about involving these creatures—it can stick in the mind in unfortunate ways. I had a couple of horrible dreams." He grimaced and rubbed his forehead as if he could wipe them from his mind that way.

Sherlock snorted. "We're in a sorry state if we let mental flights of fancy distract us from our cause. Let's keep our focus on what's real, shall we?"

The reprimand came out sharp rather than teasing—enough so that John winced. I frowned, eyeing the consulting detective. I might be wrong, but I thought I detected a whiff of "thou doust protest too much" in that abrupt dismissal. Perhaps Sherlock *had* been troubled by bad dreams too, and it was irritating him that he was bothered at all.

Something troublesome had clearly gotten into the air lately. Garrett and Bash had both seemed more hot-tempered than usual the last few days. Garrett had gotten outright cruel in some of the comments he'd made about his colleagues, and Bash... I'd never seen

Bash come anywhere near losing his cool, so even the small hints of temper he'd shown made me concerned.

I'd managed to stay in Sherlock's presence, or at least no more than a room or two away from him, for most of the time since the shrouded one had marked him, and I hadn't detected any of them nearby since then. Had one of them gotten to him—to all of them—somehow anyway? My stomach twisted at the thought.

It could very well be simply the stress of our current mission. I had to remember that the shrouded folk had been an undeniable part of my reality for my entire life. These men had only just been introduced to the idea of monsters far beyond anything they'd have considered possible. They'd witnessed horrors and seen evidence of more beyond that. I'd told them terrifying stories.

They might be experts in their fields, but nothing could have prepared them to face an enemy like this. I'd just keep an eye on them in case the emotional fraying appeared to get any worse.

John started pacing again. His mood had stayed warm and enthusiastic as usual, but he'd definitely been restless. Now he grabbed a chair by the other laptop in the room and flipped the computer open with a click to peer at the screen. "Maybe I can do some digging too."

"I think it's rather better if you didn't, John," Sherlock said, confusion as well as alarm crossing his face. "You don't have the best track record with computing devices, as I recall. I'm sure Marissa can handle it without leaving any traces that might come back to haunt us… so to speak."

John let out an impatient huff. "I just—"

"I'm in!" Marissa chirped, stirring us all into action. John sprang up, and we hustled around the table to look at the hacker's screen.

I knew my way around a computer, but not on the level this girl obviously did. The various windows with their lists of text didn't mean a whole lot to me. Marissa looked up at Sherlock. "What do you want me to bring up first?"

"Financial records," he said quickly, intentness focusing his gaze and wiping away some of his earlier melancholy. "We want to see if they had to compensate for a missing shipment any time in the last several years—and if so, exactly what and when."

Our hope was, if the pen had gotten to the commune via a theft, that we'd learn more about the commune's habits from the details around that theft. I didn't like the fact that they'd slipped out of our grasp so easily. If we could figure out their usual area of activity, where they might have gone from their original settlement...

"Let's see," Marissa murmured to herself, her hands flying over the keyboard again. "Here, these look like the right set of statements. What kind of numbers do you think we'd be looking for?"

"Fairly large, in the thousands of dollars at least," Sherlock said. "And the same value twice close together—one shipment dispatched that never reached it's intended destination, and a matching one put together shortly after."

"On it." She opened up another window and typed something into that, and the spreadsheets of data started whipping through the rows of their own accord. She paused a couple of times on spots that looked like a possibility, but one turned out to be an identical order for two different stores, and another was a swift restocking after the initial order must have immediately run out, with full payment for both.

"That's five years," Marissa said after several minutes of scanning. "Do you want me to keep going back?"

John shifted his weight, standing at a bit of an angle to reduce the pressure on his weaker leg since he hadn't brought his walking stick. "There might not be anything. This could be all a red herring."

"We told them we'd be here an hour," I said. "We might as well make use of it. Who knows when that pen was last used. Let's try another five, just in case."

Sherlock motioned for Marissa to continue, and I let my eyes linger on the screen as she continued her search. A word jumped out at me that made my pulse stutter.

"Stop!" I said, grabbing her shoulder.

Marissa stiffened, and I immediately let go, but she'd halted the search. "What?" she said.

"Go back up. Slower this time. I saw something."

"What was it, Jemma?" John asked.

"Just—let me make sure."

The entry came into view. "There," I said. "Leave it there." I pointed to the line, my heart still thumping faster than before. In the column that labeled the sources of the payments or expenses, that row simply said SHROUD.

John drew in a startled breath. Sherlock leaned closer, his eyebrows drawing together. "You don't think— A regular company wouldn't be doing *business* with this cult, would they?"

"I don't know. I wouldn't have thought so. I've never seen it happen before, but I've been pretty out of the loop since I left." I rubbed my mouth, still staring at the line. It was an expense— something provided to SHROUD from Havenboard Foods. "Are there any stores or other companies with a name that includes 'Shroud' they might have been dealing with?"

Marissa opened an internet search window in a flash. "I don't see anything like that," she said after a moment.

"I've never heard of one," Sherlock added. "But it could have some other meaning."

It could. Why on earth would this company be giving anything to the cult? What would they have been giving it in exchange for?

I wet my lips. "We might be able to get a better idea. Search and see if any other expenses like that come up."

Marissa tapped the keys. In a matter of seconds, another item came up, from about six months later. Then six months after that. Regular intervals, all the way up to a few months ago. My chest had constricted. I pulled out my phone. "I'm going to check those dates."

I looked up one and then another and then a third, my stomach sinking farther with each confirmation. After five, I decided I had proof enough.

"It's them," I said. "I don't know why, but this company has some kind of an association set up with the cult."

"Would they really label it so plainly?" Sherlock protested.

I raised my eyebrows at him. "Who would it be plain to? Other than the members of the cult, the five of us are the only people who know the shrouded folk even exist. Well, us and whoever decided on that label, apparently. What better way to keep it secret than to use a name no one knows about?"

"It could be a coincidence," John ventured, but he looked uncertain.

I shook my head and waved my phone. "All of the deliveries or payments or whatever Havenboard provided were made on the dates of the full moon. That's when the cult prefers to arrange any business where they have to involve outsiders. The folk can stay more active on the brightest nights—the commune would want to have them around for protection as need be."

Silence filled the room for a moment. Sherlock's jaw worked. "It seems this situation is even more complex than you anticipated."

I swallowed hard. "Yes. Apparently it's not just the cult and the folk we have to contend with. They have at least one real ally in the wider world as well. And someone with enough clout that they could arrange these expenses without any questions being asked."

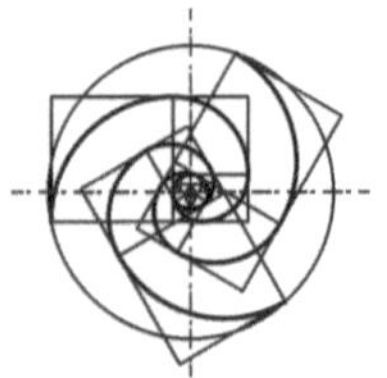

CHAPTER ELEVEN

Jemma

"I just had eyes on the meeting," Bash said through my earpiece. "They're still jabbering away."

Sitting next to me in the car, Sherlock raised his eyebrows in question. I shook my head and pressed the button on my mic to reply to Bash. "Keep watching them and let me know as soon as they look like they're getting up."

"Aye, aye, Majesty."

A smile touched my lips at the fond if teasing nickname.

Sherlock gazed out the window at the brick building across the street where MP Harvey Tillhouse had his office. His hands were clasped tightly together in his lap, and a shadow crossed his face. The moroseness I'd noticed in him at Havenboard hadn't lifted.

He turned back to me with a slight jerk of his arm. "This fellow is a talkative one, isn't he?"

"I have no idea how long is normal with these strategy meetings." I shrugged. "It doesn't matter. We'll be ready when he's leaving." We were decked out in new disguises—a blond wig for me and dun brown for Sherlock, colored contacts for both of us, a false beard straggling across his chin. I held a larger microphone on the seat next to me, ready for action, and Sherlock had a video camera with a doctored TV channel logo sitting on his lap.

My nonchalance didn't appear to alleviate Sherlock's gloom. He sighed and tipped his head against the headrest, his eyes going distant behind the bright brown lenses. His fingers squeezed tight enough around each other to turn his knuckles white.

I considered and decided to bite the bullet. It was just the two of us right now—he didn't have to feel he was admitting weakness to anyone else. We had time. And if my most brilliant crime fighter had a problem, I'd like to know about it sooner rather than later.

"What is it about this case that's bothering you?" I asked.

Sherlock's head snapped down and around. He studied me with a frown. "Who says it's bothering me?"

I rolled my eyes. "I know you well enough to see it. *Something* has been dragging at your mood. If it's not dealing with the shrouded folk, you can tell me what it is instead." I patted his leg, letting my hand linger just long enough to take the gesture from casual to flirtatious. "It's not as if I'm going to think there's anything odd about finding this whole thing difficult to take in."

For a second, Sherlock looked even grimmer. Then he let out another sigh. "I don't like cases where I can't get a sense of the full picture. There's too much about these creatures I can't fully comprehend—that I can only barely believe in the first place. And it certainly doesn't help that this latest development takes us beyond even your prior experience with the creatures."

"I can't say I'm particularly happy about that either." I made a face at the building across the street. We'd spent the last few days tracing various leads to try to figure out how Havenboard was connected to the shrouded folk. Our investigations had led us through a winding path of sign-offs and corporate shells to Tillhouse, a politician out of Yorkshire who owned the company that owned the company that owned Havenboard.

We'd determined that Havenboard's warehouse had been dropping off a large supply of nonperishable food and other supplies at a secluded storage building not far from the abandoned commune on a biannual basis. We'd also determined that the chain of commands to place that order had come from one of the few people with executive power over the company. Yesterday we'd eliminated the president of Havenboard from consideration. Now we were going to scope out Tillhouse.

"I suppose there are all sorts of benefits a politician planning on running for party leadership might get out of a paranormal ally," Sherlock said, following my gaze. Tillhouse might be only an MP now, but he was in the process of campaigning to take over as head of the Conservative Party. "The bigger surprise might be that it hasn't happened before."

"The shrouded folk don't like anyone outside their cult knowing about them," I said. "They expressly forbid revealing themselves to non-worshippers. How the hell this guy or anyone else in the company could have found out about them to even try to set up some sort of arrangement... I don't even know." All we'd been able to determine for sure was that the arrangement had been going on for nearly seven years.

"It won't matter anyway," I added. "We'll continue taking down the cult piece by piece, and there's nothing this guy can do about that. And when the cult's gone, the shrouded folk won't have the power left here to do anything for him. We just need to know who we're up against before we do anything else."

"Yes." Sherlock's solemn expression hadn't budged. He rolled his shoulders with a twitch of his neck, seeming to sink even deeper into the gloom in his head. Then, abruptly, he unclasped his hands and reached to touch my face. "Jemma?"

Even with the disguise hiding his familiar features, a flutter passed through my chest having this man train his gaze on me that intently. "Yes?"

He didn't say anything else, just drew me in for a kiss. A determined kiss, so hot it was dizzying coming out of nowhere like that. I didn't know what had gotten into him, but I wasn't going to pass up the opportunity to kiss him back just as enthusiastically.

Sherlock pulled back with a frown that wasn't at all the reaction I'd have wanted to provoke. "I thought perhaps— A different sort of stimulation— But I don't think that's the right route. I just need more answers."

"I don't know." I gave him a playful nudge. "Maybe we didn't try hard enough. You know I can offer plenty more 'stimulation' than just a kiss."

Even though he'd declared the kiss a failure, a faint flush of heat colored his skin at that remark. The sight of it lit a little fire in me. Unfortunately, this wasn't the time or place for any sort of deeper intimacy. As Bash helpfully reminded me with his voice carrying into my ear.

"They're getting up. That's your cue. Good luck!"

"Luck has nothing to do with it," I said smoothly, and shoved open the door.

Sherlock followed me out without needing any further prompting. We crossed the street and went down the alley to the building's back entrance. He already had his lockpicks in hand when we reached it. It took all of five seconds for him to force the deadbolt over.

If we'd gone in the front, the receptionist would have stopped us. This way, we slipped down the hall and up the staircase just in time to catch Tillhouse coming down the second-floor hall from the meeting room.

He looked like the kind of guy who *would* own companies that owned other companies. Square-jawed and flinty-eyed but with his silver hair slicked back in a posh style and his suit cut in the latest fashion. His staff flitted this way and that around him. One guy stopped beside him when Tillhouse stopped, the assistant giving us a cold look. "What's this about?"

I focused all my attention on the MP with a cajoling smile. "Mr. Tillhouse, we were just hoping to get a few comments on your suggested policy updates. It'll only take a minute or two. We'll give you the chance to review any clips before they air."

"I don't know how you got in here," the assistant started, but Tillhouse halted his complaint with a hand on his shoulder. He gave me a smarmy smile in return.

"I think we should reward ambition, don't you, Philip? All right.

You have a minute or two. Everyone else, carry on with what you're supposed to be doing."

Any staff lingering in the hall dispersed. Sherlock raised his camera and started recording while I held up my microphone. I wanted the man's reactions on video so I could study them at my leisure afterward to make sure I hadn't missed anything—or to analyze what I did see in the moment more closely.

"You've said you'll campaign for legislation that allows more opportunities for businesses to expand without restriction," I said, jumping in with the talking points I'd prepared. "What sorts of checks and balances would you keep in place?"

I didn't really listen to his answer, only enough so that I'd be able to react if I needed to. Instead I watched his expression, his body language, checking for any of the tics only someone who'd spent years among the cult of the shrouded folk would have noticed. Nothing overt stood out, but he rubbed his forearm at one point when he paused to decide how to phrase part of his answer. The gesture caught my eye.

I asked another question, a faster one this time, and then I let out a light laugh. "And this may sound frivolous, but many of our viewers will be curious to know—you're always so well-dressed. What designer came up with this lovely suit?"

As I spoke, my hand shot out to give his sleeve a teasing tug. I angled it perfectly so I displaced the cuff of his shirt underneath as well. For just a second, I caught a glimpse of the skin of his inner wrist and an inch beyond. Skin with a tropical tan other than a thin slash of a paler mark. My stomach turned.

Anyone else would have taken that for a birthmark, no doubt, but I'd seen that shape, that shading before. Tillhouse had been exposed to a blast of the shrouded folk's power.

The MP pulled his arm away from me with an answering laugh, not seeming concerned about the contact. He didn't have any reason to think I'd recognize that mark any more than he must have thought anyone would figure out what SHROUD referred to.

"This one's Richard James," he said, and waved for Sherlock to turn off the camera. "All right, I think you got more than the time you asked for."

I would have been fine with the progress we'd already made, but as soon as Sherlock lowered the camera, Tillhouse leaned closer to me. He tapped the neckline of my dress where it lay a couple inches below my collarbone. "I don't think what I'm wearing is half as lovely as this, though."

Understanding flashed through me. He found me attractive. I'd wrapped plenty of men around my little finger using that advantage —I'd manipulated my London trio that way, among other strategies, when I'd first met them. Peek at him through my eyelashes, ease closer to him, exchange another touch or two, and I could have all his clothes off within an hour, I'd bet. Imagine how much I might find out then.

Those thoughts crossed my mind—and jarred against my awareness of Sherlock standing next to me. Something inside me balked.

Yes, I'd used sex as a tool to get my way dozens of times in the past, when it was the *only* way I'd known how to use it and any pleasurable parts were secondary. I knew what it was like to fuck with full passion now, to get off with a partner I cared about who cared about me. To treat the act like a ploy again, with this asshole who'd conspired with the shrouded folk somehow, made my very skin recoil.

I got ahold of myself within a second. Taking down the shrouded folk was worth *anything*. I sure as hell wasn't above a pragmatic fuck along the way. I forced a smile to my lips and started to speak, but my momentary resistance must have shown. Tillhouse was already pulling back from me, his demeanor cooling. I'd rejected him without even meaning to.

"I look forward to reviewing the segment," he said. "I trust you know the way out?"

"Yes," I said, suppressing my frustration with myself. "We can handle that."

I could still use that information later, I told myself as we went down to the main floor. I could catch him somewhere when we weren't on the job and make out as if my hesitation had been professional rather than personal. It wouldn't be that hard.

And yet my skin still shivered uncomfortably imagining it.

I'd gone fucking soft. That wasn't how my alliance with the trio was supposed to work. Damn it.

A woman was standing by the front door when we reached it. She beamed at us. "He's just wonderful, isn't he?"

"Absolutely," I said, beaming right back at her and willing her the hell out of our way.

"He's gaining so much ground already," she went on, a little breathless. "I'm sure he's going to get the leadership. Just think—in less than a year he could be prime minister of the whole country."

My inner turmoil quieted under a jolt of horror. Someday soon the man I'd just talked to might rule this entire country... while carrying a debt to the shrouded folk they were no doubt waiting to fully cash in on.

CHAPTER TWELVE

John

I came home from a grocery shopping trip to find Sherlock sitting in the living room drawing his bow across his violin. The sound of him playing—and playing a song I didn't recognize, which meant he was probably making it up on the spot—wasn't unusual, but as I slid a carton of eggs and a week's worth of vegetables into the fridge, my stomach started to tighten. There was a frenetic quality to the movement of the bow and the melody he was producing that wasn't all that usual.

I hadn't heard him play like that in over a year.

He didn't stop even when I closed the fridge and walked over to the sofa beside him. His hand kept whipping back and forth, and his eyes started straight ahead with a pinched alertness, the pupils dilated. A flush colored his cheeks. He hadn't left any paraphernalia out, but I didn't need to see the tools to know what he'd done with them.

I stepped right in front of him, so close that if he'd shifted the violin an inch it'd have hit my gut. He slowed his strokes of the bow, his gaze flitting up to me now. The music quieted, but he still kept playing.

"Is my improvisation disturbing you, John?" he said in a breathless tone. I liked that voice when the enthusiasm in it came from the thrill of a case—or more intimate sorts of passion. Knowing any emotion it held today was artificial only made my stomach knot more.

"How much did you take?" I said, holding his gaze firmly.

"Oh, only a very moderate dosage. Don't worry yourself—I measured it carefully."

"You told me you weren't going to turn to the drug anymore."

He managed to make a dismissive motion of his shoulders without losing his rhythm. "I told you I'd hold off if it seemed unnecessary. I didn't promise to give the stuff up completely. Now and then my mind needs a good jolt to find the right track. We've discussed this."

We had, more than once, and I couldn't say I'd ever come away from those discussions completely satisfied. The idea that this genius of a man would insist on poisoning his brain and body with cocaine clashed with everything else I knew about him.

But there were certain other emotions, certain types of stillness and uncertainty, that he found it incredibly hard to tolerate. Even a genius had weaknesses. I'd just started to believe he was over this one.

"And have you made some additional progress under its influence?" I asked. If anything would convince him to leave off another injection, it'd be the logic he valued so highly. If the drug *didn't* help, why take it at all?

"My thoughts are much sharper now," Sherlock said. "I *can* promise you that I know my limits. This was exactly what I needed."

He said that so matter-of-factly that I didn't know how to argue with him. How could I dispute the activity of his own mind or how he'd spurred it on? I had never been the brains between the two of us. My job was to support and provide a sounding board and occasionally whack a troublesome fellow or two with my walking stick.

Sherlock wasn't looking for guidance right now. He'd found it in a dissolved white powder.

I couldn't help trying anyway. "Is there any way I can help with your newfound clarity?"

Sherlock gave a brisk shake of his head. "I'm still sorting through the concepts as they come to me. I'm sure this will lead us to a productive route soon enough. You'll be the first to know."

He shot me a smile so bright I couldn't help smiling back, even as my throat tightened too. Damn the cocaine; damn Sherlock's enjoyment of it.

Knowing what was fueling his music, I couldn't stand to stay in the flat while he played on like that. I grasped my walking stick where I'd left it by the door.

"I'll leave you to it then."

He didn't even ask where I was off to now as I headed out.

Which might have been a good thing, because I didn't have the foggiest idea where I was going. I set off down the street with the urge to find something useful to do nagging at me. I could accomplish more than just waiting around for Sherlock to figure out how he needed me, couldn't I?

I just wasn't entirely sure what. I didn't have the sort of contacts who'd be able to share information about this MP who seemed tied up in the shrouded folk's business. All our focus had been on him since we'd discovered the connection.

Well, maybe Jemma could point me in a productive direction. I dug out my phone as I walked on, my walking stick tapping against the pavement with a sound much more decisive than anything else about me at the moment.

Evening was falling, pulling the shadows long and dimming the remaining daylight between them. The air pressed down, muggy beneath the thickening clouds gathering overhead.

Jemma picked up after just one ring. "What is it?" she said, and I realized she probably assumed this was some kind of emergency. I'd normally simply have texted her unless I had urgent news.

"Nothing's wrong," I said quickly. "I just—I'm out and about, and I wondered if there was anything you needed looking into."

The explanation sounded weak when I said it out loud. As if Jemma wouldn't have told me without being asked if she'd needed me for something. But I was talking to her now. At least the impression of her presence on the other end of the phone line kept my restlessness a little more at bay.

"I'm not sure there's anything I can delegate to you at the moment," she said, her voice turning a bit wry. "Are you getting bored?"

"Maybe a little. I'm not sure it's so much that." I veered right at the next intersection at random, pushing myself a little faster even though my hip twinged. Burning off the impatient energy might do the trick. "I haven't been of much use in general with the latest developments."

"You've helped plenty," Jemma said. "Who else would corral Sherlock half as well?"

She was partly teasing, but a jab shot through me all the same at the thought of how I'd failed to stop him from doing the thing I hated most just this evening. The words to tell her what he'd immersed himself in rose in my throat, but something—maybe the guilt of that failure, maybe the sense that it was Sherlock's business whether Jemma knew what he got up to—held them back.

"I guess I'll just have to hope our next lead takes more of a medical angle," I said, matching her tone. My gaze meandered along the street and came to an abrupt halt on the fence surrounding a construction site on the opposite side of the road.

Something flickered on the other side of the fence, visible only for a moment through the chain-link gate. A piece of paper blown in the breeze, I thought. And I could have sworn I'd seen Harvey Tillhouse's photograph printed on it.

What did he have to do with whatever they were building over there?

"John?" Jemma said as I crossed the street, in a tone that suggested I'd missed something she'd said earlier.

"I think I might have a lead right here," I said. "I'll let you know if it pans out. I think I'd better get off the phone so I can take a real look."

"Take a real look? What are you doing?"

"Nothing I can't handle." I peered through the gate at the jumble of wood and steel heaped around the pit that I supposed was going to be a building's basement. The frame rose up out of it like a metal skeleton, but the construction workers hadn't gotten to the point of adding anything like floors or walls yet.

Another flash of white, a glimpse of slick silver hair, caught my eye, whisking up and then dropping behind the body of a crane. My heart thumped faster. My hand came to rest on the gate—right by the lock someone had neglected to fasten.

No one was around. Would it be so horrible for me to slip inside and grab that paper? Even if it didn't turn out to be remotely useful, at least I'd have *tried*.

An eager tingling was already spreading through my chest, deciding the answer for me.

"If I turn up anything interesting, you'll be hearing from me again soon," I said, and hung up the phone before Jemma could ask more questions. I had the feeling if I tried to explain what I was about to do now out loud, it'd sound not just weak but ridiculous.

If Sherlock could shoot himself full of drugs, I could be excused a little risk-taking of my own. At least mine wasn't going to result in bodily or mental harm.

I lifted the latch on the gate and tugged it shut behind me as soon as I was inside. Gravel rattled under my feet. I flicked a fast food wrapper away with my walking stick and headed toward the crane. When my phone jangled with an incoming call, I turned off the ringer.

The wind rose again, making one of the nearby machines creak in a menacing sort of way. The light was continuing to dwindle. I poked all around the crane, squinting, and even peered under it. As I straightened up, the paper I'd come in here after darted past my vision again in the opposite direction. It floated beyond a stack of steel beams.

Fine, then. It wanted to give me a chase, did it? I hurried over, watching in case the breeze flicked it away again.

I didn't see anything move, only felt the faint brush of the air against my cheek, but when I peered around the stack of beams, I'd lost my target again. I let out a huff of breath and scanned the wider area.

There. It must have drifted on over the ground while the beams still hid it. It was trailing along the edge of the pit now, wavering back and forth with shifts in the air currents. I gripped the handle of my walking stick with renewed determination and picked up the chase.

I got close this time—close enough to be sure even in the fading light that it *was* Tillhouse's face in that photograph, close enough to have bent down to snatch at it. The wind picked up at the last instant and whipped the paper from my grasping fingers. It flew right over the edge of the pit and into the thicker shadows below.

I stared after the white shape now skidding down the steep incline. It came to rest on part of the frame just a couple feet from the pit's side. My pulse kicked up another notch as I studied the slope.

For God's sake, I should be able to manage that. I'd tramped all around Iraq, hadn't I? This was nothing. My leg didn't slow me down that much.

I set down my walking stick at the edge of the pit and eased myself over the lip, crouched with my hands pressed against the gritty earth. After a few hesitant footsteps at almost a crabwalk, my confidence grew. I nudged myself onward at a better speed—and that was when it all went wrong.

A loose clod of dirt shifted under my left heel. My foot shot out from under me with a burst of pain through my bad hip. I skidded down the slope too fast to catch myself, the grit scraping my palms raw as I fought to at least keep myself upright.

Despite my efforts, I spun sideways. My thigh and shoulder smacked into the edge of the frame where it loomed close to the pit wall, slamming me to a stop with a fresh sear of agony.

I sat there, panting and staring up at the twenty or so feet I'd fallen, for a long moment. The sharpest shards of pain dulled, but when I adjusted my position to orient myself, my hip ached. It didn't feel as if I'd done it any serious damage, but I might if I tried to scramble back up that slope.

Even if I hadn't hurt myself, I could already tell I'd have a hell of a time making it back to the top. Shit. I couldn't even see the paper I'd been after anymore. It'd disappeared completely.

One of my hands was seeping blood where I'd scraped it. I ran my other hand through my hair, pondering how to get out of this mess. Sherlock wasn't in any real state to help. The thought of calling on Garrett made me wince.

Did I even have cell reception down here? My heart sank as I pulled out my phone. It showed a grand total of one bar, but I knew from experience that might not be strong enough to get me an actual connection. Shit squared.

I gave myself a few minutes to simply breathe and rest my leg. Any excitement I'd been feeling about this expedition had drained away, leaving only a pang of fear. I was about to give the phone a shot just in case when a voice carried down to me.

"John?"

Even distant, I recognized it as Jemma's immediately. "Over here!" I shouted, relief overcoming any embarrassment that welled up at the same time.

Her slim figure appeared at the edge of the pit, the fading daylight silhouetting her even as it caught on her fiery hair. She cocked her head as she looked down at me, her mouth twisting into a pained grimace. "How did you manage to get yourself down there? *Why* did you go down there?"

"It's a long story," I said, even though it wasn't really, only a ridiculous one. "I hit my bad leg—it's acting up. I'm not sure I can climb out on my own. But you don't want to end up stuck down here too if you—"

"I'll be fine," she said calmly. "And if I'm not, Bash is on his way too. Let's see…"

She picked her way down the steep slope much more gracefully than I'd managed it. With her grasping my arm, I managed to haul myself onto my feet. My hip still ached, but I could ignore that if it meant getting the hell out of this fix.

Jemma had brought my walking stick. She dug the base into the dirt for extra traction as we trudged out of the pit together. Her arm stayed looped around mine, steadying me.

"How did you figure out where I was?" it occurred to me to ask.

"I know at least as many people with many talents as Sherlock does. I had a bad feeling after you hung up. One of my sometime associates tracked your phone. I got rather worried when he reported that the signal had faded out, though."

"I'm lucky I have such a concerned colleague on my side, then."

"Yes, you are." She pulled me up over the edge of the pit and handed my walking stick to me. I grasped it tightly as I regained my balance on the suddenly even ground. Jemma touched my face, and I leaned toward her automatically. The kiss she offered was sweet and soft and over much too quickly.

"I appreciate that you want to explore every avenue to help with our mission," she said quietly, only pulling back a couple inches. "But I would prefer not to lose anyone along the way, all right?"

"I think I can handle that," I said with a brief laugh, but inside my gut had clenched. I wasn't sure I could fully explain how I'd let myself get that far into trouble in the first place. Looking back, the situation seemed absurd.

What had I been thinking? Or rather, why *hadn't* I been thinking? What the hell had come over me?

CHAPTER THIRTEEN

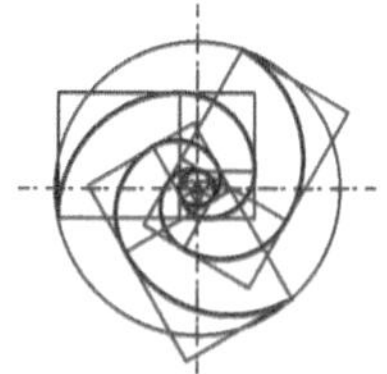

Jemma

Normally if I'd wanted to chat with Garrett—or any of the trio —I'd have picked up my phone. But after the growing uneasiness I'd felt over the last week and John's unexpected stunt last night, I found I wanted to see the detective inspector in person from the start.

There was only so much you could determine from text on a screen or a voice through a speaker. Garrett's part of our mission, on the official law enforcement side of things, was separate enough from what the rest of us were doing that I hadn't seen him face-to-face since we'd started investigating Tillhouse.

So I lingered outside the building across the street from Scotland Yard, partly hidden from the late afternoon sun by an awning, and pretending to be absorbed in the magazine I was holding. The rhythmic rumble of the passing traffic did nothing to set me at ease. Even the sweetness of the sugar cube I'd popped into my mouth only soothed me a little.

He should be finished his shift any minute now. I'd see where he headed off to, and then I'd find a good moment to join him.

My gaze came up without a twitch of my magazine when the door opened. A couple of other officers came out and headed off down the street. A few moments later, Garrett emerged.

I didn't need any detective skills to tell he was upset about something. His jaw was tightly set and his shoulders up, his eyes glowering even though he had no one to glower at right now. He set off around the building toward the parking lot.

If he was driving home, I'd need to catch him before he got in the car. I glanced around to make sure none of his colleagues were within sight and then slipped across the road to catch up with him.

Just as I reached the opposite sidewalk, he paused by a sports car halfway down the lot. His posture turned even tenser, which I wouldn't have thought was possible given how wound up he'd already looked. His hand dug into his pocket, and he drew out something I couldn't see, his gaze fixed on the car. A strange intensity had come over his face.

My pulse skittered. I didn't like that expression at all. I walked as fast as I could without making a scene of it, and his head jerked up at the sound of my footsteps, his hand jamming back into his pocket.

Garrett's eyes widened when he saw me. An even stranger cast came over his features, sickly and stormy at the same time. I didn't know what to make of it, but I could tell it didn't bode well.

"What are you doing here?" he said in a hushed voice.

"I wanted to see you," I said casually, as if dropping in on him at work were a regular thing. I tipped my head toward the car. "What were you doing? This isn't yours."

Everything else in his face faded under a flush that looked like embarrassment. "No. I—We can't really talk here. Come on. Let's get you away from the Yard."

I kept a professional distance from him as we crossed the rest of the distance to his silver sedan. Garrett motioned for me to get in. He started the engine before I even had my seatbelt on and pulled out of the parking lot swiftly, if not at quite the breakneck pace of John's usual driving.

The inside of the car smelled like Garrett, slightly smoky and electric as a live wire. Usually I enjoyed that scent, but today it made me even more unsettled.

His knuckles had paled where he gripped the wheel. I waited until we'd gotten a few blocks and put his workplace far behind us before I pushed.

"How about you tell me what was going on with that other car now? What did you take out of your pocket?"

"How long were you watching?" Garrett said, his tone unexpectedly sharp. I hadn't heard him sound angry at *me* since we'd all formed our little alliance.

I studied his profile, the flex of his jaw, the continued smolder in his dark brown eyes. "I saw you come out of the building and go into the parking lot. There wasn't much *to* watch. But I could tell you were upset, and I can tell something was going on with that car. Just so you know, the more you try to get around telling me, the more certain I am that I need to find out what it was."

He let out a rough exhalation and swiped a hand through his close-cropped hair. "I just—a few of the other detectives were taking jabs at me this afternoon. Trying to make me look bad to the chief."

I frowned, anger stirring inside me on his behalf. "Assholes. Did you put them in their place?"

"I couldn't really. They weren't saying anything right in front of me, of course. I just caught bits of it, overhearing them when they didn't realize I was close enough… That car belongs to the guy who was making the biggest deal about it. For a second—*just* for a second—I was tempted to jab my pocket knife into one of his tires. Just to slow *him* down a little."

His voice faltered on the last couple sentences, and that shamed flush came back into his cheeks. I blinked at him. "You were seriously considering damaging your colleague's car?"

"Like I said, it was only for a moment."

Even for a moment, that didn't fit with what I knew about Garrett at all. He was competitive, absolutely—sometimes to a fault. But he also had the strictest code of conduct out of the trio. That was why he hadn't been involved in the same activities we had—too much of what even Sherlock and John did in their investigations violated the letter of the law.

The uneasiness that had driven me to seek him out settled heavier in my chest. "Have you been having other moments like that in the last week or so?"

He hesitated just long enough for it to be an answer in itself. "It's just an impulse," he said. "Everyone has them. I ignore them, and it doesn't matter."

"But you've been having them more than usual recently."

"The people I work with have been much bigger arseholes than usual recently!" He caught himself with a grimace. "What are you getting at, Jemma? Are you trying to stay I can't handle this case? Because—"

"*No*," I said quickly. "Why would you even jump to that conclusion? I'm worried about you because I've never seen you act like that. You've been talking differently too... You've all been different."

My hand came to rest on the gold cuff resting against my leg under my dress pants. I hadn't been wearing it constantly like I had when I'd needed to avoid Bog's claim, so it wasn't scraping away at my essence like it had then, but I kept it on whenever I was with any of my men to make sure at least one of us would have a cool head.

Even when I'd taken it off the nights I'd slept alone or when I was working on my own in my apartment, the shrouded folk hadn't hassled me again. Because they'd decided it wasn't worth the bother when I could shut them out again so quickly with the relic?

Or because they'd decided to focus their energies on other targets?

I swallowed hard and took out my phone. "Take us to Sherlock and John's place. I think we need a general strategy meeting."

Garrett's gaze flicked toward me as he took the next right. "Is something wrong?"

"I'd like to say I hope it isn't, but hoping doesn't do much in the face of the facts." I sighed. "We'll see just how wrong it is when we're all together."

"What exactly is the emergency?" Sherlock asked when the five of us were gathered around the now-familiar dining table. His eyes looked brighter than they had the last few days, his movements more animated, but I didn't like the hint of wildness in them, as if some of his perfect control had been worn away. He took a drag from his pipe, the smoke tickling my nose, but the tobacco didn't appear to calm him.

I put a finishing touch on the Fibonacci sequence in the middle of the table—the last of those I'd laid out around the room—and dropped into my seat. I didn't know how well or how long those defenses might last us, but I didn't catch any hint of shrouded folk influence in the air now, so we were at least temporarily safe from their intrusions.

There was no point in beating around the bush. I liked every one of these men because they were straight-shooting. If they couldn't have handled the sort of declaration I was about to make, I wouldn't have been sitting here with them in the first place.

"I think the shrouded folk have determined that the four of you are helping me in my campaign against them," I said, "and they're trying to affect you in malicious ways."

Bash stirred in his chair beside me. "I haven't seen anything."

"Neither have I," Garrett jumped in.

"You wouldn't. They aren't supposed to show themselves. Even the weird lights and figure the one I had the contract with let you see —it's probably been punished for that. But they're allowed to mess with your senses and your minds in ways you wouldn't realize are supernatural."

Sherlock was frowning, and I could already see the denial on Garrett's face, but John was watching me steadily. "What exactly do you think they've done?" he said, in a quiet tone that suggested he could think of at least one example.

I could lead with that incident. I nodded to him. "You saw something yesterday that had you clambering around a construction site and nearly getting yourself stuck down a pit for the night. You could have really injured yourself—you could have even died. But you never did find whatever it was you'd gone after, did you?"

He ignored the concerned and puzzled looks the other shot his way. "No. Are you saying… it wasn't there at all?"

"A shrouded one could easily produce a hallucination. Isn't it odd that you just happened to see something you wanted that badly right when you were passing a spot that dangerous?"

His mouth twisted in a sheepish smile. "You may have a point there. I didn't even think… It never occurred to me."

"I should have warned you. I didn't think they'd go that far." I swept my hair back from my face and turned to Garrett. "And you said you've been hearing things—your colleagues talking behind your back."

Garrett started at me for a moment before he found his voice. "It sounded real enough."

"But you said they've been a lot worse recently. It started after the shrouded folk marked Sherlock, didn't it?"

His posture went rigid. "Yes. But—why would these demons or whatever care about my workplace dynamics?"

I spread my hands. "They just want to mess with you however they can. Make life difficult for you. They obviously decided that was an easy way to provoke you."

The shrouded folk had centuries, maybe even millennia of experience in observing the many negative human emotions. They might be able to read Garrett's weaknesses nearly as well as I could.

"And you," I said to Sherlock. "I don't know if you've seen or heard something, but you've definitely been in an odd mood lately."

John's gaze jerked to his friend. "You have to tell her."

Sherlock stiffened. "I don't see how it's relevant," he said in his usual even tone.

"How *what's* relevant?" I demanded.

"After all these months—it's got to be related," John said. When Sherlock didn't budge, he looked to me. "Fine. *I'll* tell you. He—"

"What John is so concerned about is the fact that I partook of a mild dose of cocaine yesterday," Sherlock interrupted. "It didn't harm me. On the contrary, it alleviated that dour mood you'd observed."

Ah, so that was why I could see a change in him—and why it didn't quite sit right. "Was that really necessary?" I asked.

"It's been ages," John put in. "And you can't be sure—it *was* a problem before."

My eyebrows leapt up. Sherlock's cool demeanor dropped, a look of betrayal crossing his face. "That was a long time ago and is hardly worth mentioning."

"The fact that you won't admit it only shows it's still a potential problem." John's hands clenched on the tabletop. He turned to me again. "When I first moved in, he wasn't as careful with his usage. There were a few times he 'indulged' to the point that he forgot to eat, or he hurt himself accidentally while going around in that state…"

"And I realized more moderation was required and took appropriate steps. I have the situation well in hand, and I have for years. It has nothing to do with these creatures."

I found that just as hard to believe as John clearly did. It didn't seem likely Sherlock would have started using right now after a long dry spell as a total coincidence.

"They haven't gotten to me," Bash said into the silence that followed. "Maybe these three need to work on their defenses if they're going to stay in the game."

I glanced at him with a pursing of my lips. The way he'd said that told me he wasn't so impervious after all. The shrouded folk were affecting him somehow too—nudging him to be more openly hostile toward the trio.

My stomach had balled into one huge knot. I didn't like this. I didn't like *any* of it. I'd known that bringing the detectives in on my quest would put them in some danger, but I hadn't meant to make their entire lives into a target. I hadn't known the shrouded folk would intrude this far.

"Maybe you should back off," I said abruptly, the words spilling out before I'd totally thought them through. "All of you. I intended to take on these fiends myself, and I can still do that. You had no idea what you were really signing up for when you agreed to help."

The offer to let them loose made my gut tighten even more. We'd made so much progress with all of us working together. Taking down the shrouded folk would be ten times harder without their resources and efforts. But I wasn't going to avenge my sister's death by leading three good men to their deaths as well.

Three, because I already knew there was no way Bash was leaving over this. He grasped my knee under the table. "Forget that. You're not getting rid of me, Majesty."

Perhaps I shouldn't have been surprised, but John leaned his elbows onto the table, his expression just as determined. "You're not getting rid of any of us, Jemma. We're in this now. There's no way we're running off scared."

He'd spoken as if for all of them, and I supposed he could. Garrett was nodding, the set of his mouth defiant.

Sherlock steepled his hands below his chin. "It seems to me that we're in a much less precarious situation now that we're aware of the possibilities and can be on guard against the creatures' influence," he said. "It also seems to me that your shrouded folk wouldn't be toeing the line of their law so insistently if *they* weren't scared. We're succeeding in pushing them back, aren't we?"

I couldn't deny that logic. "They must be worried about how much we'll accomplish if we keep going. But they could still escalate."

"Then we'll escalate right back," Garrett said, raising his chin. "Face it, Jemma. You roped us in, and now you're stuck with us."

I didn't know whether to laugh or wince at that sentiment. I *had* drawn them in—into what might be the last case of their lives. Even if we rose above everything the shrouded folk threw at us, the fiends clearly weren't going to make the fight easy.

But was this really common sense talking, or was I letting the tenderness I'd started to feel for each of these men sway me into being more afraid of the threat than it warranted? I couldn't let those emotions interfere with choosing the best path, the one that would sever the shrouded folk from this world completely.

I was Jemma Moriarty. I acted from my mind, not my heart.

What would Olivia have thought if she'd known one day I might have let the charms of a few men distract me from the vengeance she deserved?

That final thought hardened my resolve. I stood up and placed my hands on the tabletop.

"All right. We keep going, and we take those bastards down by whatever means necessary."

CHAPTER FOURTEEN

Garrett

The university registrar was being incredibly unhelpful today.

"All I'm asking for is the record from Mr. Tillhouse's admission application," I said, fighting to keep the impatience out of my voice. I spun my pen on my desk, glowering at my computer screen since I couldn't glower at the woman on the other end of the phone line. "It may relate to an ongoing case. I'm assuming there's no government-classified information in your standard application."

"There isn't, but we must keep our standards of privacy, especially regarding our more prominent alumni," the woman said. "If you provide a warrant for the information, we'd could send it to you then."

So much for maintaining helpful relations with the police. "Thank you," I gritted out, and set down the phone with a sigh I couldn't restrain.

"Tough break?" Thompson asked as he passed by my desk.

"Lots of roadblocks. I'll get around them."

I didn't mention how many had already thrown spanners into the works. Tillhouse was a difficult man to investigate. We'd already covered everything on the public record, including his nearly spotless political career, his work as a public defender before that, and a university career apparently free of any major controversy.

The strange thing was, there didn't appear to *be* any public record of Tillhouse's existence prior to his later school days. I'd tracked down a record of him attending a senior school in Sheffield for a couple years, but beyond that the trail went totally cold. It was as if the man hadn't existed until he was thirteen years old. I'd been hoping that his university application might contain more details from his earlier schooling, his family, or something else that we'd find helpful in tackling the MP. Because so far his more recent life had given us nothing to work with.

Thompson walked on, but I heard the tap of his loafers stop just around the corner of the hall. He'd bumped into one of our other constables, because a moment later their hushed voices reached my ears. I went still to pick up the words.

"...at it again," Thompson was murmuring. "As if he can ever prove he deserved to rise that fast."

"I bet it's one of Holmes's whims he's off on anyway," said a voice I recognized as DC Quimble. She made a scoffing sound. "He wouldn't have gotten anywhere otherwise. That's all he does, really —follow the real detective around like a dog."

My shoulders came up instinctively. I dragged in a breath and closed my eyes for a second, jerking my mind back to yesterday evening in Sherlock's flat. To Jemma's obvious concern for us and the suggestions she'd made about the shrouded folk misleading our senses.

Surely Thompson and Quimble wouldn't really carry on like that while I was just around the corner. Thompson had always made a show of friendliness when I was around. Maybe they were talking and some magic was altering their words. Maybe he hadn't even lingered at all and it was a complete hallucination.

I wasn't going to dignify the trick with any acknowledgment. I just had to tune it out and focus on what was important.

I clicked on my track pad, sifting through the files and photographs I'd already accumulated in my file on Tillhouse.

Technically I was supposed to be working an extortion case, but I figured saving the world from demonic fiends ought to come first. I'd done some legwork on the other case this morning.

At the desk across from mine, DI Iversley started jiggling his foot. At least, that's what I assumed he was doing. Something, presumably his knee, thumped against the bottom of his desk, making it rattle. That sound was nearly as nerve-wracking as the conversation I was now ignoring.

Someone else in the office was chewing gum incredibly loudly. My fingers twitched as I typed in a search term. Dear Lord, was all of Scotland Yard out to piss me off today? Apparently I should have brought earplugs if I wanted to get anything done.

Of course, the earplugs might not have done a thing if it was all fiendish magic seeping straight into my head.

Maybe it was the chill of that thought throwing me off, or maybe it was simply the culmination of all the irritants that seemed to have battered me at once. One of my colleagues slipped between the cubicles behind me with a muttered, "Bloody minging arsehole," that was clearly directed my way, and I found myself springing to my feet.

"Shut the *fuck* up," I snapped as I spun on the speaker.

The speaker who, from the look on the young constable's face, hadn't said anything at all. Everyone around us stared at me. Including—just my luck—the chief, who I hadn't noticed stepping out of his office.

Bloody hell.

"Lestrade!" he barked. "A word, please?"

I strode over, trying to look nonchalant even though my face was burning. Chief Higgins ushered me into his office. He didn't bother sitting down, just turned to look at me the second he'd closed the door, folding his arms over his chest.

"What the hell has gotten into you, DI?" he said.

"I apologize," I said quickly. "I was overly focused on a case and a little frustrated, and I must have misheard something."

"You should apologize to Kim," Higgins said. "As soon as you go back out there, preferably. And what is this case that's got you so frustrated? From what I saw this morning, everything's on track with that extortion situation."

I hesitated, and his eyes narrowed. "You're handling something else for Holmes, aren't you?"

"You've always said that you appreciate the strong working partnership we've developed," I said.

The chief sighed. "I do—when he's helping you with *our* cases. If he's seen some illegal activity that requires this much of your attention, he needs to bring it to us and get it officially on file. I can't have one of my best investigators going around the office with a storm cloud over his head for any longer. Drop whatever you're doing for him and stick to your assignment. Understood?"

"Yes, sir," I said. Fucking shrouded folk worming their way inside my head. Even knowing they were doing it, I'd let them get to me too much, and now I was in hot water. "I'll get right on that, sir."

"You'd better. I'm going to be keeping a closer eye on you until I'm sure you're back on track. Now get on with it."

I ducked back out of his office, hurried over to the newbie constable to offer a hasty but genuine apology, and then sank into my chair at my desk.

I couldn't hear anyone *talking* about me now, but I was pretty sure I wasn't imagining the fact that many wary glances were being shot my way. I'd made myself look like a fool, shouting like that, and now everyone knew I'd been sanctioned too. Bloody fuck on a fucking bloody cracker.

It was all right. I wasn't losing it. I'd just had a momentary slip. The kind of slip I'd managed to control before it got too bad plenty of times in the past—as recently as yesterday afternoon.

My mind slid back to that violent impulse that had come over me in the parking lot, and to Jemma, afterward, asking what had been going on. She hadn't looked horrified when I'd told her what I'd thought about doing, the way anyone here in the office would have. She'd only showed concern as she tried to figure out what might have been affecting me. It'd been obvious to her that something beyond my normal instincts had been driving me.

It was ridiculous, wasn't it? The person in my life who

understood and accepted me most was a criminal mastermind who'd broken God only knew how many laws. But that was the size of it. Even now, my fingers itched to reach for my phone, to reach out to *her*, to reset my balance.

A strange giddy ache spread through my chest. Ridiculous or not, we'd been through a hell of a lot together. I'd tried to keep my distance after the way she'd tricked us when she'd first been in London, but it hadn't worked. She drew me in far too easily. And I wasn't sure anymore that I minded. She might be a criminal, but she had better intentions and loftier goals than most of the police officers I'd met.

What was the point in denying it? I was falling for her. Hook, line, and sinker. I couldn't even blame it on her wiles, not really. I didn't think she *wanted* my adoration. She'd never shown any interest in a real romance.

That was fine. I'd simply feel what I felt and see where it took me. And in the meantime, I was going to find *something* on this bastard Tillhouse for her mission, no matter what the chief had said.

I took a surreptitious glance around to make sure no one could see my computer screen and then went back to the file I'd been sorting through earlier. The only real blank in Tillhouse's life was his childhood. People didn't erase their pasts unless there was something they didn't want discovered, did they? If I just found the right way to dig...

I paused on Tillhouse's year 10 school photograph. His name hadn't gotten me anywhere in my searches. Using our latest facial recognition software, I'd found a few new articles on him that'd been buried in the search results, but I'd offered it recent photographs for that. His adult face had changed a fair bit since his youth. What if I popped this one in?

The facial recognition searches took a while, skimming through the whole internet. I sat back in my chair as the wheel spun, still keeping a close eye on my surroundings, and popped open the paperwork for the extortion case so at least I'd look like I was working on the right thing.

Finally, an alert popped up that the results were ready. I leaned forward to peer at the screen.

The first few were photos I'd already seen from Tillhouse's later school years. Then a slightly grainy shot from a newspaper article came up. I froze in my seat.

It was Tillhouse, all right. The same high forehead and smooth straight hair, the same chiseled chin. He was being clutched to the side of a woman in a group photo with a couple of other families. I'd have guessed he was twelve or thirteen from the looks of him.

Con artists pull off massive bank scam, the article's headline read. A group of grifters had gotten together to arrange to steal a few million dollars from one of the top banks, apparently. They'd nearly managed it, too—and partly with the boy's help. He'd staged a distraction, pretending to be sick, at a key moment.

But one of the guards had realized something was wrong at the last second, and interrupted the grifters before they'd finished their ploy with the accounts. One husband and wife, according to the article, had offered their testimony in exchange for immunity.

The pieces clicked into place in my head. The couple must have been Tillhouse's parents, or he'd have had a juvenile record he couldn't simply have walked away from. No wonder he—maybe the whole family—had changed their name, though. They wouldn't have wanted this attempted crime hanging over their heads.

He'd hidden it awfully deep. It might take some convincing for anyone to believe that the boy in the photo was him after all. But if anyone was good at convincing people, it was Jemma Moriarty.

A smile crossed my lips as I saved the article for future sharing. My colleagues could say whatever they wanted about me, real or imaginary. I got the answers I needed because I was damned dogged about it, not because I'd ridden on anyone's coattails. I'd just proven once more why I'd been the youngest officer promoted to detective inspector in decades.

Now I just had to hope that the lead I'd found would be enough to get rid of Tillhouse and whatever monstrous plans he was an accomplice to now.

CHAPTER FIFTEEN

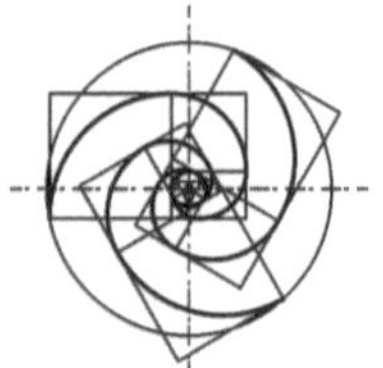

Jemma

"It was ages ago," Garrett said when I looked up from the article he'd printed out for me. "But it'll set a sort of precedent in the public eye about Tillhouse's behavior—make it more believable if we expose him for something similar."

I rested my arm along the top of my apartment's sofa and raised an eyebrow at Garrett. "But we haven't found anything similar recently to expose him for, have we?"

The embarrassed look that came over his boyish face was rather adorable. "I thought... I don't want to know *how* you do it; I don't want to be involved in that side of things at all... but you did arrange for one man to be arrested and likely sentenced for a crime he didn't commit a few months ago. We can't take Tillhouse down for helping your fiends, so it seems fair to manufacture a real crime to have justice done."

"And to clear our way." I glanced at the grainy photograph on the printout again. The man that boy had become appeared to be interfering with our best efforts to learn more about the Highlands sect of the cult we'd seen some initial signs of. Our additional investigations had produced very little information—not enough to narrow down the location in a helpful way. Records were missing. The local police had balked at helping even Sherlock Holmes. I sensed the influence of a powerful figure there.

And in a year or so, Tillhouse might be the highest authority in this entire country.

I inhaled the crisply clean air of the apartment into my lungs, willing that unnerving thought away. What Garrett had turned up was perfect. As he'd said, it gave us plausibility to make up another crime the MP was connected to. I didn't know if people would open up more if we discredited him, but at least we wouldn't have whatever unknown threat he presented hanging over our heads.

"It's perfect," I said, setting the printout on the coffee table. "And impressive work finding it. More and more I wonder how I ever expected to pull off this mission without your help."

Garrett grinned, but a nervous glint had come into his eyes. There'd been a new awkwardness to his demeanor, subtle but detectable, from the moment he'd come in. Possibly lingering shame over the incident in the parking lot yesterday? He didn't think I thought less of him for that, did he?

"Jemma," he said, "I—"

A knock on the door interrupted him. I held up my hand. "Just a second. That'll be Bash."

Garrett blinked at me as I got up. "I didn't know he was coming."

"Bash is my go-between for all dealings with characters much more unsavory than me." I winked at him. "If we're going to be doing things you don't want us telling you about, I'm going to need him here to strategize. And it won't be the sort of strategizing we'd want on any phone record."

"Right. Of course."

He didn't look incredibly pleased about Bash's arrival, but I supposed I couldn't blame him when the trio had been faced with the business end of my hitman's gun that once—and also Bash had continued to be testier than usual with the three of them lately. He definitely hadn't escaped the shrouded folk's influence. I'd have bet good money they'd been working on him somehow or other.

That knowledge made my jaw clench on the way to the door, but I managed to relax my expression before I turned the handle. "Come on in," I said to Bash. "We've got lots to do. Garrett brought me a wonderful present."

Bash gave the cop a look that couldn't be interpreted as anything other than skeptical. Garrett had tensed a little on the couch. I suppressed a frown as I returned to take my seat, Bash following me and dropping into one of the armchairs. This alliance we'd formed had worked to my benefit in all sorts of ways, but it could turn catastrophic if too much friction developed between the men around me.

"Sorry," I said to Garrett. "Before Bash and I get down to business, there was something else you wanted to tell me?"

The detective inspector hesitated, his gaze twitching to Bash and back to me. "It was something I only wanted to talk to *you* about. If we could have a moment—or it can wait—"

Bash cleared his throat ominously as Garrett moved to get up. "Anything you'd say to Jemma you can say in front of me," he said.

I shot him a chiding glance, and he eased back in his chair with just a hint of chagrin. "It's up to you," I said to Garrett. "But I think we should get in the habit of being more open with each other—all of us—unless it's information that would implicate us in a problematic way. And anything along that line that you tell me I'd tell Bash about anyway. You can trust him."

"It's nothing like that." Garrett had stayed on the sofa, but his posture was still tense. He seemed to gather himself, a hint of steel coming into his eyes. "Fine. He might as well hear it too. You've both trusted me enough to let me in on your crazy secret, and— I just want to know that you know who I am."

Bash looked as though he'd restrained an eye roll. I was pretty sure there wasn't anything Garrett could tell me that would shock me, but he was welcome to try. I scooted a little closer and patted his knee. "Go ahead."

Garrett held my gaze. "What happened in the parking lot yesterday—there were times when I was younger that I went through with acts like that. I told you before that I did some rotten things to my older brothers out of jealousy when I was younger, and I didn't mean simple pranks. I sabotaged a school project Mike had spent days working on, I let out one of their pets and because of that it got *killed*, I messed with Carl's shoes before he had a practice and they tripped him up so badly he broke his leg…"

I waited until I was sure he was done. "Is that the worst of it?" I said with a wry but gentle smile.

"It was bad," Garrett insisted, with enough pain in his expression that I knew he felt the remorse all the way down to his bones. "It took seeing one of my brothers in the bloody hospital before I realized how far I'd gone off the rails."

"You were a kid," I said. "In an intense situation where you felt nothing you could do was enough. I remember what you told me. I've *been* in a situation like that. I did far worse than you just said. You've seen what people do to each other in those communes." I swept my hand toward Bash. "And you've met my closest associate. I trust him more than anyone else in the world, and he used to kill people for profit."

He still did, technically, in so much as he was on my payroll, but I suspected it was better not to rub that aspect of our activities in the detective's face.

"It doesn't matter to you," Garret said, not a question. His posture relaxed, and a different sort of light came into his eyes.

"Did you really think it would?"

"I guess — not exactly. I just thought you deserved to know, if we're going to be working together this closely for a while."

I took his hand where it had been resting on the sofa between us. "Garrett, you don't owe me anything. Believe me, I'd let you know if you did."

The corner of his mouth curved upward. "Of course you would. I — I know I should get going so you two can get down to work, but I just — "

He cut himself off and shifted a few inches forward, close enough to tease his fingers along my jaw and tug my mouth to his.

When Garrett kissed, he *really* kissed. The live-wire smell of him filled my nose, and the intensity of his lips sent sparks crackling over my skin. If this was what he needed to trust *himself* to stay the course, I was more than happy to give it to him. I kissed him back eagerly, this good man who must barely be able to conceive of what true evil tasted like.

Bash cleared his throat softly. I ignored him, but Garrett tensed again and started to pull back. I grasped the front of his shirt before he could get very far and turned to look at my hitman.

Bash's expression was rigid. He'd known I got up to all sorts of fun with the trio, but he'd never had to see it.

An idea bubbled up inside me with a giddy energy. I might have the perfect way to undo some of the shrouded folk's influence on my men right here, right now.

I eased my hand up Garrett's lean chest to stroke his neck. "You learned not to be so jealous. How good are you at sharing?"

Understanding dawned on his face. He glanced at Bash with an audible swallow, but his expression looked wary, not disgusted or any of the other more negative reactions I might have gotten.

"Is that what you'd like?" he asked me. "To be shared?"

"I expect I'd like it *very* much. What do you think, Bash? Can you summon a little more of that generous spirit?"

Bash's gaze burned into mine. He paused for long enough that I thought he might refuse.

"It won't be the same without you," I said quietly.

Those words stirred him into action. He got out of the chair and came to me, stopping at the edge of the couch. "Then here I am, Majesty," he said in a low voice. In one swift movement, he leaned in and kissed me, hard.

Mmmm, yes, this was exactly how I liked it. I kissed Bash back with a hand tucked around the back of his neck, and Garrett eased the strap of my silky top to the side to press his lips to my shoulder. Heat kindled all through my body between those points of contact.

Bash kissed me again, his hand traveling down to skim over my breast. At my encouraging murmur, he flicked his thumb firmly over the nipple. Garrett brought his mouth to the crook of my neck and ran his fingers over my thigh. Oh, God, yes. I was caught between the two most possessively intense men I've ever met, and every inch of me was on fire.

When Bash drew back to pull my shirt over my head, I took the opportunity to share another kiss with Garrett. His tongue slipped between my lips as he unhooked my bra. I met it with mine in a hot dueling dance that left us both breathless.

"Still a firecracker," he said hoarsely, caressing my bare breast. "I don't think I'm ever going to get you out of my system, Jemma."

Something twinged, bittersweet, deep in my chest. "I don't want you to," I said with a sudden fierceness, and kissed him again.

Bash had knelt down on the floor by my legs, the perfect position to bring his mouth to my other breast. At the hot swipe of his tongue, I gasped into Garrett's mouth. Pleasure quivered over my skin in every which way.

Garrett's hand slid higher on my leg. I couldn't help arching into his touch when it reached the place between my thighs. Bliss shot through me as he rubbed my clit through my slacks in rhythmic circles. His lips trailed across my cheek and down my neck, and Bash claimed my mouth all over again.

Both of them had far too many clothes on still, but I didn't want to push their comfort levels past the breaking point. Getting naked in front of each other might be a step too far this first time around.

It had *better* only be the first time around. I could already tell I was going to want to repeat this experience.

I slid forward to make it easier for the two of them to remove my slacks, and then we all ended up on the floor, the rug thick and soft beneath us, Bash shoving the coffee table farther to the side. He swiveled his fingers against my panties and growled at the feel of the wetness already forming there. Garrett ground into me from behind, his mouth scorching against my shoulder and his fingers doing wondrous things to my breast.

"Purse," I mumbled, and he grabbed it off the couch in an instant. I reached back to yank down the zipper of his fly. Bash stripped my panties off me as Garrett readied himself.

My breath caught when the head of Garrett's cock pressed between my legs. I eased them a little wider apart, giving him access.

He dipped his fingers into my wetness with a groan and then plunged his length into me with a glorious surge of bliss that radiated from my core.

Bash kissed my mouth, and Garrett kissed my neck, the one man fondling my breasts while the other thrust inside me with his hand gripping my hip. Every nerve in my body sang and blazed at the same time. I fumbled with Bash's jeans, my hand shaky with the waves of pleasure rushing through me, and managed to free him from his boxers. His teeth nicked my lip as I gripped his erection.

"Harder," I gasped to Garrett, and he sped up his pace with a ragged curse.

"I want to make you fucking *explode*," he muttered by my ear, his hand teasing around to press against my clit. The determination in his voice combined with the press of his fingers made me do just that. As he bucked into me, my body shuddered and shattered with its release. I gripped Bash harder, pumping him faster. With a clutch of my thigh, Garrett spilled himself inside me.

He stroked his hand over my body, and then he was fishing another packet out of my purse to offer me. "Not only can I share," he said in a voice scorching enough to melt me all over again, "I can take turns too."

Bash let out a chuckle that sounded as if it'd caught him by surprise. I wasn't going to pass up a suggestion that good. I slicked the condom over Bash's length and parted my legs to welcome him.

Garrett kept caressing my side, my breasts, nibbling at my ear and the side of my neck, as Bash thrust inside me. I might have just come, but the rough strokes of my right-hand man's cock filling me sent me soaring all over again. I grasped his bicep and turned my head to kiss Garrett.

"Jemma," Bash gritted out, just my name, as if it were the only word left in his vocabulary. As his pace turned faster, wilder, the friction of his cock sent fresh pleasure searing through me. Turning my head back to him, I started to shudder all over again.

Ecstasy crashed over me. It flooded me and wiped everything else clean. Bash kissed me rough and hard and let out strangled sound as he came.

We lay there on the rug for a few minutes longer, sated and panting—and completely companionable. A smile curled my lips. The shrouded folk could throw whatever they wanted at us, but I'd proven I was stronger. I could win my men back.

Garrett nuzzled my hair and pressed another kiss to my neck. "Jemma," he said, and paused. His voice dropped to a whisper. "I love you."

My pulse hiccupped. I twisted around to face him. "Garrett—"

"I know," he said quickly, his face flushing. "I know that's not what you were looking for. I know that's not what you were offering. I don't expect anything in return. But I wanted to say it, because it's true, and it matters at least as much as the things I told you before."

I sank back into the rug, gazing back at him, but my chest had tightened. Love… that wasn't the sort of seduction I'd ever intended. It wasn't one I had any hope of ever returning. The only person I'd ever really loved had died years ago, and too much of my heart had died with her. After all this time, I wasn't sure even destroying the shrouded folk could heal the wound they'd dealt.

CHAPTER SIXTEEN

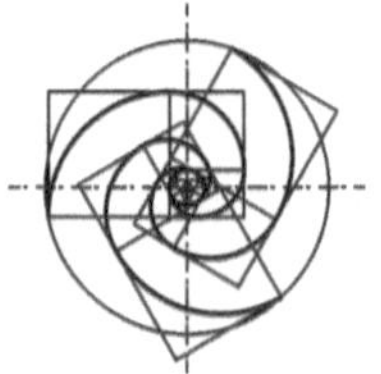

Jemma

It was a strange feeling standing surrounded by the four men I knew best in the world with none of them looking like themselves. Of course, I supposed I didn't look much like myself either.

All of us were in full costume for the complex operation we were about to carry out: wigs or temporary dye, plenty of make-up, colored contacts for some, sunglasses for others, new facial hair on all of the guys. Only Sherlock disappeared completely into his disguise with that way he had of transforming even his height and build with shifts in his posture, but I wasn't sure I'd have recognized any of my men at a distance.

I tugged a strand of my sleek blond wig back behind my ear and looked around our circle where we were sitting in the back of a rented van. The space had become humid as soon as we'd turned off the air conditioning, but it wasn't the heat that had my heart thumping faster. We might be all of a half hour from taking down Tillhouse, heading off his sinister plans, and getting a move on with clearing the shrouded folk out of this country.

"Is everyone good to go?" I said. "Any last minute concerns? Let's get them out now, because it's just about time to leave."

"I'm fully prepared and ready to start hollering," Bash said with a flash of a grin. He, John, and Garrett were heading to a political rally Tillhouse was holding here in London, just down the street. Bash had the most prominent job in that part of the operation—he'd be calling out Tillhouse for supposedly siphoning money from his company's investors, hinting that he'd uncovered the politician's criminal history at the same time to provoke a guilty reaction.

Garrett gave me a crooked smile. "My role is pretty simple. I think I can handle placing a single phone call." He was supposedly in attendance as an interested citizen, currently off duty, but he'd call in the disturbance to Scotland Yard to make sure we got a larger police presence on the scene.

"And I'll try to make sure everything stays on track," John said. "Move through the crowd, make a comment here and there to get people talking—easy enough." He rubbed his hands together, clearly eager to jump into the fray.

Sherlock and I were handling the other part of the operation, meant to launch simultaneously with the first for maximum impact. When I glanced at him, his smile looked tight, but it was hard to tell with it partially hidden behind the drooping moustache he'd fixed to his face. "I look forward to playing the supporting character to your leading role," he said in a wry voice that at least didn't sound particularly stressed. His gaze slid to Garrett. "I trust you handled the earlier aspect of your role effectively?"

"They'll be there," the detective inspector said confidently. "I heard them talking about it when I left the office yesterday afternoon." He'd surreptitiously left materials around his office about a special lunch deal for law enforcement at the restaurant where we wanted at least a few of his colleagues to show up.

Every piece accounted for. All those interconnecting elements working in harmony because I had four sharp minds working alongside mine. Sitting there in their midst with exhilaration building inside me, the sense of how much I appreciated these four men hit me like a punch in the gut.

No, not just appreciated. Maybe I couldn't say anything like the three words Garrett had offered me a few days ago, but I cared about them. I would have fought anyone who tried to hurt them. My victory over the shrouded folk would be twice as sweet because it was revenge for preying on them as well as for the many others the fiends had savaged over so many years.

I had the impulse to solidify that bond somehow, to show them how much they'd come to mean to me, but this wasn't the time for it. It wouldn't help to mess up their disguises with a kiss. I settled for grasping John's hand and Garrett's on either side of me and catching Bash's gaze with a tip of my head.

"All right then," I said. "The rally is kicking off now. The three of you get out of here. Knock this asshole out of the picture, and then we can get back to our monster-hunting."

Bash gave me a mock salute. John and Garrett returned my squeeze of their fingers. Then they stood and ducked out of the van, leaving a fizz of worry amid the eager anticipation quivering through my gut.

"Five minutes, and then we set off too?" Sherlock said to confirm.

I nodded, studying him as he leaned back against the van's wall. There was no reason for him to put on much of a false front while we were in here. That sense of gloom still hung over him, didn't it, if milder now? Was it milder because he was successfully battling it or simply because he was taking more care to disguise that too?

"Feeling better now that we've got a clear plan of action?" I asked, keeping my tone light.

"I'd be more pleased if we had any idea what this man's full connection to your shrouded folk is," Sherlock muttered, but he drew himself up straighter a moment later. "I suppose it doesn't matter in comparison to ridding the world of the menace."

"There'll always be plenty of time to question him after we've kicked their shrouded asses to kingdom come."

That remark got me a smile that was small but easier. "I certainly look forward to that moment."

I stood up, smoothed down my posh dress suit, and moved

toward the van's door. "Let's get going. We don't want to leave it too long."

We headed down the street in the opposite direction from where the other three had gone. It only took a moment to flag a taxi. The cab wove through the streets to the restaurant where both a group of police officers and some of the employees from one of Tillhouse's more upscale businesses would be taking their lunch. Sherlock sat silently, staring out the window so grimly that I started to worry again.

Before I could prod him a second time, the cab pulled to a stop at our destination. He sprang out with enough energy to convince me to put the matter to rest until we were done here. As we entered the restaurant, he walked a little behind me, as if he were more my assistant than an equal companion. Always fully immersed in his role.

I spotted Garrett's colleagues with a quick scan of the elegant interior. The officers looked as though they felt a tad out of place among the white table clothes and gleaming silver fixtures, but they were chatting away between bites of their lunches and glances at their surroundings. Our primary target, the company's CFO, was eating on his own meal with a tablet propped on the table beside him, either reading or still working while he finished his food.

The maître d hustled over. "A table for two?"

"We don't need a new one," I said in a haughty tone. "I see the person we're here to meet right over there."

I set off toward the CFO with brisk strides and my head held high. I needed to look believably like the sort of woman who might have invested a large sum in stocks for an international merchandising corporation. My footsteps and Sherlock's behind me thumped dully on the dense carpet.

The maître d had trailed after us as if to make sure we really were expected. I hoped he wouldn't cause too much trouble, but if he did, Sherlock would take care of that for long enough for me to get my piece in.

We were just one table away when the detective grabbed my elbow. I hesitated as he pulled closer to me.

"We can't use him," he murmured by my ear in an urgent voice.

I stared at him. We'd chosen the man by group consensus two nights ago. "Why not?" I asked under my breath.

Sherlock grimaced. "He's got a splotch of mud on his trousers. It's a distinctive color—one I've seen on Tillhouse's before. One I determined is specific to a country club near here. No doubt they both belong to it. There wasn't any evidence of that before. Now I'd be inclined to believe the two are friends more than distant business associates."

From anyone else, that reasoning would have sounded like a stretch. From Sherlock, I had to assume he was putting together several other minute pieces he didn't have time to get into. He wouldn't have stopped me in the middle of our operation if he hadn't thought there was a real chance we'd gotten off course.

If the CFO had a personal loyalty to Tillhouse, confronting him might not have the effect we wanted. We needed someone who'd focus more on getting to the bottom of the problem than ensuring peace of mind for the man behind the scenes.

My heart stuttering, I cast my gaze about as the maître d cleared his throat behind us. Thankfully we hadn't gotten quite close enough to the CFO for it to be obvious we were now changing our minds. Several employees from the company, which had its offices just down the street, tended to lunch here. The CFO was only the most prominent. We could just as easily use…

My gaze settled on a man I recognized from the company records we'd gotten our hands on. A couple of steps down the ladder from the CFO here, but on the accounts side of things, which worked just fine. I even remembered his name, because it fit his appearance so well: Marten. He looked like a marten, ruddy haired and weaselly.

I shifted direction with an air as if I'd taken a slight detour on purpose and marched up to Mr. Marten's table. He was sitting with a woman I didn't recognize, at least ten years younger and her clothes clearly off-the-rack rather than tailored like most of the senior employees. One of the secretaries, I'd bet. I'd put a fair amount of money on the possibility that Marten was sleeping with her too, although that had little bearing on our success here.

"Mr. Marten," I said in a sharp voice pitched to carry through the room. "I'm very concerned about the state of my accounts. The math does *not* appear to be adding up."

Marten blinked at me, his jaw freezing in mid-bite, but I'd spoken with enough authority that he had to assume he knew me even if he hadn't the slightest clue who I was.

"I'm sorry, madam," he said, fumbling. "I'm not sure what you mean?"

"My shares in Everring Marketing." I whipped out my phone open to the account—an account my and Sherlock's associates had conjured up in preparation for this confrontation. "Look at these numbers. With the percentage rise in the stock yesterday, I should have seen an increase of *twice* that much. It concerned me so much I looked back through my past statements and found *repeated* omissions across *years*. I need answers, now!"

"Ma'am," the maître d said with a wringing of his hands, and Sherlock intercepted him smoothly with some murmured distraction. From the corner of my eye, I saw the cops glancing our way.

Marten took the phone from me and peered at it. His eyes widened for a second before he caught his expression, but he clearly saw the discrepancy too. "I—I'm not sure what's going on here," he said. "If you could come into the office—"

"Into the office?" I cried. "What, so you can rob me even more? This is a disgrace. Tens of thousands of dollars taken from under my nose, and you don't know what's 'going on'?"

"Really, at this point we should call the police," Sherlock said in a high, stilted voice. "How can we trust people who've been robbing you for nearly a decade?"

As intended, a couple of the officers from the nearby table got up and strolled over. "What seems to be the problem?" the woman in the lead asked.

Marten blustered something about taking care of things internally, and the CFO slunk over to see what was going on, but I let the officers usher me off to the side where neither of the company's employees had to be part of the conversation. With much dramatics, I explained the supposedly missing money. "I wouldn't be surprised if it's all sorts of people," I finished off with. "Ripping off their stockholders left and right. It needs a full investigation."

As the woman reassured me that someone would look into it, the man with her got a call. He turned away from us to answer it and swiveled back a few moments later with a bemused expression.

"You'll never believe it," he murmured to the woman. "There's been another incident about this just now."

"Stay here in case we have any more questions, please," the woman said to me, and went off with the man to get the details. I exchanged a triumphant glance with Sherlock. At the same moment, my own phone buzzed.

It was a text from John. *All went well. Your man put on quite the show. Everyone's talking now. Couldn't have asked for a better blow-up.*

A smile curled my lips as I sent him a thumbs up in response to indicate our own part of the plan had gone off successfully despite its momentary hitch. A sense of satisfaction settled over me, tinged with not a little relief.

One major obstacle removed; one potentially horrific threat demobilized for long enough that we should be able to clear out his supernatural support and end whatever the shrouded folk had intended to accomplish here. We'd won the battle—now it was time to win the war.

CHAPTER SEVENTEEN

Sherlock

I jerked awake with a wrenching sensation around my limbs. In the dark room, I yanked against my apparent bindings instinctively. It took my exhausted brain a few seconds to register that I wasn't tied up by anything other than my twisted sheet.

I sank back into the mattress. The air conditioner whirred, turning my skin clammy with the sweat that had broken out over it in my sleep. In my sleep, and in the middle of whatever dark, ominous dream had sent me jolting out of slumber in a panic for the fifth time since I'd taken to bed last night.

The contents of those dreams eluded me. I had no idea what in them had been so terrifying. All I was left with when I woke up was the racing of my heart and the cold sweat on my skin—and the distinct impression that something essential was slipping from my grasp far too quickly.

It wasn't a sensation I enjoyed. I breathed slowly and deeply, taking my mind through the paces of a few simple meditation exercises, but my nervous system remained on high alert.

I *should* have had better control over myself. I normally did.

No doubt it didn't help matters that my sleep had been so broken. I might have gotten four hours of truly restful sleep, if that much, across the past nine of trying. Each time I'd woken up in this state it'd taken me a long time to settle myself enough to drift off again.

I stared up at my plaster ceiling, tracing the familiar paths with my gaze. My eyelids felt heavy and my head muggy, but my heart thumped on and my thoughts were whirling. Morning sunlight was seeping insistently past my curtain. I wasn't sure there was any point in trying to add to my rest for the day. If I wasn't up soon, John would become concerned, and that would only add another layer to my difficulties.

I'd functioned on less sleep before. I could manage one day like this.

And I wouldn't think about the possible causes of my nighttime disturbances. It wasn't as if I could tackle them directly as it was.

There were other things I could tackle if I got out of this bed. I shoved back the covers and methodically changed into suitable clothes for the day. Then I reached for my phone and texted Garrett.

Any additional word on the proceedings regarding Tillhouse?

I set the phone down, not expecting an immediate answer, but it rang a second later with an incoming call. Apparently Garrett had gotten into the office early—or he was monitoring proceedings from afar.

"You're not going to like this," he said grimly when I picked up. "The bastards are releasing him. He's convinced them that it's impossible he 'engaged in any wrongdoing'."

My stomach plummeted. No. It didn't make sense. It shouldn't have been possible. We'd set up everything within the accounts to make an airtight case.

"How could he possibly have done that?" I demanded.

Garrett let out a huff of breath that expressed nearly as much frustration as was coursing through me. "I haven't got a bloody clue. I can't get a straight answer—no one's keen to talk about it. But after everything we've seen... I wouldn't be surprised if Jemma's shrouded folk had a hand in it."

That possibility brought a sour taste into my mouth. Yes, why wouldn't Jemma's creatures be involved in influencing events around this case if the man was tied up in their schemes? He had to be awfully important for them to have taken a gamble on someone outside their cult.

But if that were the case... was he simply untouchable?

"There *has* to be a way we can make something stick," I said, the words coming out more vehemently than they might have if I'd been properly alert.

"Maybe Jemma will have some ideas. I'll keep prodding the detectives involved about how exactly he turned the tables. Or possibly we'll be able to circumvent him completely, if he's going to be this much of a pain in the arse."

We both knew we couldn't simply ignore Tillhouse, though. He represented the largest violation these monsters had made within our world—their most blatant grab for power. Damn it.

"I just got off the phone with someone at the station," Garrett said. "I was going to check in with Jemma, and we'll go from there. I expect you'll hear from me again before much longer."

"Yes, keep me apprised of the situation."

I tossed the phone onto my bed, walked toward the bedroom door, halted, and walked back again. Where the hell was I going? Where the hell *could* I go? For fuck's sake, the blasted shrouded folk could be in this room right now and I'd never know it. They left no traces, no clues I could easily decipher.

I came to a stop by the dresser with one of Jemma's mathematical sequences laid out across it. She'd brought decorative stones to give her patterns a more appealing look, as if I cared much about whether the things were easy on the eyes as long as they worked.

They didn't, clearly, if the creatures were sabotaging my very sleep.

The clink of dishes sounded from the other side of the door. John was moving about the common room now, making his breakfast no doubt. I couldn't summon a spot of hunger myself. And as I listened, he started humming—a slightly off-key but buoyant tune that would have made me smile fondly most other days. Today, my gut clenched in resistance.

I wasn't going to be good company for him in my current state of mind. His optimism would only irritate me, and I wasn't certain I had the capacity to completely hold my temper. Better I kept to myself as I normally did when I had a problem to work through.

A thought passed through my head as clear as my own voice. *So you finally met a case you can't crack, Sherlock.*

"I'll crack it," I said under my breath. "I just need more time."

How much time have you had already? They've gotten the better of you—there's no other way of looking at it.

It wasn't unusual for me to talk to myself while I was working my way out of a problem, but my sparring partner in those internal conversations wasn't normally so hostile. My frustrations had obviously seeped all through my consciousness.

"I'm not beaten."

Oh, no? You look an awful lot like you are. What exactly are you accomplishing right now?

My teeth gritted. "There has to be something I've missed. I *will* find it. Every crime leaves a trail behind—supernatural ones can't be any different." I refused to allow them to be.

I jerked open my work drawer on my dresser and grabbed the various printouts, clippings, and reports I'd gathered over the course of the case. The folders felt far too light in my hands. I fished out paper after paper and laid them all out across the bed, pausing just for a moment to jerk straight the covers.

There were enough pieces that they had to overlap. I squinted at them, rearranging them into clearer patterns, scowling at them when nothing new immediately emerged.

Patience. I could have patience. One at a time, read them over, study every picture. There would be a clue in there. I only had to piece it together.

Reading took longer than usual. My fatigued mind tripped over the words here and there. I rubbed my eyes and tried to focus more intently.

When my phone chimed with an incoming text, I ignored it.

Whoever wanted me, they could wait. Nothing was more important than this.

By the time I'd made it through the spread of papers at one corner of the bed, an ache was building behind my eyes.

John rapped his knuckles on my door. "Sherlock? Are you up?"

"I am. Just going over some notes."

He paused. "Garrett said he told you the news. I can't believe they're ready to let Tillhouse off without even a full investigation."

"It is a rather ridiculous turn of events," I agreed. His voice made my headache pulse harder.

"I don't know if you saw—we're going to meet up to discuss next steps. I could tell everyone to head over here—"

"No," I said, quickly and emphatically. "I'm going to bow this one out, and I can't have any disruptions. I'm—I'm close to the answer. I can feel it. Arrange your meeting elsewhere and make whatever plans you can. I won't have anything constructive to contribute until I work my way through this."

John didn't disguise the concern in his voice. "Are you sure? Your insight is always going to be valuable—"

"I'd like that period without disruptions to start now."

"Ah. All right then. I'll leave you to it. If you need any of us, you know how to reach us."

I'd expected to feel relief at his leaving. I stood stock still until I heard the thump of the outer door shutting and the click of his key turning the lock. Then I turned back to my spread of papers—the *mess* of papers, really, because it couldn't be called anything like orderly at this point—and a wave of utter hopelessness rolled over me. It pressed down on me like a boulder, heavier than I'd ever felt this sort of uncertainty before.

It wasn't the same sort of uncertainty at all, was it? Before I'd only been dealing with the habits of human beings, predictable as long as you could ferret out all the facts. Now I was dealing with the completely unknowable.

I'd pulled back the curtain to let in the sunlight, but in that moment the whole room wavered darker. The gloom had descended on me so thickly it was shadowing my vision. I was drowning in it, in dark water closing over my head. My lungs constricted as I dragged air into them.

Who was I, if I didn't have a mind sharp enough to penetrate this problem? What use was I at all—what point was there to all the studies I'd done and the exercises with which I'd honed my senses, if I couldn't stand up to the first truly expansive threat I'd ever faced?

For an instant, my throat closed up completely. Doubt suffocated me. A chill of fear prickled after it, penetrating right down to my center.

I wasn't going to think through anything when the depression settled over me this heavily. That was what the creatures would want, wasn't it—to see me incapacitated by my frustration? But I had tools they couldn't have anticipated. I could shock myself out of this state.

I *had* to.

John was long gone, but I still glanced around the common room when I came out, noting the absence of his walking stick, which he normally left by the umbrella stand next to the door, and his favorite hat gone as well. Wherever they'd ended up arranging their meeting, he shouldn't be back for some time. I could jumpstart my mental faculties in a matter of minutes and get down to work as I was meant to be doing.

I took a freshly washed glass from the dishwasher and brought it back to my room. Then I retrieved the locked box from my closet, along with a jug of distilled water. With careful precision, I poured some of the water into the glass and took the baggie of white powder and a measuring spoon from the box.

One of these spoonfuls was the dosage I'd decided on. I'd already taken it twice in the last week, and it'd only partly and briefly stirred me out of my dark state. I glanced at the scattered papers on the bed, and resolve gripped me.

I'd set that limit in consideration of the way I'd abused the substance in the past. It had been decided out of extreme caution, nowhere near any level that should be considered dangerous. What was bloody well dangerous was letting those monsters and the man they were backing roam free while I wandered in this hapless daze.

I dropped one spoonful into the glass and dug the instrument into the powder again. If there was going to be any point in taking this route, I needed to set caution aside and go all in.

Anything it took to break me free of this rut and win the day after all would be worth it.

CHAPTER EIGHTEEN

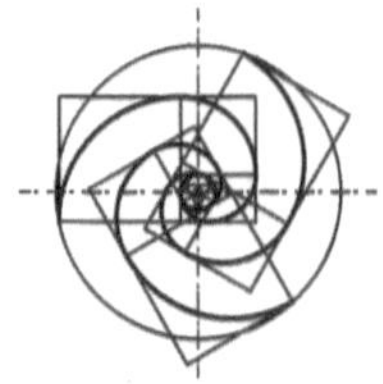

Jemma

Bash set a hand on my arm, and I looked up from my laptop's screen. Beyond the windshield of the car we were staked out in, an elderly woman was picking her way rather nimbly across her front yard between the rock garden and the ash tree. She didn't glance our way. Really, there was no reason for her to be suspicious of an old station wagon parked one house down on the other side of the street. I went back to my work.

"Do you think she knows?" Bash asked.

The woman was Tillhouse's mother. His parents had been living in this house since shortly after they'd all changed their names and gotten the heck out of dodge some forty years ago.

"About the details?" I said. "Hard to say. But even if they don't, there could still be *something* telling in here."

With advice from one of my particularly computer savvy contacts, I'd hacked into the house's home network and from there gotten access to the email accounts of the senior Tillhouses. Thank the Lord they were technologically inclined, or we'd have had to resort to digging through their literal trash.

Instead, I'd skimmed back through several years of saved emails and was now checking the spam folders.

Bash's phone dinged with a text. He glanced at it. "John says they've finished their visit to the local police station."

"Tell them to go back to that diner where we got lunch, and we'll meet them there in a half hour or so. I'm almost finished here." So far I hadn't turned up anything that looked all that useful, although I'd copied all the emails between the MP and his parents over to my hard drive for further perusing later.

There had to be something *somewhere* that could knock Tillhouse down—or at least remove him from the picture for long enough that we could make a real move on the commune that must be most directly supporting him. Our further investigations over the last couple weeks hadn't turned up any clearer patterns of activity in the country other than the ones we'd already identified. We'd taken down one sect, and another had fled. That only left our enemies in the Highlands to deal with.

Too bad there were a hell of a lot of Highlands, and apparently not all that many people in Scotland who were willing to lend us a hand.

Children laughed where they were playing somewhere down the street. I sank deeper into my seat, propping the laptop's screen against the wheel. Amazing how many junk mail messages you could manage to get in a month. None of them had anything constructive to offer, though.

My last place to consider was the digital trash. In there, I found more spam that hadn't been properly filtered and not a whole lot else. Tillhouse's parents didn't get a whole lot of expected electronic communications. I'd sucked my lower lip under my teeth, my gaze slipping down over the list of subject lines, when I stopped with a jolt of excitement.

A perfect deal for another fantastic Scottish vacation!

Bash shifted in his seat as I clicked the email open, alert to my change in mood. "Did you find something?"

"Maybe." I scanned the email's contents, and a small smile curled my lips. "Yes. It's not definitive, but—apparently the parents had a little Scottish vacation sometime last year. A country resort 'nestled in the Highlands.' It could be totally unrelated, but from what I've seen, their son pays for any luxuries they have. If he was buying them a vacation, he'd probably pick an area he's familiar with. They might even have their own part to play with the commune."

"Does it fit with the patterns of behavior the Londoners found before?"

I switched to the map and checked the resort's location. "It's within the broad area we were looking at. That could narrow things down quite a bit. At the very least, we can make a more focused effort around those parts now."

I flicked through the rest of the trash folder just in case, not really expecting another prize. Then I closed the laptop, tossed it in the back, and started the engine. "Let's see what our detectives scrounged up."

John's car was already parked in the lot of the diner where we'd eaten. A trace of berry sweetness from the tart I'd finished my lunch off with still lingered in my mouth. Maybe I'd grab another of those while we talked.

This road trip had been a rather impromptu one. We'd been discussing Tillhouse's release in frustration, and Garrett had made a comment about delving into the guy's history directly, and somehow we'd all ended up deciding to come up here and check out the area where he'd spent his later formative years.

Well, all of us except for Sherlock, who was apparently absorbed in some brainstorm he hadn't bothered to give even John any details about. I'd been tempted to nudge the consulting detective with a text and find out where his thoughts were headed, but John had forbidden any contact.

"When he gets in that state, he'll take your head off for interrupting him," he'd said. "He'll get to whatever inspiration he's chasing down faster if we leave him to it."

Now, Bash and I found Garrett and John sitting in the exact same booth, already near the bottom of their mugs of coffee and John halfway through a slice of the lemon cheesecake I'd been eyeing on the menu along with the tarts.

I plopped down across from them and promptly stole a bite of the cheesecake. John gave me an amused look as my eyes rolled upward in ecstatic appreciation. I flagged down the waitress to order a slice all for myself and then set my elbows on the table to get down to business.

"Our man's parents went on a trip to the Highlands not too long ago," I announced. "Interesting choice, don't you think?"

John perked up. "Do you figure they'd have been near the commune up there?"

I shared the same reasoning with them I'd offered Bash. My cheesecake arrived, and after I'd taken my first bite, I waved my fork in the direction of the detectives. "Did you two turn anything up?"

Garrett shook his head. "No patterns of crime or connections to Scotland that we could find—which really, we should have expected. Tillhouse wouldn't have wanted to let the criminal side of his dealings connect too closely to his home ground."

"It was worth checking, though," John said. "And obviously it's a good thing we came up here, given what Jemma found. So, what's next? We pay this vacation spot a visit and see what the word is around there?" His eyes shone with the excitement of having a mission ahead.

"If we're going to make our own trip to Scotland, I think our first stop should be the police," Garrett said. "It'll be harder for them to turn me away in person."

Bash let out a scoffing sound. "They wouldn't help you at all before—why would they change their tune now? They'll probably give you a load of bull that points us in the wrong direction just to get you off their backs."

Garrett glowered at him. The intimacy the three of us had shared a few days ago might have broken down a few hostilities, but it was hard to say the two of them had exactly become friends. Their personalities clashed too much.

"I didn't get to the position I'm in by giving up too easily," the detective inspector said. "And whatever your opinions on the police force are, we *do* tend to be loyal to each other with the right motivation."

"I think we should start with Jemma's lead," John jumped in. "It's the most concrete one we have. Then we might have more details to direct the questions we want to ask the police."

Garrett frowned. "If we start nosing around a place where Tillhouse has connections, that could tip him off that we're getting close, especially since he's probably even more on guard after the blow-up yesterday."

"How many people can he even have alerted at this point?" Bash protested. "He just got released from custody this morning, and they're off in some remote spot away from civilization. It's not like it'd take a simple phone call."

"We don't know that for sure."

"Whoa, whoa," I said, holding up my hands. The debate was setting my nerves on edge. It sounded like too much petty squabbling and not like a team working together. Possibly because we didn't have the whole team together.

But it wasn't just that, was it? Even now, even after the shrouded folk had cast a shadow over these men in various ways, the threat wasn't real to them the way it was to me. They might have seen photographs and witnessed injuries and heard my reports, but I'd seen one of those screaming violent deaths with my own eyes. I'd lived amid that violence for fourteen years.

My gut knotted. Taking down this commune, wiping out the others until the shrouded folk could no longer maintain their presence here in our realm—it wasn't just another, albeit particularly immense, case. It was a matter of human survival. There was too much at stake here to be sniping at each other over strategy.

This really was a war, and even now, none of the men around me could fully comprehend that.

"We're not doing *anything* today," I went on. "Garrett, Scotland Yard expects you back there tomorrow, don't they? And maybe we can still salvage our campaign against Tillhouse somehow once more information comes out. We need to find out what Sherlock's been up to all this time. We'll regroup, all five of us, pool our resources, and make a proper plan of attack for heading north."

Garrett winced. "Sorry," he said. "It's just so maddening that he's walking free—I got carried away."

"And we really should loop Sherlock back in," John said with a sheepish expression. "He may have wrapped this whole thing up while we've been running around."

I perked up as I popped another bite of lemon cheesecake into my mouth. "Have you heard from him?"

He shook his head. "I'll give him a nudge in warning when I'm almost back at the flat. Maybe we can have that meeting there over dinner." He glanced at the clock on the diner's back wall. "And I guess we should head out if we want to be back in London in *time* for dinner."

I jabbed at my cake. "Let me finish this, and we'll get going."

Evening was starting to settle in when Bash and I reached central London. We'd switched places in the car, him driving and me poring over Tillhouse's emails with his parents, but I hadn't turned up any clues. All I'd gotten was an ache behind my eyes. I rubbed them and closed the laptop, and my phone vibrated with an incoming call.

It was John. "Are we on for dinner?" I asked him.

"I don't know," he said with worry laced through his voice. "We're about ten minutes from Baker Street now. I texted Sherlock five minutes ago, and just called, and he's not answering."

A thread of cold wound through me from throat to stomach. "Is that unusual when he's absorbed in work?" I asked.

"I don't think he'd ignore his phone completely, especially when he knows we've been out doing our own work. For all he knows, he's missing news about Tillhouse or some other aspect of the case."

"Maybe his battery died."

"It could be. He's normally pretty fastidious about that."

My fingers tightened around my phone. "So, what are you thinking?"

"I don't know." John sighed. "It's probably nothing. He left the phone in the other room and got so caught up in thought he didn't hear it, something like that. I just don't like it."

"We'll come," I said firmly. "If he doesn't want a dinner meeting, he should have picked up the phone to tell you so." I'd rather meet an irritated Sherlock than sit with this anxiety twisted all through me.

He hadn't seemed completely like himself for a while now. The shrouded folk had been acting on him in ways he hadn't wanted to admit. They wouldn't have outright *attacked* him, would they? The possibility seemed incredibly unlikely given what I knew about them, but it also made me queasy.

"Drive faster," I told Bash. "Let's get to Baker Street."

He took the next few turns at just shy of dangerous speed, only slowing at a glimpse of a police car. We made it to Sherlock and John's building just as John and Garrett were pulling up outside.

John hustled up the stairs to the apartment with his mouth set in a tense line. "Sherlock?" he said as he unlocked the door and pushed it open. "We gave you as long as we could manage without any disruptions. I'm afraid you're going to have to put up with one now."

We got no answer. The living room was empty, the dining table bare, no sign of recent activity out here. Sherlock's bedroom door was closed.

John's posture had stiffened. He set his walking stick aside so abruptly it fell over with a clatter, but he didn't stop to pick it up. He strode to Sherlock's door with his slightly uneven gait and knocked. "Sherlock? Sherlock!"

The knob didn't budge when he rattled it. "Could he have gone out?" I said. "He might not even be here."

John's hand dropped from the door knob. "You're right. He could—" He froze, his eyes widening, and took a long inhale.

"I smell vomit," he said in a thin voice, and dashed across the apartment to his own room heedless of the wobble that speed brought into his leg. I'd already reached Sherlock's bedroom when John emerged a second later, unwrapping a set of lock picks. A faint whiff of that sour scent reached my nose, and my stomach turned.

"For the first time, I'm glad he insisted on badgering me into learning how to use these," John muttered, but his voice was taut with distress. His hands shook as he wielded the picks.

"Let me," I said.

He handed them over without protest. I inserted them into the keyhole and flipped the lock in a couple of seconds with a frantic jerk of my hands. The instant I'd pulled the picks out, John was shoving the door open.

A choked sound escaped his throat. Sherlock was sprawled on his side on the floor, his face blotchy, vomit streaking the hardwood by his mouth. John dropped at his side, grabbing his hand to check for a pulse. As I dashed after him, my pulse rattling through my veins, my gaze fell on the box lying open on the bedspread. On the baggy of white powder, nearly empty, and a syringe with a bead of liquid still poised at the tip of its needle.

This was war, all right. And the shrouded folk had found the perfect weapon to land a killing blow.

A nearly killing blow. "He's alive!" John said. "Barely. Someone call an ambulance!"

"Already have," Garrett said from the door, looking shocked.

I knelt down beside John, steeling myself against the hopeless sensation that rose up at seeing Sherlock so frail. "Tell me what we have to do to make sure he stays with us."

CHAPTER NINETEEN

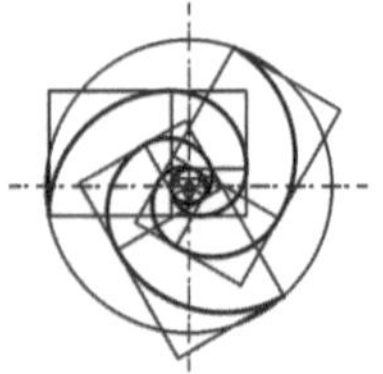

Jemma

The hospital had exactly the sort of aesthetic I should have enjoyed: straight lines and clean whites and beiges. Something in the atmosphere cast too much of a shadow over it, though—the undertone of heavy disinfectant, the beeping of machines measuring the strength of lives in peril. Or perhaps just the knowledge that one of those lives belonged to the only man I'd ever felt could match me on every front.

At first, we'd all ended up in the waiting room while the doctors did what they could for Sherlock. Bash had stayed mainly to support me, and when it'd become obvious he felt awkward lingering there, I'd sent him back to his apartment. Garrett had left a little while after that, saying the best thing he could do for the man was get to the bottom of Tillhouse's release.

That left John and me. The former surgeon had alternately sprawled on the stiff waiting room chairs and paced across the linoleum floor with sharp jerks of his walking stick, his gaze nearly always fixed on the hallway that led to the treatment rooms.

They hadn't let us see Sherlock yet, hadn't told us anything other than they were giving him the best possible care, however reassuring that was supposed to be.

I'd come across overdoses before—among junkies and other unstable characters. Even after John had mentioned Sherlock was using again after a stretch of sobriety, I'd never thought I'd find myself here waiting to find out if the world's foremost detective had survived his own over-indulgence.

How much had his own innate moods gotten the better of him in this frustrating and unnerving situation, and how much had the shrouded folk given him a direct push? Even he might not be able to tell us accurately. I knew how slyly the fiends could exert their will.

I popped a sugar cube into my mouth, my fourth of the evening, although the sweetness only cut a tiny bit of the worry souring my stomach. John marched over to the nurse's desk again.

"Is there any news at all?" he said. "Is he in recovery? When will we be able to see him?"

"I haven't gotten any updates," the nurse said in a mild but weary voice. "I'll be sure to let you know as soon as I do. From what I've seen, with cases like that, it might be a while yet. If you're going to stay, you should settle in for a long wait."

John let out his breath in a rough exhalation and meandered back toward me. The normally cheerful light in his hazel eyes had dulled to a faint, frantic glimmer. Where his appearance normally gave the impression of warmth and softness, the muscles in his broad shoulders and along his jaw had turned hard with tension. It made my own gut knot tighter seeing him like that.

I got up just before he reached me and grasped his wrist. "Why don't we find the cafeteria and get something to eat while it's still open? You're only going to feel worse if you starve yourself."

John's posture stiffened even more. "If something comes up about Sherlock—"

"We won't be gone that long. Anyway, I heard what she told you. It could be hours more before we get any real news."

He grimaced, but his stance relaxed a little, enough that I could tug him along with me.

"I'm not sure I can stomach much right now," he remarked.

Neither was I. "Well, we'll try our best," I said, attempting to insert his usual cheer into the vacuum left by his distress.

We headed down the hall toward the staircase that led to the lower level. John kept twitching his walking stick restlessly. If anything, now that we'd left the waiting room he looked even more pained than he had before.

"You know it isn't your fault, don't you?" I said.

"How can *you* know that? I live with him. I'm his best friend—practically his only real friend. I knew he was using again. I should have realized something was wrong when he put me off this morning—I should have insisted on staying…"

He trailed off as if realizing even in his furor how ridiculous that idea was. I gave him a gentle teasing nudge. "And, what, you would have sat in the living room while he worked away in his bedroom, and still not have known what he was getting up to? Do you really think he'd have agreed to hourly check-ins or anything else like that? He'd probably have come up with some quest of his own to send you on if he'd wanted privacy that badly."

"Yes." John sighed and rubbed his hand over his face. "But still. My whole job is to support him, to fill in the gaps when he can't handle everything on his own. If I can't even make sure he stays *alive*, what the hell good am I?"

Those words sent a jab through my chest. I grasped John's wrist again and turned him toward me so I could look him right in the eyes.

"He's a grown man. It was his job to look after himself. He could have told any of us if he was struggling more than he let on. And you are *not* Sherlock's keeper. You're more than just his goddamned sidekick. How many people did you save before you even met him? I don't care how brilliant or lauded a detective he is—it doesn't mean you stop mattering."

John blinked at me, clearly startled. Then he closed his eyes. "I know that," he said quietly. "I know all of that, but it still kills me that I couldn't stop this somehow, that I can't do anything now."

I drew him into an embrace, tucking my head against his shoulder. An orderly trotted by us without a second glance—no doubt people hugging out their fears or grief was a pretty common sight in the hospital halls.

John let out a shaky breath and wrapped his arms around me, pulling me closer. For a few minutes, we just stood there, locked together in the little comfort we could manage to generate between us.

When John eased back, he kept his head bowed over me, his forehead nearly grazing mine. He held my gaze for a long moment.

"It bothers you almost as much as it bothers me, doesn't it?" he said. If he sounded a little startled by that too, I suppose I deserved that.

I started to speak and found a lump had risen in my throat. "He's a spectacular man. I hadn't known there was anyone like him in the world. Now it seems like a pretty horrible thing that the world might lose him."

The corner of John's mouth quirked up just slightly. "So it's the world's loss you're concerned about, not your own?"

"It's all the same thing, really." An ache spread from my throat down through my chest. "But just so you know, the thought of losing you or Garrett upsets me just as much. If you start to feel you've been pushed to close to some edge—"

"I know." He touched my cheek. "I swear I'll tell you if anything's wrong. You don't need to worry about that."

The tingle of his breath across my face woke up other feelings far less fraught than my fears. A quiver traveled down through my core. There were other sorts of comfort, other avenues for release when there was no fully escaping the horrible situation you'd found yourself in. I suspected John could use the distraction as much as I did, if not more.

"Show me," I murmured, resting my hand on his chest. "Prove to me how much you're here with me."

The thump of his heart beneath my palm sped up. John hesitated, his gaze flicking to one side and then the other to confirm we were alone in the hall, and then he ducked his head to capture my mouth.

There was an urgency to his kiss I'd never felt from him before—

he was usually so gentle even at his most passionate. The hunger that had stirred in me before woke up completely, as if I were famished for this. I kissed him back just as hard, my fingers gripping the front of his shirt, my head tilting to allow him better access to my mouth.

John made a rough sound and shoved me half a foot back so my shoulders jarred against the wall. The impact only heightened the thrill. Our tongues dueled, and his heat soaked right through me. It might not have been able to wash away all the anxieties of the day, but it could overwhelm them while we were in the middle of this collision.

I tore my lips from his just long enough to gulp air and spot the door to a closet some ten feet down the hall. My hand still fisted in John's shirt, I yanked him with me, threw open the door, and pulled him inside.

In the brief flood of light, I saw shelves stacked with cleaning products and boxes of plastic gloves, a mop in a bucket in the corner. Then the door thudded shut behind us, choking the light, and there was nothing to see. Nothing to hear except the hitch of John's breath right before he kissed me again; nothing to feel except the solid bulk of his broad body against mine.

John nudged me up against the shelves with the patter of boxes jostling against each other. The steel frame pressed into my ass and my back, but I didn't give a shit, not when he was kissing me like there was nothing else in the entire universe.

I let go of his shirt to tease my hand up over his muscles beneath it. John let out a strangled groan and cupped my breast through my dress as he devoured my mouth. Pleasure raced over my skin with the sweep of his thumb over my nipple. I tweaked his nipples in turn, earning me a gasp. Then I let my hand slide all the way down to the waist of his pants.

I trailed my fingers over his fly, and his cock jumped beneath the thin fabric. "Fuck," John muttered against my mouth. He pulled back an inch, panting. "What are we doing, Jemma?"

"Being alive," I said firmly, and squeezed him as I stroked him through his pants. "Fuck me. Fuck me with all that life you've got in you."

A stuttered laugh escaped him, and his mouth crashed down on mine again. His hands traced down my sides and over my hips to the skirt of my dress. In one quick movement, he jerked the fabric up and caught my thighs. He lifted me against the shelves so my sex was flush against his groin.

I swallowed my moan as well as I could. If we were interrupted now, I just might kill someone.

John's mouth seared against my neck as he tugged my panties down, and I yanked at his fly. An ecstatic hum rumbled from his chest as I curled my fingers around his smooth hot length.

I'd lost track of my purse in the darkness. Every particle in my body resisted the idea of pulling apart to search for it. I'd trusted Sherlock without protection once. I trusted John just as much, didn't I? He wouldn't fuck me if he thought it would hurt me, not this sweet, good man.

He trusted me not to hurt him. Something stabbed deep down through me at that thought, but I shoved the emotion away. I wasn't going to hurt him right now. I was clean.

And oh God did I need him inside me right now.

If John had any doubts I hadn't expected, he didn't show them. His mouth reclaimed mine as the head of his cock slid against my wetness. He thrust into me so fast the bliss shot straight through my body and burst into stars behind my eyes.

We both knew we didn't have time for a leisurely roll in the hay. John bucked into me, one hand still clutching my thigh as he braced me against the shelf, the other on the shelf next to my shoulder to steady himself. I rocked to meet his thrusts, pleasure burning higher and farther with each jolt of our connection.

We *were* alive—alive and momentarily lost in it, in each other, in the ecstasy two bodies could make when they aligned in just the right way.

I felt John starting to lose control before I'd quite reached my peak, the jerks of his hips turning erratic. I growled with a hint of frustration against his lips, but his hand was already dipping between us to massage my clit. A fresh burst of pleasure flooded me with that touch, and I clenched around him with a swallowed cry.

John buried his face in the crook of my neck to muffle a groan as he came with a spurt of heat.

We stayed there for a few moments, locked together in this hasty but incredibly intimate embrace, reluctant to return to the world waiting outside. But that world seeped back into my head even there in the dark where all I could taste and smell was the man softening inside me. It must have for John too. He withdrew with a ragged sigh.

There was so much pain in that sound in anticipation of the news we might hear when we ventured back into the waiting room. Hearing it, my lungs constricted. I snatched at my panties and straightened out my dress, but my stomach sank farther with each passing moment as the afterglow swiftly faded.

What had happened to Sherlock wasn't John's fault. I'd meant it when I'd said he wasn't his friend's keeper. But this, all of this, was *my* fault, wasn't it? I'd pulled these men into a conflict they could barely understand, and in doing so I'd made myself their keepers as the only one who could properly guide them.

And now my heart was wrenching at the thought of possibly losing one of them, nearly breaking at the possibility of another's pain on top of that.

I should have known better. I couldn't simply fuck my way through this problem. I couldn't scheme through it or power my way through it either. Somehow or other, I'd come to care about my London trio far too much. And now all of us might pay for it.

"Shall we get that dinner?" John said under his breath, a hint of amusement mingling with the strain in his voice. His hand found mine and squeezed it, making the ache inside me burrow deeper.

"I think we'd better, before someone wonders why we found this closet so interesting," I said, forcing a smile he couldn't see as much more my benefit as his.

We'd just returned to the waiting room after a lackluster meal when the doctor in charge of Sherlock's care appeared. John shot out of his chair in an instant.

"Your friend is recovering," the doctor said before he had to ask. "The drugs put a great strain in his body, and now he needs quiet and rest. He's awake at the moment—you can go in and see him, but one at a time, and no excitement, please."

John glanced at me as I got up, as if there was even any question of who'd see Sherlock first. "Go on," I said. "Take as long as you need."

I followed him and the doctor down the hall and stopped outside the room. The doctor strode off, and John ducked inside. As I leaned against the wall to wait, I heard him take a harsh breath.

Sherlock's voice was thin but dry as ever. "You don't look terribly happy to see me, John."

John let out a sputter of a laugh. "I am. For God's sake, I was afraid you were going to die. I—you still don't look that far from it."

"I suppose that's a reasonable assessment, considering I don't feel far from it either."

My mouth twitched at the observation even as my throat tightened.

There was the scrape of a chair leg as John must have sat down. "I really don't know what I'd do with myself without you, you know," he said, so softly I barely made out the words.

Silence stretched for several seconds. Then Sherlock said, just as quietly, "I'm sorry. They were stronger than me."

John's voice turned fierce. "No, they weren't. You're still here, aren't you? Just... please don't give them another opportunity to come at you."

"I have certainly gained wisdom from this experience." Sherlock paused. "I meant to clear their influence from my mind. I wasn't trying to... leave. That isn't what I'd want either."

There was so much affection in his tone even if he couldn't bring himself to state his feelings more plainly. I lowered my head, my hands clenching.

I wasn't sure I'd be able to live with myself if I lost another person who mattered to me because of my own carelessness, let alone someone who mattered so much to the other people in his life too. And regardless of wisdom gained, with the way the shrouded folk were ramping up their attacks, I might already be teetering on the edge of losing not just one but four.

Bash

The moment I opened the door for her, Jemma swept into my apartment like a hurricane. She stopped in the middle of the spartan living room and set her hands on her hips. "All right. Get all your things packed."

I stared at her for a moment, trying to read her mood in her taut expression. Her tone had been cool and matter-of-fact, but tension was woven through her body from feet to face like a bow stretched back to launch an arrow. I didn't think anyone would want to be in the way of that projectile when it flew.

"What's going on?" I asked, moving toward my bedroom where I had my small assortment of possessions that traveled with me. "What am I packing for?"

"Just get everything," Jemma said with a toss of her bright hair. "You won't be back here."

"Did something happen at the hospital? You said Sherlock came through all right." She'd said it in a voice oddly detached even for her, with barely any details other than the doctor was keeping him there for rest and observation for another day. Her monsters might have launched another attack since then.

Something flickered in her expression, so briefly I couldn't identify it. "He'll be fine. Not at his best for a little while, but—he survived. That's got nothing to do with this."

From the grit that flavored that last sentence, I had the feeling she wasn't being completely truthful. But I'd followed Jemma Moriarty an awful long way without always knowing exactly how or why she did the things she did, and she hadn't led us astray so far.

Most of my clothes were still in my suitcase from when I'd moved into the apartment a few weeks ago. I tossed in the few pieces that weren't already there, along with my electric razor and toothbrush, the western novel I was halfway through, my compact laptop, and… that was really about it. I already had my phone, wallet, and a pistol on me. A concealed pocket in the suitcase hid two other handguns.

"I'm sure you've got good reasons for this," I said as I rolled the suitcase into the living room. "I'd just appreciate knowing what they are. Or at least where we're going."

Jemma jerked her head toward the door. "I'll explain on the way. Come on."

Her car was parked outside. I tossed my suitcase in the back and got into the passenger seat. The engine roared as she took off like a shot. From the sugary smell that laced the air and the icing crumbs in the cup holder, she'd clearly downed a pastry or two on her way to get me.

Considering that we were in the middle of a mission that Jemma had appeared to be incredibly invested in, it didn't even occur to me that she might be moving me all the way out of London until she pulled up outside St. Pancras International train station. She turned off the engine and shifted in her seat to face me, pulling a leather men's wallet out of her purse.

"There's a credit card in here that you can use for a month or so and fifty thousand cash," she said in that same even voice. It might have actually gotten chilly now. "I want you to take the most direct route you can to Rome and wait for me there."

I took the wallet when she handed it to me, the leather smooth as my fingers closed around it. My stomach felt as if fingers had closed around it too. *A month or so.* "Are you staying here or going someplace else? How long do you expect it to take you to follow me?"

"I don't know yet. We'll see." She motioned to me with a flinty cast to her blue-gray eyes. "I know how to get in touch with you if I think it'll be longer than you can get by for on what I've given you."

She seemed to expect me to take off just like that. My entire body balked at the idea. Something about this scenario was totally wrong.

"This doesn't make sense," I said. "If you're staying here to take on Tillhouse and the commune he's allied with, you need me here with you. What the hell am I going to do in Rome?"

"Go shopping?" Jemma suggested with the most deadpan of humor. "Eat lots of pizza? I don't think you really got your fill last time."

"So this isn't a job. Mori, what the fuck is going on? You know I'll tackle whatever you need tackling. I've got to know what I'm dealing with first."

Jemma's mouth tightened. "It's a job because it's what I'm ordering you to do—what I'm paying you to do. Because in case you've forgotten, I *am* your employer and you are my employee, and part of your job description is going where I tell you to go without asking a shitload of questions. So get going."

She spoke as steadily before, raising her chin at a haughty angle that raised my hackles automatically. My jaw clenched. "I might work for you, but we've been working *together* for seven years. We've been doing a hell of a lot more than working together the last few weeks. Shouldn't—"

"There isn't anything I should have to do," Jemma snapped, interrupting. "Get the fuck out of the car, Bash, and do as you're told —or you can consider yourself fired."

I might have stormed off then, licking my wounds and full of frustration I knew better than to throw back at her, except I noticed her hands in that moment. The one she'd set on her purse lay there easily enough, but she'd tucked the other close to her thigh. It had balled into a fist so tight the tendons stood out in her wrist.

She wasn't just tense—she was upset. And there weren't a whole lot of things in the world that could rattle Jemma Moriarty. This wasn't some cool-headed business decision; it was purely emotional.

Knowing where she'd come from, having been there when we'd found Sherlock, the pieces clicked into place way later than they really should have. She'd just taken me so much by surprise, which had probably been part of her plan in the first place. She'd known if she'd told me to pack before she'd gotten to the apartment, I'd have had more time to think through what was going on.

"Jemma," I said, quietly and calmly, "I'm not going. You are going to drive me back to my apartment, and I'm going to bring my things back up there, and we're going to raze these communes to the ground side-by-side. If that means you fire me, fine. I'll still be right there doing what I can whether you're paying me or not."

Her eyes narrowed, and she swallowed audibly. "Bash, I'm not playing around—"

"I know. And I'm not either. You know me well enough to figure out that I'm not going to run for the hills just because the going has gotten a little tough, don't you? No matter how mean you make yourself be about it."

She grimaced and jerked around in her seat. "Damn it."

Someone honked behind us. We'd been parked in the drop-off area for a few minutes now. With a growl of frustration, Jemma switched the engine back on and pulled away from the curb.

"Did you actually think that was going to work?" I asked.

"It seemed worth a try. You really are stubborn as a stack of concrete blocks."

I laughed at the mangled simile. "I'm pretty sure that's part of the reason you like me."

"Most of the time," she grumbled.

"Do you want to talk about it?"

"Not particularly."

She drove in silence the rest of the way back to my apartment, and I let her keep her own council. When we got there, though, she made no move to get out, as if she figured we could leave it just at that. I looked over at her, at this spectacular, brilliant, gorgeous woman I'd somehow managed to intertwine my life with, and a pang shot through my chest.

She was all of those things, but she was also still a human being, even if she sometimes didn't quite believe that. Even if I sometimes forgot it too.

"Come up with me," I said. "Please."

She met my gaze with a little surprise. I didn't normally bother with a lot of politeness, but I'd figured it would get her attention.

"I *don't* really want to talk about it," she said.

"Fine. There are a few things I'd like to talk about. Will you listen to me?"

She wavered, and then a little of the tension seeped out of her posture. "Yeah, I can do that."

Jemma even looked a little apologetic as I hauled my suitcase back of the stairs to the fourth floor, because none of these old buildings in central London had elevators. I chucked it in my bedroom and returned to Jemma where she was standing in the middle of the living room. The urge came over me to just hold her, to take some of the weight she was obviously carrying, but I didn't think that was what she needed. She was trying so very fucking hard to be the strongest person in the world right now.

"I'll admit it, okay?" I said. "I'm sure your monsters have been working their voodoo on me too. I've had dreams—I've been more on edge—but I have it under control. If you think I'm crossing a line, you go right ahead and smack me one. Until then, I know you're not trying to send me away for *your* benefit, so it's obviously supposed to be for mine."

"You don't know for sure that they won't push you farther than you're prepared to handle sometime when I'm not around to intervene," Jemma said. "If we'd gotten to Sherlock even a half hour later, he'd probably be dead right now."

"So what? That's the risk we all decided to take when we signed on."

"But you didn't really understand that risk." She flung her hands out into the air. "I can tell you things until I'm blue in the face, but you can't really comprehend what the shrouded folk are like, what they're capable of, until you experience it. *I* didn't even know everything they were capable of, and I lived with the fiends for fourteen years. I meant to do this on my own when I was first planning things out. I shouldn't have gotten you as mixed up in it as I did. It's my responsibility, no one else's."

"Hey." I did walk right up to her then, setting my hands on her shoulders and catching her gaze. "You've warned us as much as you could every step of the way. I have the right to make whatever decision I want with that information. I want to be here with you. I don't give a fuck what kind of danger it puts me in. I'd rather die seeing out your mission than live eating pizza in Rome while you battle on alone here. Don't you know *that* by now?"

She gave me a crooked grin, but she didn't look away. "Maybe I did and I was just hoping I was wrong."

"Mori..." I let out a breath. Part of me wanted to tell her that while she wasn't getting rid of *me*, if she wanted me to cut her trio out of our operation, all she had to do was say the word and I'd make sure they never set another foot near her or the shrouded folk. The words halted halfway up my throat.

Making that offer would only turn me into a massive hypocrite. If I could believe I was going to do her more good than harm by sticking with her, I had to admit the three of them probably would too.

"The same applies to the others," I said, "if you were planning on trying to scare them off too. They've got the right to make their own informed decision — and I think it's pretty clear what decision they're set on."

Jemma lowered her head. "I didn't mean for things to turn out like this when we first came to London. I didn't mean for any of this to happen. It's gotten so... complicated."

"Maybe in some ways. In other ways, I've found it's letting me see how simple certain facts are." I paused, holding in the other words I'd wanted to say more than once, the words that had probably been true for years now if I'd let myself examine my emotions more closely.

If a man who'd barely known her a few months could say it, why the fuck couldn't I?

I eased a little closer, one of my hands coming up to tease into her hair. "I never said this before because I thought you wouldn't want to hear it, but maybe I should have trusted you more than that. You are the meaning in my life. You may as well make the sun rise. I don't want to exist if it's not beside you. You are *never* getting rid of me, because I love you too goddamned much to ever let you go."

She raised her eyes to stare at me. "Bash..."

I stroked my fingers over her fiery hair. "I mean it. I love you. God only knows how long I have."

Her voice came out low and hoarse. "I don't know if I'm ever going to be able to say that back to anyone. I think that part of me died when my sister did."

I smiled at her, at the woman I loved with every fiber of my being, and said with totally honesty. "I don't really give a damn whether you ever return the sentiment. I'll fight with you and rise or fall with you anyway. 'The course of true love never did run smooth.' Shakespeare was right about a few things. Let's just hope we get a little more rise before the fall."

CHAPTER TWENTY-ONE

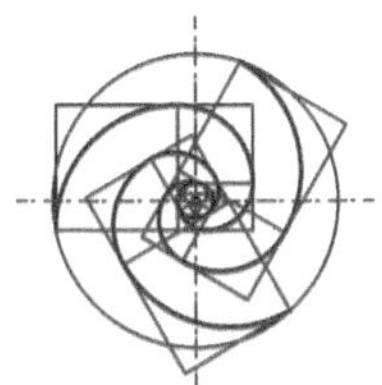

Jemma

The stretch of land around Tillhouse's country cottage was far too open for my liking. Just a broad field with overgrown grass dotted with wildflowers. I lingered for a moment in the shelter of the grove of trees on the other side of the worn wooden fence before clambering over and slipping across the yard.

In the light of a quarter moon, I could only make out the broader details of the small stone building. No vehicles were parked outside, and no light glinted in any of the windows. By all appearances, I shouldn't run into anyone during this operation. The cuff clamped around my thigh should stop any shrouded folk lingering around from noticing me too.

A twinge ran through the muscle there as I stopped near the side of the building. I'd been wearing the cuff more than I preferred the last few days—and my body obviously wasn't very happy about that fact either. But I couldn't risk tipping off Tillhouse or the local cultists before I had a new plan in place for taking them on.

I leaned against the cool stone and peered through the window beside me. Nothing but shadows waited on the other side. I stood still, my ears perked, but the only sound that reached me was the faint rustling of the night breeze over the grass.

Setting my feet carefully and quietly, I walked around to the back door. Even when the house's surroundings were totally open like they were here, people so often focused their security on the front door as if it were more vulnerable than the others.

Tillhouse intended to keep this place as impenetrable as he could, though. A glance through the window in the door showed me the red gleam of a light on an electronic security system. I could just barely make out the company name. It was one of those where you had to type in the right code to disarm it within a certain number of seconds or the authorities would be alerted.

Too bad for Tillhouse I'd come prepared. I slipped the device Bash had picked up for me out of my purse and kept it tucked under my arm as I went to work on the keyhole. It hadn't been hard to figure out what kind of security breaker I might need after I'd already penetrated Tillhouse's office and London apartment. Most people found one company they trusted and stuck with that one across the board.

It was those investigations that had led me here. I'd found a piece of mail addressed to a nearby PO Box that had fallen behind the sofa in his apartment. Tracking down the name it'd been addressed to had brought up the deed for this cottage. No actual person with that name appeared to exist, so it was almost certainly an alias. For some reason, Tillhouse didn't want anyone to easily connect him to this Yorkshire property.

I was hoping that reason would pay off with enough information to get me to my final goal.

The lock clicked over. I paused, adjusting my headset. "How does it look out there?" I asked under my breath.

Bash was staked out in our car a few miles down the road—the only road that had access to the lane that led to this cottage. "All clear so far," he said in my ear. "You know I'll alert you the second I see anything at all."

"Okay. I'm going in."

I eased open the door and darted across the tiled floor to the security panel. The plastic side popped open as the system beeped in warning of impending doom. I plugged the breaker device into a port there and jabbed a few buttons on its face.

The beeping stopped, the pane on the security panel going dark. I let out a sigh of relief and unplugged the device.

Even though the place was isolated and Tillhouse was a busy man, he must have made a point of getting out here on a fairly regular basis. The inside of the building had an airy flowery scent, not at all stuffy from being shut up. The floor turned to hardwood as I left the back hall, my shoes rasping softly over its surface.

Sherlock probably would have jumped at the chance to join this search. Breaking and entering was one of his favorite activities, as far as I could tell. I'd bet John would have been thrilled too. But Sherlock had still looked a little pale and shaky when I'd seen him this morning, and frankly, I hadn't needed any of them to pull this off.

It was a return to form—me and Bash working alone, making do with the extensive resources we'd accumulated for just this purpose. Perhaps it'd be nearly as difficult to put off the trio as it'd been with Bash, but that didn't mean I had to involve them in all of my activities. I could include them in moderation, keep them out of the riskier situations. Take a larger share of the responsibility that should have been completely mine.

I took a quick turn through the kitchen, not expecting the old-fashioned appliances and stylishly shabby wooden table to reveal much. Living rooms often proved more useful, but the one here didn't offer a single scrap of paper or telling photograph. Onward to the bedroom, then.

A faint scent reached my nose as I entered that small room— something flat and prickly like an herb left to dry too long. I couldn't place it exactly, but my pulse sped up at the smell with some memory beyond my consciousness. I peered through the darkened room intently as I started my search.

After several minutes, it appeared that initial spark of anticipation had been misleading. The wardrobe held only folded sweaters and polo shirts and a row of hanging slacks. Nothing was hidden under the mattress or behind the headboard. I was stepping back with a frown when my gaze caught on a scuffing on the floor just beneath the bed.

The varnish on the hardwood was worn down quite a bit by the legs of the bed—as if it'd regularly been pushed to the north side of the room. Bracing myself for the squeal of metal against wood, I positioned my hands and gave the whole frame a good shove.

It moved about a foot on my first attempt—far enough to reveal a line of slightly thicker shadow in the floor. There was a trap door under the bed. My lips curled into a grin. Jackpot.

I pushed the bed until it was far enough over that I could tug the trap door open. A cooler darkness waited below, laced with a stronger whiff of that herbal scent. I pulled out my phone and shone its light into the depths.

A ladder led down some eight feet into the cellar. Most of the floor was covered by a rug. A chair and table small enough to fit through the trap door stood in one corner, and a metal shelving unit that must have been constructed down there stood against the opposite wall.

Clutching my phone, I clambered down the ladder one-handed. The cool, prickly-smelling air closed around me.

Tillhouse wasn't likely to have communed with the shrouded folk down here. They hesitated to go anywhere underground, away from the sunlight. But opening the boxes on the shelf, I found a variety of artifacts he might have used in his own sort of worship elsewhere.

A blood-stained silk cloth told me he'd participated in the bloodletting ceremony at least once. He had several of the wood-and-wire tokens that the cult often sold to supernatural enthusiasts. Apparently the shrouded folk and their human devotees hadn't been upfront enough with the MP to inform him that those objects held no power or significance at all. He was a dupe just like the other collectors, just in a much more involved way.

That didn't endear Tillhouse to me at all, but it did make me even more nervous about what the shrouded folk might be planning to use him for.

The contents of the next box sent a jitter of excitement through me. He'd made notes about the commune—he'd even drawn maps. Maybe he'd duped the cult in turn. They wouldn't have approved of him having this information written down anywhere outside their domain.

One piece of paper, with multiple eraser marks as if he'd been drawing from memory, showed the layout of some twenty buildings in what must have been the commune itself. Another marked its spot about halfway between two town names I recognized from our Highlands investigations.

We had them. We knew exactly where they were now. It didn't matter if Tillhouse had gotten off the hook—when we destroyed his local base of support, he wouldn't matter anyway.

Unable to hold back a smile, I snapped pictures of both maps with my phone. Part of me wanted to get the hell out of that tight dark space as soon as possible, but my practical side won out. There were still a few more boxes I hadn't checked yet. I hadn't come all this way to rush through the job.

The next container held another assortment of knickknacks. I set that back in the spot where I'd found it and then reached for another. This one lifted in my hands with much less jostling.

It held a stack of papers. I shone my light over the sheets as I flipped through them. It only took a scan of the first few before a cold knot of horror began to swell in my gut.

The papers held notes about diversions of funds, about arranging access to supplies, about coordinating worship ceremonies... not just within the Highlands commune or between it and the other two here, but with ones noted down as *Colorado* and *Arizona*, *Granada* and *Luzern*.

If I was interpreting the figures here correctly, the shrouded folk here in Britain had turned Tillhouse into some sort of hub, connecting them with other pockets of the cult all across North America and Europe so they could collaborate more closely than they'd ever been able to from their isolated locations. Fuck.

While I'd been gathering power to take them on, they'd been gathering more power themselves, for who knew what awful purpose.

Nausea pooled in my stomach as I took photos of all the papers in the box for further examination. I climbed back up the ladder on legs that had gone slightly shaky. My head had just emerged from the level of the floor when Bash's voice crackled into my ear.

"—there? Jemma, if you don't answer me right now—"

"I'm here," I said quickly. "What's happening?" The cellar depths must have cut off the signal between us.

"A motorcycle went by about thirty seconds ago. I don't know for sure they're heading to your spot, but I'm not sure where else they'd be going. You'd better get out of there."

I swore under my breath and flipped the trap door closed. I couldn't leave the house looking like someone had poked around in it. With a massive heave, I hauled the bed back into its previous spot. Then I fled for the back door.

When I darted out into the yard, a headlight was just streaking around the bend by the stand of trees. I ran in the opposite direction so the building would hide any sight of me and threw myself down into the tall grass about fifty feet away.

The light stopped by the lane. In its hazy glow, I saw the helmeted figure on the bike turn their head as if scanning the area. Not Tillhouse, but someone he hired to keep a watch on the place? I might have been safer staying inside.

After a few minutes, the bike roared off again. My muscles went slack against the firm ground. I rubbed my eyes and patted my phone to make sure I hadn't lost it somehow in my rush to get out.

"Bash," I said into my headpiece, "we're going to need to round up and rally the trio."

Everything revolved around that commune in the Highlands. We had to take it down as swiftly and decisively as possible if we were going to actually put an end to this, and for that five minds and bodies would get us a lot farther than two.

CHAPTER TWENTY-TWO

John

I'm sorry, Mr. Holmes," the commander of the North Highland police said for what felt like the hundredth time. He folded his hands on his desk. "There isn't much we can do for you. I understand you have quite a reputation that proceeds you, but we still must follow proper procedure if we're to keep law and order."

Sherlock's lips pursed as if he'd bitten into something bitter, but he kept his voice as even as always. "I realize that. I simply wish to gain access to your historical records so that we might establish a pattern—"

"And I've told you that those records aren't available to the public. As much as you may have helped the police down in London and wherever else, you don't work for *us*, and none of your friends here do either. I'm afraid that's my final answer."

I could tell Sherlock was biting his tongue, but the drawn-out argument had clearly worn at him. He'd been more his usual color when we'd struck out on our mission this morning after a night in a nearby inn, but since then his face had started to gray. At the moment, it was unsettlingly close to the shade it'd been when he'd first gotten out of the hospital. My stomach twisted, and I resisted the urge to glare at the police commander for bringing my partner to that state.

Garrett had changed colors too—an angry flush, in his case. "Fuck," he muttered as we left the building and headed to the van where Jemma and Bash were waiting. The long-time criminals in our midst had figured it was better not to put on an appearance for the local constabulary.

"Do you think Tillhouse has some influence over them to make them so reluctant to share information?" I asked Sherlock. I'd never seen any body of law enforcement be so hesitant to help the great Sherlock Holmes.

"It could be. Or perhaps there are paranormal vibes in the air." He made a swishing gesture in the air and closed his hand when it trembled. "It could also simply be the northern Scottish dislike of most things English. Our history with them is not the most cordial, after all."

Well, yes, there was that too. Maybe the simplest explanation applied here.

Jemma took in our faces as we climbed into the van and wrinkled her nose. "No luck then?"

"The North Highland police force take the privacy of their records very seriously," Sherlock announced, and immediately sat down on one of the padded benches that lined the walls. It'd only been a few days. I wasn't sure his recovery was quite complete. He'd have denied any weakness, of course.

I sank down beside him, and Jemma shoved the box of donuts she'd bought on our way up toward us as if as a consolation prize, licking her fingers from her latest snack. Even though my gut was heavy, I picked up a salted caramel one. Sweets always seemed to sharpen her concentration. It could be worth a try.

The sticky caramel dissolved into the buttery dough as I chewed. I wasn't sure the sugar rush jostled loose any useful inspirations, but I did have to say that Jemma had excellent taste in desserts.

"Why don't we approach this the same way we did the place in the Lake District?" Bash asked where he'd turned around in the front passenger seat. His dark gaze passed over us, slightly narrowed as if he was annoyed the three of us hadn't already gotten to work on it. "Set them up for a crime, then send the police to catch them. It went off without a hitch before."

Jemma shook her head with a swish of her red waves across her shoulders. "We haven't gotten any bites for the feelers I put out, just as I suspected. We gambled on that first attempt to get Tillhouse arrested, and now they'll be on high alert. I doubt the commune will react to any bait we dangle—for now, they'll be sticking to people they're sure of."

"They might not need anything from the outside world," Sherlock put in. "With Tillhouse contributing extra supplies to whatever stores they usually kept, they may be keeping themselves set up for months at a time."

"That can't be the end of it," Garrett protested, but he hesitated when he looked at Sherlock. The overdose had clearly shaken him up too. He hadn't been quite his usual passionate, quick-tempered self since we'd discovered Sherlock unconscious. I got the impression he was afraid if he came on too strong about anything, he'd accidentally trigger some unknown sensitivity in the other man.

We'd all relied on Sherlock an awful lot over the past few years. He'd almost come to seem like a god of detection and deduction. That evening last week had been a horrible reminder of just how mortal and human the man was.

I'd flushed the rest of Sherlock's cocaine down the loo before he'd gotten home, and he hadn't complained, so I'd won at least that minor victory.

Jemma snatched up another donut and leaned back against the bench. "I still say we could take the slaughtering route. Toss some hydrochloric gas into the place. Electrocute them all. I don't care. Just get rid of them, and goodbye problem." She waved her hand.

I'd have liked to say I was horrified by her suggestion and by the fact that I suspected she honestly would have been fine with simply killing every inhabitant of the Highlands commune. The truth was, after the wrenching shock of finding Sherlock slumped in his bedroom and the agonizing hours waiting to find out if he'd even survive, I couldn't summon much if any compassion for the people who'd welcomed the creatures who'd tormented him.

No, a large part of me wouldn't mind seeing them tormented just as much in return.

I did still have a conscience, though. And there were practical concerns as well.

"You commit a mass murder, and there'll be a huge investigation," Garrett said. "I'd rather not stake my career on the police up here being too stupid to put together the evidence." He sighed and grabbed a donut for himself. "It's too bad these commune arseholes don't take the same route as plenty of other cults and mass suicide themselves."

At his words, an idea sparked in my head so abruptly and insistently that I looked at Sherlock, assuming if I'd thought of it, the same thing must have occurred to him even faster. But he was gazing toward the van's tinted window with an expression that was either thoughtful or dazed, depending on how generous you were being.

I waffled for a few seconds. If the possibility *hadn't* occurred to him, it probably wasn't a good one. I might be better off keeping my mouth shut. But maybe he hadn't even registered Garrett's remark, deep in his own contemplations.

If he and Garrett didn't have the best grip on themselves, then *someone* out of the three of us needed to keep us on track.

I wet my lips. "What if… what if we made it *look* like they did it to themselves? A mass suicide?"

Sherlock's head jerked around. He blinked at me. "Are you seriously suggesting we murder all those people?"

"No!" I said quickly, to Jemma's amused smirk. "I was thinking—we can't get them to take the bait for an actual crime. We're not sure we could convince the authorities to go after them if we simply make one up. But while the police force is hesitant to pin the locals with a crime, especially one we're presenting them with, they're a lot more likely to rush in if it's to help, aren't they? We find a way to call them in so they'll find the cultists unconscious but not yet dead—so there's still time for medical treatment."

Sherlock raised his eyebrows. "And how exactly would that play out, as you're seeing it?"

Under his scrutiny, my instinct was to bite my tongue. The idea was on the table now, and he still wasn't jumping on it, so how viable could it be?

Then I thought of the graying of his face and the tremble of his hand, and resolve hardened inside me. Jemma's voice from our talk in the hospital echoed up from my memory. *You're more than just his goddamned sidekick. How many people did you save before you even met him?*

She was right. I had to give myself more credit—starting right now. Sherlock didn't have all the answers, and I shouldn't expect him to. Maybe it was all that pressure that had pushed him over the edge, even if mainly from himself.

I glanced at Bash, who was watching me with evident curiosity. "You have military contacts, don't you? On the black market side of things? There are a couple of different gases that contain chemicals people could have taken by other means, and that would give us enough of a window between knocking the cultists out and them actually dying for a rescue team to come in and get to work."

Jemma's eyes glittered with eager understanding. "We set them up to look like they've done the whole suicide pact thing. Stick cups in their hands with residue of the same chemicals, that sort of thing. That's what you're thinking?"

Her approval gave me a renewed burst of confidence. "Exactly. We could drag out some of the most egregious evidence of their crimes too—we could plant some obvious things related to Tillhouse to tie him into the whole mess and, er, kill two birds with one stone."

Sherlock's gaze had gone distant again but in a more intent way. It shifted to me after a moment.

"You're sure about this, John?" he said. "The use of the gas wouldn't be evident? We wouldn't end up with a few dozen deaths on our hands?"

"This is my area of expertise," I reminded him. "I treated soldiers who'd inhaled one thing or another in the field. It's not a common tactic anymore, but it's still used frequently enough and in much more variety than before that we can pick our materials to suit our ends. Most of the modern forms disperse quite quickly. It won't be hard to time, either. We can alert the authorities before we even douse the place, wait until we know the emergency vehicles are close enough."

Jemma made a derisive sound as if she didn't much care whether we saved the people, which she probably didn't. I ignored that. Garrett had leaned forward on the bench, his usual energy back in his stance.

"And if there's enough evidence of suicide and their general insanity, no one's going to be looking for evidence that it was anything else. It'll be a simple case, cut and dried. They'd be able to say whatever they wanted about their supposed innocence and no one would believe it was an attack."

A slow, grim smile crept across Bash's face. "I have the contacts to get whatever we need," he said in his low voice. "Give me a list, and I can have it within a day or two."

That was barely any time at all. My heart skipped a beat at the thought of the course I was launching us into.

A hint of a smile had touched even Sherlock's face. He clapped me on the shoulder with a glint of emotion in his pale blue eyes that flared a little hotter than just admiration.

"It sounds as though you've hit on just the thing, my dear Watson. Let's get to work, then."

Even though the course I'd just set us on terrified me, I had to grin back.

CHAPTER TWENTY-THREE

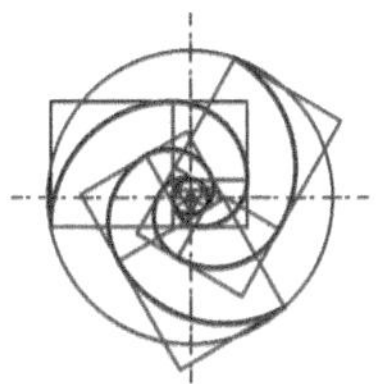

Jemma

Now that I'd tackled a few of these communes, I could predict where the guards would be stationed with great accuracy. Between my stealth, my night vision goggles, and the element of surprise, it didn't take me very long to dispatch each of them before they could give the slightest warning.

The last of the guards crumpled from my arms. I jerked back the syringe I'd used to dose him, shoved that into my bag, and arranged his body with a chemical-laced cup a few inches from his limp hand. Then I touched the button on my mic.

"They're all down," I murmured to the four men waiting in the van farther off. My gaze settled on the distant shadows up the slope between the trees where I knew the main commune lay, just beneath the mountain's peak. Some night creature rustled in the brush, and I tensed instinctively, the cool, fresh Highlands air rushing into my lungs.

It wouldn't be so fresh in a few minutes. "We're coming in with the gas," John said.

Bash's voice followed. "I'll meet up with you in the commune. All suited up and ready to go."

The two of us were going to be laying out our evidence in the settlement. I reached for my own gas mask, procured via one of Bash's ex-military contacts.

A pale shape swooped between the trees up ahead, and my pulse hiccupped. It was probably only an owl, but the image triggered too many associations deep in my brain. Olivia with her pale blond hair, spinning in a white dress. Olivia running between the stunted trees around the commune *we'd* called home.

A chill much sharper than the one in the air dug into my skin. Shit. I hadn't even thought.

My hand paused with my gas mask against my chest. "John," I whispered. "The dose you're going to be giving them all—it's enough to bring down an adult. What about the kids?"

The hesitation on the other end made my heart thud faster. When we were thinking of the cult is a bunch of sadistic demon worshippers, people who'd been indirectly responsible for Sherlock's near death, it was easy to forget the innocents among them. I had no idea how many children might be in this commune, but I had to assume there'd be at least a few. The shrouded folk demanded their sacrifices.

"I picked the levels carefully," the former doctor said. "It should be just enough to knock out a big guy, but not so much it'd do immediate damage even to someone small. They should be all right."

Should be. That wasn't enough of a guarantee for my liking. I yanked the mask up over my face and hurried through the forest toward the commune.

If anyone died tonight, it'd be the right people, at least this once.

A mist started streaming through the woods from where the guys must have parked. I picked up my pace, my breath muggy inside the gas mask. If this commune operated like the others I'd known did, I'd have a tiny window between the point when the adults had fallen and when the kids might be in danger. I just had to make it there in time.

Someone coughed in the distance. Someone else let out a shout of warning. It was too late for them. Most of the commune would have been sleeping at this hour, sucked even deeper under by the chemical cocktail, but the few who'd been on watch right in the settlement hadn't stood a chance either. The thumps of their bodies hitting the ground reached my ears a few seconds later.

I outright ran then, not bothering to worry about the crunch of twigs or the rattle of pebbles under my feet. The rough wooden buildings came into view, Bash's brawny form moving among them. He bent down to shift a body and place one of our doctored cups.

I raised a hand in acknowledgement as I dashed past him and spun around to scan the settlement's erratic layout. They tried to avoid any sort of pattern that might disturb the shrouded folk in planning the placement of their buildings, but they had other patterns of inhabitation. Usually the kids slept in one of the north buildings…

Or rather, under one of the north buildings. I threw open one door, scanned the floor, rushed to the next, and spotted the half-open trap door beside a bed where the two cultists on "parental" duty were sprawled in their beds.

The gas was already seeping through that opening into the dug-out basement room where the younger members of the cult spent their nights. The close quarters and uncomfortable surroundings gave them more motivation to harass each other for the shrouded folk's pleasure, and the door was always left partly open so the adults could hear if any conflict became too violent. Now it could spell their doom.

A small voice was coughing below, another whimpering. I dropped down by the door and leaned my face to the opening. I couldn't make out more than a few huddled outlines of small bodies, but the fragility of even that sight was enough to constrict my chest.

When the cops came, they'd be saved. They'd be placed with real families, families that wouldn't offer them up in bloody worship. I was saving them right now.

"Stay here," I told them in a voice muffled by my gas mask. "Don't come out until you hear footsteps coming in up here. Then you can yell for them to get you. Do you understand?"

"Yes," a thin voice murmured, and coughed again. "Who *are* you?"

I smiled behind the mask. "A guardian angel," I said, and shoved the trap door shut.

If the kids reported my arrival to the police or the emergency workers, they'd assume the gas had made them hallucinate an angel. That suited me just fine. I yanked a blanket off one of the slumped forms and spread it over the trap door to seal it even more from the gas. Then I jerked at the adults' bodies and set them up with their own drugged cups.

When I emerged, Bash was just coming out of another of the buildings, his face disguised by his mask. He motioned to his duffel bag, and I nodded. With swift efficiency, we unrolled the banner we'd made, the letters painted with chicken's blood, and strung it between two of the trees.

In honor of our great provider, Harvey Tillhouse, we offer up our spirits. We'd even pasted a photograph of the MP on there for good measure.

We raced through the commune, setting up the rest of the bodies, scattering our additional evidence. Notes of gratitude and more photos of the MP here. The tools of the blood-letting and other torture there. No one who walked through this place would be able to deny something deeply sick had caught hold of these people.

Sherlock's voice carried into my ear. "The police should be arriving in approximately five minutes. A couple of news teams too. Complete your work and hurry out of there."

I was just laying the last finishing touches around one of the fallen guards. We also wanted the reporters we'd tipped off to have plenty of sensational material to capture with their cameras. Tillhouse could deny all he wanted, but he couldn't stop the public commotion that would follow. No one was going to vote for a man known to associate with suicide cults.

I caught Bash's eye in a brief acknowledgement, and we took off in our respective directions. He was leaving with the guys, and I'd taken my own small car to arrive here a little ahead of them. We'd meet up back at the hotel in a couple hours.

The breeze was already dispersing the gas. It teased through my hair as I tugged off my mask. I held the bulky thing under my arm and loped on.

My thigh muscle was prickling beneath the gold cuff around my leg by the time I reached the little navy blue car. I grimaced as I hopped in, tossing my stuff on the passenger seat, but I didn't want to take the cuff off until I was well away.

The prickling expanded into an ache as I drove off down the narrow lane. The road wove back and forth through the trees down the mountain slope, with enough bumps that my stomach started to churn. I gripped the steering wheel tighter and focused on breathing evenly.

We'd done it. The commune would be shattered, Tillhouse's career would be upended—the shrouded folk couldn't possibly counteract the mess we'd just set in motion. And with that shattering, all those connections they'd been building in their international network would fray too.

The UK was clear now. Where to next? I'd have liked to tackle the fiends on my home ground now, but it'd be easier for the trio to follow me to continental Europe instead. If they were going to follow me. I'd kept in mind what Bash had said about letting them make their own decisions, and they *had* pulled this last desperate gambit off…

The pain in my thigh jabbed all the way to the bone. I flinched, my foot jerking against the gas pedal and nearly shooting me off the edge of a bend.

I managed to slam on the brake instead. The pain seared deeper as I caught my breath. It looked like I didn't have a choice about this anymore.

I yanked up the parking brake and fumbled with my pant leg as quickly as I could. The second I'd snapped the cuff off, the pain dissipated. I sagged back in the seat, waiting while the muscle gradually unclenched and the adrenaline of the moment washed away. My eyes drifted closed just for a moment.

When I opened them, a pale filmy figure was floating just beyond the windshield.

A startled squeak slipped from my throat before I could catch it. The shrouded one loomed closer, streaming its strips of faded cloth or skin or whatever that was. My hand reached for the gear shift instinctively, but if the fiend was going to try to fuck me over, maybe it was better if I wasn't operating a moving vehicle.

I rolled down the window, the cold night air flooding the car's interior. "What do you want?" I said in my flattest voice.

The shrouded one drifted around to the window, its dark void of a face even more impenetrable than the thickest shadows in the forest around us. Looking at it sent a shiver through my chest to my gut.

"You are the one that escaped the contract," it said in the dry, distant tone it shared with all the shrouded folk I'd heard speak.

I didn't see any point in denying that fact. "I am. What's your point?"

"I have a message for you. You will stop your interference, or your sister will die."

I stared at the thing until a hysterical laugh burst from my throat. "You're a little too late with that threat. My sister has been dead for years."

"She is not. She was taken but not consumed. And the one who took her wants you to stand down."

"Yeah, right. Forgive me if I don't believe you just because you said so. I'll keep doing whatever the hell I feel like doing, thank you very much." The shrouded folk didn't kidnap people and then keep them alive for years. They seared them down to their souls and swallowed them whole.

The gauzy figure wavered. A small wooden box appeared amid its flowing strips. "The one who has her sends proof. The decision is yours. Make one more move against our supporters, and there will be much blood spilled that you'd rather avoid."

It flung the box through the open window. The container dropped onto the passenger seat. When I glanced back toward the shrouded one, it had already vanished.

My stomach clenched tight. I reached for the box tentatively, half afraid simply touching it would hurt me somehow. But it felt like plain, solid wood.

I held it in front of me and popped the lid open. My whole body froze.

Lying on a bed of cotton in the middle of the box was a severed toe, so fresh it was leaking blood into the fabric.

CHAPTER TWENTY-FOUR

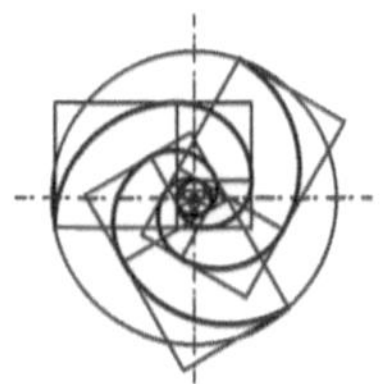

Jemma

There were too many goddamned birds twittering outside the window. I tugged the pane shut with a thump, even though it was a hot morning in the Highlands and the farmhouse Bash and I had rented didn't have any air conditioning.

After the window was closed, I gazed out it down the lane that wove between the two nearby slopes and disappeared beyond them. In the summer sunlight, the grass shone emerald green.

Bash came in with two cups of coffee. With only a brief glance away from the window, I leaned forward in the chair to accept one from him. I inhaled the steam before taking a sip. He'd put nearly the right amount of sugar in, enough that it cut through the bitterness to tingle over my tongue.

"No sign of it yet?" he said.

I shook my head. "Delivery is supposed to be by nine am. Someone's getting their ear shouted off if it doesn't turn up in ten minutes."

I made the comment wryly, but every part of my body was wound up in anticipation. I didn't know whether I was more afraid that the test would show I'd been told the truth or lied to. Both options were exceptionally horrific in their differing ways.

Bash lowered himself onto the edge of the bed next to my chair. "Assuming it's nothing—assuming it was just one of the monsters' sick mind games—you're thinking Spain next?"

"From the notes, it looks like the one commune there is larger than any we've dealt with here. I think it'd be a good next step."

"And we'd be looping your Londoners back in, or going it alone?"

"Do you really think they'd let me off the hook after all that?" I raised my eyebrows at him. "We're lucky we didn't get more argument about this little retreat."

I'd told the trio that I needed a few days of space to work out a few things before we continued our mission against the shrouded folk. Then I'd taken every possible caution to make sure the rental of this house *couldn't* be traced to me, just in case they got nosy, as had happened before. You couldn't be too careful with Sherlock Holmes in the mix.

At the growl of a motor, my back tensed even more than it already had been. A white car with a courier logo came into view on the lane. I stood up. My heart beat out a staccato rhythm at the base of my throat.

Bash got up too, watching me. "Do you want me there with you when you open it?"

I turned the idea over in my head as the car sped toward the house. "No. I think I'd like to be completely alone to work out what I'm going to make of the result before I have to figure out anything else."

He inclined his head and sat back down as I headed for the stairs.

The knock came just as I reached the pastel yellow front hall. I signed with the fake name I'd given the company and accepted the thick envelope with a stiff smile. Then I sat down in the living room and waited until the sound of the car's engine had faded away.

The envelope's seal tore easily. I slid the papers out, and my hand trembled. I'd sent away a little of my blood and a little from the severed toe the shrouded one had so graciously gifted me with to a

DNA testing facility with an extra fee for expedited results. As I looked down at the plain type printed across the stiff paper, my mouth went dry.

Analyzing the submitted samples… The results are conclusive to a high degree of validity… The two samples are a high enough match to indicate shared parentage.

My fingers twitched. The paper slipped from them. As it drifted to the floor, I stared at my empty hand.

No shrouded folk hallucination could have faked that result. A digit severed years ago wouldn't have been seeping fresh blood. My parents, if they were even still alive, couldn't have had any other children—I remembered my mother complaining about the hot flashes of her menopause a few years before I'd fled.

It was true. Olivia was alive. She was still *alive.* Oh my God.

A rush of adrenaline hit me, joy and anger mixed together. I hadn't failed her after all. I still had a chance to save her. What the hell had the folk being doing with her all this fucking time?

She hadn't been at my old commune when I'd gone back for her. Everyone there had believed she'd been taken in sacrifice. Which meant she hadn't been kept in this world. The shrouded folk had dragged her off to their own horrible realm. The tortures she must have endured—when I got my hands on their floating mummified asses—

The ring of my phone interrupted my silent tirade. I fished it out and frowned at the unknown number. It was the phone I'd used with the trio, but the caller wasn't in my contacts. I hesitated and then answered it.

"Hello?"

"Miss Moriarty." Sherlock's measured voice carried over the slightly staticky connection. "I'm glad you're up on this fine morning. Would you mind if I dropped in for a visit?"

He'd called from a different phone because he'd suspected I wouldn't answer if I'd known for sure it was him. I made a grimace he couldn't see. "I'm a little occupied at the moment, and I'm still out of town. Believe me, as soon as I'm ready to pick up the quest again, I'll let you know."

"Funny thing. I don't entirely believe you. You have been in the habit of giving us the slip. Which is why I'm currently at a hotel about a half hour's drive from that house you've taken up residence in. The Highlands rather appealed to you, did they?"

My chest tightened. He was up *here*? He knew where we were staying? Or perhaps it was a gambit to try to get the information out of me. "Nice try."

"Surely you have more faith in my investigative abilities than that by now." He rattled off the house's name and address. My stomach sank. "You employed some worthy tricks, Jemma, but I've come to know you quite well. No more sneaking off on us. Whatever you're occupied with, I want to hear about it—until those creatures we're battling are wiped off the face of this earth."

An admirable and absolutely frustrating sentiment. I closed my eyes and dragged in a slow breath.

This wasn't going to work. He wouldn't understand—the lengths I'd need to go to if I meant to rescue my sister—the trio wouldn't just stand by for that. They'd say I was taking things too far or that I shouldn't go it alone, blunder in with all their good intentions and ignorance of the shrouded folk... They'd insist on interfering like he was right now, and that could easily ruin everything. If I was going to reach Olivia, I had to keep a perfect balance of elements they barely comprehended.

I'd gotten back my chance to save my sister. To keep the promise I'd made to her ten years ago. To make up for leaving her behind to the tortures of our commune while I made my escape.

I couldn't put that mission at risk, not in the slightest way. If I failed her *again* because I couldn't keep these over-enthusiastic men at bay...

"John accompanied me, of course," Sherlock was saying into my silence. "Garrett should be up this evening for the weekend. That job of his does get in the way more often than not, as useful as I suppose it often is."

"So the gang will all be here," I said, willing my voice to stay steady. "Wonderful." *What could I do to make you leave again?*

Nothing. Not as long as they had working minds and bodies. Not as long as they believed I was still working on the most pressing problem the world had ever faced. If I could be sure of getting even a week without Sherlock tracking me down all over again… But he was far too stubborn for that, wasn't he? Far too stubborn, far too brilliant, and now he'd had far too much time to observe my habits in ways I couldn't be fully aware of.

The answer rose up in my head with cold certainty. My throat constricted, but I didn't shy away from the thought. I studied it in its brutal clarity, the gears in my mind already whirring with their usual sharp precision.

Yes. It could be so very simple. The thought made me sick, but the possibility of losing Olivia all over again was far worse.

She came before anyone and anything. That was all there was to it.

"All right," I said with feigned resignation. "You found me. I'm not really set up for entertaining here. Why don't I come to you?"

When I got off the phone, I went to the bottom of the stairs and called up to Bash. He appeared in an instant, his expression taut.

"The shrouded folk have her," I said simply. "I'm going to bring her back. But to make sure I actually get to do that, we need to accomplish one thing first."

"What exactly is it you wanted to show me up here?" Sherlock said, peering across the mountain slope.

I nudged him onward along the narrow rocky path. Our shoes rasped against the stone. "It's just a little farther. I'm not entirely sure what to make of it. It's difficult to explain without you seeing it."

"But you didn't want John and Garrett making their own observations?"

"They can come take a look later if you think it's a good idea. For now I'd like your perceptions only, without any distractions."

An appeal to ego always smoothed over a request with Sherlock. I could tell he didn't believe I'd told him the whole story, but he'd gone along with my somewhat strange invitation to see where it led anyway.

Because he didn't believe it could lead anywhere all that awful. Because he trusted that my intentions were good even when I was dissembling. That was going to be his biggest mistake.

I resisted the urge to ball my hands and strode on toward the spot I'd identified yesterday. The mountainside fell away with a nearly sheer drop at our right, gray scree spotted with tufts of grass and weeds.

It felt as if we'd left summer behind this high up. The wind whipped past me with a chilling bite. I didn't let myself shiver.

Bash was off doing his part. I'd timed the walk as he and I had discussed. If I looked back the way we'd come, if I peered for the vehicle and the figures that should be emerging from it right now, Sherlock would definitely notice that. I couldn't afford to give the game away, so I kept my gaze trained on the path ahead. On the man ahead of me who I admired so much my chest stung with it right now.

I couldn't think about the passion I'd woken in him and how delighted he'd been to provoke as much pleasure in me. I couldn't think about the thrill of matching wits with him time and time again. None of that matter. Not when Olivia was waiting for me.

My pulse was thumping hard and heavy. I kept my posture straight even though it wanted to hunch against the awful task I was about to complete.

This was necessary. It was all necessary, from the act itself to Bash bringing John and Garrett as distant witnesses. After all this time when she must have thought I'd abandoned her, I owed it to Olivia to give her everything I could.

Even if it meant sacrificing everything new and wonderful I'd discovered in myself in the last few months.

We'd reached the spot. I knew from the knob of rock that jutted from the ground beside the path. I stopped and pointed toward an imaginary object down the slope. "There. Can you see it? It's small, so it's hard to make out."

Sherlock frowned and eased closer to the edge. I watched his feet, his stance. He bent over to peer in the direction I'd pointed. "Can you give me a better idea what you're looking at?"

A way out. A severing as utter as the one that sliced my sister's toe from her foot.

One last thread of resistance trembled through me. I gritted my teeth against it. Then I smacked my hand into Sherlock's back and shoved as hard as I could down the sheer treacherous drop.

THE VALLEY OF FLAMES

MORIARTY'S MEN #4

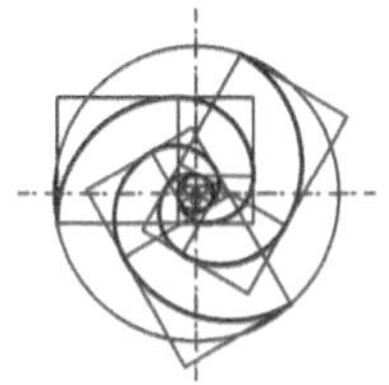

CHAPTER ONE

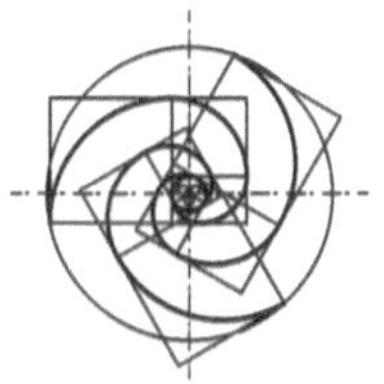

Jemma

T he hotel suite was perfectly still, perfectly silent. As it should be, considering I'd booked every room on this floor, the one below, and the one above, and left strict instructions that staff were to stay clear unless called for. Ensuring that level of service and discretion hadn't been cheap, but what had I spent all this time building my wealth for if not this moment?

This moment when I might not only get to avenge my sister but also save her.

The posh Tokyo executive hotel held all dark wood, black leather, and tan walls, soothingly refined. It was almost a shame pushing all the living room furniture off to the sides in a jumble to clear the densely woven carpet in the middle.

Bash let out a grunt as he heaved the sofa the rest of the way over, the ample muscles in his shoulders bulging. My right-hand man eyed the space we'd opened up skeptically. "Are you sure you wouldn't be more comfortable on the bed?"

"The point isn't for me to be *comfortable*." I gave the coffee table one last shove for good measure. "Ideally my body should remain on as level a surface as possible. Even a firm mattress will have some give. Anyway, I won't be conscious to care. Why shouldn't you have a proper place to sleep?"

Bash's expression turned even more incredulous when he raised his light green eyes to stare at me. "As if I'm going to sleep while you're wandering around in whatever hell those monsters live in."

"It might take me a while," I said. "You'll need to rest sometime. Besides, if something goes wrong for me, there won't be anything you can do about it. I'll be fighting my own battles. Your most important job is making sure no one disturbs me on this plane of existence."

"And reapply the dressing you talked about as necessary."

I shrugged. "It'll fade slowly. Maybe you shouldn't take a full nine hours all at once, but a few hours won't be critical. The ceremonial preparations are complicated to set up, but once they're in place, there's not much else to do."

Satisfied with the state of the room, I went back to the laptop I'd left open on the marble counter in the kitchenette to check the courier's website. "All we need is for that last delivery to get to us... And it should be here within the hour, or someone will be getting a phone call they won't enjoy."

"I'm sure it'll turn up." Bash sat himself down on one of the stools along the counter and ran his hand over the black stubble shading his tan scalp. He nodded to the computer. "Have you looked up the UK news to see—"

"No," I said, cutting him off. "I know what I intended. I don't need some outside account of the incident."

If my plans in Scotland hadn't fulfilled my intentions accurately, I couldn't do anything about that fact now. What happened to Sherlock and the rest of the London trio—the three crime-fighters I'd somehow ended up letting into my life, my mission, and to some extent my heart—didn't matter anymore. It *couldn't* matter, not when Olivia's life might hang in the balance.

I'd failed my little sister once before. I'd thought she'd died because I hadn't come back for her at our family's commune quickly enough, because I hadn't been able to escape with her in the first place. She'd deserved so much better… She deserved every particle of attention and concern I had in me until I brought her safely home.

My tongue slid against the backs of my teeth with the urge to suck on a sugar cube. The sweetness might have brought a tiny bit of comfort, but I didn't know how it might affect the ceremony ahead.

"How are you going to look for your sister once you're in that place?" Bash asked. "You're going to be on their turf—what's to stop them from capturing you however they captured her?"

"I'll figure it out once I'm there. She's my sister—we have a connection. It shouldn't be too difficult." I hoped. I'd never ventured into the realm of the shrouded folk before, and the few respected cult elders who'd gotten to make that journey once or twice had stayed tight-lipped about their exclusive experience. I didn't know what the place even looked like.

To tell the truth, I wasn't entirely certain that the ritual I was preparing was a perfect match for the ones I'd witnessed parts of in childhood. It'd been a long time. If my memory had failed me, I'd just have to track down some cult member who could give me the proper instructions with the right motivation.

"And the rules the shrouded folk follow when it comes to human beings should still apply whatever plane we're on," I added. "They can attack me, but they can't lay any claim over my soul without my agreement."

Bash grimaced. "And I'm supposed to be okay with the idea of them attacking you?"

I gave him a fond if slightly exasperated look. The ex-military sniper turned hitman had been my closest companion for the last several years—employee, friend, and recently lover. Though we didn't talk about feelings often, I knew how deep his devotion to me ran. Since our relationship had taken a more intimate turn, though, this protective streak had been coming out more and more often.

"You should know better than anyone that I can defend myself just fine," I said.

"These creatures don't fight fair."

"And neither do I." I reached out to grasp his hand on the countertop. "I know the idea of all these supernatural horrors is pretty new for you. I know you'd come with me, guns blazing, if you could. But I need you here, and I know these fiends well enough to maneuver around them. I won't be looking for a fight. As soon as I've got my sister, I'm getting out of there as quickly as I can."

"I'll do everything you've asked me to do," Bash muttered. "I still don't like that you have to take this step at all."

"But I do have to. You *understand* that, don't you?" I squeezed his fingers. "You took a big risk to save your younger siblings way back when. And they weren't in anywhere near the kind of danger Olivia is. She must have already endured so much... I can't leave her in their clutches one second longer than I can avoid."

Bash's face tensed. For a second I was worried I'd managed to offend him by mentioning his younger brother and sister. It'd been a rare moment of openness when he'd told me about how he'd brought them to live with their grandparents away from their abusive dad when he was only thirteen. He didn't generally like to talk about his childhood.

He exhaled slowly and shifted into his Shakespeare-quoting voice with its hint of irony. "'Truth is truth to the end of reckoning.' You've got me there."

"Imagine what the Bard would have made of this storyline."

"It'd have given him plenty of material, that's for sure." Bash managed a smile. "I'm still hoping it'll turn out to be a comedy rather than a tragedy."

"Well, there's not much the shrouded folk hate more than being laughed at."

Bash's phone vibrated in his pocket with a faint hum. He took it out. "Yes, he can come on up." His amusement faded as he put the phone away. "That last delivery is here."

My pulse skipped a beat. For all I'd talked to him with total confidence, I was nervous about this trip too. But there was no delaying it.

I shut the laptop. "I'll get the rest of the supplies."

As Bash accepted the box from the delivery guy at the door, I spread a spotless white sheet on the living room floor. Then I turned the air conditioning up so the suite would be appropriately cool by the time everything else was ready.

Bash brought the box over to the kitchen. I'd already gotten out a large glass serving bowl. I plopped in the softened beeswax and hemp oil I'd already acquired, tossed in a baggie of lavender, and dug into the box for the other herbs that would go into this concoction.

The final mixture let off a pungent, almost chemical smell as I mashed the dried leaves into the waxy oil with a pestle. The scent brought me back more than a decade to watching the elders prepare an honoree for the journey to the realm of the fiends they all worshipped. The man had swayed in the erratic movements meant to honor the shrouded folk, a dreamy smile on his face, as if he couldn't imagine anything more wonderful than visiting the source of the monsters that demanded blood and devoured children's souls.

I would have been one of those childhood sacrifices if I hadn't made a side deal to allow my escape. I had no idea how the shrouded folk had ended up taking Olivia. Fifteen was their preferred age to fully enjoy the energy we gave off, and she'd have only been thirteen when I'd come back three years later to rescue her. I'd always assumed the fiend who'd been eyeing me had devoured her early out of anger at my disappearance. But the shrouded one who'd brought me evidence that she was still alive had said she'd been "taken but not consumed."

They'd played that card to stop my efforts at destroying their base of human support in this world. I still intended to see them cut off from humankind if I possibly could. But I had to get Olivia back first, so that she didn't pay for my defiance any more than she already had.

I added a little more of a couple of the herbs until I felt I'd gotten the balance just right. Then I scooped about half of the mixture into another bowl and put the original one into the fridge.

"You have the pills?" I said, even though I'd already double-checked a couple hours ago.

Bash patted his shirt pocket. "Right here."

"I need to shower, and then we can get started."

I washed every inch of my body and hair with a bar of plain soap and rinsed myself thoroughly with cool water. My hair still hung damp against my shoulders when I came back into the living room naked. The broad windows on either side of the southeastern corner were bare, letting in all the sun, but I'd chosen this suite specifically because there was no neighboring building tall enough to look straight inside. If someone farther afield took a gander with binoculars, they'd get an interesting show.

Bash's gaze traveled over my body, leaving a tingle of heat in its wake. I knew how good his body could feel against mine, but that was one more distraction I had to put out of my head.

I brought the bowl of herbs, wax, and oil over to the sheet and knelt down on it. With broad swipes, I smeared the mixture into the fabric. Then I painted my skin with it, starting with my feet and working my way up. Bash took a glob to coat my back, his touch steady but gentle.

The cool air chilled my damp skin. I worked the paste into my hair and then finally wiped it across my face, not sparing even my eyelids or my lips. The pungent stink clogged my nose. My stomach lurched, and I swallowed down the bile that started to rise up my throat.

"You'll know the effect is fading if you can see spots of bare skin on my face or arms," I said. "The sheet will stop the rest from evaporating. When you notice any skin that's not shiny with the mixture anymore, just dab some of the leftovers in the fridge there."

"Now you take the pill and that's it?" Bash said.

"Everything we've done sets the atmosphere. As I go into the trance, I'll focus my mind on the shrouded folk. That should take me past the final hurdle."

I held out my hand, and he gave me the pill. It was so small I could swallow it without any water. Then I sat down on the sheet and began to methodically fold it around my legs and torso, with a twist here and a contrasting angle there, leaving no pattern to the creases. The shrouded folk abhorred any kind of mathematical arrangement.

By the time I reached my shoulders, the pill's effects were seeping through my mind. My thoughts were fogging, drifting aimlessly and colliding at random. I lay back with my head to the brightest strip of sunlight and closed my eyes.

"I'll be back as soon as I can," I managed to mumble.

My awareness of the room faded away into the haze of the drug and the herbal stench flooding my lungs. I drew up memory after memory of the commune I'd grown up in, the ashy rotten scent of the shrouded folk, the boy I'd seen them ravage in a blaze of light—on and on, sinking deeper and deeper into each moment—

With a lurch, my consciousness plunged down into a thicker darkness. My lips parted with a scream that didn't make it past my throat. Light flared through my closed eyelids, and my back hit solid ground with a jolt that radiated along my spine. The herbal smell fell away, replaced by that familiar odor of desiccated rot.

My breath caught in my throat as I warily opened my eyes. I'd arrived in the realm of the shrouded folk.

Bash

As a man of action, watching the woman I loved lying pale and motionless on the floor, knowing she was facing the most difficult trial of her life and not being able to lift a finger to help her—there was no word for it other than "agony."

I had a clear view of Jemma's whole sheet-wrapped body where I'd stationed myself on the sofa. For the first hour after she'd faded away, I hadn't been able to do much more than mark each shallow breath. They came so far apart, no more than a few each minute, and with so little rise to her chest, it'd have been easy to mistake her for dead. The greenish pallor her herbal concoction had given to her face and arms only added to that impression.

It took all my self-control not to prowl around her as if that would protect her more than I already was, or worse, to try to shake her awake. To see those brilliant gray eyes gleaming at me the way they were meant to. To know the demonic creatures she was tangling with hadn't wrenched her away from me.

She'd said it could take days. I was starting to wonder how *I* was going to survive that long.

After a while, I forced myself to go over to the kitchen counter. I could still keep an eye on her for any sudden changes from the stool there, but poking away at the computer might make the time pass faster.

I meant to use that time somewhat productively, checking up on her various business ventures and looking into arrangements for other equipment we might need. If she came out of that hellish realm with her sister—no, *when* she did, I corrected myself; this was Jemma Moriarty I was thinking about—I had to assume we'd continue our campaign against the communes that allowed the shrouded folk access to the human world in the first place.

Instead, my fingers took on a mind of their own and typed the name "Sherlock Holmes" into the search field.

Unsurprisingly, a major incident involving one of the world's foremost criminal investigators hadn't gone unreported. Several pages of results came up discussing the "horrific fall" or in one case where the headline writer got a little too clever with his alliteration, the "tragic tumble" of London's famous consulting detective. I clicked through to a couple articles that looked less on the sensationalistic side.

It appeared Sherlock's colleagues had remained tight-lipped. Even though they knew perfectly well who'd pushed the man down that cliff, the articles didn't make any reference to Jemma, only noted that investigations were in progress. When it came to the detective himself, the reports were similarly vague. He was in a Scottish hospital receiving "the highest standard of care," but no one seemed to know how critical his condition was or whether his life was on the line.

He couldn't have been feeling too spry after that fall, no matter how Jemma had positioned it.

The lack of news wasn't exactly satisfying. I skimmed through a few more accounts before accepting I wasn't finding out any more than that, and then gave up.

My fingers hovered over the keyboard for a few seconds in indecision. Jemma's comment from this morning had been running through my mind ever since she'd made it. She was off attempting to rescue her little sister. Maybe that made this the perfect time to check in on my own family.

I didn't search for information on my siblings very often. Even from afar, even just observing through a computer screen, I couldn't quite shake the sense that the life I'd made for myself might somehow tarnish theirs.

Seventeen years ago, when I'd gotten them out of our parents' house, I'd been a hero to them. That was the last time I'd seen them face-to-face. Since then, I'd become a killer and a criminal. I'd made the choices that had felt right to me in the moment, and I wouldn't have traded my partnership with Jemma for anything, but no one would have looked at me and seen anything but a villain now.

They were doing well for themselves, as far as I could tell from the public record. My brother Samuel had become manager of the hardware store he worked at. A couple weeks ago, he'd completed a marathon. It looked as though he was still with the same girlfriend who'd been showing up next to him in social media photographs for a few years now.

My sister Charlotte had finished her MA in social work this past spring. She was already knee-deep in initiatives to support abused children. Children like the kid she'd been. Now *that* was a real hero.

I considered her in the slightly out-of-focus photo, her black hair falling in tight braids around her smiling face, and tried to picture how she'd react to seeing me again. Even without knowing what I'd been through and what I'd done, I had no illusions about myself. Something would show in my expressions, in the way I carried myself. You couldn't hide certain types of history.

Would she see the big brother who'd saved her… or a man with too many similarities to the aggressive pricks she was fighting now? I was nothing like our father, but most ordinary people wouldn't differentiate between the varying ways we used violence to accomplish our ends.

The tension that had already been churning in my stomach expanded. I shut the laptop and pushed it away.

I did eventually need to eat something, or I wouldn't be much use to Jemma when she actually needed me. We had supplies for when she came to that would do in a pinch, but I'd rather not make any more noise in here than I needed to. Instead, I went down to a room on the floor beneath our main base of operations at the opposite end of the building, so there'd be as little chance as possible of the sound disturbing her, and ordered room service.

To my surprise, the concierge with whom Jemma had made the arrangements for our stay brought the cart up rather than one of the regular restaurant staff. He lingered in the hall after he'd set the tray with my meal on the room's table. His head dipped in a quick bow.

"If there's anything else I can do for you or your associate, please let me know. I hope your other colleagues have not run into any issues?"

I guessed I couldn't blame him for wondering where the hell the other people who should be occupying all the rooms we'd booked were. But we'd picked this city partly because the Japanese were a lot less likely to really pry than if we'd found some spot in, say, America.

"We have some setting up to do," I said vaguely. "No problems at all. If there's anything else we need, we'll be sure to let you know."

He bobbed his head again and slipped away. As long as we weren't disturbing any other guests or making an obvious mess, I doubted he'd intrude.

As soon as he'd disappeared into the elevator, I carried my meal up the other room. Seeing Jemma in her prone state took away any hunger that might have developed at the rich smell of the curried beef. I forced the food down as quickly as I could.

The sun was starting to sink low on the other side of the hotel. I walked into the waning light streaking through the windows to study Jemma up close.

Her concoction still shone on her face and her arms where she'd crossed them over the folds of the sheet. Her eyelids didn't so much as twitch. I suspected if I reached down, she'd be cold to the touch. With the way she'd cranked the air conditioning, I'd had to put on a sweater to avoid being chilled.

As I turned to go back to the sofa, the air between the living room and the kitchenette rippled with a wavering light. I froze, my hand leaping instinctively to the gun tucked into my jeans, but in a matter of seconds it was obvious a gun wasn't going to do anything against this uninvited visitor.

The strange light shifted into a more defined form: a humanoid figure wrapped in strips of thin, bleached fabric, only fathomless shadow where a face should have been. It didn't completely solidify but kept a filmy quality, the edge of the counter showing through its body.

I let my hand drop from the gun, but my nerves stayed on high alert. I'd never seen one of Jemma's monsters as anything more than a flash or a blur before, but I recognized it from her descriptions. I was staring at one of the shrouded folk.

One of the fiends she was attempting to trounce on their own territory right now.

A thin, faintly rotten scent tickled my nose. I folded my arms over my chest, staying between Jemma and the thing, and scowled. "Get the hell out of here. You've got no business with us."

The creature's voice came out in a dull rasp. "I wouldn't be so sure about that."

"You're not even supposed to be showing yourself to me, are you? How many rules are you breaking right now?"

"Exceptions may be made." The shrouded one drifted a foot closer, and my stance tensed all over again. If Jemma had been wearing that protective cuff of hers—but she couldn't have slipped into the shrouded realm while she was shielded from them.

They'd attacked her before when she'd broken her contract with the one monster. Was this thing going to make another go of that?

If it did, how the fuck could I stop it?

Jemma had talked about mathematical patterns repulsing the fiends. If worst came to worst, I guessed I could start shouting out my times tables.

"I repeat, get the hell out," I said in as threatening a voice as I could muster. I didn't want to make any literal threats in case those turned out to be only a bluff.

The shrouded one turned its shadowy "face" toward me. "The bloodling that was ours isn't here."

Couldn't it see Jemma lying in the living room? Or—could it only identify her from its sense of her spirit, the part of her that had traveled across the realms? A flicker of relief ran through me.

"No," I said. "She isn't. And I'm not going to give you anything."

"She is acting against us again. We warned her."

"She isn't touching your precious communes. That was the deal you made with her—leave them alone, and you'd leave her sister alone."

The fabric strips billowed farther out, and the scent of it thickened. "Where has she gone without you, then?"

As if I'd tell it. "If she wants you to know, she'll pass on the message."

It was silent for a long moment. The sense prickled over my skin that it was studying me. Then it said, in the same dull voice, "You could save her."

The prickling shot straight through my chest with a jolt of anxiety. "Save her from what?"

"She is walking a dangerous road. Do you really think she can challenge all of us and survive? But perhaps if you offered yourself in exchange, whatever she is attempting, we will let her return unharmed."

"You'd make a contract with me, huh?" I said with purposeful skepticism, but my heart had leapt. I'd always known I might die at Jemma's side. If I could give my life to ensure she kept hers, even if it was in a deal with some monster rather than a bullet I hadn't dodged, I'd take that offer without hesitation.

"Exactly. What do you think, bloodling? Are you her champion or are you not?"

The question raised my hackles, but I kept my mouth shut. Its use of the term "bloodling" only emphasized the unearthliness of the creature in front of me.

Jemma had warned me, not that long ago, never to negotiate with the shrouded folk. Not to believe anything they said or offered. No matter what they proposed, they would twist a situation to their own interests.

I wanted to fight for her, fight alongside her. I didn't want to risk giving my life up for nothing. Maybe I'd dealt with all kinds of human garbage over the years, but I had to admit I didn't know how to read the creature in front of me.

Jemma wouldn't want me to agree to anything this thing suggested. If I was acting *for* her, the only thing I could do was refuse, no matter how much I wished there really was some way I could ensure her safety.

"Her champion commits only to her," I said firmly. "I'm not drawing up any contracts with you or your friends. So I'll tell you one more time—get out of here."

"You can always change your mind," the shrouded one murmured, but it did, finally, fade away.

The hairs on the back of my neck still stood on end. I wasn't even sure the thing had left or whether it might be watching me unseen. Fucking freaks.

My fingers itched to assemble one of Jemma's spiral sequences on the nearby surfaces, but I didn't know if that would disrupt her journey, and besides, I had no idea how to construct one properly. As I hesitated, another thought popped into my head.

Mathematical patterns. Order and rhythm. Like the beats of Shakespearean dialogue, set to his favorite iambic pentameter.

A small smile crossed my lips. I wasn't sure this would have much effect, but it'd make me feel better doing *something*, anyway.

The bedroom's TV offered a wide selection of on-demand movies. I scanned through them until I found one of the more faithful Shakespearean adaptations. With a click, I set it playing, leaving the volume high enough to be audible but not so loud it would reach all the way to the living room.

Let's see if the fiends wanted to pay any more calls while the Bard's poetry filled the air.

CHAPTER THREE

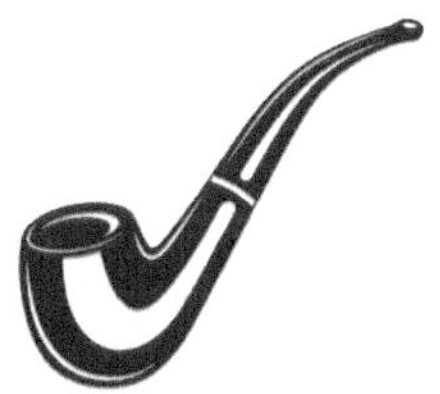

Sherlock

Waking up to the bright lights and insistent beep of a hospital room was becoming an uncomfortably familiar experience. I furrowed my brow at the stark white ceiling above me, crisply clean air filling my nose, and shifted on the firm mattress.

John's face jerked into view in an instant, his eyes wide and his mouth flying open with a hasty, "Stay still."

By the time he'd given the warning, I'd already determined its validity for myself. The second I'd adjusted my position, a flare of pain had shot down my back, up my neck, and through my shoulders as well. I clenched my teeth against the dull throbbing that continued to radiate through my body like an echo.

I could take stock to some extent while lying prone. Though sore, my awareness reached every part of my body—nothing was numbed or paralyzed. A more distant ache surrounded my right forearm, which was encased in a cast from the hand to just above the elbow. I'd been attached to a dispenser of some sort of painkiller, but one obviously not strong enough to completely offset my injuries.

Injuries. Because I wasn't here through my own imprudence this time. I'd been… walking along a mountain path with Jemma. She'd wanted to show me something. That was the most recent memory I could dredge up, and the edges of it were blurred.

"Sherlock?" John said tentatively, and it occurred to me that given the state of my body, he might have significant concerns about my mind.

"I believe that is still my name, unless someone has changed it on me," I said. Talking set off a small but sharp jabbing through my ribs. I took a slow breath before continuing. "How long have I been unconscious?"

Relief loosened only a little of the worry on my friend and partner's face. "Two days. They kept you in an induced coma for the first stretch until they were sure they'd treated all your injuries."

Another voice carried from farther across the room—the low, blunt tone characteristic of Detective Inspector Garrett Lestrade. "You survived that murder attempt rather well, all things considered. The fractured arm was the worst of it." He stepped forward to come into view, his boyish face darkened by a stormy expression.

"Murder attempt," I repeated. Was that really what had happened? The words didn't sound right.

"How much do you remember?" John asked in his gentle way. It wasn't hard to see how he'd done well with his patients before the war had left him too shaky for a surgeon's work.

I frowned. "Walking in the mountains. Jemma said there was something important I should see. The rest…"

"She shoved you off the path down a cliff," Garrett broke in when I trailed off. "As casual as anything, like she pushed people to their doom every other day." Beneath the hostility in his voice, I caught a note of confusion. Which was understandable, because that was the primary emotion his suggestion stirred up in me.

"Jemma Moriarty tried to kill me," I said, trying out the words. They jostled loose a few more pieces of memory. A hand on my back, a heave of propulsion. A flash of panic as I'd stumbled forward, my feet losing purchase as the ground slanted sharply downward. The thought that I might be about to die.

I'd been careless. I'd assumed Jemma posed no threat, and so I hadn't been keeping a particularly close eye on her movements, despite the precariousness of the path.

On the other hand... I glanced down at my aching but intact body again with a renewed wave of resistance to the idea. Jemma Moriarty might have remained a mystery in certain ways, but I'd come to know her quite well during the time we'd spent together. There'd been no denying how brilliant she was, how skilled at strategizing, at times to the point of topping my own considerable abilities. Nor had she made any secret of how ruthless she was willing to be if the situation called for it.

If the woman had truly wanted to kill me, surely I would be dead? It seemed to me it'd take an enormous amount of luck for even an amateur to fail to cause fatal damage with that kind of fall, and Jemma was anything but.

"We both saw it," John said. He rested his hand on my unbroken arm. "If we'd been closer, maybe we could have caught her—but our first priority had to be getting you help as quickly as possible, of course."

"Of course." Another source of confusion prodded me. "How did the two of you happen to be there? Jemma made a point of wanting to discuss the supposed matter of concern with me alone before bringing anyone else into it." I'd made no mention of the journey I was taking with her to either of my colleagues when I'd left the hotel.

Garrett paced out of my range of sight and back into it. "Moran came and got us, told us Jemma had been acting strange, that he was worried about what she might do. He drove us out there. And then disappeared after he saw what she'd done—couldn't stick around to deal with the consequences."

"He went with her." The answer was perfectly obvious to me. As was the flaw in his story. "Jemma's man—the man who was ready to kill us on her behalf mere weeks ago, who has shown nothing but total devotion to her—supposedly became so concerned about her apparent instability that he turned to the two of you rather than addressing it with her?"

John's mouth opened and closed again. A look of consternation came over his face. "It did seem odd. But he was insistent about it, and he did take us to her and you, and it's a good thing he did."

"Yes. For me and for her."

"What's that supposed to mean?" Garrett demanded.

I balked at saying more just yet. The theory was only starting to coalesce in my head. I preferred not to make definitive statements until I'd examined all the evidence and drawn more certain conclusions.

I moved my good hand along the mattress and carefully leveraged myself into a sitting position. A fresh throbbing spread through my torso, but it wasn't as debilitating when I was prepared for it. John made a sound of protest that I ignored. I might not always treat my body with the respect he felt it was due, but I did know its limits better than anyone else.

"I need to see the spot where I fell," I said.

Garrett stared at me. "You want to go mountain climbing two days after you fell down a cliff?"

"I want to understand how I came to fall down that cliff and end up in this particular state."

"Sherlock..." John's fingers slid up my arm to grasp my elbow. He looked at me with so much distress and fond regard that my mind, still slightly muddled by the effects of whatever medication the doctors had me on, wandered back to the last moment his lips had pressed against mine.

Something in our partnership had shifted under Jemma's guidance. I couldn't say she'd produced emotions that hadn't been there before, but she'd compelled a desire for each other into the light alongside the desire all three of us had come to feel for her. It wasn't yet clear to me exactly what John and I were becoming beyond friends and partners in our work, but I couldn't deny we *were* more than that now. Perhaps that was why his distress trickled into me. But that didn't change my objective.

"There is more to this scenario than we can comprehend from your panicked observations and my unprepared senses, both viewed through a medium as unreliable as memory," I said. "Unless there's some reason to think I'll injure myself more by taking a car ride and a careful walk out to the spot, with as much assistance as you feel you need to provide, I'd like to resolve that uncertainty as soon as possible. Bring the doctor here if you must. I'll put the matter to him."

"Stubborn as a mule," Garrett muttered, but when he paced the room again, there was more energy to his movements. He was equally eager at the thought of taking action.

From what I'd observed of the three of us, he'd fallen for Jemma the hardest and fastest. Affairs of the heart were hardly my forte. I had no idea what distress Garrett must be feeling, not only at seeing a colleague laid low but at having witnessed his lover committing what by all appearances had been a terrible crime.

John sighed. "Fine. I'll call the doctor. But in my professional opinion, a mountainside is the last place you should be right now."

It took nearly a day longer than I'd hoped, but by the next morning I'd negotiated my way back to the cliff where Jemma had arranged my literal downfall. John helped me out of the car, his expression all disapproval, but he held out his arm to take some of my weight all the same, leaning a little on his walking stick on the other side.

"I'm only coming with you because I know you'll insist on making the walk on your own if I don't," he informed me.

"Noted." Twinges of pain still ran up my legs and through my back, but my resolve to pick apart this mystery was far stronger than any physical malady. I'd swallowed a couple of painkillers in the car a half an hour ago, and their effects were dulling the discomfort without intruding too much on my mental processes.

Garrett came up to support me on my other side, and we began our slow, shuffling ascent of the path, punctuated by the rapping of John's stick.

Something twisted in my chest thinking back to the first time I'd made this trek, to the gravity in Jemma's demeanor that she hadn't been able to entirely disguise. Maybe she hadn't been trying to disguise it, knowing I'd assume it was related to what she'd supposedly meant to show me rather than a treacherous act she was planning.

She hadn't taken her action lightly, whatever her intent had been. I should have seen—if I'd been paying better attention…

I *had* been charting our progress up the mountain with some focus, in case it would prove relevant to her concern. I spotted the point where she'd asked me to stop and peer down the cliffside before the others needed to identify it.

"Here," I said, nodding to it. We came to a halt on the path right where the faint scuffing revealed the skidding of my feet three days past. I peered down the cliff. The uncertainty I'd felt faded away as the final pieces of evidence snapped into place.

I motioned to my colleagues. "What do you see below us?"

"A whole lot of rock ready to bash your head in, that you were lucky to avoid," Garrett said.

"What else?"

John picked up the thread. "A few small trees, a clump of shrubs —that's where you landed." He pointed to a small cluster of bushes, their wiry branches snapped here and there where I must have collided with them, some fifty feet down the steep incline.

"And what do you make of that?" I asked.

"Like Garrett said, you were incredibly lucky."

I turned to John and raised my eyebrows. "In all our dealings with Miss Moriarty, how often has luck been a deciding factor in the outcome of her schemes?"

He paused. "Well, not often, but why on earth would she shove you down a cliff at all if she didn't want you dead or close to it?"

"That is an important question, but one I think we've already seen the answer to in our own history."

I swept my hand to indicate various parts of the slope. "Look at the terrain. There, the drop becomes nearly sheer with nothing at all to break a fall until you hit the rocky outcropping much farther down. On that side, there are the trees, but they're at least as likely to bash a head as any rock is. A little farther along, there are a few more shrubs, but the terrain there is more uneven, with more loose stones scattered—more chance that a fall will veer in an unexpected direction or a protruding object will cause major damage."

Garrett knit his brow as he studied the landscape. "Where are you going with this?"

"Isn't it obvious? This is the only spot along this path where the drop *could* have been fatal, but isn't because of the precise combination of features. She told me to stop here specifically. A few feet to the right or left, and I most likely would have died. You can't tell me Jemma didn't realize that. But she didn't want me dead." I wet my lips. "She only wanted me—and you—to *think* she wanted me dead."

"There's no way she could have been sure the fall would have followed that exact course," John protested.

"No. It was a risk. She likely expected I'd have been more injured than I was—luck did give me a small bit of help. I don't think she'd have wanted me returning here and making this observation any time soon."

Garrett's eyes had widened. He cursed under his breath. "Bloody hell. She *asked* Moran to get us out here as witnesses—she knew how it would look—she wanted us convinced she'd taken up the villain mantle again too. Why the hell would she go that far?" His voice had gone raw.

The truth of it had already solidified in my head, crystal clear. The twisting in my gut tightened into a series of knots.

"We can't know the full story until we find her," I said. "We need to start tracing her travels from here immediately."

John clasped my shoulder. "Hold on. Even if she didn't mean to *kill* you, she still hurt you. She could do it again. We can't go rushing after her when we have no idea—"

"We do have an idea," I interrupted, more sharply than I'd intended. John's flinch made me wince inside in turn, but I soldiered on. "That's exactly how she wanted us to be thinking so that we wouldn't follow her, at least not in time. But if she wanted me dead, I'd be dead. No, she's gone off on her own again to see out some dangerous mission—something she felt would put us in far more danger than tumbling down a cliff. This was her way of *protecting* us. Of protecting me."

I hesitated, my throat constricting. "She did it because she believed she needed to. Because I proved myself too vulnerable. She didn't believe she could count on me to continue the fight."

Out of the three of us, I'd let the shrouded folk influence me the most. I'd let their shadowy compulsions drive me to overdosing on cocaine in a fit of desperation. If I hadn't—if I'd held steady in the face of their machinations—perhaps Jemma would have welcomed my assistance instead of taking this extreme step to ensure I stayed out of her next plans.

John could obviously follow my line of thinking. He gave my shoulder a gentle shake, the sun in his blond hair and glinting off his hazel eyes giving him an almost cherubic appearance.

"You were up against an unfamiliar enemy with powers beyond comprehension," he said. "No one would fault you for struggling. We *all* struggled."

Garrett nodded, a hint of shame crossing his face.

"It doesn't matter now." I drew myself straighter. "She needed our help even when she fled before. She may very well need it again, considering the creatures we're up against. We *have* to find her, and quickly—and hope it's not already too late."

John inhaled raggedly, and I met his eyes. He didn't have to speak for me to know what he was thinking.

He'd been afraid he'd lost me twice in as many weeks. The thought of racing into similar danger all over again terrified him. Not for himself—John rarely met a spot of danger that didn't exhilarate him. *He* wanted to protect me too.

I didn't know what to do with that urge of his. It warmed me and exasperated me at the same time, and I couldn't logically explain the first reaction. I wasn't sure if acknowledging the concern I saw in him would make the situation easier or harder.

Nothing in my vast range of experience and learning had prepared me for being the most important figure in any other person's life.

I reached for the right words to say and closed on nothing. He made no attempt to argue, though. He knew me, through and through. He knew when I'd made up my mind about a course of action.

I lifted my hand to touch his arm in an attempt at reassurance, and his gaze twitched with surprise. "I'll steer far away from both mountainsides and stimulants this time," I promised. "Your medical skills will be wholly unnecessary when it comes to me."

The words came out awkwardly, but they appeared to land well enough. John's mouth curved with a small but genuine smile.

"Then I suppose we'd better find out what trouble our wayward criminal genius has gotten herself into now, hadn't we?"

CHAPTER FOUR

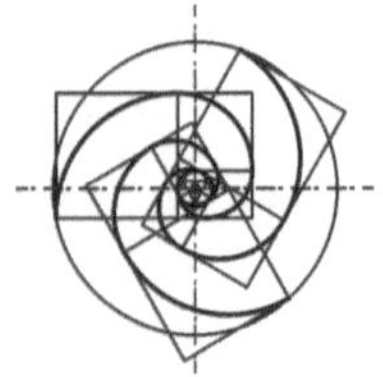

Jemma

In my first glimpse of the shrouded realm, everything blurred together into a haze of dim gray. I cautiously pushed myself upright on the hard ground, its texture gritty beneath my bare hands. A faint impression of the sheet I'd wrapped myself in had come with me, swaths of it floating around my torso and legs, though it had the same filmy quality that the shrouded folk displayed in the human world. My body was faintly translucent too.

My immediate surroundings looked like a desert lit by moonlight: cracked dry ground with no sign of vegetation other than a few shriveled, leafless shrubs, the impression of a reflected glow streaming down from above. When I peered up at the sky, which was the same dull gray shade as everything else around me, I couldn't make out the source of that pale light. It appeared to spread from one horizon to the other without ever intensifying.

No wonder the shrouded folk coveted our sun if this was the most illumination they got here. I wondered where they'd developed a taste for that kind of energy in the first place.

A breeze stirred around me, carrying a warbled sound mixed

with random clicks and hums. The erratic quality of it set my nerves on edge in an instant. The shrouded folk thrived on dissonance and disorder. I could only imagine how many I'd piss off if I started drawing out Fibonacci sequences here.

The stretch of flat ground I'd landed on ended some fifty feet away with a sprawl of structures that looked half disintegrated—miniature skyscrapers with crumbling roofs and walls, smaller buildings that might only have come up to my knees or my waist that were pocked with craters, all of them leached of any color. As I stared at the apparent wreckage, a prickle of recognition ran up my back.

If I ignored the size and the disastrous state of the buildings… that looked almost like the Tokyo skyline.

I glanced around to make sure I didn't have any company and stood up. Better to get out of this open area before any of the fiends did come wandering this way. I wasn't sure how they'd react to seeing an uninvited human in their midst or how much they could hurt me before I could wrench myself back into my natural realm, but I wasn't keen to find out the answer to either question.

When I approached the ruined city, the similarities to the one I'd left in my world stood out even more sharply. It *was* a sort of shrunken, fallen version of Tokyo. The buildings that would have been dozens of stories tall in reality stood only ten or twenty feet high here. One or two I could have stepped inside through gaping holes in the walls, but no doorway could have fit me. The "roads" were barely wide enough for me to squeeze along—where there was any need to squeeze. In many places the buildings alongside them were little more than scattered rubble.

The sight made my skin crawl. Obviously the state of this replica hadn't affected the actual city in any significant way. The buildings I saw ruined were standing just fine back in my realm. But what kind of warped alien place was this? Had the shrouded folk constructed these models and ruined them out of spite? Had they risen up naturally through some sort of parallel-universe connection? Both possibilities were equally unnerving.

As I picked my way through the bizarre city, the wavering

sounds rose and fell around me with no sense of rhythm. The hairs on the back of my neck rose. At a shiver of movement between the buildings ahead of me, I jerked back behind one of the shrunken skyscrapers.

A shrouded one came into view farther down the street, its form more solid here than they ever appeared in the human world. Even at a distance, the pale strips floating around its body looked even more like swaths of dead skin rather than the fabric I'd wanted to think they were. I restrained a shudder. Just when I'd thought the creatures couldn't get any more disgusting.

Thankfully, it wasn't traveling my way. It drifted on past the nearby structures without a sound or any clue as to its purpose here. I waited another few minutes before I ventured farther, keeping my eyes even more carefully peeled for others.

Because this Tokyo was several orders of magnitude smaller than the one I'd left—and for the most part lacking in suburbs—crossing it only took a short hike. When I reached the fringes of the city and my temporary shelter, I hesitated, scanning my surroundings up ahead.

Another long, flat plain stretched out directly ahead of me. To my left, I spotted a dense cluster of high-rises I suspected must be Osaka. Which would mean I'd originally landed at the edge of the Pacific Ocean, and the expanse ahead of me would represent the Sea of Japan.

The world map unfurled in my mind's eye. If I kept walking straight ahead, I'd reach the equivalent of Korea first, and then on to China. Based on the reduced scale, I didn't think the journey would take too long. Or I could turn around and cross the Pacific to the shrouded folk's equivalent of North America.

Where was Olivia most likely to be? They'd have taken her from our commune in the U.S., but there was no reason to assume they'd have kept her near there. They might have thought it wiser to bring her far away from the spot I'd be most inclined to look for her.

I rubbed my mouth in thought, and two of the shrouded folk glided into my line of sight. They slipped into the city farther down.

Something about their course gave me the impression they had a definite destination in mind.

It was worth discovering what they found interesting in these macabre replicas of the human world. Setting my feet carefully, I crept over to follow them.

The dissonant sounds heightened slightly, niggling at my skin. A hint of color seeped across the buildings around me. I took a turn at an intersection and peered around a skyscraper after the shrouded ones. A ruddy glow emanated from up ahead. They were heading straight toward it.

I ventured down a side street to keep some distance, the glow expanding with each block I passed. When I reached the skeletal park by what would have been Shinjuku station, I stopped and simply stared.

Where the immense train station would have been in my reality, a large spear of stone jutted toward the sky. It was shorter than many of the skyscrapers, which was why I hadn't seen it until I'd gotten closer, but at least a couple feet taller than I was. Its edges were a mix of jagged protrusions and misshapen lumps, as discordant as the warbling in the air. The warbling which had gotten even louder closer to the stone.

The sound seemed to echo a flickering red light that jerked and flared within the stone like flames whipped by the wind. Just looking at it made my stomach churn.

The shrouded folk clearly found the sight much more appealing. The two I'd been following drifted up to the stone and leaned toward it. They appeared to press the dark hollows of their faces directly to the surface of the rocky spear. Where they touched it, the crimson glow quaked.

They were absorbing some sort of energy from the stone, I concluded after watching for a few minutes. A hot, fiery energy… like the kind Earth's sun provided?

If this was what they fed on, no wonder they were so eager to cross over to the human world. Simply basking in our sun must be a hundred times more satisfying than what they could suck from one of those stones.

The shrouded folk lingered by the stone for a while longer. When they meandered off, they looked much more aimless. What did they fill their time with when they weren't drinking rocky glows or slipping into our world to prey on human beings?

I wasn't here to play anthropologist to the fiends. I was curious about this stone, though. I edged across the plaza and approached the spear.

The energy rippling off it jittered through my nerves even more forcefully. I had to grit my teeth to stop them from chattering. When I reached my hand toward the stone's surface, my stomach flipped so forcefully I nearly vomited. A wave of exhaustion washed over me.

Okay, that thing obviously wasn't going to do *me* any good. I backed up in a hurry, nearly stumbling over a low-rise.

As soon as I'd put several blocks between me and the glowing stone, the discordant energy began to fade again. My stomach settled and more of my energy returned. I dragged in a breath and considered what I'd learned.

The shrouded folk took power from those stones. In at least this case, the stone had been in the center of a major city. I hadn't seen any similar spears of rock jutting in the middle of the open plains, so maybe they were tied to the cities via whatever connection this realm had to mine.

The highest shrouded folk, the type who'd have captured my sister and been able to keep her prisoner all this time without any of the others making a sacrifice of her, would want to remain close to their power source, wouldn't they? Maybe there were different stones with different types or amounts of energy. They'd want to feed from the best.

I'd explore a few more cities and see what they offered, and then I'd be able to make a more educated guess at where Olivia might be held.

After a lot of walking, during which the sky never shifted in shade or brightness, I determined that every city that appeared in the shrouded realm did have a glowing stone, that all those stones glowed red, and that the ones in my vicinity all appeared to have about the same vibrancy. But as I ventured into the territory that mimicked mainland Asia, the crimson light began to spread beyond the stones. A faint line of it streaked along the plain I was crossing perhaps a quarter of a mile to my right. Not long after I'd spotted it, the erratic vibrations in the air had increased their effect.

I wasn't sure what the line was leading to, but it appeared to indicate more power. So I'd follow in the same direction as long as I could.

Unfortunately, the rising twitches of energy and warbles of sound were wearing at my own energy. My legs ached from the walking, and a tight pinch of tension had formed in the middle of my chest. That which fed the shrouded folk seemed to feed in turn on me. I supposed that wasn't much of a surprise.

I'd just have to hope I could find Olivia before this place wore me down completely.

The streak along the ground gleamed brighter as it reached a nearby city that I couldn't recognize on sight. I veered over to welcome the shelter of the buildings, even if the effects of that wavery red light would sap me even more. It was a trade-off. I'd passed a couple of shrouded folk at a distance out in the open now, and neither of them had accosted me, but from far away in my white sheet, I might have looked like one of their own. I had no idea how much the folk relied on sight.

Not long after I'd ventured into the city, wandering through its shrunken streets somewhat at random, a different sort of sound reached my ears—equally unnerving, but more purposeful. It was the tones of the shrouded folk's native language.

I crept around a cluster of high-rises and spied a few of the fiends in a sort of huddle not far from this city's glowing stone. The red light gave their streaming coverings a shifting pinkish tint like blood drifting in water.

The four of them were obviously discussing something without much concern of being overheard. The jerky, guttural sounds of the shrouded tongue didn't translate easily into language I knew, though

—and when they were around humans, they usually spoke in words we'd understand.

During my time in the cult, I had learned to recognize a few of the sound combinations, the ones they used most frequently when talking about us. Now, I strained my ears, listening for anything familiar.

One of them said the word for human, and my heart skipped a beat. Were they talking about their communes across the realms… or about a human who might be trapped here?

Another repeated the word and said something about light or power—I could never quite distinguish between the two concepts in the way they spoke about them. They might be leeching some sort of power from Olivia the same way they did from the people in the cult. Would the rituals work with even more potency right here in the shrouded realm?

The conversation rambled in another direction I couldn't follow. Then the four fiends went abruptly silent. One of them said something with the word for "human" again. And they turned their fathomless faces in my direction.

I ducked down behind the building I'd been peeking around with a stutter of my pulse. I couldn't hope that they'd mistake me for a fellow monster up close. However they'd sensed me, I wasn't going to wait around to chat.

"Who is there?" one of the folk called out. Instead of answering, I darted down the street and around a corner as quickly and quietly as I could. I turned right and then left, hoping the weaving route would throw them off if they followed.

After a few minutes, I sank down in a courtyard between a circle of skyscrapers and listened. The warbling breeze quavered around me. I might have caught a far-off voice of a shrouded one in its own tongue. Nothing sounded nearby… but then, the folk didn't tend to make a lot of noise moving around.

Even if they'd given up searching, they'd be more on their guard now. They might pass on word to the other shrouded folk to keep watch for an unusual figure who could be human.

And I still wasn't sure I was even heading toward Olivia rather than away.

Shit.

I pressed the heels of my hands to my forehead and dragged in a slow breath. A sudden pang of longing filled my chest—to have Bash standing by, guns at the ready, whatever good they'd have done. Hell, to have Sherlock making his observations and leaps of deduction, John providing his buoyant optimism, Garrett full of fiery determination. To know I wasn't standing alone.

But I was. In the end, this was my fight, and I'd taken the necessary steps to keep it that way. I would *not* be so weak as to wish I'd brought those weaker than me into the fray.

Jemma Moriarty needed no one. That was how it'd always been, and how it had to be now if I wanted to make it through this realm alive.

CHAPTER FIVE

John

As we strode to the hotel lifts, I bit my tongue just shy of asking Sherlock for the hundredth time if he was sure this was a good idea. At this point, determined as he was to get answers, I doubted "good" entered the equation.

I couldn't manage to stay totally quiet, though.

"What could she be doing here?" I said while we waited for a lift to arrive. "The cult wouldn't have a commune in the middle of a city, let alone one as big as Tokyo. And why would she need three whole floors to herself? It doesn't match her actions before at all."

"Which is exactly why we must discover what has changed and how that factor has altered her plans." Sherlock cast his sharp gaze over the lobby around us, unable to rein in his keen observational senses even when he believed our target was already in reach. "As for the hotel, she must have wanted a complete lack of distraction. We can assume the room she's using will be the middle of the three, with a buffer above and below, and that she'll have taken one at a distance from the lifts."

The sleek steel door opened with a chime. We got on alone. "Will we even be able to get access to those floors?" I started. "If she's taking measures that extreme…"

Sherlock brandished a plastic card he'd produced from his pocket. "I took the liberty of helping myself to a security key during our talk with the manager. That should get us all the access we need." He slid it into the opening beneath the control panel and pushed the button for the floor. The lift thrummed upward without hesitation.

Only Sherlock could have surreptitiously lifted a key card with his good arm broken. I'd be surprised if he hadn't specifically practiced that or similar maneuvers with his weaker side to prepare for this exact possibility.

Sherlock prepared for *every* possibility… until he couldn't. There was no way he could have anticipated the shrouded folk and their tactics. That didn't stop him from beating himself up for being taken off-guard, of course.

I glanced at him, searching for signs of the self-blame he'd expressed when we'd re-visited the mountain, but at the moment his pale eyes were bright with enthusiasm. There was very little the man liked more than being on the verge of solving a mystery, after all.

Before I could find myself gazing at my friend's distinctive face a little longer than was strictly *friendly*, my phone pinged with a text alert. I fished it out as the lift started to slow.

"Garrett wants to know if we got the right place," I reported. The detective inspector had unwillingly stayed behind in London after we'd finished the electronic side of our investigation. He'd already tried his chief's patience at Scotland Yard with the other schemes of Jemma's we'd gotten caught up in, and now his expertise on the cult was in demand as other law enforcement agencies worldwide began to investigate.

"One day perhaps he'll develop more patience," Sherlock said, but he sounded only amused.

We haven't determined yet, I wrote back. *Will update you as I'm able.*

The hall the lift let us out into was completely silent. Glancing in either direction, I couldn't see the slightest hint of which door

Jemma might be behind. My companion took a similar evaluation and set off to the left at a brisk stride, only a tad stiff with the battering he was still recovering from. I followed with a soft tap of my walking stick against the carpet.

Sherlock paused at the end of the hall and peered down at the carpet in front of the doors on either side. With a satisfied hum, he slid his keycard into the lock of the first door. I guessed it made sense not to give the inhabitants a chance to make a run for it, although it wasn't as if there was anywhere much they could run to this high up.

The lock clicked over, Sherlock nudged open the door—and a familiar brawny form charged into view, gun in hand.

Moran halted halfway down the suite's front hallway, staring at us, his normally impassive expression turned almost wild. His gun hand lowered but didn't drop all the way to his side. He looked over his shoulder and then back at us, his jaw working as he must have considered his options. Then he stepped toward us with a motion toward the hall that seemed to indicate he'd speak to us out there.

His silent urgency infected me. I kept quiet as he joined us in the hall, and Sherlock held his tongue too. The second the door had closed, though, my friend spoke up.

"It's mainly Jemma we wanted to speak to."

"You can't," her associate said. "She isn't here."

Sherlock gave him a skeptical look. "I could lay out all the reasons I know that's a lie, or you could let us in without the bother. I'd rather not have to force the matter."

Moran let out an incredulous sound, his gaze falling to Sherlock's cast. He shook his head. "She obviously didn't push you hard enough," he said, but his tone was so wry that I didn't bristle at the remark.

"For her ends, perhaps not, although I'm quite glad she didn't err on the other side of caution. Are you letting us in or not?"

The other man grimaced. "It's... not as simple as all that. We're better off talking out here. She *isn't* exactly in the room. She's done a ritual so she can cross over to the place where her monsters live, and I'd rather not risk disturbing her. I don't know exactly what effects a disruption might have."

His silence and the floors of rooms booked made a sudden but unsettling sort of sense. "She's gone into the place the shrouded folk come from?" I said, a shiver running down my back. I'd only had limited dealings with the creatures myself, but I'd seen plenty of what they incited their worshippers to do to themselves and others, many of those victims children. Monster was the word for them, all right. "Why on earth would she do that? We were making so much progress cutting them off from this world."

Sherlock's forehead had furrowed. "They have something that's important to her."

"You could say that." Moran eyed us for a time, presumably debating the pros and cons of telling us more. The fact that Sherlock had arrived here at all must have made a pretty convincing case that simply telling us to get the hell out wasn't going to cut it.

He'd trusted us enough to reach out to us on Jemma's behalf once. I hoped we'd continued to justify that good will in the weeks since then.

Finally, he sighed. "I don't know how much she's told either of you about this, but growing up in her commune, she had a younger sister. When she escaped, she meant to come back and get her sister out too as soon as she had the resources. The monsters don't usually gobble up the kids until they're fifteen. She managed to get back there more than a year early, and her sister was gone, taken by them —dead, Jemma had to assume. But last week, one of the things came to her with proof that her sister is still alive, that they kept her rather than swallowing her up."

My stomach clenched. I remembered Jemma mentioning that the creatures had killed her sister—once, briefly—but I'd never pressed the subject. She'd also told me once when we were first getting to know each other that she'd lost someone she cared about a lot, and that was why she'd taken up the line of work she had. It wasn't hard to see how the grief and fury over the loss could have shaped her into a woman willing to do anything to destroy those monsters' influence over our world.

"Why would they tell her that now?" I asked, my voice rough.

Sherlock gave a humorless bark of a laugh. "To manipulate her into giving up her campaign, I'd imagine. She was rooting them out, and they knew she might win that war. So they brought to bear the best card they had." He met Moran's gaze intently. "Do you think she has a chance of getting the girl out?"

"I have no idea," Moran said, and with those four words, I glimpsed the helplessness he must feel right now. "I'm not even clear on what the rescue is going to entail. I don't think she was either. She'd never traveled to their realm before—she had no idea what to expect."

"But she wanted us out of the way."

The hitman's mouth set in a grim line. "She was afraid you'd interfere in ways that would make the rescue harder for her. You *haven't* always been all that accepting of the supernatural ideas she's tried to explain to you."

That was a fair point, as Sherlock's grimace suggested he knew. He skipped addressing that point and moved on to the matter at hand. "She might need our help in this fiendish place, then?"

"I don't know how much we'd be able to do for her," Moran said, but I could hear the effort he was putting into that restraint. This wasn't a man used to sitting back and letting others do all the work.

"And you know how she arranged her passage into this realm? In theory, one or more of us could follow her there?"

"Someone needs to watch over her."

Sherlock crossed his arms over his chest, rather awkwardly with the one in its cast. "There are three of us. I'm sure that can be arranged."

Moran glanced toward the door. "We may not have enough supplies, either. There's a sort of salve she made that she smeared all over herself, and I don't think there's enough to cover another person as well as leaving extra if she needs it reapplied—and I couldn't tell you the exact proportions she used if we wanted to make more."

"I'm certain I could sort that out with a little investigation." Sherlock tipped his head toward the door. "Will you let us have a look? You should know by now we understand discretion."

Moran hesitated, but I suspected he'd already been mostly

convinced. "She's in the living room. Be as quiet as possible. If we need to discuss anything, we can do that in the bedroom."

Sherlock and I nodded, and Moran eased open the door.

The air we stepped into was chilly enough to make me wish I'd brought a thicker shirt. A tart herbal smell hung in the air, lavender and feverfew and other scents Sherlock's well-trained nose would no doubt be able to pick apart. We snuck down the hall and came into view of the body lying still on the living room rug.

Flecks of those herbs stood out against Jemma's pale skin with a waxy shine. Her bright red hair was darkened by the same stuff, slicked close to her head. As I watched, one slow breath raised her chest and slipped away.

My medical instincts clanged with alarm. I had to clamp down on the urge to run to her and begin CPR. Nothing about her state looked healthy... but she understood what she'd done here better than I could hope to.

If I rushed in and ruined her attempt to save her sister, then I'd have proven her right for trying to keep us out of this scheme.

Sherlock walked close to her body with an air of scientific examination and then followed Moran into the kitchen. The hitman took out a bowl full of the herbal mixture and pointed to a box of supplies. Sherlock gave the stuff a stir and several sniffs, rubbed it between his fingers, and riffled through the box with minimal rustling. When he was finished, satisfaction practically radiated off him. He gestured for us to join him in the bedroom.

The TV was showing some historical drama—Hamlet, I gathered after a moment. Moran switched it off with the remote and no explanation. "Well?" he said to Sherlock.

"I believe I can recreate the mixture in the correct proportions," Sherlock said. "One of us would need to grab a few supplies, but nothing it should be difficult to find in Tokyo. White sheets should be simple enough as well. Are there any other necessary materials?"

Moran's hand went to his pocket. "I have sedatives she had me pick up. She took one right before she went into that state. I think the idea is to bring the body as close to death as it can get." His mouth twisted at saying those words aloud. "The only other aspect she mentioned is that once she was prepared and in position, she was going to focus on her interactions with the shrouded folk. I guess that helps her bridge the gap between those worlds."

"Not particularly scientific, but it serves as guidance enough. What sort of monitoring has she required since going into that state?"

"I haven't needed to do anything at all," Moran admitted. "She said if the salve absorbed into her skin, to apply more, but otherwise to leave her to it."

"It seems simple enough, then," Sherlock said. "Two of us will go after her to assist as well as we're able, and one will stay behind to ensure we don't cross all the way into death or otherwise meet an unfortunate end. I believe I should make the trip. My skills will serve her better in this other realm than waiting around here making the most simple observations."

Of course he'd see it that way. With the memory of Jemma's unearthly still body fresh in my mind, every part of me balked at the idea of seeing Sherlock enter the same state. But honestly, I knew I didn't have a hope in hell of talking him out of it.

Moran met my gaze when I glanced at him. The question came down to the two of us. My throat tightened with the desire to say I should be the one to join Sherlock—I was meant to stand beside him through every challenge any villain threw at us. And I wasn't entirely sure Jemma was done playing villain with him anymore than the shrouded folk were.

This mission wasn't about Sherlock, though. It was about Jemma. And I could read how desperately Bash wanted to come to her defense in the tension etched on his face, in every flex of his muscles.

He'd devoted years of his life to her. I'd never seen anything but total loyalty in him. He was meant for this.

If her judgment became questionable again, he had the best chance to making her see reason out of any of us.

I forced the admission out. "It makes the most sense for me to stay behind. I have the medical training. I'd be most likely to notice if any of you take a turn in a bad direction—and the most likely to be able to help you survive that. I can keep Garrett updated as well." I caught Moran's eyes again. "You ought to be able to go after her."

"Thank you," he said, his voice a little hoarse. He might not have expected that generosity from any of us. He turned to Sherlock. "Let me know what you need and if there's anywhere you think I can quickly find it, and I'll pick it up. I've got a driver on call."

Sherlock rattled off a brief list Moran entered into his phone. As the hitman left the bedroom, I caught Sherlock's good arm before he could follow.

"Can we talk for a minute?" I said. "You can't start preparing until he's back anyway, can you?"

"No," my friend acknowledged. He considered me with those cool eyes that missed so little. "You'd rather I didn't go."

"I just…" I made a face at the dresser. "You've been through two major health crises in the last couple weeks. Your body isn't completely recovered. We can't know exactly what effects the herbs and the drug and the rest will have on you. It's a greater risk than Jemma or Moran doing it."

I've already nearly lost you twice. I don't want to have to face that again.

"I've suffered no internal damage," Sherlock pointed out. "I can adjust the dosage if it seems wise—and you'll be here if anything begins to go wrong."

"I'd rather not have it get to that point," I muttered.

Sherlock fixed me with that calm gaze that could be so reassuring and yet also so frustrating. "This is the life I lead, John. The life you asked to be a part of. We go up against murderers and assassins. Danger is always lurking. What we do here could decide the security of the entire human race. You must see that I can't back down from that."

"I do," I said. "That doesn't mean I have to like it."

"I won't ask you to like it then." He gave me a sly little smile that woke up a completely different emotion in me.

This impulse I didn't rein in. I stepped closer to him, my hand rising to his shoulder, bobbing up on my toes slightly so I could bring my mouth flush against his. Sherlock tensed just for an instant, but then he leaned into the kiss, his fingers coming to rest against my cheek, the warmth of his body flooding me.

God, I wanted so much more than this. The memory of our last bedroom encounter with Jemma, when Sherlock had stroked me to my release, tingled through me. But this was hardly the time or the place, and I'd only make him uncomfortable if I pushed for anything more.

I'd be honest with him, though. When we drew apart, his cheeks had turned pink in the most adorable way, as adorable as a man like Sherlock could be. "To clear our heads?" he suggested in a mildly teasing voice. It was the excuse he'd used, the excuse I'd used in turn, to justify little moments of intimacy in the past.

"No," I said. "Because I wanted to. Because I want you to know how much it matters to me that you come out of that monstrous place alive."

He didn't appear to know quite what to say to that. His gaze slipped away from mine for a second before returning. "I have every intention of returning," he said, which I knew was as close to a promise as he could give me.

CHAPTER SIX

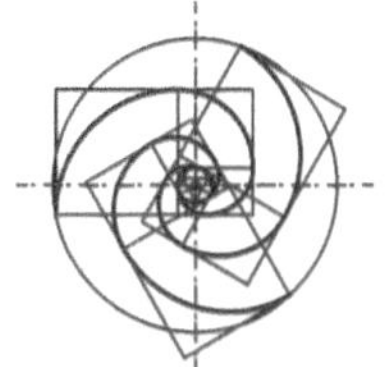

Jemma

I didn't see another significant change in the landscape of the shrouded realm until I reached a city I determined was Tehran from a couple of distinctive buildings and its relative position. The glowing red line I'd been following at a distance streaked straight into the middle of the city. I crept along the outskirts where the buildings would hide me but I wouldn't be venturing too close to this place's stone and its unsettling energy—or the shrouded folk who'd be feeding from it.

The farther I'd traveled along the line of light, the more persistent the erratic hum and crackle in the air had gotten. It itched at my skin and wobbled through my nerves. I hadn't felt any need to sleep or eat since I'd arrived here, other than the occasional pang of longing for a sugar cube to soothe my nerves, but my lungs were starting to clench around my breaths.

How much could I physically falter when my real physical form was back in the Tokyo hotel room? The body I had here might look a bit filmy, but it felt solid enough when I rubbed my arms.

Halfway around the city's edge, I came across another glowing line. The one I'd been following before veered east across the continent. This one, if my impressions were accurate, shimmered into the distance mostly to the south. If I followed that one, I suspected I'd end up in Africa.

I studied it for a while, debating whether to follow the new one and see where it led me or continue along the path I'd already been on. Unless that first path ended here? I slipped through the buildings to check, and no, the eastern line stretched onward toward the next shrunken cities.

Another thought tickled through my head. I continued around the border of the city until I came to a fourth line, this one heading north.

Hmm. So I had one line of escalating power moving to the east, and another line now bisecting it. I'd bet the two met in the middle where the stone of power stood. None of the other cities I'd passed had held two lines. What was special about this one?

I'd probably have to do a whole lot more walking to figure that out, and the wobbliness of the constant dissonant sounds was seeping into the muscles of my legs. I didn't even know if the mystery would do anything to help me find Olivia. Fuck. Maybe I should have started this journey from Scotland where the shrouded one had approached me with its warning in the first place.

I ventured toward the middle of the city to at least confirm my suspicion about the crossing of the lines. It wasn't hard to find this city's stone. The glow emanated even farther than the others had, prickling into me. This one was taller too. I stopped in the shelter of a crumbling building to study it at a distance.

The lines definitely crossed there. And that stone, maybe because of its starker glow and its size, was particularly popular with the shrouded folk. As I watched, at least a dozen drifted up to it to press their "faces" to the quavering crimson light.

None of them came along the north-south line, though. They mostly glided in from the west, some of them heading back the way they'd come, and some heading on farther east after they'd fed. That behavior suggested that if there were anything more interesting to discover, it probably lay along that line. So what was the other for?

I picked my way back through the streets, mulling over the possibilities and doing my best to ignore the shivers now running through my legs. I'd just reached the outskirts of the city when two pale forms snapped into being a few hundred feet away on the desolate plain beyond.

My first instinct was to bolt deeper into the city again. Before my legs had even started moving, though, I registered the position and details of the figures. They were lying sprawled on their backs—I hadn't seen any shrouded folk do that. And rather than faces of shadow wrapped in thin swaths of material, they had actual heads. Human heads.

Cult members—two of them joining in the ritual at the same time? I'd never seen that done before, but that didn't mean it couldn't happen. I had no interest in running into members of any commune either, even if they were less dangerous than the fiends.

I took a step backward, meaning to crouch behind a nearby apartment block to watch, and both of the figures tentatively sat up. At the sight of their movements and a fall of all-too-familiar messy dark curls, my heart lurched. I hurried forward instead, glancing around quickly to make sure no shrouded folk had lingered nearby.

So many questions and so much emotion surged up through me as I reached the two men, but making sure they didn't die in their first five minutes in this realm had to be my first priority. I motioned for them to come meet me with a jerk of my arm, and as soon as they were close, I waved them on toward the city, hustling ahead of them and scanning the landscape. Of all the ridiculous stunts they could have pulled…

As soon as we'd reached the relative safety of the city outskirts, I spun on the two of them. "What the hell are you doing here?"

I aimed my glare at Bash, because it was easier to face him than Sherlock. And anyway, neither of them could have made it here if he hadn't allowed it to happen. He was the only one who'd known the ritual I'd gone through.

Both of them *looked* a little ridiculous wrapped in their sheets like bizarre togas. I supposed I looked pretty odd too. Bash tugged at one of the folds as he held my gaze, his mouth set at a pained angle.

"You know how persistent this one is. He and the doctor tracked us down. John's watching over us back in the hotel—you know he'll have a better eye for anything going physically wrong than I would have." He paused. "It's been almost a whole day since you passed through. There has to be *some* way we can help."

"You could have ended up anywhere! This realm is huge. You could have landed right in the middle of a bunch of shrouded folk, and that wouldn't have helped me at all."

"We adapted your use of mental focus," Sherlock said in his usual even voice. "As we went under, we trained our minds not just on the shrouded folk but on your presence. That strategy appears to have had the intended effect."

I let myself meet his eyes then. There was no recrimination in his expression, no sign that he was anything like angry... but then, Sherlock didn't generally give in to such base emotions, did he? My gaze dropped to his arms, the one of them held awkwardly in front of him in a cast that had made the trip with him, and my chest tightened.

"*You* should still be in a hospital."

One corner of his mouth quirked upward. "You should have killed me better if that was the outcome you were hoping for."

The fact that he could joke about what I'd done to him sent a clashing rush of fondness and guilt wrenching through me. Fondness, guilt, and fear.

I'd pushed him, meaning to push him right out of my life, so he couldn't inadvertently sabotage my attempt to rescue my sister, yes. But seeing him here sparked a totally different sort of horror. This was the most dangerous place any human being could be. I'd wanted to keep him—to keep all the men I cared about, as hard as I often found it to admit that affection—out of this.

"Moran told us about your sister," Sherlock added in a more serious tone. "I can understand, given the situation and the unexpected way it came upon you, why you might not have trusted any of us to approach it in the most constructive way."

"And yet here you are. You should hate me."

His smile came back. "You put more care into minimizing the actual harm in my supposed murder than most people put into their attempts at assisting those in need. Did you really think I wouldn't put the pieces together?"

"I thought the damned doctors would keep you in treatment long enough that it wouldn't matter," I muttered.

"Well, they didn't, and here I am to join the search. That seems the better outcome to me."

The outcome I'd been longing for hours ago. I choked up for a second despite my best efforts. It took me a moment before I was sure my voice would come out steady. "And now I might lose her *and* you. Did it never occur to you that I might rather have you alive and hating me than dead?"

Something in Sherlock's angular features softened. "Jemma, following other people's orders has never been a particular skill of mine. I invested in this 'case' of yours, and I invested in *you*, and if I have my way, I'll see it through to the end. I'm here now, so you may as well make use of me. In future, if you tell me to stay out, I won't follow. But you're not alone in this mission, and I needed you to know that, beyond any shadow of a doubt."

Future promises didn't do me much good now, but those last words brought back the lump in my throat. I didn't know what to say in response. Instead, I turned back to Bash.

"We're here at your service, Majesty," he said with a wry lilt to the nickname. "What have you found out so far? What are the next steps?"

I exhaled slowly. They *were* here now, and they might be able to help, especially once I figured out where Olivia actually was. "If any of the shrouded folk come at you in an attack, you leave here immediately without waiting on me. Understood? All you have to do is pull the sheet up over your face to cover your eyes and focus on the room back home."

Sherlock nodded. Bash only grimaced. I gave him a stern look. "That's a direct order."

"If I can stop one of them from hurting you —"

I threw up my hands. "Fine! I'll just make sure it doesn't come to that. If my life isn't under threat but yours is, get the hell out of here. Now, let me tell you what I've determined about this place so far."

We walked the circuit of the city's edge, and I explained the way the shrouded realm appeared to mimic our world with its shrunken ruined replicas of the major human cities. I went on to touch on the stones with their unnerving energy, the line I'd been following and the new one that had appeared, and the behavior of the shrouded folk around them.

Sherlock peered intently at everything around us and broke my commentary only with an occasional question. When we came to the line that shone off to the south, he stopped and studied it for several minutes.

"From the observations you've related," he said, "I would predict that the primary line you've followed leads to some sort of central hub of greater power. Perhaps even one fueling the other stones via those lines. Which leads me to believe this secondary line may be a ring of some sort around what we might call the 'axle'."

As sharply observant as always. "I was thinking something similar," I said. "Given the distribution of cities across our world, I'd imagine that means there are likely other lines leading to that central point. The ring might connect them all the way around."

The detective rubbed his chin. "But we can't know how many or where they are without venturing along them. Where do you think these creatures would be most likely to hold your sister?"

"It's hard to know," I admitted. "I've never heard of the shrouded folk keeping a human sacrifice alive as a prisoner before, so I have no idea what might be necessary for that. My best guess was that they'd want to have her somewhere they had access to as much power as possible, but that is only a guess."

Bash shifted on his feet, gazing into the distance. "The space between the cities here is obviously a lot shorter than in the real world. I'm a big believer in getting the lay of the land before taking action. We could test out the theory about the ring and axle by following this line and seeing whether there are other 'spokes' in the cities it crosses through. If we don't have a better sense of where your sister is by the time we've explored that far, we could head on toward the center."

"Acquiring sufficient data to draw one's conclusions is a strategy I vastly prefer to any other," Sherlock said, with an approving dip of his head that left Bash a little startled looking. It was a good thing they were starting to get along, or their following me here would have been not just ridiculous but disastrous.

I brushed my hands together. "All right. That sounds reasonable. Let's get going then. I don't want to spend any longer in this realm than I have to."

I moved to walk forward, and my legs trembled under me at the sudden movement. Bash caught my arm before I stumbled. He examined my face, his own darkening with concern. "Are you all right? You haven't gotten hurt here, have you?"

I shook my head, making my best attempt at standing straight and steady. "It's the energies in this place. I'm sure they'll start to get to you too. They're constantly jarring my nerves—it's wearing me out. But I can keep going."

At least, I thought I could. I went to take another step, and my muscles wobbled again. My jaw clenched. I wouldn't be able to dodge the fiends very easily like this. I could end up being a liability to my men rather than the other way around.

"Have you found anything that counteracts the effects?" Sherlock asked.

I shook my head, fighting down my frustration. The discordant drone rattled on through my ears and into my body. My lungs constricted more tightly.

"Sit down for a moment?" Bash said, and I gave in to his suggestion. I let myself sink onto the pocked rooftop of a single-story building that only came up to my knees and dragged in a breath. Bash crouched beside me, his hand on my back. He rubbed it up and down over my spine in a ghost of a massage.

As the rhythm of the movement seeped into me, the jittering of my nerves started to fade. Even the erratic sounds themselves dulled around me. Interesting. I leaned into his touch encouragingly. "Something about *that* is helping."

Sherlock's eyes lit with inspiration. "Patterns, rhythms—anything repeated and predictable clashes with these creatures, doesn't it? It would make sense that the energy they thrive on would be repulsed the same way. Perhaps all you need is some rejuvenation time."

He sat at my other side and ran his hand over my thigh, the warmth of his fingers grazing my skin through the thin fabric of the sheet. As he stroked them down to my knee and up again, Bash continued his light massage on my back. The unsettling dissonance drew back a little more. And a totally different sensation unfurled low in my belly.

Sherlock must have detected the shift in my mood before I'd even said anything. He added a swivel of his thumb and said in an overly offhand way, "Do you suppose a more intensive physical interaction might result in a swifter recovery, Miss Moriarty?"

What a Sherlockian approach to a proposition that was. I had to restrain a chuckle, but at the same time desire flared higher inside me.

"It might. I can't see how it'd hurt to experiment. What did you have in mind, Mr. Holmes?"

He glanced at Bash as if to confirm he wasn't walking into a minefield. My hitman rested his other hand on my waist. His stance beside me tensed for a second and then relaxed. He'd gradually gotten used to the idea that I enjoyed intimacy with the trio as much as I did with him—he'd even collaborated with Garrett to satisfy me in rather spectacular fashion a couple weeks ago. Add in the element of curing me of my ills, and he'd have even less reason to hesitate.

"I think I get the general idea," he said in a low voice, and drew his hand up to cup my breast.

It was hard to say what burned away the quivers that'd been setting me off balance more—the spark of pleasure at the swipe of his thumb over my already stiffening nipple or the rhythmic intensity with which he repeated the gesture. An approving hum crept up my throat. At the same time, Sherlock shifted his touch higher to tease his fingers over my sex.

I just about growled with need when he caressed my clit, sending pulses of heat through me with each swivel of his hand. The energy of the shrouded realm dwindled to a faint drone. I gripped Bash's shoulder, Sherlock's arm, my lips flushed with the longing to collide with theirs, but I hadn't lost my head so much I'd forgotten where we were and what dangers lurked here.

Intense was good, yes, but we couldn't lose ourselves in the moment here. If I was going to give myself over to these sensations, we'd better make sure no fiends spotted us while we were temporarily... distracted.

Bash moved his attentions to my other breast, and my head started to roll back of its own accord. My wandering gaze caught on a high-rise a short distance away that was big enough to cover what would have been an entire city block in the real world. Here that made it large enough to easily hold all three of us—and one side had a hole gouged in it nearly as tall as I was.

"I think we could use a little more privacy," I said, my voice coming out breathless, and tugged the guys upward. Sherlock spotted my intended destination in an instant. We made our way over to it as if as one being, their fingertips still gliding over my body tracing patterns of heat, my legs already stronger beneath me.

The building we ducked into had been nearly completely hollowed out, only the ridges of crumpled floors marking each story. Tiny streaks of light flowed through the windows. The shrouded folk stench filled my nose for a second. Sherlock had ended up in front of me. I yanked him to me, claiming his mouth and drowning myself in the mingled scents of tobacco and astringent aftershave that I was coming to adore.

From behind me, Bash pulled the sheet wrapped around me up, gathering it by my waist. A trace of the gel-like substance remained on my skin beneath it. He slicked it over my clit as Sherlock kissed me back hard, and I moaned into the other man's mouth.

The bulge of my right-hand man's erection brushed my ass, and a sharper longing rose up inside me. I tore my lips from Sherlock's just long enough to say, "I want you both inside me. As soon as possible."

Sherlock blinked in apparent confusion, but he wouldn't need much guidance for his part. I tugged at his sheet to free his cock, and he claimed my mouth again.

Bash understood what I'd meant. He slid his hand around my hip to probe my back entrance. I might have whined, just a little, as his finger traced that ring of muscle.

The two of them were too damn tall. I gripped Sherlock's shoulders, he clasped my thigh with his good hand, and Bash steadied me from behind. With a heft, the detective had positioned me over his cock. I arched toward him, dropping my hips, and he sheathed himself inside me with a single giddying thrust.

It wasn't quite enough, but Bash was ready. He dipped his slick fingers inside me and ran them around my other opening in a blissful rhythm until I let out an impatient sound to get on with it. The head of his cock brushed my ass and slowly penetrated me with his perfect control and the most delicious burn.

Sherlock's eyes had widened. In his limited experience, this kind of joint intimacy might never have occurred to him. I kissed him through a gasp of pleasure, and any inhibitions that might have woken in him fell away. With a groan, he started to rock in and out of me.

Bash matched his pace from behind. Both of them filled me and nearly released me together, over and over. The pleasure of it thrummed through every inch of my being, chasing any last tremors of the shrouded realm's energy away.

"Jemma," Sherlock murmured, with a raw joy that shot straight to my heart. I clutched him and reached my other hand back to caress Bash behind me. The rush of bliss careened through me faster than ever before. I choked back a cry, and my body shuddered between them as I came so hard my vision dissolved into a burst of light.

Bash let out a strained sound at the clench of my muscles. He pressed his mouth to the back of my neck as he followed me.

Sherlock's breath broke. He pumped into me faster, and then he was flooding me with the heat of his own release.

My body slumped between them, tingling and sated, held by these two very different men who'd traveled across unimaginable distances to stand with me. For the first time in hours, I felt fully like myself again.

"Rejuvenation complete," I said with a smirk, and Bash chuckled against my skin. "Let's see what other surprises this realm has in store for us."

Garrett

Even if I hated being sidelined from Sherlock's investigations abroad, I had to enjoy the irony of my current situation. Just weeks ago, the chief had been hassling me about focusing too much on the cases involving the shrouded folk's cult. Now that a second commune had been revealed and raided within the UK, and with countries all across the world starting to take notice, I'd been given a small office of my own here at the Yard specifically to coordinate with the rest of an international task force dedicated to uncovering the extent of this toxic presence in our midst.

Since I was the only one on that task force who'd had direct dealing with multiple communes, an awful lot of the coordination fell on my shoulders.

"That's right," I said to the sergeant from Rome who'd started aiding investigations into the nearby hill country. "The most common signs are periodic thefts of medical supplies, food, and other essentials. You'll also want to watch for reports of any unusual violent activity—mutilated animals, destruction of property—and a higher number of missing persons than in the surrounding areas. The communes tend to choose areas at or near high elevations, often forested so they can avoid their buildings being spotted from above."

"It was a thing like that that made me concerned to start with," the sergeant said in lightly stilted English. With some of my law enforcement brethren across the world, we'd needed to rely on translators. "I can look for these other signs."

If he'd seen enough to reach out, chances were high that we had a real case there. I jotted a couple notes on my notepad. "Proceed with caution if you see more indications that you have an active commune in the area. They may be on higher alert now that we've started cracking down elsewhere. We want to bring these people in, not have them run off to start up all over again someplace else."

"Agreed." The sergeant's tone turned solemn. "I've read some of the reports, seen the pictures... We want people like that locked away."

After hanging up, I added his details to my quickly growing computer database. In just the three days since I'd returned to Scotland Yard while Sherlock and John determined Jemma's likely location and then followed her, the task force had already identified five likely commune locations in the United States, Spain, Norway, Morocco, and Peru, with dozens more suspected across the globe. If we could prove as effective at shutting down those communes as at finding them, the demonic beings egging on the cult wouldn't stand a chance.

Although from what John had relayed to me about Jemma and her sister, that might not be enough for her to declare victory.

The conflicting emotions that rose up at the thought of Jemma — the brilliant, determined woman I'd fallen for... who also thought it totally reasonable to push a man down a mountain to achieve her goals — only had a moment to stew inside me before a knock sounded on my door. At my "Come in," Chief Higgins poked his head in.

"Lestrade," he said with a strange air, his usual unshakeable authority off-balance in the face of my new, prominent assignment. "There's been an incident in Southwark I think you might want to look into."

I frowned. "In *Southwark*?" The communes within our borders hadn't been anywhere near London. They hadn't been anywhere near any major habitation. The cultists wanted to be left alone, not draw notice.

He motioned to my computer. "I've forwarded the relevant materials. It's all over the news. A small group of civilians just gave The Shard a good battering with a couple of potent homemade bombs. There are certain details about their behavior that reminded me of your bizarro cult."

A chill ran over my skin. Why the hell would the shrouded folk's worshippers suddenly be bombing major urban buildings? That didn't fit their typical MO in any way I could see, though maybe Sherlock would have had an immediate answer.

"I'll take a look," I said. "Thank you."

He gave me a curt nod and strode away.

I pulled up the files with trepidation squeezing my gut. Maybe the chief was grasping at straws trying to find a connection to my new work focus so he could stay involved, or maybe he was being overly paranoid about the slightest hint of activity that reminded him of the cult reports out of worry he'd let something slip by on his watch. It could have nothing to do with them at all.

But usually Chief Higgins was pretty level-headed. That was why I'd generally appreciated working under him. If he thought this event might be related, it was worth digging into right away.

The first photos made me wince. The Shard was aptly named considering it looked like a perfectly constructed spire of glass rising above all the nearby buildings in Southwark. Whoever this group was, their homemade bombs had shattered some of the panes and blackened others from the base to nearly halfway up the building. The effect gave it a lopsided, ravaged sort of look that was the exact opposite of its normally crystalline—if a little outlandish—appearance.

Several workers had been taken to the hospital to have burns and other injuries treated, but it didn't appear the bombs had left any fatalities. The reports suggested that the perpetrators had been focused on damaging the outside of the building more than anyone inside it. That was certainly unusual.

Then I came to a portion that described the men and women taken into custody. The officers had encountered them still in the building, "swaying in strange motions and mumbling to themselves as they bled from cuts they appeared to have sliced into their own arms and legs."

My stomach flipped over. That sounded like our cultists, all right. Jemma had said the bloodletting was part of their worship—the shrouded folk enjoyed the pain. It definitely wasn't the sort of behavior you'd expect from any ordinary bombers. What the hell were they up to?

I read through the rest of the materials the chief had sent me and then headed right out the door. I wasn't going to find out much secondhand. The real answers would be on the scene. And damn if I didn't wish Sherlock were along to make his astute observations.

He and John had gone off to handle one side of things. This part of the case was mine. I hadn't been made detective inspector younger than anyone else on the force for nothing, and I'd better prove that.

The bombing had only happened a little more than an hour ago. When I reached The Shard, the streets around the building were cordoned off with police tape. I ducked under one of the yellow strips and flashed my badge at the constables who moved to intercept me.

"This crime may be related to a special investigation I'm working on," I said. "I need to see the site of the bombing and to talk to any of the perps who are available."

The one guy nodded. "We've got a couple waiting for transport. There were a bunch of them all coordinated. I'll show you what I can of the site, and then you can have at them."

The damage looked even more offensive up close, like a massive dappled scar running up the side of the building. The constable walked me over to the base, where the panes had been completely blasted away, and pointed upward to a charred hole in the edge of the first floor ceiling.

"They had two explosives that both packed a lot of punch considering they probably bought the stuff at a gardening store. One they set off on the second floor and the other on the tenth. We haven't confirmed possible structural damage yet, so everyone's been ordered to evacuate except the inspectors."

I wasn't going to get any closer then. The sunlight slanting through the gaping openings where glass should have been caught on a reddish glint at the edge of the hole. I squinted at it. "I heard the perps were cutting themselves?"

The constable made a face. "It's a real mess up there. Blood all over the floor. From the marks on them, it wasn't the first time they'd hacked into themselves like that. Bloody lunatics."

If these people were part of the cult, he didn't know the half of it. I poked around at the rubble on the ground, shards of glass clinking against each other, but no flashes of inspiration came to me. Making obscure connections wasn't how I'd gotten this job anyway.

"Let's see these people, then."

The two who hadn't been shipped off yet were sitting in the back of a police van that needed a driver. The woman, who looked to be in her mid-thirties, glanced up with a defiant expression as I came in. The man—older, maybe fifty—shifted farther back on the bench. They'd both been cuffed, and bandages covered most of their arms, calves, and even the back of the woman's shoulder.

"Give me a moment?" I said to the constable. He drew back to rejoin his colleague.

When we were alone, I turned to the two criminals. "So," I said, as if I already knew everything, "you worship *them*, do you?"

A flash of doubt crossed the woman's face. "What we do is none of your business," she spat at me.

"I think it is when you go around blasting holes in buildings in my city." I propped myself against the wall. "I know they like you bleeding and all that, but they don't usually encourage you to draw attention to yourselves. Trying out a new approach?"

"We serve as we're asked to serve," the man mumbled.

The woman shot him a glare. "I'm not saying anything to you," she informed me.

Nothing they'd said quite confirmed it, only they were part of some barmy collective. I took a small gamble. We'd only identified three areas of cult activity in the country, and two of those

communes had been thoroughly raided. One group, however, had
fled before we'd tracked them down. Chances were, if these were
shrouded folk worshippers, they'd be that bunch, not some roaming
from across the Channel or farther abroad.

"I don't need you to say anything." I tipped my head to the two of
them. "Mostly I just wanted to see you. We know you came from
that little settlement out by Dover. Nice trick burning all your things,
but it didn't work quite as well as I'd imagine you wanted."

The man clearly wasn't as self-controlled as his companion. He
swore under his breath, hunching defensively. The woman couldn't
help reacting on a smaller level, her hands clenching in the cuffs. Her
mouth tightened.

"You know *nothing*," she sneered, but she couldn't hide the
nervousness in her expression.

"Oh, I think I've already proven that's not true. You could
enlighten me on one point, though. Why The Shard? What's it ever
done to your gods?"

The woman stared toward the little windows in the doors, and a
little shudder ran through her. This time, though, her mouth stayed
clamped shut.

I didn't think I was going to get anything else out of these two
right now. They'd given away enough. The rest I could follow up on
with the rest of the group in custody—pick out the one who looked
most likely to talk, get them alone, a little good-cop-bad-cop
routine… It might take some time, but we'd get our answers.

If we had time.

I waved my thanks and good-bye to the other officers and headed
back to my car. A cloud of uneasiness followed me. When I sank into
the driver's seat, I reached for the key, hesitated, and got out my
phone instead.

John picked up on the third ring. "No news here yet," he said,
sounding even more tense than he had when I'd spoken to him first
thing this morning. It had to be early in the morning over there in
Japan now, but I didn't get the impression I'd woken him. Was he
sleeping during the unearthly vigil he was keeping over there? I sure
as hell didn't envy him his current job.

"I didn't figure there was," I said. "Because of course you'd tell me as soon as there is. I'm calling because *I* have news. It looks like the shrouded folk are encouraging their cult to take up a new MO."

John's voice turned more alert in an instant. "What's that?"

I peered at the scarred form of The Shard through my windshield. "You remember that commune you and Moran found abandoned and scorched? I think we've found its former inhabitants. They just blew up part of The Shard while swaying and bleeding all over it in worship."

"*What?* Why the hell—they're meant to keep themselves secret."

"They used to be meant to, anyway. One of the guys I talked to made it sound as if they were asked to do it. I don't suppose you've seen anything over there or heard anything from Moran that would give you a clue as to why."

There was a rustle as John must have shaken his head. "Not at all. That's the last thing I'd have expected. Bloody hell. They didn't give you any indication of their reasons?"

"Not really. I haven't had much chance to go at them yet. I wanted to check in with you first."

"You're worried," John said. Sherlock might have been the observational genius, but the former doctor didn't miss much when it came to emotions.

There was no point in denying it. "I'm just thinking, there are dozens, maybe hundreds of these little communes we haven't taken down yet. What if this isn't an isolated incident? What if it's part of some new backlash against our efforts and Jemma's?" *What if it happens again, and next time we lose more than part of a pretty building?*

"That... that doesn't seem like an unreasonable concern." John sucked in a breath. "As soon as Sherlock, Jemma, and Bash come out of that place, I'll see what they think. But you've got your task force in place. I'd imagine you can handle this more effectively than any of us could."

I could. I'd already been thinking through how I'd reach out to my contacts, make suggestions of activity to watch out for—in major cities, around visually striking buildings and other public places...

This was the kind of work I was meant to do. I hadn't been totally prepared for John to recognize that, though.

Maybe that was unfair of me.

"If there's any way you think I can contribute, just let me know," John went on, and it hit me that I wasn't on the sidelines this time, not really. I was in the middle of the fray, calling the shots.

I'd spent so long feeling as if I was chasing along behind Sherlock's coattails, envying his easy partnership with John... but if the events of the last few months had shown me anything, it was that a hell of a lot of the bitterness I'd been holding onto was my own doing. I had to stop getting in my own way and get on with things.

"I appreciate that," I said. "I'd better get back to the Yard and start coordinating."

I *was* calling the shots—and I'd better make sure they were the right ones, or Lord only knew what kind of catastrophe the world was about to face.

CHAPTER EIGHT

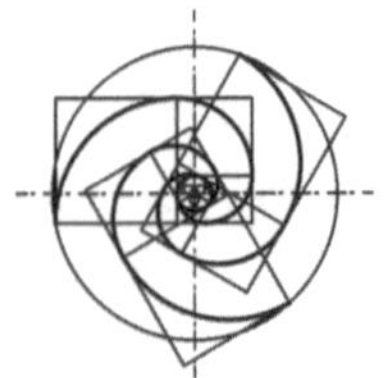

Jemma

"Another spoke in the wheel," Sherlock said with a triumphant air.

We studied our current shrunken city's glowing stone from a safe distance. Sherlock's natural pallor had taken on a yellowish cast in the hours we'd been hiking across the shrouded realm, but the sight of two lines of ruddy energy crossing at the stone brought a flush back into his cheeks. There wasn't much that invigorated him more than confirming one of his theories was correct.

I glanced around at the downtown buildings, like a crumbling toy city we'd barged into. I hadn't recognized this place as we'd come up on it, but Sherlock had immediately declared it Nairobi. We'd passed several other cities large enough to make an appearance in the shrouded realm on the way here, but the south-aiming line we'd been following had traveled through them and their stones without any intersection. I'd been starting to wonder if the detective might have been mistaken just this once.

"It could be more of a grid than a wheel," Bash remarked from behind me. He'd set his hand on my shoulder when we'd stopped, his thumb swiveling in a steady motion to push back the creeping shivers the erratic sounds around us brought on. *He* was feeling the effects too, as much as he tried to hide any shaky moments from me. I rested my hand over his to return the favor with the stroke of my fingers.

"Based on the trajectory through the cities, the line we've been tracking isn't straight but curved," I said. "At this point, I'm convinced." I turned my gaze toward the gleaming line that formed the spoke. "The real question is, what are we going to find at the center?"

I couldn't say I was looking forward to finding out. The dissonant energy of the shrouded realm had stayed at the same moderate level while we'd been navigating the ring. I suspected as soon as we headed closer to the center, it'd escalate again.

But I hadn't seen any trace of my sister or anything to suggest where Olivia might be in our travels so far. It appeared increasingly certain that the fiends would be holding her by the main source of their power. Not only would they be better equipped to control her, but the heightened energy would have sapped her strength away too. How had she even survived in this place for years when it was wearing me down after just a couple days?

The thought of all that time she'd remained a captive made me queasy. I squared my shoulders and raised my chin toward the path ahead of us. "Why don't we get going? If it takes us much longer to get back, John will worry himself frantic."

"True." Sherlock studied the pale-cloaked bodies of the shrouded folk drifting along the line of energy. "It appears we'll have more company heading in that direction. How would you suggest we avoid notice?"

"We won't walk right by the line. Better to keep a good distance, just close enough that we can still follow it. And we can adjust our sheets so they look more like the fiends' coverings." I tugged one of the folds by my back up over my head to hide my bright hair. "That also means you can escape back to our world faster if one of the creatures comes at you. Just be careful not to drop the fabric over your eyes accidentally."

We took a winding path back through the city so that we emerged a good stretch away from the line we meant to follow. It glimmered across the dull ground like a thread of flame. With the way the ring had curved, I calculated we were now heading more north than east. Up into northern Africa or even further, into Europe?

Did these crossroads have any impact on the real cities they were associated with? In my travels, I'd never noticed any urban areas that gave me an uneasy vibe, but then, I hadn't been looking for signs of shrouded folk presence amid the bustle.

Before we left the replica of Nairobi behind, Bash and Sherlock raised their sheets over their heads like I had. "The fiends have a certain way of moving that we can imitate to some extent too," I told them, and demonstrated the long, smooth strides I'd perfected while I'd been heading deeper into the creatures' territory rather than skirting it.

A dozen or so shrouded folk drifted right along the glowing line in our view. From our vantage point, they were little more than pale blobs in vaguely human form. We shouldn't look much different. When I'd traveled alone, none had come to investigate other than that bunch I'd gotten too close to early on.

Three of us making the journey together might have looked even less suspicious. Many of the fiends appeared to cluster into groups of anywhere from two to four as they made their way across the plain.

It was another long walk. Every time we passed a city, we kept to the fringes and watched for intersecting lines, but as before, the first several didn't offer anything new. The unnerving sounds constantly traveling through the realm started to ring in my ears. I felt a little childish doing it, but after a while I grasped both of the guys' hands while we walked, tracing patterns over their knuckles. They caught on and returned the gesture without any of us commenting on it. That strategy held off the discordant energy enough that my legs only twinged rather than aching.

Sherlock's eyes must have been a tad keener than my own. Before I'd noticed anything, he squinted at the next city up ahead and said, "I think we've found our axle."

I peered at the landscape around the miniature skyline as we drew closer. Within a minute, I spotted what he meant. Another glowing line to our right streaked across the plain toward that city, but at an angle sharper than ninety degrees. It could very well be the same line I'd followed into Tehran.

"That's Istanbul," I said, tipping my head toward the distinctive form of the Hagia Sophia. I'd spent a little time there for business reasons twice in the last several years — I'd found it a fascinating mix of ancient history and modern developments. The thought of the shrouded folk feeding off it even in some distant, detached way made my skin crawl.

"You haven't seen any real-world analogue for a power base there?" Sherlock asked, his hand warm and dry against mine.

I shook my head. "I never would have thought the shrouded folk interacted with our world in any significant way other than through the communes, and all of those I know about are nowhere near cities." But since I'd ramped up my campaign against the fiends, it'd become increasingly and uncomfortably clear how much I hadn't found out about them in my limited view as a child in one of those communes.

More shrouded folk were traveling toward the city along the second line. How many of those glowing trails came together in this city? We'd want to find out, but apprehension shivered through me alongside the rising erratic thrum. The place might be crawling with the fiends. We couldn't hope that we could fool them with distance once we got closer to the point where all those paths converged.

One could slip around unnoticed much more easily than three. I squeezed the guys' hands a little tighter as we reached the first of the buildings, the normal urban sprawl constricted to just the city proper as it had been in the other replicas we'd encountered. I might not have made it this far without Bash and Sherlock's support; it squeezed my heart thinking that they'd been willing to risk so much to try to help me. But the fact was that they were even more vulnerable here than I was, and I couldn't think of any way they could defend themselves, let alone me, if we got into a real altercation.

I noted a long apartment block up ahead, its ten stories looming only twice my height, and veered toward it. The entire eastern wall had caved in, leaving the interior strewn with rubble but open to intruders. I stopped in front of it and let go of the guys, ignoring the jolt of loss at the lack of contact.

"I'll scout out the city center on my own," I said in the most authoritarian tone I had in me. I fixed Bash and then Sherlock with a look imbued with the same steel. "I know you probably hate the sound of that plan, but it makes more sense than anything else we could do. I think you've done everything you can to get me through this place. We're *all* safer if we're not roaming around this city together. And I can avoid the fiends better than you two."

"Mori," Bash said, not quite a protest, with an uneasy twist of his mouth.

I gripped his arm. "I'll just take a quick look, see if I can find any sign of my sister, and then I'll come back and share my observations, and we can decide what to do next from there. I survived three years as a teenager with no real-world experience before I ever hired you. I can make it through an hour or two on my own here."

Sherlock didn't exactly look pleased, but I'd known an appeal to logic would work on him. "I would rather make my own observations. Two sets of eyes may notice more than one."

"And you can make those observations after I've taken the lay of the land," I said. "I can prepare you for the threats. Think of this just as an initial scouting mission."

He let out an impatient breath, but he stepped into the shelter of the ruined building. Bash followed him reluctantly a moment later.

"It'd better be only an hour or two," my hitman said. "If it's any longer, I'm not waiting around here."

"I'll be back," I promised. "And if the fiends stumble on you in here, remember how to get home. I'll follow you back as soon as I see you're gone."

The grimace he gave me in response didn't exactly reassure me that he'd stick to that agreement, but I could tell it was the best I was going to get.

I slunk away through the streets. We'd entered on the old town side, most of the buildings no taller than me if not shorter, but the modern skyscrapers I glimpsed over the crumbling rooftops didn't glint the way they did in my reality. Of course, there wasn't anything much like sunlight here to glint off them.

The dryly rotten stink of the shrouded folk hung so thick along the streets that within minutes it had coated the inside of my mouth. I resisted the urge to spit. At every intersection, I peered both ways before crossing, checking for a different sort of traffic. A couple of times, I caught sight of shrouded folk passing farther along in one direction or the other, and hung back until they'd drifted out of sight.

The red glow started to tint the streets up ahead as I hurried across the wider gap where rippling waters of the Golden Horn should have been. The ground rose only slightly where I remembered a steeper hill from my explorations in my own world. I passed a half-toppled Galata Tower, picking my way carefully and quietly over the fallen stones, and jerked close to the nearest building at the murmuring of fiendish voices nearby.

A clot of five or six of them passed within ten feet of me, their conversation just loud enough for me to hear, even if I couldn't understand most of it. I caught the word for *human* again, and a term that had something to do with heights. I didn't think that could be referring to my or the guys' presence here. Was my sister here—in one of the tall buildings, maybe?

As I crept after them, I scanned the structures around me for any sign of activity within or on the rooftops. Nothing stood out. The crimson light intensified, painting the street, the buildings, and the sheet that covered me.

A thicker mass of shrouded folk stood around the source of that light. I sidled carefully around the nearby structures until I found a spot where the roofs were low enough that I could see over them if I leveraged myself partway up with my foot in a smashed crevice.

The stone spear jutting up in the midst of the city was twice as tall as any I'd seen before, its light pulsing in a stuttered beat and flaring red-hot. Shrouded folk clustered all around the stone, brushing it not just with their faces but the rest of their bodies. Five glowing lines flowed into it at nearly equal intervals around the spot. A wheel with five spokes.

A tickle of curiosity ran through me at the question of what the other three ring cities might be, but it was quickly overwhelmed by frustration. I'd come all this way, I'd heard the fiends talking about a human, but there was no sign of Olivia or any kind of human prison here either. They could have meant humans from their cult or who knew what else.

I dragged in a breath and closed my eyes. She had to be *somewhere.* If I could just latch onto the slightest trace of her presence...

I drew memories up in my mind: her smiling face when I'd made her little animals out of folded paper, the closest things to toys we'd had. The way she would clutch my hand when the other kids tried to harass her. Her voice, bright and sweet, in the rare moments when no one else could hear her and she'd been happy enough to sing.

The sensations from those moments flooded me. "Olivia," I whispered against the discordant thrum. "*Olivia.*"

And like a miracle, that bright voice, though faint and ragged, floated to my ears.

"Jemma?"

My eyes popped open. Nothing lay around me except the same scene I've been watching before. "Olivia," I said again, a touch louder, straining my eyes.

The outline of a form, pale-haired and pale-dressed and the size of a grown woman — swam into view a few feet away from me. It was so transparent I couldn't make out her features, couldn't look into her eyes, but I felt down to my bones it was my sister.

Only... not really here.

"You shouldn't be there," she said in a frightened tone, the words sounding as if they'd crossed a vast distance.

"I came for you," I said. "Where *are* you?"

"On the other side. They say I'm... I'm an anchor for their stone, a bridge for the power."

My heart sank. After everything I'd risked here... "You're still in the human world."

Her head bowed in acknowledgment. Then her body twitched. "You have to go. Now. Fast. I can feel them—they're coming for you."

Her form snapped away, and I found myself staring through the spot where it'd been toward the massive stone spear. The massive stone spear and the shrouded bodies around it, several of which had turned my way.

Shit.

If I'd been here alone, I'd have jerked my "shroud" down over my eyes and willed my way home. My sister had been back there all along anyway. But Bash and Sherlock were waiting for me, and the fiends wouldn't necessarily stop searching just because I vanished from sight.

I leapt off the building and ran back the way I'd come.

The warbles of unnerving energy blared even louder, as if they were chasing after me in a wave of sound. I dodged fallen rubble and dashed left and then right between the streets. A tremor ran up my legs. I pushed myself faster—and one calf gave, pitching me across the road.

Pain and blood welled on my knees. I shoved myself back onto my feet and ran on, grasping the corners of the shrunken buildings around me for extra support.

The hiss of those swaths of dead flesh mingled with the energy's hum. I swerved around another corner and caught sight of the building where the men had taken shelter up ahead.

At the same moment, a shrouded one flew into the street in front of me.

My legs stalled. Then I hurtled forward, slamming past it with all the strength and speed left in my body. The brush of its shrouded form against my skin left my stomach lurching.

"We've got to go back home!" I called out. "Get out of here now! She isn't here!"

Bash appeared in the opening. At the sight of me and my pursuers, he moved to lunge forward. "No!" I yelled, and did the only thing I could think of that would force him to follow my orders. Shoving down the flash of panic at the thought of leaving him and Sherlock behind, I yanked the white fabric over my eyes and threw my consciousness back to the Tokyo hotel room.

CHAPTER NINE

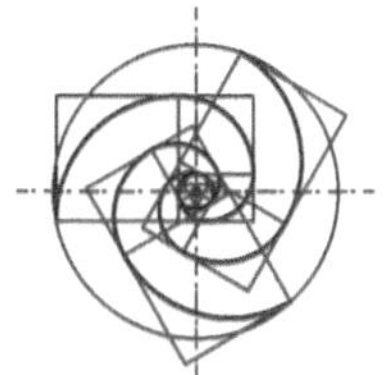

Jemma

I jolted awake on the carpeted floor with a jerk of my limbs as if an electric shock had raced through them. For a few seconds, I could only stare at the high white ceiling as the haze cleared from my head. Midday sunlight washed over my face. The sour smell of the shrouded realm lingered in my mouth. My muscles felt like jelly, and a knot of hunger twisted my stomach.

How long had I been gone from this world? The hours had started to blur together on the other side.

There was the scrape of chair legs against the floor, and then John was kneeling over me, his face tight with concern. "Jemma! Can you understand me? Are you all right?"

A form next to me shuddered and gulped air with a rasp. I managed to sit up, gripping John's hand for balance. Bash was just coming to, his face gleaming with the same herbal mixture that was still smeared all over me. Beyond him, a tremor ran through Sherlock's prone body. The detective's eyes popped open, and relief washed through me—followed by another spasm of hunger.

I opened my mouth to speak and found my throat was too dry to force any sound out. John hustled to the kitchenette. After a brief clatter of glass and hiss of the faucet, he returned clutching three cups of water. I snatched one out of his grasp and practically inhaled it.

The liquid soothed my throat but barely touched the pangs in my stomach. I set the empty glass down and wobbled onto my feet. "We should eat something," I said in a rasp. "Our bodies need to recover."

Thankfully, I'd considered that factor when we'd stocked up the suite. I grabbed the loaf of bread on the counter and started slathering it with peanut butter. Because I hadn't left my sweet tooth behind in the shrouded realm, I also drizzled it with a good portion of honey.

By the time I'd finished assembling the first sandwich, Bash had made his way over to me on legs that only swayed a little. I tried to shove the food toward him, but he shook his head emphatically. "You were over there a lot longer than us. You need it more than I do. I can make one for myself and for Sherlock."

I might have argued more if saliva hadn't been flooding my tongue and my entire abdomen clanging for relief. Dropping onto one of the kitchen stools, I shoved a good quarter of the sandwich into my mouth in one go. Oh, Lord, that was just about the best thing I'd ever eaten.

After the first bite, I forced myself to take smaller nibbles and chew slowly despite my bodily sense of urgency. John helped Sherlock over to the counter, somewhat to the detective's dismay from his expression, though he didn't fight the help. As Bash slid over a hastily prepared sandwich, I spoke up, a little more clearly this time.

"Don't take it down too fast. When you've gone a while without food, you can make yourself sick if you gorge yourself."

As I knew from personal experience. The cult's favorite methods of physical torment involved outer injuries, but my commune had experimented with various sorts of deprivation when the mood struck them.

Sherlock nodded, probably already aware of that fact, and dug into his sandwich with some restraint. John hovered beside him, his anxious gaze sliding from his friend to me and back again. With my knot of hunger unraveling, it sank in that he might be as much nervous *of* me as for me, especially when it came to the man beside him.

"Even though he showed up uninvited, I refrained from giving him another shove," I said, breaking the silence. "He isn't in any more danger from me."

John blinked at me, and I tensed with the suspicion that I'd been too flippant in my sort-of reassurance. After what I'd set him up to witness the other day, he didn't have any reason to believe me on my second point, did he?

Sherlock broke the momentary silence. "I don't believe I ever was," he said mildly, and popped the last bite of his sandwich into his mouth.

"Apparently not, considering you made it here." I glowered at him. "If you do die, it'll definitely be *your* fault for not taking the hint."

"I accept that fact without complaint."

As John watched the exchange, his expression gradually relaxed into a bemused smile. "You're both insane," he informed us. "It's a good thing you've got people on your side who are patient enough to put up with it."

Bash had recovered enough to grab us all fresh glasses of water. He set them on the counter with his eyebrows raised. "Can you imagine if the two of them were left to their own devices to work together unchecked? I'm not sure if the results would be astonishing or terrifying."

"Hey. A little loyalty?" I aimed a teasing kick at his leg, and he shot me a fond grin as he dodged it.

John shook his head at the three of us. I wasn't sure he was completely reassured, but at least I didn't feel any immediate animosity from him. My gaze slid around the room, and now that my most pressing physical needs had been met, the sense of someone missing sent a different sort of pang through me.

"Garrett opted not to join you?" I said tentatively. As much as John was wary of me, it'd mainly be on Sherlock's behalf. Garrett

Lestrade had always been the most uneasy of the bunch about my criminal inclinations in general. He took the letter of the law more seriously than the independent detective pair. He'd come to terms with my past, accepted me and opened up to me, even told me he loved me… but that was before he'd had to watch me assault one of his closest colleagues.

I couldn't say I returned the same depth of feeling he'd offered me — I wasn't sure I was capable of it — but the thought that he might be repulsed by me now sent a jabbing sensation through my chest.

"Oh, he'd have been here if he could," John said. "Duty called back in London. But he's still on the case. He's playing a key role in a task force investigating the cult's communes worldwide." He paused, his smile falling away. "That reminds me. I talked to him early this morning — he had something disturbing to report. It looks like the commune down near Dover — the one that scattered before we could catch them — launched an attack on The Shard. They blasted a large portion of the external walls, along with all the bloodletting and so on that they usually do."

My spine stiffened. "They attacked a public building in the middle of the city?" That *was* disturbing. What the hell were they up to? "Were they caught?"

"As far as Garrett could tell, they didn't make much effort to avoid arrest. One of the cultists he spoke to gave the impression that the shrouded folk had asked them to do it."

I didn't like the sound of that at all. It was probably a reaction to our attempts to shut down the cult — and it was a major escalation.

Sherlock's eyes sharpened in thought. "These beings don't care for patterns or mathematics. The Shard is a particularly… geometric building. Would that be the reason for making it a target?"

"Most likely," I said. "If just having the cult damage themselves and each other gives the shrouded folk energy, then damaging something that large and distasteful to them probably brings a whole lot more. They just wouldn't have done it before because sustaining the communes was more important than making one big smash."

"It's some kind of desperate measure to fight back?" John suggested.

Bash's expression had darkened. He knew how malicious minds worked better than most did. "Or the monsters are willing to sacrifice their worshippers because they expect to get something even better than a bunch of tiny communes in the end." He looked to me. "What could they do with a big surge of extra energy?"

"I don't know." I curled my fingers into my palms. "When I was in that last city in their realm, where their power was the strongest, I was able to talk to my sister. She wasn't fully present there—even less than we were. They've got her in this world somewhere, but she was able to reach out. She said something about them making her into a 'bridge' for their power, connecting her to the stone... They've had to rely on their cult to give them access to our world so far. Maybe with a big enough push, they could create a permanent passage between their realm and ours."

"That... doesn't sound like a happy development," John said, his jaw tightening.

"No. I'm not sure what the consequences could be, but it might mean they could act on all people, whether we let them in or not, much more freely." The horror of the possibility crawled over me as I said the words. A world where the shrouded folk roamed at will among human beings, preying on them whenever they wanted, drinking in our sunlight... I had to restrain a shudder.

"We need to round up all the cultists we can find as quickly as possible, then," Sherlock said, pushing himself off his stool as if he could stride off to do that personally right now. "If the creatures don't have representatives to act on their behalf before they've opened such a passage, they won't have the chance."

My pulse stuttered, thinking back over everything I'd seen in the shrouded realm. "The city stones gave them energy in their own realm. Those are probably the key. And the most powerful one was in Istanbul. Does Garrett have contacts there? What are the most prominent geometric-styled buildings there? Their police force needs to have people monitoring them, *now*."

John pulled out his phone and hesitated. "It's the middle of the night back in London."

"It doesn't matter. Wake him up. The fiends don't care whether we lose sleep over this. If they're starting this new strategy, that's the first place they'll strike, and one effective blow there might be enough that nothing else we do matters." I hopped off my own stool. "The rest of us should get cleaned up and then head out immediately."

Bash touched my arm. "Was your sister able to tell you where she is?"

"Not exactly." Remembering our distant conversation made my heart squeeze. "I'd bet good money that they have her somewhere near Istanbul, though, if they're trying to use her to make their 'bridge.' Especially since that's where she was able to talk to me. It sounds like that's where we'll be needed most as it is. Come on. Every second could make a difference if you don't want to see these monsters ruling over all of us."

I showered as quickly as I could while getting the oily paste off my skin and out of my hair, and then threw on the dress at the top of my suitcase. There wasn't much in the way of packing to do. I'd only brought a carry-on.

When I wheeled it out into the suite's main room, John had gathered the soiled sheets and the leftover supplies into a box. He set it on the counter as I came over.

"Moran and Sherlock went to use the other rooms rather than waiting, so we can get going sooner," he said, swiping a hand over his head that ruffled his blond hair. He leaned against one of the stools but didn't quite sit, his walking stick still braced against the floor.

"Sherlock wouldn't let you come along to assist?" I asked in a gently teasing tone. I could only imagine how much the former doctor had been fussing over his friend with the new injuries.

Injuries that were my fault.

John managed a wry smile, but his gaze slid away from me. "He's nothing if not stubborn. And independent. There's a reason I'm not only his best friend but essentially his only one."

And Sherlock was by far John's closest friend—more than friend, really—from what I'd observed. My throat closed up. I groped for the right words to convey the regret I felt without straying into disingenuous remorse. At the very least, I owed it to

John to be honest with him. He deserved to make his decisions about how far he took this quest alongside me knowing exactly who I was.

"I'm sorry," I said. "It seemed like a necessary evil to make sure I could save my sister. She had to come first—she still has to. But I didn't like doing it. I didn't *enjoy* the thought of him being hurt, or how you'd feel seeing it."

John met my eyes again. He swallowed audibly, but he didn't look half as angry as he had the right to be. "He's already forgiven you. I guess I should take my cues from him. I— It was your sister you told me about, that first night we slept together during the conference, wasn't it? The person you lost who set you on this path?"

I remembered that conversation with a dull ache in my chest. One of the first small truths I'd allowed myself to share with these men while I was still deceiving them in so many ways.

"Yes," I said. "It's all been for her. The fiends stole her life, one way or another. I hate them in general, but I mostly hate them for that."

"And you blame yourself for not saving her before they took her."

Exactly how much had Bash told John and Sherlock when they'd turned up here? He wasn't wrong, though.

I lowered my gaze, the discomfort of the admission prickling through me. "Of course I do. I was the only protector she had."

John was silent for several seconds. Then he said, slowly and quietly, "I told you a little before about my older brother, how he died. I could see him going off the rails years before the end. I tried to talk to him, to get him to cut back on the drinking, to take opportunities that would help get his life back on track, but he was difficult to be around. I could have pushed harder, been there more. And that was nothing compared to what you and your sister went through. I don't know, if I had a chance to fix things, to bring him back safe after all... I might go to some pretty horrible lengths to accomplish that."

I had to smile at him, even if the gesture felt bittersweet. "I don't think you'd do anything all that horrible. There's a goodness in you that just shines through, more than I've ever seen in anyone."

"Maybe it's easier to see that from the outside." He considered me. "You don't think you have all that much goodness in *you*, do you? But I've seen plenty."

That remark made me twice as uncomfortable as his comment about blaming myself. "Not so much recently, though," I suggested as a deflection.

"I don't know. There were a lot worse ways you could have pushed someone down a cliff." His mouth slanted crookedly. "Can I ask that you not try out any other ways in the future?"

I let out a rough laugh. "I think I've proven that I'm incapable of really hurting Sherlock even when I intend to."

"You think that's a weakness," John said. "I'd consider it a strength. You were careful with him because you recognize how important he is."

I didn't have to figure out how to answer that, because Bash hustled into the suite at the same instant.

"I've booked our tickets," he said, holding up his phone. "We'll be in Istanbul by the end of the day."

CHAPTER TEN

Bash

We stayed in the car, air conditioning blasting in defiance of Istanbul's late summer heat, peering up at the skyscraper in the city's business district that we'd gotten the address to. I wanted to think that we were barking up the wrong tree, that Jemma's monsters hadn't changed the rules of the game this much, but just looking at the building, a sense of wrongness shivered through me.

The high-rises around it stood straight and for the most part sharply rectangular, with even rows of windows or panes of glass. This one looked as if Picasso had possessed the architect partway through the designing. Floors jutted out here and there at unpredictable intervals. The windows were a hodgepodge of heights and sizes. Even the frame around the front door slanted at a slight but awkward angle.

"Construction was completed just twenty-two months ago," Sherlock said from where he was sitting next to John at the front of the rental car. I hadn't put up an argument about the former doctor taking the wheel after we'd left him behind to go after Jemma into the shrouded realm—it'd seemed only fair. "Most of the funding came from a few individuals associated with the corporation we traced those transfers of Tillhouse's to."

"Tillhouse is locked up now, isn't he?" Jemma said beside me as she contemplated the building.

John nodded. "He couldn't talk his way out of the spectacle we made at the Scotland commune. He's been taken into custody pending trial."

"I doubt he has anything to do with this situation as it currently is," Sherlock put in. "Those transfers would only make up a small amount of the cost of construction, and he passed them on more than five years ago. He may not even have known what the money was going to."

Really, we should be glad for that money, since the transactions had popped up during Garrett's digging—with the help of one of Sherlock's computer expert associates—once we'd focused our attention on Istanbul. Jemma was frowning, though.

"All kinds of people put money into that corporation," she said. "At least some of the others were probably like Tillhouse, under the shrouded folk's sway somehow. They've been extending their influence all over."

I nodded to the building. "Do you think they have a commune set up in there?"

"From the data we've been able to gather so far, the first several floors are legitimate businesses, though of course they're unknowingly funding the owners' plans with their rent," Sherlock said. "The higher floors are all apartments."

"They could have worshippers staying in those apartments, or they could even have changed the layout from the blueprints they submitted to the administrative office and opened those upper floors up more to mimic their usual settlements." Jemma sucked her lower lip under her teeth. "It's definitely going to be a lot harder to storm a secure business establishment than one of those little villages."

"The income they've been able to accumulate means we can't point to any of the usual patterns," John said. "There've been no regular thefts of supplies within the city, for example. I'm not sure we could get a warrant."

Sherlock shifted in his seat. "There are other means of detecting illegal activity. It just may take some time to dig far enough. I have people on it."

"The fiends are already escalating their attacks," Jemma said. She turned away from the window, her face even paler than usual in the bright sunlight that fell across it. "Buildings bombed in Nairobi, Paris, Houston, Delhi, and Moscow in just the last day. Some of those besides Nairobi might be part of their 'wheel' of power. I don't know how much time we have before they do something catastrophic." Her gaze lifted again. "And my sister could very well be up in that tower."

John glanced back at her. "Do you think the shrouded folk will realize we're here? They tracked us pretty well back in London."

"I wouldn't think so, not unless one of them crosses paths with one of us here and is able to recognize us. The mark that one put on Sherlock weeks ago will have faded by now. And even if they have the means to try to trace our movements, we took that last flight under false names." She paused. "On the other hand, the fiends that came after me in their realm may have put the pieces together. They won't know how much I figured out, and they were already worried about how I was interfering with their plans. Whether they know we're in Istanbul or not, they'll be ramping up whatever scheme they have underway even faster."

She motioned to Sherlock. "Make sure your people are checking for the usual signs in the more isolated areas outside the city. It's possible this building serves some other purpose or is some kind of decoy, and the cult's main activities are nearby but on more usual terrain for them."

"I already have that covered," the detective said. "I expect we'll have more answers shortly."

Jemma's expression stayed tensed. "Shortly" wasn't good enough for her in her current state.

"Why don't we scope out the place up close?" I suggested to her. I was eager to take some kind of action too, and having something concrete to do would at least break her out of her fretting. "Just the two of us, so we don't draw too much attention. We can take a look at the businesses and evaluate the building's security at the same time… and I happened to notice there's a pastry café at the back of the first floor."

Jemma shot me a thin flash of a smile. "You know the quickest way to my heart. There's definitely no point in making any plans of our own until we have a clearer sense of our options." She tipped her head to the Londoners. "We'll meet up with you and share observations back at the hotel?"

"Ring us as soon as you're back," John said with a nod.

Jemma had picked up a plain tan headscarf from a shop near the airport after we'd arrived. She pulled it from her shoulders to cover her stark red hair, hiding all but the fringe of it along her forehead. Tucking the ends around her neck, she gestured for me to follow her out of the car.

We ambled over to the skyrise as if we were heading to do our business in no particular rush. Jemma's gaze flicked intently over the front doors and around the entrance as we came in. My military instincts picked up hints in the postures of a few men in suits who lingered near the doorway. They were definitely combat trained, most likely armed.

The elevator only allowed access to the first ten floors with their offices unless you had a keycard for the higher apartments. We'd need to find someone to steal a card from or hack into the control panel. Jemma took us straight up to the tenth floor, I assumed to get a look at security just below the residences.

The tenth floor had a bright modern hall that wouldn't have held any traces of monstrous presence if it wasn't for the faint but chaotic dappling of pastel colors on the wallpaper. Jemma traced her fingers across it as if attempting to connect the dots into some kind of pattern. The monsters would love that.

We strolled along the hall and around the bend, making a show of checking the names on the plaques beside each door as if we had a specific destination in mind. When we turned another corner, the hall stretched on with only blank walls for about thirty feet after the first couple of doors, ending with an exit with a glowing sign—a stairwell for emergencies, I had to guess. Two suits were standing there. As one of them shifted his position to eye us, I caught the shape of a semi-automatic rifle dangling from the hand out of view.

Jemma glanced at both of the offices and shook her head with a rueful laugh. "We must have come the wrong way around," she said in a voice that showed no hint of tension. As we retraced our steps to the elevator, she shot me a pointed look. She hadn't missed the heavy weaponry.

"I think I might have gotten mixed up," she said for the benefit of anyone who'd been marking our travels. "Maybe it was the sixth floor."

We took a similar route around that floor, heading a little more purposefully this time toward the stairwell. Only one guard was staked out at this level, but the bulge of a holster showed at his hip. Whoever had set up this place, they weren't afraid to use some ammunition.

Jemma must have decided we'd be pushing our luck if we meandered around any of the other office floors, so she punched the button for the ground level when we got back on the elevator. "You know," she said, "I'm not sure I'm in the mood for pastries after all. I'm sure we can find something else to hit the spot if we wander a bit."

She was concerned about surveillance in any of the businesses in the building, either manmade or from the shrouded folk. I nodded. "I'm pretty sure I saw a bakery on the way over."

"That should do the trick."

She kept up that mildly upbeat demeanor as we ventured out onto the bustling downtown street. Istanbul's locals were a mix of modern and traditional, much like what I'd seen of the city's structures. Plenty of the people we passed wore clothes that would have fit in just fine on the streets of Manhattan, but here and there women had headscarves like Jemma's wrapped over their hair, and a few wore full loose robes that covered every inch of skin below their chins.

A few blocks along, Jemma glanced through a shop window and grabbed my arm. "It's been too long since I had künefe," she said, her eyes gleaming, and hustled me into the little restaurant.

Within a matter of minutes, we were sitting kitty-corner to each other at a tiny glass table eating a sort of syrupy, crunchy cake, dripping with melted cheese and topped with crumbs of pistachio. I had to admit the combination was mouthwatering, even if desserts weren't my usual food of choice.

Jemma plowed through half of her generous slice with a pleased groan before she said anything about the building we'd investigated.

"They're definitely hiding something up there," she said. "Something they *really* don't want anyone stumbling on. You don't defend stairwells with military grade weapons just for kicks."

"I thought the same thing." I sighed, my enjoyment of the snack fading. "If they were just using the building for income, they wouldn't have brought in that kind of security. It's not going to be fun getting past them. We can't get the jump on them anywhere near as easily as we could with the other communes."

"We *have* to get up there and put an end to whatever they're doing as soon as we can manage it." Jemma jabbed her fork into the cake. "They could be building this 'bridge' to their realm right now — and killing my sister to do it."

"We'll do whatever it takes," I said firmly. Thinking back to what we'd seen of the building… this might be the point where "whatever it takes" included my life. I'd sooner die than let one of those goons shoot down Jemma.

I'd risked my life for her before. I'd gone into more situations than I could count, both while in her employ and before, knowing I might not make it out. For some reason, the thought gave me a twinge of discomfort this time.

No, not just *for some reason*. Because of the other people I'd have been willing to die for, the siblings I'd been having trouble getting out of my mind since Jemma had mentioned them a few days ago.

I should have known Jemma would notice my shift in mood, no matter how slight. She cocked her head at me, pausing after she'd swallowed a bite. "What's the matter, Bash?"

"It's nothing," I said, waving off the question.

She raised her eyebrows at me. "Do you really think I'm going to accept that as an answer? Spit it out. If something's bothering you, it concerns me too."

She said that so easily, taking it for granted that my problems were hers to tackle just as much as hers were mine. God, did I love this woman. I might as well tell her, even though it was such a tiny thing it seemed absurd.

"I was just thinking about my brother and sister," I said. "With everything going on with *your* sister, it's hard not to reflect. Every now and then I wish I'd had a chance to talk to them now that they're grown up. But it's better they don't have to see what I am now, so really, it's a moot point."

Jemma's mouth bent at a pained angle. "Don't be ridiculous. Of course you should talk to them again if you have the chance. They're not going to put you through an interrogation about all your activities in the last however many years first. If it wasn't for you, they might not even be around—I'm sure they remember that. They probably wonder about you all the time."

"I don't know," I said, thinking about the busy lives they appeared to have when I looked them up, but Jemma made a decisive sound.

"The next time you're back in the States, you'll stop by to at least say hello," she said. "Promise me that."

"Is that an order?"

"It is. You haven't let me down so far—don't start now."

Her tone was lightly teasing, but her gaze was serious. It occurred to me that she'd specifically said when *I* was back in the US, as if there was much chance I'd be going there on my own instead of it being a matter of "we."

Maybe she didn't think we *would* be going back together. The same instincts that had helped me identify the building's guards prickled up my back as I studied her.

She'd seen the same set-up I had. She was talking about bursting in there and taking down the cult immediately. I'd heard how she'd talked about her sister—I could see the signs of tension in her now, running through her shoulders and the flex of her jaw.

She was bracing herself, preparing herself. To go charging in there and screw herself over to save her sister? She'd probably see that as a fair trade after all the years her sister had been held.

It didn't sound like a fair trade to me. My own shoulders stiffened at the thought.

"You should have the chance to do a lot of things after this too," I said in a low voice. "To see your sister recover, to get to know her all over again, to introduce her to the real world. To enjoy this world without the shrouded folk always in the background."

She smiled, but it still looked pained. "We'll see. First things first."

I knew better than to push the issue, but I couldn't shake the feeling that I had to do something to make sure she knew how many options *she* had.

It might be more than I could manage on my own. I knew her and I loved her, but Jemma was far from simple. It wasn't any surprise she might need more than one man to fulfill all her needs, was it? Between me and each member of the trio, we all offered something different—and she deserved to have all of that. We just had to make sure she saw it that way.

For the first time, picturing her with the other guys didn't make my chest clench up even slightly. I wanted her to have everything she needed, and the part I offered mattered just as much as anyone else's.

I just wasn't sure if she realized that what she offered us was something pretty spectacular too. That the life she had, no matter who she'd had to leave behind or what she'd been through, was damn well worth holding on to if she possibly could.

CHAPTER ELEVEN

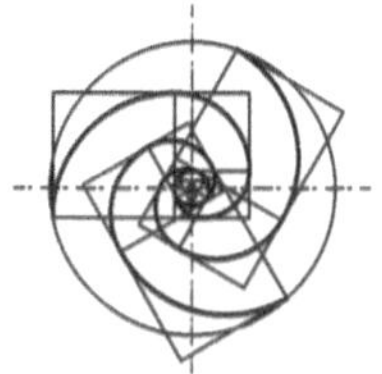

Jemma

I sat tensed in the hotel chair for a minute or so before I initiated the video chat to Garrett's number in London. Traffic rumbled by on the road a few floors below, and a warm breeze carried through the open window, where a roaming cat had come to sprawl on the wide ledge in the last of the afternoon sun.

There shouldn't have been anything stressful about the situation. I'd talked to the detective inspector hundreds of times, many of which while he'd been incredibly suspicious of me. His opinion of me shouldn't have mattered all that much anyway.

But on some level it did. I'd let John and Sherlock handle the communications with him before now. Part of me hadn't wanted to face how he'd react the first time we spoke after my horrible ruse on the mountain. I might have kept up that policy if it hadn't started to feel embarrassingly cowardly.

And if I hadn't become increasingly sure that this conversation might not be just the first since that incident, but also my last chance to talk to him at all.

I'd texted him ahead of time to ask if he was up for the video call, so Garrett was expecting me. The app connected within a few seconds. The video link kicked in to reveal his boyishly handsome face, his dark brown eyes as intense as ever and what I could see of his wiry form as tense as I felt.

"Jemma," he said in an unreadable voice. He wasn't so much emotionless as showing so many hints of conflicting emotions that I couldn't tell which was winning out. I supposed that was to be expected from a man trying to come to grips with the fact that the woman he'd believed he loved had been willing to nearly murder a long-time friend in front of him.

"Garrett," I replied in acknowledgment. "I thought I'd do the check-in this time, find out any news you have from your channels about the cult's activities."

He turned his head as if to look at something else on his desk. "Right. We've had several more reports come in today of property damage attempted or accomplished. The local police did manage to apprehend a few of the groups before they could go through with their plans. Sherlock mentioned Tehran—that was one of the spots— as well as Vancouver, Atlanta, Madrid, Algiers, and Singapore. Nothing in Istanbul yet. No changes to the MO we've seen so far."

"No bystanders have been hurt?"

"There've been some cuts, burns, and bruises, but nothing critical, thankfully." His gaze came back to me. Even through the computer speakers, I could hear his voice flatten slightly. "I guess there's been a lot of luck going around in general in that respect."

The subtle reference to Sherlock's fall made my throat tighten. I did my best to keep my own tone casual. "You're angry with me. That's reasonable."

He sighed. "I don't know what I am. I can't say it never occurred to me that you were capable of something like that. I'd imagine you've done worse to other people in the past."

He'd seen the results of my efforts in the communes, the guards I'd dispatched. There were plenty of people I *had* killed, without any remorse. But... "You never had to see it. It was never anyone like you."

"Sherlock seems to think the way you handled it makes

everything okay. I've never been able to completely wrap my head around how that mind of his works." Garrett shook his head with a small, slanted smile.

"Sherlock is certainly a unique individual." I drew in a breath and said what I really needed to say while I had the chance to say it. "If what happened changes the way you see me, I understand that. It's all right if you can't forgive me. I knew I was taking that chance."

Garrett blinked, clearly started. "Jemma—"

"You didn't make any promises," I barreled on, "and even if you had, I wouldn't hold you to them after something like that. You don't owe me anything. It really is all right. I am what I am, and I never went out of my way to drive home exactly what that means, so of course you couldn't have known everything I was capable of."

Garrett still looked puzzled. "Why are you saying all this?"

I groped for the best explanation, not even sure I could fully explain it to myself. *Because I needed to. Because I don't want to leave any more carnage in my wake than I have to. Because I may not be a "good" person, but I won't be a monster either.*

"Because I know what you're like. You're already carrying around enough guilt over ways you feel you've failed people. I'd rather not add to the pile."

He paused. His next words came out slow and careful, his gaze studying me through the screen. "And what makes you so sure I'm going to see my association with you as a failure?"

"I don't take you for the kind of person who'd tell me what you did lightly," I said. "You meant it for the woman you'd seen, but you hadn't seen everything. So... so it's all right."

Bash would still love me, because he'd known what I was all along. Sherlock and John had never expressed that deep a sentiment —Sherlock had once referred to his feelings for me as more along the lines of fascination, and I'd imagine that still applied. Garrett had put his heart on the line in a way I'd never expected and yet couldn't help feeling partly responsible for.

Garrett's expression had turned both shrewd and sad in a way I wasn't entirely sure I liked. "It would be easier for you too if I was just angry about it, if I didn't want anything else to do with you, wouldn't it?"

I opened my mouth and closed it again before I could form a suitable response. "I'm not sure what you mean. I simply wanted you to know—"

His smile came back, rueful this time... and maybe even a little fond. "You're forgetting that I do actually know you pretty well at this point, Jemma. The incident in Scotland showed a lot of things, one of which was how much in the habit you are of pushing people away—sometimes literally—when you're about to run into some horrifying situation. What are you trying to keep me out of?"

That wasn't at all the idea I'd wanted him to come away with. I summoned the haughtiest tone I had in me. "You're already apprised of as much of the situation here as we know about it. And I'd hardly need to push you away when you're already on the other side of the continent, would I?"

He didn't rise to the bait. "I think it'd be better if we waited to finish this conversation in person. I assume from what you just said that there's nothing else I should know about things in Istanbul?"

Not that I wanted him to know. I was supposed to convene with Bash, Sherlock, and John over dinner to discuss any new developments, but one of them could fill the detective inspector in as they saw fit. "You assume correctly. Garrett, there's really—"

He held up his hand with a calm firmness I hadn't often seen in him before. His experiences over the last few months had obviously changed him, perhaps in more ways than I'd realized. "When we can talk in person. It was good to hear from you, Jemma."

He ended the call without giving me the chance to respond. That showed some nerve right there. I glared at the computer screen for a few seconds before snapping the laptop shut. Something about his words and the way he'd said them left me with an uneasy impression, but I couldn't put my finger on exactly what I was worried about.

By the end of tomorrow, it wasn't likely to matter anyway.

When I slipped into Sherlock and John's shared suite a short time later, Bash had already arrived with the food: lamb dumplings slathered in yogurt sauce that set my mouth watering with one whiff of their garlicky smell. As much as I loved my sweets, I could appreciate a damn good main course.

As we ate, we also talked business, of course.

"The security personnel you saw in the tower appear to be either individual hires or supplied from within the cult," Sherlock said, checking over the notes on his phone in between dumplings. "There's no record of any security company being contracted to work there. Most likely cult members, I would suspect."

"So would I." That would fit with the way they'd protected their other communes—keeping it in the "family," so to speak.

"That means it won't be easy to displace them the way we did with the gallery heist in London," John remarked with a frown.

"We couldn't really expect it to be all that easy," I pointed out.

"What about the architecture of the building itself?" Bash asked. "Any points of access we missed there?"

Sherlock shook his head. "There is the elevator shaft, of course, with the natural dangers that comes with—and the possibility of being caught accessing it."

"We don't know which of all those upper floors we'd need to get to anyway," John said. "And they're bound to have even tighter security there, aren't they?"

I glanced at Bash. "Where you able to get in touch with that contact you thought might be able to help us with that?"

"I'm meeting with him after dinner and we'll see what we can make out first thing in the morning." He turned to the other men. "We're going to attempt to get a better sense of the higher floors using a drone with a camera to peer through the windows. Not the most elegant solution ever..."

"But we'll take what we can get." John brightened. "That's some progress, anyway. The local police appear willing to lend a hand if we can frame the situation properly. They've been keeping a close watch on the buildings that seemed the most likely targets—if the cult was planning a move here, I'd imagine the police presence has dissuaded them."

For now. I chewed my last dumpling, lingering in the rich savory flavors for as long as I could extend the sensation before I had to swallow. "Tomorrow, as soon as you have the footage, I want to look it over," I said to Bash. Whatever glimpses he and his contact managed to obtain might be all the additional guidance I needed. I'd already made a morning appointment of my own to pick up some firepower.

He bowed his head with a playful flourish. "I both hear and grant you your requests." He checked at the time and got to his feet. "I'd better not make him wait. He seemed a little nervous about the whole thing."

As he let himself out, Sherlock rose and made an attempt at clearing the takeout garbage from the table, rather awkwardly with his one arm in its cast. John swept in before he'd gathered more than a few pieces.

"You never know when to give yourself a rest, do you?" he said, chidingly but with unmistakable affection.

Sherlock grimaced at his friend as the other man took over, but he rested a hand on John's shoulder in what could only be called a caress before he stepped back. John shot him a smile filled with warmth and a spark of desire.

Watching them and the small but certain intimacies they'd become comfortable with melted most of the uneasiness I'd been left with after the call with Garrett. If John was right about the "goodness" in me, then the best thing I'd probably done outside of however much progress I'd made toward ridding the world of the shrouded folk was in evidence right in front of me. The two men hadn't even admitted their mutual attraction to themselves when I'd first met them, and now they were all but flirting right in front of me.

They would be fine without me—at least, I thought so. It couldn't hurt anything to solidify that bond even further while I was still here, could it? One final night with these two men I'd become rather fond of myself... A last hurrah would make tomorrow's plans that much easier.

When John returned to the table, I folded my arms over my chest. "I don't seem to see anything like dessert around here."

Sherlock chuckled. "A horrendous oversight. Blame your man. He brought the food."

"He's not here anymore, though. But I think there might be other ways that hunger could be satisfied."

John's gaze turned heated at the suggestive lilt to my voice, but he didn't step any closer, just gave his walking stick a sly swivel. "And what would those be?"

He was still a little more hesitant with me than he might have been before Sherlock's fall at my hands. I eased up to him and lay those hands on his chest—carefully, so that he could easily pull away if this wasn't what he wanted at all. "I think you could make a reasonable guess."

He raised his arm and traced his fingers over my hair as if refamiliarizing himself with the feel of me. Making sure I was the woman he thought he saw. My pulse stuttered as I waited, but whatever he was thinking, whatever he was remembering, a moment later he lowered his head to bring his lips to mine.

He kissed me the way only John Watson could, gently but intently, taking and offering of himself in equal portions. It'd been over a week since I'd last gotten to experience the sensation, and I hadn't realized how much I'd missed it. I kissed him back with plenty of enthusiasm but not too forcefully, still careful of scaring him off.

A hand, a little stiff from the plaster casing that crossed the palm, settled on my waist from behind. Sherlock brushed my hair to the side and ran his finger over one of the sensitive spots he'd previously discovered on my neck. I swayed against him encouragingly, and he pressed his mouth to the same spot, no doubt marking the hitch of my breath with analytical precision. The fact that he'd moved to join us at all without a conversation to justify this indulgence was a big step all on its own.

I gripped John's shirt and reached back to stroke my hand down Sherlock's side at the same time. As John kissed me more deeply, he brushed his fingers over my hair again and then teased them over Sherlock's messy curls as well. Sherlock raised his head with a ripple of hot breath over my skin. John shifted from me to his friend in one smooth movement, planting a kiss on Sherlock over my shoulder.

I couldn't say which turned me on more: having both of these men's attentions focused on me or watching them attend to each other. Especially when I got to stay part of the action. John's hand trailed down over my blouse to fondle my breast, and Sherlock pressed himself against my ass with a firm grasp on my hip, and it felt as if all three of us might melt together into a mass of bliss.

For a few minutes, I was content to simply stoke those flames. The men alternated between branding my lips and neck with their mouths and claiming each other. I lost track of whose hand was sparking pleasure where. But at the shift of John's weight on his feet, my concern for his injured leg leapt into sharper awareness.

I kissed him once more, hard now that I was surer of him, and drew back an inch. "Let's take this to my room. I have the... necessary supplies there."

The flush of John's cheeks and the squeeze of Sherlock's fingers on my thigh was agreement enough. We managed to disentangle ourselves from each other long enough to make the short trip across the hall. I grabbed a couple of condoms out of my suitcase, paused, and tossed a small bottle of lube onto the bedside table too. It might come in handy. An idea was starting to unfurl through my mind that I thought we'd all enjoy very much.

I raised my arms, and John took the cue to pull off my blouse. Sherlock unhooked my bra a second later. As John lowered his head to chart a path across my breasts, I fumbled with the buttons on the other man's shirt. A gasp slipped from my lips as John scraped his teeth across one of my nipples with a jolt of pleasure.

"Naughty," I said, not at all a complaint, and he chuckled.

Sherlock tossed his shirt aside and captured my mouth with a demanding kiss, and John sank lower, onto his knees. He might not be able to handle an operating table, but his fingers were still nimble enough to make short work of my slacks and panties. When he brought his hot mouth to my sex, fire flooded me up to the top of my head and down to my toes.

I moaned against Sherlock's lips, and he took the opportunity to test my tongue with his. As ours dueled above, John slicked his tongue over my clit and lower. A fresh wave of bliss shivered through me with an instinctive rock of my hips.

John added a finger, sliding it along my slit and then in with a pleased hum at the feel of my arousal. Sherlock cupped my breast, tweaking the nipple, and John suckled me harder. Faster than I'd expected, ecstasy rolled over me.

As the aftershock rippled through me, John looked up with a beaming smile. So goddamned adorable. I wanted him gasping with pleasure too—both of them, so satisfied they never forgot this night, never looked back on it with anything but happiness.

"Get up here," I growled, tugging him to his feet, and undid his fly before he'd even finished straightening up. I drew him onto the bed with me, Sherlock following beside us. He ran his hand down John's thighs as he helped me remove the other man's slacks, and a different sort of bliss came over John's face.

Oh, yes, I had to see that these two completely fulfilled their potential.

John grabbed one of the condoms and slicked it on at light speed. I raised my hips, and that was all the encouragement he needed to plunge into me. He kissed me, then Sherlock, and then Sherlock kissed me. The doctor moved with leisurely thrusts, patiently building to our joint release.

Which I intended to be a release for all of us... of all sorts of passions. I traced my hand down John's back and pushed myself up with my other arm so I could grip his ass. The sharper angle let his cock hit an even more perfect spot inside me. My breath broke, and it took me a second to remember my aim.

I eased my fingers to the crease of his ass. "It feels fucking amazing having someone inside you," I said by his ear. "Imagine if you could experience that too."

A quiver ran through John's body when I teased my fingertips into that crease and around the sensitive ring there. Next to us, Sherlock had gone abruptly still, his hand lingering on my breast, his gaze following the movement of my hand. He was sharp enough to know where I was going with this from just that comment.

Apparently John was too. His eyes widened slightly and then closed with a groan as I dipped a finger right inside him much as he'd done to me earlier. His gaze slid to Sherlock as he answered me. "I might have thought about that before."

"Mmm. Somehow I suspect you're not the only one." I kissed John and then gave Sherlock an amused smile. "Am I right in assuming you've done your research?"

A hint of pink colored the detective's cheeks, but he owned up to it. "Considering how things had been developing, it seemed reasonable to investigate all the possibilities."

I had to laugh. "You still need to work on your dirty talk. Give me a hand, then. And the lube."

He opened the bottle and smeared some of the stuff on his own fingers before passing it to me. Carefully, he brought his hand to the same spot I'd marked, watching John's expression carefully the whole time. The doctor let out a shaky breath. His thrusts had turned shallow, but I wasn't worried about my own satisfaction right now.

I drew my hand back, sinking down on the bed again now that Sherlock had gotten a start. John kissed me a little wildly. "Sherlock," he said in a strained voice.

The other man wet his lips, looking thrilled and hesitant at the same time. "Are you sure this is what you want?" he said in the gentlest voice I'd ever heard him use.

"God, yes." John paused, glancing back at him. "Do you?"

The color in Sherlock's face deepened. "I have been curious how the sensation would compare."

"Oh my God," I muttered in mock-frustration, suppressing another laugh. Better that I didn't push them toward the act any more than I already had. If they were going to keep on their journey together without me, they needed to be sure they'd gotten onto the path of their own accord.

Thankfully, Sherlock didn't need more confirmation. He slicked more of the gel over his cock and bowed over John as he eased inside with the utmost care. John's limbs trembled against mine, but I could tell from the catch in his throat that his reaction was all pleasure. He groaned again as Sherlock grasped his thigh, getting settled into his position. Then John picked up his pace inside me.

His body continued to shake with what must have been a symphony of sensations, bucking forward into me and back to take in Sherlock. With the first few strokes, Sherlock groaned as well. The detective's hand dropped from John's thigh to caress mine before resuming its braced position. The rhythm of their rising panting only stoked my own arousal.

I arched into John's thrusts, joining that rhythm. Becoming part of that mass of bliss all over again. John made a strangled sound, his mouth mashing against mine, and if he'd come before I hit my peak, I wouldn't even have minded. But as his hips jerked toward me with fraying control, I found myself cast across the last short distance to the edge. His cock filled me once more, and I was soaring, gasping, holding onto him as he spilled himself in me.

Sherlock let out a ragged curse, and I knew he'd followed with us. He hugged John even more tightly to him for a few moments. Then they sagged down on either side of me, their arms looping over my torso to embrace each other as well as me.

In that combined embrace, a tight, unfamiliar ache formed behind my breastbone. I nuzzled John's face and tipped my head toward Sherlock for one last kiss.

I'd started this for their benefit at least as much as mine, but it suddenly felt vital that I say something more than I had before.

"I'm glad I barged into your lives, you know," I said quietly. "I'm glad you both tracked me down after I took off on you—and Garrett too. I didn't think I needed more than I had, but you opened up so many possibilities... So many things I didn't know I could have."

John pulled himself a little closer to me and kissed my bare shoulder. "You know we could say the exact same thing to you, don't you?"

"I'll admit I find it difficult now to imagine a life that didn't include Jemma Moriarty," Sherlock said with a wry smile.

The ache turned into a pang, but I ignored that. I'd swept into their lives, and perhaps I'd changed them, but those changes were in place now. They could move on without me when they had to. And I was lucky to have gotten to experience this for as long as I had.

CHAPTER TWELVE

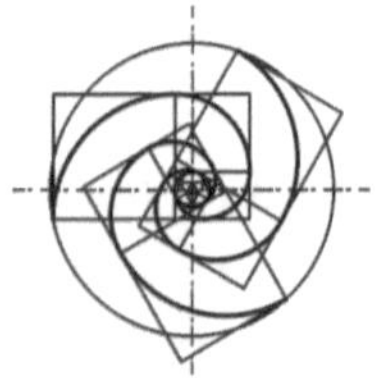

Jemma

I thought I'd have that last day to enjoy all there was to take pleasure in within the world. Pick up my munitions, meet with Bash to see the drone photos he'd gotten, solidify my strategy, and then think about anything but the task ahead for the hours remaining until the sun set.

Unfortunately, the cult of the shrouded folk decided not to cooperate with that plan.

I'd just picked up the weapons order I'd made. I was walking along the warm, arid street amid Istanbul's morning pedestrians, the thick canvas bag slung over my shoulder with a few knobby protrusions poking into my back, when an immense cracking sound split the air from somewhere in the distance. I spun around in time to see a plume of smoke streaking up over the business quarter.

My back stiffened. Despite all our precautions here and the cops' willingness to help, the cult must have managed to strike. If they were willing to sacrifice some of their local people for the effort today… did that mean they were close to their goal?

As I hurried back to the modest hotel, my heart thumped faster.

There'd be fewer people in the urban commune right now. They'd be distracted as they tracked the results of their efforts. Going now might give me more of an advantage than going at night. It wasn't even that sunny out anyway, the sky hazed with a thin layer of pale cloud.

I'd been given a chance. I had to take it.

I ducked into my hotel room and stashed the bag of weapons on the shelf in the closet. Bash had better be back with those photographs. I'd get him to hand them over and study them while I dressed and armed myself for the mission.

Before I could leave, I'd need to find some quest to send the guys on so they wouldn't be around to see me heading off. That shouldn't be too hard. I could figure that out while I was studying the photographs too.

I threw open the door to hustle to Bash's room and froze at the sight of the man just outside.

Well, actually there were four men in the hall, but it was only the one right in front of me that made my pulse stutter. Garrett's hand had been raised to knock, his jaw set at a familiar determined angle. He startled briefly at the swing of the door. I stared at him, momentarily lost for words, only vaguely registering the rest of the London trio and my right-hand man in their semi-circle behind him.

"What are *you* doing here?" I finally managed.

The detective inspector gave me a grim but not unfriendly smile. "Hello to you too, Jemma."

"Fine. Hello, greetings, good day, isn't the weather lovely, I hope the family's well, etc." I waved my hand in the air. "Now answer the question—what the hell are you doing here? Aren't you supposed to be coordinating a global cult takedown from Scotland Yard?" It was easier to focus on that than to wonder how this fit in with our fraught conversation last night. I'd considered this loose end tied up, but here he was in the flesh, impossible to ignore.

"I'd been wanting to join the efforts here since I first heard what you all were up to," Garrett said. "After our chat yesterday, I decided it was time to get on with that. There was a seat available on an overnight flight direct."

"Wonderful. And now you're here. You're all here." I lifted my gaze to really take in the rest of the guys. Apprehension trickled through me. "Why did you all come over to my room? Is there a problem? I saw some kind of attack happened downtown—it looked about the same as the others, but if it was more serious—"

"We're not here about the bombing downtown," Sherlock said evenly. "Although that is a concern. We're here because it only took a short discussion for us to determine that we've all seen reason for concern in *your* behavior."

"My— What is this? Some kind of intervention?" I narrowed my eyes at the bunch of them, but even Bash held firm. "I don't need one."

"We'd just like to talk," John said softly. "Would you come over to our suite, just for a little while?"

"We can look over the footage the drone was able to capture too," Bash said. "It's probably best if everyone sees that."

I didn't think so. I didn't want any of these four setting one foot in that building again. But obviously I wasn't getting much say in the matter.

I let out my breath in a huff and stepped out of my room. "All right. Talk away." I didn't have to tell them anything I didn't want to. It wasn't as if I had a shortage of practice dodging private topics.

The table in John and Sherlock's suite wasn't really big enough to comfortably seat five, so we ended up in the sitting area with its long narrow sofa and two arch-backed armchairs. I dropped down at the end of the sofa where it wouldn't feel as much as if I was in the hot seat. Bash sat beside me, studying my face.

He knew me better than any of them. Of course, I'd also expected that he knew better than to share any more sensitive observations he made with the rest of them. They were forming a regular conspiracy, apparently.

Garrett sat in the armchair closest to me, and John and Sherlock took the spots at the other end of the living room. For a few seconds, none of them seemed to know how to start. Then Bash said, in his low smooth voice, "Where did you go this morning, Mori?"

If he'd noticed I'd left, he might have noticed my cargo coming back, so I couldn't offer too obvious a lie. "I was just picking up some supplies that might help us take on the cult. I'm not going to sit around twiddling my thumbs while the rest of you do all the work."

"What kind of supplies?" Sherlock asked.

I gave a casual shrug. "Pieces that'll mess with the shrouded folk's energy. Equipment for climbing the elevator shaft. That sort of thing. Why was an interrogation about that necessary?"

I intended to glance around at them with an air of confusion, but when my eyes caught on Garrett's, I found it hard to look away. He was watching me with that almost sad air I'd sensed from him briefly through the computer screen yesterday.

"And what's your plan, Jemma?" he said. "What part do we play in it?"

"I assumed we'd figure that out once we had a look at Bash's pictures." Impatience wriggled through me. If I was going to take advantage of the cult's distraction, I needed to get out there soon.

"The thing is," John said, leaning forward on the sofa so he could see me better, "we've *all* gotten the impression in the last couple days that you're preparing for something you're not including any of us in. That you've been saying good-bye in your own way. And I don't think I'm convinced yet that we were wrong."

My instincts screamed for me to get out of this conversation immediately, but I couldn't do much of anything without Bash's data. I kept my expression placid. "I'm sorry if I came across that way."

Sherlock let out a sound like a restrained snort. "I'd imagine you are sorry you *came across* that way, since you'd obviously rather we hadn't caught on. Haven't you dashed off on your own enough times, Jemma? We've accomplished the most when we've pooled our resources and talents, not when you've gone rogue."

A wave of exhaustion washed over me. What was the point of continuing to dissemble when even Sherlock was sure of my intentions—and right? If I'd revealed too many of my cards, he wasn't going to let this go. And I wasn't going to get to my goal by pushing him or anyone else in the room to their theoretical deaths this time.

"This is different," I said. "This is the fiends' ultimate plan. This is the center of their influence in our world. This is my *sister*. If it's just me, I know I can get in, I can pretend to negotiate with them—I can save her and destroy everything else they're working toward. That's all that matters."

Bash's mouth twisted, but he didn't look surprised. "You're not counting on getting back out."

"That's where there's the most chance for failure. If I just go and get it done, then that's... that's enough. The rest doesn't matter. If I start pulling my punches because I'm worried about coming out alive, then I'm screwed." I gave each of the men around me a sharp look. "But that's *my* sacrifice to make. In a way, it's the sacrifice I was supposed to make ten years ago, only it's on my terms this time, and I get to make them pay. That's the most I could ask for. It's *more* than I expected to get to ask for." I'd never thought I'd rescue my sister along with avenging her.

"But what if you could have even more than that?" John said. "You haven't given us a chance to strategize. We could save her and destroy them, and you'd still get the rest of your life."

"Or you might all end up dead instead of it only being me. We might not pull off anything. The more complicated the plan, the harder it is to pull it off."

"So you're going to push yourself off a cliff this time," Garrett said.

My gaze jerked to him. "That seems a lot more fair, don't you think?"

He looked straight back at me unwaveringly. "Wouldn't you rather have a future—with your sister? With us?"

My chest constricted. "What does that even mean? Whatever we've had, it's all been around this quest to get rid of the shrouded folk. It'd fall apart as soon as that's over anyway."

John raised his eyebrows. "Because you wouldn't want it anymore, or because you assume that we wouldn't?"

"I—" I started, groping through words through the rush of emotion that question provoked, and Bash took my hand in his, twining our fingers together.

"We're not asking you to give up your quest, Mori. None of us would do that. Believe me, I wouldn't be sitting here with this bunch if I didn't know they respected you that much. We just want you to give the future a chance. To give yourself a chance. To give *us* a chance to really be something other than a monster-fighting unit. All we want is the chance to see if there's a feasible way we can take these creatures down that doesn't end with you dying. And if there is… wouldn't you take that route?"

When he put it that plainly, when they all waited for my response the way they were right now with that air of hope, something twisted inside me. To imagine being as satisfied as I'd found myself in the last few months, challenged and invigorated and adored, even after the menace of the shrouded folk was no longer looming over us… That sounded like fucking heaven.

It also sounded so impossible that my heart shuttered at the thought.

I gripped Bash's hand. "I know you'd be here for me no matter what. You always have been. But…" I looked around at the London trio again. "Even if we banish the shrouded folk from this world forever, I'm not going to transform in a shower of pixie dust into some kind of fair maiden. You've seen what I am. I'm still going to be that woman. I'll break the law, I'll twist what you see as morality, I'll be most at home on the side of darkness. It won't be as easy to ignore when we're not up against a threat to all humanity."

Sherlock gave a dry laugh. "Do you think we'd want a fair maiden? The way you are, the way you think — it's brilliant. If I'd dispute some of the details, we could hash that out in good time. I've met plenty of 'fair maidens' in my time, and none of them had the slightest appeal to me."

"Because you're insane," I informed him, thinking back to John's remark in the Tokyo hotel.

The detective's lips curled into a smile I couldn't call anything other than a smirk.

"If he's insane, then we all must be," Garrett said. "I… I can't imagine you being any other way, Jemma. And I can't imagine not being part of whatever dark and brilliant life you'd lead on the other side of this, if you'd still have me."

His voice dipped with the last part, as if he really thought *I* might reject *him* after I'd gone to such lengths last night to give him an out.

"You can say whatever you want about yourself," John added. "But I know what I've seen. And what I've seen in the time I've spent around you is not only brilliance but more generosity than just about anyone I can think of. Like Sherlock said, the details can be worked out later. I want to work them out. We work well together, the five of us. I want to see what we can be when there isn't some urgent threat for us to fight."

The ache that'd come over me lying between him and Sherlock yesterday expanded through my chest.

I believed they meant all this now. I didn't know if I could believe they'd still mean it when they were faced with the reality. But... these were the smartest and most devoted men I'd ever met. If anyone could say what they were saying, it was them.

And hell, I *wanted* to believe them, so fucking badly.

Really talking through a plan, considering all the possibilities, and letting them be a part of it would be more complicated than sneaking into the building alone and blasting the cult and their instruments to smithereens. It would be harder and more painful, with the lives of these four men to worry about in ways I didn't quite worry about my own. But damn it, I wanted that chance.

I didn't let myself think about what I might be owed very often. Didn't I owe it to *them* to give it a try, though, after all the faith they'd just offered me?

I dragged in a ragged breath, and the words spilled out. "All right. Let's see what we can come up with when we put our heads together. But we need to get this plan worked out *fast.*"

CHAPTER THIRTEEN

Sherlock

The commander from the local police was one of the more agreeable law enforcement officers I'd spoken to in my time.

"We appreciate you lending your wisdom and experience to this situation, Mr. Holmes and Mr. Lestrade," the portly fellow said as he flipped through the images of the dark-paned office building that had been damaged by more of the cult's homemade bombs. "There've been some political problems in this country over the years, but we haven't seen anything quite like this."

"The perpetrators you brought in—could you confirm them as local citizens?" Garrett asked, leaning forward to study the photographs.

"None of the four of them had any sort of ID, and they've refused to give even their names. We were able to match one of the men to a record using photo recognition, but he hasn't shown any activity under that identity in several years. The others we couldn't find matches for at all."

"From what we understand, it isn't unusual for this cult to keep to themselves and handle even births within their communes without involving any of the standard procedures," I said, but Garrett was frowning.

"Only four?" he said. "Were there others on the scene who managed to escape?"

The commander shook his head. "All the witness accounts mention only the individuals we brought in. They made no attempt to flee. It appeared to my officers that they wanted to extend the amount of time they could be carrying out their strange ritual with the blood and so on for as long as possible."

I glanced at the detective inspector. That detail hadn't stood out to me, but Garrett had been much more heavily involved in tracking the international incidents committed by these people. He might not connect the dots quite so swiftly as I preferred to, but he was still sharp enough that having him here was a benefit.

"Were there more present for the other bombings?" I asked.

Garrett nodded. "Generally eight to ten. Occasionally even more than that. They've never needed that much assistance to carry out the explosive aspect, so I'd assumed they wanted as many people involved in the ritual as possible for maximum effect."

"So it's odd that they'd hold back here. Unless they're saving their manpower for future efforts." Ah, yes, I could see why that possibility would disturb him. It rather disturbed me.

The cultists themselves were difficult to predict given their isolation from regular society. The "gods" they worshipped were inscrutable on an even higher level. With an ordinary criminal, I might have made a reasonably accurate guess as to their next move. In this case, I could think of several equally likely scenarios… and I recognized that the outcome might be none of those.

"Exactly." Garrett motioned to the commander. "How many of your people can you have monitoring activity in the business district and around those other buildings we've pointed out as likely targets? I know it's a lot of territory to cover, but the change in the pattern makes me concerned about what else this group might have up their sleeve."

"We've implemented regular patrols and kept the officers informed of the signs to watch for. After this crime, I can justify bringing in some reinforcements from farther abroad. We've also spoken with the private security present at most of the buildings to help them prepare. Unfortunately in this current case, the perpetrators were able to disguise their intentions until it was too late."

"This particular building didn't have a bag search or similar security protocol," I said to confirm.

"No, it hadn't been necessary."

"That's probably why they picked that one," Garrett said. "Any of the other buildings meeting the usual criteria that don't search visitors should add that to their protocol for the time being if at all possible. If not, I suppose doubling the police and other security presence at those locations would have some benefit."

Exactly what I would have suggested. I gave my colleague an approving smile. "I fully agree with that approach."

"I'll see what I can do," the commander said. "People often complain about increased monitoring, but when we have an example of what we're trying to guard against, it may be easier to convince them."

"There were no casualties from the bombs, were there?" Garrett checked.

"We had several civilians hospitalized, but none of the injuries have been serious. The perpetrators seemed to be focused on hurting the building more than anyone in it."

"That fits with what we've seen elsewhere, at least. Have you been able to find any further information on the owners or inhabitants of the building we've identified as the likely local cult headquarters?"

"Nothing beyond what we were already able to produce. If we come up with something else, I'll be in touch immediately."

"We appreciate that," I said, standing. The meeting had obviously fulfilled its usefulness. Time to move on. It wasn't likely the police could discover more using their official channels than my internet-savvy connections had been able to procure for us.

"I don't like it," Garrett said as we left the police building. "I guess it's good in the short term that the cult hasn't made a larger effort here, but I don't think we'd want to find out how they plan on escalating the situation."

"Agreed. Well, we're pulling together our own plans as swiftly as we can. They won't be able to anticipate everything *we'll* do."

I paused, an unexpected compulsion coming over me. Perhaps it was simply brought on by our conversation with Jemma earlier this morning—by seeing how thoroughly even her genius mind had been able to convince her that in spite of all available evidence, we wouldn't have any interest in her once this case was over.

To ensure some things were understood, you couldn't rely on actions and observations. The words themselves needed to be said. And Jemma was hardly the only member of our team I valued.

"You've done solid work handling the communes abroad," I said to Garrett. "There's a lot of data to sort through and an abundance of people to keep organized, and you've stepped up admirably while we were occupied with our more specific quest."

I knew at once that putting my respect into words had been worthwhile from the brightening of the other man's expression. Perhaps I'd been rather harder on him than he'd deserved at times in the past. Although if I hadn't been, he might not have been able to step up the way he had now, so no point in dwelling on that.

"High praise from the great Sherlock Holmes," he said in an amused tone, but his smile showed how much he genuinely appreciated it. "Unless that's a hint that I should get back to my post in London?"

"No, not at all. At this point, I think this is the best place you could be. There aren't many people in this world I fully trust, and I'd like to have all of them on hand for what may be the final confrontation with these... monsters."

"You're still not totally comfortable with the idea of them, are you?" Garrett said. "It's not as if we can deny their existence."

"No. I'd just greatly prefer it if they didn't exist at all."

My phone vibrated with a text alert. I stopped on the sidewalk to check it and immediately looked up to search for a cab. "John has some leads on the equipment we might use. He wants to go over it with me. Were you still going to see if you can get anything out of the cultists they have in custody?"

"As much good as it might do us. None of them elsewhere have been much for talking, but I'll see if I can find some leverage to apply. If we could get them to talk, it'd certainly be worth the effort."

"It would." I gave him an awkward clap on the shoulder that I meant as a friendly gesture and waved to the cab I'd spotted. "We can reconvene to discuss our progress at the hotel in a few hours."

John was waiting for me at a table outside a café not far from the hotel. At my first glimpse of him, I allowed myself the momentary indulgence of noticing the gleam of the sunlight in his bright hair, the sparkle in his hazel eyes that looked green when he wore that moss-colored shirt. As ridiculous as it seemed to care about those aspects of him, it also seemed ridiculous that somehow I'd gone years before without noticing them at all.

Or perhaps I had and some part of me had simply refused to acknowledge it.

He'd already procured himself a lemonade with a sprig of mint and a plate of small pastries that gave off a buttery scent as I sat down across from him.

"Picking up Jemma's tastes in cuisine, are you?" I said wryly.

He nudged the plate toward me. "They're really very satisfying. Might as well enjoy the local dishes while we're here."

I bit into one and found it wasn't as sweet as I expected, filled with a fruity tartness and a hint of wine that was quite enjoyable. The rest of that pastry disappeared into my mouth in a flash. It had been rather a long time since breakfast. Mind and body needed their fuel.

"What did you come up with?" I asked my friend.

He had a journal on the table beside him. As I ate another pastry, he flipped it open. "I focused mostly on what you said about your experiences in the shrouded realm and how elements of the environment affected you. If we're going to create the opposite effect so the shrouded folk who might be hanging around the tower can't interfere, we'll want to focus on opposite sorts of stimuli, right? Patterns and orderly sensations."

"That sounds reasonable enough." I leaned my elbows onto the table, eyeing his notebook with curiosity. John's mind worked in a much more meandering and fanciful way than mine generally did, but over the years I'd come to value the unique contributions he could make from that perspective.

"I've started with the idea of visuals, just because we have to start somewhere." John turned a page in his journal to consult the notes he'd made there. A few rough sketches marked the space between them. "It shouldn't be too difficult to come up with the means to project patterns like Jemma's favorite Fibonacci sequence onto the outside of the building. Creating consistent visual stimuli *inside* will be harder, but we could bring smaller projectors and set them up in places the cultists aren't likely to stumble on them—or perhaps we could quickly have decals printed that we could stick to the walls?"

My thoughts had already turned to which of my nearest associates I might be able to call on to accomplish each of those things. "The decals would be more compact and more difficult to disrupt once in place. We'll simply need the patterns we want drawn up for the printing."

"I figured Jemma would want some input on that subject." John turned another page. "I started making some initial research into auditory stimuli, but that's a pretty complex area. I'll need more time. I thought I'd head back to the university library this afternoon—it's got a good collection."

"I suppose your medical expertise should be useful in this area," I said. "There are certain visual and auditory stimuli that can alter the mental states of regular human beings as well."

"There are. I was going to look into those too, although they'll depend somewhat on the individual people and their mental state. There isn't a catch-all beyond blaring sounds loud enough to be distracting or that sort of thing."

"Well, it's a start. Shall we see if we can get Jemma's thoughts on your initial ideas?"

"If she hasn't already charged off on her own despite our talk this morning," John muttered with a crooked smile.

From what I'd seen of Jemma's demeanor, I didn't think she'd have changed her mind again so quickly, but she was a difficult one to anticipate. Perhaps we really should get going.

We each grabbed one of the last two pastries, and John waved a waitress over to get the bill. As we walked back toward the hotel, John gazed around him, eagerly absorbing the sights of the city that as far as I knew he'd never visited before. It was something impressive about him that he could still take such delight in a relatively ordinary walk, even after the trials he'd been through in the military and beyond.

Another compulsion ran through me, even stronger than before. I held myself back in a brief hesitation, but for fuck's sake, less than twenty-four hours ago I'd been as intimate with the man beside me as any two people could be. I knew he'd be pleased by the gesture. The only reason for me to balk was my own discomfort at shows of affection I'd generally thought of as facile.

But what was so facile, really, about making a concrete statement of what another person meant to you? John had to have been nervous making any gesture of that sort to me, but he'd put his feelings out there regardless.

I suppressed the flicker of nerves and reached out to take his hand.

Surprise flashed across John's face, but his fingers closed around mine in an instant. He didn't remark on the gesture, didn't even look at me, but I could sense the contentment that hummed off him all the same. *He* knew me well enough to understand that this one small action said more than any words I could have produced would have.

We were partners, yes, but more than that too. Much more than that, in ways that I still found somewhat inexplicable. But I had to admit my life felt fuller now than it had, even if I hadn't been aware I was missing anything until this unexpected flatmate had fallen into my lap.

We would face these literal demons and their sycophants together, and I would not let myself be shaken by uncertainty while this man stood by my side.

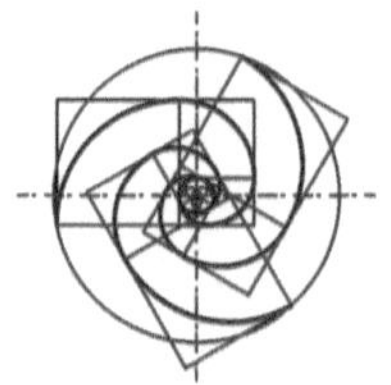

CHAPTER FOURTEEN

Jemma

For some reason, I'd expected the elevator shaft to be cold. Maybe because the few times I'd found myself in one in the past, it'd been in much chillier climates.

The tall, ridged passage above me was gloomy, the maintenance lights on the top of the elevator car only providing a dull glow that reached partway up it, and the air had a slightly damp metallic smell. Still, I was already sweating from the heat in the enclosed space within a couple minutes of clambering through the panel I'd opened from inside the car. Obviously the air conditioning didn't penetrate the walls.

The surface beneath me vibrated as the car hummed upward on someone's command. I kept myself braced, watching the doorways slide by, ready to flatten myself to the roof if we appeared to be heading for the top floor. I wasn't sure exactly how much of a gap I'd get up there, but I'd rather not find out by slamming my head into the ceiling.

At the same time, I watched the video feed I'd patched into my phone from the tiny surveillance camera I'd added to the corner of the car. I wanted to see exactly how the building's inhabitants got access to the residential floors—and what those residents looked like.

They didn't venture out of their territory very often, I quickly gathered. In a normal apartment building, people would be coming and going all through the day. In the first hour of my surveillance, no passenger went any higher than the tenth floor of offices, and no one higher above summoned the car so they could come down. It was a good thing I'd worn the gold cuff that hid me from the shrouded folk's awareness, or any of the fiends hanging around here would have descended on me by now.

How long was I going to have to sit here to make my observations? And it wasn't only data I'd come to gather. My sister had managed to reach out to me across the divide between this world and the shrouded realm. If I got close enough to where they were keeping her in this building, assuming they had her captive here—if I could make her aware of my presence somehow—maybe we could communicate again.

Bash's drone photos had given us some sense of the interior layout on the upper floors. The first several above the tenth appeared to have kept to the blueprints with fairly standard apartment layouts, although in a few I'd been able to pick out tools of the cult's worship. They were definitely being used by a commune, if not the type I was used to.

The floors above those had mostly been hidden by curtains or shades, but the drone had managed to capture a little footage that showed large rooms with no dividing walls within view, markings on the floor—some of which looked like blood stains—and more of those tools scattered around. My best guess was that the cult members spent the more normal parts of their lives in the apartments and went up to the common areas above to conduct their more focused worship.

The very top few floors, we hadn't gotten even a peek at. I suspected if Olivia was being held in the building, it'd be up there. They might have an entire floor dedicated to keeping her captive and working whatever awful rituals they were using on her. Chances were it'd be the penthouse at the highest level, as close to our sun as the tower reached.

But I didn't know for sure, and as much as I wanted to scramble up the maintenance rungs and smash my way in there, I could recognize that the group plan I'd started to form with my men this morning gave me a better chance at seeing not just me but *her* out alive. Without any definite signs of where she was, I couldn't leap in with guns blazing or tossing explosives, or I'd be as likely to tear her apart as our enemies.

The elevator glided back down to the ground floor. I peered at my phone, and a smile crossed my lips as a middle-aged woman with gray-streaked hair got on. There was something about the hitch in her step—and yes, there it was. As the door slid closed, she swayed in a halting fashion to one side and the other: a cult motion of worship.

She slipped a keycard out of her tiny purse and pushed it into a slot on the control panel. While it was still inserted, she pressed the button for the fifteenth floor—one of the apartment levels. The elevator whirred upward, and she retrieved the card.

If the cultists left the building as infrequently as it appeared, it'd be difficult to get our hands on one of those. Between Sherlock's and my connections, we could probably find someone reasonably local who could make a working facsimile, but only if the security system was generic enough. I wouldn't put it past the cult to have commissioned a custom system that a person would need direct access to in order to figure out the programming. We weren't likely to get away with that.

Of course, climbing the shaft was still a viable option.

And one I intended to make use of. I wasn't going to sit around all day hoping someone sent the elevator up to the top floors.

When the woman got off, I did too—grasping hold of the maintenance rungs and hefting myself upward. It only took a few heaves before I found my rhythm. Listening for any sound of the elevator rising after me, I clambered up the shaft one floor at a time.

The car dropped below me. Its lights dwindled in the distance.

The vertical passage felt suddenly perilous, although I was sure of my grip. If I lost it, I wasn't going to survive the fall.

Climbing was definitely an option, but we'd need additional equipment if Sherlock with his cast or John with his weak leg were going to make it safely up the tower this way.

It was almost completely dark in the shaft by the time I reached the highest floors. I sensed more than saw the end of the passage above me. The heat had faded some as I'd climbed, but the effort had left my shirt sticking to my skin anyway.

I adjusted my position, looping one arm around the metal post that rose between the shallower rungs. With my feet steady on the rung beneath me and that arm solidly in place, I could relax enough to concentrate on things other than avoiding falling. I trained my attention on the wall in front of me and let the shadows wash through my mind.

"Olivia," I called in a low voice, as loud as I dared without risking that any regular person would hear me through the walls. Whatever the fiends had done to my sister, her awareness could slip across worlds. She'd been able to notice my presence near her before. I had to make myself as obvious to her as I could.

"Olivia. Olivia." I chanted her name over and over at intervals, like a sort of meditation. I was starting to feel a little hazy when a faint tingling sensation brushed over my face.

"Jemma?"

It was the same voice I'd heard in the shrouded realm, still with a faraway quality but not anywhere near as far as before. My heart skipped a beat.

"It's me, Olivia. I'm going to get you out of here. You're in the tower, aren't you?"

"Jemma... You shouldn't be here."

The mournfulness of her tone made me choke up. "Of course I should. I promised I'd come back for you, and I meant to do it years ago. I have friends. We can make it work. But it'll be easier the more I know about where exactly you are and how they're holding you."

"You don't know... Their plans are all wound through me. It's too tangled. As long as I'm here, they'll use me."

I leaned closer to the wall as if that would bring her to me, the ache in my throat running right down through my chest. If I could have just touched her, hugged her, shielded her the way I'd tried to so many times when we were kids…

"That's why I'm taking you away from here. We'll ruin their plans and take you someplace where you'll never have to deal with the bastards again. I swear it, Olivia. Do you know what floor you're on, even?"

Her voice took such a long time coming again that I started to think she wasn't going to answer. "High," she murmured. "So close to the sky. I can taste it through the roof."

She hadn't sounded that spacy even when she was ten. I hoped the effects of the shrouded folk's manipulations would fade once she was away from them. It sounded like she was on the top floor, as I'd suspected, at least.

"Are you near any windows?" I asked. "Do you see the elevator when people come up?" *Help me find you.*

Her voice was little more than a wisp now. "No windows. It's all dark. So dark when I open my eyes. The light is all inside. Sometimes it burns."

My hand tightened into a fist. If I could have punched every one of the fiends to Kingdom Come, I would have right this instant. My gaze traveled to the doorway across from me, meant to open for the elevator car. How crazy would it really be to force that open right now?

While all I had was my fists and the single pistol tucked in the back of my jeans? Pretty fucking crazy. The shrouded folk might not be able to see me while I wore the cuff around my thigh, but the cultists wouldn't have any trouble, and they were the ones with the semi-automatic rifles. There'd be plenty of them guarding this treasure their masters had preserved for so many years.

Gritting my teeth, I stayed in place. "I'll come for you as soon as I can," I said. "Do you know how soon the shrouded folk are hoping to complete their plans? Or what they're going to do in the city to add to their energy?"

If her inside knowledge could protect the people outside the tower too, I might as well find that out.

"I don't know. They want it all." A sound like a muted sob reached my ears, and my jaw clenched even harder. "Something's been gathering. It's all connected, here and there, inside me. Everything's tying together and pulling tight. The bridge is almost solid—days. It can't be more than days now." Her voice broke completely. "I don't want to help them. I want this to be over. I don't want them to use me like this."

"I know," I said fiercely. "I won't let them. I promise you that."

"Jemma..." All at once, her tone sharpened. "They're coming. They'll hear. I have to—don't let them find you. Please."

"Olivia!" I whispered.

She didn't respond. My stomach felt as if it'd twisted into one huge knot. I leaned my forehead against the cool metal pole and fought back a scream of frustration.

All the horrors and all the pain they'd put her through, and she was worried about them hurting *me*.

The shrouded folk were close to their goal. Just days away, from what she could feel. That matched the urgency I'd sensed. It was better than hours, anyway.

She was waiting for me. I'd made a promise back then, and I'd made it again—I wouldn't let the fiends take her. And that meant we'd better get on with figuring out how to end the shrouded folk for good.

Dragging in a breath, I shifted my position to begin the long climb down to the bottom of the shaft.

CHAPTER FIFTEEN

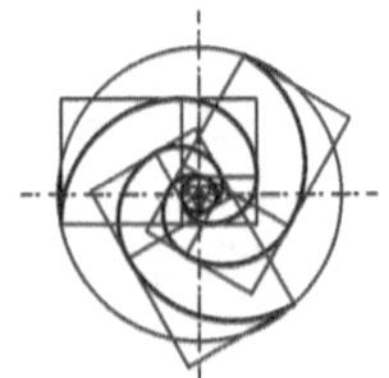

Jemma

"Well, I'm pretty sure that fellow thinks I've gone barmy," John said as he hung up the phone.

I glanced up from my laptop where I'd been working at making my own arrangements on his suite's sofa. All of us had gotten down to work at gathering whatever necessary equipment we could lay our hands on after our most recent strategy discussion.

"He didn't think requisitioning a bunch of high tech medical equipment in a rush for a supposed police operation was a normal request?" I said wryly.

"Not particularly." John rubbed his forehead. "He may still come through. Or our other options for getting the right kind of auditory effect may turn out to be equally effective." He looked to Sherlock, across the table from him. "Have your contacts offered much so far?"

"I've begun with the visual side of things," the detective said. "I believe I should be able to come up with projectors and mounts that will cover at least the majority of the tower's exterior. It is rather a tall order, though. I've gotten some bemused comments."

I took a sip from my coffee as I studied the two of them, letting the sugar-laced bitterness soothe a momentary twinge of anxiety. "It's going to be something of a spectacle when it all comes together. This isn't going to be a peaceful raid. Are you sure you're not getting yourselves into more trouble than you'll be able to get out of, calling in all these favors?"

Not that I wanted to turn away their help—I might have been able to get my hands on just as much equipment alone, but it'd have taken a hell of a lot more time. I was merely highly conscious of the fact that most of my and Bash's arrangements in the last couple hours had involved items designed for slaughter.

I wanted to see my men, my sister, and me out of that building alive, yes, but every other person residing in it could meet their maker as far as I was concerned. If no one was left alive, then there'd be no one to make another stab at carrying out the shrouded folk's warped plans.

"Let us worry about how to handle the authorities on our side of the law," Sherlock said, his voice dry. Then he went back to frowning at the diagram he'd been studying.

They were grown men. They could look after themselves, make their own decisions. I'd been up against the shrouded folk on my own for so long, not even telling Bash the real reasons behind the connections and wealth I'd accumulated, that it was still hard to let go of the sense that the fiends were my responsibility and no one else's. Especially when I'd seen so much more of their horrors than anyone else here had.

A text popped up on my phone from Bash, who'd been making his inquiries in person. *Supplier agreed to make a deal for most of what was on your list. Hand-off scheduled for five, outside the city. I'll just need the money.*

Of course, I wrote back. *Why most and not all? Did you tell him we'll double the price to get things shipped across borders?*

This has all been through a middleman so far, but I got the impression he's leery about the size of the order. I think he's coming to the hand-off personally.

As if it was any of the black-market businessman's concern how much I bought from him, as long as I paid. I grimaced at the phone in momentary hesitation and then wrote, *I should come too then, just to make sure it all goes smoothly. Where should I meet you?*

For the last few years, I'd let Bash handle almost all of my face-to-face transactions. The type of people I dealt with on *my* side of the law tended to respect a brawny ex-sniper a hell of a lot more than a skinny young woman who didn't look like she could snap them in half—even though I could. But if this asshole was going to give even Bash a hard time, maybe he needed a reminder of who exactly he was dealing with. I'd be happy to give him a demonstration.

Bash knew better than to argue the idea. He just texted me a spot at the north end of town. I took a little more time in the suite to arrange the cash I'd need, which I could pick up on the way, and then got up.

"I should have most of my part of the inventory covered. Off to collect it with Bash now."

John gave me a playful salute on my way out. I stopped in my own room to drop off my laptop and arm myself with a pistol and a knife. As I stepped back into the hall, Garrett was just coming down it toward Sherlock and John's suite.

He slowed when he saw me, and I paused, feeling unreasonably awkward. We hadn't talked one-on-one since he'd showed up out of the blue this morning. I had the sense the conversations we'd had since that moment on the mountain weren't exactly finished, but I wasn't sure how to resolve them.

"Heading out?" he said, in a casual tone as if nothing all that momentous was going on, but his gaze was serious as he waited for my response.

"Making sure the crooks I have to deal with don't screw us over," I said with a small smile. "Are you only just getting back from the detention center?"

"Yes. Unfortunately the cult members here are as tight-lipped as anywhere else. I could tell they didn't like the fact that I was poking at the possibility of there being more destructive plans in the works, but I can't say I have any better idea what those plans might be." He let out a breath. "I guess my next job will be making sure the local police don't interfere with *our* plans. Can I assume these 'crooks' you're seeing won't be directly involved in those?"

"It's just the five of us who'll be seeing things through," I said. "So, only the crooks you already know."

The joke fell flat with the tightening of Garrett's mouth. The sight made my innards tighten in turn.

"I don't really have time to talk right now," I added. "But perhaps we should, when we both have a moment, just the two of us? To clear the air?"

His expression relaxed a little. "I think that would be good. But Jemma?"

"Yes?"

He moved closer to me, with that electric intensity none of my other men could quite match. His hand came up to touch my cheek. "I don't look at you and see a crook," he said quietly, and tipped his head to bring his lips to mine.

When he kissed me like that, like he'd never wanted anyone more, I wished I didn't have some idiot supplier I needed to deal with. I'd much rather have given all my attention over to the man who was giving me his forgiveness with the heat of his mouth and the caress of his fingertips over my skin. I leaned into him for a moment, but he would still be here when I got back, and the supplies might not be if I didn't make sure of it. Reluctantly, I drew back.

"We'll definitely have to have that conversation—soon," I said, and a smile flitted across his face in answer.

By the time I reached Bash's meeting spot, I had a car with a locked case full of cash and a film of dust coating my throat. As I ditched the car and carried the case over to the delivery truck Bash had gotten his hands on, I gulped from a bottle of lemonade I'd picked up. The sour sweetness only left my mouth sticky.

"I'm not looking forward to this," I muttered as I got in. Navigating city streets on four wheels rarely put me in a good mood.

"I can still do the hand-off myself," Bash offered.

"No. Part of the reason I'm not looking forward to it is I have a feeling there'll be some kind of trouble."

We left the dense urban sprawl behind quickly, heading farther north past shabby-looking warehouses behind even shabbier concrete walls and patches of sparse forestland. "Do you think we have anything major to worry about from this guy?" I asked Bash.

"His people didn't seem hostile. There was just a lot of back and forth working out the deal, and he definitely balked over a few requests." Bash shrugged. "Who knows what's gotten into him. Maybe the blast downtown yesterday has him jumpy, even though it should be obvious we didn't have anything to do with that."

"We've been investing in his operations for a while. I really can't see how I've given him anything to complain about—or any reason to think we won't make good on any arrangements we make."

"Of course you haven't, Majesty," Bash said affectionately. "And if he isn't a total moron, he'll be there with the goods when he said he'd be, and you won't even need to get out of the truck. You've been good to people, and most of them know what's happened to the idiots who didn't appreciate that."

His confidence didn't completely reassure me. Even John's and Sherlock's contacts were giving them some grief over this operation, and I didn't exactly have the same kind of rapport with my business connections.

Bash pulled into the yard of one of the more distant warehouses. Around the back of the aluminum-sided building, a couple of guys were waiting by a truck of their own. One of them held up his hand, partly in greeting and partly to motion for us to park about a dozen feet back. A prickle ran down my spine. They were treating us like uncertain associates rather than long-established allies.

Bash hopped out, leaving the case with the money with me. An older guy got out of the other truck and sauntered to meet him in the middle of the yard. His gaze twitched to me behind the windshield and then back to my right-hand man. I rested my arm in the open window, watching and listening intently.

"Do you have all the items we agreed on?" Bash asked with a jerk of his chin toward the truck.

"I was able to get it all together, pretty impressive given the time window you gave me." The guy folded his sinewy arms over his chest. "What are you going to do with all that shit anyway? You starting a war or something?"

Ending it was more like it. I restrained a smile.

Bash glowered at the man. "I don't see how that matters. We need the equipment. We're paying you for it. The rest is our business, not yours."

"I just want to be sure there isn't going to be some big blow-up that comes back to haunt me. You've got to understand, as one businessman to another."

"We keep our books clean. You don't need to worry about anyone connecting you to anything."

The guy swiped his hand over his ratty beard. "All the same, I think I need a little insurance, considering the extreme nature of this deal. You want the full load? I'm going to need double the payment we talked about before."

The fucker. We were already paying a hell of a lot more than the stuff would have cost him to get to make up for the short notice.

"We've brought what we agreed on," Bash said. "That's what you're getting."

"I can wait while you get together the rest. Or you can leave with just half the stuff. It's up to you."

Before he'd even finished that last sentence, I pushed open the truck door. The guy stiffened as I strode across the concrete with sharp raps of my shoes.

"Teppo, isn't it?" I said, coming to a stop beside Bash. "You know who I am. You know you wouldn't have your fingers in half as many pies as you've managed without my assistance. So what's all this bullshit now? When have I given you any indication I'd screw you over?"

His eyes went twitchy again. "I— You've got to see— It's not about screwing over. I've never delivered a load like this to anyone. I don't even know what you'd do with some of the stuff in there. And if you're doing to do something crazy, then I've got to cover my ass."

"Watch how you talk to her," Bash said in a growl, taking a menacing step forward.

I caught his elbow to hold him back and gave Teppo a thin smile.

"*I've* been covering *your* ass for the last four years, making sure you have a leg up over competitors, settling disputes in your favor, only asking a very small portion of your earnings as payment. I don't believe I've let you down once. And the thanks I get is the suggestion that *I'm* going to be bad for your business? I'll give you one more chance to reconsider your stance. The money is in the truck."

The guy's mouth opened and closed a few times like a fish drowning in air. Finally he mumbled, "Look, I've got to do what's best for me, and I need that extra cash to make this right."

The emotion that came over me wasn't even anger. It was simply resignation shot through with a dollop of irritation.

I didn't need this guy anymore. All the plans I'd been building up to were culminating within the week, and then... if I survived... I wasn't even sure how far I'd keep up the business. So if he wanted to be a jackass about it, let him find out what jackasses got.

"I think you've forgotten who you're dealing with, Teppo," I said, low and clear. "The only person here acting crazy and fucking up your business is *you*. To make sure you remember what kind of respect is due in future, I'm imposing an asshole tax on this transaction. Everything in that truck is mine, and I'll keep the cash too, thank you very much."

Teppo's eyes widened. One of his men reached for a gun at his side, but Bash was faster. He had his pistol in hand in an instant, aimed at Teppo's head.

"Try it, and say goodbye to your boss," he said.

"Now, just wait a—" Teppo said, starting to sputter.

I cut him off with a wave of my own pistol. "Keys. Now."

"There's no way I—"

I shot the ground, so close to his foot that smoke wisped from the toe of his shoe. "Keys." When he simply stared at me, I shot again, this time aiming for the side of his calf.

The bullet tore through his cargo pants and flesh with a spray of blood. Teppo cried out and crumpled onto his ass, clutching at his leg. I walked up to him, gun still at the ready.

"Keys," I said. "Or I'm going to keep working my way up. And believe me, the damage will quickly become permanent."

Teppo made an anguished jerk of his hand toward one of his underlings. The younger guy, his face tensed, fished out a car key and tossed it to me. I pitched it to Bash, who caught it without his gun wavering even half an inch.

"We're not going to leave you stuck out here in the middle of nowhere," I said, heading back to our truck. I grabbed the case with the money and left the doors open. "Get your boss to a hospital before he loses more blood than he needs to. And don't mess with me again unless you want to see how much worse the consequences can get."

Bash and I circled the three men on opposite sides. One of the underlings had wrenched off his shirt to press it to his boss's wound. The other scrambled to the truck. Bash threw the key after him with a clink as it hit the pavement.

The punishment had been brutal, efficient… and I wasn't enjoying the moment at all. From the cab of Teppo's truck, I peered down at the limping man and the splotches of blood marking the concrete, and weariness swept through me.

I was bored of these clashes, the power plays, the asserting of dominance. More than ten years of it, all to climb high enough to challenge the shrouded folk, and I was ready to step back from all this crap. If I ever got the chance to make that choice.

CHAPTER SIXTEEN

John

The pile of books on my "finished" side was finally higher than on my "to read" side, but I still didn't feel as if I'd made a lot of headway. I made a face at the text I was currently skimming through, the author of which kept hedging his suggestions with uncertain language about how most of his propositions were only theoretical. The rasp as I flipped the page sounded loud in the quiet of the university library.

A rustle of fabric approached my table. I glanced up, and my pulse skipped a beat with a mix of happiness and guilt. Happiness because Jemma's form sinking into the chair across from me was a welcome and unexpected sight, and guilt because I'd meant to have more to tell her when I did see her again.

She was carrying a plastic bag, which also rustled. With a sly grin, she slid it across the table toward me.

"Still buried in the books, I see. Sherlock told me you'd probably still be here. It's past seven, you know. I'm going to guess you haven't had any dinner yet." She nodded to the bag, which was giving off a spicy, meaty smell that had already set my mouth watering. "I picked you up some kofta kabobs from that restaurant you liked so much the first night."

"You figured I needed looking after, did you?" I said, but she wasn't wrong. My stomach gurgled at the smell. I looked at my current book and pushed it to the side. "I don't think eating's allowed in here."

"Afraid to break the rules now?" Jemma teased with a glint in her lovely gray eyes, but she got up at the same time. "I'm sure we can find a good enough spot somewhere on campus. Whatever you're mulling over, taking a break from the books will probably help the ideas come together anyway. And even if it doesn't, we can't have our doctor starving himself to death."

"I'm not exactly a medical practitioner anymore," I couldn't help pointing out, but I got up, taking the bag of food and my journal full of notes with me.

We ended up sitting on the grass beneath the campus's huge stone gate with its impressive arches. Jemma, naturally, had picked up a pastry full of custard for herself. She nibbled at it, appearing to savor each bite, while I worked through the kababs. As I polished off the last one, she licked the sugar and flecks of cream from her fingers with flashes of tongue that stirred a different sort of hunger in me. Then she sat back on her hands and gave me a pointed look.

"All right. Let's hear what you've come up with. I want the chance to try out the strategies we're considering using ahead of time, so we've got to get moving with any more equipment we need to gather."

I nodded. The texts had repeated the same themes enough that I didn't even need to consult my notes to go over the general concepts.

"Sounds, especially loud and unexpected ones, can have an adverse effect on heart rate and blood pressure," I said. "Continual noise elevates cortisol levels, which results in fatigue, irritability, difficulty concentrating, and sometimes more acute physical symptoms like headaches. Those are the most definite effects we could count on. If we can work a pattern in while also making the sound disruptive, I assume we'd be interfering with both your fiends' and the cultists' ability to fight back."

"So we want an irritating rhythm," Jemma said with obvious amusement. "I think we can manage that."

"Another factor is actual talking," I said. "Bash mentioned that he helped keep the shrouded folk away in Tokyo by playing Shakespearean movies—he figured something about the rhythm to the dialogue repelled them. There's also been research suggesting that hearing conversations going on around you hinders mental processes like short-term memory, which makes it harder to complete tasks."

The corner of Jemma' mouth quirked upward. "Tasks like 'Let's tackle these intruders who've just broken in'? I don't see why we couldn't give that a try too. Was there anything else?"

I shook my head, a pang of my earlier guilt returning. "Those are the connections that've been researched the most and shown consistency. I'm not sure how much we'd want to gamble. I was going to keep looking, though. And I've taken notes on specific kinds of sounds that showed the most detrimental effects, that sort of thing."

"I'm not sure we'll need more than that." Jemma exhaled slowly, her gaze going distant for a moment. The sinking sun was casting the sky overhead with a rosy hue only a little less vibrant than her hair. "I suppose the difficult part is going to be finding equipment that will effectively conduct the sound through walls and so on, and getting it all up to the higher floors of that building without them noticing. Maybe if we could set up some things outside, by the windows... I'll have to look into the sound conductivity of glass."

"You might ask Sherlock. I'd say there's a fifty percent chance that's one of the many subjects he's decided he needed to investigate for one reason or another in the past."

Jemma gave a short laugh. "He is something of a repository of knowledge, isn't he? I'll start there. It'd certainly be easier if he's done the work for us ahead of time."

I chuckled. "Well, easy depends on how much you enjoy listening to him pontificate rather than consulting the books for yourself."

"Yes." She lay back on the grassy slope, tucking her hands

behind her head and considering the streaks of cloud that crossed the sky. Then she shifted her gaze to me. "You enjoy his pontificating."

It was a statement rather than a question, but she said it mildly, without any sign of where she was going with the observation.

"I'll be the first to admit he can go on too long," I said. "But the energy that comes over him when he latches on to a subject—it really is something to see."

"It is." She was silent for a minute or so, long enough that I started to wonder if she expected me to take my leave, and then she said, softly but succinctly, "Are you sure you wouldn't be happier with just him?"

I blinked. "What do you mean?"

She arched her eyebrows at me. "I mean... you all went to a lot of trouble to convince me to stick around, painted a picture of this future where we'll all keep on having whatever exactly relationship we have right now. That's no surprise coming from Bash, and I could see Garrett wanting that too, but you and Sherlock have each other. Doesn't adding me to the mix just overly complicate things?"

I hesitated, at a loss for words as I tried to sort through the feelings her words had stirred to the surface. There was a quiver of excitement, yes, at the thought that Sherlock and I had anything that could really be called a relationship. But the way Jemma seemed to think she could be so easily cut from that dynamic made my chest clench.

She was brilliant, no doubt about it, and those glinting gray eyes saw a lot. They clearly didn't see everything, though. Somehow she'd missed the way I looked at her, the way every part of me responded to her. Somehow she couldn't see how right now just taking her in, from the waves of her scarlet hair against the green of the grass to the creamy paleness of her skin, the narrow lips I'd come to know the shape and taste of so well, the slender curves of her sprawled body that contained so much condensed strength... It kindled not just a fire in my loins but a heady warmth that filled my heart.

This beautiful, brilliant, complicated woman had crashed into our lives with startling grace and care, had twisted us around her finger and yet woken us up at the same time. I wouldn't have Sherlock the way I did now at all if it wasn't for her. I probably still wouldn't have admitted to myself what mattered to me.

And one of the things that mattered to me was her.

"I'd have thought you knew me well enough by now to realize that complications are a feature, not a defect, as far as I'm concerned," I said with a crooked smile. "I like a little trouble along the way. That's what makes it fun."

She rolled her eyes at me. "There's trouble and then there's 'likely to get you killed in half a dozen ways in any given month'."

"I don't see how that'll be much of a concern once we've dealt with these monsters. Unless you're planning on bringing violent criminal associates around to our doorstep."

She grimaced. "No. I'd rather not have them even at my doorstep."

"Then what's the problem?" I asked.

"I just don't want you to feel some sort of obligation because of what we've been through and what we've shared, if your heart's more elsewhere already. I won't be offended. I'm *glad* the two of you have each other the way you do."

"Jemma…" My throat tightened with emotion. "Do I really need to tell you that you mean more to me than that? I can't imagine living my life without Sherlock in it, no, but it'd seem awfully drab without you in it too."

"You managed fine for years without me in it."

"I managed without being more than Sherlock's completely platonic colleague too." I let out an exasperated huff. "You spark something in me no one else does, not even him. Something I don't want to lose. I'm head-over-heels in love with you, Jemma. Has it really not been obvious?"

She stared at me for a second. Then she pushed herself back into a sitting position, her gaze never leaving my face. "No. Not — I mean — it's not an area I have a lot of experience in."

Her startled uncertainty brought an even sharper warmth into my chest. She knew how to tackle everything except tenderness, didn't she? "I forgave you for pushing my best friend down a cliff. I've followed you everywhere you've let me follow." I paused.

"Maybe I can't offer Sherlock's genius or Garrett's fervor or whatever else, maybe I can't make the most impressive confession ever, but—"

"John," she said, cutting me off. She set her hand over mine and squeezed, her eyes searching my face, and for the first time I noticed the sort of desperation that colored them, as if she were both afraid of what she might see and afraid she wouldn't see it at all. "You're wonderful the way you are. I think you're what keeps the rest of us from falling apart. Don't ever, *ever* suggest you're somehow worth less than anyone else."

"I could say the same right back to you," I said quietly.

She went still. "Yes. Well." Then she leaned in and brushed her lips to mine so quickly I barely had time to react.

"Thank you," she murmured by my ear. I caught her before she could pull back and hugged her to me. She leaned her head against my shoulder, and for one fleeting moment I felt her relax against me, like all the weight in the world had lifted off of her.

The business side of her took over before long. "You'd better get back to those books if you're going to finish before the library closes," she said, but her tone had a gentleness to it that hadn't been there before.

"Very true," I said, getting to my feet.

She gave me a peck on my cheek and a squeeze of my arm before she loped away. It occurred to me as I watched her disappear into the dwindling evening light that I wasn't completely sure what she'd been thanking me for. That was all right, though. It was enough that I'd said something she'd thought it worth thanking me for at all.

One more offering that might hold her back from throwing her whole life on the pyre to make the shrouded folk burn.

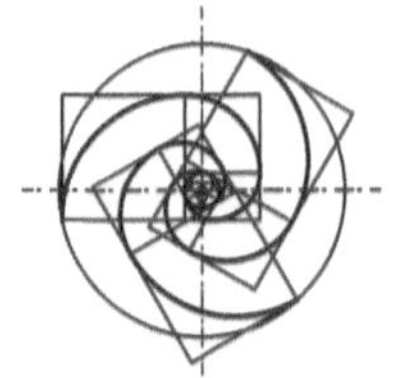

CHAPTER SEVENTEEN

Jemma

When Garrett answered my knock on his hotel room door, he looked as if he'd already started to turn in for the night. He'd unbuttoned his light blue dress shirt halfway down his chest, and his hair was more rumpled than usual, in a rather appealing way.

"Is this a good time for our talk?" I asked with a cock of my head.

He ran his hand over his hair a little self-consciously, but he stepped back to let me in. One of the pillows on his bed was propped upright with his ever-present notepad lying on the covers beside it — he must have been relaxing there while he went over the case.

I nodded to the notepad. "Any new developments since this afternoon?"

"A good one, actually," Garrett said, his usual energy coming back to him as he shut the door behind me. "The local police have agreed to monitor the comings and goings from the tower and to tail anyone who shows indications of being a cultist. Right now, there's an officer watching a small group that left about an hour ago. All they've done is get dinner so far, but if they start preparing to cause any trouble, someone should be able to intervene."

That was a welcome development—although it depended on the police's ability to ID the actual cultists. If the commune noticed the surveillance, they'd be more careful about their behavior leaving the building.

"I suppose getting bugs planted inside the apartments would be too much to ask," I said.

"If we could draw a definite connection between crimes already committed and the inhabitants, maybe not, but even in that case, it'd still take more time than it sounds like we have."

"Yeah." I sank down on the end of the bed, all the events of the day from the "intervention" to talking with John at the library pressing down on me with a sudden weight. We'd accomplished so much in just one day… but there was still so much we'd need to do before we could destroy those fucking fiends, or at least their connection to our world.

I didn't want to think about what would happen if we weren't fast enough.

Garrett sat down next to me, close enough to be companionable without being overly familiar. As if we could get any more familiar than we'd already been. But we hadn't really talked, hadn't touched more than that kiss in the hall, since I'd nearly destroyed any trust I'd gained from my trio of detectives, and his tentativeness sent a twinge through me.

How much was he being respectful of my space and how much was he asserting his own need?

It should be easy enough to tell. I slid my hand across the bedspread toward his, waiting for his reaction. Without hesitation, he met me halfway and grasped my fingers with his.

All right, then. The space was for my benefit. He was looking out for me like he had been this morning, like he'd been by coming here at all.

I couldn't leave it alone, though. Poking at the subject felt like picking at a scab, but the fact was, a wound like this couldn't really heal if we just ignored it. If I tried to pretend nothing had ever been amiss, it'd only fester in both of us. Better to drain any lingering poison out of it now.

"You couldn't have been feeling this forgiving right after I gave Sherlock that shove."

"No, I'd say that's an understatement." He let out a rough laugh under his breath. "I was furious. And hurt. I should admit that too."

"Because you expected better of me."

His hand stayed clasped around mine. "Because I didn't know the full story, and in the moment it looked as if you really meant to kill him, and…"

"And?" I prompted him when he trailed off.

"Honestly, because it reminded me of the worst parts of myself."

I gave him a quizzical look, and he offered me a sheepish smile in return before lowering his gaze.

"I've told you about all the anger that drove my behavior when I was a child, out of jealousy and frustration. You caught me struggling with the urge to slash my colleague's bloody tires not that long ago. If anyone should know anything about tackling problems with unnecessary violence, it's me."

"You didn't slash those tires," I pointed out. "You'd already gotten a hold on yourself before you even realized I was there."

"And you didn't really try to kill Sherlock," Garrett replied. "You were trying to go off on your own like you've done before, and he'd proven how dogged he'd be about following you… and you had your sister's life and freedom to consider. Hell, for all we know, we'd have met a worse fate than a tumble if we'd come charging right after you."

My throat tightened. "You still might."

"You see?" He lifted my hand to rest it against his thigh and raised his head to meet my eyes again. "*That* is who you are. Who you've shown yourself to be with every honest gesture and comment you've offered the entire time I've known you. None of this has ever been for *you*, especially once you ended that deal. You could have lived the rest of your life without giving the demons a second thought. You could have thrown us into the fray ahead of you. But every step of the way, you've been fighting to stop them from hurting more people the way they hurt you and your sister, you've been trying to leave us out of it so we won't get hurt too…"

"I'm not a martyr," I protested.

"No. I'm not saying you are. But in spite of being a criminal mastermind, you're still one of the most selfless people I've ever met. When this is over, when we kick them off the face of this Earth and get your sister out of their clutches, then are you finally going to let yourself have a few things that are just for you?"

Staring back into his dark brown eyes, I couldn't say I completely agreed. "I've indulged myself now and then. If I were really so selfless, I'd have gone and stormed the tower by myself no matter what the bunch of you said."

Garrett raised an eyebrow. "Why didn't you, then?"

"Because I want this more than I probably should."

I leaned in, and he met my kiss, his mouth hot and tender all at once. No, I wasn't selfless when it came to these men. I was fucking greedy. Deep down, I wanted all of them, everything they'd give me, even the parts I couldn't give in return.

Garrett slid his free hand along the side of my neck, brushing my hair back over my shoulder. He cupped my jaw and kissed me again at an even better angle. The soft but eager press of his lips set off that familiar flame running down through my chest to smolder low in my belly. I ran my fingers up his chest to the open V of his collar to trace the lean muscles there.

He pulled back an inch, resting his forehead against mine, his breath ragged. "I missed you, firecracker," he said. "Even when I was furious with you, I missed you."

My pulse stuttered with an emotion that was both hopeful and pained. But I could return that sentiment.

"I missed you too," I said softly.

"Even with Sherlock and the rest around to keep you occupied?"

"The group doesn't feel complete without you there." I paused. "I don't feel complete. There are ways we understand each other that I don't have with anyone else." That was true for each of the guys, really. So perhaps I couldn't be blamed for wanting to keep all of them by my side.

It must have been the right thing to say, because Garrett kissed me even harder, his arm looping around my waist to pull me right up against his wiry frame. I eased one leg across his lap, half straddling him, so we could fit even more tightly together, and a groan caught in his throat. He smelled as delicious as he always did, like a flare of electricity, smoky and potent. Irresistible. How could I not devour this man?

But some small fragment of me wasn't entirely satisfied by the forgiveness and affection he'd already expressed. That selfish particle of longing that held me back for a second even as I unbuttoned the rest of his shirt.

The request slipped out. "Say it again?"

Garrett had just tugged my blouse free from my skirt. He stopped with his hand on my bare skin below my breast and peered at me searchingly. "It?"

An embarrassed warmth crept through my chest, but that didn't prevent me from continuing. "What you told me, that day with Bash. If it's still true. I know I can't say it back, but I—I think I'd like hearing it."

For a second, I felt ridiculously awkward, like a schoolgirl confessing her first crush. What was wrong with me? But any regret that'd come over me at asking washed away with Garrett's softly beaming smile.

"I love you," he said, tipping his head so close his lips brushed mine a hair's breadth from another kiss. They teased across my cheek toward my ear. "I love you, Jemma."

I *couldn't* say the words back. Even as my heart swelled with affection for this man, too much of it was devoted to my sister and the cause I'd spent my whole life working toward. But I could show him a sort of love I expected he'd very much enjoy.

I nudged him higher on the bed as I peeled off his shirt. He tugged off my blouse in turn. While he eased down the straps of my bra, his mouth branding my collarbone with a blissful heat, I opened the fly of his slacks. I curled my fingers around his already rigid cock and was rewarded with the hitch of his breath.

"Jemma," he murmured, all hunger now. I slipped from his grasp and sank over his hips with a swipe of my tongue over the head of his cock. His voice turned choked. "Fucking bloody hell."

"I'll translate that as, 'Please do go on'," I teased, and took him right into my mouth.

His only response was an inarticulate sound. He slumped back on the bed, but he kept one hand on my shoulder with a continuous caress, growing shakier as I swirled my tongue around his velvety flesh. I hadn't attended to Garrett like this before. His cock tasted like the rest of him, only sharper, as if I was drawing a live current into me with the movements of my lips.

I was never going to be a normal girlfriend. I'd never be made of sweetness and light. But I could damn well give it good in some respects. I didn't think any of my men would look back on our time together with disappointment, however things worked out in the end.

Garrett's hips jerked as I sucked him down harder. A groan escaped his lips. He gripped my shoulder harder and then pulled at me to stop. When I raised my head, he urged me up the bed beside him, rolling onto me when our bodies aligned. The feel of his weight pressing down on me sent a fresh wave of desire through me from head to toe.

"We haven't done it in a bed yet," he said, kissing my cheek and then my jaw. "This will be an interesting experiment. If you don't think it's too outrageous."

I laughed, squirming so his erection would come to rest against just the right spot between my legs. It was true, we'd made use of desks and dressers and rugs but never an actual bed in the past. "I think I can handle this," I said, and gasped as his cock slid against me.

He fumbled along my hip for my skirt's zipper, and together we peeled it off of me. A growl of frustration slipped out of me when I realized my purse wasn't in reach. Garrett let out a soft chuckle.

"Call me optimistic, but I came prepared," he murmured, and reached to grab a packet out of the bedside table's drawer.

He paused before opening it to dip his head to my breasts, lavishing them with the attention he hadn't gotten the chance to offer earlier. My fingers curled into his hair as he flicked his tongue over my nipple with a flare of pleasure. For a second, I was torn between lingering in that bliss and careening onward to the greater ecstasy ahead. Then I pulled him back up to claim his mouth—or maybe he was claiming mine—it didn't really matter when his cock was penetrating me a few moments later.

I arched upward so he could plunge in all the way to the hilt. Garrett gripped my thigh and bowed his head. As he plowed into me hard and fast, he nipped my shoulder with a smaller spark of pleasure.

It wasn't the most outrageous sex I'd ever had by a longshot, not even in the past week, but the desire in his touch and the urgency of his thrusts brought a different sort of high. We were in sync, in more ways than one—in ways I'd never have thought I could connect with a man so devoted to justice and the law.

I crossed my ankles behind him and cried out as he hit the most sensitive spot deep inside me. My head lolled back with the rush of my coming release. Garrett clutched me to him, keeping his strokes firm and fast, the intensity of his lust as giddying as the ecstatic burn of him filling me.

I came just seconds before he did, with another cry and a quiver that ran through every inch of me, flooding me with bliss.

Garrett eased me down on the mattress, but he stayed braced over me, gazing down at me. I gave him a pleased smile in return. He'd better be able to tell just how much *I'd* enjoyed that. But something else, something slightly nervous, darted through his gaze.

"It's a big bed," he said cautiously. "I wouldn't mind sharing it for the night. And then you'd be right on hand if the police have any updates for me."

Oh, this dear, lovely man. Emotion caught in my throat, recognizing what the invitation meant to him and how uncertain he was of how I'd receive it. The truth was that a few months ago, maybe even a few weeks ago, the thought would have made me edgy. Now it only melted me even more.

I could do this much. I could let myself have this much. Hell, it might be my last chance.

"In that case," I said, "I'm not going anywhere."

CHAPTER EIGHTEEN

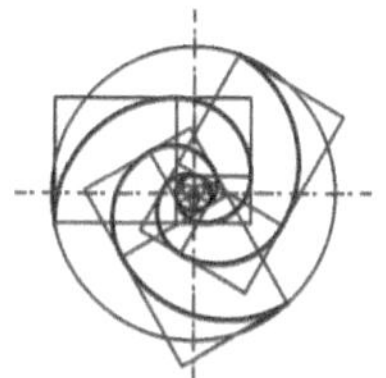

Jemma

I was meandering through a dreamland Istanbul, streets merging with one another, a single turn taking me from the middle of one neighborhood to a totally separate one, when a voice drifted to me as if carried on a faint breeze.

"Jemma," it whispered. "Jemma, can you hear me?"

I spun around outside a temple and found myself by the shop where I'd picked up last night's dessert. The voice came again—from a different direction? Or from all around and yet whisper-soft at the same time.

"Are you there, Jemma?"

It was Olivia's voice. The recognition shot through me with a jolt of adrenaline—and I jerked awake in Garrett's bed, sweat forming on my skin and heart thudding.

Garrett stirred at my sharp inhalation, reaching to touch my side from where he was sprawled under the covers beside me. "Okay?" he mumbled, still half asleep.

"I—I don't know. I have to…" My thoughts were muddled. I

shook my head and burrowed it back into the pillow. As I closed my eyes, I strained my ears, but my sister's voice didn't reach me again.

She hadn't projected it to me physically. She'd touched my mind somehow—some way she only could when I was in that in-between world of dreams?

I willed my breath to even out and tried to let my mind drift back into slumber. Unfortunately, my senses were far too much on high alert now. My muscles wouldn't quite relax; my thoughts spun restlessly in my head. After a few minutes that only made me more tense than I'd been to start with, I pushed out of the bed.

Garrett woke up more as I padded across the room, pulling my clothes back on in the hint of dawn light that was just starting to seep past the curtain. He squinted at the clock, which read 5:47, and then at me. "Jemma, what's wrong?"

"I think my sister was trying to tell me something while I was sleeping. So I have to get back to sleep. And it's not happening on its own."

He heaved off the covers and grabbed the thin hotel bathrobe. "Are you sure you weren't just dreaming?"

No. But... "It didn't feel like part of my dream. It felt like when I talked to her in the shrouded realm." I grasped the door handle. "I need to talk to Bash."

There wasn't much Garrett could contribute to the situation, but I didn't argue about him following me either. Because he'd come to Istanbul later than the rest of us, he'd ended up on the same floor but at the other end of the hall. I slipped past the closed doors where other patrons were sleeping and knocked as loud as I dared on Bash's.

The hitman never slept all that deeply. He was at the door within a matter of seconds, peering at me a little blearily but more alert than Garrett still looked. His gaze slid past me to the other man, but if he had any qualms left about the fact that he was sharing my affections with other lovers, it didn't show in his expression.

"What's going on? What do you need?" he asked.

I motioned him back into his room, and Garrett and I joined him there. I glanced around the darkened space. "Do you still have the leftover pills from the ritual we did in Tokyo?"

"I wasn't sure if you'd want to pass over again," he said, frowning. "They're in my suitcase. Are you going back right now?"

"No, not exactly. I just need to get back into a state like sleep. I'll take half a dose."

"She thinks her sister was trying to talk to her in a dream," Garrett offered by way of explanation.

Bash nodded as if that were an everyday occurrence and fished the pill bottle out of one of the hidden compartments in his suitcase. I poured one of the tiny pills onto my hand, eyeballed it, and managed to crack it almost perfectly in two with a jerk of my thumbs. One half, I popped into my mouth and swallowed with just saliva.

I might not have been thinking as straight as usual with my early waking and my impatience to get back to my sister. "You should lie down," Garrett reminded me.

I headed toward Bash's bed, and the medication's effects rippled through me. My balance wobbled. The men caught me and helped me the last few steps. I slumped down on one side of the mattress with the vague thought that I needed to leave room there for the two of them, they might want to get more sleep too, and then my mind tumbled away from me into a shifting haze.

A vague awareness of the room and people around me lingered, but I couldn't have tracked their movements or spoken to them if I'd wanted to. My consciousness drifted deeper into the haze, on a plane somewhere between meditation and sleep. *Olivia*, I thought, but I didn't know how to speak to her across the distance the way she'd spoken to me.

I didn't need to. She was waiting for me. The haze solidified around me into vague shapes of buildings and streets, and that faint whisper tickled my ears again. "Jemma. You came back."

"I'll always come back," I said. "How did you—no, it doesn't matter. What did you need to tell me?"

"They're doing something," my sister said. "They're—I can feel the energy rising—I can feel—"

"What?" I said, my stomach knotting.

For a few seconds, she was silent. Then a sensation brushed over my arm, delicate as a moth's wing, and a set of impressions that weren't mine trickled through my body.

Little electric jolts twitched through my nerves. There was a vast dark space and a sprawl of gray land that I recognized as the shrouded realm. Mixed between those came hints of moving traffic and sunlight reflecting off of windows—fragments of the city around us.

All of it flowed through me as it must have been flowing through Olivia, as if she were all those places at the same time or connected to beings who were. With a distant slash of a knife and welling of blood came a sharper flash of energy. It twined all through her being, winding around her throat, creeping across her lungs, penetrating her gut. The ruddy glow of it set my nerves jittering the way the light in the shrouded folk's stones had.

They'd tied her up in their schemes in a totally literal way. Their essence ran all through her like a conduit. They were making her into a bridge, she'd said. It felt as though the construction were almost complete, with her body and soul strung all through it. Anguish rose up inside me, overriding the sensations she was sending to me.

How the hell could I pull her away from that without hurting her even more?

"There," she murmured, and an image flitted through my head of a tall, glittering office building. Something heavy and ominous rested in a pair of hands. Exhilaration rippled in the air as figures marched toward the place together.

"And there." A public square I recognized from the business district, with tramway tracks running along one side. A few café owners were just setting out their signs and wiping off their patio chairs. A malicious glee reached me with the thudding of a pulse in anticipation.

The cult was making another move. Getting into place to wreak more havoc—right now, right here in the city.

"We have to stop them," I said, urgency flaring in my chest.

"I can't," my sister said, her tone so hopeless it tore at my heart.

"I'm buried under, broken. I can't do anything. They want to rip me even farther open—but maybe you—if you can get to them—"

Yes. I had to get out of here, out of this daze, and bring hell down on the cult before they did the same to us.

My dream arms flailed out in the sleep-like haze. I clawed toward consciousness. Up, out, eyes open, mind clear—if I just reached far enough, strained hard enough…

I flung myself right back into awareness with a gasp for breath. My body knifed upward on the bed. Bash grasped my shoulder to steady me, and the words tumbled hoarse from my throat.

"The cult is planning more attacks—getting in place right now. I'm not sure about one of the spots, but the other's near here." I spun to find Garrett straightening up in the room's chair. "You have to tell the police to get over there, catch them before they do anything."

He jumped to his feet. "I'll get my phone. Do you know what the people look like? What exactly they're going to do?"

I shook my head with a clench of my gut. "All I know is the places." I described the building I'd caught a glimpse of and told him the name of the square, and he hustled out of Bash's room.

My pulse hadn't stopped thudding. I slid off the bed, still a bit dizzy from the pill but with adrenaline cutting through its effects.

"We should go too. To the square. I'd probably recognize the cultists before the police do. I don't know how much time we have."

"Of course." Bash grabbed a car key off the bedside table. He'd dressed while I drifted in my artificial sleep, maybe anticipating that I might need more from him soon.

When we came out, Garrett was heading back down the hall toward us, speaking in a low but intense voice into his phone. He'd thrown on a pair of slacks and a shirt he hadn't yet buttoned. At the sight of us, he picked up his pace to catch up, with a nod as if he'd guessed what we were doing.

"I understand that the chief isn't there yet," he said into the phone. "You still have officers in the field and on call, don't you? Get them out there. We're lucky we got any advance information at all."

I glanced at the door to Sherlock and John's suite, but it'd be a tight fit with all of us in the one car, and Bash and I alone should have been able to take on a handful of cultists if need be. Let them get a little more sleep.

As we hustled down the stairs, skipping the wait for the elevator, Garrett hung up with a grimace. "They're sending people over. I don't know if they believed the situation was quite as urgent as I tried to tell them. Are we going to try to beat them there?"

"Better than sitting around doing nothing," I said. "I could feel my sister when I was talking to her—feel how the fiends have been working on her, manipulating her body to their ends... I don't think it's going to take much for them to push through with their plans. If we can even stall one of this morning's missions, it could buy us time we'll need."

On the street outside, Bash dropped into the driver's seat of the used car he'd bought cheap for our activities here that didn't involve much cargo. Garrett didn't object to my taking the other front seat. Bash gunned the engine as the detective scrambled into the back.

I consulted my mental map of the city. "Take the second left. That street should get us there the fastest."

Bash pulled onto the road, quiet in the expanding dawn, and took off with a roar that sounded thunderous. I scanned the sidewalks as we sped along, watching for any figures who pinged on my cult radar. Should we swing by their tower in case there were more sneaking out on similar errands? But the figures Olivia had conveyed to me had already been getting into place. We couldn't risk wasting any time.

Lord only knew what the bastards meant to do. My stomach turned at the memory of the vicious impression I'd gotten from the emotions that had briefly grazed mine.

Bash tore around the corner and swerved around a few slower cars rumbling along ahead of us. I leaned forward in my seat. It shouldn't take more than five minutes to reach the square at this time of day, especially at the speed he was going. Then we just needed to spot the perps, and—

Garrett's phone rang. He yanked it to his ear. "Yes?"

There was a long silence with nothing but the rumble of the

engine. My heart started to sink. Then Garrett let out a curse so choked that my hopes slipped away completely.

"It's too late," he said to us. "It's already happened. They weren't going after the buildings this time, not really. Three different sites around the city, including that square—they just opened fire on everyone in the area, on the windows of the shops and the apartments overhead... The police are only just arriving on the scenes, but at least a dozen people are dead."

CHAPTER NINETEEN

Garrett

The local police commander's accent grew thicker when he was frustrated.

"I can't order a raid on an entire business complex just because a foreign officer said so, Mr. Lestrade," he said over the phone. "The culprits weren't traced from the building, and we've found no identification that would allow us to connect them to it. I want to see an end to this violence as much as you do, but my hands are tied."

I was starting to see why Sherlock often got irritated with my insistence on staying within legal bounds. I sank back into the sofa in his and John's suite, grimacing at the wall. "Between the three attacks, you've now got nearly forty deaths that happened in the space of a few minutes. They've already escalated their attacks once. Do you really want to find out what they'll do next if we don't step in?"

"We're doing everything we can. If you can provide a clear link to the building, we'll act immediately. I have superiors to answer to."

Didn't we all? Maybe it *was* easier for me to argue with him when mine were thousands of miles distant. That didn't ease the anxiety tangled in my gut. But this conversation wasn't getting us anywhere.

"I'll see what I can do," I said, and hung up with a sigh.

"No luck?" Jemma said from where she'd been pacing the living area. For a brief while last night, she'd looked content. She'd looked *happy*. Now her face was as clouded as her pensive gray eyes.

She hadn't said it, and I doubted she'd admit it out loud, but I'd been in enough fraught situations like this to recognize the signs. She blamed herself for not figuring out sooner what the cultists meant to do, for not getting there fast enough to stop them.

"They can't prove the perps from the shootings had anything to do with the tower," I said. "So they can't justify any kind of building-wide action. If their people had been watching the place more closely…"

"As everywhere, we can't count on official channels for the most effective action," Sherlock said in his matter-of-fact way.

Normally a comment like that would have raised my hackles, but at the moment I couldn't help agreeing.

"What steps can we take at this point?" John asked, coming over to the dining table with a cup of tea he'd just poured. "We've treaded outside the law to take down communes before."

Bash scowled where he was leaning against the sofa near Jemma, his gaze following her movements through the room. "It's a lot easier setting a community up for a fall when they're out in the wilderness without walls or security systems and all that protecting them. All we needed before was stealth and good timing, and we didn't have to worry about any neighbors spotting us and getting nervous. This is much more complicated."

"And the tower commune must have noticed the increased police presence by now." Jemma stopped in the middle of the room with a frustrated exhalation. "They *couldn't* have all snuck out without alerting anyone unless they realized the building was under surveillance and purposefully took steps to evade the cops. Which means they'll be on high alert inside, too. If I'd taken a stab at it a couple days ago…"

My chest tightened. She wasn't just blaming herself for this morning—she was convincing herself she should have gone on what would essentially have been a suicide mission, alone and without half the support we'd arranged.

"You might not have gotten more than two steps beyond the lift," Sherlock said baldly. "They may have increased their defenses, but we've come up with several techniques for breaking those down. I expect the balance will lean in our favor." He glanced at his phone and then at John. "Speaking of which, aren't we due to gather that order from the warehouse shortly?"

The doctor mumbled a curse and took a large gulp from his tea before leaving it on the table. "I lost track of the time." He nodded to the rest of us. "It shouldn't take more than an hour. This is the last of the equipment. Then we can lay out the full strategy and be ready to tackle them by tomorrow."

Neither Jemma nor Bash looked all that comforted by his comment. As they ducked out, Jemma started pacing again.

"We don't even know how well most of those techniques are going to work," she muttered. "I've never tried them before. We could *all* be walking into a total slaughter."

I hesitated for a second and then got up from the sofa. We were in this together now. She'd agreed to hold off on the self-sacrificing approach, trusting that we had a better chance working as a group. She'd come to me last night—she'd wanted that connection. And God, I'd wanted it too. Why the hell should I hold back on showing how I felt now?

I caught her in mid-pace, gently grasping her hands as I looked her in the eyes, knowing better than to assume a full embrace would comfort her.

"Hey," I said. "You've been doing everything you can. There might have been even more attacks today if we hadn't alerted the police as quickly as we were able to. We're going to kick these bastards right out of our world and throw away whatever key has been letting them come back in. They don't stand a chance against the five of us."

Her laugh came out rough. "There's a hell of a lot more than five of them. And they've been preparing for this moment for an awfully long time, from what I can tell. I had no idea—I never thought—"

She pulled away from me with a strangled noise and stalked to the other end of the room. Bash's gaze continued to follow her, but he didn't try to stop her. I guessed he could tell it wouldn't help.

"We've got the tools to completely fuck with their set-up now," he said instead. "You haven't used those strategies before? That's a good thing. It means they can't expect them. We'll shock the hell out of them. That gives us plenty of advantage."

"And how many more people are going to die before we get the chance to try?" Jemma said, glaring at the mirror over the desk. "There were three kids this morning—one of them was only five. If they launch another attack in the middle of the day instead of that early, there'll probably be even more."

Oh. I hadn't even considered that dimension to her distress. In every kid the shrouded folk or their minions hurt, she saw her sister.

"You're right," I said with a rush of conviction. "There has to be something more we can do to protect people." I was a goddamned cop—out of the bunch of us, I should be able to figure out how to get the local law enforcement on our side.

If only we could have come up with an angle like in Scotland, where we'd gotten the police to raid the place out of concern for their well-being rather than evidence of crimes. But that had required a set-up we couldn't pull off in the middle of a city without being caught.

The whole scenario had been different, though. We hadn't needed to worry about anyone's immediate safety outside of the commune. Here, the cultists had innocent people working right below them, maybe even living among them for all we knew.

An idea sparked in my head with a ripple of exhilaration. I sucked in a breath. "Jemma, it doesn't matter if the cult knows we're onto them, does it? Because you believe they already know that?"

She turned to study me. "I don't think we should show too much of our hand, but no, I don't think it'll be any surprise to them to know we've marked their location and that we're probably planning *something*."

"Then why don't we set the police on the people who *aren't* part of it?"

Bash gave me a puzzled look. "What are you talking about?"

I made a vague gesture in the air. "The Istanbul police can't take the actual criminals into custody because there's no proof they're criminals right now. Fine. So let's remove the commune's most immediate potential targets. If we present the police with a course of action that's about saving people's lives rather than arresting them, they're less likely to balk. All they need to do is make up an excuse to evacuate the building. Tell the tenants there's an issue with the electrical system or the plumbing or whatever makes the most sense. I doubt they'll go around banging on people's doors forcing people to leave, but—"

Jemma's eyes widened, but she was smiling. "Everyone who doesn't have a higher agenda wrapped up in the building won't need to be forced. They'll go because they're told. We'll get all the innocents out of the way before we go after the commune."

Her obvious approval brought a grin to my own lips. "And it'll also make it harder for the commune to arrange any further attacks. Once the tower is officially evacuated, the police monitoring it will have to assume *anyone* who leaves the building is part of the cult."

"What are you waiting for, then? Get them on it."

The commander wasn't exactly happy to hear from me again, but when I laid out the plan and emphasized the potential carnage avoided, he gradually warmed to it. "I'm not sure how long we can keep up the ruse," he warned me. "There are limits to how much we can deceive people even for their own safety."

"I understand," I told him. "We're hoping to have a more permanent solution very soon." One he wouldn't approve of, but he wouldn't need to know the details—or anything at all about it until after we were either through to the other side or dead.

By the time I'd hung up, tomorrow's looming mission had overshadowed most of my triumph at the gambit I'd come up with. Evacuating the building really was just a stop-gap measure. And Jemma was right: We didn't know how well any of our experimental techniques would work against the cult or their masters.

But maybe there was a way to find out.

I grabbed my laptop from where I'd left it on the side table and brought up my files from the task force. Police forces from all over the world had sent in data that matched the patterns I'd laid out to get outside confirmation that they had cultists in the area—and what exact area the commune was likely to be in. I'd gotten some from officers in this region before I'd even shown up here. Not for anything within the city, but...

There. My grin came back. I looked up and found Jemma watching me, warily but with obvious interest.

"You want to make sure we can crash the party in the tower tomorrow?" I said. "We can give all this equipment we've been gathering a trial run tonight. I'm pretty sure there's a commune just a few hours outside Istanbul."

Hope lit in Jemma's eyes. "All right. Let's get warmed up."

CHAPTER TWENTY

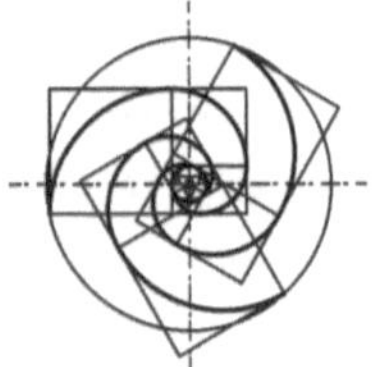

Jemma

Because there was only one shrouded folk-deflecting cuff and I was the one most used to wearing it, a lot of the heavy lifting for tonight's endeavor fell on me. Carting the sound system and the projectors around the spot where we'd identified a tiny mountainside commune would have been easier with a vehicle, but that would have caught someone's attention. So I carried the equipment a couple pieces at a time on foot through the dry forestland that covered the slope.

A crisp sap smell tickled my nose in the cooling night air. I scanned the forest around me and set the amplifier and its power source into a nook between two tree roots, the volume turned up as high as it would go. Hopefully that would be loud enough to blare all the way to the commune. I hadn't let myself go close enough to need to deal with whatever guards they had staked out around the place.

That was the last speaker in the ring around the commune. I straightened up with a roll of my shoulders, both to stretch the muscles and to try to release the tension that had gathered in them.

If this didn't work, if the strategies we'd come up with barely affected the shrouded folk and their worshippers, then we were back to square one when it came to tackling the creeps in the tower. It was better to find that out now rather than in a much tighter situation, but the thought still made my stomach knot.

I loped back to the truck we'd parked at the edge of the forested area. My men were waiting for me there, John and Garrett already stirring restlessly as they waited for my return, Bash keeping his usual cool composure. Sherlock was standing out beside the truck too, but he didn't have anything to be anticipating. While the four of us tackled the commune, he was hanging back here. Partly to activate the speakers on cue, but also partly because John had insisted.

"Even with your fighting experience, that arm is going to hold you back too much," he'd said on the drive over. "From the activity around the place, there can't be many people living there. The four of us should be able to handle them just fine." And when Sherlock had started to protest, he'd added, "I didn't kick up a fuss when you insisted that *I* stay back while you and Bash put yourselves into comas to go after Jemma."

Sherlock had grumbled a little, but he'd accepted his friend's judgment after that point.

Now, I gave them an all-clear gesture as I approached. We'd already discussed how we'd position ourselves for the raid, each of us carrying stun guns and tasers, but before they headed off my nerves compelled me to make a final reminder.

"We don't want to let *anyone* make it out of the commune. The guards go down first, then the sound and lights display kicks off once we're in the settlement and can keep track of the other inhabitants. If any of them slips away and warns the commune in the tower about what we're doing, we could be screwed even if this works."

The guys nodded and set off to form a loose circle around our target. I stayed at the truck with Sherlock, which was a welcome rest after all the trekking around of various equipment.

I hopped up on the hood with my radio ready for the guys to let me know they were in position. Sherlock leaned his good arm onto the truck next to me, studying the forest as if it might tell him ahead of time how this encounter would play out.

"I'm sorry," I said. "Technically it's my fault you have to sit out."

He glanced at his cast and gave a rueful shake of his head. "It's because of you I'm a part of this mission at all, so I'd have to say on the balance I still owe you."

"For getting you sucked into a case that's a hundred times more dangerous than anything you've faced in the past?"

Sherlock made an incredulous sound. "I don't evaluate the value of a case based on how little peril I personally risk. My life's work is finding the ones where my expertise and intellect is necessary to unraveling the mystery and where the greatest number of people stand to benefit from that unraveling. This scenario is both incredibly obtuse and exceptionally catastrophic. I'll consider it the pinnacle of my career if I contribute in any meaningful way to preventing that catastrophe."

"Let's certainly hope there aren't greater heights for you to reach in the future, then," I teased.

"I think perhaps I might enjoy a few more pedestrian cases in the aftermath, if only to cleanse my palate," the detective allowed.

I looked at him in the twilight, watching his expression carefully. The question had been niggling at me for a while, but this line of conversation brought it to the forefront. "When you joined in with the others to convince me we should tackle this situation together... Am I really going to hold all that much interest to you once we're finished with the shrouded folk? Or was *your* goal mainly about getting to play a part right now?"

Sherlock blinked at me with a bemusement that reassured me more than I'd realized I needed. "Why would you think that?"

"*I'm* not much of a mystery anymore, am I? You've unraveled me. What's left to be fascinated by?"

He let out a bark of a laugh. "I find it hard to believe you'll fail to find new ways of engaging my attention. Besides, John is hardly a mystery, and I haven't stopped appreciating his company." His eyebrows rose slightly. "Are you asking because you're finding yourself becoming bored with *me*?"

Every part of me protested at how ridiculous that idea was. In who else would I find a mind this precise and agile, that could keep me on my toes and meet every feint and parry I made with one of his own?

Which, of course, was obviously the same point he'd been making in relation to me.

I scooted back to lean against the windshield, mostly satisfied. But his question still deserved a thoughtful answer.

"No," I said. "But to the others, it's more of a romance. They've all expressed, in their own ways, a certain… depth of feeling that fits with a long-term commitment. You and I aren't people inclined to make our decisions based on emotion, are we?" I thought of Olivia. "Other than in rare circumstances. At least, I assume I won't be getting any declarations of love from you."

Would I want to? I wasn't entirely sure. It was so difficult to picture it happening that I had trouble judging how I'd feel about it, both bizarre and a little thrilling at the same time.

"Perhaps not," Sherlock said with a nod. "But what is 'love' other than a word that means different things to every speaker? It's hardly an objective stimulus that one can identify with certainty. I'd propose that it means much more that I can say I look forward to every conversation we have, that I find myself constantly stimulated—in one way or another—in your presence, and that I've come to understand you well enough that I can easily accept even an apparently horrifying transgression."

It was such a perfect response, and perfectly Sherlockian, that an unexpected flutter passed through my chest. Right then, if only for a few seconds, maybe there was enough room in me that I could have said I loved him. Those seconds were fleeting, though. Instead, I said, "I believe it does. And in case there was any doubt, all those sentiments are returned."

"I don't recall ever making any horrifying transgressions on you," he said dryly, but the glint that came into his eyes was pleased.

"You interrupted my quest to rescue my sister very clearly against my desires," I pointed out. "And without really having any idea how much trouble you could be causing for me."

"A gamble I made with much the same confidence in my abilities to mitigate that damage as you had when you pushed me down that cliff." Sherlock smiled at me. "So yes, I suppose there is an equivalency there."

My earpiece crackled, and Garrett's voice traveled through. "I'm in position now."

I straightened up on the hood, checking my weapons. It was only a few more minutes before John spoke up too. "I've arrived."

Bash had the farthest to go, taking the spot at the complete opposite end of this area, but he was also the fastest of the guys. I'd only just finished making a final examination of the broadcasting equipment in the truck when he called in too. "Ready to go."

I tugged my light jacket down to my hips. "All right. Let's move. Call in again when you're sure you've disabled any guards in your range."

"I'll be waiting for your signal," Sherlock said. He hopped into the back of the truck.

I kept my breaths slow and even as I set off into the woods again. Based on the data Garrett's associates had uncovered, I doubted this commune held more than twenty people total. They wouldn't have more than a few on guard. They might even be more complacent right now, thinking our attention was focused on the urban incidents.

About five minutes past the ring of speakers I'd set out, I spotted my first guard. I slowed, setting my feet carefully, and flexed my fingers at my sides.

I expected John and Garrett would stick to stunning any they came across. I had no qualms about snapping their necks. The shrouded folk might have commanded their followers, but the people had minds of their own, and with those minds they'd decided to torment each other and any kids born into the place. People from this spot might even have traveled to Istanbul to help with the shootings there.

The guy ahead of me held a revolver at his side. I slipped around him and slunk up behind him, my body tensed for the maneuver. He started to shift his weight—and I grasped his head with a sharp twist of my arms.

His spine cracked. I guided his limp body down to the ground so it wouldn't make too loud a thump.

"One down at the south end," I murmured into my mic.

"I just took down one here in the north," Bash said.

There was silence from the other two for a short time as I crept closer to the actual commune. Then Garrett said, in a tight voice that didn't hide his discomfort, "One down here in the east. I haven't seen anyone else around."

"I haven't come across any guards at all," John said. "I can see a building now through the trees. Maybe there were only the three."

"Let's be sure." I started to veer to the side. "Bash, head west, and we can check the edges of his section."

I didn't come across any other guards in my prowl, and neither did my hitman. "Pretty small outfit," he remarked.

"As we expected," I said. "All right. Up to the edge."

We eased through the forest toward the area where scattered trees had been cut down to make room for the commune's buildings. It wasn't exactly a clearing, because they'd left some vegetation for cover, but once out there, we'd be able to see anyone who tried to flee. I stopped a few paces from the nearest building, the silence thick around me, and whispered, "Here."

One after the other, the men reported in. I braced myself, popping out my earpiece to replace it with plugs as the others should be doing and slipping my fingers around my taser. Then I said, "Sherlock, let them have it."

The soundtrack we'd put together blared from the planted speakers so loud that I flinched even though I'd expected it. Drums pounded out a beat composed of multiple patterns; voices pontificated in iambic pentameter; a rhythmic stomping overshadowed it all. The noise blended together into a weird sort of harmony that any shrouded one should be repulsed by—and any human being without any ear protection should be disoriented by. Overhead, projected lights formed a gigantic Fibonacci sequence against the sky.

As cultists started bursting from their huts, I lunged into the commune. I zapped a woman with a rifle first. As she fell, I grabbed the gun and spun to slam the butt into the head of a man who'd charged at me.

Shouts penetrated the onslaught of sound faintly. I stunned another man who stumbled out of his hut bleary-eyed and dashed deeper into the settlement.

The noise was definitely affecting the cultists. A woman in front of me swayed as she swiveled on her feet, her face scrunched with discomfort. She barely seemed to see me before I knocked her down. If any fiends had been lurking around their worshippers, they'd been driven away—I didn't catch so much of a whiff of their putrid scent.

I sprinted around another hut and found Bash and Garrett shocking two cultists who'd emerged from neighboring buildings. Then whatever teamwork that effort had involved fell apart.

Bash motioned for Garrett to drag the cultists into one of the huts. Garrett frowned and shook his head with a wave toward the other buildings.

He was right—the plan had been that we'd make sure we'd caught all the cultists before we worried about confining them. But Bash stepped toward the detective inspector with a menacing look that made my jaw grit. I hurried over to snap him out of whatever macho mindset he'd gotten into, and the crack of a gunshot split through the blaring rhythms.

The bullet slammed into Bash's shoulder, making his whole torso jerk. My lips parted with a cry, but his military-trained instincts took over in a snap. He threw himself back against the closest building, his head leaping to his real gun in the same motion. His sniper-trained eyes narrowed. Ignoring the blood streaking over his shirt, he fired at someone I couldn't see from where I stood. I knew he'd landed the shot from his grim but satisfied expression as he lowered the gun.

Garrett hesitated and then hurried off to check the rest of the commune. I caught Bash's eye, and he indicated I should keep on with the plan with a brisk gesture before pressing his hand to his shoulder. My gut clenched, but I jogged on to check for stragglers.

It wasn't a life-threatening wound. He'd be all right. But all the relief I'd felt in seeing our gambits succeed had drained away.

He'd gotten distracted with his posturing, his momentary refusal to let one of the other men stick to our plan. The bullet *could* have blasted through a lung or his heart.

How the hell could I be sure we'd make it through an invasion of the tower tomorrow if the five of us still couldn't totally trust each other?

Bash

My goddamn shoulder still ached. I sank a little deeper into the chair at my hotel room desk and grimaced.

Even when I wasn't moving, a dull pain throbbed right below my shoulder cap where the bullet had passed through. I'd taken a Tylenol 3 I'd had on hand, but I didn't want to risk getting too dopey before our mission-to-end-all-missions tomorrow.

No, I'd already fucked things up enough without that. As much as I disliked the pain, the worst part of the injury was the reminder of how close the shot had come to striking something I couldn't just bandage up and grit my teeth through. And it'd been my own carelessness that'd done it. Caught up in the moment, wanting to take charge and make sure the job was done right *my* way… and failing to notice the enemy just fifteen feet behind me.

Jemma hadn't said anything about it to me while we'd shut the cultists up in one of their huts or during the drive back. She'd made sure the wound was cleaned and well-bandaged and then leaned against the window to doze through the deepening night. But even when she'd been half asleep, the worry lines had remained on her forehead and at the corners of her mouth.

So much depended on what we did tomorrow. Whether we could pull it off. Whether we could work *together*, as a unit, not some hotshot maverick who thought he was better than teamwork.

I hadn't worked with a full team since my army days, ages ago, and I hadn't really liked it even then. No, being out on my own with my sniper rifle in hand and target in mind had been vastly preferable. But I should damn well be able to cooperate when I had to. I wasn't that nineteen-year-old jackass anymore.

I was better than that. Jemma had believed it. But maybe it was more important that I convinced myself to believe it too.

After tomorrow, I might not be around to be anything at all. Going up against that piddly commune had been nothing compared to launching an assault on the monsters' tower. Before that could happen… there were a couple other people in my life I might owe something to.

I opened up my compact laptop, barely more than a tablet with a keyboard. That was how I liked my computers: small and straightforward. The street beyond my window was pitch-black, the time well past midnight, but that was perfect for a call back to the US. They'd just be getting home from work.

I checked my shirt to make sure the bandage on my shoulder was covered, and then I typed the number I'd gotten via one of our hacker cohorts into my phone. Texting my little sister.

Hey, Charlotte. It's Bash. I'm sorry for the long silence. Can we talk—maybe a videochat over the computer? I'd like to be able to see your face.

I hadn't seen her in motion since I'd left her and Sam at our grandparents' house all those years ago. Still photographs didn't quite cut it. She might still say no, though. She might think it was some kind of prank.

Tapping my fingers against the side of the phone, I waited. And waited. Impatience started to prickle up my spine. Then, finally, an answering message popped up.

Bash? Are you kidding me? Of course. I just walked in the door —give me a second to get everything set up.

I thought I could read enthusiasm in that response, but it was hard to tell with plain text. My heart thumped heavily as I typed in my account info so she could try to connect. And then I waited again.

It only took a couple minutes this time. The app sounded an alert for the incoming call. A flash of panic washed over me—did I look presentable? What if I said the wrong thing? —but I forced myself to hit the button to accept the call.

And there was my sister staring back at me, her face narrower without its former childhood softness, her eyes not quite as wide but still framed by long lashes, her expression slack with shock. She must be making a similar assessment of me.

I hadn't seen her since she was seven. She hadn't seen me since I was thirteen. I'd grown up a lot since then too.

Not so much that she had any doubts, clearly. "It's really you," she said in a halting voice. She leaned closer to the screen as if she could reach right through it to this room. "Oh my God. Where have you been? Sam and I were worried you were *dead*, that Dad—or some other way— It's been *seventeen* years."

My throat constricted. "I know," I made myself say. My fingers itched to cut off the connection, to slam down the laptop as if that would sever the guilt and the fear too, but I clenched my hand and held it in place. "I'm sorry. At first I just thought it'd be easier for you, staying with Gram and Gramps, if you weren't thinking or worrying about me, and then I got caught up in a bunch of stuff, and… I let it go too long. I didn't want to let it go any longer."

"Well, I'm really, really glad that you're okay." A shimmer came into her eyes that looked like a hint of withheld tears. "And really glad that you tracked me down. How pissed off was Dad after he found out you'd taken us away?"

I didn't often think back to those last few years with my parents before I'd conned my way into the army underage. The truth was Dad had raged about it for a few days and then fallen into his usual routines as if it'd always been just Mom and me around to act as punching bags, verbally or physically. I didn't think it'd help

Charlotte any hearing the details. That wasn't what I wanted this conversation to be about anyway.

"He was… Dad," I said. "But I survived, and I got out of there myself pretty soon after, and Mom got away too eventually. Has she been in touch at all?"

"A couple times. I think she was embarrassed that it went on so long, that you were the one who got us out instead of her." She swiped her hand over her mouth and then peered at me more avidly. "Tell me what you've been doing all this time—whatever you can tell me. I want to hear everything."

I wasn't going to tell her *everything*, of course, or even half the things I'd gotten into, but I managed to put an acceptable spin on most of my activities over the last decade and a half. When Charlotte looked satisfied, I prodded her to tell me the things I already knew about her life in her words, plus a few things internet searches hadn't been able to reveal.

The conversation had an awkwardness to it, pauses where one or the other of us grappled with what we'd say, hesitations when we weren't sure how to take a comment, but I couldn't have expected it to go perfectly smoothly. Talking to her still felt *good*, in a way I hadn't even imagined.

I'd done okay by her. Look at this woman she'd grown up to be.

"Are you going to talk to Sam?" she asked before we ended the call.

I nodded. "I figured I owe him too. Maybe… Maybe if I'm back in your area sometime, we could grab a coffee or something."

She smiled. "Yeah. I'd like that."

The call with Sam went a little more awkwardly with a little more frustration on his part over the long silence, but he didn't vent much anger, just pent-up worries. After we signed off, I climbed onto my bed and lay down on top of the covers, letting my mind process everything I'd just experienced.

My siblings didn't hate me. They didn't look at me and automatically see a criminal. I was still their big brother, somehow or other.

The thought both reassured me and gnawed at me. I'd stepped back into their lives, and I might vanish all over again tomorrow.

Well, I simply couldn't let that happen then, now could I?

The pain in my shoulder had faded a little more, but I couldn't have said I was anywhere near drifting off when a knock sounded on my door. I sat up in an instant.

"Yeah?"

Jemma's voice traveled through. "It's me."

I got up and let her in, that more recent, sharper guilt jabbing through me all over again. She looked tired, her red waves swept back into a braid which left her eyes looking even larger in her pale face, but she walked over to perch on my bed with a typically determined air.

"We can't let what happened tonight happen again tomorrow," she said without preamble.

Had that worry been keeping her up? I swallowed hard. "I agree. I got distracted in the moment—I should have kept better control over myself."

She looked up at me with the same frank, assured gaze she'd had since the moment I first met her years ago, when she was still a teenager. "I need you in there with me. You're the one with the most combat experience. That isn't negotiable. So whoever we need to ask to stay out of the mission so you're not thinking about their performance instead of yours, you have to tell me. We'll figure it out."

I could just imagine how Garrett—or John—or even Sherlock would feel about that. The guilt dug in even deeper. "I know to watch for it now," I said. "I won't react the same way. We're going to need all hands on deck, won't we?"

"Better fewer hands who are all fully focused."

This was my fault. That understanding sank in and settled like a stone on my gut. *I'd* created a fissure where we'd been building a force to be reckoned with.

That wasn't what I wanted to be for her. I wanted to be the solid foundation she could stand on, the one who held her... and everyone she needed with her... together.

The impulse hit me, sudden and potent enough that I didn't second-guess it. I motioned to the bed. "Relax a few minutes and wait for me. I'll be back. All right?"

Jemma gave me a curious look, but she scooted farther onto the bed so she could sink back against the pillows. "What are you up to all of a sudden, Bash?"

"You'll just have to wait and see, Majesty," I said with all the good humor I could summon through my dampened mood. Then I stepped out into the hall.

My little brother and sister weren't the only family I had left, or the only family I needed to connect with. Jemma was my family more than anyone else in the world now. And it was time I admitted that whatever strange family the two of us had formed had grown in the past few months. It was time I showed her that I could handle that, in every possible way.

I rapped on Garrett's door first. He opened it looking rather tired himself but still in his clothes, so obviously he hadn't been having the easiest time getting to bed. Despite the way I'd hassled him in the commune, when I said, "Come on. There's something we need to do," he trusted me enough to follow. Which maybe was all I had to know.

When John opened the suite's door, I could see Sherlock standing by the table, where two glasses of what I'd bet was sherry sat. They'd stayed up hashing over tomorrow's plans, no doubt.

"What's this about?" Sherlock asked when I repeated the request.

"Jemma," I said, and that was enough to shift him the two doors down the hall to my room.

Jemma sat up from her lounging pose when we came in, her gaze sliding over all of us with an expression both puzzled and intrigued. "You thought we should have a group meeting?" she said. "There's more room for that in the suite."

"No," I said. "I think we all need to be one hundred percent clear on how committed we are to collaborating. On how committed we are to *you*. I'm not out to have you all to myself, Mori." My mouth went slightly dry. "Not when I knew everyone in this room brings something into your life. Makes you happy. If you're up for it, I want to see how just how satisfied you can be when you've got all of us at your disposal." I glanced around at the other men. "Unless any of you has an objection."

Garrett swallowed audibly, but a spark of excitement had already lit in his eyes. "None here."

A flush crept over John's cheeks. "Well, I... I guess it would be good to find out how well we can, er, work together."

As usual, I found Sherlock difficult to read, but it was clear from his answer that he wasn't against the idea anyway. "An interesting proposition," he said. "It has seemed that two can provoke more pleasure than one, so *four...*"

Jemma wet her lips. She shot me a quick but brilliant smile that melted most of the guilt still lodged inside me. "I think I'm ready to find out."

She stayed where she was, waiting for us to come to her—understandably, since she was already on the bed. I didn't want to step in right away in case it looked as if I were staking some kind of claim despite everything I'd said.

To my surprise, John moved first. He leaned his walking stick against the bedside table and climbed onto the bed next to Jemma. She tipped her head, and he took the invitation to kiss her.

That kiss jolted everyone else to action. Garrett came around the other side of the bed to sit at Jemma's other side, slipping a hand around her waist and kissing her shoulder. Sherlock settled himself near the end of the bed and eased one of Jemma's socks off before beginning to massage her foot.

I hung back for a moment, deciding where I best fit in. Jemma was beaming with an exhilarated flush as she turned her head from John to Garrett, and part of me would have liked to stay there and simply watch her immerse herself in the other men's attentions. But I was part of this bizarre family too, and that meant taking my place alongside them.

Jemma had pushed herself away from the pillows. I tossed a couple of them aside to make more room and dropped down behind her, running my hand up her back. She leaned into my touch as she kissed Garrett and stroked her fingers down John's chest, and even though I'd thought going through with this might be hard, instead I felt nothing but how right this was. For her to be admired and cherished—and, yeah, *loved*—in every possible way.

She'd spent so long having to shut everyone around her out to protect herself, and now she was letting four of us in. And I had the honor of being one of those four. That was pretty fucking amazing.

I teased my hands down her sides and grasped the hem of her sleeveless blouse to lift it off her. The other men shifted as I tugged it over her head. Then I was sliding my hands around to the bare skin of her belly, and John was claiming her mouth again, and Garrett was snapping her bra loose before lowering his mouth to her breast. Jemma hummed encouragingly, so low it was almost a purr.

Sherlock had just finished tending to her other foot. He fondled her legs from calves to knees, slowly working his way upward. When he reached her upper thigh, she made an impatient sound with a buck of her hips. He chuckled and reached to undo her pants.

Jemma sat up on her knees to shed her slacks and her panties. She glanced around at us with an imperious look. "If I'm calling the shots here, I'd like to see a lot less clothes on all of you."

We all took a moment to shed shirts and pants. I scooted to the side so I could claim Jemma's mouth for myself, and she kissed me back hard, her fingers gliding up over my scalp in the most delicious caress.

Garrett cupped her between her legs until she was swaying and moaning at his touch. Then he bent down on the bed to bring his mouth to her clit. As I lowered my head to provoke her breasts with the heat of my mouth and swipes of my tongue, Sherlock leaned in for a kiss, and John ran his hands over her ass.

"Condom?" he said in a ragged voice.

"In the drawer," Jemma said with a vague motion and a gasp as Garrett tilted his head. "Be quick about it."

John chuckled and did as he was told. Her breath hitched as he slid into her from behind. Between him inside her, Garrett's oral attentions, and Sherlock and I trailing our hands over every other inch of her, she was already trembling in that way I knew meant she was close to coming. And God, what a spectacular coming I expected it'd be.

Jemma gripped my arm, her hips rocking between her one lover's thrusts and the other's lips. Sherlock nipped her shoulder and rolled her nipple with his thumb, and she yanked his mouth back to hers. Then she was urging him upright with one hand while the other traced a tantalizing path down my chest to the bulge tenting my boxers.

I could feel her muscles quivering with the building bliss, but she held on to bring us with her. As she freed Sherlock's rigid cock and sucked it into her mouth, she dipped her hand inside my boxers to grasp my erection. I mumbled a curse and kissed a path along her shoulder.

For all the sensations that must have been rushing through her, her grip stayed steady. She pumped me firmly but tenderly, swiveling the heel of her hand over the tip in a way that made me groan.

It didn't take long before my balls tightened. I stroked her breasts and her back, willing every ounce of pleasure I could into her body to offer back what she was doing to me. Her fingers pressed against the underside of my cock, and I came with a choked sound and a giddy rush that shot right through the top of my head.

Somewhere during my hazy afterglow, Sherlock's breath caught with the shudder of his own release. Jemma's head tipped back toward John, he sped up his pace, and her body shook with the force of her orgasm racing through her. I got half hard again just seeing it. John bowed his head next to hers from behind as he must have reached his own peak.

As Jemma's body started to slump with satisfaction between us, she looked to Garrett, who'd raised his head with a pleased grin. "I'm good, Firecracker," he told her. "This was about you, not us."

That was true, but it had been about the four of us at the same time. About sprawling around her without feeling in any particular hurry to go anywhere else. About not getting uptight if my arm brushed Sherlock's shoulder or Garrett's knee bumped my ankle. About seeing how spectacular this interlude had been, *because* we were all here.

The other three men hadn't just contributed to Jemma's happiness. If I was being honest, they'd each given a new dimension to my life too. When I set anything like jealousy aside, I had to admit I appreciated Sherlock's smarts, John's generosity, and Garrett's stubbornness.

If we were her family, then we were each other's too.

"We'll all be there tomorrow," I said to Jemma, stroking her hair. "You can count on all of us."

This time, she didn't argue with me, only snuggled deeper into the nest between us as if we'd always been so united.

CHAPTER TWENTY-TWO

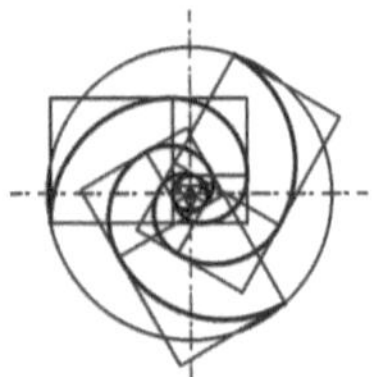

Jemma

One benefit of having the tower's offices evacuated was we didn't have much competition for the use of the elevators. I popped the maintenance hatch in the ceiling of one car and scrambled up onto its roof without needing to worry about onlookers.

Bash and Garrett clambered after me. John gave us a playful salute that contrasted with his tense expression before he helped click the hatch back in place. We'd decided that since we'd probably need people on the ground running interference with the regular citizens and possibly the police once our lights and sounds display kicked into gear, it made sense for the two members of our group who'd have the most trouble climbing a couple dozen stories to take that role.

We still might not have much time once the show started. The three of us were all carrying custom decals and portable speakers in our backpacks, but most of our equipment we'd had to put in place using the surrounding buildings and other city structures. The general population probably wouldn't be too happy once we started blasting our bizarre soundtrack.

I adjusted the pack's straps on my shoulders over the padding of my bulletproof vest, exchanged a nod with the other two to confirm we were ready, and gripped the cool metal rungs to start my upward climb. This part, the pure physical exertion with the uncertainty of what exactly we'd find on the other side of the elevator doors above, was my least favorite part of the plan. The sooner we could get to kicking cultist ass, the happier I'd be.

My muscles remembered the tempo I'd found when I'd climbed higher in the shaft before. This trip from the ground floor might be twice as far, but I could handle that. I kept a steady pace, centering my weight on my legs as much as I could, taking deep breaths of the cool still air.

The maintenance lights formed an eerie glow around us. The only sound right now was the murmur of our breaths and the rasp of our shoes against the rungs.

We were starting our assault at the very top, because I was almost certain that was where the shrouded folk were holding Olivia, but that didn't mean we could forget about the floors below. The second this urban commune realized they were under attack, we'd face a counter-attack from every person on hand. I was going to plow through anyone who got in my way until I found my sister and the bridge the fiends were building through her. Bash and Garrett would cover me.

Garrett had balked a little at the rifle Bash had handed him when we'd been suiting up, but he had a stun gun too. "Don't pretend you can get away with just knocking them out if the fighting gets too fraught," I'd said to him. "You want me to get through this alive? I want you to survive it too. If you feel any guilt, just remember the kids you've seen at the other communes, the photos and all that. The people here have done as much or worse. They want to give the monsters free access to our world to turn it into their bloody playground."

The reminder had brought the resolve back into his expression. I didn't think he'd hesitate when the bastards came at him.

I'm coming, I thought to my sister now, even though I didn't know if she could sense anything inside my head while I was awake. *I'm finally coming back for you the way I promised.*

As we reached the highest floors, a hint of the shrouded folk scent, dry and sour, tickled my nose. My shoulders stiffened. I climbed faster. It could be just a lingering odor from their periodic visits to the commune, or —

The smell thickened at the same moment as a vibration echoed through the wall. My head jerked down in time to see Bash swing to the side, only keeping his hold on the maintenance ladder by one hand. My pulse stuttered, and I slammed my hand on the device dangling from my belt.

It sent a signal directly to Sherlock and John outside. A second later, the cacophony of sound we'd inflicted on the forest commune yesterday boomed through the walls. Thank God for the ear plugs we'd carefully equipped ourselves with ahead of time. My eardrums ached even with that layer of protection.

Bash regained his balance with no sign of another blow. The rhythmic noises and the patterns that'd now be projected on the outside of the building must have done the trick to repel the shrouded folk. We'd lost any of the surprise element in our attack, though. I hauled myself up the last distance to the elevator's top entrance as quickly as I could, my muscles straining, and smacked a small explosive against the seam in the middle of the doors before ducking out of range.

The explosive went off with a crash to rival the racket from outside. The force wrenched the doors apart with a gush of smoke to momentarily disguise our arrival, although the cultists would figure it out soon enough. I leapt up the rungs and sprang through the opening, the guys right behind me.

Gunfire crackled through the smoke. I dropped to the floor and swung out my leg to topple a figure that staggered toward us. With a sharp kick, I cracked his neck. Spinning around, I wrenched one of the portable speakers from my pack, shoved it against the wall, and hit the power button. The sounds from outside flooded the hazy room even louder than before.

Garrett had just zapped a woman who'd lunged at us with a carving knife, and Bash fired his pistol at someone farther into the room. I clapped a few decals onto the walls and threw myself back onto my feet.

The smoke was clearing. I took down a couple other armed figures with my own pistol as I scanned the room. It was wide open if dimly lit from the shuttered windows, the vacant area stretching across the entire top floor—other than a room built in the center of the space.

My fingers tightened around the gun. I ran for that room, trusting the guys to have my back.

I didn't see any sign of the shrouded folk themselves intervening again, and the noise was obviously affecting the cultists here just like it had at the other commune last night. One guy with a rifle stumbled as he tried to swing it toward me and then collapsed with one of Bash's bullets in his skull. A woman burst from the stairwell across the room and promptly tripped over her own feet and sprawled on her hands and knees. A couple of older teens hunched in one corner, their hands clamped over their ears.

That didn't give me completely smooth passage, though. As I raced toward my goal, a figure charged toward me. I dodged to the side in time for one of my men to get in a shot—and plowed straight into a woman who'd flung herself around the side of the central room.

She was holding a pistol, and she'd have needed to be essentially dead to miss at that range. Her first shot fired right against my side, jolting me enough through the bulletproof vest that I lost the grip I'd tried to get on her arm. I managed to smack at her hand just as she pulled the trigger again, but I wasn't quite fast enough. The bullet tore through the flesh of my inner thigh. Pain seared along the its path.

I bit my tongue against a cry and shoved the woman to the side before she could make another attempt. My gun hand whipped up at the same time. I shot her between the eyes.

I limped on toward the room as fast as my legs would carry me, searching for the entrance. My thigh kept burning and the fabric below the wound dampened with a steady flow of blood. She might have nicked an artery. I didn't have time to stop to bandage it. That could wait until I got Olivia the hell out of here.

More shots rang out behind me, mingling with shouts and the blare of our recordings. I tuned it all out when my gaze caught on the outline of a door in the room's far wall.

A heavy padlock held it shut. I had to fire two shots at it to break through. My jaw clenching against the agony spreading through my leg and pelvis, I pushed it open and shuffled inside.

The door swung shut automatically, and the sounds from outside fell away. The sickening stench of the shrouded folk flooded my lungs, so thick I had to stop myself from gagging. A ruddy glow filled my vision. As I leaned on my good leg, I popped out one of my earplugs. Even then, all I could make out was a warble, but I should be able to hear if anyone tried to come after me.

I blinked in the crimson light, trying to clear my eyes. My gaze stalled on the form in the center of that room, the air in my lungs congealing with horror.

The glow was coming from that... thing. A thing that was a column made of lumps of skin and tattered cloth, melted like tree roots into the floor and stretching up to touch the room's low ceiling. The red light rippled through it in an erratic pulse that set my nerves on edge even as my stomach turned. Glowing streaks arced across the ceiling—five of them, like the ring of five keystones in the shrouded realm.

The form shifted, and I made out two pale eyes in the middle of the mass.

I couldn't hold it back then—my gut heaved, and I vomited the small lunch I'd forced down. The liquid mess splattered the floor with a sharper throbbing through my thigh and the sting of stomach acid in my throat.

"Jemma?" the thing said in a quavering rasp.

It was my sister. Or at least, my sister was part of it. When I forced myself to look at it again, I made out the outline of her face, the knob of a chin, the streaks of flaxen hair merging with the column of flesh. Were those her arms, lifted over her head and stretched toward the ceiling, melded together and expanded to encompass that glow from within? Was that a knee partway down the tattered trunk?

The glow flowed through her with its dissonant flickering, even flashing behind those pleading eyes.

"Olivia," I said, barely managing more than a croak. "What did they do to you?"

"I'm the bridge," she said. Her voice wavered with the glow. "I'm here and not. I'm human and them. I bind the worlds together. It's —" A breath rattled out of her. "It's almost complete."

The door behind me started to open. My heart lurched, and I flung myself back against it. It slammed shut, blood pattering onto the floor from where it had saturated my pants. Each thump of my pulse came with a stabbing like shards of glass.

Someone pounded on the door from the other side. I braced my feet against the floor as solidly as I could and clutched my pistol in case I had to shoot whoever was trying to enter.

"How do I get you out?" I said, ignoring the wave of nausea when I looked at my sister again. "I don't want to hurt you." She was so tangled up in whatever the hell the shrouded folk had turned her into, so fused with the room, I couldn't even see where the monstrosity ended and she began. I pictured trying to carve her out and blood gushing forth in a torrent.

"Jemma." Olivia sounded a little choked now. "You can't. I'm here. I'm this. You have to end it. You have to end *me*. That's the only way I can escape."

The horror before was nothing compared to the revulsion that swelled inside me now. "No. I came here to *save* you. I promised I'd come back for you, get you away from them. There has to be a way."

The door shuddered behind me. My feet slid an inch in the pool of blood creeping across the floor.

"This is how you save me," Olivia said. "You have to let me go. Please. I don't want to be what they've made me into. I want to be done."

She'd said something like that before, but I hadn't realized just how final the statement had been. Every bone in my body balked. "I can't. We'll figure it out. We'll kill all the bastards out there and then we can talk it through—"

"There's nothing to figure out. I know. Please, Jemma."

Her voice broke in a way that brought tears to my eyes. The door lurched behind me again. My feet skidded with a hitch of my pulse before I managed to shove it shut again. My head was starting to spin with the pain and the loss of blood. I opened my mouth to form another protest, and Olivia's eyes caught mine through the ruddy gaze.

"You promised me you wouldn't let them *use* me," she said. "Stop them. Free me. Please."

Any hope I'd been holding onto plummeted like a stone tossed into a well. All I was left with was resignation and the memory of a promise given more than ten years ago that I'd been fighting all that time to keep, a promise I'd renewed just two days ago.

Yes, I had promised her that. I hadn't wanted to fulfill that promise like this, but— *Fuck.*

Maybe I had to let go, but I couldn't just yet. "Do you remember the good times?" I found myself saying. "When we'd get away from the others and go wandering? Searching for snakes in the shadows of the rocks. Picking flowers to chain into crowns." Petals stark white against her bright hair. I'd told her she looked like a princess.

Something glimmered in Olivia's eyes. "Of course I do," she said. "That's where I've gone every moment I could since you left. You were always here with me. You always will be. That's where I'm going to go when I leave this place—into the good times."

I didn't know if that was even possible, as nice a thought as it was. And I *hadn't* been with her, not when it had really mattered, not in the way that counted. My throat tightened. "I should have gotten here sooner. I should have gotten *there* sooner. I'm sorry, Olivia. I'm so, so sorry."

The planes of my sister's face shifted, and just for a second I saw the bright smile that had always warmed me in our childhood. I saw her, the way she was meant to be.

"I'm not sorry," she said. "This is the best I could have asked for

—to die ruining their plans, with my sister guiding me along the way."

A sob sputtered out of me. "I love you," I said.

Someone bashed against the door behind me, sending me stumbling forward, but I was already raising my gun. I brought it to rest against what should have been Olivia's forehead as gently as I could, and closed my eyes with a gasp as I pulled the trigger.

The crimson light flared and snuffed out, both within Olivia's "bridge" and in the glowing lines that had stretched out into the world. In the sudden darkness, the figures who'd rammed open the door swayed uncertainly. I spun around, swaying a little myself, and put bullets in two of them just before Garrett barged into view, toppling the third with his stun gun.

I ran my fingers down my sister's form, whatever of her remained in that monstrous mess. The flesh was already chilling. She might have been dead for a long time, only the shrouded folk's energy keeping her alive. Tears dripped down my face to mingle with the blood on the floor.

I'd saved her. I'd kept my promise. I'd foiled the shrouded folk's most horrible plan. But I couldn't imagine this moment every feeling like a victory.

Could they still use her—revive her, restore her torment? My chest hitched. I couldn't take that chance.

Garrett's gaze slid past me to the mass behind me. He couldn't have made out much in the darkness, but his mouth twisted anyway.

"Is she—" he started, and didn't seem to know how to continue.

"It's over," I said. "I just need to—"

I fumbled in my pack for the flammable explosives I'd brought with me. To cover the evidence, if we needed to. Or to make sure the shrouded folk's toxic presence was burned clean from this place.

I pulled the pin from one and dropped it at the base of Olivia's mutated form. As I lurched backward, my whole body made of pain now, flames burst up, crackling over her and then across the floor in an instant.

Garrett's eyes widened at the sight of my wound. "Fucking hell, Jemma," he said, grabbing my arm. As he helped me out of the room, one last gunshot rang out, and Bash loped into view. Seeing me, the bloody mess of my clothes, and the fire raging hotter behind me with every second, his expression tensed.

"We've got to get out of here," he said, hurrying over.

"I can walk," I tried to say, but my mouth didn't move on command. My thoughts swam in my head. The last thing I was aware of was holding on to two of my lovers as they carried me from the crackling heat of my most recent act of destruction.

CHAPTER TWENTY-THREE

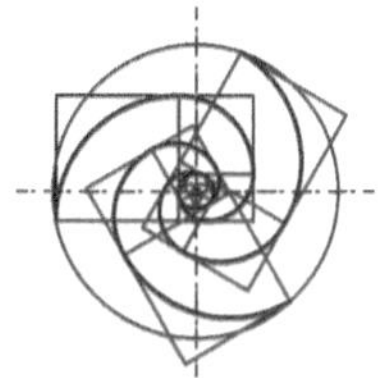

Jemma

It felt like a very long time since I'd set foot in Sherlock and John's Baker Street apartment. Years. Perhaps decades. Although in truth it'd only been a matter of weeks.

As always, the place smelled like the smoke from Sherlock's pipe, which he was enjoying right now in the armchair across from me. John had set out a box of donuts on the table, with a meaningful glance at me that said they were for my benefit, although Garrett had taken one as well.

I leaned forward carefully in my chair to grab a cinnamon sugar one. The bullet wound on my thigh was all patched up now, but still a little raw. I'd discovered a couple days ago that if I moved too quickly, that area would start to throb all over again.

Bash, who'd barely left my side since we'd left the tower in Istanbul, let his elbow rest on the arm of the sofa with his hand against my chair, as if to indicate he was right there should I need him. It wasn't as if my injury had been *that* horrible. If I hadn't spent so much time bleeding before doing anything about it, I'd have been perfectly fine.

"Just in the few days since I've been back, the task force has taken down more than two dozen of the communes," Garrett said, apparently deciding it was on him to start the discussion. "The reactions my colleagues abroad have reported sound... promising."

"There haven't been any more bombings or shootings related to the cult," Sherlock observed. "Is there more to it than that?"

"Yes, actually." Garret gave a puzzled frown. "Some of the reports have mentioned the cultists seeming confused or out of sorts, or even mournful. One that came in this morning mentioned some of them complaining that a 'they' had abandoned them and wondering where 'they' had gone."

"The shrouded folk?" John suggested.

"That would be my best guess. I get the impression the creatures haven't been in any sort of contact with their worshippers."

A sense of satisfaction trickled through me. It was tinged with grief and regret, but at least I knew that in saving Olivia in that horrible way, I'd saved a whole lot of other people in a much more literal sense.

"That matches what I saw in the shrouded realm," I said.

Garrett stiffened. "You traveled through again?" He shot Bash a disapproving look.

My hitman raised his hands. "I follow the orders; I don't give them. I'd like to see you argue her out of an idea when she's set on it."

"I'm none the worse for it," I broke in, glowering at both of them. "I only passed over for a few hours this time. But it was enough to confirm—the energy the shrouded folk have been consuming and, it seems, building their 'bridge' out of has almost completely faded. The stones only had a tiny flicker, and the 'spokes' of their wheel were completely gone."

Sherlock leaned forward in his chair. "Can we conclude that this is the result of your actions in Istanbul?"

"I think so." The memory of my Olivia's distorted body, of the shot I'd had to fire and the flames I'd left her to, made my lungs clench up for a moment before I could speak again. "I think the energy in the stones was fueled at least in part by the worship here that allowed the fiends to cross over. And they must have been channeling a lot of it into my sister to try to form that permanent gateway. When she died, that energy dissipated into this world—it was lost to them. She was connected to both realms. Who knows how much slipped away without them being able to stop it?"

"Then they're shut out from this world," John said. "They can't hurt anyone or incite anyone to cause harm again."

"Maybe. For the time being." I nodded to Garrett. "Your task force's efficiency is a great help. Without the communes, they'll have no way to build up that energy again. I hope."

"We can't know for sure," he said.

"No. They crossed over to our world on their own some time back in history. And we may not get to all the communes in time. We can't assume it's over. We should all keep watch... for the rest of our lives, really, for any sign that menace has returned."

"Naturally," Sherlock said without hesitation. The others murmured their agreement. I hadn't really thought that proposition would be the difficult part of the conversation.

"There hasn't been any fallout for your careers after the mess in Istanbul?" I asked.

"Between Sherlock and I putting our spin on the publicly known events and the upper floors of the tower gutted by the fire, there've been some disgruntled comments, but nothing that I think will be an ongoing problem," Garrett said. "Especially since the violent attacks in the city have stopped now."

Sherlock chuckled dryly. "It's easier to redirect the questions when they can hardly comprehend what went on in the first place."

"Well, at least there's that." I sank a little deeper into the cushions with some relief.

"So, with the immediate threats all conquered, how will the great Jemma Moriarty pass the rest of her time from here on?" John said in a teasing tone.

There, that was the difficult part. I took another bite of my donut, rolling the sweet doughy goodness around in my mouth before I answered. "I still have business interests to keep track of. I do feel, though, that I'd prefer to keep things much more low key and relaxed than they might have been before. It was a lot of hassle, really. You can assume I won't be involved in any indiscretions you'd feel it necessary to pursue."

I wasn't going to tell them I'd never engage in criminal activity again. I'd just overseen a couple of deals this morning. I needed to keep some of my finances and network alive in case the shrouded folk made a return, after all. But I had a broad enough foundation that I had no need to expand on it.

"And you'll be managing those interests from London?" Sherlock asked.

It wasn't an invitation or a request. I looked around at the London trio, uncertain in a way I wasn't used to and didn't entirely like.

When we'd talked about a future together back in Istanbul, we hadn't touched on any of the specifics. Perhaps they'd rethought the commitment they'd offered now that the catastrophe was averted. Now that they'd had a little time to settle back into their regular lives that they'd been content with before I'd ever meddled with them.

"I hadn't thought that far just yet," I hedged. I wasn't going to force them to stick to their offer, even if the thought of giving up the closeness we'd come to share made me feel sick.

John glanced at Sherlock with an oddly enthusiastic expression. Sherlock smiled in response, amused but warmly enough that my uneasiness started to fade.

"I happened to hear," the detective said, "that the building next door has a flat that will be available at the end of the month. A large one, I believe quite acceptable to your needs. If you wouldn't find that to be a closer quarters than you prefer, it would certainly be useful having you so near at hand. Perhaps you could even lend a thought or two to our cases as need be."

Next door. *They* wanted me that nearby, that much a part of their lives. And there was no denying the hopefulness in Garrett's eyes as he waited for my response.

A smile of my own crossed my lips with a flutter of joy in my chest. "I think that would be quite satisfactory. I'll speak to the landlord today."

CHAPTER TWENTY-FOUR

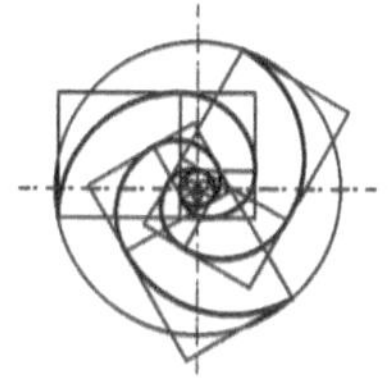

Jemma

Several months later

I poured more water into the glass vase with its small bouquet of lilies of the valley and paused there by the window to brush my fingertips over the delicate petals. The sweet scent drifted up to my nose.

"That bunch is still going strong, huh?" Bash said from where he'd just come out of his bedroom.

"Yes." I smiled as I gave the bouquet one last caress.

The flowers weren't exactly the same as the little white ones Olivia used to pick around the outskirts of our childhood commune, but they reminded me of those... and maybe they reminded her too. I'd been setting them out on the little table beneath the living room window like an offering since we'd moved into this apartment last autumn, and they always stayed fresh and vibrant for weeks longer than any cut flowers should naturally.

It wasn't definite proof. If some part of my sister's spirit did linger on in the world, taking pleasure from little gestures like this, she hadn't communicated with me in any clear way. But if the shrouded folk could exist, if my spirit could travel from this world to theirs without my body, then I didn't see any reason why she had to be completely gone. I was happy to keep setting out flowers for her either way.

Bash came up behind me and wrapped his arms around my waist, still a little tentative with the first contact to give me time to stop him if I didn't want the embrace. I leaned into him, absorbing the solid feel of his body against mine, reveling in the fact that I could enjoy the gesture of intimacy so easily now.

It'd taken time to completely adjust to the change in our relationship from colleagues to lovers—with each other, and with the other three men in my life—now that we weren't in the middle of a desperate struggle with malicious supernatural foes. Every now and then, I was struck by a tiny flash of panic, as if I might have made a huge mistake. But those flashes came much less frequently than they had a year ago when I'd first embarked on this path. I'd gotten practiced at ignoring them.

"Will the trio be here at the usual time?" Bash asked.

"Of course—unless some urgent case comes up, I suppose."

Bash and I had been sharing the apartment next door to Sherlock and John's from the beginning, which had also been an adjustment. I suspected our arrangement was a lot like theirs was now: a common area when we wanted each other's company and separate bedrooms when we needed our privacy—but which could be shared when we were in the mood.

I saw the other men separately here or at their apartments at least once a week, but Friday nights—often blurring into Saturday mornings—were reserved for all five of us to have dinner together and whatever else we took a mind to do. Since we'd started the tradition, work had only called away one or more of the trio a handful of times.

And today... today was special, though I wasn't entirely sure any of my men would have taken note of the fact.

Bash went out to take care of a business errand, and I showered and assembled my clothes with particular care, slipping into a dress I'd picked specifically for this occasion. The air conditioning was whirring at a low level, but the silky fabric still felt delightful against the underlying July heat. I checked on the items I'd prepared and then set the table. I trusted John to choose each week's takeout, since of my lovers he had the most appreciation for a good meal.

My heart thumped away a little faster than it normally would have for a regular Friday night dinner. I closed my eyes for a second by the table, willing my nerves to settle.

It would be fine. I'd given tonight's plans more thought than I had any recent business endeavor I'd engaged in, and the men involved in that plan were a hell of a lot less treacherous than my usual associates. I just wasn't entirely sure what reaction to expect. And that reaction meant more to me than anything had since Olivia's death.

Bash returned not long before our guests were due. Sherlock arrived first, only needing to stroll a few feet down the street. He waved his phone at me after he'd stepped inside.

"A new case has come to my attention that I think you might have an interesting perspective on. I've emailed you the specifics."

I grinned. I might still have my fingers in all sorts of not-entirely-legitimate pies, but it was a pleasure matching wits with the consulting detective even when we were on the same side—seeing how closely our theories aligned, what we each might notice that the other hadn't, who could hone in on the answer to the mystery first.

"I'll take a look tomorrow, if there's not any particular rush," I said.

"No, this one has a trail some seven years cold, so I can't imagine a day will make a great deal of difference." He settled himself onto the sofa, looking quite at home. "No need to interrupt our other activities."

I couldn't resist ambling over to curl my fingers around the collar of his well-pressed shirt and steal a kiss, as a taste of the "activities" to come.

John showed up next, laden with takeout bags and with Garrett at his heels. The detective inspector helped the former doctor set out the cartons and tubs, Indian spices tickling my nose. My mouth was already watering when we sat down to eat.

The usual sorts of conversation carried on around the table—talk of each other's latest cases, recent international news, wry observations, and the possibility of taking a trip abroad this fall. Other than the few minutes when we all confirmed, as we did every week, that we hadn't seen any reason to suspect that the shrouded folk had reinvaded our world, my attention might have strayed. I obviously wasn't participating as much as usual, because when Garrett and Bash got up to clear the table, Sherlock turned to me with his piercing gaze.

"You've got something on your mind that you haven't brought up yet," he said. "How long will we need to wait before you impart that information?"

"It's nothing unpleasant," I said quickly at John's concerned glance. "I actually—I have something for each of you. Why don't we sit down in the living room, and your wait can be over?"

I got curious looks from all of them at that statement, even Bash, who I'd managed to keep all my arrangements secret from. They sat down on the sofa and armchairs where we usually had our after-dinner conversation before the tone shifted in a more bedroom-ward direction. John took the spot next to Sherlock with a casual caress of the other man's knee that gave me a flutter of pleased warmth despite my nerves. At this point, neither of their companions so much as blinked at the show of affection.

I ducked into my room to get the four packages I'd carefully wrapped this morning. "Let's start with Sherlock, since he prompted this along," I said in as even a voice as I could manage, and handed his package to him.

He turned the gift over, no doubt able to tell it was a book in less than a second. When he eased off the paper and saw the ancient leather binding and the title embossed on the cover, though, I wasn't sure I'd ever seen him quite so surprised. His head jerked up, his eyes wide as they met mine.

"Franz Sauer's analyses of criminal psychology and pathology.

I've seen it referenced but—I was under the impression there were no copies left. I always wondered…" He touched the pages reverently.

I smiled with a rush of relief that my first effort had hit the mark so well. "I know. You've mentioned it once or twice. As far as I know after doing some digging, there's only *one* copy still in existence— that one you're holding right there."

He stared at me again. "The amount it must have cost you to obtain this—"

I waved him off. "Money is not an issue—and there were favors owed that defrayed some of the cost. Just don't ask for the details of how exactly I got my hands on it."

From the awe in his expression as he cradled the book, I didn't think he was likely to get nitpicky about my methods.

I turned to John next and handed him a much smaller package. "For you, I wanted to honor the side of you that you rarely let yourself completely indulge."

He raised an amused eyebrow at me and tore open the wrapping. The box inside opened to reveal a key on a fob. When he looked at me again, I tipped my head toward the window. "It's parked outside. You probably drooled over it on your way in."

From the flicker of astonishment that crossed his face, that guess had been right. He hurried over to the front of the apartment, not bothering with his walking stick, and leaned close to the glass. A brilliant smile curled his lips.

"Sherlock's not going to thank you for that," he said, but there was no mistaking the glee in his voice.

The detective tore himself away from his adoration of his own gift for long enough to ask, "What's she done now?"

John dangled the key. "She got me a motorbike. One of the new Ducatis." His gaze slid to me. "I never told you I admired those."

I rolled my eyes at him affectionately. "The way you drive your car, it's pretty obvious you could use another outlet for that need for speed."

He chuckled with a hint of a flush in his cheeks. "It *is* a lot."

"Don't you start thinking about the money either. It was a drop in the bucket."

Picking out something that would really matter to Garrett had been harder. I suppressed the urge to fidget after I gave him his gift, which was the largest of the bunch but perhaps not as objectively impressive.

He opened the box and paused before lifting up the piece on top, a dark silk suit jacket, gingerly as if he were afraid of ruining the fine fabric just by touching it.

"It's for the conference next month," I said. He'd been asked to speak and receive an honor for his work on the task force at a major police function where all the top brass, even the prime minister, would be present, and he'd been quietly fretting about whether he'd look up to snuff ever since he'd gotten the invitation. "If it doesn't fit quite right, I can get some more tailoring done, but I think I know your body rather well by now."

Even the prime minister was unlikely to have a suit quite that well designed, though I'd gone for understated rather than flashy in consideration of Garrett's tastes. He looked at the pants folded beneath the jacket and the gold cuff links I'd tucked into the corner in their smaller box and then back at me with a shimmer in his eyes.

"Thank you," he said. "I can't imagine it's anything but perfect already."

Bash had watched all the goings-on with bemused interest. When I held out the last gift to him, little more than an envelope covered in gift paper, my hitman shook his head at me before he dug his thumb under the folds. "You know I've already got everything I could want, Mori."

"I know you *could* have everything you want," I said. "But you have a bad habit of putting what you think I need over what you do."

Before he could question that comment, two plane tickets were falling out of the envelope into his hands. He blinked at them for a few seconds as understanding washed over his face. "Jemma," he started, and then didn't seem to know how to go on.

"I can spare you for two weeks," I said. "You've been talking to your brother and sister for almost a year now—it's time you got to see them again, properly. Or if I've been mistaken and you'd *really* rather not, we can exchange them for a trip to Fiji or wherever. But you won't be with me in London for those two weeks. You deserve a break, too."

He managed to keep his expression relatively impassive, but I heard the emotion in his voice. "Well, if you insist... Thank you."

John glanced around at the other men, still lit up with excitement over his own gift. "Why all this now, Jemma? There's still five more months until Christmas."

My gaze lifted to Sherlock, who I figured was the one most likely to connect the dots if any of them did. His small smile in return told me he already had.

"It's exactly one year since the day in Rio de Janeiro when we all agreed to join forces with Jemma to tackle the shrouded folk," he said. "The anniversary of our official partnership?"

"That sounds like a reasonable way to put it," I said.

Garrett had closed the box with his suit, his arms resting on it in a protective stance. "I didn't realize—we don't have anything for you."

My throat constricted, but my heart only pounded harder. My heart that had felt so inaccessible for so long, with no room in it for anything except my sister and the vengeance I meant to deal out for her.

My love for her, and the pain and grief that came with it, hadn't shrunk. No, that wasn't it at all. What I'd felt over the past year had been more as if my heart were growing, bit by bit, to have more and more capacity for affection and devotion with every day I spent with these men.

I swallowed hard. "You've given me so much. For months, you've all offered me your love when I couldn't respond in kind, when I wasn't sure I ever would be able to... So in a way, I've kept you waiting a very long time for this. It seemed only fair to show it as well as say it."

Even though I was sure of them, even though I'd planning for days how I'd say them, the words stuck before I could propel them out of my mouth. "I love you. All of you. There isn't any way I'd rather spend the rest of my life than what we have now."

The flash of panic hit me, for what I hoped would be the last time. In that instant, I couldn't look at any of them. Someone sucked in a breath, and then all four of my lovers were getting to their feet, surrounding me, wrapping me up in a joint embrace. They didn't need to say the words back right then for me to know they felt the same.

I was Jemma Moriarty, devoted sister, cult escapee, criminal mastermind, attached beyond what I could ever have believed to these four incredible men. Our arrangement might have looked odd to outside eyes, but what any outsider thought didn't matter. It worked perfectly for us. And it was far more of a happy ending than I'd ever believed could be mine.

ABOUT THE AUTHOR

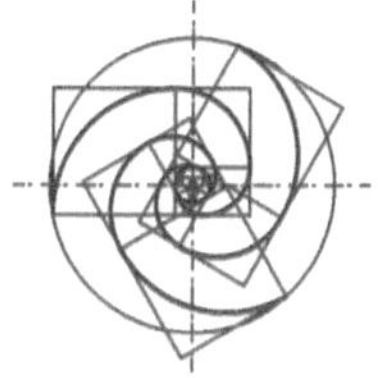

Eva Chase lives in Canada with her family. She loves stories both swoony and supernatural, and strong women and the men who appreciate them. Along with the Moriarty's Men series, she is the author of the Bound to the Fae series, the Flirting with Monsters series, the Royals of Villain Academy series, the Looking Glass Curse trilogy, the Their Dark Valkyrie series, the Witch's Consorts series, the Dragon Shifter's Mates series, the Demons of Fame Romance series, the Legends Reborn trilogy, and the Alpha Project Psychic Romance series.

Connect with Eva online:
www.evachase.com
eva@evachase.com